RANDOM HOUSE
LARGE PRINT

Also by Richard North Patterson

THE LASKO TANGENT

THE OUTSIDE MAN

ESCAPE THE NIGHT

PRIVATE SCREENING

DEGREE OF GUILT

Richard North Patterson

Published by Random House Large Print
in association with Alfred A. Knopf
New York 1992

Published in the United States by Random House Large Print,
New York, in association with Alfred A. Knopf, Inc.,
and simultaneously in Canada by Random House
of Canada Limited, Toronto.
Distributed by Random House, Inc., New York.

ISBN 0-679-42211-0
LC 92-54446

Manufactured in the United States of America
FIRST LARGE PRINT EDITION

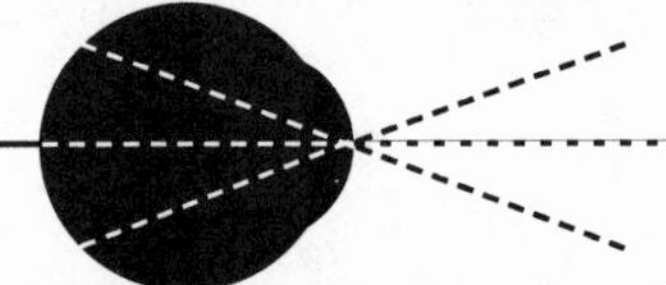

This Large Print Book carries the
Seal of Approval of N.A.V.H.

FOR LAURIE,
FOR EVERYTHING

DEGREE OF GUILT

PART ONE

THE KILLING

January 13

ONE

THE WOMAN FROZE in the hallway, staring at the numbered door-plate.

For a moment, she felt uncertain that this was the same suite she had left perhaps a minute before. Then she turned the knob slowly, wincing at its metallic click.

The door cracked ajar, a pallid sliver of light coming from inside. She paused, looking over her shoulder, less from fear of being seen than the desire to stay suspended in time, outside the room.

Time. She glanced at her gold wristwatch. When had it happened? she wondered. No way of telling now. Thirty minutes, she decided arbitrarily. Thirty minutes, and she had not decided what to do. Her mind was sluggish, numb with disbelief. She felt drugged.

Her fingertips were damp, she realized. With every thought, her choices seemed to narrow. She fought the impulse to stop thinking, to run. It took all her will to do nothing.

The chime of an elevator rang.

She flinched. Quickly, she tried to remember arriving in the elevator, how far it was down the hallway. Afraid to turn, unable to recall the corridor right behind her.

She straightened, squaring her shoulders, and pushed open the door.

The rectangle of light from within captured her like a photograph, a slender woman with long black hair, standing motionless in the door frame. The elevator opened. A second chime penetrated her shock.

She stepped inside and shut the door behind her.

Closing, it sounded heavy. Final, she corrected herself. It sounded final.

She turned to face the room.

Her eyes sought out details. Drawn blinds. Her black leather purse on the floor. The gold neck of an empty champagne bottle, above the rim of a silver ice bucket on a glass coffee table. The two crystal glasses. The heavy oil painting of San Francisco Bay she had remarked on, slightingly, when she first entered. Her panty hose on the carpet, ripped in one leg.

She touched her throat, feeling for scratches. She had broken a nail; it was that, oddly, which made her remember her own fragility.

Finally, she looked at him.

There was blood on the carpet now, beneath his chest. His pants were pulled below his knees.

A sudden jumble of images: Legs splayed at crazy angles. Blue argyle socks. A curly shock of red hair. Thin craggy face, turned to chalk. Eyes open as if to stare at the black handgun, lying near his head where she had left it.

For an instant, she was paralyzed.

She breathed in deeply, once, and exhaled. Then she took three steps, standing over him, and stared down at his bare buttocks.

The wave of revulsion hit her again, rose to her throat. She felt sure she would vomit; some cold, distant part of her brain wondered how that would look to them. Perhaps they would see her fear, see how afraid he had made her. Then the hatred ran through her again, hard and deep and raw.

She shut her eyes, remembering. What he had done. What he had wanted to do.

When they opened again, she felt stronger, more ready. More like the woman who had come here. More like the woman she had always been.

The nausea had passed. She sat beside him on the carpet.

There was no hole in his back, she saw; the bullet had not gone through. The flabby skin of his buttocks was turning gray. She could hardly see the scratches she had left there.

In her new resolve, she tried to summon a clinical dispassion. Perhaps forty minutes before, she realized, his heart had stopped pumping blood. The great man, bottom in the air, pale as a fish. It was almost comic.

The smile, small and involuntary, hurt her bruised mouth. The dark mirth vanished.

The rest of her life, she resolved, would not be about him. She would not let him do that to her. She would leave this day behind her.

Starting now.

She looked down at her watch. Too much time had passed. She must think quickly.

She stood with a kind of awkward dignity, preparing herself.

Walking carefully around the dead man, she knelt again on the other side, to pick up her panty hose. She left the gun where it was.

She held the hose dangling in one hand, reflecting. Then she hitched up her skirt, examining her legs. The scratch on her left thigh traced the tear in her panty hose.

They would ask to see her legs, she was certain.

Long, slender from the twenty years of exercise since college— running in the morning, gyms at night. Twenty years of willpower: like everything else in her life, her body was as nearly perfect as she could make it. But today, it had seemed, not perfect enough.

Struggling into the hose, she realized that her shoes were still under the coffee table.

What mattered? she wondered. It was hard to know.

She walked to the coffee table, staring down at the tape recorder.

Small and black, it stood upright near the glasses. Through its plastic window she saw that the tape had played until it stopped. And, with it, the woman's voice. Low and smoky, damning in a monotone a man whom she had never met and yet had believed in. Until now.

It was a moment before she realized that her fists had clenched. Another before she could move again.

As if in her sleep, she straightened her dress, put on her shoes. Looking around the suite, she saw that the bedroom door was shut. Strange, she thought, that he had not shown it to her.

She looked back toward the room.

The desk drawer was still open. She walked across the room, past the body, and closed it.

As she turned, the mirror above the couch caught her face.

It stopped her. With an odd detachment, she realized that the cameras would magnify the bruise beneath her eye.

She found nothing else. Neither the years since Washington, nor the past hour, had changed her much. No matter what he had said or done, or could not do.

She studied her reflection.

A face that photographed well, filmed well. A strong face, high cheekbones, clear brown eyes. It had always helped her, whether or not she had wanted that kind of help. She did not know whether it could help her now.

Turning, she took one final look at him, then at the room around her. To remember. Simply to remember. It would be a long day, she knew, a long night without sleep. Perhaps many nights until she slept. But she would need to remember, not forget.

Briefly, she thought again of the boy, and was ready.

The telephone was on an end table, next to the couch. She picked it up, standing stiffly, listening to the dial tone. Then her gaze caught the tape recorder.

They would record her, she knew. Listen to her words over and over. Listen to her tone of voice.

She swallowed once, clearing her throat. Her mouth tasted bitter.

Willfully, she stabbed the numbers.

The dial tone broke, became a ringing on the other end. She listened, steeling herself for the answering voice. But the man's brusque tone startled her. How foolish, she thought, to have wished for a woman.

"San Francisco Emergency," the male voice snapped again.

She found herself staring at the man on the floor, fixated on the black gun by his head. A foreign object, she thought. Foreign in her life. Foreign in her hand.

"There's been an accident," she said simply.

Teresa Peralta glanced at her watch. It was close to five, and he still had not sprung the trap.

The deposition had been going for seven hours. It was like watching a cat-and-mouse game where the cat had his eye on a second mouse; what lent the game its fascination was the smugness of the second mouse, who sat watching the cat toy with the first mouse, secure in his delusion that the cat had not seen him.

"Perhaps I can refresh your memory," Christopher Paget said pleasantly, and handed the first mouse a document. "Can you identify Defendant's Exhibit 13?"

This particular cat wore a navy double-breasted pinstripe of soft Italian wool. With that came a silk floral tie; a white cotton shirt; square gold cuff links. As with other things about Christopher Paget, Terri wondered whether the careful dress was a form of camouflage, meant to deflect attention from who he really was.

They sat in a large conference room with a view of San Francisco Bay. Two lawyers on each side of the table, a witness and a court reporter. Terri was next to Paget, watching. The document—which seemed to have transfixed the witness—was his last.

"Please take your time," Paget suggested calmly.

Time, Terri thought again. Through the window, dusk was falling across the bay; lights were beginning to glimmer from the city and, across the gray swath of water, from Marin County. Five o'clock; the day care center would close at six. It was on the other side of the Bay Bridge, for Richie's convenience, near where they lived because Richie liked Berkeley better than the city. Next to her was a message, brought in at four-thirty. Richie was having dinner with some "business associates," to work on his new software "deal"; Terri must pick up Elena.

Forget it for a moment, she told herself. Learn something. Watch him do this.

Her metaphor, she decided, was better than she had thought. Paget had a cat's patience, a cat's still blue eyes. And there was a look of fineness to him, the result of great self-discipline and much exercise. The copper hair, ridged nose, and clean angles of his face seemed little different from the classic photograph, taken fifteen years before.

Christopher Paget had been famous so young, she knew, that some saw his career since then as an afterthought; the picture had been on the cover of *Time,* when he was twenty-nine.

She had found it in the library, as she was about

to interview for a job as his associate. It was a well-known cover: a young lawyer testifying before Congress, the portrait of idealism and risk. Curiosity had led her from one article to another, relearning things she had heard about but had been too young to remember clearly.

The case had involved William Lasko, a close friend and financial supporter of the President. Paget was an investigator for the Economic Crimes Commission, assigned to check out Lasko's stock transactions. A key witness—one of Lasko's employees—had died in a hit-and-run "accident," leaving behind one ambiguous memo and the suspicion in Paget that someone within the ECC was betraying his inquiry.

Slowly, Paget had begun to uncover corruption within the ECC, which, he came to suspect, reached all the way to the White House. Then a second witness was kidnapped. When Paget persisted, someone had tried to kill him, just before he pieced together the meaning of Lasko's transactions.

The transactions, it turned out, were meant to funnel one and one-half million dollars to the President's campaign. And the man who had been leaking information about the investigation to Lasko was the chairman of Paget's agency. A man named Jack Woods.

It was never clear, Terri had found, whether Paget had entirely uncovered the corruption within the

ECC itself. But he had taken the story to the Washington *Post* and then to Congress. A second witness had come forward—a young woman lawyer who was Woods's chief assistant. The results were prison sentences for Woods and Lasko, and political ruin for the President.

Christopher Paget was the first twenty-nine-year-old, a columnist wrote sourly, to bring down a President without using sex. The columnist seemed slightly nettled; Paget refused all requests for interviews.

As far as Terri could tell, he had never spoken of the Lasko case again.

The strain must have been enormous; everyone wanted a piece of him. The young woman witness, Terri knew, had become a television journalist. But Paget seemed to want no part of it. And, much more than the woman, he had earned the undying enmity of partisans of the President, who felt that he had tampered with the scales of history. He had left Washington and returned to California for good.

He had started his own firm, turned down requests to enter politics, made a specialty of white-collar crime. Within the office, Paget's time in Washington was treated like some private trauma, which people were too tactful to mention. In six months, she had learned almost nothing about him except that he was very good at his job.

"Mr. Gepfer?" he asked politely.

Across the table, the witness was staring at several pages of handwritten figures, seemingly unable to move or speak. He *looked* like a mouse, Terri decided: thin, sharp face, sandy hair combed to cover a bald spot, small eyes that shifted between avarice and fear. Had he not been so dishonest, and the moment so sublime, she would have felt sorry for him.

"I don't recall this document," opposing counsel broke in. "I'd like to know what this is and where you got it."

It was with Starr that Terri's conceit of cats and mice broke down. He had a basilisk face, slicked-back gray hair, and an air of deliberate shrewdness; it had not surprised her to learn from the skinny associate who sat next to Starr that he treated his staff like serfs.

Ignoring him, Paget turned to the court reporter, a young woman who sat watching from the end of the table, fingers poised over her machine. "In Mr. Starr's excitement," he said, "the witness may have forgotten the question. Perhaps you should read it back."

Starr leaned across the table. Terri scrutinized him, trying to figure out how much he understood. Not quite enough, she concluded; he looked like a man who was prepared for a setback but not for a disaster.

''Oh, go ahead.''

''Thank you.'' Paget's tone held the barest trace of irony. He nodded to the reporter.

''Can you identify Defendant's Exhibit 13?'' the reporter read out.

Almost inaudibly, Gepfer answered, ''Yes.''

Paget took up the questioning. ''And is that document in your handwriting?''

''Yes.''

''Could you read the heading at the top center, please.''

Gepfer's eyes shut. ''Liberal Accounting Adjustments,'' he said in a monotone.

''How did you come to call it that?''

''David Frank suggested it.''

''When he was still chairman of Lyon Industries?''

''Yes.''

''Did you also get the figures under that heading from Mr. Frank?''

Starr watched the questioning without changing expression. What Terri noticed was how intent he was.

''He set the direction,'' Gepfer answered miserably. ''I came up with the numbers for him.''

''And what do these numbers represent?''

''The amount of additional income Lyon needed to show a profit in fiscal 1991.''

''Additional, or imaginary?''

Gepfer frowned, as if pondering a complex thought. ''We didn't make the money,'' he finally answered, ''if that's what you meant.''

''But the figures on the document,'' Paget said, ''became the figures on Lyon's financial statements, correct?''

''Correct.''

''And were used to raise $53 million in the public offering?''

''Yes.''

''Mr. Frank sold stock in that offering, correct?''

''Yes.''

''And made several million dollars.''

''Yes.''

''And you also sold stock in the offering?''

''Yes.''

''And made roughly $670,000.''

''Yes,'' Gepfer said again.

Paget had him in a rhythm now. ''Whose idea was it to change the books?''

Gepfer's voice turned accusatory. ''Mr. Frank's.''

''And you just went along.''

''Yes.''

''Did my client, Steve Rudin, know about this?''

''Objection,'' Starr cut in. ''Calls for speculation.''

Paget's eyes widened. ''Really, Mr. Starr, I'm

proving your entire case. I'd think you'd be more grateful. . . .''

''Come off it. Frank killed himself. How can this man know who Frank talked to?''

Paget looked at him a moment. Not for the first time, Terri had the sense that nothing surprised him; that something had taught him not to show what he felt; that he expected very little from anyone. ''You mean you haven't asked him?'' he asked Starr softly. ''You're prosecuting this case against my client, this man's cooperating with you, and you haven't asked him yet?''

Starr leaned back. ''I'm not the witness here,'' he retorted. ''I'm not telling you what I've asked or haven't asked. That's work product.''

''I'll try another question,'' Paget said agreeably, turning to the witness. ''Before today, when was the last time you saw this document?''

Starr's face said everything; too late, he saw where this was about to go. Could hear the next five questions before they were ever asked.

''July,'' the witness said. For Gepfer, Terri knew, the worst had already happened; the questions were now worse for someone else.

Paget sat back, looking at both Starr and the witness. ''At that time, did you give this document to anyone?''

''Yes.''

Paget had stopped looking at Gepfer now. When

he asked the next question, his gaze was fixed on Starr.

"And who was that?"

"Objection!" Starr stood up. "That's work product."

The court reporter's head had begun moving back and forth, following the voices.

Paget turned to Gepfer. "You may answer."

"Press on," Starr snapped, "or we're walking out."

"That hardly seems reasonable." Paget had yet to raise his voice. "Let me suggest this, Mr. Starr. Why don't we call a magistrate and get a ruling by telephone."

"Fine." Starr spoke with more assurance. "But the courts close at five—there's no one there to give us a ruling. I'm busy the next few weeks. Maybe sometime in February."

Terri suppressed a smile.

"Curiously," Paget said to Starr, "I anticipated this problem and called Magistrate Riordan's office this morning. He'll be available until six."

Starr stared at him. Paget pointed toward a telephone table. "The telephone is over there," he said. "Just dial nine for an outside line. I believe Ms. Peralta's written the number down for you, if you haven't yet committed it to memory. . . ."

"This is an abuse. You're trying to invade the tactical decisions of opposing counsel. That's the classic definition of work product."

"Hardly. In fact, I'm fascinated to know how the identity of the nameless person with whom Mr. Gepfer shared this document could be *anyone's* work product. Really, Mr. Starr, it seems you have but two choices. The first is to call Magistrate Riordan and present an argument that, quite likely, is without precedent in the annals of Western jurisprudence. That's the option I favor, if only for the sheer interest of listening to it.

"The second and more mundane choice is to take a ten-minute break and see if we can resolve this matter without compelling Mr. Gepfer to answer any more questions."

Starr was impassive. Finally, he waved Gepfer and the court reporter from the room.

"If you have something to say to me," Starr said at length, "I'll give you ten minutes."

Terri could not help but admire the gall that made a trip to the abattoir sound like a concession to good manners.

"Ten minutes," Paget responded, "is all I'm giving you to drop this lawsuit."

"What kind of crap—"

Paget reached beneath the table, pulling a typed agreement from his briefcase. "This is a stipulation of settlement. It recites that you have become aware that your charges against Steve Rudin are mistaken; that Mr. Gepfer has confirmed the error; that you are dismissing this lawsuit; and that your firm is paying Mr. Rudin $250,000 to compensate him for his time and expenses.''

''I won't sign that.''

''For at least six months,'' Paget went on, ''you've had this document. Which means that you've known for at least six months that my client was innocent of fraud.''

''You can't hold me responsible for what Gepfer says now.''

Paget looked at his watch. ''Why don't we save eight minutes and ask Gepfer what you knew?''

''The man's admitted falsifying documents. Now you want him to give false testimony. Whatever he says, no one will believe it.''

''Won't they? Frank was bankrupt when he killed himself. That leaves only two defendants with money. Gepfer has less than a million; but my client is *very* wealthy *and* covered by insurance. So you make a deal with Gepfer: if he doesn't give anyone else the document and doesn't tell anyone what really happened, you let him keep the money he stole and try to extract a settlement from my client by tying him up in an endless lawsuit you know to be a fraud.''

Starr folded his arms. ''You can never prove that.''

''Care to find out? Because if the case against Steve Rudin goes one question longer, you'll find out more than that. Whether we can prove it. Whether we can win a suit for malicious prosecution. Whether the legal press will enjoy watching us try. Whether the Bar Association will let you keep your license. Whether every judge in this district will start looking at you like some evolutionary cul-de-sac. And the only person who will enjoy that more than I is Steve Rudin—the man you charged with fraud.'' Standing, Paget looked at his watch again. ''You have five minutes, it seems.''

Terri followed him to his office.

It was sparsely furnished: bright modern prints; two plants; a glass table; a single picture of a dark-haired boy. Paget collected art, she knew; one of the prints was a Miró. She had no idea who the boy was.

Paget stood staring out the window.

''Will they go for it?'' Terri asked.

''Yes.'' He answered without turning. ''Starr is driven by sheer self-interest.''

''I can hardly believe he knew.''

''Oh, he knew. Always expect people to be what they've been in the past. That way, they don't surprise or disappoint you.'' Paget shoved his hands in his pockets, sounding suddenly weary. ''Being surprised is a sin, professionally. But it's the disappointment that can be so soul-wearing.''

The remark was uncharacteristic; it was almost, Terri thought, as if he were talking to himself.

"How *did* you get the document?" she asked.

"I promised not to say." He turned, smiling faintly. "But Starr really should treat his employees better."

There was a knock on the door. Starr's associate came in, holding the settlement papers. He paused, glancing at Terri. She wondered if the associate, who seemed a little too interested in her, realized that she was married. It wasn't as though he *knew* her at all, and lately it was harder to believe that men could find her attractive. What could you say about a nose that she thought was a little too sharp, crescent eyes a little too small for her liking, straight brown hair that she shared with fifty million other Hispanic women in the Western Hemisphere alone? You could say what Richie said in that ambiguous tone of voice—that she looked smart.

"He signed them," Starr's associate said, and handed the papers to Terri.

"Thank you," Paget answered civilly. The associate looked at him, then at Terri, and left.

Terri felt a rush of triumph, although the triumph was not hers. Without really thinking, she said, "I thought maybe the watch trick was overdoing it a bit. At least on top of handing him the agreement."

He shrugged. "Apparently not."

"Did you ever do that before?"

He regarded her a moment. "Once. Years ago."

"Did it work?"

"After a fashion."

There was distance in his tone, perhaps preoccupation. Feeling awkward, she looked at her watch.

"I have to run. A kid emergency."

"I have somewhere to go too. We'll call Steve Rudin in the morning."

The telephone rang. Distractedly, Paget answered it. Terri paused in the doorway, thinking it might be something about the case. But what kept her there, forgetful of herself and time, was the stillness that came over him.

"Where are you?" Paget finally asked.

He listened for another moment.

"Don't talk to anyone," he said. "I'll be right down."

Paget sounded quite calm. Only when he put the telephone down, with almost exaggerated care, did she notice he was pale.

She looked at him quizzically.

Paget seemed surprised to see her. Then he said simply, "Mark Ransom's been killed."

It startled her. She did not know why someone would be calling him or how he was connected to the famous writer. Finally, she asked, "Who was that?"

He paused a moment. "Mary Carelli."

"The TV interviewer?"

The description seemed to surprise him. Suddenly it came to her: the woman in Washington, the second witness against Lasko. Then, as if correcting her, Christopher Paget replied, "My son Carlo's mother."

TWO

CHRISTOPHER PAGET had not imagined that the mother of his only son, a woman for whom he had felt much more passion than trust, would be accused of murder within twenty-four hours of appearing in their lives for the first time in eight years.

They had been in the kitchen of their house in Pacific Heights. It was four o'clock: through the floor-to-ceiling window, the failing sunlight lent the trim Victorians and stucco mansions a pale Florentine pink and white; the bay a slate blue; the Marin headlands beyond a tawny brown. Paget was slicing lemons for chicken piccata. Carlo was sitting on a barstool, slender frame leaning against the counter, complaining about his girlfriend's parents.

"She's *fifteen,*" Carlo was saying, "and they're absolutely paranoid. They've done everything but have her tubes tied."

Paget smiled at the hyperbole; he was fairly confident that Carlo did not yet warrant such drastic measures.

"Like what, exactly?" he asked.

"Like they won't even let her out on weekends."

"At all?"

"At all."

Paget began chopping scallions. "That's a bit medieval. Are you sure there isn't some history there?"

"She *has* no history, Dad. They've never let her out of the house at night. They're afraid her morals are going to get corrupted or something, and all *I* want to do is introduce her to my friends and do stuff with everybody."

For the moment, Paget guessed, that was pretty much true; Carlo and his friends hung out in groups, and the easy interchange of boys and girls as friends struck Paget as infinitely saner than the rituals of his own teenage years, when girls were a mystery and dates took place in cars.

"They're afraid of *something*," Paget finally said. "Perhaps from their own lives."

Carlo pondered that a moment. Not for the first time, Paget examined his son with a kind of wonder. To be so uncertain still, he thought, yet so suddenly close to manhood. Paget could recall like yesterday carrying Carlo on his shoulders. Now Carlo was taller than he, a handsome black-haired boy with a crooked grin and startling blue eyes. The eyes were regarding him with that opaque look which, Paget knew, often concealed thoughts too close to home. "They're pretty young," Carlo ventured, "to be parents of a fifteen-year-old."

Paget refocused on the scallions. "And Jennifer is an only child?"

Carlo nodded. "After her, she says, her parents gave up sex."

"Kids always think that." Paget smiled. "The alternative is too grotesque for any teenager to imagine."

"I don't know." Carlo's voice took on a teasing edge. "I've never had much trouble with that."

"I suppose it's that I'm single." Paget took a light tone, trying to decipher the meaning of his son's remark. "I guess that makes my social life a little more conspicuous and makes it somewhat less likely you'll confuse me with Ward Cleaver. Back to Jennifer: is your homework done?"

"Yes—for hours. We've got a basketball game tomorrow, and I want to rest up. Anyhow, what does my homework have to do with Jennifer?"

"If you have time, perhaps we could invite her to dinner this evening. I can make more chicken, and maybe Jennifer's parents will feel better about letting her go somewhere they know there's another parent and perhaps a few house rules."

Carlo grinned. "Like safe sex and a two-drink limit?"

"If I were you, I would keep *that* line in the family." Paget looked over at him. "I sometimes wonder, Carlo, what lessons you've learned from me."

"What do you mean?"

Carlo looked genuinely puzzled. Perhaps, Paget thought, there was less beneath the conversation than he had feared. "There's enough to choose from," Paget finally said. "Your life hasn't precisely been the Disney Channel."

"Did I ever accuse you," Carlo said, deadpan, "of murdering Mickey Mouse?"

Paget put down the knife. "You are absolutely determined to make this hard for me. Okay, the message goes like this: The subject of the moment is sex. It can be wonderful—as long as you treat it with respect, it's part of a friendship, and you're as honest about your feelings as you would be with any friend when the subject truly matters. Sometime, making love will be there for you. When it is, don't lie, don't push, and don't sleep with anyone you won't care for next month. Is that succinct enough?"

Once more, Paget saw the question in Carlo's eyes. But his son let it go unspoken, as he had for eight years. "Maybe," Carlo said simply, "our generation will do better with all that."

"I think you'll do better with everything." How, Paget wondered, to steer the conversation from this precipice. "The most important thing," he added, "is to listen, to be fair with each other, and to speak your heart without attacking your partner. But my own parents could neither show nor tell me, and I've only been able to tell you.'' And, Paget thought silently, I've been all you had. ''Maybe,'' he finished, ''you can show *me*.''

When the doorbell rang, his son was still regarding him, as if forming a thought or question. Paget smiled. ''Dorothy Parker once asked, when the doorbell rang, 'What fresh hell is this?' But in this case, someone's just saved you from 'Father Knows Best.' ''

Carlo raised an eyebrow. ''Guess you want me to get that.''

''Please.''

Paget heard his son head past the dining room, feet padding on the hardwood floor. The living room was large, with a sprawling Persian rug and a ten-foot ceiling that tended to eat up sound, muffling Carlo's footsteps as he moved toward the door. Paget resumed thinking about chicken piccata.

''Dad?''

''Yes,'' Paget called out.

''There's someone here.''

Carlo's voice sounded thin and a little strained. Paget put the knife down and headed for the living room.

She stood with her back to him, looking at the prints as she had that morning in Washington, fifteen years before.

He watched her, silent.

Without haste, she finished her scrutiny of the last

print, an exotic African landscape by Jesse Allen, lush trees and surreal birds that existed only in the artist's imagination. Turning, she said, "It's rather like your apartment on East Capitol. Of course, I recognize several of the prints." She smiled almost imperceptibly, pointing out the red-and-blue print of a geometric ball that seemed to roll as one approached it. "That's a Vasarely, I believe you once informed me."

Speak of the devil, Paget thought, looking from the woman to his son. But they had not been speaking of her, not directly, and Paget found himself speechless with surprise and withheld anger.

"Carlo," he finally said, "I believe you recall your mother."

Carlo stood as if caught between them, uncertain of what to do or say. Flashing the boy a warm, almost intimate smile, she moved to him. "Oh, yes," she said dryly to Paget. "We've met."

Paget was struck by how alike they were: dark hair, olive skin, chiseled faces, a slimness that combined strength with a certain delicacy. In Carlo, her grace was still a tentative teenage dignity, which, Paget knew, might well mature into the stylish ease that can capture a room. As she could.

"What brings you here?" he asked.

"Work," she said dismissively. "Perhaps an interview."

If she had any further explanation, her tone said,

it would not come in front of Carlo. The boy shifted from foot to foot, like a matchmaker watching a blind date go sour. Paget felt desperately sorry for him.

"Don't worry," Mary said to Carlo, taking his arm. "He's always like that around me—completely mesmerized. When he was twenty-nine, it was all he could do to ask me out. But then it was all *I* could do to accept."

Carlo grinned, still embarrassed, but relieved at her banter. "Then why did you?"

"Oh, I was waiting for Kevin Costner to mature. And your father had a certain indefinable charm."

Paget stood there, grateful that she had put Carlo more at ease, unsettled by the artificiality of it all. "I'm not speechless. Just cooking. I can either skip this celebrity roast or burn the chicken." He paused at the look in Carlo's eyes. "Can you stay for dinner?"

"I can't, really." Her half smile reflected how tepid he had sounded. "Go cook. Perhaps Carlo can show me the house."

Her voice was different, Paget realized. The trace evidence that she was second-generation Italian—a sort of Mediterranean intensity that underscored certain words—had become the studied diction of a stage actress. Television, he thought: flipping channels, he had seen her once by accident and stopped, bemused by her genesis from lawyer to "personality.'' Abruptly, he had snapped off the picture; some moments later, he had found himself staring at a blank screen.

''Carlo's room alone,'' he said now, ''should make the tour worthwhile. There's been nothing like it since Chernobyl.''

She smiled again. ''I'm Carlo's guest,'' she said. ''I'll let him pick his spots.''

Awkwardly, Carlo led her upstairs.

Paget walked to the kitchen, still suspended in time.

So much like Washington, she had said. Remembering the Vasarely as Paget remembered her standing in front of it, studying its patterns, wearing nothing at all.

It was the last weekend they had ever made love.

The Lasko case had not yet broken, and Paget had been certain that it never would—that he was at the end of things, that Lasko had killed a witness with impunity, and that Lasko's source within the agency, the one who had monitored Paget's progress, would never be detected. Trapped in a deep and solitary anger, feeling that Mary was opposed to him, Paget had meant to spend the weekend alone. Then Mary had come to his apartment unannounced, as she had come today.

They were both in their late twenties, Paget reflected now, so sure of what they already knew, so disastrously unknowing. Alone in his kitchen, with

Mary and their son upstairs, he felt the blindness of the moment as they lived it then.

At first, the sense of things unspoken had hung between them. They played backgammon, drank wine, smoked dope. They did not speak of Lasko.

Finally, gradually, they talked about themselves.

"What do you want in a woman?" she had asked him.

Her voice wasn't intrusive, just curious. Paget felt stoned enough to try to answer; drugs, and defeat, seemed to have lowered his defenses. "A lot of what I look for in anyone, I guess. Curiosity. Dislike for the easy answer. That in a good moment they can imagine what it's like to be an old woman or a small child. That they are more than what they do or what they are."

Mary smiled through the haze. "You don't ask much."

"Not much at all."

They slid down the couch, heads resting on opposite arms, legs parallel on the pillows. The next record fell on the stereo.

The Starship began singing.

Paget's limbs felt numb. The darkened room became images in a field of black, suspended in black: the spotlit Vasarely ball rolling toward them; the two empty glasses; the last roll of the dice faceup on the backgammon board. Her eyes.

He began to feel lost in them. The notes of "Miracles'' came to him one at a time, from some great distance. He did not know or care how many moments had passed since anyone had spoken.

Her voice broke the quiet.

''You know, Chris, you've been very lucky. You've never wanted—or needed—anything.''

It sounded like someone else, not him. But all he said was, ''I keep hearing that.''

''No, I mean it. Half the girls I knew growing up were married at eighteen. Sometimes I hate looking back.''

Her words seemed to hang in the air. Paget realized that he had forgotten the bitterness she seemed to carry: about being Catholic; about her parents' stillborn emotions and lack of encouragement; about the ex-husband who had wanted her to quit law school and have babies. Forgotten, more surprisingly, how much she needed to succeed. Forgotten her fierce pride at being assistant to the chairman of their agency, the ambition that had caused her to clash with Paget as many nights as they had made love.

Tonight he wanted none of it.

''No need,'' Paget answered smilingly. ''You've done a lot. That's something else I like in a woman.''

She smiled back. Paget reached for her then. She looked at him with a clear black gaze. Then her arm rose in a graceful arc and pulled him down.

They undressed each other slowly, mouths and

fingertips stopping where they cared to. For a long time, they lay in a cocoon of touching, finding, sounds that were not words. From one thing to another, mouth on her nipple, hand grazing her wetness, her hips rising, body twisting into him. Warm skin, thick clean hair against his face. Moments of suspended time, the absence of haste, the banishment of their ambitions and anything else that mattered in the daylight.

Perhaps an hour passed before he was inside her.

Even that felt different. Especially that.

Her stomach and hips rose, pressing against him as if desperate to pull him inside, to touch as much skin with her skin as she could. When they moved together, it was without hesitance, subtle changes in rhythm passing between them without words, suddenly faster, almost desperate, until she shuddered as their mouths found each other and a half cry rose from her throat and met his.

Afterward, no one spoke.

It was as if, Paget thought, their bodies had learned something their heads did not yet know. Neither of them wanted to spoil that. Neither wanted to ask for anything.

"You wanted to ask me something?" she said now.

He turned from the stove.

She stood in the doorway, without Carlo. Paget sensed that she had been there for some moments and that, unusual for him, he had been too abstracted to sense her presence. He looked past her, toward the living room.

She followed his thoughts. "Carlo's waiting outside," she said in a quiet voice. "I told him I wanted to say goodbye."

"I might have wished," Paget answered with equal quiet, "that you'd bothered saying hello."

"He's my son—"

"A cat's a better mother," Paget cut in. "You performed a storage function, that's all. And we both know whom you did *that* for."

"Do we, Chris?" Her smile was bitter. "Do *we,* really? Because I doubt you'll ever know or understand."

Paget's gaze was cold. "I've come to understand a great many things. About you, and about myself."

"Including why *you* did things? Or are *your* motives as pure as ever?"

Paget stared at her, silent.

"It seems," Mary said with muted irony, "that we're beyond the help of a family counselor."

Paget kept watching her. "What I was going to ask," he said more evenly, "is why you're here."

"As I told you, I'm here to do background for an interview."

"You could have come and gone. As you have a dozen times."

"I wanted to see him." She gave a small, almost

helpless shrug; it was sufficiently unlike her to give Paget pause. "Needed to. For reasons of my own."

"What about *him?*"

"Is it really bad," she retorted quietly, "for Carlo to think I care a little?"

"Why now?" Paget shoved his hands in his pockets. "You could have called. I could have prepared him. I wouldn't have stopped you."

"Then call it a moment of weakness, Chris, and trust the good outweighs the bad." She smiled faintly. "We've had those moments before."

Paget looked past her "He's a nice boy," he said finally. "Normal. I think quite happy, for the most part."

"I can see that." She paused, then spoke with more feeling. "It was what I *wanted* to see."

Paget nodded. "Now you have."

She turned to leave. Turning again, she paused in the doorway. "You look well, Chris."

"And you."

She smiled again, as if some private thought amused her, and was gone. Paget stood there, suddenly quite certain that she intended never to see him again.

Now, a day later, she had called.

"If you need me," Terri Peralta was saying, "I can call a neighbor, see if someone can pick up Elena."

They were standing in the elevator on the way

down to the parking garage. He had been lost in memory; it took him a moment to respond.

"Thanks," he answered. "Just go home, be a mom." He saw her puzzlement, realized how dismissive he might sound. "She'll want a referral, that's all."

"Are you sure?"

"Positive. It's never good to represent someone you know, and she's far too smart to want that. Plus I haven't done a homicide in years."

Terri was studying him intently. She doesn't miss much, he thought, but this is more than she will ever understand.

The elevator opened. Paget said good night and walked quickly to his car.

THREE

MARY WAITED IN a witness room on the sixth floor of the Hall of Justice.

The room was spare: a bare table, white cinder-block walls, gray linoleum floors. A squat female cop watched through a glass window to ensure that Mary did not harm herself.

She turned her back to the guard.

The monastic simplicity helped her concentrate. He would want to know what happened; unless the years had changed the way he thought, no detail would be too minute.

He would not, she was determined, find her desperate and without resources.

What would help most was to trace what the police had done. To remember, moment by moment, the four hours that had passed since she stood staring at Ransom's body, telephone in her hand.

"What happened?" Emergency had asked.

She had envisioned the tape spinning, capturing her words and tone of voice. "There's been an accident."

"What kind of accident?"

She hesitated. "A gun went off."

"Someone's been shot?"

"Yes." The stain was spreading on the rug. "I think he's dead."

It sounded so foolish that the tremor in her own voice startled her. "Where are you?" Emergency was demanding.

"The Hotel Flood." She went blank. "I can't remember the room."

"Who is this?"

"Wait. . . . It's registered to Mark Ransom. A suite."

"Who is this?" the voice repeated.

"Just come," she said.

When the two police officers and three paramedics burst through the doorway, they found her sitting in front of the tape recorder, legs crossed, staring fixedly across his body at the drawn blinds of a window.

The paramedics ran to the body. They flipped it on its back, opened the bloodstained shirt, placed pads on its chest. To her, their near frenzy seemed close to pantomime, like practice for a paramedic class. It was standard procedure, Mary supposed; only she knew how very dead he was.

"It's a coroner's case," one of them said.

The others nodded. Much more slowly, they turned Ransom on his stomach, as he had been before. When they rose, stepping back from the body, she saw that Ransom's eyes were still open. With a rush of nausea and anger, she remembered how he had looked at her in the moments before he died. Once more, she hated him.

"What happened?" a policeman asked her.

He was a big man, with a creased young-old face and light-blue eyes that looked immensely sad. He seemed to know who she was; for a moment she wanted to talk to him until she had nothing more to say. Then she caught herself; like the 911 tape, everything she said would be sifted by the police, the district attorney, the media.

"He tried to rape me," she answered.

The cop looked her up and down, pausing at the bruise on her cheek. She became aware that the second cop, a small, wiry man with glasses and a brown mustache and a notepad, was staring at the tape recorder. "Did he?" the first cop asked.

"Did he what?"

"Penetrate you?"

"No." She realized that she had folded her arms.

"Do you need a doctor?"

"No. Please. It's the last thing I want—someone touching me."

Slowly, he nodded. "Could you tell us your name, ma'am?"

The respectful "ma'am" carried a certain irony: she did not date the loss of youth from her fortieth birthday but from the first time the salesgirl at the Saks cosmetics counter had called her ma'am.

"Mary Carelli."

"I've seen you on TV." He hesitated. "And *his* name was Ransom?"

"Yes." Her voice was flat. "Mark O'Malley Ransom."

He paused, perhaps in recognition of Ransom's name, perhaps wondering how much he could ask without giving her Miranda warnings. He seemed to be feeling some new hesitancy, a concern about mistakes.

"Whose handgun is that?" he finally asked.

"Mine."

Her interrogator looked briefly at the second cop. "Thank you, ma'am," he said.

She nodded.

He glanced back at the body. "We'll need to keep you here for a while."

The second cop went to the door and stationed himself outside. The first went to the phone.

The next hour was a jumble that Mary struggled to understand. Several men in plainclothes arrived. They videotaped the body, took pictures. Blinking at the flashbulbs, she watched as a slight blond woman she took to be from the coroner's office glanced quickly at her and then bent over Ransom.

The woman flexed Ransom's arms, felt his forehead and beneath his armpits. Then she examined the surface of his shirt where the bullet entered; inspected his hands; slid an instrument under his fingernails; applied some type of swab to his penis. The woman's cool meticulousness made Mary feel sick. Her throat was dry.

Two more men arrived, one white, one black. The black man had short grizzled hair, a shambling frame that half concealed a paunch, gold wire-rimmed glasses, and an impassive face that seemed never to change. He took in Ransom, then the room.

The woman had turned Ransom on his stomach, examining his back. "It didn't go through," she said to the black man.

She sounded faintly disappointed, as if that were a problem. The black man nodded, and she resumed her inspection of the corpse.

She paused at Ransom's buttocks, eyes narrowing. She traced the scratches with her fingertip.

The black man was speaking to Mary. "Inspector Monk," he said. "Homicide."

She looked up at him, startled. He nodded toward the woman. "There are some things we'll need to do." Like everything else around them, his rich baritone seemed too methodical to be human.

How long must I stay here? Mary almost asked, and then caught herself. Much better that she stayed, she realized. She asked simply, "Can I have some water?"

Monk went to the bathroom and returned with a

glass of water. As he placed it in her hand, the woman appeared next to him. ''This is Dr. Shelton,'' Monk said. ''The medical examiner.''

The woman had level blue eyes and wore no makeup. ''Elizabeth Shelton,'' she amended. We're sisters, the clear voice conveyed; I recognize you. As the woman knelt by the couch, Mary felt a moment's gratitude.

''He didn't penetrate you?'' her new friend asked.

''No.''

Shelton nodded. ''Do you care to see a doctor?''

''No. I don't want to be touched.''

Shelton paused. ''Can *I* look at your neck?'' she asked.

Her expression seemed as sympathetic as her voice. Silent, Mary leaned forward.

Gently, the woman raised Mary's chin with her fingertips. ''How did this happen?'' she asked.

Mary swallowed. ''He did it.'' She hesitated, and then added, ''When he was on top of me.''

''Are you hurt anywhere else?''

Mary touched her cheek. ''Here.''

''What happened?''

''He slapped me.''

Shelton looked at her. ''With his palm open?''

''Yes.'' Mary's voice fell. ''He just kept hitting me.''

''How many times?''

''I'm not sure.''

Shelton hesitated. "Are there other places?" she asked.

Mary looked down at her legs. "Yes."

"Where?"

"My thigh."

Shelton nodded. "Can you show me?"

Mary said nothing. Shelton glanced up at Monk. Wordless, he retreated to the other side of the room.

Gently, Shelton said, "It will help us."

Mary glanced around her. Monk was pulling up the closed blinds. Monk's partner—a pale, balding man who reminded Mary of a priest—was stooped over her black gun. The first uniformed cop watched him with an expression of infinite melancholy.

Slowly, Mary pulled up her dress.

The welt seemed more raised now, a red jagged line beneath her panty hose. Shelton tilted her head. "What happened here?"

"He was trying to pull down my panty hose."

Shelton contemplated the welt. "You had them on, then."

"Yes. Of course."

Almost solicitously, Shelton pulled down Mary's dress. Only after a moment did Mary realize that she was examining the fabric.

"May I look at your hands?"

When Mary nodded, Shelton took each hand in hers. Once more her tone was cool, gentle. "I'd like to take samples," she said. "From your fingernails."

She went quickly to a black bag and reached inside. Then she returned and knelt again, holding a slim metal instrument and a small white envelope. "May I?" she asked.

After a moment, Mary nodded. Shelton slid the instrument under the forefinger of Mary's right hand. As she did, Mary noticed her gold hoop earrings.

Mary still said nothing. Finger by finger, the woman took samples. Suddenly, oddly, Mary felt naked.

"I'm tired," she murmured.

"Just three more." The woman sounded like a pediatrician now, talking to a child. "I'm almost done."

Mary just sat there. She seemed unable to do anything.

"Thank you," Shelton said.

She paused, glancing at the tape player, an unspoken question forming in her eyes. Mary imagined Shelton's surprise when she listened to the tape. Then Shelton rose, breaking her thought, and went to Monk.

Standing beside Ransom's body, they spoke too quietly to be heard. Mary felt utterly alone.

Monk nodded to Shelton and came back. "We'll need to take you down to Homicide, go through what happened."

Mary felt herself stiffen. "How long will it be?" she asked.

"A few hours. You'll have to wait while we clean up here."

He never apologized, she noticed, as if she were the grist for some impersonal machine. "He *abused* me," she said.

"You can tell us that." His voice was neither indifferent nor impressed. "You can tell us all about that."

Something in his tone bespoke hour after endless hour. When Mary stood, her legs felt shaky. She was all right, she told herself. It was just that she had been sitting too long.

"Officer DiStefano will take you," Monk was saying.

The sad-faced policeman took her arm. Haltingly, she let him steer her toward the door. How many hours, she wondered, had it been since she had first entered, taken the glass of champagne from his hand? Listened to the woman's voice on tape, telling her what Ransom wanted?

Turning, she half hoped to see an empty room.

The tape recorder still rested on the coffee table.

The second cop was putting the two wineglasses in a bag. To his left, Shelton had turned Ransom on his back again. Ransom stared emptily at the ceiling as Shelton examined his shirt, then his fingers. She slid two glassine bags over Ransom's hands.

Suddenly, irrationally, Mary felt that she could not leave them alone with Ransom.

"Come on, Miss Carelli."

The door closed behind them.

Downstairs, the lobby felt strange. A concierge, a few tourists, a middle-aged man with his arm around someone who looked like an expensive prostitute. No one else. Some watchful part of Mary's mind registered that the media did not yet know.

Outside, it was cool. As they walked to the patrol car, she was only half aware of the city surrounding Nob Hill. Then a car door slammed behind her, and it was cramped and dark.

In the back seat, Mary found herself staring at the metal grille between herself and DiStefano. He started the engine.

"Just stay here for a moment," she said. "And open the windows. Please."

The Hall of Justice was a featureless monolith, longer than a football field. The lobby was as bleak as the emergency room of a city hospital: dim light; bare walls; green vinyl tile worn by countless footsteps. A few refugees from the urban underclass drifted through the hallways on their way to some business with police. Mary had the surreal feeling of having passed into another life.

They took her to the sixth floor, through a door marked HOMICIDE in forties-style black letters, and put her in an eight-by-eleven room without windows. Someone brought her coffee with powdered cream and a stir stick. She examined the room: a long table, hard wooden chairs, yellow walls, green carpeting. The coffee tasted thin and bitter.

Mary waited for two hours.

What were they doing? she wondered. Staring at the bare walls, she reviewed what Shelton had done: her inch-by-inch examination of the body, her finger tracing the scratches on Ransom's buttocks, her stillness as she studied Ransom's wound. What had she seen?

Reflexively, Mary touched the bruise beneath her eye.

It felt puffy, hurt to the touch. The scratch on her neck made it painful to turn.

Fingernails. Shelton had looked at them. Looked at Ransom's. Looked at the wound again. Sent Mary away.

Monk appeared in the doorway.

"Are you comfortable?" he asked.

"Yes."

"Feel up to talking?"

"Yes." Mary felt new energy. "I want to get this over with."

Monk left, and then he returned holding a tape recorder. He placed it on the table between them.

Mary stared at it. "What's on that tape?" she finally asked.

Monk appraised her. "It's a blank tape," he said. "We record all interviews."

Somehow she had not expected that. Eyes fixed on the tape recorder, she nodded.

He pressed the button. Mary watched the tape begin slowly turning.

"This is an initial homicide investigation." Speaking into the tape, Monk's voice was deliberate, uninflected. "It is January 13 at 4:45 p.m. The victim is Mark Ransom. The interviewee is Mary Carelli. I am Inspector Charles Monk."

Monk took a small white card from the inside pocket of his suit coat. "Miss Carelli, we are obligated to advise you of your rights. I am going to read your rights from this card. Please respond in a clear voice."

"All right."

"You have the right to remain silent. That means you do not have to answer any question I ask. Do you understand that?"

"Yes."

"Anything you say can and will be used against you in a court of law. Do you understand that?"

Mary watched the tape turn one rotation, then another.

"Miss Carelli?"

"Yes. I understand that."

"You have the right to have an attorney present.

If you cannot afford an attorney, one will be provided for you. Do you understand that?''

''Yes. Of course.''

''Do you want an attorney present?''

''No.''

''Do you wish to answer my questions?''

''Yes.'' Raising her eyes from the tape, Mary sat straighter. ''He tried to *rape* me. Does anyone here care about that?''

A moment's hesitation, and then Monk's impassivity returned. ''Did you know Mark Ransom?'' he asked.

''Only in the way that everyone knows Mark Ransom.'' She caught herself. ''Mark Ransom courted celebrity. But I'd never met him before today.''

''How did you come to be in his hotel suite?''

''It was work.'' She paused, and then asked, ''How much about myself do I explain?''

Monk regarded her a moment. ''I recognize you,'' he answered. ''But the tape doesn't, and this is *your* story.''

''All right.'' Mary shrugged. ''I'm a television journalist, for ABC. Since last fall, I've been doing interview segments for *Deadline.*'' Suddenly Mary wanted Monk to confirm her existence outside this room. ''You've seen it—on Tuesday nights?''

Monk considered the question, as if it would change the dynamic between them. ''My wife watches,'' he said at last. ''Go on.''

"That was why I was meeting with him. To discuss a possible interview."

"Who arranged the meeting?"

"It was *his* idea." Mary could hear her own bitterness. "He *called* me."

"Where?"

"He left a message at my office. In Manhattan." She paused. "I called him back from home."

"What did he say?"

"That he thought I'd be interested in the book he'd just finished."

"Did he tell you what the book was about?"

"Laura Chase." Monk did not ask who she was; presumably, Mary thought, the tape recorder was more familiar with dead movie goddesses who had put revolvers in their mouths and pulled the trigger. "Ransom claimed to have new information about her suicide."

Monk looked slightly puzzled. "How long has Laura Chase been dead?"

"Almost twenty years."

"What kind of information did Ransom have?"

Mary paused, keeping her tone level. "About her affair with Senator James Colt."

"James Colt?" Monk said the words softly, as if to himself. For a moment, he seemed to lose the thread of his question.

"James Colt," Mary repeated. "It's part of the whole mystique about her suicide: 'Who Killed

Laura Chase?' and all that folklore about the mysterious woman who called the police to say that Laura had killed herself. It never seems to stop: just last month, someone insisted to me at a cocktail party that the Colt family had murdered Laura Chase to save his chances to be President, and that the unknown caller was the senator's wife.'' Mary's voice turned bitter. ''But Ransom said he had something new that no one knew but him. Something he would share with me.''

''What was that?''

''Ransom claimed that James Colt met her in Palm Springs about a week before she died. She got drunk, took pills.'' Mary paused. ''After Senator Colt got through with her, Ransom told me, he passed her on to two friends.''

Monk's impassivity seemed now to take an effort. ''Passed her on?'' he repeated quietly.

''Supposedly, Colt watched them do it to her.'' Mary looked at her lap. ''Laura Chase remembered him through some sort of semialcoholic haze, sitting in a chair by the bed and sipping a martini while his friends took turns.''

Monk was quiet for a time. ''I don't understand,'' he said finally. ''How does a dead woman 'remember' anything?''

Mary found herself staring at the tape recorder. ''Ransom had a tape of Laura Chase. Talking to her psychiatrist." She paused again. "That was what Mark Ransom called to tell me."

For the first time, Monk's inflection changed. "When you said she *remembered* . . ."

"It's on the tape." Mary hesitated. "The one on the coffee table."

Monk studied the tape recorder, as if newly fascinated by its workings. Mary could see him imagining the tape: the husky voice of a famous actress, describing her abuse by a senator from California—a man who millions wished had become President and whose death in a plane crash was still widely mourned. A man whose son was now poised to become governor.

"You could hurt people," Monk said softly, "with a tape like that."

The words held the resonance of feeling, reminding Mary that Monk lived a life outside this room and that some image of James Colt was surely part of that. Mary had images of her own: James Colt marching with migrant workers; speaking with passion on the Senate floor against the tragedy and waste of Vietnam, yet demanding of college students that they give up their deferments to "fight against a war the less advantaged are fighting in your place." Looking now at Monk, Mary reflected that James Colt occupied a special place for blacks: he had been the last potential President to speak for social justice without apology. The people Ransom's tape would "hurt," as Monk had put it, were not just James Colt's family.

"Yes." Her eyes rose from the tape recorder. "Tapes like that could hurt people."

Monk seemed to settle in his chair; something about him, Mary thought, seemed more tired than before. "Did Ransom say how he got the tape?" he asked finally.

"He bought it." Mary felt the edge in her voice. "From Dr. Steinhardt's daughter. She wanted to keep the house in Beverly Hills."

"Dr. Steinhardt."

"The psychiatrist. He's dead."

"But aren't there rules about that? In this state, we have a psychiatrist-patient privilege."

Mary shrugged again. "Laura Chase and Steinhardt are both dead. Who's left? Only Steinhardt's daughter and . . ." And Ransom, she had been about to say.

"Are you all right?"

"Yes." Mary realized that she had touched her eyes with the fingertips of one hand. "It's just that I saw him for a moment."

"Him?"

"Ransom. When he died, he was staring at me."

"Yes," Monk said. "We'll get to that."

Beneath his voice, she heard the faint whirring of

the tape recorder. "Let's do that now," she said. "I'm tired."

"We just need to cover things."

She opened her eyes. "May I have some water?"

"Sure."

He got up, went out, returned with a Styrofoam cup of cold water. The tape kept spinning.

Monk leaned against the wall. "You've mentioned conversations—he called you at work, you called him at home. Before the interview, were there any more?"

"He called again. To tell me where and when he could see me."

"He chose San Francisco."

"Yes."

"Was that convenient for you?"

"No."

"Why did you do it?"

Mary flushed. "He said he might play the tape for me," she said finally. "If I came alone."

Monk's eyes widened, almost imperceptibly. "That was what persuaded you."

Mary sipped water, selecting her words. "I wasn't interested in destroying James Colt's memory—or in Laura Chase's death, for that matter. I was interested in the ethics of it. Buying and selling people's most intimate secrets, things they wouldn't tell you."

"How did you feel about that?"

"That he shouldn't use the tape." Mary paused. "But I'm also a journalist. Ransom told me that truth was more important than privacy or sentiment, for the dead and for the living."

"Did you agree?"

"No." Mary examined her broken nail. "But it was impossible not to see him."

"Did he say why he contacted you?"

"Yes."

"And why was that?"

She felt herself stiffen. "That he liked watching me on television. And that the 'subject matter' might interest me."

"Did he elaborate?"

"No." Her voice cooled again. "Not until I saw him."

Monk sat down and contemplated her across the tape recorder, hand touching his chin. "What happened," he finally asked, "when you came to his suite?"

Mary looked past him at the wall. Think about each detail, she told herself, one sentence at a time.

"I got there at eleven-thirty." Her voice turned cool. "I expected him to have a publicist. But he was alone."

Monk sat back. "Instead of me asking questions, why don't you just go through it. We can go back over any details later."

Mary found herself watching the tape recorder, mute.

"Maybe," Monk prodded, "you can start with what he was like."

Mary raised her eyes, looking straight at Monk. "He was disgusting."

"In what way?"

"*Every* way." She exhaled. "To really understand, you would have to be a woman."

Monk seemed to smile without changing expression. "Try me," he said.

Mary looked down. "To start," she said finally, "he was repellent physically. He was a tall man, and he tried to be so patrician—his Anglo-Irish accent, the way he would stand, as if posing for a portrait. But it was like watching a figure in a wax museum. Even his skin looked cold. He had this soft white stomach . . ." She stopped herself. "That wasn't until later."

Monk's eyes narrowed. "Take it from the beginning."

Slowly, Mary nodded.

"At the beginning, it was the *way* he looked at me. He was Irish, of course, but he had these ice-blue eyes and kind of Slavic features—a face with a lot of surfaces, and eyes that seemed to pull up at the ends, maybe from plastic surgery. And even when he smiled, his eyes never changed." She turned away. "I remember suddenly thinking that he looked less like an intellectual than like a Russian general at a May Day parade. One whose grandfather had raped his grandmother in some peasant uprising . . ." Mary found that she was clasping her wrist. Quietly, she finished: "I thought that before I even sat down, and congratulated myself on what a clever observation it was."

Monk waited, letting her collect herself. "What did he say when you first got there?"

"That I was a beautiful woman." Monk looked up again. "That the camera didn't capture all of me."

"What did you say?"

"I thanked him." Her voice was ironic. "Of course. Then I changed the subject."

"To what?"

"To his writing. What else do you talk about to a writer who has already proposed his own obituary: 'More than anyone, he saw and wrote the truth about his times' . . . ?"

Monk said nothing. He was waiting her out, she realized; she was digressing, trying to avoid the essence of her story. "It was while we were talking," she said, "that I noticed the tape recorder."

"Tell me about that."

Mary nodded again. "It was on the coffee table."

"Yes?"

"At first I didn't understand. When I sat down, I asked him what it was for."

"You didn't know?"

Mary realized that she was staring at the tape recorder. "I thought he might be recording us for some reason."

"What did he say?"

"That it was the tape of Laura Chase. He was going to give me an exclusive opportunity, he said."

"What did he mean?"

"What he *said* he meant was that when the book came out, I could do the first television interview." She paused again. "All about Laura and James Colt."

Monk folded his hands. After a moment, he asked, "Did Ransom say why he'd brought the tape with him?"

"As bait. He said he might let me listen." She stared at her wrist. "The tape seemed to excite him—he kept looking at it."

"What did *you* say?"

"Nothing. He said that he wanted to talk first, about the book. That we should have some champagne."

"Did you?"

"I didn't want to. But it was a story, and I was there, and champagne was part of his pretense of elegance. So I let him order champagne from room service. We sat on the couch, talking, and I had one glass."

Monk raised his eyebrows. "The bottle was empty," he observed.

"He drank the rest." Mary closed her eyes. "While we listened to the tape."

Monk was silent. "You listened to it?" he finally asked.

"Yes. At some point, I realized that was why I was there. He wanted to *share* it." She paused, speaking more slowly. "He needed me to hear what James Colt had done to Laura Chase."

Monk seemed to search for another question. Then he asked simply, "What happened?"

Mary felt cold. "It was horrible. The last time I had heard Laura Chase was at the movies, or perhaps on her early records. It was the same voice, but there weren't any pictures. Instead I was sitting in a hotel suite with Mark Ransom, while an actress who's been dead for twenty years described how a senator I remembered admiring watched two of his friends take turns with her." She found herself staring at the tape recorder again. "I'm not sure, at first, that I even felt his hand on my knee."

"Ransom fondled you while the tape was playing?"

She nodded. "At first, I thought it was a mistake. I mean, it was more like grazing than touching. Then I stopped and looked at him.

"He just stared back at me. When he knew he

had my attention, he looked down at his lap. Slowly, to make sure I would follow him."

"And."

"He had an erection. That was what he wanted me to see."

The gold-rimmed glasses seemed to magnify Monk's eyes. "He had his penis out?"

"No. It was obvious enough."

"Did he say anything?"

"He offered me an 'arrangement,' to play the tape on *Deadline*."

"Did he say what kind of arrangement?"

"Are you serious?"

"Just what he said."

"All right. What he said, exactly, was, 'I like fucking women I've seen on film. It's as if I've made them real.' "

Monk touched his chin. "What did *you* do?" he finally asked.

"I told him I was much too smart to fuck him, and took his hand away. Then I said to him, much more calmly, that I was willing to deal with him as a news professional and make some other kind of 'arrangement.' "

"What did he say?"

"That *his* arrangement was the *only* arrangement. That I'd like it." Mary paused again. "All this time, Laura Chase is still talking on the tape, about having sex while James Colt watches."

The room was silent. Mary could hear the whisper of the tape.

"What happened next?" Monk asked.

"I stood up, grabbed my purse off the coffee table . . ." Her voice trailed off.

"Yes?"

"Ransom caught me by the arm."

Monk waited for a moment. "Take your time."

"Can I have more water?"

"Sure." Monk stood again. "Anytime you want something, just tell me."

Mary picked a spot on the wall. Don't think about Monk, she told herself. Concentrate on the words. When Monk returned and handed her the full cup of water, she kept her eyes on the wall.

"Go ahead," Monk said.

She nodded. "Ransom spun me around and clasped both of my arms. It threw me off balance . . ."

"Yes?"

"He pushed me to the floor. It was so sudden—I was still holding my purse. And then he was on top of me." She drank water. "Really, I can't remember all of it."

"Why don't you tell me what he did."

"He was grunting, almost—for me to stay still. That he was going to fuck me, no one would know. His face was against my neck. He was hot and smelled like champagne and men's cologne." She stopped for a moment. "Somehow, he pulled open my legs. That must be when my thigh got scratched."

"Go on."

"It was like the wind had been knocked out of me. I remember feeling sick, the room getting dark for a moment, Laura Chase's smoky voice in the background . . ."

"The tape was still on?"

"Yes." Mary nodded. "For some reason, I could hear it clearly. She was talking about the second man, doing whatever he wanted."

Monk examined his tie clasp. "What happened then?" he asked.

Mary touched her face. Coldly, she said, "That was when I started fighting."

"How?"

"I made fists. Hit his face, arms, anything."

"And then?"

"He put one hand on my chest and leaned on it to pin me to the floor, propping himself over me. His face was red, and his eyes were fixed and full of hate. It stopped—just for a second. I half raised my head to look at him." She paused, took one breath, and finished: "Then he raised his arm, very slowly, and slapped me across the face."

"What happened then?"

"I cried out." Mary paused. "So he hit me again."

"And then?"

She looked away. "I stopped fighting."

"Is that the bruise?"

"Yes." Mary kept staring past him. Her voice had become a monotone. "My head hit the floor. Pain shot through my neck. For a moment, it got dark again. I think maybe he was choking me."

"You're not sure."

"No." She swallowed. "The next thing I remember is that my skirt is around my waist and my legs are spread apart, with the panty hose still on."

"What is Ransom doing?"

"He's kneeling between my legs, staring down at me. His pants are around his knees." She paused. "It's so crazy—somehow it shocks me that his pubic hairs are red. There's a red birthmark on his thigh . . ."

From the corner of her eye, Mary saw Monk pause, absently pushing the gold-rimmed glasses where they touched the bridge of his nose.

"What does he do then?"

"He stops for a moment." Mary's voice grew quieter. "I think he's listening to Laura Chase."

"And then?"

"I feel the strap of my purse in my left hand. It's funny: I've never let it go." Mary spoke more softly still. "And then I remember the gun."

Monk's own voice had become quiet. "Go on," he said.

"All this time, I've never spoken. Now I say, 'You can take me. I'll let you do it, any way you want.' His eyes seem to light up." Mary paused, permitting herself a bitter smile. "Then I tell him, 'But only if you use a rubber.' "

Monk's impassivity had become a stare. "What," he asked at length, "did Ransom say?"

"He laughs—kind of a short bark. 'No,' I say, 'there's one in my purse.' It seems to startle him. Before he can answer, I twist and reach into my purse. . . .

"When he pushes me on my back again, the gun is in my hand.

"When he grabs for it, I knee him. His hands are on my wrists. He gives this cry; his body seems almost to twitch. . . ." Mary closed her eyes. "That's when the gun went off."

"What else do you remember?"

Mary bent forward. "Just his face. He looks softer, almost disappointed, as if I had hurt his feelings. I catch him in both hands, an inch or two from my body. His breath still stinks. All my strength, and I can barely push him off." She paused once more, and finished. "That's when I noticed that Laura had stopped talking."

There was silence. Mary felt herself slump in the chair. Over, she told herself. It's over.

She opened her eyes. "Can I go now?"

Monk watched her. "I'd like to ask you a few more questions. Just about what you've told me."

Mary felt a surge of anger. She sat, irresolute, replaying the tone of Monk's voice. His face showed nothing.

"The gun," he said. "Why do you carry one?"

She sat back, drained. "I've had threatening phone calls, she said finally."

"When did they happen?"

"The past two months . . . I don't know, exactly."

"Male or female?"

"Male."

"At work?"

"No. At home."

"Are you listed?"

"No."

"Did the person seem to know who you were?"

"I don't know."

"Could it have been Ransom?"

Mary hesitated. "I don't think so."

"How many calls?"

"Two, I think."

"What did they say?"

"Not much. Just that they were watching me."

"Did you report them?"

"No."

"Did you tell anyone?"

"No. Not that I remember."

"But you bought a gun."

"Yes." Mary summoned a tone of weary patience. "I'm a public person. Those calls reminded me that there are strange people out there, and that I'm a woman living alone."

"When did you buy the gun?"

Mary shrugged. "About two weeks ago."

"Was that before, or after, you first heard from Ransom?"

Mary stared at him. "After, I think."

Monk leaned slightly forward. "You flew here from New York, correct?"

"Yes."

"When?"

"Sunday morning."

Monk cocked his head, as if to consider her from another angle. "Who made the hotel and plane reservations?"

"I did."

"Did you make them through *Deadline*?"

"No." Mary paused. "I paid for them myself."

"Doesn't ABC pay for business travel?"

"Of course." Mary's voice grew impatient. "Why is this important? They can either pay me in advance or reimburse me."

"Did you tell anyone at ABC about seeing Ransom?"

"No. I wouldn't have to."

"Or about his calls?"

Don't be defensive, Mary told herself. "No," she answered.

"And you brought the gun with you?"

"Yes."

"How did you get it out here?"

"In my luggage."

Monk's eyes seemed never to move. "Did you tell the airport people you had it?"

"No."

Monk paused for a moment. "Today," he said, "did anyone see you in the lobby?"

"I don't know. I went right to his suite."

"Once you were inside, did anyone come to the room?"

"Not that I remember."

"What about room service?"

"Yes . . . that . . ."

"Was the person a man or a woman?"

"A man."

"Can you tell me what he looked like?"

"I don't know . . . short. Hispanic, I think."

Monk leaned back. "When you got to the room," he said, "were the blinds closed?"

"I think so." Once again, Mary paused. "Yes, I'm sure."

"There were scratches on Ransom's buttocks. Do you know how they got there?"

"Of course. When I was struggling with him."

"You'd mentioned your fists being closed, and I don't remember anything about scratching his buttocks."

Mary recalled Dr. Shelton, tracing the scratches with her finger. "I don't know," she said wearily. "Maybe it happened when I was pushing him off me. After the gun went off."

Monk nodded again. "When you were struggling with the gun, were Ransom's hands on it?"

Shelton had inspected the dead man's hands, put them both in glassine bags. . . .

"I don't remember."

"When the gun fired, Miss Carelli, how far was it from Ransom's chest?"

She had touched his wound, the torn cloth around it. . . .

"Very close."

"*How* close? Was it touching him?"

"No." Mary could hear the tape recorder whirring. "Two inches . . ."

Monk leaned forward. "Not two *feet,* or three feet?"

"No."

"The scratch on your throat—it happened after Ransom slapped you?"

She had taken samples from her fingernails, then his. . . .

"Yes."

"And then he pulled his pants down."

"Yes."

"Did he have an erection?"

She had taken swabs from his penis. . . .

"Miss Carelli?"

The tape kept spinning.

"Yes." She reached for the empty cup of water. The tape still coiled, slowly, repeatedly.

"The erection." Monk's voice seemed far away. "What do you remember about it?"

"I don't know. It was an erection, that's all. I didn't have time to think about how special it was."

Monk folded his arms. "After the gun went off, what did you do?"

"I don't know. . . . I was dazed."

"How long did it take for you to call 911?"

She had reached under his armpit, felt his skin. . . .

"I don't know. As soon as I was able."

The tape turned again. Once, twice.

"While you were at the suite, did you leave at any time?"

Mary looked up.

"Miss Carelli?"

"Could you stop the tape a moment? Please."

"I can't do that." Monk said calmly. "It's regulation."

The tape turned again, recording silence.

Mary reached out and pushed a button. The tape clicked off.

"I want to see a lawyer," she said. "Now."

FOUR

THEY TOOK PAGET to the witness room, opened the door, and closed it again, leaving them alone.

The way she looked startled him.

The fluorescent light captured with pitiless clarity the change since the previous day: puffy eyelids; a yellow pallor to her skin; the slack beneath her face. Slumped in the chair, her slender frame looked drained of energy, much older and too thin.

He gazed at the bruise next to her eye, then at her eyes themselves. They had a haunted, fearful look she would hate if she could see it.

It was that—the sense that some essence had been taken from her—which made Paget want to touch her. And then feel, in the next moment, that this was the last thing he should do.

"I'm sorry this happened," he said.

She studied him. "Don't feel sorry, Chris. It happened, and it's done. I just want to get out of here."

"Are you all right?"

"Yes. Please, just help me."

Paget nodded. "The first thing is to persuade the D.A. he doesn't have a case."

"How do I do that?"

"I'll help you find a first-rate criminal lawyer—someone who's tried these cases a lot and whom the D.A. respects. He or she can sit down with the prosecution and tell them why they should drop this."

Mary gazed through him, as if she had not heard.

"If you want," he said, "I can probably get someone here to see you within an hour. Get them started."

Slowly, she shook her head.

Paget sat across from her. "I know you're tired . . ."

"You don't understand, Chris. *You* have to do this."

Paget felt a kind of dull surprise. It was as if, he thought, her own shock was a contagion.

"Look," he said at length, "I know you can't believe what happened, that it doesn't seem real. But it is. You need a real lawyer."

"And you're not one?"

"Not for this. I don't do homicides anymore."

"Do this one."

Paget stared at her. Were it not for what she wanted, her new animation would have made him feel better; some life was back in her face.

"If I were going to resume an old career, Mary,

yours would be the last case I'd choose. You don't try cases for someone you know.''

''Is that what I am?'' she said with irony. ''Someone you know?''

Paget leaned back. ''I would have a very hard time defining,'' he said at length, ''all the things you are to me. You know as well as I do the reasons I can't take this.''

Mary seemed to gauge his strength of will. ''They're the very same reasons,'' she said finally, ''that you have no choice.''

Paget felt a rush of anger. ''You're in no position—''

''No choice at all,'' she interrupted. ''As you know all too well.'' The irony stole back into her voice. ''After all, there is so very much that binds us.''

Paget fought for self-control. In a lower key, he said, ''Carlo, you mean.''

She looked away. ''Choose whatever reason you like, Chris. The one that makes you feel best. Just do this.''

''Damn you,'' Paget snapped. ''Think. Think of *him* for once. Even if you walk tomorrow, Ransom's death will be news for months. Whatever else you and I may have done, we've at least kept Carlo's life to himself. But 'The Return of Chris and Mary' will be the stuff of TV movies. You're not just asking me to do something for you. You're asking me to risk changing Carlo's world forever.''

Mary looked up again, her gaze level. ''How do you know,'' she finally said, ''that I'm *not* thinking about Carlo?''

''Because you couldn't be.''

''You are so very good at believing the worst of me.''

''It's hardly a natural gift, Mary. I came by these feelings the old-fashioned way—you taught me.''

Her face closed against him, as if she were withdrawing all feeling. Then she shrugged. ''Have it your way, then. I am, as usual, a cold-blooded bitch. I'm forcing you to put our son through publicity hell to spare me the minor inconvenience of a trial—or, at most, life imprisonment. Because I know how hard you'll work to spare *Carlo* the further trauma of having a murderess for a mother.''

Paget watched her face. ''Why?'' he asked softly. ''Why force me to do this? Just tell me that much.''

''Because I know you'll do whatever it takes to win whatever you decide to win.'' Her voice was quiet, bitter. ''Isn't that what every client wants?''

Paget found himself looking at the scratches on her neck, then at the table. ''No,'' he finally said, ''there's something else. I need to know what's really happening here.''

For a moment, Mary was silent. Paget could not

tell whether she was considering what he had said. Then she sat straighter, looked him in the face.

"What's really happening here," she answered crisply, "is that Mark Ransom was a pervert and a swine, who at the moment that I shot him was especially deserving. Or, as I put it more neutrally to the police, at the moment that the gun went off."

Paget stared at her. "The police," he repeated. "Why did you stop answering Monk's questions?"

"Because I was *tired,* half in shock. Because, however good my reasons, I'd *killed* someone. You can't know how that feels—you don't believe it, and yet you're scared to death nothing will ever be the same." She paused. "For the first time in my life, I stopped coping, that's all. I think I have a decent excuse."

"That's a reason not to talk to them at all, not tonight anyhow. But once you've started . . ."

"I wanted to persuade them, don't you see. Wanted all this over with—to get out of this building without ever needing you or anyone." She paused, exhaling, head bent forward. "The questions became confusing. I couldn't recall things clearly, couldn't follow him anymore. I was afraid of making a mistake."

"How can the truth," Paget asked quietly, "be a mistake?"

"I don't know." Mary shook her head, as if to clear it. "You feel like someone in a Kafka novel.

Like they're going to misunderstand something you said, or did or didn't do, or something you didn't remember quite right. That tape . . ." She paused, touching her face with the fingers of one hand. "I was dislocated. I just had to stop talking, that's all."

Paget folded his hands. "Do you have the wherewithal to talk to me? Monk told me only a little, on the elevator up."

Mary gazed at him. "You'll do it, then?"

She seemed unsure again; it was as if she were too vulnerable to be sure that she had won.

"What I'm agreeing to do," Paget said, "is find out what the D.A.'s thinking. For that I'll need to know precisely what it is you told them."

Mary nodded. "All right," she said.

She seemed to reach within herself. When she spoke again, it was in a monotone—repeating her litany of a dead actress; a squalid weekend in Palm Springs; the dark side of a famous senator; a celebrated but perverted writer; a brutal attempted rape; the gun firing; a spreading bloodstain—as if she were dictating a recorded message. When it ended, an hour had passed, and Paget felt exhausted.

He was quiet for a time, organizing his thoughts. It was odd, he realized; one of the things that slowed him was a recurring image of the day James Colt had died. Paget had told the story to Carlo more than once. He had gone to cash a check and heard the news from a bank teller; tears had begun running down her face as she tried to count out money. He pushed the memory aside.

"Do I know," he finally asked, "everything the police know?"

Mary gave him a look of quiet understanding; he had not asked her about the events themselves. "What you know," she answered, "is everything I told them."

He watched her. "Would you like to finish up with Monk—once you're rested?"

"No." Her voice was clear and cool. "I used to be a lawyer, you may recall. Any tape I give is evidence at trial, mistakes and all. I want you to talk for me. Persuade them there should be no trial."

Paget's eyes met hers. Let her know, he thought, that I'm studying her face. "What about a lie detector test? Those aren't admissible, and they'll likely want one, if only to cover themselves if they drop the case."

"I don't believe in them." Mary's gaze remained steady. "I don't believe they can measure guilt."

"We can do it in my office. If we don't like the results, the D.A. never sees it."

"No," she repeated. "He abused me, and I killed him. I told them that. The only question they're facing is the degree of guilt. I want you to persuade them that they already have the answer."

Paget watched her. A minute, perhaps more, waiting for his silence to work on her. She said nothing.

"Tell me about the medical examiner," he finally said. "Everything she did."

Mary did that, eyes narrow with concentration. When she finished, he asked, "Were there powder marks?"

"Where?"

"On Ransom's shirt."

She leaned back in her chair. "Is that important?"

"I'm not sure yet."

She studied him. "They'll tell you, right?"

Paget let that hang a moment, unanswered. "I expect so," he said finally. "I suppose I'd better go see them."

"They'll be in now?"

"For this—yes. The D.A. himself will be in." Paget stood. "They hate cases like this, you know. Ninety-nine percent of what they get in, nobody gives a damn about. But there are too many ways that something like this, with well-known people, can go bad on them."

"What does that mean for me?"

"Politics, for openers. You have a dead Pulitzer Prize winner, accused of attempted rape by the celebrity who shot him. There isn't a voter with a pulse who won't have some reaction to this, no matter what the facts are or what the D.A. does. It means they're going to be very careful, and that nothing will happen very fast."

It seemed to deaden her; he could watch her imagine days, or even weeks, without an answer. In any other context, Paget would have felt too much compassion to press his advantage. "Which," he told her, "brings us once again to Carlo."

She looked up at him. "Forget," he said coldly, "that you're going to have to tolerate publicity that would make Liz Taylor vomit, or that Court TV will fight to televise your testimony in all its intimate details. You're going to have to *want* that. Because it's not just about who you are, or who Ransom was, or even the terrible stuff about Laura Chase and our late and sainted senator. Your defense lays out as a feminist cause—a fight for justice for all the powerless victims of date rape. No competent defense lawyer would try to win this case at trial without first trying to win it in the media. Including me.

"There's only one difference. Any other lawyer would love that. I'll hate you for it. Because of the son I'll be living with every day. You should think very hard about having *that* kind of lawyer defend *this* kind of case."

When he finished, Mary was gripping the table.

"You were always good," she finally said, "on television."

Paget simply stared at her. In a softer voice, she added, "I'll try to make things right with Carlo."

Paget did not answer her. Instead he opened the door, said briskly to the matron, "We're through here,'' and let them take Mary to her cell without saying anything more.

The district attorney occupied the corner office of a bleak green maze that housed two lawyers in cubicles that a rabbit would resent. Paget's guide, a wiry woman in her mid thirties who had introduced herself as Marnie Sharpe but said little else, steered him through the door. Her air of humorless containment suggested to Paget that she was a lawyer, not the D.A.'s secretary, and that she was already feeling the weight of some responsibility for Ransom.

The D.A. had claimed one of the few decent spaces in the building. There was nothing one could do about the three small windows—neo-Stalinist architecture, Paget thought—but McKinley Brooks had twice as much room and no roommates. There was an Afghan rug, a leather chair, one potted palm, and a wall big enough to house the usual photo collection of a public man: Brooks with several judges, two mayors and, of all people, Luciano Pavarotti. His leather briefcase sat unopened on his desk, as if Brooks had returned hastily from home.

Brooks rose from his chair with a professionally amiable smile and the fluid grace of an ex-athlete still in his early forties and only now running to fat. The carefully trimmed gray Afro, slight double chin, and liquid eyes made him look, at first glance, like the slicker black version of a pleasant Rotarian.

"Christopher," he said in a gravelly voice that managed to make every word sound like a performance as Othello. "What are *you* doing here, nice uptown lawyer that you are?"

"Visiting a sick friend," Paget said easily. "Anyone seen Mark Ransom lately?"

From the corner of his eye, Paget saw Marnie Sharpe's mouth tighten.

"The medical examiner," Brooks answered. "Even as we speak. And you've met Marnie, I assume."

Paget nodded. "Just now."

"Please sit down, both of you. Marnie will be handling this for the office." Brooks looked over at Sharpe, adding, "Chris and I are old friends."

What that was intended to convey, Paget suspected, was that he should be accorded the respect due someone who had given money to Brooks's campaign. The good-humored civility was routine: even in a city as liberal as this one, it had taken a black man as smart and supple as Brooks to win election to a law-and-order post. What was not routine was Marnie Sharpe. Paget knew enough to know that Sharpe was not on the D.A.'s homicide team; it had taken Brooks a few short hours to think through the politics of dealing with Mary Carelli and to decide that it played best with a woman prosecutor.

As if reading Paget's mind, Brooks said, "Marnie's from our rape unit. She's ideally situated to be attuned to all the aspects of this matter."

That, Paget thought, was a particularly neat touch: a prosecutor who could reasonably claim to identify with Mary as possible victim, or could deflect charges of callousness if they decided to prosecute. Paget said evenly, "I appreciate your sensitivity."

Brooks smiled a moment, as if acknowledging the subtlety of the compliment. Something in the smile reminded Paget that, beneath his geniality, Brooks was as sentimental as a Venus's-flytrap. Paget, Mary, and even the pressures on Marnie Sharpe would get as much or as little consideration as Brooks's circumstances required.

Brooks's smile faded. "What *are* you doing here?"

Paget shrugged. "Miss Carelli is a friend of mine."

"The Lasko case." Brooks nodded. "Of course."

Paget felt Sharpe watching from the side, her wary, suspicious look seeming somehow to include both men. "I don't suppose," Paget said, "that either of you doubts this is traumatic for her. Even without all the publicity, stretching it out will make things that much worse."

"It's just a mess," Brooks agreed. "I'm sure you've already told her how little we enjoy things like this."

"Of course. But she's a little beyond the standard consolations. She's been beaten, forced to kill a man to keep from being raped, and thrown in a jail because she wanted to see me. The first two things you can't do anything about. The last one, you can."

Brooks held up a hand. "Please understand. We're not going to shove her in some cell with a bunch of drunks. She'll be as comfortable as we can make her here."

"That's the key word: 'here.' " Paget appraised him. "Right now she's under arrest. Within forty-eight hours, you've got to file a complaint charging her with something, or let her go. You can rearrest and charge her anytime you want. But nothing that happens in the next forty-eight hours is going to turn this into a case. And making someone like Mary Carelli wait two days for you to spring her is bad practice and worse politics."

Brooks spread both hands. "We have to be *cautious,* Chris. We've got a corpse on the first floor who was America's most famous living writer when he checked into the Flood this morning."

Paget turned to take in Sharpe. "How much of Ransom's work have either of you read?"

Sharpe stared at him in silence. "A few of his books," Brooks answered.

Paget kept looking at Sharpe. "Then is either of you really surprised that Ransom tried to rape someone? Because a lot of literate women in this country won't be.''

Sharpe seemed to tense; there was, Paget thought, something brittle about her. It would make her harder to deal with, and the only place it might ever work for him was if they went to trial. ''We have to go on the evidence,'' she said. ''Not on what he may have written. Or was planning to write.''

''Which brings us,'' Brooks said quietly, ''to this nasty tape about Laura Chase and Senator Colt.'' He paused. ''Millions of people still love the man. Including me.''

Paget nodded. ''You met him, as I recall.''

''I *campaigned* for him.'' Brooks shook his head. ''When his plane crashed, two friends and I drove three thousand miles across the country in a state of shock to see them bury him. It was like we couldn't let go.'' He gazed at Paget. ''The country,'' he added softly, ''has never quite let go.''

That was right, Paget thought. Perhaps it was that Colt's plane crash at night in the California desert, three months after Laura Chase had died, had seemed so arbitrary and irrational. With his blond hair and grace of movement, his smile and quick wit, James Colt had seemed at forty impossibly young to be President; yet there had been something bracing in the thought, as if only a country whose best moments lay ahead would choose him. One had not thought of James Colt and thought of death; perhaps that was why the shock of it remained imprinted on the mind like the images of his memorial service: his ash-blond widow, painfully stoic; the unformed face of his teenage son, transformed by the wishes of those watching into an eerie replica of the father.

"Is it true," Paget finally asked, "that James Colt junior plans to run for governor?"

Brooks nodded. "So I understand."

Paget appraised him. "You certainly *do* have your troubles," he said finally. "Which you might do well to leave behind."

"If only we could, Christopher. If only we could."

Paget considered him. "All right," he finally said. "So the M.E. doesn't like the powder marks."

Brooks's eyes widened in mock surprise. "Very perceptive," he answered. "There *were* no powder marks. No gunshot residue of *any* kind. Nothing."

"And so?"

"So it's a problem. The M.E. can't always tell us what *did* happen, but she can pretty much always tell us what *didn't* happen. And what didn't happen here is that Miss Carelli shot Mark Ransom from two, three inches. Not even close."

"That's surprising," Paget said. "Mary's usually so precise. I guess she forgot her ruler."

Brooks's smile was a narrowing of the eyes,

quickly passing. "Nice jury argument. But with Ransom eight hours dead, we can't ignore that. And it's going to keep us thinking for a while."

"Come off it, Mac. Ransom was *attacking* her at the moment the gun went off. Mary could have been wrong. Ransom could have been shrinking back from the gun. Consider the possibilities."

"And I'm sure you'll suggest all that to her. Just as possibilities, of course."

Paget shrugged. "When she thinks about it, I doubt she'll be able to swear to a distance."

"But then," Brooks went on, "there's cutting off Monk's questions. It just doesn't sit right with some of the people you're asking to believe her. And she *did* ask for a lawyer."

"Law school graduates are funny like that. And she didn't ask for a lawyer—she asked for me. It was more like calling a friend, or a priest."

"A priest?"

"Someone who would feel sympathy," Paget said coolly, "as she has every right to expect."

"She will certainly get sympathy. But just like you're not a priest, I'm not an ostrich. One possible construction of pulling the plug on Monk is that she saw she was in trouble."

For the first time, Paget felt a moment of fear. "A far more humane construction," he retorted, "is that she was a bit under the weather." He turned back to Sharpe. "How many rape victims ever report what happened? Maybe fifteen percent, even people like Mary Carelli. They feel ashamed, they feel guilty, they feel alone, and if they report it, then they get to explain it all to some man they've never met, while they're still semitraumatized. Mary Carelli got to explain herself within three or four hours of killing the man who tried to do it, sitting with Monk in an environment where she was utterly lost. So she felt disoriented, attacked, ashamed, and, yes, probably as 'guilty' as any normal person would feel who has just shot someone to death. Even though she's innocent under the law."

Sharpe's face was taut; Paget realized that it was herself, not Mary, whom she saw as under attack. "We know about rape," she answered. "*I* prosecute any case that's righteous. Even if I think we'll lose."

"I'm well aware of that." Paget looked back to Brooks. "You have a fine record on sex crimes, Mac. The people who care know that. Don't throw it away by coming out on the wrong side of a bad case."

Brooks's gaze was cool. "Give me a reason to spring her, Chris. One I can explain to people."

Paget had a bleak, wasted feeling. "I have a reason," he finally said. "But not one I'd like explained to anyone."

Brooks looked curious. "What is that?"

How little, Paget thought, he wanted to say this, with or without Sharpe in the room. "My son, Carlo.

He's fifteen now and lives with me." Paget exhaled. "He's also Mary's son."

Brooks stared at him. "Sweet Jesus Christ," he murmured. "So *that's* why you're here."

"That's why I'm here."

Paget felt shamed; he had expunged Brooks's debt to him by cashing in his personal life, and that of his son, in the hope of a favor. "There are aspects of Carlo's life which have been . . . difficult. But those things have been private. This won't be. He'll get to work through whatever his mother has done with the help of the media. It would help if he didn't wake up tomorrow to find her still in jail."

Sharpe seemed to have removed herself. Brooks gazed at his hands. "What is it," he asked, "that you want us to do?"

"Just listen. Give me every chance to show you this isn't a case before you decide to bring it. And in the meanwhile, let her go."

Brooks looked up. "Will she take a lie detector test?"

"No. On my advice."

Brooks raised an eyebrow. "Of course," he finally said, "she could finish up with Monk."

"She could. But for the moment, I'd like to handle this."

"Because nothing *you* say to us can be used at trial."

"Because that's the way *any* competent defense lawyer deals with your office."

"But you're asking—"

"And because," Paget finished evenly, "the prosecution has the burden of proof. I don't think you have a case. If I'm right, then I'm doing *you* a favor, simply by pointing out why. Plus you get some notion of what I'm thinking."

Brooks looked to Sharpe, then to Paget again. "Okay," he said. "Full disclosure. We decide to bring a case, we'd have to lift our skirts anyhow."

"Better find another metaphor, Mac. At least for press conferences."

Brooks gave Paget a wintry smile. "I wish this case weren't so unpleasant, Christopher. You and I would have such fun. . . ." Abruptly, he picked up the telephone, dialed a number he already knew. "Are you about through with him?" he asked into the telephone, and then said, "We're with Ms. Carelli's lawyer—please come on up," and put down the phone.

"The M.E.," he explained. "She's finished making nice with Ransom."

A moment later, a slim blond woman came through the door and extended a cool hand. "I'm Elizabeth Shelton," she said. "The medical examiner."

"It seems," Paget said, "that you've been quite busy."

She gave him a quizzical smile. ''It's been a very long day,'' she responded, and she pulled up a chair between Paget and Sharpe.

''We've been having a candid chat among friends.'' Brooks waved a hand at Paget. ''Chris understands your problem with the gunshot wound. Maybe you can tell us what else you found.''

''Very little. Almost nothing, in fact.''

''What do you mean?'' Paget asked.

She looked quickly at Brooks and, when he nodded, back to Paget. ''One thing I mean is that there's an absence of the physical evidence I'd like to have. Bullet angle, for one thing. If the bullet goes through, we can trace the path from the body to where the bullet lodges and tell you not only the angle but where he got shot within a couple of feet. But here, the bullet lodged in his spine.''

She spoke with a cool precision, clinical but not unpleasant.

''What else?'' Paget asked.

Shelton considered him. ''The other thing,'' she said finally, ''is there is almost nothing about Ransom's body that confirms what Miss Carelli told us.''

''Well,'' Paget said mildly, ''he *did* have his pants down. That's not standard dress for interviews.''

''No.'' Her eyes and voice were cautious. ''So I swabbed his penis and tested for traces of seminal fluid. You'd expect fluid on a man who'd recently had an erection, even without ejaculation. Nothing.''

"Is that test one hundred percent reliable?"

"Almost no test is. But I'd expect results." Her look grew more intent. "As it happens, I'm no fan of Mark Ransom. But I can't tell you he's a rapist, or even an attempted rapist."

"All right. What else did you find?"

"Miss Carelli said that Ransom reached for the gun before it fired. But there aren't any powder marks on his hands. Again, it depends on how it happened, but powder marks would tend to confirm what she told us." She hesitated. "And of course, there's the fact that she didn't fire from two or three inches or, in my opinion, anywhere within two or three feet.

"In short, Mr. Paget, there's very little about Ransom's body to tell me that Miss Carelli didn't shoot him while they were strolling in the park."

"There were," Paget said evenly, "a few things about Miss Carelli."

Shelton nodded. "Scratches, for example. I took samples from both of their fingernails. There was skin under Miss Carelli's nails, but none under Ransom's."

"What's the reliability there?"

"Low," she concluded. "And we can't even tell *whose* skin it is—in fact, we usually can't. But one of the things we try to do is rule out possibilities. Here, I can't rule out the possibility that Miss Carelli scratched herself and broke a nail in the process."

Shelton's calm was unnerving; she knew her field,

conceded what she had to, and seemed utterly dispassionate. In the right case, she would make a devastating witness.

"You also looked," Paget prodded, "at that rather nasty bruise."

For a moment, Shelton looked puzzled. "Yes." She nodded. "Miss Carelli's left cheek."

"Then did she pistol-whip herself? Or is she just allergic to champagne?"

To the side, Brooks gave the perfunctory smile of a lawyer who appreciates a problem. "No," Shelton conceded. "It looks like a slap."

"With an open hand?" Paget asked.

"Yes."

"Relatively recent?"

"Yes."

"And Ransom, I assume, was right-handed. So that he could have struck Miss Carelli on the left cheek."

"Yes."

"A couple of blows like that," Paget said to Brooks, "and I'd have shot Ransom myself. And if Ransom slapped her, it makes everything she told Monk a lot more plausible and renders the notion that she later decided to scratch herself impossible to explain. Add the tape of Laura Chase and James Colt, which gives Ransom's own sexual problems the awful ring of truth, and you've got no reason to doubt her.

''Which gets me to the last thing—motive. *Our* motive is simple: the man was trying to rape her, and she shot him. The bruise on her face supports that. But if he *wasn't* trying to rape her, why on earth does someone like Mary Carelli shoot a man she only knows through books?''

Brooks nodded. ''No motive.''

''None at all,'' Paget responded crisply. ''No motive, no witness, no case. Leaving the only possible disposition a decision by the D.A. that Mary acted in self-defense.'' Paget finished more slowly, his gaze covering Sharpe and Shelton. ''There are a lot of people out there, a lot of them women, who will know intuitively that's what happened once they see Mary Carelli on television. Gunshot residue won't mean a damn to them. Because they'll *know*. And because after Clarence Thomas and Willie Smith, they *also* know how easy it is for a man to walk away.''

Sharpe frowned; Shelton stared at the rug. ''The women's movement,'' Sharpe finally said, ''is too important to too many women for any of us not to do our job.''

Beneath her didactic tone, Paget sensed as much pride as principle. ''I understand,'' he said mildly. ''But my point was that part of your job—and Mac's—is not to waste moral or political capital on a case that you can't win. Forgive me if I made the point inartfully.''

Sharpe stared at him, unbending and unmollified. "Artfully enough," Brooks said finally. "Can we agree, for the moment, to leave Laura Chase and James Colt out of this? At least as far as the press is concerned?"

Paget nodded. "I imagine so."

"All right." Brooks seemed to expel a short breath. "If you care to wait upstairs for a while, you can take Mary Carelli home."

Paget felt more tension easing from him than he had known was there. "Thank you," he said.

"Just part of my job, Christopher, as you point out. But there are other parts. I assume that what might be called the Paget family will forgive us if we finish the job before signing off on self-defense."

"Of course."

Shelton stood up. "I'll walk you up there," she said. "Perhaps it will move things along."

"I'd appreciate that." Paget shook hands with Sharpe and then Brooks. "I'll be back in touch. Perhaps in a couple of days."

"Do that," Brooks said, and then Shelton whisked him out the door.

In the hallway, she said, "Better me than Marnie Sharpe, I thought."

Paget smiled. "Is that 'M-a-r-n-i-e,' as in the Hitchcock film?"

"Yes. And it's perfect for her. Marnie has two obsessions—her job, and movies." She pushed the elevator button. "You know, I really did look for things to support Mary Carelli's story. I just want an answer."

Paget nodded, and then recalled something Mary had said. "Didn't you examine scratches on Ransom? On his buttocks?"

Shelton paused. "I'm still working on that."

Her voice had a faint troubled undertone. As he waited for Mary, it was that, rather than Sharpe's antipathy, that stayed with him.

FIVE

THE GUARD BROUGHT Mary to a small open space at the front of a row of cells housing spaced-out hookers, chattering druggies.

"Bye-bye, Rosebud," someone jeered, "pretty boyfriend," and then the elevator door closed behind them, and they were alone.

She slumped against the wall. "How," she asked wearily, "did you get me out?"

Paget pushed the button. "Just reminded them of what they didn't have. They'd have gotten there without me."

She was silent. The elevator creaked downward. Both of them, Paget thought, would be content to stay sealed in this space, as long as no one bothered them.

The elevator opened.

Through the glass doors of the entrance, a crowd of reporters was waiting, cordoned by police. Their muffled voices echoed in the lobby.

Mary recoiled. Paget stopped walking; for all that he had said, he was not prepared for this so soon.

"What do we do?" she asked.

Paget saw a cameraman spot them through the glass and then jostle for position. His movement spread through the crowd. Paget felt a flash of anger, at the media and at Mary.

"I'll make a brief statement," he said finally. "Then we'll go. Just be the dazed but dignified victim." He turned to her, heard the bitterness in his voice. "This is the first time anyone will have seen you since Ransom was shot. Your face will be the lead for every news flash. All that people will remember—what Carlo will remember—is how you looked."

She nodded slowly, as if only his words mattered, not his tone. Then she took his arm.

Paget looked down at her hand. "This is the first time anyone will have seen *us,*" she said quietly, "since Washington. What they'll remember is how *we* looked."

Her voice and gaze were level now. Paget had the sudden weary certainty that the separation of their lives since then had been an illusion; decisions once made, he thought, can never be unmade, and debts to the past can never be discharged.

The night before they had testified in the Senate, Mary had called him.

"I have to see you," she had said.

It was almost one o'clock, and Paget had been

unable to sleep. Two months before, they had shared the bed he lay on, but now that was impossible.

"Why don't we just talk," he said.

"I need to see you, Chris. In person."

"Exactly what is it you want?" he asked. "It's all been said."

"This isn't about Lasko." Her tone was cool, determined. "It's personal."

He looked out at the darkened room, at nothing. "Where?" he finally asked. "Here?"

"I don't want people to see us together—the two key witnesses, right before we testify. Someone might think we were deciding what to say." Her voice held a trace of irony. "Meet me at the Jefferson Memorial. You told me once you liked it there."

The night was chill with autumn. Framed by a half circle of cherry trees, the outer shell of the dome was dark; in the pale light within, Jefferson was a solitary stone figure, gazing outward as if waiting for visitors who might never come. Paget turned, walking toward the cement plaza that faced the Tidal Basin. The water was inky black; beyond, centered within a grass rectangle perhaps a mile long, the Washington Monument was a darkened obelisk, tip disappearing into the night. At the far end of the rectangle the Lincoln Memorial was so distant that it looked like a tourist's replica. Paget was alone.

"Hello, Chris."

He turned. Mary wore dark wool slacks, a silk

blouse, a tailored jacket over her shoulders, silver earrings. In the moonlight, her face looked tan and her hair glossy, as if newly washed. She could have been going on a date.

"From what I read," she said, "you've had a busy two months. Since last we spoke."

"As have you, I hear." He paused, examining her face. "What's curious is that it seems to have agreed with you."

"Oh, I'm all aglow."

Paget almost smiled in spite of himself, and then he took a second look at her.

"I'm pregnant, Chris."

He paused, stunned. "You're sure of that?"

"Very."

He turned, staring at the darkened pool. Then he looked back into her eyes. "Whose is it?" he asked.

She stiffened, almost imperceptibly, and then gave a thin smile. "That's hardly flattering."

Paget shrugged. "The last two months," he answered, "have beaten the romantic clean out of me."

Mary looked away. "So much so that our last weekend slipped your mind?"

He was silent. "You know better," he said finally.

She moved closer to him. "The sad truth is, Chris, that a lot of things slipped our minds that weekend."

He folded his arms. "Why are you telling me this tonight? *Especially* tonight."

"Because sooner or later, I'd have had to tell

you." She paused. "I thought later you might appreciate having known it now."

"And why, I'm forced to wonder, is that?"

She squared her shoulders. "Because I'm keeping it."

Paget stared at her. "You must be joking."

"No." Her voice had a determined edge. "I'm Catholic, you'll remember."

In his confusion and astonishment, Paget almost laughed. "All I heard from you was how much you wanted to escape the 'trap'—parents, church, your troglodyte ex-husband who wanted you to have children and 'use your education in the home.' If you were driven by profound religious feelings, it certainly escaped me. Or did you experience an epiphany while we were making love that Sunday morning, and wish you were at Mass?"

Mary frowned. "You were always very clever. But I *am* a Catholic, happy or not. You never know what something means until you're there. There are a thousand things I wouldn't expect you to understand."

Paget found himself gazing past her. "Mary Carelli," he murmured. "The Bride of Christ." When he turned back, her face held nothing but watchfulness. "Forgive me if I suspect some other agenda."

In the darkness, her body seemed to slump. Paget wanted to ask how she felt, and then she straightened again.

"At this point," she said coolly, "it hardly matters what you think."

The words made it sound final, irretrievable, pushed him into another realm: this woman, of all women, might have his child. In their silence, he found himself looking for changes in her body that could not yet have occurred.

"Do you get tired?" he finally asked.

She looked down. "A little. But not sick."

He nodded. "Maybe you should sit."

They sat on a bench overlooking the pond, several feet apart. The night seemed colder yet.

"What is it you want from me?"

In profile, she smiled at the murky water. "Marriage, of course. A ranch house in Potomac."

He waited, silent, until the smile faded.

"Nothing," she said. "Just for you to know. Whatever you do in the future, you do."

Paget watched her. " 'In the future'?" he repeated. "If I follow your logic, timing is everything."

"If you think it is." She stared fixedly at the pool. "I suppose it depends on what value things have for you, one over another. The only thing I'm sure of is that I'm going to have a baby."

Paget felt his eyes narrow. "And," he said, "that you're testifying before the Senate tomorrow."

"Yes." Still she did not look at him. "I don't

think that particular men's club gives exemptions to unwed mothers.''

Paget realized that he was facing in the direction of the White House, shrouded by night and leafless trees. ''We'd better go, then.''

Mary turned, searching his face.

''Yes,'' she finally answered. ''We'd better go.''

Her Volkswagen was parked in the darkness beneath the half circle of trees. Paget walked her there, hands in his pockets, waited as she unlocked the door.

Sliding into the seat, she looked up at him again. ''It's going to be a long night yet. At least for me.''

He watched her taillights until they disappeared.

The next morning, entering the hearing room, she looked as if nothing had happened.

She broke away from her lawyer, came toward him at the back of the room. Her carriage bespoke poise and serenity; Paget was certain that he alone noticed the trace of sleeplessness beneath her eyes. The reporters and photographers taking their positions, the senators and staffers gathering at the raised wooden bench, ignored them both.

''Will you be watching?'' she murmured.

Paget nodded, glancing around them. ''You realize,'' he said quietly, ''what all of this could mean.''

Mary drew closer, looking up at him. ''My life

has changed already,'' she answered with equal quiet. ''And not because of Lasko.''

She turned and walked toward the witness table.

He found Carlo in the library, watching them on television.

The room was dark; the colored images of Paget and Mary came through the glass doors of the Hall of Justice as if emerging from a cave. Gazing at his parents on film, Carlo did not turn or speak.

Paget touched his shoulder. ''I'm so sorry. There wasn't time to tell you.''

Carlo raised his hand, asking for quiet.

On the screen, Paget and Mary were surrounded by reporters, cameras, police. The lens zoomed in for head shots; as if by instinct, Mary leaned against his shoulder, gazing back at the camera. Her face held pain and vulnerability and a kind of wounded strength.

It was perfect, Paget saw. But, at least in this way, Mary no longer surprised him.

Fifteen years ago, he had learned that her face was made for the camera.

The picture changed, recapturing that moment as he remembered it.

A dark-haired woman in her late twenties, leaning forward to speak into a microphone, gaze calmly raised to the row of senators looking down at her. Waiting in the witness room, Paget had seen her on television as if for the first time: wide-set dark eyes; high cheekbones; full, even mouth; a faintly cleft chin whose clean lines finished a kind of sculpture. A face even more vivid on-screen.

The newsman's voice-over echoed in Paget's library. "It was as a young lawyer," the narrator was saying, "that Mary Carelli first came to national attention. In televised hearings of the Senate Commerce Committee's investigation into the William Lasko scandal, Ms. Carelli confirmed charges by Christopher Paget—now her attorney—of corruption against the chairman of the Economic Crimes Commission."

On the screen, the voice-over was replaced by the bourbon drawl of Senator Talmadge of Georgia. "Miss Carelli," Talmadge said deliberately, "I would ask you to describe for this committee, as precisely as you can, how you first became aware of the possibility that Chairman John Woods was leaking Mr. Paget's investigation to William Lasko in order to save the President from embarrassment—or worse. In addressing this pivotal question, I must caution you that as far as we can determine, you alone know whether Mr. Paget is telling the truth about Chairman Woods's involvement."

Paget felt Carlo's shoulders tense; it was as if, Paget thought, even the outcome of events before his birth was once again in doubt.

"I wish I could tell you, Senator," Mary was saying on the screen, "that I would be happy to. But the night of August twenty-seventh contained the most frightening and disillusioning events of my life, and my strongest desire is to leave them behind."

Mary paused. In the silence, the camera panned the hearing room. Suddenly she was a small figure in an oak paneled cavern with ornate chandeliers, confronted by a panel of thirteen senators, staffers at their sides, reporters and photographers jammed into the seats behind her.

As the camera returned to her, Mary seemed to square her shoulders, as she had the night before. "Nonetheless," she finished quietly, "I will do my best."

For the next hour, Mary had held the country transfixed.

Alone in the witness room, Paget had been utterly still, watching television with millions of others. Not knowing what she would say, knowing only that when she was done, it would be his turn to testify.

The events she described were dramatic enough: the death of a witness; the attempt to kill Paget; the night that Mary and Paget had found Jack Woods, the chairman of their agency, about to destroy the evidence Paget had hidden in his desk. But what Paget found so riveting was Mary herself: not simply the tension of what she would say, but the wonder of how she said it. Her voice and expression ranged through sadness and humor, idealism and failed ambition, to fear and resolve and, finally, fatalism. She had lost much and learned much, she seemed to say, and now had come to speak the truth.

Watching her, he at first felt mere surprise, then felt a kind of wonder. It was as if, Paget thought, he had never truly known her.

When at last it was over and she rose from the witness table, Paget heard the door open behind him.

It was Talmadge's aide, a bespectacled man hardly older than Paget. "You're on next," the aide had said.

Paget felt an odd surprise. He followed the aide into the hearing room, still lost in what he had seen and heard.

Mary was walking toward him, followed by reporters hoping for a quick quote. Reaching Paget, she stopped.

Surrounded by reporters, their faces were perhaps two inches apart.

"Did you see me?" she asked.

"Yes," Paget had said simply. "I saw you."

Now, on television, their son saw the moment.

Captured at a distance, her lips moved silently, then his. Faces close, a portrait of intimacy.

"Before the death of Mark Ransom," the narrator was saying, "the names of Christopher Paget and Mary Carelli had not been associated for over fifteen years."

Abruptly they were in close-up again, standing outside the Hall of Justice. Paget could still feel the chill, see faces shouting from the semidarkness as if in a kind of nightmare.

A mustached reporter thrust a microphone at them; instinctively, Mary leaned back. Her hair touched Paget's face.

"Are you representing Miss Carelli?" the reporter asked.

"I'm *helping* Miss Carelli. She doesn't need a lawyer."

"Then you and Miss Carelli have a personal relationship."

Watching, Paget saw Carlo stiffen, felt the life he had constructed for them slipping away. On the screen, he answered evenly, "Yes—we're friends," and, facing the crowd, held up one hand.

"I have a brief statement. All that Miss Carelli asks is that you listen and then let her begin what you surely understand must be a long process of healing."

Paget had gathered his thoughts, searching for a sound bite. Now, with his son, he watched himself.

"At approximately twelve o'clock this afternoon," he began, "in a suite at the Hotel Flood, Mark Ransom attempted to rape Miss Carelli."

There was an eruption of sound, flashbulbs popping, shouted questions. Paget ignored them.

"It was under the pretense of business," he continued, "as these things often are. It was unexpected, as these things often are. And it was undeserved, as these things *always* are."

Paget paused. They were quiet now, waiting for more.

"There was a struggle. A gun fired. What resulted is that rarest of tragedies—an attempted rape where the result is tragic for both the rapist and the victim."

Mary looked down, as if stricken, and then silently back into the camera.

"Mark Ransom's death *was* tragic. Mary Carelli no more wished this talented but tormented man to die than she wished him to assault her. And that is *her* tragedy—that she must forever live with the memory of his assault and the memory of his death.

"That there will be no charges I am certain. But what I deeply hope is that those who know Miss Carelli only as a public figure will now extend to her the same compassion as those of us who truly know her."

On the screen, Mary was in close-up. Paget saw with astonishment that there were tears in her eyes.

As the police had hurried them to the limousine, Mary had taken his hand. She did not let it go until the door had closed.

They were alone then, behind the darkened windows of the one-way glass, separated from the driver by a glass shield.

"That," Mary had said, "was close to perfect."

Paget looked past her. Reporters and cameras pressed blindly against the windows, unable to see. "Yes," he answered. "Just like always."

She drew back. "I suppose we've had enough togetherness. At least for now."

"Yes. I suppose we have."

They said nothing more. The limousine circled the block twice, losing the reporters, and then dropped him at his car.

Carlo pushed the Mute button. In the glow of the television, he looked older than he had that morning. Behind him, pictures flashed without sound, mouths moved but spoke no words.

"Why isn't she *here,* Dad? Why didn't you bring her home?"

"ABC sent a limousine and got her to a hotel, with guards to protect her privacy." Paget hesitated. "She's better than you might expect—it's just that she's so tired."

Carlo shook his head. "But she's alone."

"I know. But I also know *her*. It's what she needs."

Carlo paused and then sat straighter, as if tensed against a blow. "Tell me what happened," he said. "Everything."

Paget sat next to him. Then, as clearly and simply

as he could, Paget repeated what Mary had told Monk.

Carlo's eyes seemed never to move. For Paget, their fixity was worse than tears. "Do they believe her?"

"They don't know." Paget gazed at the silent television. "From their perspective, no one knows the truth but Mary."

Carlo seemed to search his face. "Do *you* believe her?"

Pausing, Paget replayed his son's tone of voice; the question was not about Mary but about Paget himself.

"Yes," he answered. "Essentially."

Carlo was quiet. "Since I've lived here," he asked, "have you ever done a murder case?"

"No."

"Then you should tell her you can't do it."

Paget felt weary. "It's more complicated than that."

"But you can't represent her, Dad, if you don't even believe her."

"You misunderstand me, Carlo. I appreciate we're talking about your mother. But we're also talking about a human being, charged with murder and scared to death. When you're facing *that*, you forget things. Or your story isn't coherent. Or you don't say something because it will make you look less attractive, even if it doesn't mean you're guilty.'' Paget tried to speak more gently. ''Being your mother is a real argument for canonization, but even saints aren't perfect.''

Carlo seemed to search his words for meaning. Finally, he asked, ''You did love her once?''

Paget looked at him. How to talk about this, he wondered, when every word might carry an unspoken subtext: Carlo's life was an accident.

''I thought she was beautiful, Carlo, and even more than that, I thought she was an extraordinary woman.'' Paget paused. ''Did I love her? Did she love me? I honestly don't know.''

''Why not?''

''Circumstances came between us before we had a chance to know. We were two very willful people, who didn't really trust each other. We disagreed violently about politics, and then we were thrust into a situation that was very public and very painful—congressional testimony that destroyed Jack Woods, a man she worked for and deeply admired, and ruined the President they both supported. Our relationship simply became impossible.''

Carlo cocked his head. ''Did you even try?''

Paget heard the question that Carlo had not spoken: Didn't I make it worth trying? ''I know it's hard to understand,'' he said at length. ''You would have been the reason, but we didn't *know* you then. I'm sure that sounds strange now, but you were just an abstraction—you weren't *you* then.'' Paget hesitated. ''We had no plans to marry, no real basis for believing that it would work, and a lot of reasons to think that it wouldn't. That kind of marriage is no favor to a child.''

Carlo's voice turned stubborn. ''Then why didn't she have an abortion?''

''I'm not sure. She could have done it, and I'd never have known.'' Paget paused again, searching for an answer that Carlo could accept. ''But the ultimate answer is that—even if we didn't know you—we both loved you too much already to miss out on who you would turn out to be.'' Paget touched his shoulder. ''We wanted you. We just didn't want to be married and didn't particularly think you'd want us to if you'd had an informed vote.''

''Did you ever talk about it?''

''Not really. Most affairs like ours end with little to show for it. We've been lucky—we've got you, which is much more than either of us could ever have expected.'' Paget tried to smile. ''As for you, you got a whole life out of the deal, and me for a father at that.''

Carlo did not smile. Paget heard his son's next question before he even asked it.

''Why did she give me up?''

Perhaps a hundred times, Paget thought, he had

prepared for this moment, discarding a hundred different answers. ''She didn't really want to,'' he said finally. ''Basically, I forced the issue.''

''Why?''

''You were with your grandparents more than Mary—she was traveling a lot. Your grandparents were loving people, but they were *old* people. She knew that.'' Paget looked at him intently. ''Perhaps I was selfish. But I was pretty adamant on the subject, enough to go to court over it. She knew that too.''

''What did *she* say about it?''

''In the end, she agreed that it was best you be with me. But it was very hard for her to let you go, and harder still to stay away.''

''Why did she?''

Paget paused. ''To let me be your family,'' he finally said. ''To not be the fantasy perfect mother, flitting in and out—to let you and me work things out when things got tough. However complicated my feelings about her may be, I know that Mary Carelli has character, and you should admire her for that.''

For a long time, Carlo just gazed back at him, doubt struggling with the desire for resolution. ''It's pretty confusing—if you're me.''

''I know.''

''Then she comes back, and now this. . . .''

Carlo's voice trailed off. As if reciting a catechism, Paget murmured, ''It's okay, son. It's going to be all right.'' Said that, and then heard himself saying these same words to a frightened seven-year-old boy, eight years before.

But Carlo, of course, did not remember.

''I'm pretty tired,'' he finally said.

Paget knew the conversation was over, at least for a time. ''Sure. But if you want to talk, wake me up.''

Carlo nodded, and stood to leave.

Paget hesitated. ''How was your game?'' he asked.

For a moment, Carlo looked blank. ''Oh,'' he answered. ''Fine.''

Briefly, Paget considered asking who had won and how Carlo had done, wanting to know but afraid his son would see this as indifference to his mother. The moment passed. Silent, Paget watched Carlo climb the stairs.

He felt more tired than he could remember. But then lying had always done that to him, especially to Carlo, and long before this.

PART TWO

THE INVESTIGATION

January 14 – January 22

ONE

"THE WAY TO shut this down,'' Paget told Teresa Peralta, ''is to show Brooks that Mark Ransom was who Mary Carelli says he was.''

For Terri, the moment possessed an eerie normality. They were sitting in Paget's office the next morning. The ten lawyers and staff could talk of little else. Reporters prowled the lobby, and the receptionist fended off requests for interviews. But Paget was having his calls held, and his office was quiet.

Seemingly well rested, Paget had reprised Mary Carelli's statement to Monk with the professional detachment of a lawyer who had been handed the defense of a total stranger. The only apparent difference was the newspaper folded on his desk: the headline read: MARK RANSOM SLAIN; the subheading added: ''TV Interviewer Claims Rape Attempt''; and the photograph was of Mary Carelli in close-up, swelling beneath her left eye, head resting against Christopher Paget's face.

He followed Terri's gaze to the newspaper. ''This

is difficult, obviously. All the more reason to start thinking like a lawyer."

The remark was a concession to feelings that preempted any discussion of them. What he needed, Terri saw, was to deal with Mary Carelli as if she were not part of his life.

"It's pretty simple," Terri answered. "We need some prior acts of abuse. Something we can get before a jury."

Paget nodded. "If we can show that Ransom raped someone before, McKinley Brooks would toss this case quicker than a dead mouse on his kitchen floor. Assuming that the judge would let us prove that."

"There *is* the bruise." Terri paused, surprised at her own anger. "I mean, aren't blows to the face good enough? Or does some creep unilaterally deciding you want him inside you qualify that as foreplay?"

Paget shook his head. "Hardly. But we have to look at this from Brooks's perspective. He's got a case that could ruin his career, not a clue what really happened, and the only witness, Mary, saying what any woman would say who didn't want to go to jail."

"But what if we don't find anyone? What if Mary's the first?"

"Then it's a problem."

"I feel sorry for *any* woman who's some guy's first victim. Who's going to believe *her?* Maybe, after a while, she doesn't want to believe it herself.

Maybe, day after day, she has to see this guy again.'' Terri stopped herself. ''Even if there *is* someone, I think we'd have a tough time getting her to talk about it.''

Paget considered her. ''You were a rape counselor, I recall from your résumé.''

Terri looked away, surprised. ''Just for a semester,'' she said, ''and more in helping with the legal than the emotional side of things. I don't think I was very good at it—I was busy, and it seemed to take a lot out of me.''

Paget gazed at the photograph of Mary. ''It just struck me,'' he ventured, ''that a woman with a bad experience might talk more easily to you. And that in the remote event this thing ever goes to trial, it might be better if you did the questioning as well.''

''I haven't got that much trial experience. A few misdemeanors with the public defender, and that's it.''

Paget nodded. ''That would bother me,'' he said, ''if you were someone else.''

The tacit compliment surprised her. Mary Carelli was Carlo's mother; at a time when Paget must surely feel great anxiety, however he might hide it, he had enough confidence to trust Terri and enough perception to treat her with some tact.

''Do you really believe that?'' she asked, and then felt more embarrassed. The Richie effect, she thought; she was no longer used to compliments.

"Not a word of it," Paget said. "I'm just shopping for a feminist lawyer that everyone on the jury will want to adopt. Someone to offset Marnie Sharpe's warmth and humor."

Smiling, Terri wondered if Paget was helping her cover her own awkwardness. "Then I want to help," she said. "I'm sorry if I sounded funny about it."

Paget seemed to appraise her. "No matter," he said finally. "Rape's a subject that anyone normal feels funny about."

Especially, Terri thought, when it happens to someone you know. She searched for a change of subject.

"What," she asked, "did you think of Marnie?"

Paget leaned back in his chair. "Distrustful, I suppose. And brittle."

"Try steely. I've seen Marnie quite a bit, in court and because she's on the board of the Women Trial Lawyers." Terri paused. "Can I give you some advice?"

"By all means."

"First, don't make her angry. Somewhere inside Marnie Sharpe is a little girl who knows the boys don't like her and wants to hurt them back for it. And she can't make McKinley Brooks the enemy, even though he's kind of set her up. Which leaves you.

"Speaking as one professional to another, you're the kind of man—attractive, polished, seemingly secure—that Marnie despises most. It will be easy for her to feel that beating you would make her whole somehow. And like a lot of unhappy people who can function in the real world, she'll find a socially acceptable way to rationalize her own needs. Not just to Brooks but to herself."

Paget nodded. "I've often thought that a lot of lawyers would be tower snipers if they'd failed the bar exam."

Terri shook her head, wanting to make sure he understood. "Don't make her into a caricature. And *never* underestimate her, 'cause Marnie Sharpe was *always* first in her class. This may sound like pop therapy, but sometimes it helps me to see people as not too much older than Elena, my five-year-old. To me, Marnie is the kid who always did better than everyone else, even though she wasn't the smartest, because working by herself gave her the only sense of mastery she ever had." Pausing, Terri realized that Paget was close to smiling. "Sometimes I take this stuff a little far. It's just that I can imagine you thinking that maybe Brooks made a mistake if Marnie ever had to take this case to trial, and I'm not so sure he did."

"I was just thinking that you read my mind. How do *you* suppose Sharpe will be in court, then?"

"Tough. Hard cases don't scare her. Rape prosecutions *are* hard; she's used to trying cases like this one, where there aren't any witnesses and the evidence is circumstantial. So she's won some cases she should have lost.

"There's something very admirable about her, really. She's made rape her issue—not just prosecution but better counseling and support—and she's earned a lot of gratitude from the women she's helped. And she'll have thought of absolutely everything, down to the sixth permutation, because that'll be all she ever thinks about. To a jury, that comes off as trustworthy and professional. They may not love her, but they'll absolutely believe her."

Paget walked to the window, to stare down at the bay. The water was slate beneath gray skies; there were a couple of sailboats, a luxury liner, and a Honda freighter bringing cars in from Japan. "I liked my version of Marnie better," he said.

For the first time, Terri heard a note of worry. "Of course," she observed, "this time Marnie's going after Mary Carelli."

"I wonder," Paget said quietly, "how that cuts."

Terri tried to read his mood, gave up. "From my perspective," she began, "Mary Carelli is the whole case. So it's a good thing she's a defense lawyer's dream."

"How so?" Paget turned to her again. "I mean, from *your* perspective."

Terri nodded. "When I was at the P.D.'s office," she began, "we represented a lot of people who could hardly speak their names: drugs, alcohol, mental illness, simple illiteracy—you name it. Most of them couldn't even lie well. I tried to keep myself from getting too excited when I found out some client had told me the truth—I might begin to expect it. That was when I started wondering what practicing law did to the psyche.

"But Mary Carelli is more than just credible. She's successful, well educated, articulate. She's a role model for women. She has a very sympathetic story to tell, and there are a lot of people who are ready to support her. She understands the legal process. She's even TV trained, and she was a natural before that—I mean, her testimony before the committee was sensational."

"Yes." Paget looked out the window again. "I saw they ran that again last night."

"She was great," Terri finished. "And of course, she's absolutely beautiful."

Paget did not answer. Terri paused, wondering how he felt about this woman, whether part of him still loved her. "Is Mary all right?" she finally asked.

"More or less." Paget seemed to hear her first, unspoken question. "Forgive me if I sound cold. I'm just trying to see Mary as I would any other client. To me, precisely because of all the things you mention, Mary's someone a judge or jury might turn on if Sharpe could give them a good enough reason. And if I understand Sharpe at all, she'll be deeply offended if she thinks that Mary's using *her* issue as an alibi.''

Terri considered him. ''How bothered are you with the gaps in Mary's story? The bullet, for example.''

Paget shrugged. ''I'm less concerned with whether *her* story is completely right than with what Brooks and Sharpe can prove. Or what they can't prove, such as that Mary had any other motive than rape.''

Terri hesitated. ''I can see you have to detach yourself a little.''

Paget nodded. ''There is one area,'' he said finally, ''where detachment fails me. Carlo. He knows who his mother is, but almost no one else does. We never wanted to bring any publicity down on him.''

''I understand.'' Terri paused again. ''Isn't that going to be kind of hard now?''

''It is.'' Paget stared down at the newspaper. ''I wasn't expecting to represent her.''

Nor, Terri was suddenly sure, did Paget want to. And if that was true, it made no sense that he *was* representing her.

''Before,'' she said quietly, ''I didn't think you were being cold.''

''I appreciate that.'' For the first time, Paget sounded tired. ''I just want to bury this thing. Quickly.''

Confused, Terri searched for something to say next. ''How do we do that?''

"First, we hire a detective named Johnny Moore." Paget sat, crisp again. "When Johnny was an FBI agent in the sixties, he spent three years with the Weather Underground as a double agent, so he's used to looking strangeness in the eye. The white-collar stuff I do bores him to tears, so it'll be a relief to Johnny when I ask him to turn Ransom's sex life upside down.

"Beyond that, we should at least consider speaking to Dr. Steinhardt's daughter. Find out if she had any idea that Ransom was using Laura Chase's psychoanalysis as an aphrodisiac."

Terri looked across at the picture of Mary, imagining what had happened. Her stomach felt tight. "Does the media know about that part yet?"

"No."

"That tape gives me the creeps. With or without James Colt." Terri folded her arms. "Mark Ransom's little version of 'virtual reality.' "

"That's why it may be useful, from our point of view." Paget considered her. "For now, that seems like a place to look."

Terri nodded. "What do you want *me* to do?"

"Didn't I tell you?"

"Not specifically."

"Talk to Mark Ransom's one and only ex-wife. They were divorced five years ago, with an astounding lack of publicity." Paget gave a fleeting smile.

"You might ask if it was just his books she didn't like."

Within two hours, Johnny Moore had called Terri with a Manhattan telephone number for Ransom's ex-wife.

"Melissa Rappaport," Moore said. "Took back her name. She's a free-lance editor, works at home."

"How'd you find her?"

"She was hiding out in the white pages, just like a real person. Maybe she figured divorcing Ransom would buy her a normal life."

Moore's voice was less sardonic than matter-of-fact—mild, pleasant, and faintly Irish. Terri trusted him instinctively.

"How do you think I should approach her?"

"Oh, I wouldn't wear a mustache or anything like that. The best way is what you'd probably do on your own—call her up, tell her who you are and that you want to talk with her. Just be ready for an answering machine: she's probably been called by everyone from *The New York Times* to *Women's Wear Daily,* asking how she feels about the great man dying with his pants off. Keep your message short, clear, and professional."

"I keep thinking Chris should do this."

"No, he's right. Chris is hotter than Warren Beatty after being on those TV clips, and if she's already press shy, a call from him would make things worse. Besides, you'll be an island of feminine calm in a sea of media maggots whose idea of a story is screwing and death—preferably in that order, although for some publications it's not a requirement."

Terri found herself laughing. "I'm sorry," she said, "this really isn't funny."

"Of course not. That's why I make jokes about it."

Terri thanked him and hung up.

She found herself staring at Melissa Rappaport's number, and then at what little else there was to stare at. Her office began to annoy her—it was half the size of Paget's, and she'd put nothing in it but a preschool picture of Elena. Time to stop living like a transient, at work as well as with Richie; maybe she was doing okay here. A couple of posters, something like Picasso or Kandinsky, might make things feel permanent.

Just call the woman, Peralta. Quit stalling. You were always good at talking to people, and at least they'd listen to you.

Anyone but Richie.

Best not to think about that. Richie loved Elena, in his way, and Terri's job now was to make sure that they raised Elena to be as secure as she was smart. If Terri tried hard enough, she and Richie could make it so.

What would Christopher Paget think, Terri suddenly wondered, if she couldn't get Mark Ransom's ex-wife to even return a phone call?

It would help, Terri decided, to have an image of the woman she was calling. But it was hard to picture Mark Ransom's wife. All she could come up with was that Melissa Rappaport would feel far too shocked to carefully weigh the messages of strangers, distinguishing one from another. And all that she could do, Terri decided, was to say what she herself might respond to.

She composed a speech for the answering machine, committed the basics to memory, and dialed the number Moore had given her.

The telephone began ringing. One ring. Two. Three. Four. Terri was not sure what would happen if a real person answered.

"Hello," the cool voice said. "You have reached 501-7216. You may leave a message at the tone."

Melissa Rappaport, Terri thought, wasn't one for insincerity, such as that she was glad to hear from whoever called, or for false promises, like that she'd call back soon or ever. The voice had the crisp economy of someone who got to the point: Terri suddenly envisioned a thin woman, restlessly pacing her apartment, and began mentally editing her message.

The beep sounded.

"This is Teresa Peralta," Terri began. "I'm an

attorney in San Francisco. Our office represents Mary Carelli.''

Terri imagined the woman stopping to listen, surprised at who was calling, poised on the edge of hostility.

''It feels foolish to tell you how much I hate bothering you about something this painful, and then to ask you to call back anyhow. I'm asking because this is so painful for Mary Carelli. I need to help her make sense of this, emotionally as well as legally.

''You may think that you can't help, or just that you don't want to. All I ask is that you not decide until I've told you all I can about what Mary says Mark Ransom did.''

In her mind, Terri saw the woman standing over the machine, caught between the wish to know and the desire to be left alone.

''You can listen,'' she continued, ''and then not tell me anything. Anything you do choose to tell me will be confidential unless you say otherwise. I'm not the press, and I don't think people's lives are entertainment—yours, Mary's, or Mark Ransom's.

''I can be reached at work, (415) 939-2707, or home, (415) 232-5455.

''Thank you for considering this.''

Slowly, Terri put down the telephone.

She checked her watch, saw that it was eleven-forty-five, and decided not to go to lunch for fear of missing the telephone. She wasn't hungry anyhow.

No one called. At two-thirty, her stomach felt concave, her blood sugar seemed to have gone into deficit, and she had begun debating whether it was all right to ask her secretary to get her a sandwich.

In Manhattan, Terri realized, night had fallen.

When the telephone rang, Terri was certain it was Richie.

"Terri Peralta."

"Hello." It was the cool voice of the tape. "This is Melissa Rappaport."

Terri sat upright. "I'm so glad you called me," she said. "Really, thank you."

"Really," the voice answered, "I'm not sure why I did."

The voice was cultivated and very cautious. Keep this going, Terri thought, engage her. "I promised to tell you what happened," she tried.

There was silence.

"Would it be better," Terri asked, "if I came to New York?"

"Just to satisfy my curiosity?" The voice paused again. "What *is* it you want?"

Terri gazed out at the bay, unseeing. She imagined Melissa Rappaport in the darkened bedroom of her apartment, weary from a day's worth of calls she had not answered, connected to Terri by a thread she could break simply by hanging up.

"I guess part of what I'm asking," Terri responded, "is whether the Mark Ransom that Mary describes is anyone you recognize."

"And if it were?"

"Then I could at least tell Mary Carelli she's not alone—that she's not the only one who can imagine what your ex-husband did to her." Terri's voice grew softer. "It's awfully lonely to accuse someone of trying to rape you."

There was silence. "In other words," Melissa Rappaport finally said, "did Mark ever use force."

"I was going to ask that, yes."

"No." The voice was toneless. "He never used force."

Terri tried to replay the words; heard something careful, literal. "Was there something else?"

"Yes." The word had a certain edge. "You said that you would tell me what happened. Or, more precisely, what Ms. Carelli says happened."

Terri felt deflated. "Where would you like me to start?"

"Perhaps," Melissa Rappaport answered, "with how Ms. Carelli happened to find herself in Mark's suite."

Terri stood, striving to remember all that Paget had told her. "He said he wanted to talk to her. About an interview."

"She knew him, I assume."

"No."

"Then why did Mark contact her?"

There was a moment's pause. Terri hesitated, trying to track the careful cross-examination. "What he first told Mary," she answered, "is that he liked watching her on television."

This time, the silence was much longer, the voice a little flatter. "Watching her on television."

"Yes."

"Really. I'd have thought her a bit dark for Mark's tastes. But then I hadn't seen him in several years."

"What were his tastes? That is, when you knew him."

More silence; Terri froze, fearful that she had gone too far. "I'm sorry," Melissa Rappaport said. "That last was a pointless remark. It may take me a couple of days of living with Mark's death to get the emotional range just right."

Terri had begun to feel the long-distance voice as if connected to her nerve ends. For the first time, she was certain that the rigid self-control sealed off some well of feeling.

"*I'm* sorry," Terri answered quietly.

"No matter. The etiquette for this conversation has yet to be written." There was another pause. "Tell me, how is it that Mark is supposed to have—to put it politely—introduced the subject of sex?"

"He suggested that she sleep with him in exchange for an interview."

"For an interview?" Over long distance, Melissa Rappaport's mirthless laughter was close to eerie. "We are *not* discussing Garbo or Howard Hughes. Mark Ransom was hardly a rare commodity. If the price of far too many words from Mark was sleeping with him, then he's screwed every talk show host but Regis Philbin."

Terri felt humiliated. "What he said, to put it *less* politely, is that he liked to fuck women he'd seen on film."

She heard the edge in her own voice a moment after she spoke. Perhaps, Terri thought, that had caused Melissa Rappaport's latest silence; she was about to hang up.

Tonelessly, Melissa Rappaport said, "What a very charming story."

"Our client didn't think so."

"No. I suppose she wouldn't have." There was another pause. "But what makes it so implausible is the idea of Mark offering his face on television as if that gave him sexual leverage."

Terri hesitated. "Not just his face. He was going to talk about a new book."

"Less plausible yet. We in what the more precious among us might call the 'literary community' may find it rather melancholy, but the publication of a novel is rarely the stuff of prime time television. Even a novel by Mark."

Again, Terri heard some buried emotion, a faint rueful edge. "I think," she answered with studied calm, "that *this* book might have been different."

"Different? I must confess that I don't even know what *this* one was about. I suppose I'm feeling a little left out." Rappaport hesitated, and then spoke more quietly. "You see, on top of everything, I used to edit his novels."

Terri thought she heard the last vestige of widowed intimacy. "It wasn't a novel," she said. "It was a biography."

"Biography?" Rappaport sounded surprised. "Not autobiography? That *is* a departure. Who was it that Mark found so uniquely worthy?"

"Laura Chase."

There was silence. Terri waited, heard nothing. Decided to speak again, go for broke. "He had a tape. Of Laura Chase talking to her psychiatrist. He asked Mary there to hear it."

"I see." Rappaport's voice seemed oddly detached. "What is on the tape?"

Terri hesitated. Paget had instructed her not to discuss the tape unless it was a strict necessity: knowledge of the tape would cause a scandal, outraging James Colt's family and those who loved him still. "This part isn't public," she said. "I don't think anyone wants it to be."

Terri's own words came back to her as tentative,

untrusting. ''What makes you suppose,'' Rappaport said in a cold voice, ''that *I* do.''

Terri felt the tension run from Rappaport to her, the thread between them close to breaking. ''It's about Laura Chase and Senator Colt,'' she finally said. ''A weekend in Palm Springs just before she died, where she drank too much and took too many pills.'' Terri paused. ''Colt brought two friends with him. On the tape, Laura Chase describes what they did to her.''

There was more silence. Then Rappaport asked quietly, ''Did Mark actually have her listen?''

''Yes.'' Terri heard the tightness in her own voice, paused once more. ''That excited him, Mary says. He tried to rape her while the tape was still playing.''

The silence lengthened. It was more than seconds, perhaps close to a minute, before Melissa Rappaport spoke again.

''I think perhaps I should talk with you,'' she said. ''In person.''

Paget picked up the telephone. Without preface, she asked, ''Is Carlo all right?''

For a moment, Paget did not respond. Dark had fallen, and the lights of the city were bright and clear; it reminded him of the moments, only an evening ago, before her telephone call had changed everything.

''Terrific,'' he answered coldly. ''Not only are both his parents famous once more, but this morning there were reporters outside when he went off to school. He'll never be lonely again.'' Paget paused. ''Of course, his friends don't know where to call, given that we've had to change our telephone number. But I'm sure the press will ferret it out.''

Mary ignored his tone. ''Do they know about me?'' she asked.

''Not yet. But think what a career-maker that'll be for our son. I rather like imagining Carlo's face on the cover of *People,* superimposed on his birth certificate.''

There was quiet. ''Do you have to be like this?''

''Oh, I certainly think so.'' Paget stared out the window. ''Someone once told me that sarcasm is the safe alternative to expressing anger. And I'm far too civil to be angry at such a difficult moment in your life. To invert what I said to our TV friends last night, those who truly know you should try to extend the same compassion as those who know you only through the media.''

Paget sensed, rather than heard, a sharp intake of breath. ''You know, Chris, you really are a bastard.''

It was curious, Paget thought, that any words from her could still carry the memory of hurt. ''You already told me that, Mary. On a particular disenchanted evening, fifteen years ago.''

Mary was silent for a moment. "All right," she said dismissively. "Then let me be redundant on a subject I care much more about. How *is* Carlo?"

Paget found himself gazing at Carlo's picture. "How Carlo is," he answered, "is worried and confused. Not just about you but about us, in the past as well as the present. This has opened up a lot for him that you and I both know would be far better buried."

There was another silence; it came to Paget as the sound of something Mary had decided not to say. "You may not believe this," she said at last, "but if there were anything I could have done to stop Mark Ransom from doing this to all of us, including jump from the twenty-third story of the Hotel Flood, I would have done it."

Paget leaned back in his chair. "Well," he said at length, "it hasn't been a dead loss. You certainly have Carlo's sympathy, even if you find my response a little wanting. In fact, *Carlo* seems to find my response a little wanting."

"What does he say?"

"Very little. Sometimes, with Carlo, you have to read between the lines. But he seems to want me to exhibit more compassion, and us to act more like his parents than two strangers." Paget realized that his gaze had not moved from the picture; Carlo, a year younger, smiled back from a time of seeming innocence. "I suppose there are certain archetypes that arise from something deep in all of us, like it or not. Such as those involving mothers and fathers."

"Yes." Mary's voice was drained of feeling. "Mothers and fathers. Which brings us back to what I, or we, can do for Carlo now."

"It's quite simple. Get me off this case."

There was more silence. "Other than that," she answered quietly.

It was a moment before Paget felt his own anger. "Then why," he said, "did you ever ask the question? Had you read somewhere that caring was good form?"

She did not answer. Paget sensed her framing some retort, then repressing it with effort. "I have my reasons. And they *are* mine."

Paget felt his eyes narrow. "When, Mary, were your reasons ever anyone else's?"

Paget heard her exhale, the sound of impatience. "This gets us nowhere. I asked about Carlo, not you."

Paget stood, angry, then found his self-control. "All right," he said. "Short term, the only thing I can think of is for you to give him some reassurance that you're okay and, as you put it during your unexpected visit, that you care a little."

Mary was silent. "You asked me for dinner," she said coolly. "Maybe I should accept. That way you and I can pretend for Carlo that we're not the Addams Family.''

Paget hesitated; the image of Mary inside his home felt more invasive than the cameramen outside it, the pretense it would require far more wearing. But he had already lost control of things, and the sole remaining question was how Carlo would respond.

''Let's do it on Friday,'' he said at length. ''By that time I'll have revisited Brooks. If we can get some time alone, we can talk about whatever's happened without your coming to the office.''

''Fine,'' she answered briskly. ''I certainly wouldn't care to invade each and every one of your private spaces. Incidentally, what *has* happened?''

With surprise, Paget absorbed the fact that she had killed a man yesterday and yet had talked mainly of their son. ''My associate's going back east to see Ransom's ex-wife. Terri thinks there's something there but has no idea whether it's helpful stuff or just emotional confusion.''

''And you're sending some associate—this Terri—rather than go yourself. How old is she?''

''Twenty-nine.'' Paget paused, then added softly, ''The exact age you were when the Lasko case went down.''

With equal quiet, Mary answered, ''That means nothing.''

Paget began pacing. "You wanted me to represent you, and you won. Now you'll have to start trusting me, just like any lawyer you were desperate to have."

"Do you trust me, Chris?"

"No." Paget gazed out the window. "But then I wouldn't anyhow. I only trust my clients when long experience has taught me that I can."

Mary did not answer. Something in her silence made Paget feel less than human and then wish for a way out.

"Has the press bothered you much?" he asked.

She seemed to consider whether to even respond. "Not much. The guards have kept them away. And room service has exceeded my expectations."

How was it, Paget wondered, to be a prisoner in a strange hotel room? "A few days," he said, "and we should be able to get you out of town. In the meanwhile, don't talk to the press until we've both worked out a script."

"Then we should do that." Her tone was businesslike again. "I may be going on *60 Minutes* this Sunday."

"You've *already* talked to them about it? The day after Ransom dies?"

"Not me," she said coldly. "My agent. As you said, this is now a problem in public relations. And that's who deals with public relations when I'm too devastated to speak for myself."

The uneasy mix of irony and truth made Paget feel a kind of shame. "How *are* you?" he asked.

"Fine. Wouldn't you be?"

"No."

"Then you have one more reason to admire me," she said, and hung up.

"Why New York?" Richie asked. "I thought there was no travel in this job."

Bringing Elena home from day care, she had found him intently focused on the computer in the bedroom of their apartment, creating a complex graph that represented his imagined new enterprise. The computer, Terri realized, symbolized the differences between them: Richie looked at the screen and envisioned his ideas turning into money; Terri remembered what the screen had cost them. Forty-five hundred dollars, sitting on their charge card.

They had argued for two days, until Richie had worn her down, and then spent another three days while a newly energized Richie had dragged Elena, Terri, and her MasterCard through a half-dozen computer outlets, excitedly querying salespeople about the latest options. At the end, Terri was exhausted from watching Elena, and Richie had a laser printer and the best new color graphics.

"I said not *much* travel," she told him now. "Almost any law job has *some* travel."

"But why you?" he queried. "It's *his* girlfriend."

Once more, Terri was glad that she had not told Richie about Paget's son; her own confidences to Richie had a funny way of coming back with a little twist at times when she felt most vulnerable.

"Not girlfriend, old friend. And I feel good that Chris trusts me to do this."

"So it's 'Chris' now." Richie gave an exaggerated shrug. "Absolutely, then . . . whatever 'Chris' wants."

"Don't be an ass, Richie. Do you want me to call him 'Mr. Paget,' like Mary Tyler Moore used to call her boss 'Mr. Grant'?"

She felt Richie watch her, saw him choose a lower key. "What it is," he said, "is I've got plans, dinners with people who might invest in Lawsearch. I can't be baby-sitting Elena."

" 'Baby-sitting'?" Terri repeated. "You mean the thing teenagers do with kids who aren't theirs?"

"You know what I mean," Richie snapped. "Tied up."

"Maybe you can talk to them during the business day."

"Can't. They've all got jobs."

Terri searched his face for conscious irony, saw none. "Yes," she said. "A surprising number of people do."

Richie flushed. "That's abusive, Ter. How can I share my plans with someone who uses them to hurt me?"

For a moment, Terri found herself just observing him. Thin, wiry, with curly brown hair and intense black eyes, which had always made him seem consumed by some compelling inner vision. When she first met Ricardo Arias, he was only twenty-two. But he had struck her as different from anyone she'd ever met—full of ideas, yet always in motion, driven to make his best dreams real. Between Richie then and now were a law degree, the MBA she had helped him pay for, and three jobs he had not kept, and the endless motion seemed less that of an achiever than of a wind-up toy Terri had placed before Elena in the living room, to distract her while they talked.

"I'm sorry," she said. Partly for the thoughts. Partly to deflect him.

"It's okay." Richie kept his voice deliberately flat. "Maybe you don't always hear the way you talk to me."

The words were meaningless. Did she imagine, Terri wondered, the triumph in his eyes whenever she backed down, or had he taken so much out of her that she, like him, had begun to believe that every hurt was meant to help steal from the other some essential self. "I guess I worry about the dinners," she said finally. "Our credit's at the limit."

"It can't be helped. I can't get their attention during the day. Besides, dinners are a better place for them to get a feel for me."

Terri said nothing. In Richie's mind, a fancy restaurant, and not their bare apartment, spoke to who he was. Only Terri seemed to see Richie at the dining-room table they had never owned, the down-payment money lost on his last deal, the new dresses she too seldom bought Elena. The night before their latest move, when the last place had gone condominium, she had found herself staring into a packing box and thinking that the fruits of their marriage were their old college yearbooks and two honeymoon albums, complete with funny captions that seemed to have been written by some other woman.

"Mommy," Elena asked, "can we have macaroni and cheese tonight?"

She was standing in the doorway, holding her wind-up duck. A beautiful five-year-old with Richie's eyes. The real fruit of their marriage.

"Sure, Lainie." Richie scooped Elena up in his arms. "Mommy'll make that. Daddy likes it too."

Terri went to the kitchen, Elena and Richie chattering behind her.

That night, she did not sleep. The next morning, she left money for a baby-sitter, drove Elena to day care, and caught an eight-thirty flight to New York.

TWO

MELISSA RAPPAPORT WAITED in the doorway of her apartment.

Terri had not expected this. And something about Rappaport herself put Terri on edge; a too-slim woman in her forties with a thin face and marmoset eyes that shone with a bright intelligence. She wore little makeup, and what might have been unruly black hair was tamed by a hairstyle short enough to be severe. Her clothes enhanced the impression of someone too serious to care about frills—gray slacks, turtleneck sweater, flat black pumps, no jewelry at all. Even Terri's wool suit and white blouse felt inappropriate and overdone.

Rappaport's hand, extended to Terri, felt fragile. "You've come so far," she said. "Mark would have been flattered."

"I appreciate your seeing me."

"Yes?" The word held a note of denial, as if Rappaport wished to forget her own suggestion that Terri come. "Well, please step in."

They walked through an alcove, past a library with

bookshelves from floor to ceiling, and entered the living room.

The room was spacious, furnished with spare iron sculpture and abstract prints. The hardwood floors were a bleached white, and the furnishings were white Italian leather; the absence of color lent the sensation of someone who had bled the emotion from her life.

''May I bring you some coffee?'' Rappaport asked.

Terri sensed that she would rather busy herself than talk; she projected the neutral and slightly distracted air of someone who had been snatched from thought by a visitor of no great interest.

''Black coffee would be nice,'' she said, and Rappaport left the room.

The front wall was virtually consumed by a rectangle of glass. Through the window, Central Park in winter looked like a moonscape—grass shrouded in snow, empty paths, a pond frozen to an icy mirror. Clouds darkened the distant towers of the East Side, casting shadows across bare trees; their naked branches reminded Terri of the sculpture in the room itself. Staring into the park, Terri wondered how a free-lance editor could afford the view.

As if to answer, Melissa Rappaport spoke from behind her. ''This apartment was Mark's originally. Of course, the furnishings are quite different now.''

Terri nodded; there was little here that matched her sense of Ransom. "The view is lovely," she said.

"Thank you." Rappaport handed Terri a china cup and saucer, gesturing toward the couch. "Please sit down. You won't mind if I stand—I sit all day."

"Of course."

Rappaport stood with her hands in her pockets. Her posture lent a certain mutability to the moment, as if a change of mood would send her to the door. Terri decided to say nothing.

"Your telephone call," Rappaport said at length. "I suppose it shook me." Her tone was neutral, as if she were speculating about the emotions of someone else.

"I'm sorry," Terri said.

"We were married for almost six years, you know. I sometimes hear people say divorce is easier without children. . . ." The woman shrugged, cutting herself off.

"How did you meet?" Terri asked.

Rappaport's lips formed something halfway between smile and grimace. "I was Mark's editor. At Doubleday."

"That must have been quite interesting."

"Challenging. Mark had such talent—he was like a volcano, spewing words in wonderful bursts and torrents. There was life on every page. It was just that he loved each phrase too much, could never slaughter his babies.'' Rappaport's voice had a staccato intensity Terri had not heard before. ''I suppose I gave him the structure he needed, a sense of where passion became excess.''

''That's important,'' Terri said. ''For me, sometimes it's the difference between finishing a book and picking up something else.''

Rappaport looked at Terri more closely. ''Have you read anything Mark wrote?''

''The novels, mostly.'' Including, Terri did not add, the one she had reread on the flight east, to refresh her memory.

''What did you think?''

Terri sipped coffee, considering her answer. ''I liked the lush way he used language—for another writer it would have been too much, but Mark Ransom could immerse me in a world where I didn't want to turn the pages too fast. Also he seemed to feel his male characters from the inside, even the worst ones, so that I could believe that they were particular human beings and not types.''

There was life in Rappaport's eyes now, a hint of challenge. ''And?''

Terri met her gaze. ''And,'' she said slowly, ''the way he wrote about women made me uncomfortable.''

The strange semismile reappeared, as if this were familiar ground. ''Why, exactly?''

''Because he never wrote from a woman's point

of view. They were always seen from the outside, either as bitch goddesses or as something for two men to compete for. The sex was conquest. . . ." Terri paused. "I didn't get the feeling Mark Ransom liked women, that's all."

"When I met him, that's not quite how it seemed to me." Rappaport's tone held the trace of ancient argument, with someone else than Terri. "Writers need understanding; fear impairs it. Mark had great understanding of everything but women because we frightened him so much."

"But why?"

Rappaport shrugged. "I think it happened to Mark the way it happened to other men I've known—their mothers. I never met Siobhan Ransom, but my sense is that she made Mark live his boyhood under a sort of military occupation of the mind and heart—no privacy, much guilt, few male activities, and tremendous pressure to succeed or lose her love. And his father was a cipher." Rappaport turned to the window. "Mark was sterile, you know. He couldn't have children."

"No. I didn't know."

"No one was supposed to. It hurt him very badly." Rappaport became pensive. "I used to think Mark believed that somehow his mother had stolen his manhood. And that beneath Mark's sexuality was an anger born of fear."

Terri nodded. "They ran an old tape of him on

television last night, denouncing the pro-choice movement. He tried to be ironic, but he seemed to feel such anger. Not just at abortion but at the women who spoke up for abortion rights.''

''Oh, I think Mark took all that personally somehow.'' Rappaport clasped her hands; Terri had begun noting the small aimless gestures of a woman trying not to reach for a cigarette. ''I tried not to feel any anger of my own but to understand why Mark had become the way he was.''

Terri looked at her curiously. ''Was that hard?'' she asked.

''Yes.'' Rappaport turned to her. ''But *I* cared. For Mark's sake, and for the sake of what Mark wrote.''

''Did you feel that his writing became better. I mean, in *that* way?''

''In *that* way, I did nothing for him, in his writing or in his life.'' Rappaport's voice was quiet, bitter. ''But then Mark's writing didn't kill him, did it? Your client did. That's why you're here.''

Terri was silent, unnerved by the shift in mood. Then she asked, ''Did Mark ever watch Mary Carelli? Or talk about her?''

''No. Of course not.''

''Why 'of course not'?''

''Because she's neither interesting nor appealing.'' Rappaport frowned. ''I understand that she's quite beautiful and that people watch her interviews, but to me she's all surface and calculation.''

But what did *he* think? Terri wondered. ''Plus she wasn't Mark's type, you said.''

''It was a cheap remark—or wounded, perhaps.'' Rappaport snatched a black purse from the coffee table in front of Terri and reached inside for a cigarette. ''Really, I'm a bit sorry I troubled you to come. You called me at a moment of disequilibrium.''

Her tone was dismissive. Terri felt something akin to panic; Rappaport seemed to be slipping away, as if she had taxed her own patience. Instinctively, Terri said, ''I felt you reacting to Laura Chase.''

The cigarette paused in front of Rappaport's lips. ''Was that what it was?''

The question sounded rhetorical. ''Yes,'' Terri repeated quietly. ''I think it was Laura Chase.''

Carefully, Melissa Rappaport picked up a silver lighter, snapped forth a flame, and took one deep drag of her cigarette. She smoked hungrily, Terri thought, like a man.

Terri broke the silence. ''Did Mark ever talk about Laura Chase?''

Rappaport sat at the other end of the couch and placed an ashtray in her lap. She looked not at Terri but at a Kafkaesque print, distorted rectangles and broken lines. ''Mark,'' she said finally, ''was obsessed with her.''

"Obsessed?"

"I chose that word with care. Mark read everything there was about her, had a scrapbook of publicity pictures, knew all about her marriages and the hundreds of men she'd slept with, all the apocrypha about Laura and why she died—a preoccupation so morbid that, in my mind, it became a sort of mental necrophilia. And he'd heard the rumors about James Colt, of course. I think he even *imagined* himself as Colt: to him, it made sense that one of the most powerful men in America would take a woman who, Mark once wrote, 'was the primal image at the heart of every male, half goddess and half slave.' " She gave a mirthless laugh. "Mark even made me watch her movies, over and over, until I knew every line as well as he did."

"Made you?"

Terri saw Rappaport nod slightly. "Not literally. I *wanted* to, you see, so that I could understand what went on inside him." Rappaport took another drag. "I was in my early thirties when I met him, but I hadn't that much experience with men."

"What did you expect to learn?"

"How to be a woman, of course. I was less than certain of myself that way—sexually." Her tone was still ironic, but her mouth was set in a line. "I was trying to learn what so appealed to Mark about Laura Chase, and he was going to learn to love that part of me that wasn't her at all. Or so I thought."

Terri shifted in her chair. She had begun to feel Rappaport resonate with the echoes of a long-ago psychic explosion, from which the current woman had been reconstructed with great care. "Laura Chase," she said, "was not much like you or me or anyone else I know."

"Do you mean bleached blond and voluptuous, with a mock-sexy voice and an air of undereducated precocity? Or do you mean alcoholic, nymphomaniac, and wholly lacking in self-esteem?" Rappaport paused, as if listening to herself. "In the end," she continued more softly, "all I shared with Laura Chase was a lack of self-esteem. And that, it now seems clear, was exactly what I'd started with."

Terri's coffee cup was half full; she had not touched it in some moments. Finally, she asked, "Was that because of how he treated you?"

Rappaport shook her head. "He treated me that way because that was who I was. Toward the end, when he lost interest in me, I grew more desperate."

"Lost interest?"

"Physically—he wouldn't react to me. It made me *try* harder, as it were. I'd always believed that I was smart but not that I could make someone love me. During the day, I'd slash words, scenes, whole chapters, imposing enough discipline on his talent so that people would want him." She paused, staring fixedly at the print. "At night, I would do anything Mark asked."

Terri's voice felt tight. "But he didn't mistreat you."

"No. He simply pretended to."

It was a moment before Terri understood. "He invented scenes of some kind?"

"Of a particular kind." Terri saw that the cigarette had burned close to Rappaport's fingers. "He would pretend to rape me."

Silent, Terri reached over and took the cigarette from Rappaport's hand. The woman seemed not to notice. Placing it in the ashtray, Terri saw that her own hand was shaking.

"How did he 'pretend'?" Terri asked.

"With my cooperation, of course." Rappaport's words, measured and toneless, had the inevitability of catharsis. "Every night I would call him from work, to tell him that I was leaving. Then I would ride home on the subway, wondering whether it would happen. It was part of our game.

"You see, what made it work for Mark was that he would never tell me. I would open the door and find a darkened apartment, not knowing whether he had gone out or was inside, waiting.

"I never knew until I felt Mark smother my mouth.

"I never knew how, or which room. All I knew was how worthless it made me feel." Rappaport's profile was still and white, and her gaze seemed directed at something outside the room. ''Sometimes he left without saying anything at all. Like a stranger who had raped me.''

Terri was conscious of her own body, small, taut, leaning forward. ''Did you ever tell anyone?''

''No. It was just a game we played.'' Rappaport's eyes shut. ''But he's dead now, isn't he.''

Terri's throat was dry. ''When we spoke,'' she said finally, ''something connected all this with Mary Carelli. I thought then it was the tape.''

''The tape?'' Rappaport touched her eyes. ''Of course, you had no idea what you were dredging up.''

Terri watched her. ''Can you talk about it?''

Rappaport nodded, silent.

Terri waited. When Rappaport spoke again, her eyes had opened, and her voice was dry and precise.

''The apartment was dark, as if it might happen. But he had been going out more, playing our 'game' less and less. I didn't expect him to be there.

''When I saw a faint glow from the bedroom, and then a shadow crossing it, I was almost grateful.

''I was alone in the hallway, bracing myself, when he came through the door.

''All I saw was a flash of red hair.''

Abruptly, Rappaport stood, as if at a sound that only she heard. ''He threw me over his shoulder, too hard. I remember my head snapping back, being dazed. Before I knew what was happening, he had thrown me facedown on the bed, pulled up my dress, torn my underwear and stockings from behind.

"Mark took me that way.

"I still didn't understand. Then he grabbed the hair at the nape of my neck and wrenched my head up. To show me.

"The light was from the television screen. He had a stag film on the VCR.

"It was Laura Chase.

"She was very young, before she became a movie star. There were two men with her. It looked like she was crying.

"Mark's face was next to mine, watching the two men take her as he had me, from behind. I didn't know that I was watching too, until I began to cry."

Rappaport paused, tears in her eyes. "When the film was over, I knew that I would never be with Mark again. But I didn't know why Laura Chase had killed herself until I spoke to you."

Terri looked away. "I'm so sorry."

Melissa Rappaport turned to her. "Don't be. It was the last time I was ever with a man." Her smile seemed more painful than her tears. "You see, *that* was what I learned from Mark."

"That," Paget's voice said, "sounds like what we needed."

From a telephone booth, Terri watched the baggage carousel spin. Drained by a long flight spent thinking of little but Melissa Rappaport, she still held the scrap of paper with Paget's new telephone number. "If she's willing to testify," she answered. "And if the judge will let it in."

For a moment, Paget did not answer; the sound of someone paging a John McDermott echoed in the cavern of an airport at night. "Would you mind dropping by here?" Paget asked. "I hate to keep you, but I'm seeing Brooks and Sharpe tomorrow morning, and it would help to know exactly what she told you."

Terri hesitated. It was seven-thirty and the sitter had said that Elena was asleep. Paget sounded anxious, and something about Rappaport had made her feel more alone.

"Give me directions," she said.

A half hour later, Terri found a three-story white Edwardian with bay windows, a slanted roof, and a spotlit palm tree that seemed to have migrated from Los Angeles. She stopped to examine the tree, struck by its incongruity.

"I keep hoping it'll die," Paget's voice said. "But the thing's obnoxiously healthy."

As Terri looked up, he rose from a lawn chair on the front porch and came down the stairs, dressed in jeans and a white Irish fisherman's sweater.

"I like it," she told him.

"You and Carlo." He gave the tree a look of mild

bemusement. ''That foolish palm is why I bought this place.''

''Because of a tree?'' She turned to look again. ''This must be the world's most expensive palm.''

''Tell that to Carlo.'' Paget stood next to her, contemplating the tree. ''After he came to live with me, we went out one day to look at houses. Nothing interested him until we saw this place, and then I could hardly get him to leave. He told me we had to live here because the tree looked like home.''

Terri glanced at him, surprised. ''Where had he been living?''

''Boston, of course. The date palm capital of Massachusetts.''

Terri smiled. ''Kids' minds are really funny. Elena once asked me why Richie and I hadn't taken her on the honeymoon.''

Paget cocked his head. ''That's one question that Carlo's never asked.''

Terri was quiet. ''So,'' she finally ventured, ''whose idea was the spotlight?''

''Mine. Or so Carlo informed me.'' Paget turned to her. ''Ever notice how literal little kids can be?''

This was not, Terri thought, a conversation she had ever imagined. ''Sure. I try to be pretty careful about what I say to Elena.''

Paget nodded. ''We drove away from here, Carlo still chattering about the palm tree. The whole thing was so bizarre I could hardly keep from laughing—

I was about to spend a million dollars to buy a tree I couldn't stand. So I turned to Carlo and said with utter seriousness, 'Don't worry, son, not only will your doting father buy this house, but I'll get the lighting on the tree just right.' It was one of those remarks you make to a kid which is really for the amusement of another adult—or, in my case, because I was laughing at the idea of myself as a father." Gazing up at the spotlight, Paget shook his head. "It was also a mistake. Carlo remembered every word."

Terri smiled at him. Silent, Paget kept his eyes on the tree; she had the sense that he needed to talk about his son but seldom did, so that now he felt embarrassed.

"We'd better go in," he said. "I'm keeping you."

"It's all right. Richie's out, and I wanted to tell you about Rappaport."

Opening a beveled double door with a brass knob and door kick, Paget led her inside.

The interior made Terri's preconceptions seem foolish. She had vaguely imagined the movie-set trappings of inherited wealth—the oak paneling, brown leather, and oil paintings of dead ancestors more appropriate to some private men's club. The actual decor was light: white walls and blond hardwood floors, with track lighting and bright splashes of color everywhere—a deep-red Persian rug, vases and silk flowers in various hues, an eclectic assortment of vivid prints and oils, which somehow enhanced each other rather than clashed. Passing the library, Terri saw a long marble fireplace and then a shelf full of games, which, like geologic periods, seemed to trace Carlo's passage from seven to fifteen. Terri felt a moment's envy, for Elena's sake more than for her own: Christopher Paget's house felt as if the same people had lived here for a while, adding pieces of themselves over time, secure in the knowledge that this was their home.

"That's a lovely fireplace," Terri said.

Paget nodded. "Carlo always liked me to build a fire for him, read stories in front of it. When he was younger, the library was his favorite room."

"Your whole home is beautiful, really. Did you do all this yourself?"

Paget nodded. "That's what explains all the primary colors," he said. "Carlo and I have a complete lack of subtlety no decorator could match."

Smiling, Terri felt the seemingly light remark bring Paget into focus: he was clinging to a life that might now change irreparably, and for the wrong reasons. It lent an unsettling note of worry to this lightness about Carlo.

"Where is he?" she asked. "I've never met him."

"Studying, I hope." Paget glanced up the staircase. "If you don't mind, perhaps we can chat in the kitchen. I was just cleaning up."

Paget looked slightly uncomfortable, as if concerned that his manners had lapsed. Terri realized that he preferred that his son not walk into the middle of the kind of conversation this was likely to be; thinking about Mark Ransom and his mother, she was sure, had already been hard enough.

"That's fine," she said. "I like any kitchen that I don't have to cook in."

The kitchen was what she now expected: high-tech, track-lit, spacious, light. On the other side of a bleached wooden counter were two white leather-covered barstools, where, she guessed, Paget and his son ate breakfast. Terri declined a glass of wine and sat with her hands folded in front of her. Paget leaned casually against the counter, as if to help her relax.

"Just tell me about Rappaport as it happened," he said. "From beginning to end."

For forty minutes, Terri did that.

At odd intervals Paget would interject a question, as often about how Rappaport looked or acted as about what she said. Terri sensed him piecing together this woman from whatever Terri gave him, adjusting the picture here or there, with the dispassion of an archaeologist reimaging a long-dead creature from a few scraps of bone. His face showed nothing save a slight narrowing of the eyes; Terri could not tell whether this reflected a reaction to what Rappaport had told her or to Terri herself.

When she had finished, Paget walked to the refrigerator without a word, poured a glass of white wine, and held it out to her. "If you don't want this," he said, "I'll drink it."

Terri realized that she wanted it. When she had sipped awhile, Paget said, "A few more questions."

"Sure."

He leaned back on the counter, regarding her. "Did she say Ransom had other women?"

"I assumed that." It sounded foolish, Terri felt, and was. "She didn't say so."

Paget nodded. "When she said Ransom had lost interest, did she mean that literally, or was she talking about some failure of performance?"

Terri hesitated. The question had not occurred to her. "I'm not sure."

"Did she know anything about Ransom's sex life outside her own experience—from Ransom himself, or anyone else?"

"I didn't ask her that." Terri stared at her wine. "I should have."

Paget smiled faintly, shaking his head. "Perhaps at a deposition. Not when you're watching a self-possessed woman unravel because she's telling you things you want to know but wish had never happened to her, until you're no longer sure you even want her to keep talking."

Terri felt surprise, and then something like relief. "I felt ashamed," she said. "Like I was taking something from her."

"I think not, in the end: it's what Ransom did to

her that's awful, not the facing up to it. What strikes me is how much she seems to have taken out of you.'' He paused for a moment. ''Do you always fool yourself when something's bad?''

Terri hesitated. ''This shouldn't be.''

Paget shook his head. ''What she told you is quite extraordinary, and it connected you to what she felt. That's how you know you're not a sociopath, or dead.''

Terri kept gazing at the glass. ''It was unbelievable,'' she finally said.

''I really don't know how you got her to say all that.'' Paget poured himself some wine. ''But by doing it, you've given Mary far more credibility than she could ever have on her own.''

''Do you think they'll drop this now?''

''Quite possibly. One problem with Mary's story is that Ransom's connection to her is so arbitrary—it's like deciding to rape Barbara Walters because you saw her on *20/20*. I can understand Brooks and Sharpe thinking that there must be something more.'' He paused, as if trying to imagine himself as Sharpe. ''What the D.A. has to accept,'' he finished, ''is that, like Melissa Rappaport, but for reasons only Mark Ransom could ever have explained, Mary Carelli became the object of his Laura Chase fetish.''

Terri finished her wine. ''There *is* one difference. Which got Mary where she is.''

"Which is?"

"She wouldn't play the game."

Paget considered her. "Mary Carelli," he said, "has never played anyone's game but her own."

His voice had a faint sardonic edge. Terri was still trying to decipher that when she discovered with surprise how very much Mary Carelli resembled their son.

"Am I interrupting?" Carlo asked them.

How long, Paget wondered, had Carlo been standing there, and what had he heard?

Carlo looked from his father, to the wineglasses, to Terri. With perfect composure, Terri slid off the barstool, extended her hand to Carlo, and said, "I'm Terri Peralta, your father's associate. So all you're interrupting is your father attempting to make sense of things, and me attempting to listen with my usual respect. Unfortunately, I'm doing better than he is."

Carlo's air of uncertainty eased a bit; through intuition or sheer luck, Paget saw, Terri knew that the surest way to disarm Carlo was to poke fun at his father.

"That explains the wine," Carlo answered. As he turned to Paget, his expression was more equable. "You guys were talking about my mother."

Paget nodded. "Terri's trying to help me prove

that Mark Ransom was what your mother says he was.''

Carlo looked at Terri again. ''Do you think you can?''

Paget watched Terri appraise Carlo's face, react to the confusion she saw there. ''Speaking strictly for myself,'' Terri said, ''I think Mark Ransom did stuff like this long before he made the mistake of picking on your mother. If I'm right, then there are other women out there who didn't have the wherewithal to protect themselves the way your mom did. We've been trying to figure out how to find them, and what made your mother more able to take care of herself.''

Terri, Paget realized, had neatly covered their conversation, putting a benign spin on the ambiguous comment Carlo might have overheard. The boy began fidgeting, as if not wishing to talk more but afraid of missing what else might be said.

''I assume,'' Paget ventured, ''that your original purpose was not to meet Ms. Peralta, but to raid the refrigerator. Ice cream, or milk?''

''Both, actually.''

Terri glanced at her watch. ''I should be going.''

The comment sounded perfunctory, Paget thought; Terri had the relaxed posture of someone with nowhere to go. ''Why don't you have some ice cream,'' he suggested.

Carlo nodded. "I can spare a little."

"What? And create another chubbette?"

Paget looked at Terri's small frame, slim wrists. "In which life?"

"This life. I'm absolutely convinced that somewhere in Latin America, there's another Hispanic woman named Teresa Peralta who's wearing all the doughnuts I ate in high school." Terri turned to Carlo. "Because of me, she weighs at least three hundred pounds, and no one asked her to the winter prom."

"It's okay," said Carlo. "Our winter prom was awful. No one danced."

"So have some ice cream," Paget said.

Terri gave a theatrical sigh. "When I'm this tired," she said, "I've got no social conscience."

Carlo sat next to Terri, while Paget dished out two bowls of ice cream. "What about you?" Terri asked Paget.

"Never touch the stuff. Especially now."

"Why not now?"

"So I can recognize myself when they run old clips of the Lasko hearings. . . ."

"The truth," Carlo interjected, "is that my father runs five miles every morning and weighs himself six times a day. He wants to make the cover of *Seventeen.*"

"*American Bride,* Carlo. And every parent needs

a hobby to help compensate for disrespectful children. I've selected vanity, and I'll thank you to respect that."

Terri laughed. "Do you two always carry on like this?"

"Only when Carlo gets gratuitous reinforcement." Paget looked from his son to Terri. "Unfortunately for me, he seems to have found his natural audience."

Terri grinned at Carlo. "I guess he's right," she said, and then turned to Paget. "I don't want to hurt your feelings or anything, but during the Lasko hearings I was an eighth-grade cheerleader."

Paget looked at her in mock horror. "Tell me," he said, "do you even remember Paul McCartney's group before Wings?"

Carlo pointed to Paget. "Do you even remember *him?*" Carlo asked.

"Vaguely," Terri said. "But your mother has aged quite well."

Carlo burst out laughing. "Your move, Dad."

"I was just thinking, Carlo. Before I yank the barstool out from under her, you might want to ask Terri all the questions I'm too old to answer—stuff about dating, acne, things like that. You might even ask her why a superficially presentable fifteen-year-old, despite living in these modern times of which I am so dimly aware, can't get a couple of mere parents to let their daughter go out with him. Although, on reflection, Terri may only be able to help you with the daughter.''

''What is this?'' Terri asked Carlo.

Carlo put down his spoon. ''I've got this girlfriend, Jennifer, only she's more like my girlfriend at school. Her parents won't let her go out on weekends.'' He frowned. ''It can't be *me*—they don't even know me.''

''Then maybe that's the problem.''

Carlo turned to her. ''What do you mean?''

Terri finished her ice cream and put aside the bowl. ''I had the world's greatest mother, all right? She wasn't the way these people sound—I could talk to her about anything, and she trusted me a lot.'' Terri propped her chin on her hand. ''But it was an unwritten rule that nobody took me out until they spent a little time around the house.''

Carlo looked curious. ''Did she ever say why?''

''I think mostly so my mom would get some handle on who they were.'' Terri paused, reflecting. ''Also,'' she went on, ''I think she wanted the boys who took me out to remember I had a family, someone who cared. Like Jennifer's parents, she had a lot invested in me.''

Terri, Paget thought, had a gift for talking to Carlo on equal ground.

"True," Carlo said. "It's just that being *those* people doesn't sound like a lot of fun."

Terri nodded. "Probably not. But what my mom said it told her was whether a boy thought I was worth the trouble." Terri's expression turned questioning. "Do you think Jennifer's worth the trouble?"

Her tone held neither challenge nor reproof, as if the right answer was whatever Carlo felt. Watching Carlo reflect, Paget began to believe in Terri's mother.

"Yes," Carlo said. "I really think she is."

Terri smiled. "What's she like?"

"Really nice. Good sense of humor." Carlo paused. "She's just really nice to be with."

"Carlo," Paget observed mildly, "can make Venus de Milo sound generic. Jennifer probably has an IQ around one fifty and looks something like Winona Ryder."

"No," Carlo answered. "She's just nice."

" 'Nice,' " Terri said lightly, "is a hard concept for your dad to grasp."

"I get 'nice,' " Paget protested. "That's like Santa Claus, isn't it? Or Harvey the Rabbit?"

Terri and Carlo smiled at each other. When she was truly amused, Paget saw, Terri's grin cracked white and sharp. Carlo's smile in return was more genuine than Paget had seen it lately; with foolish surprise, he realized that his fifteen-year-old son not only liked this woman but thought she was attractive.

"Hopeless," Carlo said.

Turning, they both looked amiably at Paget. "Hopeless," Terri agreed.

Paget smiled. "That's what shock treatments are for." He turned to Carlo. "At the risk of introducing a grim note of realism, how is your English paper going?"

Carlo gave a comic wince. "It's going. And so am I." He turned to Terri, hesitated, and then said seriously, "Thanks for helping with my mother."

"I'm happy to. But it's really your father." She touched Carlo's shoulder. "All kidding aside, she can't do any better."

Carlo seemed to consider that. "He certainly works hard enough," Carlo answered. Saying goodbye to Terri, he went back upstairs.

Paget turned for a moment, as if listening to his footsteps, and then looked back at Terri.

"I appreciate that," he said. "Things have been a little tough around here lately."

"I'm sure." Her face was thoughtful again, and then she gave a small smile. "This much is true—ten years ago, *I* was a teenager."

Paget smiled back. "Now I *do* feel old. Perhaps I should be consulting your mother." He leaned back on the counter. "Do you still talk to her a lot?"

"A fair amount." Terri hesitated. "There are a few things we find it hard to talk about."

"I guess that happens. You get married and develop a zone of privacy."

Terri looked away. "I suppose that's it," she said, and glanced at her watch. "God, it's nearly ten. I really should go."

"Sure." Paget felt embarrassed. "I'm sorry to have kept you."

"You didn't. This last was nice, after Melissa." Terri gazed at her wineglass. "Part of me," she added finally, "wishes I only knew about Mark Ransom through books."

Paget nodded. They walked together to the door.

The night air was cool and crisp. "This may not be the time to mention it," Paget said, "but there's Dr. Steinhardt's daughter. Specifically, whether she had any sense of how Ransom was using the tapes."

Terri looked up at him. "You'd like me to go see her?"

"I'd like you to go see her." Paget paused. "Hard or not, you did well today."

Terri smiled faintly. "All right."

Turning, she stepped onto the porch, gazing down at the tree-lined street. At night, the three-story homes were covered by darkness. In the streetlights some distance away, a woman with a large dog moved from light to shadow, shadow to light, reappearing and then vanishing again. Terri folded her arms, as if against the cold.

"Where are you parked?" Paget asked.

She did not turn. "Just a little way. Maybe a block and a half."

Paget watched her. "Would you like me to walk you to your car?"

Terri was silent, and then said simply, "Please."

THREE

SHARPE AND SHELTON were waiting with Brooks in his office. Feeble morning light came through two windows with a view of several parking lots and a highway overpass. The room, Paget thought, had looked better at night.

"I understand," Brooks said briskly, "that you have a little something to share with us."

Paget nodded. "My associate saw Mark Ransom's ex-wife. It turns out that Ransom had some peculiarities that should sound quite familiar."

Brooks raised an eyebrow. "Then we're all anxious to hear about them."

Their anxiety, Paget thought, registered in distinctly different ways: Brooks's expression was one of calm neutrality; Shelton looked interested but somewhat uncomfortable; and Marnie Sharpe folded her arms and sat straighter, as if extending a courtesy for which she had little patience and little time to someone she had little inclination to trust.

"The short is this: Ransom had rape fantasies and

a sexual obsession with Laura Chase." Paget paused. "Mary Carelli got to see them converge."

Brooks's gaze came as close to a stare as he ever permitted. "The wife says all that?"

"More or less."

"You'd better lay it out for us."

Paget kept it succinct, letting the story speak for itself. No one interrupted. At the end, Brooks whistled softly. "That, Christopher, is truly disturbing."

Shelton, Paget saw, was examining her hands. Sharpe's unwelcoming look had become one of intense concentration. "*I* thought so," Paget said. "And it explains what Ransom did to Mary better than she ever could."

Sharpe gave a short shake of the head. "Not to my satisfaction," she said slowly. "Even assuming that Ms. Rappaport wants to come forward, which you haven't said, I doubt it's admissible."

"Admissible?" Paget turned to Sharpe. "We're not at trial yet. What we're discussing is an issue of fairness."

Sharpe's face closed against him, and her tone became didactic. "The issue *I'm* raising is relevance, which also happens to govern admissibility. You're suggesting that her story involves a prior similar act. But Melissa Rappaport *consented* to this particular practice. That is *not* a rape and therefore does not suggest that what your client says happened was part of a pattern of nonconsensual sex. The reason a judge wouldn't let it in later is the reason it doesn't satisfy us now."

The "us," Paget thought, was an assertion of authority. He paused to ensure that he responded with sufficient tact. "That's far too literal, Marnie. There is such a thing as psychological truth. Two different women, five years apart, confronted something in Ransom that is *very* particular. The reason to believe Mary Carelli is the same reason I get this into evidence at trial—because it makes what Mary told you *feel* right. Which is exactly what you'd argue if this were a rape prosecution."

Sharpe gave him a thoughtful look. As Brooks watched her, silent, Paget realized that Sharpe had started to invest in the case and that Brooks had moved from prosecutor to referee, carefully weighing his own interests.

"*Will* she testify?" Brooks asked.

Paget turned. "I don't know, Mac. I hope never to ask. It would be fairly uncomfortable, and not just for Rappaport."

Brooks considered him. "If you mean would we *enjoy* that," he said finally, "of course not."

Brooks, Paget saw, had followed him perfectly; his pretense of opacity was meant to force Paget to speak their understanding aloud.

"Actually, I was thinking of James Colt."

Brooks's mirthless smile came and went. "The one who's dead," he asked, "or the one who's running for governor?"

"Both," Paget answered, "and all the people who admired the father and support his son. Including the widow Colt and her very wealthy family. None of whom, as you've already conceded, will be eager to watch you add Laura Chase's less than glowing memories to the family annals."

"That tape," Sharpe cut in, "will be in the public domain as soon as Ransom's publisher gets someone to finish the book. Whatever your client's motives, she has virtually guaranteed that the Laura Chase biography will sell a million copies. The damage to the Colt family will already be done, and it won't be the fault of this office."

That was right, Paget knew. And if Mary was indicted, her story could merge with Laura Chase's, creating a media event that would lead them straight to Carlo. Once again, he felt the trap in which Mary had placed him: his best chance to protect Carlo was to prevent an indictment.

Slowly, Paget turned to Brooks. "You *have* listened to the tape, I assume."

Brooks nodded. "I have."

"Then speaking strictly as a human being," Paget continued, "how did you feel hearing Laura Chase's voice when she describes James Colt watching as his two friends had her?"

Brooks was quiet for a moment. Shelton turned toward a window with no view; Paget guessed that she, too, had listened to the tape.

"Speaking strictly as a human being," Brooks answered slowly, "what I was—God help me—was fascinated and repelled."

"And do you think simply *reading* about it would be quite the same experience as *listening* to it?"

Brooks's eyes narrowed. "No. I don't."

"Nor do I. And while we're about the business of calculating audience shares in the millions, how many million people watched the Willie Smith trial?"

"On Court TV," Brooks said flatly.

Paget nodded. "On Court TV. Because I would absolutely do that, Mac. If this case goes to trial, I'd insist that the judge let them show it nationwide. Then, like any defense lawyer in his right mind, I'd ask to play that tape. I don't know about your standing in the polls, but your Nielsen ratings will go right through the roof."

Brooks folded his hands in his lap. "And James Colt's family?"

"I've never been interested in politics." Paget paused, then finished softly. "That family means nothing to me. As I mentioned the last time, I have my own."

Paget heard Sharpe's curt intake of breath. Brooks looked from Paget to Sharpe and back again.

"There are problems, Chris. New ones."

Brooks's reluctant tone troubled Paget more than bluster. "Such as?"

Brooks looked to Sharpe. "More discrepancies," she said. "At least one seems quite serious."

Don't seem anxious, Paget thought. Turning to her, he assumed an expression of polite inquiry. Her lips tightened, as if she was nettled.

"To begin with," she said finally, "Mary Carelli told Inspector Monk that the blinds were drawn when she came to Ransom's room. Monk thought that sounded peculiar. So he asked the waiter who brought the champagne from room service. The blinds were open—he's quite sure of that."

Paget tried looking puzzled. "From which you extract what, exactly?"

"We're not sure, obviously. But it raises the possibility that Ms. Carelli closed the blinds for reasons of her own."

"Can you suggest a reason that makes her indictable?"

Sharpe looked at him closely. "We don't indict people," she said in cold tones, "for closing their blinds. But people sometimes close blinds so other people can't see what they're doing."

"Which," Paget answered, "raises the possibility that Ransom closed the blinds because he was planning to rape Mary Carelli and that she didn't notice or didn't recall. Assuming, that is, that the waiter remembers the precise status of each individual window shade in each of the many rooms he no doubt visited that day—a question you might care to ask him before making too much of this.''

Behind Sharpe, Elizabeth Shelton smiled faintly.

''I did,'' Sharpe retorted. ''He distinctly remembers Ms. Carelli. He thought Mr. Ransom was a lucky man.''

''He certainly *tried,*'' Paget said. ''But then, as Somerset Maugham once observed, 'luck is a talent.' ''

Sharpe flushed; Shelton's smile was replaced by a closer scrutiny of Sharpe. In quick succession, Paget had two impressions: that Shelton did not care for Sharpe, and that something was troubling Shelton that Paget did not know.

''Forgive the levity,'' he said to Sharpe. ''I'll ask Mary about the blinds, of course. Is there something else?''

''Yes.'' Sharpe looked distinctly unmollified. ''Ms. Carelli says that she never left the suite. But another guest believes that he saw her enter the suite as he got off the elevator. I should say *reenter;* the guest was returning from lunch at about one o'clock, well after Ms. Carelli says she arrived.''

For the first time, Shelton spoke. ''One o'clock,'' she said carefully, ''is the approximate time of death.''

Paget turned back to Sharpe. ''Is this guest certain it was Mary?''

"He only saw her from behind. But it was a dark-haired woman, around five feet eight or so, who carried herself like Mary Carelli."

Paget considered her. "Assuming that it was Mary, I expect what he saw was Mary arriving, perhaps earlier than he thinks."

A brief triumphant expression crossed Sharpe's face. "She wasn't arriving," she answered. "No one came to the door. The woman let herself in."

Sharpe had gained confidence, Paget realized. It was as if she knew that the same calculation which had caused Brooks to stick her with Mary Carelli gave her much more leeway than usual. He decided to speak for Brooks's benefit.

"But what does it mean?" he asked. "Ransom's rape fantasies and the Laura Chase tape *mean* something."

Without responding, Sharpe turned to Shelton. Her look was a curious admixture of deference and command; Paget perceived that Shelton had been summoned to speak on cue.

"There's one more thing," Shelton said slowly.

"What is it?"

Shelton turned from Sharpe, speaking to Paget as if they were alone. "Do you remember that night, on the elevator, when you asked me about the scratches on Ransom's buttocks?"

"Yes."

"I've gone back over them, thought about it quite

a bit more." She paused, then added quickly, "I don't think they were made until after Ransom died."

Paget stared at her. "After?"

"Yes. Not seconds after, or even a couple of minutes. Appreciably after."

Paget tried to organize his thoughts, found none. "On what do you base that?"

"The scratches themselves." Shelton's gaze held his. "The normal scratch, such as those you saw on Mary, are like a red welt. The red color comes from bleeding under the skin, broken capillaries. But Ransom's scratches are white."

Paget noticed that Brooks had gotten up and was standing behind Shelton. Reluctantly, Paget asked, "What does that tell you?"

"Ransom's skin was damaged, just as Mary Carelli's was. But there was no bleeding, no burst capillaries. Because, in my opinion, his heart had stopped pumping blood." Shelton leaned forward, hands clasped in her lap. "It's really just a matter of gravity. A dead person's blood ends up in the lowest extremity, like a garden hose after you turn off the spigot. By the time the buttocks were scratched, most of Mark Ransom's blood had gone to his chest."

Paget touched the bridge of his nose. "Are you certain of that?"

"Not certain. No."

"But it *is* your opinion," Sharpe interjected.

Shelton gave a reticent nod. "What I would testify, if asked, is that what I have just told you is more probable than not."

"Which means," Sharpe said to Paget, "that Ms. Carelli waited at least thirty minutes to call 911. Before which she left several scratches on the buttocks of a corpse, quite possibly to make Ransom's death look different than it really was."

Paget gave her an incredulous look. "That's bizarre. This is San Francisco, not Transylvania."

"That may be." Brooks stepped between them, as if he had heard enough. "And it may be too little to indict on. But it's too much to ignore. For now, we're going on with this."

FOUR

TERESA PERALTA OPENED the door of Mark Ransom's suite.

She hesitated; for a moment, Terri felt that if she did not enter, nothing would happen to Mary, and Ransom would still be alive. Then she stepped inside and saw the bloodstain on the carpet.

She was still staring at it when Paget and Johnny Moore came in behind her.

It was a moment before she turned. "Could you see me from the elevator?" she asked.

Paget nodded. "Clearly enough."

It was a little after eleven-thirty in the morning, roughly the time that Mary had arrived, four days prior. The door bore a sign that read: CRIME SCENE—CITY AND COUNTY OF SAN FRANCISCO. KEEP OUT. A policeman had broken the tape sealing the door; he waited for them by the elevator.

Terri looked around the room. The furniture was unremarkable—two end tables, a bookshelf, a small desk. The two windows of the sitting room faced east, across the city and toward Berkeley; there was enough morning sun left to make the room somewhat bright.

"You couldn't have seen my face, though," Terri said.

"No, the angle's wrong, and there's also the distance. Johnny and I paced it off at about sixty feet. But even three or four seconds would be enough to describe height, weight, and hair color." Paget looked down at the bloodstain. "Put it this way," he finished slowly. "I could tell the difference between you and Mary Carelli."

A sudden shadow fell across the bloodstain.

Terri and Paget looked up. Johnny Moore had pulled down a blind and was walking toward the second window. "Makes a difference," he said, and yanked down the other blind.

It was like instant dusk: a bright room, suddenly dark enough to sleep in. Johnny Moore's ruddy face and white beard had turned gray.

"It's depressing," Terri said to him.

"Unless you're Edgar Allan Poe." Moore walked to the end table by the far side of the couch and switched on a lamp. The effect was dim and unnatural, like a lamp in one corner of a windowless cell. "Maybe it was Ransom's idea of romance."

"Ransom's idea of romance," Paget answered, "was 'Mutant Cheerleaders in Bondage.' "

Terri shook her head. "There's no way," she said slowly, "that I'd have felt comfortable in this room."

Paget gazed at the stain and then at Terri. His look was curious, reflective. "Of course," he observed, "you know what happened here."

"That's not it." She looked around the room. "This just doesn't feel right. If it had been me, and Ransom had pulled down the blinds . . ."

She stopped there. "You'd have left?" Paget asked.

She folded her arms. "I don't know."

Paget regarded her another moment. "In any event, it seems that it would have made an impression on Mary."

Moore walked to the middle of the room. "Probably so, before she shot him. *After,* telling it to the cops, what happened might have gotten pretty confused. Like reading *Ulysses* for the first time."

Paget smiled faintly. "You like the Irish writers, don't you?"

"The Irish who *stayed.*" As he glanced down at the stain, Moore's Irish lilt became slightly more pronounced. "Personally, I always thought Mark Ransom's work would gag a vulture."

Paget ceased to smile. "Not unlike Marnie Sharpe's theory of this case."

Moore considered him and then nodded toward the couch. "Why don't we three rest awhile," he said, "on the Mark Ransom memorial love seat. You can explain why Miss Carelli defaced the poor man's arse *after* she shot him."

"Oh, that," Paget said. "Because then he couldn't complain, of course."

Terri realized that she was hugging her shoulders. "Would you two mind," she asked quietly, "if I pulled up the blinds?"

"I'll do it," Moore said. He opened the blinds and looked back to Terri. "It was becoming a bit like a séance, wasn't it?"

Paget stood to the side, watching her face. "Johnny's spent far too much time among the dead," he said finally, "and I spent too much time with Ms. Sharpe this morning. I'm a little off my feed."

Staring at the coffee table, Terri imagined the tape of Laura Chase. After a moment, she asked, "What's Sharpe thinking?"

The two men sat on each side of Terri. Paget was quiet, ordering his thoughts. Resting his feet on the coffee table, Moore gazed slowly around the room.

"It's pretty simple," Paget said. "Sharpe's been arranging and re-arranging the facts—or the absence of facts—until Mary comes out a liar.

"First, Mary says Ransom tried to rape her. To which Sharpe, or Shelton, says that there is no sign of seminal fluid and hence no evidence of sexual arousal. And as we know, there was no penetration.''

Terri felt cold. ''Mary kept making mistakes. She should have let Ransom deposit the evidence.''

''You're beginning to sound like me,'' Moore told her. ''That is, of course, the irony of Sharpe's scenario.''

''Granted,'' Paget said. ''But fact two, according to Shelton, is that Mary's statement that she shot Ransom from two or three inches isn't even close.''

Moore nodded. ''I ran that one past my forensics guy at Berkeley. Take a Walther .380, and the absence of gunshot residue, and he says Shelton has to be right. Liz Shelton's a professional; to get someone to testify against her on *this* point, you'll have to find a whore.''

Paget shook his head. ''If I put on some hired gun, Shelton would kill him. I'll have to find another way around it.''

''In other words,'' Moore said carefully, ''things happened much too fast for Mary to be sure.''

''Of course.'' Paget paused. ''But there's also the lack of gunshot residue on Ransom's hands. Mary says they struggled and the gun went off. Residue would help confirm that. There wasn't any.''

''And needn't be,'' Moore answered. ''Depends on how it happened.''

Paget shrugged. ''The next thing is the blinds.

Mary says they were drawn when she got here. But the room service waiter, who has no ax to grind, says they were open. It's hard to miss the difference. From which Sharpe no doubt posits that Mary drew the blinds, presumably after she shot him, and presumably because she didn't want to be seen.''

Moore got up from the couch without responding, looked through one window, then another. Arriving, Terri had seen that the Flood was not a perfect rectangle but a courtyard surrounded by two wings that faced each other. Ransom's suite was near the center of the top floor; through the window, the city and the bay were framed by wings on either side.

Moore pointed to the right. ''I'll have to check it out,'' he said. ''But from here it looks like the last couple of windows on that wing could see into this room. At least it's something you'd think about if you were standing here, wanting privacy.''

Paget considered that. ''It works best,'' he said, ''if this waiter isn't sure. That way, the blinds are drawn when she gets here, which makes better sense for us than Mary *or* Ransom pulling them down.''

Moore sat again. ''I'll find the waiter.''

Watching them, Terri was struck by their total absence of sentiment. Moore did not ask if Mary was telling the truth; Paget's focus was on what the prosecutor could prove. Neither showed passion or outrage. Which, Terri thought, was more to be expected in Johnny than in Paget: Mary Carelli was the mother of his son.

"That gets us," Paget continued, "to Mary's fingernails as compared to Ransom's. There are scratches on both Mary and Ransom, but Shelton was only able to find traces of skin under *Mary's* fingernails, not Ransom's. To Sharpe, the least that means is that Ransom didn't scratch her."

Moore leaned back on the couch. "Interesting," he said, "but not very compelling. It's kind of like listening to someone's theory about life on other planets. Maybe, you think, but you can argue it a thousand different ways, and who knows?"

"Until we get to Sharpe's little surprise. The scratches on Ransom's backside." Paget's face was so expressionless that, to Terri, it reflected some deliberate effort. "Shelton's theory is that the scratches weren't made until a half hour or so after Ransom died. If you believe that, it gives them two things: the passage of time, and the calculated alteration of a crime scene in the most cold-blooded way—the disfigurement of a corpse. And that pulls it all together for them."

Terri felt reality slip from her grasp. The day before, listening to Melissa Rappaport, she was certain that she had found the truth. But in the suite where Ransom died, truth had become a kaleidoscope: the pattern kept shifting, as did her sense of Paget himself. That, and the strangeness of the room, put her off balance.

"The case Sharpe is making," Paget said, "is that Ransom died in another way than Mary described, for some other reason than rape." Paget gazed at the bloodstain. "Then Mary pulled down the blinds and for over a half hour worked on Ransom's body, and her own. She pulled down his pants, scratched him, scratched herself. And when she'd done all she could, she called 911 and kept on lying until she got too lost. After which," he finished softly, "she called me."

The last words seemed to have taken him somewhere else. As if to reclaim him, Terri said, "Ransom *hit* her."

"Oh, something happened in this room. Just something quite different from what Mary described. That is, if you're Sharpe."

Moore considered him. "How sure is Liz Shelton about *this* one?"

"Sharpe's pushing her some, although I expect there's only so far she gets pushed." Paget shrugged. "I think I could get her to say she's not sure."

The last phrase jarred Terri again; it was the pragmatic calculation of a defense lawyer, not the musing of a friend or lover.

They fell silent. "Give me a *reason,*" Moore said at last.

"Sharpe has none," Paget answered. "She can make up a how, but she can't figure out a why."

He stared out the window, chin propped in his hand. After a time, he asked Moore, "Have you seen what you needed to see?"

"Pretty much." Moore stared, spent another minute checking the drawers of the end table and desk, and then said, "Let's go."

Outside the room, they stopped for a moment, looking around the corridor. There was little there: more doors; a smoke alarm; a mail slot across from Ransom's suite. No telephone, Terri thought, nothing of interest to anyone who was thinking clearly.

She paused, making sure that the policeman who waited could not hear.

"What's Sharpe's point," she asked Paget, "about Mary being in the hallway before she called 911?"

"No idea—just a discrepancy. But I'm sure Sharpe's working on it." Paget nodded toward the mail slot. "Probably figures Mary found herself with a half hour to kill, scribbled a few postcards on Ransom's rear end, and then mailed them to all her friends."

Moore gave Paget a quizzical look; all at once, Terri felt how shaken Paget was.

"By the way," Paget asked her, "will Steinhardt's daughter talk to us?"

Terri nodded. "For a fee."

"A fee? What on earth for?"

"A research fee, she says. She keeps her father's papers."

Paget shook his head in disgust. "I suppose she needs money," he said, "now that Mary's spoiled the sequel," and then turned to Moore.

Moore shrugged.

"Pay her," Paget said.

FIVE

CARLO CARELLI PAGET gazed at his parents, two profiles in the candlelight.

They sat in the dining room, poised between salad and dessert, at the end of the long mahogany dining table where he and his father always sat. The chandelier was dim; two white candles in brass holders created a pool of light that made the Persian rug seem richer, the crystal brighter, the room closer and more intimate. At his father's suggestion, Carlo sat at the head of the table, one parent to each side.

He watched them, trying to pretend that he was not doing so. The talk between them had been strained. His father, dressed in a white silk shirt and black wool slacks, was even more self-contained than usual. His mother seemed subdued, less electric than the woman he had seen on Sunday. She still looked beautiful, Carlo thought, but a little sad.

"Do you always eat like this?" Mary asked him. "By candlelight, I mean."

Carlo nodded. "When it's dark. I guess it's kind of a tradition."

"How did that start?"

"Dad?" Carlo turned to Paget, wanting to bring him closer to the moment. "You remember these things."

"That's because you were seven." Paget smiled. "Parents spend all this time building memories, and then they're devastated to find out that what their children remember about being little is when they backed up the car without looking and ran over the cat."

"*Did* you run over the cat?" Mary asked.

As his father turned to her, Carlo thought he seemed almost reluctant, as if forced from the familiar refuge of teasing him. "No, someone else did," Paget said. "But it was an awful day—the car was going quite fast, and Fluffy was, shall we say, unsuitable for viewing. I had to take care of it before Carlo got home, and then explain that Fluffy had gone straight to heaven without passing go. I felt like a murderer."

Carlo flinched inwardly. Mary stared at his father; Carlo saw the careless phrase come back to him in a narrowing of the eyes. A moment's signal seemed to pass between the two adults, a rearranging of their gazes in which his father apologized, Mary accepted. It put Carlo even more on edge; his father, whom he thought of as so graceful, did not seem himself.

"What did Carlo say?" Mary asked politely.

"He asked me to describe heaven, and then a few days later we got Fluffy the second."

Mary smiled. "That must have been hard for you."

"The part about heaven, or the cat?"

"Heaven." Mary tilted her head. "Not anything you used to spend a lot of time on."

"That's not fair. Believing as I do in the perfectibility of man, I simply assume that heaven can be realized here on earth, through the achievement of a balanced budget and a comprehensive program of national health insurance."

Carlo was silent. To him, they seemed like two actors, speaking lines they neither felt nor cared about, but expert enough not to be awful. He wished that he could imagine them without this veneer: younger, maybe the age of his dad's associate Terri, and in love with each other. But he could not understand them, or even explain to himself why it was so hard to think of Mary as his mother.

Lightly, she asked him, "What do *you* believe?"

She had no idea, of course—she couldn't have. That was part of why this seemed so difficult; his parents must have talked so little about him that she had to learn about his life as if he were the son of a business acquaintance.

"Nothing," Carlo said flatly. "I don't believe in

any of that stuff. I could never get how Jesus' mother comes home, pregnant, tells this guy that God did it, and he buys that."

Something flickered in his mother's eyes. Now it was *his* turn, Carlo thought; he hadn't even sounded right to *himself*. But he couldn't tell what had hurt her, or how to get out of it. All at once he wanted dinner to be over.

"Well," his dad put in, "Joseph did get a son out of it all, if only on loan." His father turned to Mary, smiling a little. "My failures as a parent are worse than you imagine. Religion is one thing, but what's truly disturbing is that Carlo doesn't want to be a lawyer."

"Too many lawyer jokes?" Mary asked him.

Carlo felt a touch of gratitude; even a return to banter was better than where he had just been. "My dad *is* a lawyer joke," he said. "Always working, and always on the phone. I call it 'Lifestyles of the Rich and Compulsive.' "

"Well," his father answered mildly, "your mother gave it up, so I suppose there's precedent. And I expect she likes what she's doing now far better."

"Do you?" Carlo asked her.

She smiled. "Oh, yes."

"What is it you like? Being on television?"

Mary considered him. "It depends," she said finally, "on how you mean that. I've gotten to live lots of places—New York, Los Angeles, even Rome for a time. But what television really does is take you far beyond your own life. It's like plugging into this enormous current: suddenly you can meet almost anyone you want, ask them almost any question you want, and they *want* you to, because they want to be part of the current. Television gives me a license to be part of things. And instead of just watching other people help me know what to think, *I* help other people do that."

Mary's voice was animated. Carlo saw his father looking at her; for once, the look was without facade or wariness, as if she had spoken some deep truth about herself.

"Who did you like meeting most?" Carlo asked.

Mary smiled. "Well, lots of them are at least *interesting;* I've known the last three Presidents, and interviewed people like Gorbachev and Mitterrand and Margaret Thatcher—whom I absolutely admired, by the way; she had her own program, and people reacted to *her,* not the other way around." She paused, remembering. "But the best was Anwar Sadat, and his death was a tragedy."

"Why him?"

"Because he was an unquestionably great man—everyone who met him knew that, almost at once." She leaned forward, as if trying to help Carlo feel what she had felt. "He was so *himself:* visionary, but plainspoken and completely honest. He seemed to transcend time or place, which was why he was able to envision peace with Israel while everyone else stayed trapped in their own history. I could feel that even in how he treated *me*. A lot of Arab men have trouble talking to women, but Sadat talked to *me* directly, like an equal, as if I were the most important person in the room. He was like that with everyone."

There was life in Mary's face now. Carlo felt a kind of closeness; she did not know how to act like a mother, but she could talk to him as herself.

"It's hard to imagine," Carlo said. "Being you, having everybody know you."

"They don't really *know* me. They have an *image* of me, or maybe they like my work—it's nice when people come up and tell you that. Although," she added with a sardonic smile, "the last few days, I could have done without people knowing me at all. So it depends, I suppose."

Carlo hesitated; she seemed objective enough that it might be safe to talk about it. "Aren't people going to sympathize more," he asked, "because they like you?"

"Some do. ABC's getting lots of wires from people giving me support, and various women's groups want me to speak out—less about *me,* really, than the whole issue." She paused. "Maybe it'll help me get through this thing."

Carlo felt his father retreat within his own thoughts. He wanted to reach out to her.

"Are you doing okay?" he asked her. "I really kept wishing I could see you."

Her smile seemed genuine, even grateful. "I'm all right now," she said. "For the most part anyhow—I spend a lot of time thinking about it." Her voice became quieter. "It's odd, Carlo. I've been so used to controlling things, and this thing just happened. It still doesn't seem like a part of me. But it is, for the rest of my life."

Carlo had the sudden sense of a lonely woman, speaking to him alone.

"I'll help you," he said. "Any way I can."

From the corner of his eye, Carlo saw his father's gaze, abstracted and unfathomable, directed at the candles. But his mother's returning look was intent. "The best way you can help me," she said, "is to keep living your life. It's how *I've* always been, and it'll make me feel better if you can be that way now." She reached out, touching his wrist. "Your father and I are two very capable people."

Her fingers felt warm, light. It was good, Carlo thought, to have his mother touch him.

"Okay," he said finally. "But I'll bug him about it."

Her hand tightened around his wrist, as if feeling something she could not ask in words. "That much," she said softly, "would be nice."

* * *

Watching them together was so strange, Paget thought. As strange as the moment he had first seen them: a woman he knew but did not know, her two-day-old son.

Mary lay in the hospital bed, pale and drained of energy. The baby, this stranger with matted black hair and an old man's face, wrinkled its features and yawned without sound. The baby's wristband read "Carelli."

"Does he ever make noise?" Paget asked.

She nodded. "Short squalls, mostly. He doesn't seem to be a complainer."

"Just as well, considering." Paget hesitated. "Does he have a name?"

Mary nodded. "Carlo. At least that's what's on the birth certificate."

"Carlo Carelli?" Paget looked at the baby. "A bit ethnic, don't you think?"

"It's my grandfather's name." Her voice was quiet. "The man I most remember loving."

Paget gazed at her. "Whose name," he finally asked, "is on the birth certificate?"

Her answering gaze was cool and level. "Yours."

Paget turned to the window. The room was cold and spare; it felt like prison. "I suppose," he said finally, "I should be grateful that you didn't name him Frank. After your ex-husband."

Mary did not smile. "No chance of that," she said. "Any more than there'll be more husbands."

Paget found his eyes drawn to the baby, stretching, hands making random fists. Funny, he thought; they don't really do anything, and still you watch them. "Who will take care of him?" he asked.

"My parents. At least for a while."

"Your *parents.*" Paget shook his head in wonderment. "You can't stand them—with good reason, you once tried to persuade me."

"It's only for now." Her voice turned bitter. "I may be a disgrace, but I'm one of theirs."

"That hardly seems best."

"Neither does day care. And he *is* my son."

Paget's voice was soft. "And mine, I'm given to understand."

Mary stared at him. "Had it been up to you, Chris, Carlo wouldn't have lived past gestation."

Silent, Paget gazed at the baby, resting against Mary's shoulder. Finally, he asked, "What will you do?"

"I don't know yet. Just not practice law."

Paget put his hands in his pockets. "I'd like to help."

She gave him a long look of appraisal. "I'm grateful for what you've done. Really. But I don't need you anymore." She looked down at the baby's head. "From time to time, we can talk."

"I'd like to *see* him, Mary."

She gazed back up. "How often?"

He hesitated. "I'm in California now. But whenever I can."

She watched his face a moment and then nodded. "All right."

Paget could find nothing else to say. Wordless, he looked at the baby and then at Mary again.

Slowly, she held Carlo out to him.

Paget took him from her. Carlo's hair was soft against his face; the baby's skin smelled fresh and new. Paget had not known how this would feel.

"Time to go back," a brisk voice interrupted.

It was a red-haired nurse behind him. She took Carlo from his arms. "You the dad?" she asked.

"Yes," Paget said. "I'm the dad."

Walking alone to the car, Paget realized that there were tears in his eyes. He did not know for whom.

"Well," Mary said, "I think it went pretty well tonight. At least at the end."

Paget turned from her, closing the glass doors to the library so that Carlo could not hear them.

"Sit down," he said.

They sat facing each other, Mary on the couch, Paget in an armchair to the side, the spotlit palm tree filling the window behind them. Mary felt tense; the polite tone he had assumed for Carlo's sake was gone.

"What is it?" she asked.

Paget did not answer. His expression was so devoid of sentiment that she recalled again that Christopher Paget was the man who had most frightened her since she had left her father's home.

"This is *me,*" she said coldly. "Save the ice-blue stare for witnesses and unruly spaniels, where it works."

His expression changed but slightly. "Are you going on *60 Minutes*?" he asked.

The indirectness of the question unsettled her. "Yes," she finally said. "We should seize the moral high ground."

"Ah, yes," Paget said. "The moral high ground, our accustomed territory. Just be careful to remember when you're lying."

The insult was so casual that it was as though he had slapped her in slow motion; it took Mary a moment to realize that she was taut with anger and apprehension.

"Spit it out, Chris, whatever it is. Or do you still enjoy pulling the wings off flies?"

He raised his eyebrows. "Was I too subtle? All right, then: you're still a liar, but you've lost your touch. Your story's getting threadbare."

"Damnit, tell me what's wrong."

Paget shook his head. "I'm going to ask you a few questions. If you can't bring yourself to tell me the truth, at least don't insult me by lying."

Mary paused, then she saw she had no choice. Folding her arms, she said, "Have it your way."

Paget leaned back in his chair, appraising her. Finally, he asked, "How long did it take you to call 911?"

"I don't know. Really."

"Less than a half hour, or more?"

She hesitated. "Perhaps more."

Paget's eyes narrowed. "What about Ransom?"

Mary gazed at the rug. Quietly, she answered, "He was dead."

"How did you know that?"

"Because he never moved." She infused her tone with the slightest edge: "I guess you had to be there."

"You're not a doctor," Paget shot back, "and that answer won't do. Why didn't you call for help?"

"I suppose I was in shock."

Paget watched her. "Were you? Or are you trying shock on for size?"

Mary looked back up at him. "We're all different," she said coldly. "That night in Washington, when you nearly killed Jack Woods, your first reaction was to call the Washington *Post*. But I don't recall you phoning 911."

Paget looked at her. "You had it right about one

thing,'' he said in clipped tones. ''I didn't give a damn whether your good friend Jack was dead or simply had a dental problem. Any more than he, among other people, ever cared about whether I lived or died.''

Mary stiffened. ''That's not fair.''

''I am so sorry. Tell me, was there some reason you preferred *Ransom* dead, as opposed to merely disheartened?''

''No.'' Her voice rose. ''Of course not.''

''Then let's return to the question you so neatly avoided by turning the spotlight on me: why so much time passed before you called 911.''

Mary stood, eyes averted, gazing out at the palm. ''This may not sound attractive,'' she finally said, ''but I was frightened for myself.''

''Why, exactly?''

''Because I felt as if it were my fault. That I could have avoided it.'' Mary paused, remembering her own fear, then finished quietly, ''And that people wouldn't believe me.''

''What did you do?''

She shook her head. ''My brain felt sluggish—it was like trying to run when you're waist deep in water. I couldn't think—you can't believe it's real. It takes time to accept—''

''What did you do?'' Paget repeated.

Mary closed her eyes. ''I really don't remember.''

She heard Paget get up, walk close behind her

until she felt him through her nerve ends in the back of her neck.

Softly, he said, "Someone saw you outside the room."

It startled her. "Is he sure?" she asked.

"Yes. The only question is why."

Mary realized that her eyes were still shut, her arms folded again. "I can't answer that," she said.

"Can't, or won't?"

Make him stop, she told herself. Turning, she looked straight at him. "I was confused. You're going to have to accept that, and make the district attorney accept that."

Paget's face was inches from hers. "Four days ago," he said quietly, "you didn't tell Inspector Monk that you left the room."

"That was four *hours,*" she retorted, "after Mark Ransom's death. I was a mess. I mean, can you think of any rational reason for me to be out in the hall?"

"Not unless you knocked on doors, trying to get help."

"I didn't." Mary paused. "As I said, I was confused."

"Were you also confused about the blinds?"

Mary stepped away from him, sat down. After a moment, she repeated, "The blinds."

"They were open when you got there—despite what you told Monk." Paget still stood, looking down at her. "Who closed them, Mary, and why?"

"Why?" She hesitated, feeling helpless, unable to explain. Finally, she said, "Because I felt ashamed."

Paget sat beside her. "Ashamed?"

"Yes." She turned to him. "I didn't want anyone to see."

"To see what? Ransom?"

"Everything." She turned to him. "After I shot him, I thought about running, hoping no one had seen me—crazy things. I couldn't say that to Monk."

"So you lied about the blinds."

Mary leaned back from him. "The term is 'confused,' " she said coolly. "I was confused."

"Too confused," Paget asked, "to kill Ransom from a safe distance, pull his pants down, leave scratch marks on his buttocks, scratch your own neck and thigh, and then dream up a rape attempt detailed enough to fly?"

Mary felt numb, and then the terrible knowledge of how alone she was came over her. "They can't believe that."

"Why? Because you're so eager to help them out?"

"No," she said dully. "Maybe some of what I said was a mistake. But they can't believe I'm a murderer."

"They believe that you defaced a corpse a good half hour after his death. That makes murder a bit less of a stretch."

As if by reflex, Mary touched the bruise beneath her eye, now blue-green. "Do they think he was dead," she asked, "when he did this?"

Paget did not answer. "Tell me," he finally said. "Did you already know Mark Ransom?"

She stared at him. "God, no . . ."

"Because Sharpe's next step will be to look for some connection between Ransom and you. If there is one, tell me now, or I really will leave you to twist in the wind."

Mary felt her anger turn to fear. "Before he called," she said, "I'd never met him. I swear it."

"That had better be right. It's quite enough that Monk has on tape several answers that are either implausible or, as you now admit, inaccurate. Not to mention that you and Shelton's autopsy are essentially at odds." Paget's voice grew quiet. "I can't say you've done very well this time around."

Mary's face grew cold. "It's hard to choose what's more offensive—Mark Ransom or you, afterwards, grading my performance."

"So hire Melvin Belli, Mary, and restore your faith in men."

All at once, Mary felt drained. "You don't believe me at all, do you?"

"Not true. I believe about every other word. Assuming, of course, that you throw in the commas."

Mary stood again. "You know, I've had about enough of this."

Paget shrugged. "You should count your blessings, Mary. Your fifteen-year-old son believes in you. As for me, *I* believe in sparing Carlo needless pain, which is all the motivation I require."

"Fine." Mary reached for her purse. "Are we through here now?"

"For the moment. But take my advice: no specific comments on TV—just heartfelt generalities about your ordeal and that of victims everywhere. I don't want yet another 'mistake' I have to clean up later."

Silent, Mary watched him. "I'll say good night to Carlo," she said.

The limousine was outside when she returned. Paget walked her to the door. Outside, she turned back to him, uncertain of what she was looking for.

His face was without expression. "Enjoy *60 Minutes*," he said. Then he softly shut the door, and Mary was alone.

"It was a nightmare," Mary said softly. "I've heard women say that, but I never really knew."

In the library, Carlo and Paget watched her, their only light the glow from the television. The camera panned her hotel suite, framing Mary and her interviewer, then moved in until Mary's face filled the screen. Her expression was troubled, inward, as if too caught in painful memory to remember the lens.

The interviewer became only a voice. "Can you describe your feelings?" he asked.

Paget glanced at Carlo, tense and still, the Sunday paper on the couch beside him. The headline read: RANSOM DEATH UNRESOLVED.

Sharpe, Paget knew, had preempted Mary's interview.

The article was plainly Sharpe's idea. The reporter quoted her as being "concerned with discrepancies between Ms. Carelli's statement and the physical evidence"; "puzzled by Ms. Carelli's cessation of her interview"; "resolved that the concern with rape which has defined my own career not foreclose a neutral inquiry"; and "hopeful that the public will not forget that a gifted man died in this city." The sole photograph was of a younger, much more appealing, Mark Ransom.

Paget had managed to insert a quote. "Puzzling over tests and slides," he said, "should not distract us from a central truth—Mary Carelli was forced into a tragic act for which there is no reason but attempted rape." But it could not change the pressure Sharpe had shrewdly put on Mary: to respond in detail and on television, or look evasive.

On the screen, Mary gazed down. She seemed mute, battered. "It still seems unreal," she finally answered. "One minute, it's as if it must have happened to someone else. Then I feel my own terror as a physical thing—his breath on my face, body pressing down on me, hands tearing at my clothes." She paused, touching her cheek, and then finished softly, "The shock when he hit me."

"Did he say anything?"

"Yes. I can't repeat it. Not yet." She stopped, then murmured, "I'm sorry. I can't even call him by his name."

"Would you like to stop?"

"No." Slowly, she shook her head, seemingly less for emphasis than in confusion. "Perhaps I'm doing this too soon. But no." She looked up, eyes imploring. "It's like that, you see. You're all right, and then . . ."

"Perhaps this isn't timely," the interviewer said, "but I thought perhaps you might care to comment on certain questions that seem to puzzle the district attorney's office."

Mary's face froze for a moment, and then she looked bewildered. "I'm not sure I even know what they are. Or why they have them. He tried to rape me. . . ."

Once more, her voice trailed off.

"Perhaps," the interviewer prodded, "this will be an opportunity to put some of those things to rest."

Mary nodded.

Carlo leaned forward. "What are they doing?" he demanded.

Paget felt his own tension. "I'm not sure yet."

"For example," the voice went on, "the district attorney suggests that the bullet which killed Mark Ransom traveled from at least three feet, in contrast to your claim that the gun went off while he was on top of you."

For a moment, Mary looked surprised. To Carlo, Paget murmured, "The D.A.'s fed him questions."

On the screen, Mary had composed herself. "What they don't seem to understand is how quickly things happen and how stunned you are." Her voice was calm again. "It was over in seconds. He had just slapped me. I was hurt, frightened for my life. At the instant the gun went off, he must have been falling back—from one split second to another, a bullet could have traveled a few inches, or more than that. Some nights, that's all I think about—the moment he died—but it's so hard to see it in terms of distance. It's more—I don't know—impressionistic than that, and far too shocking for clarity." She paused. "I don't wish to offend anyone, but for someone to blame me for imprecision is really quite callous."

"Damn," Carlo said. "That's good."

Paget did not answer; he could imagine too clearly Sharpe's reaction as she watched.

"The D.A. also suggests that you did not call 911 for at least thirty minutes."

Mary shook her head. "I really have no sense of

time about that day. As I told a friend, shock makes your brain sluggish, as if you're trying to find your way through a darkened house that isn't yours. The one thing I knew clearly was that this man was dead." Mary looked back at the camera. "If that weren't true, I could never forgive myself, no matter what he'd done to me."

"Do you recall what happened during that time?"

"No, only fragments." Her voice was soft, puzzled, as if explaining to herself. "I really think what happened is that I came out of shock and called 911."

Watching, Paget felt relief. "I think she's gotten through that," he said.

Carlo turned to him. "You sound as if she's guilty."

Paget mentally cursed himself. "Not guilty," he said. "On trial. The D.A.'s put her there, and she's doing well."

"Our sources indicate," the reporter was saying, "that you've refused to take a lie detector test."

Paget stood. "That bitch . . ."

Carlo turned. "Who?"

"Sharpe." Paget looked at him. "Sorry. Let's just watch, okay?"

Turning back to the screen, Paget saw Mary's look of tired resolve. "As you know," she said, "I began my career as a lawyer. Lie detector tests are so notoriously inaccurate that no court, anywhere, will allow them to be used as evidence. Every district attorney in this country knows that, and every D.A. *should* know that anything which can't be used in court shouldn't be used to damage someone's reputation.'' She paused. ''You know, it's hard to believe what's happening here.''

''I don't mean to suggest that you did something wrong.''

''Good,'' she said firmly, ''because I'm not the one who's done something wrong. I don't blame you for asking questions. But I *do* suggest that you have to evaluate your sources, and their motives.'' Her voice turned cold. ''Whoever they are.''

''We always try to do that,'' the interviewer said. ''One way is to get your response, as I'm doing now.''

Mary nodded. ''I understand. I'm just very disappointed in the use of selective truths, by anonymous sources, to create a false impression of something that was so simple and traumatic.'' She paused, as if belatedly astonished. ''My God, does anyone think I *wanted* this to happen? Does anyone think I *wanted* this man to die? Does every woman who is raped have to endure snickers for being victimized and insinuations for fighting back?''

''Don't go too far,'' Paget murmured.

''That certainly is not our intention,'' the interviewer responded. ''By asking these questions so close to Mark Ransom's death, we run the risk of offending you and countless others. But however uncomfortable this may be, for us as well as you, it's unethical to sit on questions when they're brought to our attention.''

Mary frowned. ''I'm a journalist, as you are. But I've also become the victim of an attempted rape. And I know, and you know, that our society is still unfair to women who are victims of rape.''

''I agree.'' The interviewer paused. ''May I ask you one more question—as a journalist.''

Watching, Paget recognized her expression: to anyone else it might seem thoughtful, but Paget knew it as deep wariness. ''Of course,'' she answered.

''What we have been told,'' the interviewer said, ''is that another guest at the hotel, looking through his window, saw you pulling down the blinds in Mark Ransom's suite.''

Paget felt Mary's surprise like a contagion, knew that Sharpe had concealed this fact from him for just this moment. Duck this, Paget instructed Mary mentally, any way you can.

''Let me ask *you* a question,'' Mary retorted. ''Has the district attorney told you *why* I went to see Mark Ransom?''

''Why do you ask?''

Mary nodded. ''No. I didn't think so. And *I* won't tell you, although it would explain a great deal. Because it involves the reputation, and the feelings, of people other than myself.'' She paused, looking directly to the camera. ''What you should demand of your sources is full disclosure: that they tell you exactly what was found in that room. And once *they* refuse to tell you, the one thing you will know is that *you* have been very badly used.''

Despite himself, Paget laughed aloud: Sharpe had warned Mary, and now Mary was warning Sharpe.

''What's she talking about?'' Carlo asked.

''The tape,'' Paget said. ''As a good Democrat, McKinley Brooks does *not* want to answer to James Colt's family. Your mother just took that tape and stuck it in Marnie Sharpe's ear.'' In two days, Paget thought but did not add, no one will remember that Mary used it to avoid a question.

''I have *more* questions,'' Mary went on, ''that people should ask themselves.'' Her gaze was steady, her voice crisp and clear. ''Why is it,'' she asked, ''that in the case of a sex crime, so many people remember the sex and not the crime?

''Why are the victims of rape, already so devastated in their own hearts and minds, cheapened in the eyes of society?

''Why does the justice system treat them as if they have committed a crime?

''Why are these women so often made to feel like they asked for what no sane person would want?

''Why, tonight, is this happening to me?''

Her voice had thickened. Carlo leaned forward, as if to help her finish.

"I'm not sure," she said to the interviewer, "that you can ever know how that feels. But hundreds of thousands of women know, and now *I* know."

On the screen, her picture froze in close-up. Her eyes shone with tears.

SIX

For Teresa Peralta, Beverly Hills was a mirage.

It seemed far too lush for winter: the manicured sweep of lawns, the tropical mix of vegetation, the surprising bursts of pink and white, were like false spring. The sun was bright, the sky blue and crisp, the palm trees lining Santa Monica Boulevard seemed to float and vanish in the shimmering subtropic light. It made calling on Steinhardt's daughter seem even more unreal.

At the end of a winding driveway on Canyon Drive, tucked behind shrubbery and green trees, Steinhardt's white stucco home was a collection of rectangles and jutting squares; almost as high as it was wide, it looked as if it had been constructed by an imaginative child with a sense of light. There were many windows and skylights; the trees had been pruned to admit sun from every angle. When a Hispanic maid led her to the living room, Terri found herself beneath twenty-foot ceilings, surrounded by shafts of light.

In Spanish, Terri said, "This is a beautiful room."

The maid seemed surprised. Then she answered in the same tongue: "It is just as Dr. Steinhardt left it," and went to find his daughter.

Terri looked around her. Something in the decor was too calculated, she decided: the prints were too carefully selected, the vases too perfectly placed, and the sculpture—African here, Asian there—seemed chosen to reflect their place of origin rather than a passion for the things themselves. It was more like visiting an art museum than a place where someone lived.

"It always struck me as a room full of specimens," a husky voice behind her said. "Rather like a butterfly collection, but even less alive."

Turning, Terri saw a sharp-featured woman in her thirties, tall and slender in a coppery silk jumpsuit, with tinted ash-blond hair and long red fingernails. Her eyes were a vivid green; beneath this chic veneer, her carriage had the tensile alertness of a greyhound. Terri's first impression was of a woman who trusted no one.

"I'm Jeanne-Marc Steinhardt," the woman said, adding dryly, "My mother was French."

There was something bloodless in the reference, as if she were speaking of a vase and not a person. Terri extended her hand.

"Teresa Peralta." Smiling, she added, "My mother was Guatemalan. Still is, actually."

"How nice for you." Jeanne Steinhardt looked past her at the room. "Mine slashed her wrists when I was five. For years, I thought it was the art."

What, Terri wondered, should she say to *that?* "Then I'd change the decor," she finally answered.

Steinhardt turned to face her. "Oh? And what would your mother favor? Although I'm afraid an oil of the Madonna and Christ child would be incongruent with my background."

Terri felt herself tense; the sole ambiguity in Steinhardt's remark was whether its bias arose from class or race. "Many of us," she said evenly, "used to favor a framed portrait of James Colt. Preferably one that glowed in the dark."

Jeanne Steinhardt looked surprised and then moved her lips in an expression of chill amusement. "I take it," she said at last, "that you know what's on that tape."

Terri nodded. "I've stopped lighting candles for James Colt, if that's what you mean. And so did Mary Carelli, after Mark Ransom played it for her."

Jeanne Steinhardt stared at her openly, as if appraising and reappraising. "Yes," she said. "I saw her on *60 Minutes* last night. Impressive. Please sit down."

Silent, she led Terri to a long couch in the middle of the room, a white cotton fabric with an Aztec design. Terri sat at one end, Steinhardt at the other, hands folded, legs carefully crossed.

It was time, Terri thought, to soften her tone. "Your mother," she ventured. "That must have been hard."

"I barely remember her." Steinhardt gave an elegant shrug. "It's less a loss than an absence."

Terri tried to imagine her life had Rosa Peralta been "absent." It was, Terri found, like imagining that she herself did not exist. In that moment, she saw the emptiness she sensed at Jeanne Steinhardt's core as the absence of love.

"As you say," Terri answered, "I've been fortunate."

Steinhardt made a dismissive gesture. "You came about my father, and his tape."

Terri nodded. "About the tape, and about Mark Ransom."

Steinhardt gave her a curious look. "What is it that you care to know? Seeing that your client has already killed him."

Terri was silent for a moment, gazing out the window. There was a pool outside, a long oval that contrasted with the lines and angles of the house itself. A Hispanic poolman stretched over it with a long wire net, reaching for a tropical leaf that marred the blue surface of the water.

"How was it," Terri asked, "that Mark Ransom acquired that tape?"

"That part's quite simple." Steinhardt gave a thin smile. "I called him."

That, Terri thought, was no surprise. "For what reason?" she asked politely.

The question was perfunctory; Terri was quite certain that she already knew the answer: money. Steinhardt was silent for a moment. "Because," she answered coolly, "I found listening to it so educational."

Terri hesitated. "Wasn't it confidential?"

"That was certainly my father's intention. He left instructions that all tapes were to be destroyed by his executor." Steinhardt permitted herself another cold smile. *"I'm* his executor."

Terri tried to choose a neutral voice. "Don't you have problems with the psychiatrist-patient privilege?"

"Oh, I think not. Laura Chase moved beyond my father's ministrations, as it were, when she put the gun in her mouth and pulled the trigger." The husky voice seemed to drop a register. "Perhaps Laura felt she'd graduated."

Terri paused again, off balance. Beneath this woman's icy air of intelligence and self-interest, Terri felt another emotion which she could not identify. "Still," she said carefully, "people might argue that Laura would have wanted to protect her privacy."

Steinhardt shrugged. *"They* might. But I don't expect to hear from *her* about it. Which left me quite free, my lawyer confirms, to contact Mark Ransom."

Steinhardt seemed to be speaking by rote, Terri thought: there was a certain relentless quality to her indifference, as if she wished to ensure that it was noticed.

"What did you tell Ransom?" Terri asked her.

"Just enough." The clipped words had a faint derisive edge. "That I admired his work. That I'd read an article he'd written about Laura Chase—'Flesh Become Myth,' I believe he called it. That I shared his interest in Laura's death. And that, were he interested, I might let him listen to my father's tapes." She smiled at the coffee table. "At a price to be negotiated, of course."

"What did he say?"

"That he wanted to meet me." The strange smile reappeared. "So we did. Sitting in my father's office, with the door locked, surrounded by his tapes."

The image of their meeting, Terri found, unsettled her. "Where is his office?" she asked.

Steinhardt gave her a look of surprise. "Here, of course, in my father's home. So very private, so very *him.*"

Terri hesitated. "May I see it?"

"If you like."

Steinhardt led her through a hallway hung with Flemish tapestries and opened a white door. She stood in the doorway, arms crossed.

Terri entered the room. It was sparely furnished, almost entirely in white—including the couch for patients to lie on and Steinhardt's leather chair at its head. The empty couch and chair were haunting, Terri thought; they reminded her that Steinhardt could not help Laura Chase.

"As sterile as an operating room," Jeanne Steinhardt said from the door. "But then someone once called my father 'The Surgeon of the Mind.' "

Terri turned. "Where are the tapes?" she asked.

Steinhardt pointed. "Through here."

In the wall, between the couch and the chair, was a door Terri had not seen. Steinhardt walked quickly past her and unlocked it.

The second room was dark.

Steinhardt switched on a black desk lamp. Terri saw shelves, books on psychiatry, a single desk, two black chairs, no prints or vases anywhere. The room was wholly impersonal.

"The inner sanctum," Steinhardt said in a mocking stage whisper. "My father's cerebral cortex. Or, perhaps, his essence."

Terri walked toward the bookshelf on the far wall. It was honeycombed with slots, as if for tapes of someone's favorite music. But these tapes, in white plastic cases, were coded with Roman numerals, numbers, years, dates. Removing one, Terri felt unclean.

"It could be anyone," Steinhardt said behind her. "How does it feel to hold someone's life in your hands?"

Staring at the tape, Terri replayed Steinhardt's words, her tone of voice, sensed some feeling she still could not grasp.

"How did you know which tapes were of Laura Chase?"

"My father had an index." Once more, the voice turned sardonic. "I showed it to Mark Ransom when we met. Rather like a shopping list."

It was difficult, Terri found, to look at Steinhardt. She edged along the shelf, her gaze sweeping hundreds of tapes. Then found a gap; one shelf, then half of another, were empty.

"That space represents Laura Chase," Steinhardt told her. "Her cure took quite some time."

Terri was silent for a moment.

"Ransom took them?" she finally asked.

"Yes. That was part of our negotiation." Steinhardt sounded almost amused. "He wanted to work at home."

Terri stared at the last shelf of tapes, less to inspect them than for something to do.

There was, she saw, another gap. It was small, two empty slots where tapes would fit. She placed her fingers there. "And this?" she asked. "Also Laura Chase?"

"I don't know." Steinhardt paused. "If so, they would have been out of order."

Terri looked at the tapes on either side. If she understood Dr. Steinhardt's code at all, they belonged to two separate patients; the numbers and numerals were different, and the dates overlapped.

"*Was* there anything in this space?"

For a moment, Steinhardt looked puzzled. "I'm not sure. I noticed that the other day. But I couldn't remember."

"If there *were* tapes, could Mark Ransom have taken them?"

Steinhardt shrugged. "It's possible, I suppose—once or twice I let him listen in here, alone. You know, when he couldn't wait." Steinhardt's voice turned dry. "He seemed to like communing with Laura in the room where she had most exposed herself—figuratively speaking, of course. How he must have wanted to *be* my father."

Terri felt a kind of chill. "Would the index show if tapes were missing?"

There was a moment's silence. "It would have. Yes."

Terri began to turn, then was stopped by a black and white photograph, the ascetic face of a man in his sixties.

It hung on the wall by itself. The man's face was thin, his skin like parchment; his eyes, pale and translucent, betrayed no feeling.

"Your father?" Terri asked.

Steinhardt nodded. "I hung it myself, just before Mr. Ransom's visit. It seemed somehow appropriate."

Terri was quiet for a moment. Turning, she asked, "Can you tell me about that?"

"Of course." Steinhardt took one chair, Terri the other. "It was really quite amusing, in its way."

The dimness of the room, Terri realized, was oppressive. "In *what* way?" she asked.

"The way he changed. When he arrived, Mark Ransom projected this restless energy—a prisoner in his own skin, a red-haired Irishman wrestling with his devils. It was something you could feel if he'd never said a word." Steinhardt gazed around her, profile almost leonine. "But once he got here, in *this* room, it was like he'd entered a cathedral. When I showed him the tapes, all he could do was stare.

" 'Play one for me,' he asked." Steinhardt's voice became almost teasing, as if replaying the moment. "So I did. Just one."

"The one he played for Mary Carelli?"

"Oh, no. Like Laura herself, I wanted to save the best for last." Steinhardt flicked back her hair. "For him, the sound of her voice was enough—Laura Chase, returned from the dead."

"What did he do?"

"He just sat there, hunched forward, listening. He hardly moved." Steinhardt smiled. "And when it was over, he offered me a hundred thousand dollars.

"I told him, more in sorrow than in anger, that his offer was deficient. And then I told him about

Laura's last tape.'' The strange smile returned. ''The one with James Colt.''

It had been a game between them, Terri realized. Quietly, she asked, ''What did Ransom say?''

''Oh, it was more how he looked that confirmed my sense of value. His face was—how should I say it—so *avid.*'' Steinhardt's voice took on the jaded tone of a woman mocking a discarded lover. ''It felt as if I had offered him Laura Chase herself.''

Terri imagined the moment with something close to horror. In return for money, Jeanne Steinhardt had set far more in motion than she could ever have imagined.

''What happened?''

''We reached an agreement, sitting here in this room. Two hundred and fifty thousand dollars, plus thirty percent of any royalties.'' Steinhardt gazed up, as if addressing her father's picture. ''The last ten percent,'' she said in a mordant tone, ''was for letting Mark take Laura home with him.''

Terri watched her face. ''Did he say how he would use the tape?''

''No. But I assumed that he would use it to promote the book. The tape goes far toward explaining her suicide, don't you think?'' Pausing, Steinhardt still gazed at her father's photograph. ''Laura's, that is.''

For a moment, Terri found she had lost her train

of thought. Then she asked, "Did he ever talk about playing the tape for Mary Carelli?"

"No." Steinhardt turned back to Terri, her voice edged with contempt. "But then he also failed to tell me that he saw the tape as foreplay. With my limited imagination, I merely saw it as the basis for a number-one best-seller regarding Laura's suicide. You know, the book that finally tells the world 'Who Killed Laura Chase.' "

Terri paused. "In connection with Laura Chase," she asked, "did he mention *any* other women?"

Steinhardt paused. "I do recall him mentioning Lindsay Caldwell," she finally said. "Although the connection wasn't clear to me."

Terri hesitated, surprised at this mention of the distinguished actress, still beautiful at forty, and as well known for her social causes as for the Oscars she had won. As an undergraduate at Berkeley, Terri had heard Lindsay Caldwell speak on women's issues. Drawing on her own painful evolution from "Barbie Doll to Superwoman," as Caldwell dryly put it, the talk had been surprising for its candor and universality. She was, Terri thought, the polar opposite of Laura Chase—the kind of woman whose politics and persona Mark Ransom would most resent.

"What did he say about her?" Terri asked.

"The first reference I don't exactly recall. I do

remember Mark asking if I knew her. Which I don't.''

''Did he ask whether she had some connection to Laura Chase?''

Steinhardt shook her head. ''He didn't, and I don't know. But unless I'm wrong, Laura died when Lindsay Caldwell was barely out of her teens.''

Terri's gaze moved across the shelves to the space where two tapes might have been. ''Did Lindsay Caldwell ever see your father? Professionally, that is?''

''I didn't memorize the index, if that's what you're asking.'' Steinhardt hesitated. ''When I listened to the tapes, I confined myself to Laura Chase. The last tape, really.''

''Why was that?''

Steinhardt's expression turned cool, her voice cooler. ''The circumstances of her death intrigued me.''

Terri paused again, decided not to pursue it. ''A moment ago,'' she said, ''you mentioned Ransom's 'first reference' to Lindsay Caldwell. Was there another?''

''Yes. He called me from New York. I had asked to read what he had written, to be sure he truly understood the implications of Laura's tape. He was going to be here, he explained, to see Lindsay Caldwell. He sounded quite pleased with himself.'' Steinhardt gave a faint smile. ''I never saw his draft, and he never met with Caldwell. He was scheduled to meet with her one day after Mary Carelli.''

Terri paused. Quietly, she asked, ''May I see the index?''

''No.'' Steinhardt's voice was level. ''I'm afraid you can't.''

The woman's gaze was watchful, impenetrable—rather, Terri thought, like the cold face in the photograph.

''Perhaps,'' Terri said, ''you can look at it yourself. All I want to know is whether Lindsay Caldwell was a patient of your father's.''

Steinhardt's look turned curious. ''To what end?''

''I'm not sure, quite. Perhaps she knows something about the tape.''

''Well, you'll have to ask Miss Caldwell about any relationship to my father.'' Turning, Steinhardt gazed at the rows of tapes. ''After Mark Ransom and I made our arrangement, I burned the index.''

Once again, Terri was surprised. ''Why?'' she finally asked.

Steinhardt's eyes moved to her father's picture. ''For the same reason,'' she answered coldly, ''that I now intend to destroy these tapes. Because I had done what I set out to do.''

All at once, and for the first time, Terri understood what Steinhardt had done. And then she saw, as Steinhardt still did not, how pointless all of it had been. Softly, she said, "This was never about money, was it?"

"Oh, it was." Steinhardt's smile was bleak. "If I made Mark Ransom pay dearly for that tape, I thought he would have no choice but to use it. And I dearly wanted him to use it."

Terri nodded. "Because of your father."

"Yes." Steinhardt's eyes became fierce. "Have you ever listened to that tape?"

"No."

"It was a revelation to me. For almost fifty minutes, Laura Chase talks about how worthless James Colt had made her feel. By the end, she was sobbing convulsively. My father spoke only to ask for more detail about what they did to her. And then he told Laura that her time was up." Steinhardt's voice became so raw that it sounded painful. "By the time the tape was over, I knew that my father was a collector and we were his specimens. Every one of us."

But no one else, Terri thought, would hear what Steinhardt heard. Quietly, she asked, "When did your mother kill herself?"

"Thirty years ago. She died quite anonymously. No one remembers her, including me." Steinhardt's face had turned to stone. "But now, because of me, no one will ever forget who murdered Laura Chase."

* * *

"I find it refreshing," Johnny Moore told Terri, "that this case offers us at least one celebrity who's still alive."

Terri sat on the balcony of a suite at the Beverly Hills Hotel, courtesy of Christopher Paget, speaking into the first cordless telephone of her experience. Moore would make her smile, Terri thought, if she weren't so depressed.

"Do you have a number for her?" she asked.

"Just her answering service. I took the liberty of leaving a message on your behalf: 'Call Teresa Peralta, attorney for Mary Carelli, regarding Mark Ransom.' " Moore laughed softly. "An adequate attention getter, I would think, even in la-la-land. Otherwise, I'd have left a message from Ransom himself."

Terri gazed across a courtyard filled with flowers, watching the sun fall into an ocean she could not see. "I wonder if she'll call me."

"That may depend," Moore answered, "on why Ransom wanted to see her. Or she *him*—although I find that harder to understand."

His voice was sardonic. "Jealous?" Terri asked.

"You've caught me out, Ms. Peralta—what a man we have lost in Mark. Of course, I'm quite put out with *her* too. All that feminist propaganda decimated my happy home."

"Really."

"Oh, yes. Surely it had nothing to do with my rotten hours, sporadic drinking, mysterious absences, and dubious friends. After all, Harriet Nelson would have understood."

"Those were the good old days," Terri gibed, "before they started giving women jobs."

"Now, that," Moore answered lightly, "is what's ruined the American family. Millions of women can actually leave their odious husbands and not starve to death. It's a poor society that pins its hopes on marriage counseling."

Terri smiled. "My only question is whether Richie can afford to leave *me.*"

"The family meal ticket, are you? Then go make partner, and you'll inspire the love that lasts forever. In the interim, just be sure he's on your health plan."

Terri felt a touch of shame; even joking about Richie was like a betrayal of their secret. "It's not that bad," she said. "I'd never let it be."

Strange, Terri thought, asking Johnny to believe what she could not believe herself.

"Oh, Terri," he said gently, "is there no romance left?"

It was as if Moore understood her and wished to make her smile again. But his feelings would not be hurt, she thought, if he could not see her.

"Thanks for everything," she answered, and said goodbye.

She was watching the sunset when the phone rang again.

Tense, she answered, "Teresa Peralta."

"Hi, Ter. What's this message about your not coming home?"

She slumped in the chair. "I've got more business than I thought. Another witness—at least maybe."

Richie sounded put out. "Yeah, well, we really need you here."

No questions about her day, Terri thought—not that she'd feel comfortable telling Richie other people's secrets. "I'll be home tomorrow night," she said. "Unless this person can't fit me in until later."

"So tell him to see you tonight."

"I'll try." Suddenly Terri felt tired. "Can I talk to Elena?"

"She's not here. When I got your message, I asked Janie to keep her for the night."

"Why?"

"I've got another investor dinner. Janie said it was fine, that Lainie and Tess do well together."

For a moment, Terri wondered whether sending Elena to a neighbor's was some obscure form of punishment, not for Elena but for her. "I thought I told you that Elena doesn't like Tess all that much."

"Really? I guess I forgot."

"You were at your computer." Terri stood, watching the falling sun become a ribbon of orange. "Maybe you didn't hear."

"I guess not. Anyhow, getting out makes kids

more independent.'' Before Terri could retort, he shifted subjects. ''Listen, Ter, there's something I was wanting to talk to you about.''

Why, Terri wondered, did she feel a knot forming in her stomach. ''What is it?''

''It's about capital. We're still a few thousand short of seed money.''

''Maybe we can sell my body.''

''I'm *serious.*''

Terri rubbed her temple. ''So am I. We don't have money—just a new computer I can't seem to pay off. Maybe you can sell that.''

''I need it for my business. Besides, it's all deductible—you've got to factor in the tax benefits.''

''We don't have any more money,'' she said slowly. ''It's that simple.''

There was a long silence. ''That's what I wanted to talk with you about.''

The headache, Terri realized, started in the cords of her neck and ended at her eyes.

''What, exactly?''

''Your pension plan.'' Richie paused. ''We can borrow against it.''

Terri touched her eyes. ''I'm not sure we can.''

''We can, though. I checked with your accountant, at the firm.''

''You *called* her?''

''You weren't *here,* all right? Lighten up, Ter. I

didn't take the money or anything. Nothing can happen until you sign the papers.''

Until, Terri thought. Finally, she said. ''I haven't been here that long. It's probably only about five hundred dollars.''

''Nearly thirteen hundred.'' Richie began speaking faster. ''You can borrow up to *half* of that, at a cost of less than eighty dollars a month. No monthly payments, even—they just take it off the top of your check.''

''You mean, like having your wages garnisheed?''

''Listen to yourself.'' Richie's voice rose. ''This is what I mean about complete nonsupport. Except it's even worse—you try to humiliate me to control me.''

Terri sat down. ''I'm sorry,'' she said. ''I don't want to humiliate you. I just want us to get a grip on our life. I can't *predict* anything, Richie—there's always something else.'' She paused, struggling to explain. ''You begin to talk, and I feel paralyzed. My stomach gets like this fist.''

Richie's tone softened. ''I'm sorry, babe. I forgot how rules-oriented your mom was. All those limits.''

Why was it, Terri wondered, that so often with Richie she did not know how she felt. She might be angry, somewhere, but all she felt was numb. ''It's not my mother, Richie. It's me.''

Richie gave a knowing laugh. ''Okay, *you*. Then ask yourself whether a few hundred bucks is worth all this time on the phone. You're eating into our profits, Ter.''

It was dark, Terri suddenly realized; she had not seen night fall. ''I'll think about it,'' she finally said. ''Okay?''

''Great.'' Richie was upbeat again. ''We can talk about it as soon as you get back.''

Terri paused. ''Listen, if for any reason I'm home late tomorrow night, please keep Elena home, all right?''

''Sure. I'll take her out for dinner at some place she really likes, then maybe for an ice cream float.'' He paused, as if struck by a new thought. ''Listen, why don't the three of us go to Tilden Park this weekend—take a picnic, ride the train. Great family day.''

Something in his energy, Terri thought, made her wearier yet. Then she remembered how much Elena liked the train. ''That sounds fine,'' she told him, and said goodbye.

For a while, she simply sat in the darkness. Terri thought about room service, wondered about Lindsay Caldwell, about Richie and herself; did nothing. She felt unreal—adrift in a tropic night, away from her daughter, waiting for a call from someone she had seen only at a distance or on film.

The telephone rang, snapping Terri to alertness.

“Hello,” she said.

“Hello. Is this Teresa Peralta?”

The voice was clear, unadorned; Terri had always thought of it as stylish midwestern. “Yes,” Terri answered. “Thank you for calling.”

“You’re welcome,” Lindsay Caldwell said. “But then you knew I would, didn’t you?”

SEVEN

"IS THIS ABOUT Mark Ransom," Lindsay Caldwell asked Terri, "or Laura Chase?"

They sat on the deck of Caldwell's glass-and-redwood beach house at Malibu Colony, watching the morning sun dance on the ocean. Wearing blue jeans and a white sweater, Lindsay Caldwell seemed smaller than the woman Terri remembered seeing; with her tawny hair, clear blue eyes, and look of watchful intelligence, she appeared less like a film star than like a casually affluent suburban mother who did graduate work on the side. The sole difference was the businesslike authority, neither flaunted nor concealed, of a woman who produced her own films and thought her own thoughts; at whatever cost, Lindsay Caldwell had found out who she was.

"I'm not sure," Terri answered. "On the telephone, you said that I must know that you would see me. I don't even know why Mark Ransom wanted to see *you*."

Caldwell's expression mixed appraisal and surprise. "You don't," she said flatly.

Terri shook her head. ''What I thought,'' she ventured, ''is that you might have been a patient of Dr. Steinhardt's.''

''It's a decent guess.'' Pausing, Caldwell turned toward the water. ''There was a time when I ran through therapists like some women run through lovers, although what *I* was shopping for was a father. But no, I never tried that particular Freudian.'' Caldwell's tone became quiet, reflective. ''Although I've told myself often enough that no one could have saved her, or helped Laura save herself.''

The last caught Terri by surprise. ''You *knew* her?'' she asked.

This time, Terri thought, Caldwell's look had a certain furtive quality, as if her answers were themselves a form of probe. Slowly, she nodded. ''I was quite young then. Nineteen, in fact.''

Terri paused a moment. It was difficult to accept that Lindsay Caldwell would give her time, harder still to ask her about a legendary actress without knowing what the point was or why Caldwell would care to answer. Terri felt less lawyer than star-struck voyeur.

''Was that what Mark Ransom wanted to see you about?'' she asked.

Caldwell raised an eyebrow. '' 'That' being . . . ?''

''Laura Chase?''

Caldwell nodded. ''Yes. That was why Mark wanted to see me.''

Caldwell's tone was neither helpful nor hostile; Terri had felt more warmth from the woman who had spoken on the Berkeley campus than from the one sitting next to her. She decided to pursue a different tack.

"I heard you speak at Berkeley once," she said. "What was so effective was that you used what had happened to you, like sexual harassment or trying to get artistic control, to bring you closer to things that bothered me and all the other women I knew. But it's hard for me to relate to Laura Chase at all."

Caldwell's look became interested, more personal. "It's because you don't *want* to—none of us does. Laura was an exaggeration of everything women most fear in ourselves: a needy victim, full of short-sighted guile, who played into male fantasies and traded a sense of herself for any form of 'love' that would keep her from feeling alone." Caldwell paused. "If you've never, ever, had those thoughts about yourself, then you're either delusional or have such remarkable strength of character that you need to tell me how you've done it."

There was no edge in Caldwell's words, simply an unsparing self-knowledge that embraced them both. "I'm more delusional," Terri said simply. "Some days it works better than others."

For the first time, Caldwell smiled. "It's like trying to be a feminist—some days it works better than others. But, at least in my experience, it beats the known alternative.''

Terri nodded. ''Unless you're Mark Ransom.''

''Iron Mark.'' Caldwell's tone was flat. ''A man truly in touch with his primal self.''

Terri hesitated. ''Did you know him—I mean, before he called?''

''Oh, yes. We met at a symposium at Yale on 'Women in Film.' Someone thought it would be entertaining to invite him.'' Turning, Caldwell gazed out at the water. ''We had a disagreement, it's fair to say, regarding Laura's place in the pantheon of role models. It was hard to gauge Mark's strongest emotion—his passion for Laura Chase or his instinctive dislike for me. I was less confused: I remember calling him 'the poet laureate of the centerfold.' '' Caldwell frowned, shaking her head. ''What a complete waste of time. It's so much more effective to speak for your own beliefs than to ridicule someone else's.''

The breeze picked up, rippling Caldwell's hair. She looked clear-eyed, a little younger than she was, yet etched with the self-knowledge that time brings. Terri felt momentarily at peace; she watched the ocean, the line of white where waves struck the sand and, farther out, long strands of kelp undulating with the ebb and flow. A lone runner grew small in the distance, vanished. The air was heavy and smelled of salt.

Finally, Terri asked, "Why did you decide to see him?"

Caldwell kept watching the water, as if she found it soothing. "He discovered I'd known Laura."

"What did he say?"

"That he wanted to talk to me about it. Personally."

Caldwell's answers were becoming terse again, a little distant. Perhaps, Terri thought, another direction would help things flow.

"Laura Chase was much older," she ventured, "and even then, you couldn't have been much alike."

Caldwell shook her head. "More alike than you think. I'd been locked up in boarding schools for years, rebelling against my father through the usual well-considered means—drinking and boys." Caldwell paused. "There got to be a lot of boys. The angrier my father was, the less it mattered who I did it with, even boys I hated. Back then, they called it promiscuity. I forget what Radcliffe called it when they threw me out."

Terri had not known this. But Caldwell spoke the words with a tired familiarity, as if she had traveled this road many times before, in search of understanding.

"How did you meet Laura Chase?" Terri asked.

"That part was easy. As you may or may not know, my father ran Paramount then, so they stuck me in the family business." Caldwell's voice became dry. "Eventually, I developed a perverse desire to be more important than he was. But my first job was a minor role as Laura Chase's kid sister, for which my major qualification was to be more or less flat-chested."

"I've never seen that one, I guess."

"It never got made." Caldwell's voice grew softer. "Laura killed herself just before our biggest scene."

For a moment, Terri was silent. Then she asked, "What was she like?"

Caldwell's eyes narrowed. "In retrospect, I suppose the most obvious thing about her was a kind of ruined sensitivity—she wanted to love and be loved but was far too needy to find that in any way that wasn't self-destructive. One day, she would sleep with an extra for the most fleeting sense of security. The next day, she'd stay in her trailer until the director begged her to work. But she could never find enough within herself to figure out how to get things right." Caldwell's tone turned rueful. "What she did have was an uncanny sense of what was wounded in other people. Especially when the wounds were like her own."

It was best, Terri decided, to see where this might go. "It's funny—I've read a lot about your parents or your politics or how you got to make your own films. But I don't remember you saying anything about Laura Chase.''

''I've never talked about her.'' Caldwell gazed toward the water. ''Not in public, at least.''

Terri paused. ''Why was it,'' she asked, ''that you were willing to talk with Mark Ransom?''

''He said that he had tapes. Of Laura, talking to her psychiatrist.'' Caldwell paused. ''It came as a surprise to me.''

''Is that how he became aware that you knew Laura Chase—something on the tapes?''

Caldwell turned to her. ''Can I ask why you care?''

The question was edgy, guarded. ''Ransom had a tape,'' Terri answered, ''from a few days before she died. It's about a weekend in Palm Springs—Laura Chase meeting James Colt and two of his friends. What happened to her was bad enough that it may explain her suicide.''

''And she mentions me?''

Terri was startled. ''Were you there?''

''In Palm Springs?'' Caldwell turned away. ''God, no.''

Her voice held a hint of pain. ''As far as I know,'' Terri answered, ''Laura didn't talk about you on that tape. Ransom must have had another one.''

Caldwell looked at her again. ''He told me he had all of them.''

Terri nodded. "What he tried to do with Mary Carelli was trade the tape for sex." She paused, and then added, "That particular tape seemed to excite him."

Caldwell stood and walked to the railing of the deck. She leaned there, palms flat on the top rail, staring out at the ocean. "What you're trying to establish," she finally said, "is that when Mark met Mary Carelli, he had some sort of premeditated sexual agenda and that the tapes were a part of it."

"Yes."

Caldwell shook her head. From the back, the gesture suggested not denial but weariness. When she turned, she seemed a different woman, vulnerable and self-doubting. "You simply don't know what you're asking. But then Mark Ransom did know. And if I understand what I saw on *60 Minutes,* Mary Carelli could use a friend." She hesitated, looking intently at Terri. "If I tell you what happened, I decide whether and how it gets used."

It was a statement, not a question. Terri nodded. "All right."

Caldwell searched her face. Finally, she asked, "What is it that you want to know?"

Terri reflected. "Maybe where to start is what Ransom said was on the tape."

Caldwell looked at her for another moment. "Just enough to convince me to see a man I loathed."

"What were you afraid of?"

"Several things." Caldwell's voice and gaze were steady now. "Beginning with the week I spent in Laura's guesthouse."

Terri said nothing. She was learning to know when words were needed and when silence was better than speech. Lindsay Caldwell seemed in control of herself; if she had decided to talk, it was for her own reasons, and all that Terri needed to do was listen.

"I was a mess," Caldwell began. "Drinking every day, screwing more or less at random. Some days I'd wake up pretty close to a black-out drunk, uncertain whether the fragments of memory were real or some twisted dream. A couple of times men called me and I couldn't remember who they were or what I'd done with them." Caldwell paused. "Even when they told me.

"That was how I was when I met Laura—drunken, careless, and lost. Like Laura herself."

The words came easily, as if Caldwell had said them to herself a thousand times. But speaking them aloud produced a rough edge in her voice Terri had not heard before, on-screen or in person. "Laura knew that," Caldwell continued. "She had radar for the wounded. Before the first scene we did together, she seemed remote and hardly real, as if she were another species of woman. But she was the one who realized that my hands weren't shaking out of fear but because of what I'd done the night before.

"'It was an adaptation of a William Inge play—she was a glamorous woman from Chicago, returning to her tiny hometown, and I was the bookish sister, too scared to leave. The first scene was supposed to be in my bedroom, both of us putting on makeup for a dance while we talked about her life.'' Caldwell shook her head. "I knew my lines well enough, but eyeliner was beyond me. My hands shook too much.

"So Laura improvised. She took the eyeliner from my hand, said, 'Here, let me show you,' and applied my makeup while we finished the scene. It was instinctively perfect, just right for the relationship between the two sisters, and the lines flowed from there. The director loved it.

"Afterwards, I thanked her. She gave me that funny smile she had—like she knew your worst secrets and didn't care—and said, 'If you're going to drink like that, wait until they need you enough to clean up after you.' And then she went off to her dressing room.

"That night, when I was walking to the parking lot, I felt a hand on my arm. It was Laura. 'Are you at least taking the night off?' she asked. I wasn't, of course—I'd been semi fixed up with a bit actor who I knew in my heart wanted to tell his friends he'd fucked Leon Caldwell's daughter. Which was exactly why I was going to let him do it.'' Caldwell shook her head. "I don't know why, but I couldn't tell

Laura that—it was like she knew me too well. After a moment, she said, 'You'd better come home with me.'

"I didn't think about arguing. I just went."

To Terri, the words sounded like a fissure between one part of Lindsay Caldwell's life and another. Caldwell turned to her. "Laura took care of me," she said simply.

Terri hesitated. "In what way?"

"Every way." Caldwell looked past her. "She had a beautiful house in the West Hollywood Hills, with so much luxury it was almost a spoof—a deliberate one, I think, like Laura's film persona. But Laura herself became a different woman. Off came the dress and cosmetics, up went the hair, and Laura suddenly looked something like a homemaker. It was as if, for Laura, coming home, and having company who wasn't a man, was a relief.

" 'I always wanted a sister,' she told me, 'and now I've got one. Thanks to William Inge and Twentieth Century-Fox.'

"Before I knew it, she'd fixed up the guesthouse, found me some clothes to wear, and we were sitting at a table by the pool, nibbling Caesar salad and watching the sun go down, while Laura told me all about her childhood. No drinks in sight, either—just iced tea."

Caldwell paused. "It was funny," she went on. "I felt taken *over,* like I was a blank screen on which

Laura was projecting her need of the moment. But I also felt taken *care of,* without being judged, which my father had never made me feel. At some point in the evening, I just gave in to it.

"I told Laura things I had never said to anyone."

Even at twenty years' distance, Terri thought, the words sounded lonely.

"And then," Caldwell said in a flat voice, "Laura lit the candles on the table and told me about her father raping her, repeatedly, until she blacked out."

Terri froze, staring up at her. "It was plain to me," Caldwell said. "Even then. What had happened with her father was more shock than any adolescent could handle, and it changed the way she felt forever. She was worthless, men were a frightening mystery, and the only thing she took from it was an instinct for pain. Which she would experience, again and again, without ever comprehending why.

"When she finished, I was crying." Caldwell hesitated. "It should have been for Laura," she said softly. "It wasn't, really. For the first time, I had begun to understand myself.

"When I looked across the table, I realized she thought it was for her. She stood up, came closer." Caldwell paused. "When she kissed me, I felt too selfish to object.

"We went to the guesthouse then, Laura carrying the candles." Caldwell began walking in random circles. ‘‘She was very tender, not like the boys I’d known. I suppose she’d pleased so many men, wished for so much she’d never gotten, that she knew just how to be with me.

‘‘I let her undress me, kiss my nipples, do everything she wanted. That first time, it was all her, and she took care of me.’’ Caldwell stopped, turned to Terri with a look of pain. ‘‘Just like she wanted someone to take care of her.

‘‘Afterwards, she told me she had never been with a woman before. That it was like inventing her own language instead of speaking someone else’s. And now we could invent it together.’’ Slowly, Caldwell shook her head. ‘‘For a time, I just lay with my head in her lap, listening to her talk. Until turning my face didn’t seem very far to go.

‘‘It was like that for a week.’’

Caldwell looked away again, her gaze following a lone gull that had swooped down on the beach. ‘‘We would go to the studio together, come home and cook dinner, drink nothing but milk. Every night, we would swim together, in the nude. Afterwards, she would towel me off and help me practice my lines. Almost as if I were a child.

‘‘She asked for very little. Just to take care of me, as she wanted to be taken care of, and to get affection in return.’’ Caldwell paused. ‘‘For that one week, I gave that to her.’’

Terri was silent. How many lives, she thought, have their painful private moments, too intimate to be shared with strangers, too powerful to forget. Finally, she asked, "Is that what Ransom knew?"

Caldwell watched the gull. "Part," she said. "Perhaps not all."

Terri hesitated. "What did he want from you?"

Caldwell's eyes grew cold. "A private interview. In his hotel suite."

"What did you think that meant?"

"Some private indignity. Something far less tender than occurred with Laura." Caldwell's voice was quiet. "If I had any doubts about that, they ended with Mary Carelli."

"Were you going to go?"

"I was going to *listen* and then deal with him somehow." Caldwell's tone grew crisp. "I have two children now, a husband whom I very much love and don't care to hurt. I'm sure they'd try to understand, but still . . . And what about the others, who see me as a symbol of the women's movement, pro and con? Did you catch the furor when the president of NOW admitted being bisexual?"

Terri nodded. "Yes. I did."

Caldwell paused. "Twenty years ago, I learned that at any given time, some people can be one thing or another. But that's harder for a lot of other people to understand than equal pay for equal work, and I don't want to help some yahoo like Jesse Helms confuse the two—as cowardly as it may be to skip this chance to educate the public.''

Terri was silent, sensing something left unsaid. ''What else,'' she asked quietly, ''did Ransom know?''

Caldwell's searching gaze became a stare. ''What makes you ask?''

''Because you wanted Ransom to tell you something that you didn't know.'' Terri watched her. ''Just as you've hoped that *I* can.''

Caldwell's face seemed to pass through a series of changes, from surprise to resignation to a deeper level of anguish. Then she looked at Terri again, even more closely than before. ''You have a kind of gift,'' she said. ''A silence, almost a stillness, while someone talks to you. You've drawn them out before they learn how much you see.''

Terri felt her own surprise; what Caldwell said sounded true, and yet she had not quite known it. ''It's not meant to harm,'' Terri answered.

Caldwell studied her in silence. Finally, she said, ''Let's walk, all right? I feel like a prisoner.''

Terri kicked off her heels. They followed the redwood steps down to the beach and began walking on the sand, Caldwell looking like a woman on vacation, Terri like a yuppie on a lunch break. They would have been an amusing pair, Terri thought, except for the look on Caldwell's face.

"It was during that week," Caldwell began, "that Laura told me about James Colt."

Terri glanced over at her, surprised.

"How long was that before she shot herself?"

Caldwell knelt, rolling up the bottom of her jeans. Quietly, she answered, "Ten days or so."

From her tone, Terri knew that she need ask no further questions. They resumed walking, both silent.

After a time, Caldwell spoke again. "I had heard the rumors, of course. About how she and Colt would meet in secret, even how she fantasized about becoming First Lady—which was impossible, of course. But it was still strange to hear Laura talk about making love to 'the future leader of the free world,' as she mockingly called him, the blond handsome man we saw on television talking about courage and sacrifice and social justice." Caldwell looked over at Terri. "Somehow, knowing made me feel lousy. James Colt was a hero to me—I wanted him to be a little better than the last six guys I'd slept with. Too good to be taking advantage of Laura's weaknesses like some sleazy producer banging her on the couch and then going home to his wife and son.

"But what was worse, I realize now, was how Laura talked about him.

"He was this mysterious force she didn't understand. Laura wanted to believe in him, but she felt a deep resentment too—she referred to him as 'God almighty' as often as she used his name. The one thing that was clear to me was that Laura was at his beck and call. Even her jokes about him were the wisecracks of a slave.'' Caldwell paused, shoulders hunched forward. ''It made me think about my life.''

Terri looked over at her. ''Then Laura taught you something.''

''More than you can imagine.'' Caldwell looked away. ''I was there the night James Colt asked her to meet him in Palm Springs.''

Surprised, Terri said nothing. Simply watched her.

Caldwell turned toward the water, standing where the waves, dying at their farthest ebb, met the sand. The wind rippled her honey hair, glistening in the sun. The ocean lapped at Terri's feet.

''We were in the guesthouse,'' Caldwell said in the same quiet tone, ''in a pink bedroom with mirrors on the ceiling one of her husbands had installed. I was lying with my head on her shoulder, watching my own reflection as Laura stroked my hair.''

For a moment, Caldwell's voice had a dreamlike quality. ''I was neither happy nor sad. I felt peaceful and at the same time sort of lost. Like this wasn't really me, just sort of a space I was occupying until something changed in me and I started on a different life than the one I'd brought to this house.

''Then Laura began to talk.''

The rhythm of Caldwell's speech changed again,

quickening. "What was so good between us, Laura said, was that it was so gentle. There wasn't any taking, only giving to each other, because all we wanted was to love and be loved. I had given her something that she'd never had before." Caldwell's voice grew lower. "In the mirror, I saw that Laura's eyes had filled with tears.

"I turned to her then, confused and somehow frightened." Caldwell paused. "She thought I was turning out of love. So she smiled, even with the tears, and then kissed me.

"When the telephone rang, she was saying, 'I love you too.' "

For a moment, Caldwell's voice had caught. Terri tried to imagine the moment: Lindsay Caldwell lost at nineteen, Laura Chase reaching out to her. To her surprise, what she felt most clearly was how overwhelmed Caldwell must have been.

"It was Senator Colt," Caldwell said. "Laura held the phone out so I could hear his voice.

"It was so strange. I was lying naked in bed with another woman, perhaps the most famous actress in the world, listening while someone who might become the next President asked her to spend the weekend in Palm Springs."

Caldwell looked down. "He talked for a while—I couldn't hear him clearly. In the mirror above me, Laura's face got very clouded, and then I felt her draw up her knees.

" 'Who are they?' she asked."

Caldwell shook her head. "She didn't have to say anything more—I could see her eyes reflected back at me. No matter how he'd put it, Laura knew what he had in mind for her, and *I* knew she knew.

"Suddenly my skin felt cold, and then Laura reached for my hand.

" 'I'm not sure,' she told him. 'I'll have to think about it.'

"He started talking again. As she listened, her fingers clasped mine tighter. Just before she hung up, Laura said, 'Suppose I'm not available. Just suppose, Senator Colt, that *I've* found someone else.' "

Caldwell knelt to scoop up a sand dollar, inspected it in silence. "It was a moment before I realized," she said at length, "that Laura was talking about *me*."

Terri glanced at her again. As the path of her story moved toward its end, Caldwell's voice seemed to be losing resonance. Even her steps had slowed. "When Laura hung up," Caldwell said, "I felt as if I'd made a commitment.

"I should have been glad for her—that she hadn't said yes right away. But what I felt was this kind of suffocating pressure. That Laura might reject James Colt for me. That if she stayed away from men, or drinking, it would be for me. That it all depended on *me*.

"I'd given myself over to Laura, and now, suddenly, I wanted to be away from Laura.'' Caldwell paused. ''And while I was lying there, thinking that, Laura laid my head between her breasts.

''That night I almost ran away.''

Caldwell shook her head. ''I couldn't,'' she added softly. ''When Laura fell asleep, her arms were still around me.''

Terri gazed ahead, walking in tandem with Caldwell at the edge of the water. The sun was in midflight now, the sky winter blue, the light-streaked water aqua gray as it reached the whiteness of the sand. But Caldwell's story of Laura Chase made it all seem surreal, a dream.

''How did you leave?'' Terri asked.

Caldwell gave her a sidelong glance. ''In the only way possible,'' she said at last. ''I told her the truth.''

Terri said nothing. After a time, Caldwell continued as if she had not stopped. ''Sitting at breakfast, with Laura holding my hands. Not because I was honest. Because I was selfish, and scared, and couldn't think of any other way.

'' 'Why?' she kept asking, with tears running down her face, sobbing, until I told her everything.'' Caldwell's speech quickened, as she was drawn back into the moment. ''That I was confused. That she frightened me. That I was too much like her. That being secret lovers was no life. That I had to find my own life.'' Caldwell paused, drew in one sharp breath, and then finished quietly: "That I could never love her as she wanted to be loved."

There was silence, and then Terri realized that she was walking alone. Caldwell had stopped behind her, touching her forehead. "It was like if I told her everything," she murmured, "Laura would let me go."

Terri waited a moment. "What did she do?"

"I got my wish." Caldwell looked up, face ravaged with pain. "It was as if I'd shot her.

"She dropped my hands. Just looked at me. Mouth half open, no sound at all. Only her eyes moved." Caldwell paused, voice slowing for emphasis. "I've experienced a lot before and since, including things my father said or did that were crueler than people can imagine. But I have never seen a face that wounded.

"I don't know how long we were sitting there, a few inches apart, saying nothing. And then she whispered, 'I'll have to go with him now.' "

" *'No,'* I said. 'It's not about *me*. I don't *want* it to be about me. Don't go for *you*. Because you don't want *anyone* to treat you like that.' "

Caldwell gave a humorless smile. "Great advice, right from the self-help library—I was ahead of my time. But I was the only one who heard it. For Laura, I could have been speaking Swahili." Caldwell's voice became bitter. "And, of course, I knew that."

"But it's true," Terri said. "You can't supply

some other adult with something they don't have. Any more than you can sustain a relationship by offering up your sense of yourself as a kind of bribe. In the end, everyone loses."

Caldwell gave her a complex look of irony and understanding. "Are you talking to me, Teresa, or to yourself?"

Terri hesitated. "To you, at least."

"I see." Caldwell paused, searching Terri's face. "Well, then, if you're talking to me, then there's a little more to the story, and the ending is a little more dramatic.

"The night Laura died, she called my apartment."

Caldwell turned toward the water. "It was an hour or so before she shot herself. I hadn't needed to be on the set, hadn't seen Laura at all, had tried not to imagine her weekend in Palm Springs. I was thinking about going out and picking someone up." Caldwell paused. "To prove to myself that I was straight.

"Somehow, I knew it was her.

"She was drunk, and alone." Caldwell folded her arms. "As people will when they're drunk, she kept repeating herself. And what she said, over and over again, was, 'I need you tonight.' "

A tremor seemed to move through Caldwell's body. "She scared me. Her voice was like a child's. It made her sound so insatiable.

" 'Please,' Laura said. 'I went with him.'

"The way she sounded—I just didn't want to hear. I didn't know who I was more frightened of: Laura or myself.

"All I knew was that I had to stop her from saying 'I need you.' " Caldwell's eyes shut. "I told her I had a date."

Inwardly, Terri winced.

"After I said that," Caldwell went on quietly, "Laura began sobbing. Hurt, almost animal sounds. It was like I could feel her shiver through the telephone.

"There was only one thing I could think to do. I told her goodbye and hung up." Caldwell had begun pacing in half circles, as if confined by the apartment she was remembering. "Then I turned out the lights. As if I were afraid that Laura might find me."

Caldwell stared down at the sand. "The telephone rang, again and again. I sat there in the dark perhaps an hour or so, afraid to answer. Just listening to it ring.

"Then it stopped."

Caldwell turned to Terri. "I'd never known that silence could be so profound. Perhaps it was the darkness. For I'm not sure how long, I couldn't move. Then, without realizing why, I got up and drove to Laura's.

"There were no lights. When I rang the doorbell, no one answered—no Laura, no maid. The door was locked.

"I was relieved." Caldwell shifted slightly, turning away from Terri. "I thought Laura had gone out. Then I remembered the guesthouse.

"There was a moon. I found the path around the house, through the flowers and shrubbery, which came out by the pool.

"The pool was dark. I stared into it for a moment, looking for something, hoping not to find anything. Then I noticed that the lights were on in the guesthouse.

"When I reached the door, it was ajar.

"I stood there, suddenly afraid. And then I knew why I had come."

Caldwell paused, gazing down. In Terri's imagination, her posture mimed that of a nineteen-year-old girl, twenty years before, deciding whether to step through a half-open door. And then Caldwell said, "I went in.

"The bedroom door was open.

"Inside, the light was pale yellow. The first thing I saw was the telephone by the bed. It was off the hook, dangling by the cord, which stretched to the floor until it disappeared in shadows. The receiver made a throbbing sound that seemed to echo in the room.

"Laura was on the bed.

"She was naked, her hair was wet, she was lying on a bath towel. For a second, I thought she'd just passed out after going for a swim. Then I saw the revolver in her hand, blood and hair scattered across the pillow. The back of her head was gone."

Terri flinched. "I turned away," Caldwell said softly. "After that, I never looked at Laura again. Except on film."

Terri wanted to reach out to her, then felt that this would be pointless. "What did you do?" she asked.

"I was in a trance. I stood there, my back to Laura, as if I'd been anesthetized. What penetrated, finally, was the relentless screeching of the telephone." Caldwell's voice had steadied. Each word was precise and clear, as if she were describing a picture she had memorized years before. "It kept beeping until I couldn't stand it anymore. All I could think of was to stop the sound. When I hung it up, and the sound stopped, it was like my brain reconnected to some sort of reality.

"Someone had to know." Caldwell paused. "It was foolish and empty, but I couldn't leave her alone like that.

"I picked up the telephone. When the Emergency operator came on, I said, 'Laura Chase has killed herself.'

"There was this long silence—I'm sure she thought I was some sort of crank. Finally, she asked who I was. I realized that I didn't want to say. So I answered, 'Just a friend.' " Caldwell shook her head. "It sounded so miserable.

"She kept asking who I was. Somehow, it made

me angry. 'Damn you,' I snapped. 'She's put a fucking bullet through her brain,' and slammed down the telephone.

"After that, I just walked out.

"I didn't look back and didn't run. It was like turning away from Laura had taken all the energy I had. I walked to the car like a robot, switched on the ignition, and started down the driveway.

"When I got to the end, I had to stop for a moment, to remember where I was going, which way to turn. Then I started home." Caldwell paused. "I'd gone perhaps a quarter mile when I saw the ambulance, lights flashing, coming toward me in the other lane."

Caldwell looked at Terri. "That's when I knew for sure that the whole thing had been real.

"I just kept driving.

"That night, I couldn't sleep. The next day, when I could finally stand to open my door, Laura looked up at me from the morning paper."

Remembering, Caldwell's eyes seemed uncomprehending. "I kept waiting for them to come. They never did. No one had taped my call. They didn't have my fingerprints. No one knew about me and Laura." Caldwell looked away. "No one knew I was even there."

Terri said nothing. There was a long silence, and then Caldwell raised her head. She looked determined, almost defiant. "For years," she said, "I've read articles about the mysterious caller, about 'Who Killed Laura Chase.' But I'm the only one who ever knew the answer." Turning back to Terri, she finished in a steady voice. "*I* killed Laura Chase."

"No," Terri answered. "You didn't."

Caldwell looked at her. "Oh, I know all the right answers. I've had years of therapy to master them. Laura killed Laura. Or society, or Hollywood, or her father or Senator Colt or a thousand men in between. Even swine like Ransom, who built their fantasies on an idea of Laura which has damaged countless other women almost as badly as it damaged her. I *know* all that. But there's still one question for which those answers don't work at all.

"I keep asking myself, What would have happened to Laura if she'd just gotten through that night? For *that* there is no answer."

Terri shook her head. "But that was twenty years ago. You have a whole life to look at now. Not just the senseless thing that Laura did when you were nineteen and even your own life made no sense."

"My own life," Caldwell echoed. "I'm still sorting out how much of *that* I owe to Laura. After that night, I hardly drank again. I didn't go out for almost a year, and when I did, the sport fucking was over. Laura's death was like a fault line. Did she make me a feminist? Or a mother? Or a filmmaker? Or a wife? Or some or all of them? I'll never know that, either."

Terri waited, then asked quietly, "What is it that you thought Mark Ransom might tell you?"

"Part of it was what he might tell my husband, or my children. But there was more." Caldwell frowned, as if struggling to articulate something too enormous to be captured in a few words. "All this time, I've talked to Laura in my head, asking why she did it, what I meant to her. But when she answers, it's in my voice." She paused. "I wanted to hear *her* again, talking *about* me but not *to* me. I thought I might learn the truth."

"Do you think Laura really knew the truth, whatever it is?"

"Perhaps not." Caldwell turned to Terri, as if in search of understanding. "But how could I know the tape existed and run away from it?"

Terri studied her face. "So Ransom promised to bring a tape. Where Laura talks about you."

Caldwell nodded. "I suppose the police must have it now."

"No." Terri hesitated. "When he died, Ransom only had one tape. The one he played for Mary, about James Colt. The second tape he described to you, he didn't have."

Caldwell looked surprised, and then her eyes went cold.

"That bastard," she said.

EIGHT

"So far," Moore said to Christopher Paget, "it would appear that Ransom was either celibate or had taken up the 'solitary sin,' as my old priest used to call it. At least for the last two years."

They sat on a bench at the foot of California Street. To their right, the cable car line swept up California to the top of Nob Hill, where Ransom had died; ahead and to their left, Market Street ended at an open plaza, behind which stood the Ferry Building, its venerable clock tower showing a little past 2:30. Behind them were the four adjacent towers of Embarcadero Center, each housing about thirty floors of offices; the crowd around them seemed equal parts tourists and professionals, with a scattering of street people and three or four strutting pigeons, looking for food. On a nearby bench, a harmless lunatic, dressed in the jeans and seaman's jacket he had worn every day for years, shouted his usual mix-and-match fragments about conspiracies: today's special seemed to feature the CIA, Mary Lou Retton, and the New York Museum of Modern Art.

Moore, who could not stand to lunch indoors, consumed the last bit of his salami sandwich.

Paget looked at him. ''Nothing?''

''Nothing. And I don't just mean a laudable absence of attempted rapes. I mean the virtual absence of attempted dates.'' Moore made a short, choppy gesture of emphasis. ''Nothing in the columns. No trips with women. Not a single female person, so far, who will admit to screwing Ransom anytime this decade. Either the act was so dreadful they've repressed it, so forgettable they thought dear Mark was merely sneezing, or sex just wasn't on his agenda for the nineties.''

''That simply can't be. Not after his call to Lindsay Caldwell.''

''I know, I know.'' Moore's eyes narrowed. ''Poor woman. I always liked her.''

''I still do.''

Moore nodded. After a time, he said, ''*Our* little girl's done well.''

''Terri, I assume you mean. My only question about Terri is whether she knows how good she is.''

Moore became quiet for a moment. ''There's something sad about her, don't you think?''

''I *think,* yes. But I honestly don't know what, or why—it's more a sense, like quicksilver, which comes and goes in an instant. Terri's very private, and she holds on tight.''

''Unlike you,'' Moore said sardonically. ''The

Mr. Rogers of white-collar law, so warm and fuzzy. It goes without saying that you've not met the husband."

"No." Paget found himself squinting at the sunlight. "Why do you ask?"

"Just a sense of my own. Something she said in passing."

Paget examined him. "Ah, Johnny," he said lightly, "you're not falling in love, are you? Not with my twenty-nine-year-old married associate."

Moore shook his head. "Too old," he said. "There's just too much sadness in the world, that's all, and it's far too late for either of *us*."

Paget smiled. "Personally, I've pinned my hopes on Carlo. It keeps me from becoming maudlin when I start performing mental tricks like doubling my age or adding up how many years I've already lived past Mozart. When I turned forty-five, the results of either calculation were rather melancholy."

"Still," Moore said, "you at least owe Ms. Peralta a pat on the back when she returns. This Lindsay Caldwell thing—"

"This Lindsay Caldwell thing," Paget put in, "reeks of sexual blackmail. It's a weird variant of what Mary says happened to her: trading tapes for sex, except that Ransom had tremendous leverage on Caldwell and none at all on Mary. Which, one assumes, is why he resorted to rape. And why Mary felt free—however inadvertently—to spare Lindsay

Caldwell a private meeting with someone who no doubt had given considerable thought to her debasement.''

''Except,'' Moore retorted, ''that there *was* no second tape, and Mark Ransom has been living the life of Saint Augustine.''

''Oh, there was a tape about Caldwell, all right—Ransom must have listened to it before he called her. Which leaves the question of where it is.''

''I've no idea.'' Moore turned to him again. ''If it comes to a trial, Chris, can you get Caldwell's story into evidence?''

Paget shook his head. ''In justice, I should. But I probably have even less chance than with Melissa Rappaport. Nothing happened: Ransom scheduled an interview and then died first. The only consequence to Lindsay Caldwell is that somewhere, perhaps in one of Ransom's homes, exists a very nasty tape that will give Marnie Sharpe hours of listening pleasure.''

Moore considered that. ''Jeanne-Marc Steinhardt,'' he finally said, ''paid her dear old mum a real tribute. So meaningful to the dead, so helpful to the living.''

Paget was silent for a moment. ''No price,'' he answered softly, ''is too great for the truth.''

Moore looked at him. ''If there's any dirt on Ransom, Chris, I'll find it.''

* * *

At seven-fifty, Paget found Terri in her office, looking drawn in the fluorescent light.

"Why aren't you home?" he asked.

Terri brushed back her hair. "By the time I got in from Los Angeles, Richie had taken Elena out to dinner." She smiled faintly. "Father-daughter night, he called it. So I decided to take a little more time to process things."

There was a hesitancy in her voice; except to see Elena, Paget guessed, some part of her was not eager to go home. "In the past six days," Paget said, "you've interviewed Melissa Rappaport, Jeanne Steinhardt, and Lindsay Caldwell. Processing *that* should take some time."

Terri watched him. "I suppose, for me, it will."

"For you?" Paget smiled. "As opposed to whom—the truly insensitive in general, or Johnny and me in particular? Or have your glaring personal inadequacies prevented you from noting that you've gotten three strangers to tell you things they've never told anyone else and perhaps never would have."

"That's part of what bothers me." Terri's shoulders drew in. "Knowing this stuff—it makes me feel responsible for them."

"You made them promises, Terri. I promise you I'll keep them." Paget watched her face. "Somewhere along the line, I've started trying to notice the damage I'll do before I do it. I do have a couple of questions, though."

Some of the strain seemed to vanish from Terri's face. "Sure."

"Are you hungry? Because I am. And have you ever eaten at Piano Zinc?"

Terri looked surprised. "What about Carlo?"

"He had a game. So I fed him on the way back, to save homework time, and then watched him shuffle up the stairs toward his English paper like a prisoner on death row. Which is close to how I'm feeling about being here now."

Terri smiled. "Then the answers are 'yes,' 'no,' and 'I'd like to.' "

Le Piano Zinc was a crowded art deco café with mirrors on two sides, light-pink walls, framed Parisian posters. The slender, mustached maître d' and Paget spoke briefly and amiably in French, and then Paget introduced Terri in English. The maître d' smiled, shook her hand, and led them to a table in a quiet corner. The minute or two spent doing this reminded Terri of how little she knew about Paget's life.

"I didn't know you spoke French," she said.

"College French, and poor at that. I practice on Robert, who indulges me. It's the last vestige of my first ambition."

"Which was?"

"To live in Paris and be Hemingway. Problem was, there'd already *been* a Hemingway."

"Why didn't you try someone else?"

Paget smiled. "That was the ultimate problem—I couldn't 'find my own voice,' as it were. When I didn't sound like Hemingway without the machismo, I sounded like Faulkner without the genius. And too few people read the Faulkner who *was* a genius."

Terri appraised him. "You know, sometimes I can't tell when you're serious."

"Believe me, it's completely intentional." Paget smiled again. "Some of the things I'm serious about embarrass me."

Somewhere in the flippant remark, Terri thought, was an element of truth. "You're serious about Carlo," she said.

Paget nodded. "About Carlo I'm absolutely serious." He paused, then added lightly, "Poor kid."

The throwaway line hung there for a moment. What was it about Christopher Paget, Terri wondered, that so often made her feel as though they were having a two-track conversation: the first level what Paget said, the second and much more obscure level what Paget might communicate if she ever got close enough.

"How has it been," she asked, "raising him alone?"

Paget's eyes narrowed; Terri could not tell whether this was in contemplation of the question itself, or of why she had asked it.

"In a way," he said finally, "that's like asking what it's like to be me: it's all I know, so I've got no perspective on it. I suppose raising Carlo makes me acutely aware of all my deficiencies; I'm sure that makes me much more anxious than I'd be if I were married, and much more a burden to Carlo." He paused. "Although, in my own childhood, I learned that a rotten marriage is also rotten for the kid, and in ways more subtle and insidious than Carlo's teenage resentments of me."

"Is that why you never married?"

Paget looked surprised and then laughed. "I *was* married. Just not to Mary Carelli."

"To whom?"

The waitress, Terri realized, was hovering near their table. Paget turned to her with a wry expression, as if in search of rescue.

"Will you be having wine this evening?" she asked.

Paget turned to Terri. "*I* will," he said, "if you insist on having this particular conversation."

Terri hesitated and then saw that, in some small way, Paget's remark was to signal his acceptance of her as something more than just a lawyer. "Sure," she said.

"Do you care what we're eating in terms of red or white?"

"No." She smiled. "Richie and I drink from jugs, not bottles, and according to what's already open."

Paget turned to the waitress, said, ‘‘The Meursault, please,’’ and then faced Terri again.

‘‘As I remember,’’ she said, ‘‘I'd just asked who you were married to.’’

‘‘Oh, that. Her name was Andrea Lo Bianco.’’

Terri cocked her head. ‘‘Why does she sound so familiar?’’

‘‘She was a principal dancer for the San Francisco Ballet.’’ Paget smiled briefly. ‘‘After we divorced, she joined the ballet in Paris, funnily enough.’’

‘‘Was it funny?’’

‘‘Not terribly. But divorce rarely is.’’

Terri hesitated. ‘‘Was that before Carlo came?’’

Paget shook his head. ‘‘A year or so after. The two events were not unrelated.’’

The last remark, delivered matter-of-factly, had an undertone of regret. ‘‘She didn't want him?’’ Terri asked.

Paget gazed at the tables around them, almost idly. ‘‘It was far less personal than that, and more complex. Andrea had never wanted children, because of her career and temperament, and I didn't really care—I'd never thought that much of myself as a putative father. Her dancing was demanding, and when she was home, Andrea could pretty much count on having my attention.’’ Paget paused. ‘‘She knew about Carlo, of course, but when he actually came to live with us, our marriage changed quite a lot. In fairness to her, Carlo required a good bit of attention then, although that was hardly his fault, either. And for my own part, I felt I had no choice at all.''

Buried somewhere in the last two sentences, Terri thought, was a piece of the puzzle that was Paget's relationship to Mary Carelli. ''Why was that?'' she asked.

Paget looked off into the distance. ''He had some emotional problems,'' he finally answered. ''Today's shorthand, I suppose, would be that Carlo lacked self-esteem.''

The remark carried a painful trace of understatement. In the time it took the waitress to pour their first glass of wine, Terri decided to bury two questions she badly wanted to ask: ''What problems?'' and ''How did Carlo come to live with you?''—the second of which, she was somehow sure, would drive Paget back within himself.

Smiling, Paget raised his glass to her. ''To a marvelous career,'' he said, ''for a lawyer who's already better than most.''

Terri felt pleased and embarrassed, all at once. ''Hardly. But thanks.''

Paget gave her a droll look. ''Someday, Terri, you'll learn to accept a compliment. Perhaps your friend Johnny and I should take turns forcing them on you, until you acquire the knack. It'll be a lot easier for us than for you.''

"I don't mean to be like that. It's just that when people say nice things about me, I feel as though I've fooled them."

Paget smiled in acknowledgment. "The impostor syndrome. I know it well. Inside every self-assured professional lives a frightened neurotic who prays that he can somehow succeed before his clients discover the fraud. It's the guilty secret that drives us all."

"You too?"

"Me too." Paget grinned. "Even though, viewed from the outside, I'm clearly an incredible talent."

"Not to mention," Terri added, "Marnie Sharpe's forbidden fantasy."

Somehow the image piqued Paget's sense of the absurd. He started laughing and couldn't stop. "God," he said, "the mental pictures . . . ," and began laughing again. There was a sudden carelessness about his smile that made Terri want to keep it there: for a moment, she could imagine the young man he had been, before time and circumstance had changed him. And in that same moment, she realized how attractive he still was. The perfect match, she thought foolishly, for a prima ballerina.

"Mary, Andrea . . . ," she said, smiling. "Do you ever fall in love with Wasps?"

"Never; it's the tragic flaw that keeps me apart from Marnie. Ever since I was young, I've had the deep-seated fear that I'd grow up to marry an eastern type named Muffy, and then she'd give birth to twin loaves of Wonder bread.''

Terri shook her head. ''You can relax,'' she said. ''Carlo is not your white-bread kind of kid. More like an Italian film star.''

''Takes after his mother,'' Paget said lightly. ''Goes to show what careful planning can do.''

Again, Terri sensed something unspoken. It changed her mood ever so slightly; perhaps he had made her think of Elena. She finished her first glass of wine. ''What I can't understand,'' she said finally, ''is why you didn't think you'd be a good father.''

Paget poured them both more wine. ''For the same reason that I didn't think that *I'd* had a particularly great childhood. Too often, people do with their children what their parents did with them. *My* parents had parents too—who was I to think I was any better?''

''You are, though.''

Paget shrugged. ''Sometimes people can rise above themselves. If the need's extreme enough.''

''And Carlo's was?''

''Yes.'' Paget hesitated. ''Carlo's was.''

The reluctance had crept back in his voice. Terri realized that, for whatever reason, Paget had been more candid with her than was his custom; perhaps it was safe to give something in return.

"*My* parents fought," she said. "Or, more accurately, my father fought, and my mother tried to protect us."

"From what, exactly?"

"He drank. And when he drank, he got violent." Terri looked up at him. "It's something I've never really talked about."

Paget considered her. "Why not?"

"I'm not sure." Terri hesitated. "When you're young, you realize the family doesn't want people outside to know. It gets to be a habit." She touched her chest. "Intellectually, you understand all that. But it's what you feel here . . ."

Paget sipped his wine. "Your mother never left him?"

"No. She's Catholic and believes in the rules, no matter what." Terri stared at the table. "And there were five of us. I was the oldest—there are two still at home, and Mom's still watching out for them."

"How did she do that? Protect you, I mean."

"I don't know." Terri exhaled, began again. "I guess part was that she was so watchful, pretty much all the time. When my father drank, he heard insults where there weren't any. You never knew when it would hit. When I was little, I remember closing my eyes, covering my ears." Terri folded her hands. "Sometimes my mom had to stand up for us. But mostly she kept us out of the way, tried to calm things, kept up with our classes and activities. My father saw it as some sort of conspiracy, almost. But it was just my mom taking care of things the way she had to do."

Paget gave her a reflective look. "What did you learn from all that?"

"That there's nothing I can do for her."

"What I meant was: for yourself."

Terri touched her wineglass, tracing the circle at its rim. "To avoid fights," she finally answered. "And to take care of things myself."

"It stands to reason." Paget's tone changed, as if to signal a change of subject. "Tell me about Elena."

Terri felt a knot in her stomach she had not known was there. "Do you mean: what has Elena learned from me?"

Paget shook his head. "That's your question, Terri. It wasn't mine. I've got no right to strip-mine your personal life."

She looked up at him, surprised. His gaze was even, almost gentle. The tears in her own eyes startled her. "I'm sorry . . ."

Christopher Paget, Terri realized, had reached across and briefly touched her arm.

"For what?" he said. "You're my friend, okay? I've decided that arbitrarily, because Carlo likes you. It's an awesome responsibility, but since there are two of us, we can probably handle it."

All at once, Terri felt relief course through her,

warm and sudden. Lightly, Paget resumed the conversation. ‘‘Sometimes, as Freud once said, a cigar is only a cigar. I really did want to know about Elena.’’

Terri smiled. ‘‘Oh, Elena’s wonderful. She’s very imaginative, poetic almost, and she has this incredible fantasy life. She’s much more like Richie that way—I’m so literal, and about as poetic as a pair of Birkenstocks.’’ Talking about Elena, Terri realized, made her feel more like herself. ‘‘This is probably a mother speaking, but I’m sure that Elena will be someone out of the ordinary—a sculptress or a terrorist or something.’’

‘‘Maybe she’ll content herself with vandalism.’’ Paget thought for a moment. ‘‘What are you going to do about her schooling?’’

Terri frowned. ‘‘I’m not sure. I’d like to pick somewhere permanent to live, with good schools. But we really can’t afford a house.’’

Paget looked surprised. ‘‘I can’t swear to it, but the last time I looked, we paid our associates a living wage. In fact, although you were gracious enough not to say it, I had the distinct impression you left the P.D.’s office less for my charisma than to double your salary.’’

Terri smiled. ‘‘It *was* the money. And I’m not complaining. It’s just that Richie works at home right now.’’

‘‘What does he do?’’

"He's trying to start his own company." Terri paused. "He's very bright, really, very inventive. Like Elena, Richie sees things that I really don't. It's just that sometimes, I think, someone like that finds it difficult to work for other people."

"Are you ready to order?" the waitress asked.

As Paget finished ordering, Terri looked around them. The tables were filled with couples and foursomes, some smiling, some serious and intent, their profiles reflected in the mirrors. These days, Terri and Richie seldom ate out alone; when they did, Terri enjoyed looking at the other faces and imagining their lives. Sometimes she would pick a man and woman, trying to figure out which date this was or why they were together. It caused her to wonder now what she would think were she someone else, watching herself with Christopher Paget. "A penny for your thoughts," Paget said. "Or would you like a raise?"

Terri smiled. "I was just thinking that I liked this place."

Paget nodded. "I like rooms with a little animation. This way I don't feel like I'm communing with my ancestors." He seemed to hesitate. "On the subject of raises, we review our compensation every year. You're doing well with us, and it might make the joys of ownership look a bit more doable."

Terri looked at the table. "Thank you. It's nice of you to take an and interest. But there's daycare, too, and I can see some other expenses coming up."

Paget looked quizzical. "Does Richie watch her in the afternoon?"

"No." Terri paused. "He's busy at home."

The quizzical look vanished, replaced by the blank expression that, Terri had come to realize, concealed thoughts Paget did not wish to show.

"Perhaps you can work it out," he finally said. "Elena sounds like a special kid. I know when Carlo came to me, I decided that education and stability were what he needed most. It was worth the pain of paying for it."

Terri hesitated. But there was no point in discussing her fights with Richie, his insistence that children were flexible and could be happy anywhere. "When it comes to money," Terri joked, " 'pain' is a relative concept. I mean, don't you own a railroad or something?"

Paget laughed. "The *government* owns America's railroads, including Great-Great-Grandfather Kenyon's. As for the money I inherited, I never touch the stuff."

Terri looked at him a moment, trying to decide whether he was serious. "You're kidding."

"Of course not." Paget smiled. "Are you familiar with the theory of devolution? That's what happens when your great-great-grandfather passes down a ton of money, creating three of the most useless generations that ever walked the planet. It's like a curse. Shortly after college, I decided that my only hope was to make my own money. Which I have.''

``So when Carlo talks about how hard you work . . .''

Paget nodded. ``Sad but true. That didn't help with Andrea, either.''

For a moment, Terri felt dull-witted, trying to process how this changed her idea of him. The thing that came to her was that, more than most people, Christopher Paget had his own idea of himself and had never wished to tamper with it. Finally, she asked, ``What do you do with all the money?''

``Except for the occasional gift to worthy causes, it's in trust for Carlo and my theoretical other children, who grow more theoretical by the day.'' Paget smiled again. ``The dirty trick I've played on Carlo is that, for purposes both legal and philosophical, the money actually goes to *his* children—which is as far into the future as I can postpone the curse. Carlo gets a more than comfortable life income, but only after I die. By which time, I trust, he will have developed what used to be called character.''

Terri laughed. ``That's appalling. Does Carlo know?''

``Oh, I've told him. Just last year, once he was secure in the more spiritual aspects of my paternal devotion.''

``What did he say?''

"As I recall them, his precise words were, 'Then there's no point in putting rat poison in your cabernet.' I nearly choked up with real tears." Paget smiled again. " 'Don't worry, son,' I said. 'You've still got me.' To which Carlo responded, deadpan, 'Then you're just going to have to work a little harder.' "

"He really said that?"

"Absolutely. But the truly frightening thing was that his grades shot up next quarter."

Terri smiled. "I liked watching the two of you—the joking back and forth."

"It's my way of showing affection, and I fear I've passed it on." Paget's tone was dry. "But then I had to give the boy *something*. As matters stand, Carlo's the last of the Pagets."

"You never wanted more?"

"I just never had the right situation, and now I'm pretty much out of time." Paget glanced at her. "Are you and Richie planning on another one?"

Terri sipped her wine. "I don't know yet." She paused a moment. "We didn't plan Elena, really."

Paget nodded. "Birth control is tough these days, given that IUDs and the pill can kill you. If I were Johnny Moore, I'd say something like: 'The marvels of medical science—condoms to condoms in a single generation.' And once you're pregnant, the options aren't so hot."

"I really couldn't have done anything else." Terri stared at her wineglass. "It was time, I guess. Richie wanted a commitment—we'd have gotten married anyhow, he said, and he really wanted children. And I'd always had this strong sense of wanting to build a real family, one that's intact and free from conflict. That still means a lot to me."

Paget appraised her for a while. "This may be presumptuous," he said, "but have you ever wondered if you're still trying to fix your family of origin?"

Terri looked up at him. "No," she said quietly. "But sometimes I've wondered if I'm too much like my mother."

Paget paused, as if sensing that he had gone too far. "Perhaps *I'm* too much like someone who's divorced and has spent far too much time thinking about why." His voice was dismissive. "Probably the biggest gulf between my generation and our parents is that self-examination frightened them to death, whereas we're attuned to every quiver of the id and ego. It's tiresome, I'm sure."

It was uncanny, Terri thought: Paget seemed to know what questions to ask, when to talk, when to listen, and when to retreat under cover of self-deprecation. Either he was more sensitive than he cared to show, or he was getting a better fix on her than she herself had or wanted anyone else to have. It was unexpected, and somewhat unnerving.

"Not tiresome," she said lightly. "It's just that I'm too tired for all this stimulation."

Paget laughed. "Tell that to Carlo. The other night, when I was philosophizing about something or another, I heard him murmur, 'Get the hook.' "

"Like in vaudeville?"

"Uh-huh. The kid's ruthless. But it may be a line worth remembering."

Paget, Terri realized, was telling her that she controlled the depth and rhythm of their conversation, was free to pick and choose. All at once, she felt relaxed again: grateful for the evening and for everything that he had said.

"This was nice of you," she said.

He smiled. "I thought you and Carlo said I didn't get 'nice.' "

Terri raised her glass. "No," she said. "You get it."

Almost in spite of himself, Terri thought, Paget looked pleased. Lightly, he said, "I'll put that one in the bank, Terri," and changed the subject to work.

Dinner arrived; ahi tuna for Terri; cassoulet for Paget. The food was wonderful, Terri thought; they shared a little, and went over Steinhardt and Caldwell again, all the way through crème brûlée and a glass of port.

"Do you have any idea," Paget asked as they finished, "who the other two tapes belonged to? The ones Steinhardt couldn't identify?"

She shook her head. "No way to tell that they even existed, except to find them: the index is gone, and for all we know, it's just a gap. Does it matter?"

"Probably not. I'm just curious, that's all." Paget thought for a moment. "If they do exist and Ransom had them, Sharpe will find them soon enough. She's probably at home right now, baking cookies and listening to Troy Donahue tell Dr. Steinhardt about his mother."

" 'Ids on Tape,' " Terri said. "Poor Lindsay Caldwell."

Paget nodded. He finished his coffee, asked Robert to call a cab for Terri, and paid the bill.

It was drizzling outside, a cool wetness that felt good on Terri's face, a pleasant complement to the glow of wine and port. Standing next to Paget, it occurred to her, suddenly and by surprise, that she had liked the last few hours of her life.

From the row of headlights cruising up Market Street, a battered yellow cab peeled off, heading down the side street where they waited.

"Your limousine," Paget said, "has arrived."

She turned to him. "Thanks for dinner."

"The least I could do." He smiled. "Short of a raise, which is coming."

There was mist in his hair, she saw. Suddenly, impulsively, Terri stretched to kiss him on the cheek, and then stepped back again. She felt like a kid.

Paget was giving her a quizzical smile. "What did I do," he asked, "to deserve that?"

Terri felt herself grin. "It was the wine," she answered, and got into the cab.

The next morning, while Paget was still at home, McKinley Brooks called.

It caught Paget by surprise. " 'Lo, Mac," Paget said. "What's up?"

"Any number of things." Brooks paused. "You'll want to see me, I think."

His voice was somber, almost hesitant. "Can you give me a preview?" Paget asked.

"Yup. We found another tape."

For a moment, Paget thought of Lindsay Caldwell. "What's on it?"

"She starts out talking about you taking Carlo. But then she changes the subject, it seems. To the Lasko case."

Paget stiffened. "What in hell are you talking about?"

"You really don't know?" There was another, longer silence. "Mary Carelli was a patient of Dr. Steinhardt."

NINE

MARY HAD STARTED, Brooks said, with Paget taking Carlo.

It made what had happened sound almost brutal, as if Paget had coldly planned to deprive Mary of her son. But on the warm spring afternoon that Paget had come to the Carellis', he had intended to stay for an hour or so and then resume his life.

Mary's parents lived in the North End of Boston, just off Hanover Street, in a brick walk-up distinguished from its neighbors by green shutters that needed paint. John Carelli had run a corner grocery store, while his wife, Francesca, raised seven children, of whom Mary was the last. They were both in their seventies, the store had long since been sold, and, at least to Paget, any life in the house had decamped with their last daughter, so different from the others.

Now Carlo lived in the home that his mother could not wait to leave, while Mary traveled incessantly. In two or three more years, she had told Paget, her new career as a journalist would be stable enough to let her stay in one city, pay for a live-in person to help her raise Carlo. Meanwhile, she said, her parents were at least better than her older brothers and sisters. Paget knew only that two of Mary's brothers drank too much; that an older sister had refused to raise Carlo; and that the distance Mary had traveled made relations with her siblings as bad as with her parents. Some of that, Paget guessed, was the result of her relentless drive. But it was as hard for Paget to imagine Mary bounded by this world of parochial schools, male dominance, and rigid structure as it was for him to realize that her oldest sister still referred to Carlo as "Mary's bastard."

When John Carelli opened the door, he stared at Paget as if he were a derelict. He was a short man with a face like a walnut, all knots and crevices, a stooped body, and sharp, suspicious eyes. Nothing about him suggested warmth or laughter; Paget sensed a soul in life's harness, living so fiercely by the rules of his church and culture that it had killed something inside him. Whoever remained, Paget guessed, had just enough life to despise Paget for being like his daughter.

They stood in a cramped alcove. Behind John Carelli, a dark hallway stretched past a series of doors; like a ghost, Francesca Carelli appeared in the hallway, opened one of the doors, and closed it behind her. In three prior visits, Paget had not met her; he could only sense that once she might have looked like Mary.

John Carelli ignored his outstretched hand. "She said you were coming."

Paget nodded. "To see Carlo."

Carelli did not move; everything in his posture said that were he younger, he would throw Paget out. Finally, he grunted, "He's in here," and led Paget to the living room.

Its only adornments were heavy drapes that were completely drawn, a crucified Jesus, a still life of a pear and apples, and family pictures from which Mary was missing. The dark room smelled stale, as if no one had opened the windows for some time. There was nothing of Mary, save for the slim, dark-haired boy in front of the television, eyes vacant, watching reruns of a cop show. In profile, the boy had long eyelashes, delicate features.

"Carlo?" Paget called.

The boy did not look up. Paget knelt beside him. "I'm Christopher," he said. "I've come to see you."

Hesitant, the boy turned to him; as before, Paget was startled by the clear blue eyes. But they held neither recognition nor interest: two years was a long time in the life of a seven-year-old, and the boy did not remember him.

"Would you like to go outside and play?" Paget asked.

The boy did not answer. Paget touched his shoulder. ''Maybe we can go to a park.''

Quickly, the boy shook his head. ''I want to watch this.''

Paget looked up at John Carelli. ''Do you have a baseball or anything?''

Carelli scowled. ''This is what he likes to do.''

Paget glanced at the boy, still intent on the television, and then back to Mary's father. ''I'll just be here, then. Don't let me keep you from whatever you were doing.''

John Carelli was silent for a moment, and then he left the room. Paget sat next to Carlo.

The show was about the California highway patrol. ''Who are the good guys?'' Paget asked.

The boy pointed at the television. ''Him, and him.''

''What are their names?''

''John and Ponch. They're on TV every day.''

''Do you watch them every day?''

The boy nodded, eyes not moving from the television.

''Why do you do that?'' Paget asked.

''Because John is my best friend.'' The boy hesitated. ''Sometimes Ponch is too.''

''Do you ever play with other friends, outside?''

Slowly, the boy shook his head.

''Why not?''

The boy looked vaguely frightened. Finally, he said, "I'd miss John and Ponch."

The answer had a bewildered sound, as if the idea of doing something else was overwhelming. Paget had the sudden desire to rip down the blinds, throw the windows open. Instead he watched television in the gloomy room, saying little, sitting beside Carlo Carelli.

On the television, the two highway patrolmen helped a mother and father look for a small boy named Timmy, who had gotten lost in a mountainous state forest. At least, Paget thought to himself, they had let Timmy play outdoors.

He forced himself to settle back, miming the boy's attentiveness.

After a time, he felt Carlo's shoulder touching his. He glanced over. The boy's gaze at the television was more intent than ever, as if he was afraid to acknowledge what he had done.

Paget said nothing. Then, without speaking or looking over, Paget lightly put his arm around him. The boy was very still. As they watched John and Ponch look for Timmy, Paget felt the boy lean into him, ever so slightly.

On the screen, Timmy had encountered a bear.

"Maybe," Paget said gently, "you'd better sit in my lap."

The boy seemed to hesitate. Without saying anything more, Christopher Paget picked him up.

When the bear went away, Carlo remained in Paget's lap. He was still there at the end, as Timmy and his parents hugged each other.

"My daddy's dead," Carlo said.

Paget rested his face against the top of Carlo's head. "Who told you that?"

"Papa."

"Who's that?"

Silent, Carlo pointed down the hall.

"What does your mommy say?"

The boy shrugged. The small gesture, like the boy himself, felt fragile.

Looking up, Paget saw John Carelli standing in the entryway. The hard look in his face said that Paget's time was up.

"Is there a park around?" Paget asked. "I was going to ask Carlo to play with me."

"He doesn't have time," John Carelli said. "We eat at five-thirty."

How, Paget wondered, had Mary ever escaped this, and how could she stand to think about Carlo here? "That's nice of you," he answered pleasantly, "but I wouldn't want Mrs. Carelli to go to the trouble of feeding me. Thank her for me, though." Paget paused, allowing himself a moment's petty enjoyment at the old man's look of anger, and then added, "I'll just feed Carlo after we've played. Is seven-thirty all right, or did you have something special planned?"

John Carelli stepped forward, blocking his path. "We didn't know you were staying."

For the dead, Paget thought but did not say, time is a never a problem. Then he felt the boy stiffen in his arms, as if aware of his grandfather's disapproval. He stood, scooping Carlo up in one arm, so that the boy could not see the warning look he gave John Carelli as he walked toward him.

"Well, I am," he said in a cheery voice meant for Carlo. "It's not every day that I have a boy to play with."

Carelli did not move. As they reached him, Paget politely said, "Pardon me," as if stepping into a crowded elevator, and firmly pushed the old man back with his free hand. Slung against Paget, the boy saw nothing. "I'll let myself out," Paget said over his shoulder. "Do enjoy your dinner, and thank Mrs. Carelli for her hospitality."

"Well," he said to Carlo when they got to the car, "where do we go from here?"

The boy shook his head; Paget realized that he had not seen him smile.

"What *I* figured," Paget said, "is that we'd go to a playground and then to dinner. What do you like to eat?"

The boy hesitated. "Pizza?" he ventured.

"Pizza it is. All we need now is a playground. It's been years, Carlo, since I've been on the slide."

The boy pointed to his suit. "You can't go like that."

"Oh, that just makes it more fun." Paget eyed him. "Do you ever do things you're not supposed to do?"

Again, the boy shook his head. "Papa won't let me."

Paget nodded. "Papa just wants to take care of you. But I'm thirty-seven years old, so I get to slide dressed any way I want to."

Carlo looked at him. "You're as old as my mommy, I think. She's thirty years older than me."

Paget smiled. "That's really not very old. At least your mommy doesn't seem old."

"Do you *know* her?"

Paget nodded. "Your mommy and I are friends."

The boy hesitated. Finally, he asked, "Did you know my daddy?"

Paget looked at him, and then he smiled again. "Why don't *I* be that, just for today, and you can help me find a park."

The boy's eyes changed, as if trying to remember how the subject had shifted. "What's your name?"

"Christopher." Paget turned the ignition. "And I'm ready to play."

The playground was small, cramped, but filled with mothers and children and a few old men on benches. Paget took a red rubber ball from the car. "Ever play catch?" he asked.

Carlo shook his head. "Only at school. They don't let me much—I'm not very good."

"I'll bet you're better than you think." He pointed to a swath of grass. "Here, I'll help you practice."

Haltingly, Carlo backed out onto the grass. Paget tossed the ball underhand. The boy flinched; when he clutched at the ball, it had already hit his chest.

"We'll start over," Paget said. "From closer."

He knelt a few inches away and tossed the ball more softly. Carlo dropped it again.

"That's okay," Paget said. "When I was a kid, I had to practice a lot."

"Were you good?"

"Not at first. But in the end, I got good."

On the fourth try, Carlo caught the ball.

He moved like his mother, Paget saw; he would be a tall boy, and even now the length of his arms and legs caused a little awkwardness. But his hands were quick enough; his problem was not reflexes but confidence and opportunity.

Carlo caught the ball again.

"You see," Paget said. "You're good."

Once more, Carlo shook his head. "I'm not good. You're just letting me be good."

Paget smiled. "It's you who's catching the ball. Not me."

"They'll never let me play." Carlo's voice was flat. "I could ask them for a million years, and they'd always tell me I'm not any good."

In these few words, Paget saw Carlo's life. He knelt beside him on the grass. "What's wrong?" he asked.

For the first time, Carlo spoke in a flippant voice. "I hate myself," he said. "I want to kill myself, that's all."

The boy's expression was so curious, Paget thought; half teasing, half searching. All at once, he felt despairing, at sea. By a kind of instinct, Paget said lightly, "If you killed yourself, Carlo Carelli, I'd have to eat the pizza alone."

The boy watched him for a moment. Then, for the first time, Carlo almost smiled. "Then I won't until later," he said.

"You would appear to have a problem," Larry Colvin said to Paget. "Or more accurately, Carlo does. At least on the basis of two visits."

When, Paget wondered, had his college friend Larry become so soft-spoken, his words so measured. And then it occurred to him that he had almost never known a mental health specialist who, at least in a professional mode, did not seem gentle to the point of sedation. Even his office—an upstairs room in his brick town house near Beacon Street—was subdued.

"I'm no child psychologist," Paget answered, "but I did take 'I hate myself, I want to kill myself' to be some sort of clue."

Colvin nodded, his fine, sensitive face reflecting sadness and a little curiosity. "To speak in shorthand, he's emotionally deprived—too little warmth, too few stimuli, not many reasons to feel good about who he is. The biggest problem with the conditions in which he lives is that he's internalized them all. Because he doesn't get much love, Carlo believes he's not worth loving."

Paget shook his head. "Short term, I really don't see that changing."

"Can you talk to the grandparents?"

Paget felt a moment's anger. "For God sakes, Larry, these people live in some other world. Mrs. Carelli won't speak a word—for all I know, she's been autistic for the last seventy-five years. As for the odds of meaningful dialogue between the father and me, one of us would have to die and be reincarnated." Paget paused. "When I came back to the house and asked if Carlo had report cards from school, Mary's father wouldn't answer. I had to threaten him with a court order even to get Carlo here."

Colvin nodded. "Do you think *I* could talk to them?"

"You can try. But you'd be talking in Morse code across a cultural Grand Canyon—you're young, highly educated, and, even worse, believe in insight-oriented therapy. These people are in their mid seventies, pickled in the Catholicism of the late Pope

Pius, and members of a generation where even the well-educated believe that asking themselves any questions will destroy the foundation of their lives. It would be like Mozart meeting Genghis Khan for drinks.''

Colvin got up, walked to a shuttered window, and threw it open. Outside, the cobblestoned street looked fresh-minted in the sun of a spring afternoon; the leafy branch of an oak tree, stretching toward the window, rippled with a fitful breeze. Colvin stared out the window.

''This city,'' Colvin murmured, ''was a great place to grow up. I still love it, especially on days like this.''

''But it's no good for Carlo. Not the way he's living.''

Colvin nodded. ''The thing is, he's really quite a bright boy. And, somewhere inside there, quite a sensitive one. For someone with so little stimuli at home, he follows things, even has something of a capacity for humor.''

''I can feel that. Even in the little time we've had together, I've noticed that irony is something he gets and that it's safe for him. But the Carellis don't bring any of that out.''

''How is he with you?''

Paget hesitated. ''He doesn't show a lot of emotion—I'm sure that's true generally. Each time I visit, Carlo seems a little gladder to see me. But he doesn't like being touched, and I can't hug him at all. It's sort of sad.''

''Everything you say, Chris, is pretty much what I'd expect.'' Colvin paused for a moment. ''How about the mother?''

''I finally tracked her down in Rome—you may have seen her on the evening news when the Red Brigades killed Aldo Moro. It's going well, she says: two more years, and she'll be back in New York and able to rescue Carlo from her parents.''

Colvin turned to him. ''That takes him to nine years old, at least.''

''I know.'' Paget hesitated. ''I can see the pattern in the report cards I got from school. He's going downhill.''

''It's not just school, Chris. It's pretty much everything. Self-esteem, ability to relate, even comfort with his own body. The next two years are critical.'' Colvin permitted himself a final note of irritation. ''Does the mother know what she's getting into with this boy? I mean, does she have some sort of plan?''

Paget shrugged. ''To have an au pair, I assume. Preferably someone with a working knowledge of English.''

Colvin sat down again, expression curious and intent.

''Forgive me, Chris, but I think I'm permitted liberties with a friend that I would never take with a patient. How is it that two bright, obviously sophisticated people like you and the woman I watched during the Lasko hearings ended up with an unwanted child?''

The phrase ''unwanted child'' pierced Paget's heart and mind: the image it left was Carlo in front of the television, alone. ''I can see why you don't usually take those liberties,'' he answered. ''People in your business aren't supposed to make their clients feel guilty.''

''Guilty? You look miserable.'' Colvin's voice softened. ''Which is part of why I ask.''

''*I* was a lonely kid—I never wanted to create one.'' Paget paused. ''Although I've been reminding myself for the past four days that I survived.''

Colvin leaned forward. ''Are you happy with that answer? I mean, for yourself.''

Paget shrugged. ''Spare me, Larry. Next you'll have me drawing pictures to see whether I include arms and legs and have smoke coming out the chimney.''

''Spare *me* the deflective wit, all right? You can even skip Carlo for the moment. What I'm saying, pal, is that this is important to *you*.''

Paget smiled faintly. ''My God, you're sounding like a human being again. I should have 'unwanted children' more often.''

Colvin gave an impatient shake of the head. ''Cut the shit, Chris.''

''All right,'' Paget said. ''The cold truth is that

had it been my decision, Carlo would never have been born. I feel terrible about that, and even worse about how he's living.'' He paused, adding quietly, ''As for Mary, she wanted him for reasons of her own. In that way, Carlo may already have served his purpose.''

Colvin looked puzzled. ''What do you mean?''

Paget paused. ''It's a personal thing. Really.''

Colvin searched his face. ''All right,'' he finally said. ''We'll stick to current events. Have you told your wife—Andrea, is it?''

''Not much about the last few days—she's touring Europe right now.'' Paget hesitated. ''As a general matter, Andrea treats the fact of Carlo like something that happened in another world, perhaps because she finds it painful. Denial, I think they call it.''

Colvin seemed poised to ask a question, then did not. At last, he asked, ''Do you think Mary has a clear impression of how Carlo's living now?''

How, Paget wondered, to explain Mary as fairly as he could, yet leave out those things that Colvin did not need to know. ''Mary has a clear impression,'' he answered. ''She just doesn't *feel* it the way you and I might feel it.''

Colvin leaned forward. ''I thought, from what you said, that she despised her parents and pretty much hated her whole childhood.''

Paget nodded. ''All true. After seeing Chez Carelli at first hand, I'm amazed that she accomplished all she did. But becoming who she is took pretty much all she *had*. Mary's very tough now, in a cut-and-dried sort of way. She doesn't process bad experiences; she just leaves them behind. Just like rules. She learned that her parents' rules were a trap, so she invented her own and still does her damnedest not to care about anyone else's. If you have a problem, Mary would say, fix it however you need to. Don't feel sorry for yourself, and don't whine to *me* about it.

"Mary's so completely practical that it's become a form of ruthlessness. And like a lot of self-invented people, the distance she's come, and her success in getting there, has made her judgmental in a social Darwinist sort of way." Paget paused. "Although I would guess that it's part of Mary's creed never to pass moral judgment on herself."

Listening, Colvin watched Paget's face. "You seem to know her well," he finally said, "for so short a time spent together."

Paget found himself staring out the window. "Mary Carelli," he answered, "is someone to whom I've given a great amount of thought."

"Does she ever ask you for anything?"

"It's worse than that: she won't *take* anything. I don't know why."

Colvin seemed to reflect. "Okay," he said. "So why doesn't she feel Carlo's situation?"

"It's simply this: some part of Mary must think that Carlo can survive all this. Because she did."

Colvin paused for a moment. "Do you think that?"

Paget stood, walked to the window. "No," he answered. "Carlo's not a clone of Mary. There are other things inside him."

Colvin was quiet. After a time, he joined Paget, and the two friends gazed out the window together.

"You're right," Paget said. "This *is* a great city. I've liked it since you first showed me around, in college."

Colvin turned to him. "What are you going to do?"

Paget shook his head. "I have absolutely no idea."

Standing in front of the door, John Carelli shook his head. "You can't see him," he said.

"Why not?"

"Because this is my home." His voice was rough. "I'm sick of you hanging around."

"Next time, I'll see him elsewhere. Is Carlo here?"

John Carelli folded his arms. "You make my daughter pregnant, you think that gives you rights? *Anybody* can make a girl pregnant if she lets him. That doesn't make him a father, *or* a man."

Paget stared at him. Quietly, he said, "How true."

Carelli flushed. "You're a rich, spoiled boy. Carlo's never going to be like you—or Mary."

There was only judgment in this house, Paget thought. Carlo would see himself only in the Carellis' eyes, the son of a flawed woman, another person not worth cherishing.

"Have you given any thought," Paget asked, "to what *Carlo* will be like when he grows up? Or is it more rewarding to hate a daughter than to love a grandson? Because I've looked at you, Mr. Carelli, and there's no love in you." Paget paused. "If there *were,* you'd see that Mary's real sin was not sleeping with *me* but leaving her son with *you*."

John Carelli raised his hand to slap him. Paget grabbed his wrist; suddenly he felt exhausted. "I'm sorry," he said softly. "I had no right to say that. Please, I've just come to say goodbye."

Slowly, John Carelli reclaimed his hand. "Leave him be," he said. "You've done too much harm already, stirred Carlo up for nothing. Now leave him be."

"Papa?"

It was Carlo, standing behind his grandfather in the alcove. He had left his television program; from the living room, Paget heard the disembodied voices of John and Ponch. The boy looked up at him, eyes the shape of his mother's, their color as blue as Paget's own. "Northern Italian recessive," Mary had called them, as if dismissing any father at all.

"Hi, Carlo," Paget said, and then looked to John Carelli.

"Five minutes," the old man said. "Then I call the police."

Silent, Paget nodded, and then Carelli moved aside.

Paget knelt by Carlo. "Will you watch with me?" the boy asked.

Paget shook his head. "I'd like to. But I can't."

Even to his own ears, the words sounded empty.

"Are you going away?" Carlo asked.

Paget nodded. "I have to go now."

"Why?"

"Because I have to go to my house." Paget hesitated, trying to explain. "I live in California, where John and Ponch live."

Carlo looked down. "That's far away, isn't it?"

"Yes."

The boy nodded. "My mommy goes away."

"I know. But she'll be back. Mommies always come back."

"Will you come back?"

"Uh-huh. Someday."

Carlo went to the living room. When he returned, he was holding the rubber ball that Paget had given him. He put it in Paget's hand. "When you come back," he said, "bring this."

"But I wanted you to keep it."

Carlo shook his head. "We can play with it. If you come back."

Paget felt Carlo press the ball into his palm. When Paget closed his hand, Carlo did not let go of the ball; Paget's fingers curled around the boy's.

There were tears in Carlo's eyes. "What's your name?" he asked Paget. "I forget."

"Christopher." Paget paused, gazing at the boy, and then spoke before giving himself time to reflect. "I'm your father."

Carlo looked blank for a moment; Paget thought he saw a faint spark of hope, and then the boy glanced over his shoulder, as if afraid.

Paget picked up the boy and held him close. Carlo was stiff, uncomprehending. Then, slowly, his arms went around Paget's neck.

"I'm your father," Paget murmured again, "and it's going to be all right."

Paris was as beautiful as Paget had remembered.

It was a fresh spring afternoon, two days after he had left Carlo. Paget sat alone at Les Deux Magots, the outdoor café on the Boulevard St. Germain that he had haunted during his college year in Paris. He had liked it then for the boulevard's walking street show, and the corner café still offered a glimpse of every variety of Parisian—street jugglers, elegant women, would-be artists, older people who walked their dog and would stop for a glass of wine at this café or next door at the Café Flore. Near the entrance were the sculptures of two Chinese merchants from which Les Deux Magots derived its name; across the street was the forbidding stone mass of the twelfth-century cathedral of St. Germain-des-Prés, its small garden surrounded by an iron fence and graced by Picasso's bust of the poet Apollinaire. Paget watched a tall, dark-haired woman cross the street with the self-conscious grace of a runway model; it reminded him again that he had missed Andrea by one day and that she would dance tonight in Prague, six hundred miles away.

Idly, reflexively, Paget touched the briefcase full of papers.

"Basking in nostalgia?" the familiar voice asked. "Or imagining an evening with that slightly overdone brunette I saw you watching?"

Paget turned. "Nostalgia," he answered. "I was counting the years since last we met."

"Five," Mary said. "Would you like to talk here? I wouldn't mind a glass of red wine. I'll buy, of course, given that you've come all this way."

Paget nodded. "In that case, I'll have one too."

It wasn't until Mary had slipped off her coat and sat across from him that he started to absorb the changes in her. She was a woman in her thirties now, whose assertiveness had become self-possession. Her clothes and makeup were perfect as well: not too much of anything, but enough to suggest taste and an eye for detail. Even her speech, now well modulated for television, was clearer and more polished. Paget didn't know whether the better analogy was to a fine wine or a chameleon: there was nothing about this woman that suggested she and John Carelli belonged to the same race, let alone the same family. Even to Paget, she felt like a stranger.

"Why did you pick this place?" she asked.

"When you said you'd be in Paris, I thought of it." Paget glanced toward the street. "Not only is it good for people-watching, but this corner has a rather rich history—street battles of various kinds, even a few beheadings."

Mary smiled faintly. "And naturally, you thought of me. For my taste, though, that cathedral is a bit grim. I can't imagine spending any time there."

"Be respectful. In the thirteenth century, clerics died there, defending it from attack by students from the Latin Quarter. Not to mention the Huguenots who had their tongues yanked out for heresy."

A short, bustling waiter, officious and classically French, interrupted and took their order. When he left, they were silent for a time.

"You came about Carlo," she said at length.

"Yes." Paget paused. "I want him to come live with me."

Mary raised an eyebrow. "Just like that."

"No, *not* just like that. As I said on the phone, I've visited him several times lately, taken him to a child psychologist, gotten enough sense of your parents that I don't require any more. Carlo needs a father—or, more accurately, needs a parent. I told you how unhappy he is, how he reached out to me."

She made a brief dismissive gesture. "Chris, you can't possibly know what you're doing."

"In what sense?"

"In every sense." Her tone was impatient. "You can't just declare yourself a father and start making decisions."

Paget leaned forward. "I didn't declare myself a father, *you* did—the night before we testified. So here I am."

Mary shook her head. "I've asked you for nothing. Or haven't you noticed?"

"That's not true, Mary. You asked me for a great deal. Just not since Carlo was born."

Her eyes widened. "Is that what this is about? Making yourself feel better? Because what's done is done, and you'll just have to live with that. It's far too late for regrets."

"I know that very well," Paget said coldly. "But it's not too late for Carlo. In two years, it will be."

The waiter brought two glasses of red wine. The wine sat before them, untouched.

"Since when," Mary asked at length, "did you become such an expert in child development? I already know there are problems, because I know my parents. Believe it or not, it bothers me to leave him there for a couple more years, until my career gets straight. But I'll be able to change that. What suddenly makes *you* the one right answer?''

Paget decided to change tactics. ''Look,'' he said quietly. ''I'm not. And this isn't some sort of contest between the two of us. It can't be, for Carlo's sake.''

''He's *my* son, Chris. I can't give him up. It really is that simple.''

''It isn't, though. Because Carlo's not an inanimate object. Although if he keeps living in your parents' home, he may well become one.'' Paget's voice rose. ''Damn it, the night I called, I *told* you how things are—as if you should even *need* that.''

''I *am* coming back.'' She gave him a look of disbelief. ''Really, this is grotesque. You never wanted to be a father, never wanted Carlo, and, until this moment, paid him less attention than one of your precious paintings. This conversation must be happening in a dream.''

Paget stared at her. ''Make up your mind, Mary. Am I the bad parent who never wanted Carlo, or the man you effectively disowned as a father the moment Carlo was born? Because 'whatever suits my need of the moment' cuts no ice with me. Not, at least, on the question of this boy.''

There was a subtle change in Mary's expression, as if she had deliberately forced patience on herself. ''How much thought,'' she finally asked, ''have you actually given this?''

"As much as I could, in the time allowed. Not as much as I will." Paget stared at his wineglass. "It's obvious that Carlo needs special tutoring, physical activity, and, most of all, consistent love and attention." He looked up at Mary. "Someone, every day of his or her life, has to make Carlo believe that he's the most important thing in it."

She smiled slightly. "You make it sound like a form of atonement, or a crusade. Of course, you used to be good at crusades."

"Not a crusade. Just a lot of time spent, and a certain sensitivity." Paget paused again. "In other words, the things neither of us got from our own parents."

"Which you alone have to give." Mary leaned forward. "Tell me, is Ms. Pavlova aware of your new ambitions?"

Paget hesitated. "If you mean Andrea—no, not in detail. But I'm sure we'll work it out."

"Oh, I'm sure." Mary gave him a sardonic smile. "I can so easily imagine it. 'Back from six straight days in Pittsburgh, my love, dancing *Giselle?* Carlo and I are going out to his Little League game, but you can meet us later at McDonald's.' Assuming, of course, that they have Little League in San Francisco. Do they?"

"They must."

Mary shook her head. "Honestly, it doesn't sound like you have much of a clue. You had an emotional reaction to my parents and caught a plane to Paris, *both* of which I completely understand. But that is *not* much basis for changing Carlo's life.''

Suddenly Paget had the feeling that Mary was testing him, or perhaps just tormenting him—he could not tell which. It created feelings of hope and desperation.

''I'm *good* with him,'' he said. ''I don't know why, but I am. The rest will come.''

She gazed at him. ''Are you so desperate,'' she asked, ''to be good with someone? If so, maybe you should start closer to home. How *is* your marriage, I'm forced to wonder. Given that you propose to sandwich my son in the middle of it.''

It's fine, Paget wanted to say. And then, because she was Carlo's mother, he told Mary something closer to the truth. ''Andrea,'' he said slowly, ''has more emotional requirements than some. It's all right as long as I'm available.''

''Don't you think you should talk to her a little more before bothering *me* with all this?''

''I have.'' Paget paused. ''The best way to describe her reaction is 'distant.' ''

Mary frowned. ''Then I suggest you withdraw your application and resume your former life.''

Paget shook his head. ''I've seen too much of Carlo,'' he said. ''It may sound cold, but this is *not* a decision Andrea can make for me. Because if she did, and Carlo suffered for that, it would end our marriage. And *that* is what I've told her.''

Mary watched his face. Around them, as the afternoon moved toward evening, men and women in business suits had changed the mix of the crowd, and the waiter seemed to wish that Mary and he would drink their wine or leave. Paget ignored him.

''No,'' Mary said finally.

Paget tensed. ''Why not?''

''Because if Carlo does come, you'll have as good as ended your marriage. Which would make you a busy single father with a young son bearing the weight of a divorce. Carlo would feel guilty, and you might well resent him.'' Mary's gaze hardened. ''What makes that a better life than the one I'll give him in two years?''

''Honestly?''

''Of course.''

''Because he's in deep trouble, for all the reasons I described to you on the phone, which I know you understand too well.'' Paget's voice slowed. ''And because I'm the right parent for that boy. If I didn't know that, I wouldn't be here.''

Mary shook her head. ''Go home, Chris. Save your marriage. In two years, I'll rescue Carlo from my parents. As I told you when Carlo was born, you've already done enough.''

Paget looked into her eyes, as coolly and directly

as he could. ''Which gets us,'' he said, ''to the bottom line of this discussion.''

Silent, Mary watched his face. ''What, precisely, are you referring to?''

''To the papers I've had prepared, awarding me legal and physical custody. And, of course, to the reason that you'll sign them. For the sake of politeness, we'll call it 'career considerations.' ''

Her eyes widened, almost imperceptibly. ''You're joking.''

''No. Like many women, you've come to value your work. After an honest self-appraisal, you've seen the tension between career and motherhood, and recognized the expanded role a father can play. In this case, me.''

She smiled coldly. ''You seem to forget, Chris, that the same 'career considerations' affect us both.''

''They don't, though. Because we're nothing alike. For one thing, as you once were fond of pointing out to me, I'm rich.'' Paget leaned forward. ''Seven years ago, I just stopped caring. I don't give a damn what happens to me now. So I'm content to sit here until you tell me that same thing—that *you* don't care what happens to *you*.'' He finished quietly: ''Perhaps, while I wait, we can have a bottle of wine.''

It was odd, Paget thought, that her smile lingered, becoming a smile of appraisal. Even as she said, ''You really *are* a bastard.''

Paget felt tired. "I'm not, though," he said slowly. "I hate doing this. Just as I hate you for making me do it."

Mary shook her head. "That you hate *me*—that's no surprise to me. That you hate doing this the *way* you're doing it *would* be a surprise, if I believed it." She stared at her wineglass. "No, the real surprise is that you *are* doing it. Never, seven years ago, did I see this day coming. Never did I imagine you wanting to raise him."

She was pale, Paget saw.

"I'm sorry," he said. "I truly am. But if you don't do this, we'll be in court, with me waving Carlo's birth certificate and asserting my paternal rights by any means I can. Any at all. And that will do you no good at all. Nor Carlo, either."

For an instant, her eyes shut. "No doubt."

"No doubt," he softly echoed her. "And don't ever doubt I'll do it."

"Oh, I believe you." Her voice was thin, remote. "You have the papers with you, I imagine."

Nodding, Paget reached into the briefcase, placed the papers on the table. Mary read them carefully, like the lawyer she once had been.

"What do you intend to call him?" she asked. "I don't think 'Carlo' should change."

" 'Carlo Paget,' I thought."

She looked at him. "Carlo *Carelli* Paget."

Paget nodded. "All right."

Quickly, almost carelessly, she scrawled her name wherever it was needed.

"Did you know," she asked, "that Carlo likes blueberry waffles?"

Paget shook his head; it was surprising, he thought, how painful this felt, and how enormous.

"Well," she said, "I'm sure he'll tell you."

Abruptly, Mary stood. Paget saw a change come over her face, a shocked, wounded look—pain, anger, disbelief at what he had done. She seized her untouched wineglass, staring down at him; for an instant, Paget was sure that she would throw the wine in his face.

Turning, she drank until the glass was empty, and placed it down before him.

"Congratulations," she said. "You're Carlo's father now."

She turned, never looking back, and walked quickly away.

TEN

WHEN PAGET APPEARED in Brooks's office, there was a tape recorder on the desk, and Marnie Sharpe was with him. No one shook hands.

"You'll want to hear this," Brooks said.

The drizzle streaking the windows seemed to pervade the room. The D.A. did not smile; there were none of the usual graces. To Paget, Sharpe had the gaunt, angry look of a bitter saint.

"Where did you find it?" Paget asked.

Sharpe leaned forward. "At Ransom's home in Key West," she snapped. "Just how stupid do you think we are?"

"Not stupid, Marnie. Paranoid, perhaps."

Her mouth compressed. "It's hard to believe that you didn't know about this. And once they hear what's on the tape, no judge will believe it, either."

Paget tried to control his temper, and his nerves. "Why on earth would I conceal something so easy for you to find?"

"That's simple. You knew Carelli was Steinhardt's patient. You just weren't sure that Ransom had the tape. So you tried to shut us down, quick, before we figured things out.'' Sharpe paused. ''The only other possibility is that your client lied to *you*. As to that, I *do* believe that Mary Carelli is a congenital liar. But it now appears that you're the perfect couple.''

Paget stared at her. ''Grow up,'' he snapped. ''No one asked if Mary was a patient, so no one lied about it. This isn't kindergarten—the job of a defense lawyer isn't to tattle to the principal. Nor is this case a personal thing between you and me.''

Brooks raised his hand for silence. Quietly, he said, ''We should play the tape.''

Paget nodded. ''I thought that was why you asked me here. Because if your purpose was to permit your staff to instruct me on my character, or that of Mary Carelli, you should know that the only person I answer to is me.''

''Consider us instructed.'' Brooks placed his finger on a button. ''I've fast-forwarded over the preliminaries, like who she is and what she does, so you can get right to the meat.''

Brooks pressed the button.

There was a moment's silence, and then Paget heard the voice of a man, emotionless and disembodied in the gloomy room.

''Was there something in particular,'' he asked, ''that made you come here?''

More silence.

''Yes,'' she answered. ''Three years later, I still

can't leave it behind. I keep having this dream." There was a pause. "It's as if I shut it off by day, but at night I lose control."

Paget could identify the speaker—not the woman he had first known, but the more polished woman he had met in Paris. But without her face and gestures, there was something naked, almost haunting, in her voice. Some part of him, much deeper than the lawyer, did not wish to hear more.

"Can you describe the dream?" Steinhardt asked.

"Of course." Mary's voice sounded parched. "It's the same every time."

Paget became aware of Sharpe's stare, angry and intent.

"Tell me about it," Steinhardt prodded.

"I'm in Paris," she said, "at the church of St. Germain-des-Prés. In life, I've never seen it, except from across the street. But in my imagination, the inside is as gloomy as I remember the outside being on the one day I was there—dark and vast, so that the inner walls as they rise above me disappear in shadows. Behind the altar is a sculpture of Jesus, crucified and suffering, like the one my parents had." The voice became sardonic. "Except, of course, much larger."

"In the dream, why are you there?"

Paget became aware of Sharpe and Brooks, gazing fixedly at the tape. As it turned, Paget could imagine Mary in the white room Terri Peralta had described to him, staring at a blank ceiling, with Steinhardt sitting behind her, an unseen voice.

Mary answered softly. "To ask forgiveness for my sins."

"Are you alone?"

"I've left my son, Carlo, across the street, sitting at an outdoor café. Even in the dream, I feel guilty about leaving Carlo by himself. But this is something I must do, and I never want Carlo to know my sins."

"Are they forgiven?"

Mary's voice became muted, subdued. "At first, I have no sign. There is no one else there. I hear nothing, feel nothing. For a moment, it's as if the dream is telling me what I always told myself when I was young: that the Church is as empty as the Latin Mass became when I first heard it in English. That God either has left it or was never there." Her voice grew lower. "Then I go outside and receive His answer.

"Carlo is gone."

Voice thickening, Mary paused. Paget folded his arms, staring at the floor. He no longer knew, or cared, whether Brooks or Sharpe was watching.

"In his place are two empty glasses." She paused. "One for me, and one for Chris. And then I know."

"What do you know?"

"That Chris has taken Carlo, and that I must let him." Her voice became ashen. "That my sins are past redemption."

There was silence. "Who is Chris?" Steinhardt asked. "And what are your sins—in the dream, that is?"

More silence. "Do you know Christopher Paget?"

"I know *of* him. The young man who testified at the Lasko hearings."

"Yes." Mary paused. "Chris has Carlo now."

Paget could imagine Steinhardt making choices, deciding whether to pursue reality or dream. His hands clenched.

"And your sins?" Steinhardt asked.

"In the dream, or in real life?" Her voice became cooler, almost defiant. "Because in real life, sin has little meaning to me."

"The dream, then."

"You can't understand them," she said, "without some background. Did you actually watch the hearings?"

Paget realized that his posture was as it had been in the witness room, as he watched Mary fifteen years before: taut, leaning forward, living from word to word.

"Yes," Steinhardt said. "Like millions of others, I was fascinated."

Mary's voice was bloodless now, that of a lawyer describing someone else's case. "And did you watch my testimony?"

"With great interest."

"Then we need to start with one essential fact."

"What is it?"

Mary paused. Then, in a cold, flat voice, she said, "I lied."

There was a long silence. Brooks stared fixedly at the tape; Sharpe at Paget. "Concerning what?" Steinhardt asked.

"Several things." Mary paused again; Paget could only wait. "I'm sorry," Mary said, "but that tape makes me nervous."

Abruptly, Paget, reoriented, became aware that Brooks and Sharpe were watching him.

"Why is that?" Steinhardt asked.

"Isn't it obvious?" Mary sounded impatient. "If it got out, what I'm telling you could ruin me. Really, I don't know if I should be here at all."

Paget touched the bridge of his nose; somehow, the reflexive gesture helped him shut out everything but Mary's voice.

"But you felt you needed to come," Steinhardt said.

"Yes."

"Why, precisely?"

"The dream." Mary's voice was flat. "As I said, I don't like losing control."

"Then let me reassure you. The tapes are for my use only, and only to assist me in your therapy. By state law, they are subject to the doctor-patient privilege, which I would ardently insist on even were there no such law. So whatever you tell me is as confidential as if there *were* no tapes.''

There was a quiet vehemence to Steinhardt's words that Paget found disturbing. Perhaps, he thought, what troubled him was Jeanne Steinhardt's comment about ''specimens''; more likely, it was listening to Steinhardt's assurances to Mary, five years later, in the office of the district attorney. He looked first at Brooks, then at Sharpe, making the point without words.

''All right,'' Mary told Steinhardt.

There was more silence, and then Steinhardt spoke again. ''You mentioned lying to the committee, as you put it. Perhaps you could tell me what you meant.''

Paget leaned forward. Then Mary said quietly, ''Some of what I told Senator Talmadge was true—the parts about Jack Woods. The chairman. My boss.'' She paused, and then her voice became clipped and systematic, as if reciting a litany.

''It was true that Jack spied on Chris for the President.

''It was true that Lasko had Chris's witness killed because Jack told Lasko that Chris was meeting him in Boston.

''It was true that Jack helped cover up the reason for the murder.

''It was true that Jack tried to stop Chris before

he found out that Lasko had funneled money to the President.

"And it was also true that, because of Jack, Chris was nearly killed.

"All in all, I told the truth a good deal of the time." Mary paused. "What I didn't tell Talmadge is that *I* had helped Jack do every one of those things."

Paget felt the silence on the tape merge with the silent stares of Brooks and Sharpe, directed at him. He tried to focus on the tape recorder.

"You wanted to protect yourself?" Steinhardt ventured.

Mary sounded almost amused. "I wanted to stay out of prison. Even without that, the life I had worked so hard for would have ended if I had told the truth." She paused, voice softer. "And of course, I was pregnant."

Sharpe, Paget realized, was wearing a strange smile.

"Did Chris know about you?" Steinhardt asked.

"Know what?" Mary answered, and then the tape clicked off.

Sharpe leaned forward. "*My* question exactly." Her voice mimicked Steinhardt's: " 'Did Chris know about you?' For example, when *you* testified before the Senate."

Paget looked at her coldly. "I take it there's a second tape. Why don't you just listen and find out?"

"Don't bullshit me. You *know* there's a second tape, and you know that *we* don't have it."

Paget paused, feeling a moment's respite from his sense of vertigo, of things spinning out of control. "I don't have a second tape," he said. "And if I did, the only person I'd give it to is Mary Carelli. Who's the only person entitled to it." Paget looked from Sharpe to Brooks. "As for *this* tape, it will never become public—at least in a court of law—and both of you damn well know it."

Sharpe shook her head. "Only if Mary Carelli doesn't screw up on the stand, and only if her lawyer makes absolutely no mistakes. And, you surely agree, that lawyer can't be you."

Paget looked quizzical. "So that's what you're after—me out of the case."

Sharpe frowned. "Don't flatter yourself. We're not talking about my personal preference in defense lawyers; we're talking ethics. This case isn't about Mary Carelli—it's about *you* and Mary Carelli, and perhaps even your son, as I think you knew all along. I can't even begin to count your ethical problems."

Paget turned to Brooks. "Mary's conduct is at issue here, not mine. I'm not charged with anything, nor am I a witness to anything. Whether I continue to represent her is *my* decision, not yours."

Brooks shook his head. "You're walking a *very* fine line here. For two weeks now, you've told us that Mary Carelli had no motive for killing Ransom but self-defense. Now we've got a motive: Ransom had a tape that could ruin her for the rest of time, as she herself admits.'' He nodded to Sharpe. ''And *I've* got the M.E. and the head of my rape team telling me this case has zip to do with rape, except the one your client tried to fabricate as cover. Which, if proven, may help us get to murder one.''

''As far as the jury goes,'' Paget retorted, ''you've still got no motive. That tape is subject to doctor-patient privilege. No judge in his or her right mind can listen to Steinhardt promise Mary that the tape is confidential and then let you put it before the jury.''

''We've considered that,'' Sharpe put in. ''Now you consider *our* case. There's no question Carelli killed him—the only question is why. So first we put on the tape recording of her interrogation by Monk. Then we bring on Liz Shelton to show how Ransom couldn't have died the way she said and how the physical evidence suggests a cover-up that includes defacing a very dead body. The room service waiter and the guest who saw her give us a couple more lies. And just as Carelli really begins to smell, we rest.'' Sharpe paused for emphasis. ''Without ever saying a word about Steinhardt.''

''Also without,'' Paget answered, ''ever making it past reasonable doubt. I file a motion, the judge throws your case out, and we all go home.''

Sharpe shook her head. ''You file the motion, and

you lose. We also keep out Rappaport, because she *consented* to whatever Ransom wanted. That leaves you with only two alternatives.

"The first is to argue reasonable doubt, keep Carelli off the stand, and let the jury wonder why your feminist heroine has chosen to hide behind her lawyer. You will no doubt conclude, as I would, that choice one involves a very big risk.

"The second, of course, is to have Mary testify in her own defense and let me cross-examine her.

"Maybe, although I doubt it, she can survive all the inconsistencies arising from the Monk interview, Liz Shelton's analyses, and the two witnesses. But there is nothing in the doctor-patient privilege that prevents me from asking *whether* she saw Steinhardt as a patient, *why* she didn't tell Monk that, and *if* Ransom had a tape that would end her career.

"If she says 'yes' to that last question, she's merely hurting. If she says 'no,' she's history. Because the judge already knows she's lying and, I'm pretty damn sure, would let me find a way to get the tape in."

It was strange, Paget thought, how this relentless woman could make him think of the pain of Mary's dream and not the coldness of her lies. "Assuming," he said quietly, "that the tape hasn't already found its way into the morning papers."

Sharpe shrugged. "I'm not responsible for what they print."

"Why not?" Paget snapped. "You were the last time." His voice grew cold. "And if you play games with this tape, any games at all, it won't be Mary who's history. Because first I'll get a mistrial, and then I'll nail you to the wall."

Sharpe flushed. "I can certainly understand," she said, "why *you* want those tapes concealed."

"Do you? Then you should have no trouble believing me." Paget turned back to Brooks. "Are you enjoying this?"

"No." For the first time, Brooks looked uncomfortable, as if he wished he were somewhere else. "Under the circumstances, no."

Paget paused. "Under *what* circumstances?"

"We're charging her with murder." Brooks shook his head, as if hearing bad news for the first time. "We've got no choice."

Beside him, Sharpe looked triumphant. Paget felt stunned. "That's a real mistake," he said.

"The only mistake," Sharpe put in, "would be turning down our deal."

"Deal?"

Sharpe nodded. "Your client pleads to voluntary manslaughter, and we recommend the minimum sentence. A few years' prison, and this tape never comes out."

Brooks leaned forward. "Think about it, Chris. It protects Ms. Carelli from far worse."

Keep your head, Paget told himself. "And, with

all respect, protects you from the political consequences of a backlash in Mary's favor. Not to mention the considerable distress of the Colt family."

Brooks summoned an equable expression. "I prefer to think the ends of justice will have been satisfied. And on a less ethereal note, I'm not as worried about 'backlash' as I used to be. Such an ugly word anyhow, I think we would all agree. As for the ire of James Colt's family, I would argue strenuously that the Laura Chase tape isn't relevant anymore and should never see the light of day." He spread his arms. "Besides, I can't imagine that a trial could be good for anyone—for Ms. Carelli, for you, or for your son. So talk to her, Chris, and get back to me. We won't indict until I hear from you, and if she signs on, we'll handle this with all the civility we can manage."

The D.A. was massaging him, Paget thought, as he would any defense lawyer with a guilty client in a mildly troublesome case. He stood, numb with disbelief. "This isn't a month's stay in a Best Western," he said. "It's the end of Mary's life, and she'll surely understand that."

"A conviction for murder one," Sharpe answered, "is the end of Mary's life. Compared to that, this is a sabbatical. Tell her that."

Paget turned to her. "Could you write that down for me? I don't want to miss a word."

Silent, Sharpe got up and opened the door for him.

It was, Paget thought, the ultimate gesture of dismissal.

"Good luck," he said to Brooks, and walked through the door.

When Sharpe and Paget were on the other side, she shut the door behind them, as if to say something she wished Brooks not to hear. "When you first came here," she said in a flat voice, "I had some sympathy for you, believe it or not. Now I know you're just another user. So I want *you* to know that you're using the wrong issue, for the wrong woman, in the wrong case. That's what I'm going to prove."

She turned and stalked back to her office, the brisk click of her heels sounding on the tile floor.

ELEVEN

"DID CHRIS KNOW?" Steinhardt had asked.

Alone in his office, Paget imagined the second tape.

He was certain that it began with the night in Washington, fifteen years before, when Mary helped him evade Lasko's men at the airport. The night they had found Jack Woods rifling Paget's desk, clutching the memo that would destroy William Lasko and the President. The memo of a dead man. The witness Lasko had ordered killed, Alec Lehman.

For an instant, Paget remembered, Woods's face had frozen in surprise. Then it had settled into closed-off pride, looking from Paget to Mary and back again. His broken nose lent a hint of violence.

"What the hell are you doing?" Paget had demanded.

Woods had remained silent, giving the room a searching glance. Only the desk was between them. The overhead light cast a sickly yellow tint on the bare walls.

The desk touched the wall to Paget's right. But

between the desk and the left wall was a four-foot space. Woods gauged it, then turned back to Paget.

Paget felt a sudden wave of anger. ''Give me the memo.''

Woods shook his head. Paget's anger began turning to disbelief. ''It was you all along,'' Paget said.

Woods stared at Paget with contempt. ''Nothing justifies the fuck-up you've made. You're a fool, with no sense of proportion.''

''And you're a low-rent John Dean, Woods, with the ethics of a war criminal.''

Woods answered in a smooth, indifferent voice. ''Lehman's dead. I didn't want that, but there it is. There's only you to say this memo ever existed. And there's no one over me for you to say it to.''

They were both to the side of the desk now, three feet between them. Woods was framed by the darkened window, Capitol Hill spotlit behind him. The two men watched each other.

''If you want to walk out of here,'' Paget answered, ''you'll have to kill me yourself. I know it all now. Most important, I know where the money was going.''

''I'll bite,'' Woods said negligently. ''Where?''

''The President.''

For five minutes, still tensed and watchful, Paget had spelled it out: a one-and-one-half-million-dollar ''contribution'' to kill an antitrust case, the one witness who could prove that, Alec Lehman, whose memo Woods now held—whose death Woods had caused.

Woods's response was unnaturally calm. "You've lost," he said simply. Without this memo, no one will believe you."

The words covered Woods's careful slide toward the door. Paget slid back his right foot, to brace himself.

Woods suddenly dipped his shoulder and shot forward, knocking Paget against the desk. Paget bounced off and punched up from the rib cage. Woods's teeth clicked.

Pain ripped through Paget's forearm. Woods rocked, then caught himself against the wall.

Paget lunged for the memo. But Woods was too quick and too strong. He sidestepped as Paget stumbled past, off balance. A fist cracked into Paget's cheekbone. He staggered, then sprawled facedown on his desk, seeing a sudden purple haze. The haze cleared. In front of him was an onyx bookend, a squat hunk of rock. He grabbed it left-handed and spun.

What Paget hit was teeth.

Woods's hands jerked up to clamp his mouth, as if to hold it together. Paget cocked the bookend, then hacked at Woods's forehead.

Paget heard Mary scream.

As Woods tottered on his heels, Paget hit him again.

Woods staggered, eyes glazed. Then he slid slowly down the wall. Paget gaped at him, breathing hard.

Mary stood in the doorway, staring. Woods was sprawled gracelessly on the floor, like the victim of a sudden stroke. His mouth was oozing blood.

Mary looked up from Woods, and then saw Paget's face.

She froze, irresolute, turned to run. Paget caught her and threw her against the wall. She made a little sound, like a hurt cat. Her fingers covered her mouth.

Paget moved toward her.

She shook her head like a mechanical doll. "No. No, Chris. You can't believe . . ."

Paget shook her hard.

"Lehman," he demanded. "It was you and Woods."

Mary stared at Paget.

"Tell me, damn you, before I mash your fucking face into the wall."

Her words escaped in twos and threes. "That night . . . the first time we went out . . . you said you were going to Boston. To meet a key witness." She caught her breath. "I called Jack, after I got in. Jack called Lasko."

Paget clamped her shoulders. "Goddamn you."

Her voice jumped. "No one knew Lasko would kill Lehman. I could hardly sleep."

Paget shook her. "I was there, remember?"

The personal thing was close to the surface, passing unspoken from Mary's eyes to his. ''Please, Chris,'' she pleaded, ''let me talk.''

Paget slowly eased his grip. Her mouth worked soundlessly, then started. ''I never talked to Lasko or anyone at the White House. I never wanted you hurt. I didn't know, really. I didn't know what I was into. I just tried to help Jack control the case. I couldn't expose him after the Lehman thing. He said we were both in trouble, because I'd known what he was doing. That's the only reason I kept helping him.''

''Including tonight, when you called him from the airport? That *is* what happened, isn't it?''

''Yes, damn it. Now let me go.''

''Did you call anyone but Woods?''

She shook her head. If that was true, Paget thought, perhaps he had some time before Lasko's people, evaded at the airport, figured out where he was. He let his hands drop.

Mary straightened and smoothed her hair, seemed to retrieve some of her poise. Something in Paget had admired that, even then.

Her eyes softened. She spoke quickly, looking at him. ''Chris, you think I was with you because of the case. Maybe I used that a little. But I didn't have to come to you this weekend. And I didn't have to stay. I did that because I wanted to.''

Two days before, Paget remembered, they had

made love. It seemed much longer. "I've had the privilege of listening to your speeches about politics, remember? You were just another weapon they could use. To pry the memo out of me, and give it to Woods."

She nodded her concession. "All right. But if I'd kept you away from Lasko, or gotten this memo, you'd be safe. I cared for you. You were good at things, gentle underneath—and so free. Money does make you free, you know."

"No, I don't know."

"Chris, please let's not lose this too."

It was no good, Paget realized. Slowly, he shook his head. "What I very much don't want to lose," he answered, "is my life."

A touch of panic crossed her face. "Give me the memo, Chris, and I can protect you. There isn't anywhere you can go with this. Not Woods, the White House, or anywhere else."

She was right, Paget knew. He looked over at Woods. He was still unconscious, but Paget's time was running out. He turned to Mary and pointed to the chair behind his desk. "Sit over there."

Paget reached for his telephone. In quick succession, he made two phone calls. When he had finished, a police lieutenant in Boston knew about everything except Mary, and a reporter from the Washington *Post* was hurrying from home to meet him outside.

"Why didn't you tell them about me?" Mary asked.

"I have my reasons."

Woods moaned but didn't move. Mary glanced at him dispassionately. "You know, he was right. You don't have enough proof to do to him what you've done to Lasko."

Paget shrugged. Her eyes were imploring now. "Chris," she said urgently, "there has to be some way to make this better."

Paget did not answer. His watch showed 9:43; in a minute or so, the reporter would be parked in front of the building.

Paget picked up the telephone and placed his last call.

An operator answered. "Police Emergency."

"Yes. I'd like to report an incident. The address is the ECC Building on D Street, Northwest, room 327. I've just caught a man trying to burglarize my desk. I knocked him unconscious, possible concussion. I'll need a couple of officers and maybe an ambulance."

Mary bolted upright. The operator repeated the address. "We'll have someone there within three minutes," she said.

"Thank you."

As Paget put down the phone, Mary lunged for the door, half tripping over Woods.

Paget caught her by the wrist.

She struggled, then stopped. Paget pulled her back. "The cops will be here in about two minutes. I have to leave. I'm giving you a choice—stay or go."

Mary stared at him furiously. "I want to leave."

Paget forced himself to be very calm. "Choice one is to stay and tell the truth. That Woods said he called Lasko about Lehman, that you called Woods tonight, and that after that he broke into my desk—"

"I didn't know he was going to do that," she interjected.

"And along with that, you can do your Miss Innocence routine and try to wriggle out. If you can pull that off, I won't stop you."

Her eyes were black pools. "And if I leave?"

"Then I give your name to the *Post*."

She clutched Paget's shirt. "Do you know what that would do?"

"I figure disbarment at the very least. You've got about a minute to decide."

She dropped her hands. "I'll stay, damn you."

"Good. Tell the police I'll be by in the morning."

Woods was moaning, the blood caked on his mouth. The memo still lay by his hand.

Paget picked it up and started to leave.

"You're a bastard, Chris." She said it in a clear, quiet voice.

Paget turned back. She was watching him, with an odd, expectant look. "My reporter friend will be calling the police," he said, "at exactly midnight. To check your statement on Woods, for his article. If you change your story or tell the cops where I am, you'll be reading about yourself tomorrow morning."

Mary's mouth parted. It was strange, Paget thought; he had never seen her more beautiful.

He turned and walked out.

He glanced back, once, as he rounded the corner. Mary was staring down at Woods. The yellow light was surrounded by darkness. The room looked like a cell.

"Did Chris know about you?" Steinhardt had asked Mary.

Chris knew everything.

There was a knock on the door, and Terri Peralta came in. "What's wrong?" she asked.

"Did you find Mary?"

"Yes. She'll be here in about an hour."

Paget nodded. "Close the door," he said. "There are a few things I have to tell you."

It was somehow touching, Paget thought, to watch Terri's attempt to listen like a lawyer, devoid of judgment or emotion. It made his own feelings a bit more bearable.

When he had finished, Terri simply sat there for a moment. ''Why did Mary tell you she was pregnant?'' she finally asked. ''At least when she did.''

''Insurance, I would guess. That night in my office, neither of us could know what we were getting into—a Senate investigation, national television. We were both improvising, with Jack Woods lying there on the floor. I was trying to save my life and, as Mary saw it, she was trying to save *her* life.'' Paget paused. ''By the time we got to the hearing, I guess Mary wasn't sure I'd still protect her.''

''Would you have?''

''I had hoped that no one would ever ask about her.'' Paget leaned back, remembering. ''When Talmadge did ask, there were so many things going through my mind.

''The hearing room was quite imposing: leather chairs and a long wooden bench, raised so that you had to look up from the witness table; thirteen senators staring down; cameras everywhere.

''Millions of people were watching me. I had come so far with this since I'd seen Alec Lehman run down on a Boston street, since William Lasko had tried to do that to *me*. In the last two hours of testimony, I had settled my accounts with Lasko, with a President I didn't even know, and, most personal of all, with Jack Woods—who represented everything in government that I despised.

"I had to decide whether to go all the way, or to end it with a lie.

"In a way, it was Woods who put me there.

"Mary had finished him, of course—I couldn't have nailed Woods without a second witness. Skipping the question of morality, her testimony that morning was a thing of beauty. With complete self-confidence, she had told the truth about Woods by claiming that he had 'confessed' what Mary in fact already knew. Then she covered for herself, absolutely certain that Woods could never implicate her in any convincing way without implicating himself."

Paget watched his words register in Terri's eyes: their client was a liar and worse, and Paget had always known it. "Which brings us," he said slowly, "back to me.

"Talmadge asked a question with a lengthy preamble, as senators seem prone to do on television. But when he finally got to the question, it was, 'Did Miss Carelli have any involvement in the death of Alec Lehman, the obstruction of your inquiry, the leaks to William Lasko, or the alleged cover-up of illegal contributions to the President himself.'

"I remember looking up at him, composing my answer. Thinking about Woods, and Mary, and the baby she would have.

"Just as I began to answer, a camera flashed."

Paget gazed at Terri. "I lied, of course. *Time*

magazine captured the moment in mid-sentence and put it on their cover.''

Terri met his gaze, impassive. ''Is that why you've never talked about it?''

Paget nodded. ''I don't know,'' he said softly, ''whether it was that so many people thought I was a hero, or the lie itself. Whatever, the Lasko case had done something to me, and I was through with it.''

''Does anyone else know?''

''Only Mary.'' Paget hesitated. ''And now you.''

''Not Carlo?''

''Definitely not Carlo. Not, at least, until someone finds the second tape.''

All at once, Terri's shoulders slumped. ''Oh, Chris,'' she said quietly. ''I'm so sorry.''

''Don't be,'' he said. ''Mary and I both made our choices. We're the perfect couple, and Carlo is a lucky boy.''

Terri shook her head, almost angrily. ''He *is* lucky. What you did was out of love—it's something a parent does for a child.'' She finished more gently: ''It's something my mother would have done for me.''

''That's the most attractive view. But I didn't do it just for Carlo.'' Paget turned, watching the rain spatter his windows. ''Perhaps, to some degree, I did it for Mary herself. But I don't think it was just that, either. Maybe it comes down to this: I needed

Mary to tell the truth about Jack Woods, so I helped her lie about herself.''

Terri's gaze was steady again. ''That doesn't explain raising Carlo.''

''If you believe Mary, I was searching for atonement.'' Paget looked away. ''I know this much: the day in Paris, when I threatened her with the truth unless she gave up Carlo, was one day Mary thought would never come. And today, listening to her confess on tape, was a day *I* thought would never come. For any of us.''

Terri was silent. Finally, she said, ''If that tape gets into evidence, Mary doesn't have a prayer, does she?''

Paget shook his head. ''Not only does the tape give her a motive, but the motive is to conceal that she's already committed perjury. After *that,* no jury will believe her about anything.''

Once more, Terri hesitated. ''Do *you* think Mary planned to murder Ransom?''

''I have no idea.''

Terri looked pensive. ''What I don't understand is why she wanted you to represent her. Of all people, you're the one least likely to believe her.''

''Oh, Mary's reason's clear enough to me.'' Paget turned to her. ''I'm the only person alive that Mary absolutely believes to be as ruthless as she is—at least if I want something badly enough. She's seen that twice: that night in Washington, when I wanted to finish Woods, and that afternoon in Paris, when I felt I was saving Carlo.'' Paget paused. ''Because of Carlo, I have something to lose now. It was Mary's turn to play the perjury card. To force me to represent her.''

''With what's on the tapes, though, why would she want you?''

Paget gave a bleak smile. ''They're the best motivator of all. The first tape damages me by implication, the second no doubt finishes the job. If I don't manage to suppress either or both—not so coincidentally giving Mary her only hope of beating this—Carlo will get a rude surprise regarding *both* his parents.''

Terri touched her eyes. ''What are you going to do?''

''I don't know that, either.'' Paget hesitated. ''I may not have a conflict in the literal sense—I'm no longer chargeable with perjury, and I have no personal knowledge regarding Ransom's death. But in the deepest way, my own interests are very much at stake.''

''Or Carlo's interests.''

Paget shrugged. ''In a family, it's hard to keep them separate: what the parent does, or doesn't do, invariably affects the child. That's why Mary was right to give up Carlo. For whatever reason.''

''Have you thought of telling him?''

"A thousand times. And the answer I keep coming up with is 'not unless I have to.' "

Terri hesitated. "He's not a frightened seven-year-old anymore. He's a different boy."

Paget considered that. "How different, I wonder. Most kids, when they learn some hard truth about a parent, make their peace with it in private. That's a bit easier than learning in the full glare of publicity that your mother—who's already charged with murder—obstructed justice fifteen years before, was morally implicated in the killing of a government witness, and went hand in hand with your father to lie about it to the United States Senate." Paget shook his head. "What would your mother do with *that* one?"

Terri gazed at the floor. "I don't know, Chris. I really don't."

She sounded tired, distant. "I'm sorry," Paget said quietly. "I know how disappointed you must be."

"In what?"

"In me." Paget found it painful to say more. "Look, I'll take you off the case, help you find another job—"

"*No.*" Terri stood. "You just don't get it, do you?"

Paget stared at her. "Get what?"

"You said I was your friend. All right, I get to

care about you as a friend.'' Her eyes were alive again. ''You're a much better person than you allow yourself to believe, so this hurts me that much more. But that's all you're seeing, damn it. *I'm* not fifteen.''

Paget watched her face, unsure of what to do. ''You owe me nothing, Terri. I chose *you* as a friend. You didn't choose me.''

The smallest smile appeared at the corner of her mouth. ''Sometimes,'' she said, ''you really *are* hopeless.''

When the telephone rang, Paget was still looking at her.

''Mary Carelli,'' the receptionist said, ''to see you.''

For a moment longer, Paget gazed at Terri. ''Send her in,'' he answered.

When Mary entered, turning to Terri with open curiosity, Paget realized that the two had never met.

It was strange to see them facing each other: Mary nearly a half foot taller, with her air of sophistication and command; Terri, still young, with that look of level intelligence, of seeing things clearly. They seemed very different.

Terri extended her hand. ''I'm Terri Peralta,'' she said. She did not smile; it was no doubt difficult, Paget thought, to first encounter a client within moments of learning that she was amoral, a gifted liar, and, quite possibly, some form of murderer. Add that Mary was Paget's ex-lover and the less than stellar mother of a teenage boy whom Terri seemed to like, and Terri's poker face was an achievement.

"Yes, of course." Smiling slightly, Mary gave Terri a quick once-over, which Paget thought less than polite. "Chris, as is so often the case, seems to have forgotten his manners. Including any explanation of why it was so urgent to see me."

"Now that you're here," Terri answered, "I'm sure that Chris will make it up to you."

Terri's tone, cool and undeferential, transformed her from Paget's associate into a woman with thoughts of her own. It seemed to bring Mary up short.

She turned to Paget, as if to dismiss Terri from the room. "Are the two of you through?" she asked him. "If not, I can wait outside."

Beneath the polite inquiry, Mary's message was clear: Whatever Paget had in mind, she did not wish to discuss it in front of Terri. "Oh, no," Paget said casually. "We're ready to meet with you now."

For an instant, Mary looked off balance. "Perhaps," she said, "it would be better if we talked alone."

Paget took his time. "I have no secrets from Terri," he answered. "And neither do you."

Mary stared at him. "What do you mean, precisely?"

"That as long as she works on this case, and whatever it turns out to involve, Terri will know everything."

Something new crossed Mary's face, doubt and a trace of humiliation. How much does she know? the expression asked. Turning to Terri, she said, "Chris must have great confidence in you."

Terri nodded. *"He* can, so *you* can. But I have things I can be doing." She turned to Paget. "Think you can handle this alone?"

Paget felt himself smile. "I think so." He paused, then added, "Thanks for your help."

Mary looked from Paget to Terri and back again.

"Sure," Terri said easily. She went to the door, gave Paget a final glance, and left.

Mary watched the door close. Then, as if to dispel her own tension, she said lightly, "There's something a little proprietary in how she looks at you, don't you think?"

"Something a little human. I'm trying to get used to that."

Mary continued, as if impervious to his tone. "I'd guess she has a crush on you, actually. But then I'm sure that even the mailroom boy pines for you hopelessly—"

"Is this your idea of diversionary patter?" Paget interrupted. "Because if you're auditioning for *Private Lives,* I wouldn't expect a long-term contract."

She stopped abruptly, sat down. "All right," she said quietly. "What's wrong?"

"Why don't *you* tell *me?* For once."

Mary turned to the window. Waves of rain hit the glass, a drumbeat of sound. Her tone was subdued. "Do I get a clue?"

"Just one. Think of something a client with any intelligence would tell her lawyer." Paget's voice grew softer yet. "Or something a mother with any decency would tell a father."

Mary could not seem to turn from the window. "They found a tape."

"Yes."

She leaned back in the chair. "Where?"

"At Ransom's apartment."

Mary's eyes shut. "What, exactly, is on it?"

"It's *your* tape, Mary."

She shook her head. "It's been five years. I was in somewhat of a state."

"So was I, listening to it."

"Please, Chris."

"All right. It begins with your dream, in the cathedral of St. Germain-des-Prés." Paget paused. "It ends with your perjury before the Senate."

She expelled a short breath, eyes still closed. "I never meant you to hear that."

"Why? Did you think I'd forgotten?"

She shook her head. "The dream."

"It enhanced your image. Really, I was pleased to discover that your subconscious believes in sin."

Mary swallowed. In a trembling voice, she said, "And your associate knows all this."

"You have an odd sense of priorities. The *district attorney* knows all this." Paget's voice went cold. "They're issuing an arrest warrant."

Slowly, Mary nodded. Her eyes remained shut.

Paget leaned forward. "If I retained any sense of humor about this, I'd say we were having a crisis of confidence."

"I'm sorry." Her voice was soft. "I truly am."

"So am I. Particularly because there seems to be a second tape out there, one that is no doubt worse for me."

"Yes," she answered dully. "Far worse."

"Would you mind looking at me while you admit to screwing me and, potentially, our son? After all, they say that the eyes are the windows of the soul."

Mary turned and opened her eyes. It was a look more naked than he had seen that night in Washington. The night when he had found out who and what she really was.

"What would you like from me?" she asked.

"Some approximation of the truth. Because if *you* lie now, *I* walk—no matter what."

She stared at him, silent.

"Tell me about Steinhardt," he demanded.

"I saw him once. Five years ago, for two hours. I never went back."

"Why not?"

"Perhaps it was like confession: tell it once, and it's over." She gave a small shrug. "There was something haunting about it—him, the room, the tape. Talking about it at all." She paused. "You know how Indians used to believe that a photograph would steal your soul? When I left, that's how I felt about those two hours."

"Did you stop having the dream?"

Mary's face hardened. "That," she said, "is none of your concern."

Paget watched her. "Why are there *two* tapes?"

"Because I was there so long. As I recall, he had to change tapes."

"What's on the second tape?"

Mary shook her head. "Some of what I said is *my* property, as *all* of it was meant to be until Mark Ransom started pawing it. I don't feel the need to discuss it with you, and I won't."

"There is, I assume, more about the Lasko case."

"Nothing that should make *my* situation any worse—I'd already confessed to perjury. To the extent that it concerns you, the missing tape tells what you knew." She paused, adding quietly, "It also concerns the circumstances of Carlo's adoption, as it were."

Paget appraised her. "Where's the second tape?"

"I don't know." She turned away. "For your sake, and for Carlo's, I hope they never find it."

"Ransom didn't say?"

Mary hesitated, as if deep in thought. "No. He didn't say."

Paget waited until she looked at him. Quietly, he asked, "Did you murder him?"

Mary turned back to him, composed. "He tried to abuse me," she said coolly. "I executed him."

Paget could think of nothing to say. At length, he asked, "Why did Ransom call you? The truth, this time."

She nodded. "To tell me he had the tape."

"Your tape, or the tape of Laura Chase?"

"Both." She paused. "He made it clear that his interests were both professional and personal."

"How so?"

"Professionally, he wanted to use the Laura Chase tape to promote his book." She looked down. "Personally, he felt we should have a 'private interview' about my past."

"Was he more explicit?"

"He didn't have to be." Her eyes raised. "His tone of voice was worse than anything he could have said."

Paget paused. "What did he say about the tape itself? Your tape, that is."

"He described what was on it—in detail. To leave me in no doubt he had it."

"Did you ask him to bring the tape to San Francisco?"

Her eyes filled with anger. "Yes."

"But he didn't?"

She stared at him. "It seems to me," she said coldly, "that you and your friends at the D.A.'s office just finished listening to a tape. I suppose my good friend Mark just forgot to bring it out."

"But he did remember to bring the Laura Chase tape."

"Of course." Her voice was edged with contempt. "As I told Inspector Monk, it seemed to excite him."

Paget watched her face. "Why San Francisco?" he asked.

"He told me that he had a private interview with another famous woman." Contempt turned to bitterness. "That he wanted us 'back-to-back.' That he wanted to 'compare notes.' "

That, Paget realized, had the ring of truth—but only if one knew about Lindsay Caldwell. "Did he mention any names?"

"No. He was going to be 'discreet,' he said." She paused. "Even on the telephone, I could feel his hands on me. That was why I bought the gun."

"So you lied to Monk about receiving threatening calls."

"Of course." Mary looked pensive. "If I had told him the truth—that Ransom was blackmailing me—then I'd have a motive for murder, wouldn't I?"

"Not to mention that purchasing the weapon begins to sound more than a bit like premeditation."

Mary shrugged. "Anyhow, they can't prove I got no calls. I'm better off with that than I am with the truth."

Paget smiled faintly. "Getting by with one lie out of six or so leaves something to be desired. Whatever made you think you could go one-on-one with someone like Charles Monk and come out ahead?"

"I didn't want to look guilty." She gave him a sardonic returning smile. "I suppose my past success had made me overconfident."

"That's unfortunate. The average homicide cop is smarter than the average senator, and much more attentive to detail." He paused. "Just for fun, why don't you tell me exactly what *did* happen in that room."

Mary searched his face. "Does it matter?"

"What do you mean?"

"The tape of Monk questioning me is admissible, isn't it?"

"Yes."

"Then that's the story I'm stuck with."

"True," Paget said. "And that's unfortunate as well. You didn't tell Monk about Steinhardt. You didn't admit to blackmail. You forgot about closing the blinds. You got the gunshot distance all wrong. You denied leaving the room after Ransom died, which you clearly did. And as far as Liz Shelton is concerned, you have no respect for the rear end of a corpse. Compared to all that, making up nonexistent phone calls is a stroke of genius.''

Mary's gaze was level. ''Too bad. Because the essence of what I told them was true.''

''Define 'essence.' '' Paget's voice went cold. ''I can hardly wait.''

Mary breathed in again. ''Ransom abused me,'' she said slowly. ''And I killed him.'' She touched her cheek. ''If that weren't true, *this* wouldn't have happened. Please, trust me this far.''

''What *did* happen?'' Paget asked again.

''What I *said* happened. Insert the tape of *me* with that of Laura Chase, add the blackmail that came with it, and what I told Monk is pretty much the truth.'' Mary paused. ''With allowances for shock and a few omissions.''

''Like the blinds?''

''Yes. *I* pulled them down.''

''Why?''

''Because Ransom asked me to.'' She looked down. ''Things hadn't come to a head.''

''And leaving the room?''

Mary folded her hands. ''I thought about getting help. Then I figured I hadn't thought quite hard enough.''

"About what?"

"About what to say and what to leave out."

"Is that why you delayed in calling—because you were refining your story?"

"It was hard for me to think, that's all. Looking back at it, I really *was* in shock." Her voice lowered. "A lot had been done to me, emotionally and physically, and then I'd killed the man who'd done it."

Paget waited for a moment. "You should know," he said at last, "that they'll take a plea of voluntary manslaughter."

She faced the window again. The clouds had thickened, blocking the view; the rain spattering the window seemed to come from a wall of gray. "And if I don't agree?"

"Then you go on trial. For murder one."

For a long time, Mary was quiet. "What are my chances?" she asked.

Paget hesitated. "It's a tough case," he finally said. "For both sides."

"Why tough for them?"

"They can't get the Steinhardt tape in. Unless, possibly, you take the stand."

"And for us?"

"If you *don't* take the stand, they play the tape of what you said to Monk and then show all the problems with your story. After that, the jury will wonder why they should believe in a woman who's lied to the police and then declined to testify.'' Paget paused. ''Frankly, to the extent that I believe you at all, it's only because Melissa Rappaport and Lindsay Caldwell lend you some credibility. Granted, the jury doesn't have the advantage of knowing you as well as I do, but they probably won't have the advantage of seeing Rappaport or Caldwell, either. I doubt the judge will let the jury hear them.''

Mary turned to him. ''Which means I have to testify.''

''I think so.'' Paget gazed at her. ''More specifically, you have to explain your misstatements to Monk, admit the blackmail you forgot to mention, and then persuade the jury to believe you anyway.''

She smiled slightly. ''That's all?''

''Not quite. You will also have to admit the Steinhardt tape was damaging, while avoiding any mistakes that would strip you of the psychiatrist-patient privilege and allow Sharpe to play it for a jury. Because if they get to hear you admit lying to the Senate, it's over. And Marnie Sharpe will be looking for any way she can, including tricks as dirty as she can get away with, to make sure that happens.''

''Why?''

''Because she's ambitious. As ambitious as you were.''

Mary's face turned grim. ''Ambitious, perhaps. But she doesn't have nearly enough to lose.''

Paget shook his head. ''In the middle of the night,

when she's alone with her private thoughts, I think Marnie Sharpe has as much to lose as anyone.''

''And you, Chris?''

''If that tape comes in, I may have a lot to lose. And so may Carlo.'' Paget paused. ''Which is why McKinley Brooks suggests that I sell you this deal.''

Mary considered him. ''I plead guilty, and the tape stays buried. Is that the deal?''

''Yes.''

''How neat.''

''Whatever,'' Paget said softly, ''made you think they wouldn't find it?''

Mary's eyes narrowed. ''Because *I* didn't know where it was. And if I didn't tell them about it, the police wouldn't know to look.''

''Bad judgment, Mary. As I said, you're losing your touch.''

Mary sighed. ''All right,'' she said finally. ''What would you do?''

''I won't say. Brooks and Sharpe want me to make a choice for you, and their choice at that. I refuse.''

''Despite what you and Carlo have at risk?''

''Despite that. *You* put me here, because you thought I'd play to win. That's the 'essence' of *you*—manipulative and completely without conscience—and I despise you for it. But I won't let the D.A. turn your trick around on me and make me play to lose.'' Paget shrugged. ''Your killing, Mary. Your choice.''

She was quiet for a time. "If I go to trial, will you defend me?"

"What about Carlo? After all, he *is* our son."

Mary looked down. "The way I see it," she said slowly, "is that Carlo's mother is either an admitted murderer or a potential perjurer with a chance to be innocent of murder. Which I am." She looked up again. "So the only question is: Will you represent me?"

Paget got up, walked to the window. Again weighed Melissa Rappaport, Lindsay Caldwell, the odds that whatever Mary had done was not premeditated murder. And, finally, thought of Carlo.

He went to the telephone. "I'll call Brooks," he said.

Mary looked relieved. But all she said was, "I'm sure you'll think of something."

Brooks's secretary answered on the second ring. Paget told her who he was, and waited.

"Hello, Christopher," Brooks said. "Long time no speak."

"No deal, either."

Beneath the opening banter, Brooks had sounded tense; now Paget could measure by his silence how little more he relished this trial than Paget himself. "You needn't be precipitous," Brooks said. "Really, I didn't expect you back so soon. If you want more time to think, take it."

"Don't need it. I'm bringing her in for photographs and prints. All I want is a few courtesies."

He could hear Brooks exhale. ‘‘All right. Anything else?’’

‘‘One suggestion. Keep Ms. Savonarola under control. For both our sakes.’’

‘‘I read you,’’ Brooks said, and hung up.

Paget turned to Mary.

She looked hopeful, watchful, scared. The look reminded him of the moment before she had testified in the Senate, first pregnant with Carlo, when she had gazed into his face.

He did not need to tell her what was coming: the reporters shouting questions, the flashbulbs popping, the cameras. Nor did he need to hear the voice-over that night, as he and Carlo watched alone:

‘‘This afternoon in San Francisco, television journalist Mary Carelli was charged with the murder of America’s most celebrated writer, Mark Ransom.’’

PART THREE

THE WITNESS

January 27 – February 10

ONE

Five days later, Mary Carelli was in court.

Terri and Paget stood next to her, facing Municipal Court Judge Caroline Masters, Terri's former boss at the public defender's office. The occasion, the arraignment of the accused, was the most humdrum grist of the criminal mill. Paget would plead Mary innocent, and Judge Masters would set another meaningless date: the preliminary hearing in municipal court, where all that Marnie Sharpe had to establish was that there was "probable cause" to believe that Mary Carelli had committed a crime, an event as routine as singing the national anthem before a football game.

The arraignment, Terri knew, was likely to be Caroline Masters's first and last appearance in the case; another municipal court judge would likely preside over the preliminary hearing. After the prosecution showed probable cause, the muni court and its judges would have finished their work, and the case would be dispatched to the relative grandeur of the superior court, the forum of higher jurisdiction, to be tried by a superior court judge.

The sole reason Judge Masters had borrowed such an impressive courtroom was that this time the mill was grinding on Mary Carelli, and space was needed for all the media people who wished to watch it happen. The sterile courtroom where Caroline Masters usually processed the minions of muni court—traffic violators, parking scofflaws, and petty disturbers of the urban peace—could barely accommodate the defendants and their sport-coated lawyers; the more spacious courtroom specially assigned for *People v. Carelli* could absorb a greater crowd, and its oak bench, high ceiling, and wood-paneled walls would show well on television. Watching Caroline Masters and knowing her aspirations, Terri was certain that she enjoyed this respite, however fleeting, from processing the dregs of the justice system in a room that looked like public housing.

"How do you plead?" Judge Masters asked.

Paget paused. "Not guilty," he answered calmly.

Judge Masters gazed at the participants, stretching out the moment. At one long table, both dressed in gray, were Marnie Sharpe and a young male assistant D.A., who Terri guessed had been selected for his ability and inexperience, so that Sharpe would have competent help without being challenged by a seasoned homicide prosecutor with ideas of his own; McKinley Brooks was nowhere in sight, for what

Terri was certain were reasons of political prudence. At the other table were Paget, Terri, and Mary Carelli, Mary in a simple black dress, Paget dressed with a bit less dash than usual. Even Caroline Masters seemed to have given her appearance some thought: her black robe looked freshly pressed and her straight black hair newly cut, and her gold-and-onyx earrings and red-orange lipstick nicely complemented a deep tan acquired at her time-share in Puerto Vallarta. But as with other things about Caroline, Terri had no idea whom she might have vacationed with or what she might have done; in two years of work, Terri had learned little more about Caroline Masters than that she was quite ambitious and very smart.

It was not, Terri thought now, that Caroline had not been pleasant to her—in her incisive way, she had quickly concluded that Terri had enough talent to make her worth Caroline's time. But the advice she had given had been strictly professional; Caroline, Terri learned, drew a wall around herself. What, if anything, she was protecting, Terri did not know; Caroline acknowledged her passion for privacy only by making it seem impersonal. "The way for a woman to survive," she once told Terri, "is to make men see you as a lawyer. If they see you as a *woman*—someone with fears or a troubled marriage or a lover who's broken your heart—they'll start seeing weakness that they'd never see in a man. It's sad but true.'' To Terri, the comment seemed too stark, the flip side of some hurt that Terri could not see. Since she had been appointed to the court, Caroline had not changed; Terri would see her come alone to bar functions, nursing one drink carefully, determined to be nothing but a judge. By consensus, Caroline Masters was a good one.

``The defendant,'' Judge Masters repeated for the record, ``has entered a plea of not guilty to the charge of murder.'' She stopped a moment, allowing the court stenographer to catch up, and then turned again to Paget. ``Has the defendant arranged for bond?''

``Yes, Your Honor,'' Paget answered. ``Five hundred thousand, by agreement with the district attorney.''

Judge Masters nodded. ``In that case, Mr. Paget, we are required by statute to set the preliminary hearing within thirty days. Do you wish to waive the ten-day period?''

It was, Terri knew, the standard inquiry. In practice, the preliminary hearing was worthless to the defense; by waiving the right to a hearing within ten court days, the defense lawyer typically lost nothing of value, and in exchange gained time to prepare by putting off the setting of a trial itself. From her expression and tone of voice, that was what Caroline Masters expected of Christopher Paget.

"The defendant," Paget answered pleasantly, "chooses not to waive time."

For the first time, Judge Masters registered surprise, her raised eyebrows making her thin face seem longer, her expression more intent. At the prosecution table, Marnie Sharpe had turned to look at Paget.

"Might I inquire," Judge Masters said to Paget, "as to why you want the prelim so promptly? As you may know, our docket is stacked up like planes at the airport. If you're going to discommode the court, it ought at least to serve your client's interests. It's not apparent to me, Mr. Paget, that this does."

Already on edge, Terri began to lose hope. The question was vintage Masters; it was Caroline's habit to decide what lawyers should do, and lawyers who did otherwise affronted her sense of strategy. But that she was so direct in saying so told Terri that Paget was not among those defense counsel who, by virtue of their experience in murder prosecutions, might get some slack from Caroline Masters. Sharpe, who had shown a moment's surprise and annoyance, now looked pleased.

Tense, Terri watched Paget frame his answer. But Paget seemed unaffected; perhaps only Terri could tell how uncertain he was that he could draw Judge Masters into a plan that had little precedent.

"There are several reasons," Paget responded.

"But one, I think, should suffice. My client is a television journalist. She does *not* make her living in the state, but in New York and around the world. Yet at the insistence of the district attorney's office, in the person of Ms. Sharpe, Ms. Carelli is not allowed to leave the state until the case is over." He paused. "Apparently, Ms. Sharpe is concerned that Ms. Carelli is going to escape justice. In truth, all Ms. Carelli wants to do is escape Ms. Sharpe's misguided charges. But if what Ms. Sharpe requires for Ms. Carelli to resume her life is to get this trial over with, that's what Ms. Carelli wants—just as quickly as these charges warrant." Turning to Sharpe, Paget inquired amiably, "I assume, Ms. Sharpe, that you're prepared to show probable cause within the statutory period."

Caroline Masters did not appear sympathetic; she did not yet see, Terri realized, what Paget was about to do. As for Sharpe, she was openly annoyed.

"Of course," she told Paget with asperity, and then turned to the judge. "If it would make Mr. Paget happy, the People could show probable cause by the close of business today."

Judge Masters gave her a curious look. "That won't be necessary," she said. "Just as I wonder if it's necessary to keep Ms. Carelli on quite so short a tether."

"*We* think so." Quickly, Sharpe sought the cover of her office, making her judgment institutional.

"Mary Carelli has considerable resources, and the charges pending, in our view, make her a serious flight risk." Sharpe turned to Paget and Mary, speaking with a certain bite. "The court will remember, as will Ms. Carelli and Mr. Paget, the case of William Lasko. After Mr. Lasko's conviction, with his appeal pending, he fled to Costa Rica. It took several years for the United States government—with all its legal and diplomatic resources—to secure Mr. Lasko's return. Where the district attorney has not insisted on prohibitive bail, the least we can do is not facilitate that kind of risk." She turned again to the judge. "We therefore join Mr. Paget in requesting the promptest prelim possible."

Terri knew that the gratuitous reference to the Lasko case, and therefore to the tapes, was meant to put Paget on edge. But his face showed nothing. "We appreciate Ms. Sharpe's endorsement," he responded pleasantly, "if not her analogy to William Lasko. And for the record, Ms. Carelli prefers Bolivia."

Sharpe stared at him; for the first time, there was laughter from the press. Caroline Masters raised her gavel with a look of annoyance, signaling her intent to run a tight courtroom, and the noise subsided.

"All right," she said crisply. "We'll need an estimate on time. How long, Ms. Sharpe, will you require to show probable cause?"

The usual prelim, Terri knew, consisted of a couple of witnesses and lasted one to two hours. For an important homicide case, it might run on for the morning; for someone as careful as Marnie Sharpe, it might extend to midafternoon.

"One day," Sharpe responded. "Max."

"All right." Judge Masters turned to her courtroom deputy, Charlie McWhorter, a paunchy factotum who seemed to predate the courtroom and, perhaps, the court itself. "Charlie, find out from Department 20 when they can hear this."

"Pardon me, Your Honor." Paget stepped forward. "Might I be heard on the question of time?"

This time, Masters showed genuine surprise. As she paused before answering, Terri watched the judge begin to wonder where Paget might be heading. "The prelim is the D.A.'s show," she said flatly. "Were you intending to cross-examine?"

"What we're intending," Paget answered, "is to challenge the D.A.'s entire case."

Sharpe spun to look at him; Terri heard another, deeper murmur from the press. There was no laughter at all.

The judge's aquiline features had rearranged themselves into a stare of incredulity. "You intend to challenge probable cause?"

Paget nodded. "Specifically, we intend to *refute* probable cause and to ask this court to dismiss all charges against Mary Carelli."

In the silence, a reporter murmured, "Jesus

Christ!'' There was a babel of sound. Paget glanced at Terri, as if to say: It's all right, and then Judge Masters's gavel cracked like a whip.

''How long,'' she asked in hostile tones, ''do you expect that process to take?''

''Two weeks,'' Paget responded blandly. ''Give or take a day.''

''*Your Honor,*'' Sharpe cut in angrily, and then Judge Masters waved her silent; to Terri, the gesture said: I'll take care of this myself. Terri wished she did not have to watch.

''This is unheard of,'' the judge snapped at Paget. ''And two weeks' cross-examination is absurd.''

With whatever effort, Paget looked unruffled. ''Not just cross-examination, Your Honor. We intend to challenge the admissibility of certain prosecution evidence; to put Ms. Carelli on the stand; to put on other witnesses and evidence; and to proffer the testimony of at least two further witnesses in closed sessions in the chambers of the court itself.'' Paget turned to Sharpe. ''And now that Ms. Sharpe knows our plans, I expect she'll want a bit more than one day. Our two-week estimate includes several days for the prosecution.''

For the first time, Masters's look of irritation betrayed a certain interest. ''As I said, Mr. Paget, I've never seen this done. The role of a preliminary hearing is *not* to replace a trial—even if the prosecution loses for lack of probable cause, they can refile if they find more evidence. Nor does the defense have an automatic right to put on its case in advance of trial.''

Paget nodded. ''That's correct, Your Honor, as a general matter. But my understanding of the law is that at a preliminary hearing, the defense *is* entitled to establish an affirmative defense. Self-defense is an affirmative defense to murder, and preventing rape is a form of self-defense.''

Caroline Masters examined him for a while, suspended between annoyance and intellectual fascination, and then permitted herself a thin smile. ''That's also *my* understanding of the law. Which may or may not be terribly fortunate for you. Seeing that you propose to give Ms. Sharpe a preview of the entire case.''

Paget smiled back. ''If I'm right, Your Honor, a preview is all that Ms. Sharpe will ever get.''

Masters looked dubious. ''There's a big difference between 'probable cause' and 'reasonable doubt.' In my experience, the D.A. *never* blows 'probable cause.' It's hardly a daunting standard.''

''Daunting enough,'' Paget answered, ''if the D.A. doesn't have it.''

''I would like to be heard,'' Sharpe demanded. When Terri turned, she saw that Sharpe had grasped the table with both hands. ''Mr. Paget's ten-day ploy has now become transparent. He means to rush the prosecution into a minitrial before the case is ready.''

"And you bit, Counselor, didn't you?" Masters's tone was dry. "Do you still think Ms. Carelli's such a flight risk, or are you willing to loosen her bonds?"

Sharpe shook her head. "The People will not change their position on flight. We *will* be ready within the ten-day period, and simply ask that the prelim be set at the end of that period."

"Very well." Turning back to Paget, Masters used her most ironic tone. "Is there anything else, Counselor?"

"Just one more thing, Your Honor. The matter of Court TV." Paget paused. "I've had several discussions with their representatives, the short of which is that they very much want to televise all public sessions of the prelim. On behalf of Ms. Carelli, I request that they be allowed to do so." Glancing over at Sharpe, Paget added, "The prosecution purports to bring these charges on behalf of 'the People.' We believe that 'the People' should be allowed to watch."

Masters was silent for a moment, examining Paget with an opaque expression, and then looked to Sharpe. "Ms. Sharpe," she asked, "have you some thoughts on this?"

"Yes," Sharpe answered succinctly. "This trick is worse than the last. Having invented an unnecessary hearing on the question of probable cause, Mr. Paget now proposes to use it to generate so much prejudicial publicity that it will be impossible to ever select a jury once we *do* prove probable cause. The People are opposed.''

''Mr. Paget?''

''My reaction is that having invented an unnecessary charge of murder, Ms. Sharpe now proposes to hide it.'' Paget paused. ''The primary concern regarding pretrial publicity is the *defendant's* right to a fair trial. Ms. Carelli believes that fairness is best served by full disclosure.'' Once more, Paget looked at Sharpe. ''Indeed, listening to Ms. Sharpe, I'm reminded of Justice Cardozo's dictum that 'sunlight is the best disinfectant.' ''

When Sharpe began to retort, the judge cut her off. ''Enough, both of you. I think I understand the argument. I will say to Ms. Sharpe, without prejudging what should be done here, that a defense request on this issue is entitled to great weight.'' Masters turned again to her deputy. ''Now I really would like to see the calendar.''

McWhorter brought a bound logbook to the bench. Masters motioned him closer. Bending over the logbook, they murmured to each other. Then Masters turned to McWhorter, said a few final words; he nodded and then retreated to his desk at the side of the courtroom, looking bemused.

Caroline Masters surveyed the courtroom. To Terri, she seemed to sit straighter, look even more like a judge. ''All right,'' she announced. ''The preliminary hearing will begin on February 10 and will continue five days a week until concluded.'' She paused, looking from Paget to Sharpe. ''Generally, this would go to Department 20. But it's my current intention to delegate my normal caseload to a judge pro tem and to handle the prelim myself.''

With that, Terri knew, Paget had achieved what he wanted. ''Thank you, Your Honor,'' he said.

Masters nodded to each side. ''Mr. Paget, Ms. Sharpe. See you in two weeks. And thank *you* for this morning's entertainment.''

''All rise,'' the deputy called out. As the courtroom stood, Caroline Masters walked from the bench.

In the eruption of sound, Terri felt the release of tension. Mary uttered her first words in an hour. ''Congratulations,'' she murmured to Paget. ''For a single father, you're remarkably well prepared.''

''Congratulate Terri,'' he answered coolly. ''The reason I'm so well prepared is that after two straight nights of research, she knows more about preliminary hearings than God *or* Marnie Sharpe.''

Mary turned to her. After a moment, she said, ''Thank you.''

Terri nodded. ''You're welcome,'' she said. But Mary had already turned away; Terri stood there, wondering what it was about her that Mary so disliked.

Marnie Sharpe broke into her thoughts.

She had walked briskly up to Paget, reaching him

before the press did. "Never," she said, "have I seen someone cut their own throat with such aplomb. At least not since Peter Sellers stopped playing Inspector Clouseau."

"Peter Sellers is dead." Paget smiled. "That's the wrong joke, Marnie, from the wrong woman, about the wrong movie. The film I had in mind was called *Les Misérables*. You know, the one where a maniacal policeman pursues the innocent for twenty years." He paused, adding lightly, "*This* film, at least, promises to be shorter."

When Sharpe turned and walked away, Terri knew that Paget's nonchalance had only fed her anger. Which was, against Terri's better judgment, precisely what Christopher Paget had set out to do.

Christopher Paget's sailboat knifed the water.

Terri watched him. She knew nothing about sailing or the boat itself, a trim twenty-footer. But Paget knew what he was doing; slim and alert, he gazed intently at the water ahead, weight shifting easily with the waves. Johnny Moore, who had clearly done this before, helped with the sails. Terri leaned back against the inside of the boat; it sliced the bay at a forty-five-degree angle, tilting her forward. She looked out at Angel Island and the Golden Gate, breeze cool on her face.

It was the morning after Mary's arraignment, and unseasonably warm. The three of them needed to talk. Johnny Moore, who hated meetings and liked the outdoors, had told Paget that in this weather he preferred to meet in the middle of San Francisco Bay; when Paget had called to ask her about it, Terri volunteered to pack sandwiches. "That clinches it," Paget said, and asked what she wanted to drink. The only person who did not like Johnny's plan was Richie.

"What kind of job is this?" he had demanded as she pulled out blue jeans and a sweater.

"The kind that supports us," Terri had answered. Then she had dressed Elena and driven her to day care, Richie's nameless irritation trailing after her.

After an hour or so, they docked at Angel Island. Wooded and green in winter, the hilly island rose above them and curled around the waterfront. The only sound was the wind and the cries of gulls; behind them, more gulls walked stiffly down the dock, searching for scraps of food. They sat hunched inside the sailboat, looking out at the terraced hillsides of Sausalito and, beyond that and to their left, the distant skyline of the city, white and sparkling. Paget and Terri drank mineral water; Johnny sipped at a long-necked bottle of Beck's beer, looking contented in the sun.

"This is better," he said. "I feel mummified in offices. Especially yours."

Paget shrugged. "My view is nice."

"I suppose. The problem is that the building

works me over. I step inside, start breathing air that's been filtered by God knows how many machines, and then surrender to an elevator that's run by remote control instead of by a person. By the time I've risen twenty floors, I've given up all control over my destiny, and the only reminder of normal life is when I look about a quarter mile down through your window, and I can't even open that. I feel like a fish in an aquarium.''

Paget turned to Terri. ''Remind me,'' he told her, ''to look for space in a trailer park. Something human scale, for Johnny's sake.''

There was an unwonted edge in Paget's voice; Terri decided the moment needed some lightness. ''I like it this way,'' she answered. ''You provide a decent office, and Johnny takes me sailing. Between the two of you, you're almost satisfactory.''

Moore smiled at her fondly. ''That's my most fervent endorsement,'' he said, ''since my ex-wife passed up our anniversary dinner for an evening of group therapy. And to think that all I needed to make her happy was to bring Chris along.''

They stopped talking for a moment, gazing out at the city, each with their own thoughts.

''Would someone please tell me,'' Moore inquired at last, ''why you two are challenging probable cause? That's like standing in front of a bullet and asking it to stop.''

As Paget leaned back, squinting slightly, Terri

could read how uncertain he still was. He looked not at Moore but at the city.

"This case," he said, "is going south. I want to try and end it before it crosses the border. The prelim is our best chance."

Moore regarded him. "You don't want them to find the second tape."

"That's very much part of it," Paget answered. "Do you have any idea where it could be?"

"No. But even the police have had no luck—it's like dear Mark mislaid it." Moore paused. "Am I correct in understanding that this tape is worse for you than her?"

Paget shrugged. "Aside from whatever it says about me, and whatever it might do to Carlo, I have the strange feeling that it would do Mary no good at all. In spite of what she says."

Terri watched Moore hesitate, take in how difficult Paget must find this conversation. "I wouldn't think worse of you, Chris, if you *were* just looking out for yourself and Carlo. She's put you in a terrible place, and long ago."

Paget's eyes narrowed further. "But *I'd* feel worse. As I did then, lying to serve my own interests, as well as Mary's. It surely has come back to haunt us all."

It's haunted *you,* Terri thought, all along. A single lie, for better reasons than you can believe of yourself, changed the course of your life.

"Ah, well," Paget said. "The problem now is to deal with it. Whatever I have at stake, our client is Mary Carelli."

Moore appraised him. Finally, he asked, "You still don't believe her, do you?"

"No. She's hiding something from me. But I don't know what, or why, and there's no point in even asking. I just don't want Sharpe to find whatever it is."

"But do you really think there's any chance to beat Sharpe at the prelim?"

"After the arraignment, yes. *Some* kind of chance."

Moore pulled on his beer, plainly skeptical. "Because you sucked Sharpe into an early prelim?"

Paget nodded. "That, and Caroline Masters. I counted on her being intrigued enough, and ambitious enough, to handle the prelim herself. It was obvious that she'd prefer doing this to cases of sidewalk spitting. What was less obvious—but I think very much on her mind—was that two weeks on television could shoot her up the judicial ladder." Paget paused. "Which, although I was far too circumspect to even hint at it, was precisely what I offered her."

"But why would you *want* her?" Moore asked. "In my observation, the woman's a real piece of work. Piss her off, and what she'll offer *you* is two weeks in the eighth circle of hell, and on television at that. I can see the promos now—'Watch Christopher Paget, turning on a spit.' "

Inwardly, Terri winced; perhaps better than Moore, she could feel the pressure of a televised hearing bearing down on Paget. But Moore was too honest and professional to withhold his doubts for the sake of tact. Paget turned to Moore with an expression of weary patience. "Why did I want her? Because Terri told me I should. Does that make you feel better?"

"That makes me feel a *little* better." Moore looked over at Terri. "Please, reassure me."

Terri hesitated; inadvertently, Moore and Paget had reminded her how much was riding on her judgment of Caroline Masters, and how much Paget had begun to trust her. "I used to work for her," Terri said at length. "The first thing you notice about Caroline is that she has immense self-confidence, and an overwhelming—and generally justified—belief in her own intelligence. She's smart enough to see where Chris is going, and one of the few judges with guts enough to throw this out. Assuming that she *buys* where Chris is going. Which she's more likely to than most."

Moore looked curious. "Why is that?"

The wind shifted, rippling Terri's hair. She leaned back, gazing at a sailboat that cut across her line of vision. "Because like any judge," she answered,

"Caroline is a real person, with real opinions. Her personal life is an enigma, but her personal *beliefs* aren't: if you'd taken off her robe and introduced her to Mark Ransom, she'd have told him to go fuck himself. And she used to be a defense lawyer. You can make yourself a judge—and Caroline's a good one—but you can't make yourself a whole different person."

Moore nodded. "But you can," he ventured, "make yourself a *Superior* Court judge."

"Or, even better, an *appellate* judge." Terri paused. "Everyone at the P.D.'s office knew *that* was Caroline's goal. At some point, the politics of letting Mary off are going to cross her mind. Depending, of course, on how Mary looks on the stand. And, Chris tells me, on the publicity Mary intends to generate."

Moore frowned again. "Before we leave Judge Masters's more human qualities, there's something else about her." Moore glanced over at Terri. "Perhaps it's just that she's so determined to be in charge, and therefore a sexist reaction on my part, but I've the funny sense that Judge Masters may not like men much. Of which variety our friend Christopher is indubitably one."

"And so was Mark Ransom." Terri paused, intent on showing Johnny that at least they had thought this through. "Chris and I parsed this until, as he put it, we felt like a couple of soothsayers reading the entrails of a goat. Because she's a woman who's new on the bench, Caroline is very sensitive on the issue of bias, both other people's and her own. She strives not only to *be* fair but to *look* fair. What I can't tell you is how that cuts. Will she bend over backward not to show favoritism to the female defendant, or to the female prosecutor? It's probably a wash.

"Anyhow, I'm not sure that Chris and Caroline won't have better chemistry than Caroline and Marnie Sharpe. Caroline likes to be on the cutting edge of the law, and she admires creativity almost as much as she does intellect." Terri smiled over at Paget. "For sheer creativity, what Chris did yesterday is hard to beat. In her own way, Caroline seemed almost grateful."

Moore pondered that. "You seem to have put Judge Masters through everything but a Rorschach test."

"It's the trial lawyer's favorite game," Paget observed. "Psychoanalyzing the judge. I've been wrong so many times that I figured it was Terri's turn."

Moore studied him. "Now that you have Caroline Masters, you must also have a plan to impress her."

Annoyance crossed Paget's face; it was a sign, Terri knew, of how worried he was. "Eat your sandwich," Paget answered, "while I try to figure out some way to keep your excitement under control."

For a while, they fell quiet. Terri sat between Paget

and Johnny, eating her lunch, content. The water lapped at the boat. In the distance, the city looked like a dream.

"It would be a lovely world," Moore observed at length, "if life were as gentle as this."

Paget nodded, silent. For an instant, Terri imagined she read his thoughts: I hope Carlo's will be. Idly, he tore the crust of his sandwich into bread crumbs, lobbed a couple to the sea gulls. Finally, he said, "At least let's try to make the world safe for Mary Carelli, shall we?"

Moore turned to Paget, face troubled again. "Let's hear it, then."

"To start, our defense is an evidentiary nightmare." Paget leaned back again. "We all know what rings true about Mary's story—something between Mark Ransom and women was very badly wrong. That's what this whole obsession with Laura Chase suggests and what, in their different ways, Melissa Rappaport and Lindsay Caldwell made clear to Terri. To me, they help make Mary's version of Ransom credible. The problem is that—as the law now stands—Judge Masters isn't likely to let them testify before the jury." Paget paused. "If that's true, then what happened to Rappaport and Caldwell will be like the proverbial tree falling in the woods: in the jury room, Rappaport and Caldwell won't exist."

Moore thought for a moment. "But they'll exist for Caroline Masters."

"One hopes." Paget tossed another bread crumb, watched a gull scoop down to skim it off the water. "If Terri can persuade them, we ask Rappaport and Caldwell to tell their stories. Sharpe will insist that the judge hear them first in chambers, so that she can argue that their testimony should be excluded. Should Judge Masters decide against us, neither woman will have to face the ordeal of public testimony. But while the judge may erase them from the hearing, there's no way that she can erase them from her mind. And it's Masters who decides whether this case goes to trial."

Moore examined him. "You're going to need more than that."

"I know, I know, but it's at least a start." Paget paused again. "Even the smartest of judges likes to appear evenhanded. If Masters turns us down on Rappaport and Caldwell, we'll ask her to split the baby. Specifically, to rule that Mary's tape is inadmissible, and to order that any misuse of the information therein will result in the dismissal of the case. And if *that* doesn't work, there's the tape of Laura Chase. I don't want to reveal it now, if for no other reason than because it would look so gratuitous. But in chambers I'll insist that the Laura Chase tape is at least as relevant as Mary's tape—given that it's part of Mark Ransom's sexual pathology—and ask that it be played in open court. The Colt family notwithstanding."

Moore gave a low whistle. "All that," he said, "would make Sharpe *very* angry."

"Yes. I'm counting on her."

A gull swooped, capturing a bread crumb without breaking the speed of its flight. Moore watched it rise again, as if toward the sun, and then turned to Terri. "I thought the idea was not to engage Sharpe's pride."

"This is *my* call," Paget cut in. "Not Terri's. For whatever reason, Marnie Sharpe disliked me on sight. Perhaps for my own sake, perhaps because she thinks I'm helping Mary rip off the rape issue for her own self-preservation. That means that charming her is hopeless, but it also means that she's carrying around some psychic baggage. My guess is that if I'm careful about how I do it, I can goad her into a mistake." Paget turned to Moore. "The only advantage I have over Marnie is that, smart as she is, I'm some sort of symbol to her. Whereas to me, she's simply a technical problem. Like quantum mechanics."

Moore hesitated. "If goading Sharpe is a positive benefit," he said finally, "then you're off to a flying start. Or so it appeared from the peanut gallery."

Paget seemed to contemplate the whiteness of the city; in the distance, the afternoon sun made its buildings shimmer with light. "I understand that it's risky," he answered. "But we don't have many cards. At the least, we'll find out before trial just how good Sharpe really is. And in a hearing like this, without a jury, my lack of recent practice in trying homicide cases should hurt a little less."

Moore gazed out to the city. "What happens," he asked finally, "if Judge Masters goes along with you? Suppose she rules 'no probable cause.' Can't the D.A. just dig up more evidence, satisfy probable cause, and take Mary to trial then?"

"It depends. If the prosecutor fails for lack of evidence, they can refile if they come up with new facts. The tape, for example." Paget sipped his mineral water. "But until and unless they do that, Mary walks. Forever."

"You're taking a pretty serious chance, it seems." Moore looked from Paget to Terri and back again. "If this strategy is so inspired, why don't real defense lawyers use it?"

Paget smiled faintly. "Because they know better."

"You make it *sound* good enough."

Paget turned to him. "What it is, Johnny, is a terrible risk; Caroline Masters saw right away how desperate we are, no matter what face I put on it. Masters hit the nail—probable cause is far too easy to make out, and if I lose, we'll have previewed our case so thoroughly that Sharpe will crucify us when it comes to jury time. And on the evidence that now exists, I lose."

Moore seemed to squint. ''Am I correct in assuming that the purpose of this little outing is to make me feel the heat?''

''Of course.''

''In other words,'' Moore said slowly, ''you need a real live act of rape. Within the next two weeks, no facsimiles accepted.''

Paget nodded. ''Sometime, somewhere, Ransom has to have crossed the line. The problem is that women don't report these things.''

Moore turned to Terri. ''Do you agree with that?''

Terri gazed at her feet. ''Yes. I do.''

''Then all I can do,'' Moore said, ''is try.''

For another moment, they were silent. ''I'm sorry to be so bald about it,'' Paget offered in half apology, ''but I need to give Judge Masters something to hang her psychic hat on when she's thinking about Rappaport and Caldwell, whose testimony she may never acknowledge and whom the press may never see. If I can, maybe we win. If not, Mary loses.''

And you, Terri thought. And, more important to you, Carlo. Once more, she admired Paget's stoicism and felt his fear.

Moore was looking at her. After a time, he asked, ''Would you consider going on television?''

Interrupted from thought, Terri felt confused. ''To do what?''

''To ask for witnesses.'' Moore hesitated. ''Try as men may, I suppose something like this strikes a chord in women that we simply can't replicate. *You* obviously feel it.''

''I still don't follow.''

Moore shrugged. ''Perhaps it's a bad idea. I just wondered if some appeal for information about Mark Ransom, perhaps on CNN, might scare up a witness. A request for help from women, by a woman lawyer, on behalf of a woman defendant.'' He glanced over at Paget. ''Is that insane?''

Paget, Terri realized, had been looking at her for some moments. ''I hadn't thought of it,'' he said. ''It's hard enough to ask something so intimate of someone sitting right in front of you—which Terri's done so well—let alone of an audience of women you can't even see. We'd likely learn nothing, and look desperate in the bargain.''

For a moment, both men were silent. Neither looked at Terri.

''If you want me to,'' Terri finally told them, ''I'll do it. God knows we need a break.''

TWO

"THAT'S A TRICKY ONE," Elena Arias announced to Carlo Paget.

They sat hunched over a black onyx coffee table in Paget's library, arranging small odd-shaped blocks in a precarious high-rise. The purpose of the game was alternately to place the blocks one upon the other, without causing the edifice to fall. Dressed in jeans and a T-shirt, Carlo sprawled with his long legs stretched on the rug; Elena, pretty in a pink dress, with her hair freshly combed, was on her knees; the pile of blocks they had constructed—a rickety multicolored tower with angles jutting everywhere—violated every rule of aesthetics and, as far as Terri could see, of gravity. Elena, who had just placed a round peg on top of the block beneath it, was delighted with herself. Carlo looked bemused.

"I never lose to five-year-olds," he said in mock frustration. Carlo glanced up at Terri, who sat on the couch sipping wine. "Do you see any way out for me?"

"You're on your own," Terri answered. "I thought you were the house champion."

"For eight years running." Carlo smiled. "But that's against my father, who has the spatial-reasoning capacity of a primitive fern. He didn't prepare me for Elena."

But he had, of course, Terri knew; the pile of blocks was a tribute to Carlo's deftness at selecting moves that would keep Elena in the game, as all the while he acted as if she had forced him to the wall. The tower Carlo and Elena were creating was like a minihistory of Paget's relationship to Carlo; the younger player gaining confidence while the older, groaning and protesting, lost at great length and with great ingenuity. Elena, who played with more daring than sense, had stretched Carlo's gifts to the limit.

"Your mother won't help me," he told Elena.

"She can't help *you.*" Elena jabbed her chest. " 'Cause *I'm* her kid."

Carlo raised his hand for silence, signaling his awareness of all that was at risk. With utter gravity, he trained his eyes on the rickety tower. The windows of Paget's library cut the late-afternoon sun into squares of light on the black onyx table and inside the marble fireplace; across one of the squares fell a shadow of a frond from Carlo's palm tree. Carlo's wrist caught the light as he suspended his block over the tower, moving downward with excruciating slowness, block pinched between his thumb and index finger. Terri held her breath.

Slowly, carefully, he placed the block on Elena's peg. The peg leaned one way, the block beneath it another. The tower began to teeter.

With the terrible inevitability of a chain reaction, the blocks crashed in a heap.

Carlo stared at the rubble as if galvanized. "Total devastation," he said to Elena. "I can't believe it."

"But you *tried.*" With sudden concern, Elena touched his hand. "I bet you can still beat your daddy. That means you're the *second* champion. Next to me."

Carlo laughed out loud. "Five years old," he told Terri, "and she's already learned condescension."

Terri smiled. "It's not condescension, it's codependency. Elena's taking care of you."

Carlo gave her a look of exaggerated concern. "Are you codependent," he asked, "if you go to a movie that your girlfriend wants to see?"

"Only if the movie's terrible." Terri appraised him. "Does this mean you got Jennifer out of the house?"

"Yeah." Carlo grinned. "Like you said—I went over there a couple of times and sat around and talked with them."

"Was that okay?"

"It was fine." Carlo's face clouded. "Except half

the time they wanted to talk about my dad's case. At least that's what they called it—'your dad's case.' "

Terri's eyes flickered to Elena, who was beginning a new tower with a child's unselfconscious concentration. "Jennifer's parents don't know who your mom is?"

Carlo shook his head. "No."

He looked down, silent for a moment. Terri decided to say nothing, just to wait. She sipped her wine.

"The whole thing," Carlo said at last, "makes me feel weird. Like I'm hiding her. Like I'm hiding *out.*"

Terri glanced at her daughter. "Elena," she asked, "could you help Chris with the hamburgers? He's all alone on the deck."

Elena considered this. "How do I help him?"

Carlo smiled at her. "Tell him not to cook the hamburgers on high, because it makes them dry inside." He turned to Terri. "It drives me nuts."

Terri looked at Elena. "It sounds like Chris needs help."

"Definitely," Carlo affirmed to the little girl. "Just tell him 'no dry hamburgers.' "

Elena stood straighter, as if affirming the importance of her mission. " 'No dry hamburgers,' " she repeated, and scampered down the hallway.

Carlo grinned after her, clearly pleased at the notion of his father being instructed by an officious five-year-old, aware that Carlo was the source of her message. Terri smiled as well, and then realized with sudden guilt how glad she was that Richie had not come.

It had been awkward at first; Paget's invitation had been for all of them, and what it had finally come down to was that Richie had asked Terri to refuse. Richie didn't feel like it, he said; he'd be bored. Terri could only guess the deeper reasons: that Richie resented her friendship with Paget; that Richie was too proud to spend time with someone he could not impress; that Richie did not care for social settings that he could not control.

In this case, Terri at first had acceded to his wishes, and then their pointlessness had made her angry. The upshot was that Terri had pleaded business reasons to Richie; offered Paget a lame excuse for Richie's absence; and come because she wanted to. Alone, she did not have to fear that Richie would try to solicit Paget as an "investor," or dread the exaggerated politeness on Paget's face as he mentally took Richie's measure and filed him away. But to be ashamed of Richie made her feel guilty; what made her feel better was the chance to talk with Carlo about something that mattered.

"Don't your friends," she asked him, "know who your mother is?"

He shook his head. "Not really. I'm in a new

school this year, and she's never around for people to know about.'' A pained expression crossed his face. ''I mean, what do I say? Butt into the middle of some conversation and say, 'Have I told you that Mary Carelli's my mother?' Especially with all this stuff on television, and then the way some people at school talk about her . . . *I'm* not afraid, but I'd only make *them* feel bad.''

For a moment, Terri tried to imagine not telling people that Rosa Peralta was *her* mother, and then she saw that what divided her from Carlo was what he could not bring himself to say: that Mary as a mother did not seem real to him, so that claiming her would feel like pretense.

''What *do* your friends say?''

Carlo reflected. ''Some people don't say a lot,'' he answered with irony, ''because it's my *dad's* case. Other people feel sorry for her.'' He paused. ''I guess a few think she did it.''

''You 'guess'?''

Carlo's handsome features hardened. ''One guy on the team said she was probably sucking him off and then Ransom just got out of hand.'' His eyes narrowed. ''You know—like she was going to let him beat her up too, only it got too real for her to like it.''

Terri watched his face. ''Do you believe that?''

''No.'' He hesitated. ''I don't know her, really. But she just doesn't seem like that to me.''

Terri put down her wine. ''Like what?'' she asked.

Carlo looked away, as if struggling for words. ''Like someone who wants to be pushed around, or would even *pretend* to want that.'' He turned to her. ''Look, I know there's stuff I don't know . . .''

What, Terri thought, do I say to that? For a moment all she wanted was to pass the buck to Paget, whose buck it rightfully was, and not make some snap judgment that might hurt both father and son. But that, she concluded, was the coward's way out, and Carlo deserved better—even from her.

''*I* don't know,'' she answered evenly, ''what you know or don't know. But yes, I imagine there are things your mother and father haven't told you.''

Carlo's eyes turned stubborn. ''I'm not some kid. I'm old enough.''

Terri nodded. ''I understand, and so does your dad. But what makes you think that he's protecting *you?*''

''Because he always does. Too much, sometimes. It's like he *worries* about me so much.''

Terri could imagine too well how a seven-year-old who spoke of killing himself would tear Paget apart; the painstaking years of care when Paget battled the boy's self-hatred; the constant habit of watchfulness, too ingrained for Paget to dispel. Could see perhaps better than Paget that, whatever his lingering wounds, Carlo no longer was that fragile boy and had no conscious memory that he ever had been. And that without this understanding—which Paget would never wish to give him—Carlo might feel weakened by a primal sense of his father's fears for him.

"Do *you,*" she asked Carlo, "tell your *dad* everything you do? Or think, or feel?"

Carlo shook his head emphatically. "No."

"Why not?"

Absently, he began putting blocks back in their box; his fingers seemed to know from memory where each piece fit. "Because," he answered, "there's some stuff you don't want anyone to know—especially a parent. I don't know how to explain why something feels private—it just does. Not even 'cause you feel ashamed always, or even embarrassed. It's just *yours,* that's all, and it's important not to talk about it unless it's even more important that someone know."

"But what's the test for when that is?" Terri spoke more quietly. "That's the problem *I've* always had."

Carlo looked up from the blocks. "I don't know. I guess when talking will help you more than hurt you—that is, if you really need to talk. And when the other person is a person who needs to *know* and won't be too hurt by what you say."

Terri gazed at the shadows from the palm tree, falling across the room. "What makes you think," she finally said, "that your father's any different? Suppose he hasn't told you everything he knows, or everything he's afraid of. That doesn't mean that he lacks confidence in you or doesn't think that you're adult. All that may mean is that he's protecting your mother, or even himself. Sometimes, adults need privacy even more than teenagers—they've had a lot more time to do things they're embarrassed about or ashamed of. And as far as your mother goes, it's not your dad's place to talk about her life. Or mine. *She* makes those calls, and we all have to respect that."

Carlo stood, turning to the window, hands in his pockets as he stared out at the palm. The stance was so much like Paget's that Terri wondered, not for the first time, about the line between genetics and simple emulation. Once again, she tried to imagine the seven-year-old boy as Christopher Paget had found him.

Carlo turned to her. To Terri, his face looked suddenly older. "I want to go to the hearing," Carlo said at last. "To be with them. But I've been afraid to ask."

Surprised, Terri felt she had exceeded her limits, searched for the temporizing question. "What about school?"

"They're my father and mother, and she's on trial for murder. That's a little more important than school." His voice became intent, persuasive. "I wouldn't find out any more by being there than anyone else who's there, and isn't even in this family. But it would mean I'm there for her, instead of hiding out in school. What either of them tells me about their lives is up to them.''

Terri watched him, suddenly sure that—at this moment—Christopher Paget would be proud of his son. And, Terri hoped, could also manage to be somewhat proud of himself.

``All you can do,'' she said simply, ``is ask him. Silence isn't fair to either one of you.''

Carlo considered that. ``He's just so sure he's right, sometimes.''

Beneath Carlo's plaint, Terri felt the tension in Paget that was making him seem peremptory, even to her. But she could not tell Carlo about Paget's fears that Sharpe would find the second tape; or the days in which Johnny Moore had not found a single witness; or the nights Paget spent trying to find a way to cross-examine Monk and Shelton; or the mock courtroom session in which Paget had torn Mary's testimony apart until her eyes blazed with anger; or the endless pressure of trying to give interviews that would do more good than harm.

``That's just how it looks,'' she finally answered. ``You know the strain he's under. In a week, we're going to court.''

``I know.'' Carlo shifted from one foot to another. ``But this case seems to be changing him.''

``How so?''

``He's got a really short fuse with me.'' Carlo hesitated. "I think part of it is my mother. He never really says anything. But somehow I don't think he's very fair to her. Really, I don't know why he ever wanted to defend her."

How, Terri wondered, to be fair to Christopher Paget and still conceal the facts? It made her appreciate the painful intersection of Paget's lawyering for Mary with his parenting of Carlo, in which the truth could not be spoken. "It's easy to misread your dad—especially when he spends more time looking out for other people than caring how he looks to them." Terri paused. "But there are two things that I'm sure of. The first is that he desperately wants to win this case. The second is that he loves you very much."

"I love him too, and I respect him a lot." Carlo paused, as if to say more, and then chose to end with a throwaway line. "I just don't want it to go to his head."

Terri watched him, realizing that Carlo had said all he cared to say. She decided to join his attempt at levity. "It won't go to his head. Not with Elena deflating him. I can imagine her out on the deck, saying 'No dry hamburgers' like a talking parrot. Your poor father."

Carlo smiled back. "You'd better go save him. I'll clean up the blocks to preserve his sense of order."

When Terri came to the deck, she was surprised to find Elena sitting on Paget's lap, alternately monitoring the hamburgers and gazing out at the bay, blue-gray with failing light.

Standing behind them, Terri decided that the backs of their heads made a nice picture: Elena's straight brown hair next to the copper waves at the edge of Paget's collar. They did not see or hear her.

"What do you do at home?" Paget was asking.

Elena thought. "Play," she announced. "With toys. Sometimes Daddy's there and Mommy's not. On vacation days from school."

"You go to school?"

"Course. Mommy takes me to Explorer Preschool. It's good except for Janie."

Paget turned to her. "What's Janie's problem?"

"She pulls my hair." Elena's voice turned indignant. "The teacher made her take two time-outs the other day. *Two.*"

Paget smiled. "Bad day for Janie."

"Bad day for the *teacher,* you mean. She said she had a headache." Elena paused. "Sometimes Mommy gets headaches. Daddy says she worries too much."

The two of them looked out at the bay. It was past five, and the sun had begun setting behind the Golden Gate; the bay was silver, the sailboats were flecks of white. "What *I* think," Paget said, "is that your mommy works very, very hard. Sometimes people who work hard get headaches."

Elena considered that. ‘‘My mommy’s not home, always. But Daddy’s home.’’

Paget seemed to reflect. ‘‘That’s because your mommy works with *me,*’’ he answered, ‘‘so she can make money for food and clothes *and* your house. Sometimes that happens in families—one person takes care of everyone else.’’

Elena looked at the hamburgers. ‘‘Mommy cooks dinner too.’’

‘‘Then maybe sometime you and your dad can cook it for your mom.’’ Paget smiled. ‘‘Because your mom is very nice, and both of you are lucky to have her.’’

‘‘It’s true,’’ Terri interrupted, smiling. ‘‘I *am* wonderful, and the whole wide world is lucky I was born.’’

Paget turned, surprised. ‘‘I was going to cover that,’’ he said. ‘‘But the hamburgers would have turned to carbon.’’

‘‘Hi, Mommy,’’ Elena said. ‘‘Chris says you’re nice.’’

‘‘But I only say that behind her back,’’ Paget told Elena. ‘‘It’s easier that way.’’

Although Elena did not understand, she knew that Paget had made a joke and that she was included in the spirit of it. Elena smiled up at her mother, as if she were a third adult. ‘‘That’s right,’’ she told Terri. ‘‘You’re nice. It’s easier that way.’’

Terri laughed. ‘‘You know what’ll be nice, Elena?

Dinner. But only if you go to the bathroom first. Better go ask Carlo where it is.''

Elena ran back down the hallway, happy to have a question to ask Carlo.

''Thank you,'' Terri said to Paget.

''For what?''

''For telling Elena that her absentee mom is not so bad.''

Paget gazed at her. ''Someone else,'' he said, ''should be doing that job.''

Terri gazed past him, at the bay.

''What I meant,'' Paget amended quietly, ''is that sometimes it's hard to speak for yourself. Especially in families.''

Terri turned to him. ''Actually, there was something I wanted to talk to you about. If you have time after dinner, can Carlo watch Elena for a minute?''

''Sure.'' Paget hesitated. ''If it's about going on TV, you don't have to do that. Let Johnny keep digging for a witness. After all, it's *his* job.''

Terri paused a moment; the hearing was so much on Paget's mind that, much more than usual, he had begun projecting his thoughts onto others. ''TV's okay, really. But this isn't about that.''

''Can I ask what it *is* about?''

Terri gave a small, embarrassed shrug. ''Carlo,'' she said.

THREE

"WHEN YOU ANSWER a question," Mary Carelli murmured, "never look at the person who asks it. Gaze directly at the camera." She paused, adding dryly, "That's how the audience knows you're sincere."

Terri nodded. "All right."

Mary raised an eyebrow. "You sound a little dubious."

"It seems artificial, that's all. Now that I'm here, it's difficult for me to imagine talking some other woman out of her home, long distance, and into a courtroom to describe herself being raped. Assuming that Mark Ransom ever did that."

Mary shrugged. "That's why *I'm* here. When it comes to television, or Mark Ransom, I can imagine almost anything."

They sat on an empty soundstage that CNN had borrowed from ABC's San Francisco affiliate, waiting for the interview. In nine days, Johnny Moore had found nothing that would tie Mark Ransom to a sexual assault—no reported incidents or even rumors. The preliminary hearing was five days away.

It was that which had pushed Christopher Paget into letting Terri go on television. Even then he had seemed reluctant; only when she insisted was the interview set.

Involving Mary had been Paget's idea. "You're the lawyer," he said, "but Mary's the supposed victim. Besides, she's famous and does this all the time. For Mary, a touching plea for help will be just another star turn." His voice turned cynical and a little weary. "Just keep her off the 'facts,' for lack of a better name."

"But aren't we assuming," Terri asked, "that her story is basically right? Isn't that the point of looking for another victim?"

Paget had shrugged. "All that *I'm* assuming is that Ransom was a pig. The only question is whether he was this particular kind of pig."

"And whether," Terri answered, "anyone will say so."

Now, sitting next to Mary Carelli, Terri wondered who might watch. She envisioned a lonely woman who had hidden an assault from friends and family, perhaps buried it so deep that it seemed a vague memory she no longer quite believed in, real only in the fear she felt when she walked alone at night, or when she experienced that first unwanted glance from someone she'd misjudged. The woman that Terri imagined would not talk to anyone.

"You look pensive," Mary told her.

Once more, Terri had the sense that Mary was examining her, and with little liking. It put Terri even more on edge. "I was just imagining our audience," she answered. "I mean, would you come forward?"

Mary smiled. "I *did* come forward."

Terri turned to her. "You had no choice," she said simply. "Ransom was dead. If he'd lived, and simply raped you, *then* you'd have had a choice."

Mary glanced around the soundstage—its blank partitions behind them, three chairs, two cameras pointing at them like armed guards. "You don't believe me," she said.

Terri examined her. "I don't *understand* you," she said at last. "So I don't know whether I believe or disbelieve you." She paused, adding softly, "All I know is that it doesn't really matter."

Mary gave a sardonic smile. "Because you're a lawyer? Or because of Chris?"

"Because I'm a lawyer. That's part of who I am." Terri paused, adding pointedly, "Just like being a wife and mother is part of who I am."

"You make it sound like you've signed on for life."

"I signed on for life," Terri answered, "the day I had Elena. In that way, I'm a pretty simple person."

Mary's smile turned skeptical. "How many people have underestimated you, I wonder."

"It depends on the person." Discussing herself, Terri felt an odd detachment. "For some, there was nothing to understand. They had me pegged just right."

Mary looked at her curiously. "If I've touched some nerve," she finally said, "I'm sorry."

"You didn't touch anything. I just want to get this over with."

"You seem as tight as a spring." Mary smiled. "Look at it this way—it's like going to court, but the questions aren't as intelligent. It should be no problem at all for anyone as smart as Chris thinks *you* are."

Chris again, Terri thought, and then wondered if this cool, detached woman had so distanced herself from her own emotions that she no longer knew what they were. Any sense of Mary Carelli seemed to slip from her grasp; beneath the self-preserved veneer, Terri saw only glimpses—pride, solitude, and, most elusive of all, a hint of wounded puzzlement, as if Mary could not understand why no one understood her. As for Mary's true feelings for Christopher Paget, or for their son, they were hidden from view; Terri felt them only in the sense that they were connected to Mary's resentment of her.

"Did you know," Terri asked, "that Carlo wants to go with you to court?"

Mary's face changed utterly. "Surely Chris won't let him."

"I think he may, and hope he does. Carlo very much wants to. Particularly for your sake."

"He *can't*." Mary's voice turned hard. "He simply can't. Really, I don't want him to hear this."

Terri paused again. "What would be worse for him," she answered, "is for his mother and father to treat him like a child."

"That's not for you to decide." Mary's voice was tight with urgency and anger. "You have no idea what this is all about. You have no idea what *Carlo* is all about. None at all."

Terri stared, startled at the visceral intensity she saw on Mary's face. And then, like a cold finger on her spine, she felt for an instant that Mary Carelli was capable of murder if something pierced to the core of her. But what that core was, Terri could not know.

"At this point," Terri answered softly, "it's really for Chris to decide, isn't it? Whatever you won't or can't say to me, perhaps you should say to him. Assuming, of course, that there's something *else* Chris doesn't know."

Mary hesitated, as if surprised, and then gave Terri a long glance of appraisal. "You're a very perceptive woman, Terri, and a bright lawyer. But this isn't a lawyer's problem, and *I'm* the only woman who owns it. Don't tamper with this, please. I'm asking you not to.''

Tamper with *what?* Terri wondered, and then the interviewer came onstage.

A brisk, slender man in his forties, Greg Cook looked like someone who burned calories just by standing around. In quick succession, he reacquainted himself with Mary, was introduced to Terri, and had ushered them back into their chairs, with microphones clipped to their blouses. Terri drifted through it all like an automaton, still suspended in her conversation with Mary.

''We're running this on the nightly news,'' Cook explained. ''You can watch yourselves at seven this evening.''

The filming started. After a few preliminaries—introductions, Terri's office telephone number—Cook demanded of Mary, ''Why are you here?''

Mary leaned forward, focused on the camera. ''Because we believe that what Mark Ransom tried to do to me, he may have done to someone else. If so, I ask them to come forward now, to testify on my behalf.''

''How would that help you?''

Mary looked grave. ''Because it's a sad fact of life that any woman claiming to be the victim of a sexual assault faces a high threshold of disbelief.'' She paused, her expression open, candid. ''That's all the more true when the woman is charged with murder, and attempted rape is her sole defense.''

Cook nodded. ''But this, you would agree, is an extraordinary step.''

''I would. But what is truly extraordinary is that four out of every five rapes go unreported.'' Mary's voice quickened, became more urgent. ''We believe that hidden behind these statistics—this collective fear that society has too long fostered in *all* women—at least *one* woman may be watching whose life Mark Ransom changed.''

To Terri, she seemed too crisp, more political than personal. Behind tortoiseshell glasses, Cook raised his eyebrows. ''But—and I speak as a matter of psychology, not morality—why should a woman who is too traumatized to help herself relive that trauma by helping you?''

Exactly, Terri thought. She turned to Mary, as if she were the nameless woman in the audience, fearful and waiting for an answer.

''Because,'' Mary said calmly, ''the issue transcends what happened to me. True, my life and freedom are at stake, as is the public reputation I am fighting to maintain: I'm either a victim and exonerated, or guilty of some degree of murder.'' Mary paused, as if daunted by her personal abyss. ''But the ultimate issue is whether victims everywhere will speak out against rape and thus diminish the number of victims to come. True, I ask for help, and I need it. But it is also true that anyone who helps me offers hope to countless others.''

''All surface and calculation,'' Melissa Rappaport had said of Mary. Perhaps this cut too deep for objectivity, but to Terri, Mary's answers were the slogans of a movement, not simple words of pain.

On impulse, Terri asked, ''May I say something?''

Cook and Mary turned, as did the cameras. Cook looked curious, Mary perplexed. Then Cook said, ''Surely, Ms. Peralta.''

Terri found she could not speak; her few seconds of confusion seemed infinite. ''For someone who's been raped,'' she began at last, ''rape is not a cause.'' Terri paused, searching for words; suddenly it was not hard to look into the camera. ''It's deeply personal, and it can make a woman feel cheap, and damaged. We're not talking to 'women' about 'protecting' other women. We're asking a lone woman to remember something she never reported to anyone, something she has tried very hard to stuff somewhere and never think about.'' Terri paused again, then spoke, her voice softer. ''Because after it happened, that was the only way she could think of to protect herself.''

At the corner of Terri's vision, Mary's face was cold. Cook seemed surprised. ''You seem to be arguing against the purpose of this interview.''

Terri gazed down, feeling chastened and exposed.

When she looked up again, it was at the camera. "I'm not arguing with anyone," she answered quietly. "I'm not even talking to anyone here. I'm talking to someone I don't know, who may be watching by herself, or with a husband, or with children, or her friend. But no matter whom she's with, she's completely alone. Because *she's* the only one who knows."

"Are you saying that she should *not* come forward?"

"No." Terri inhaled, forcing herself to speak slowly and clearly. "I'm saying that if she *does* come forward, it should be to help herself. Because, as if she were partners with the man who raped her, she's hidden the rape inside her until she's become a different person."

Cook nodded. "You obviously have some empathy with the people you're seeking out."

Turning from the camera, Terri felt cut off from the woman she had imagined. "I was a rape counselor," she told him. "In law school."

Cook gazed at her a moment. Then he said, "Teresa Peralta, Mary Carelli, thank you for appearing on CNN nightly news," and the interview was over.

Mary looked startled, and then composed herself. "Thank you," she said. Terri said nothing.

In the elevator down, Mary finally spoke. "No wonder you were nervous. You have no idea of television, or how to help me."

Terri turned to her. Very softly, she said, "But it didn't happen to you, did it?"

Mary stared at her, as if to respond. Then she said only, "I have a rally at two o'clock. I should change. Please drive me to the hotel."

Now, six hours later, Terri sat with Richie on the couch, watching the news. Elena played nearby with the blocks, which Carlo had given her.

There was a clip of Mary Carelli, addressing a crowd on the steps of the Hall of Justice. Dressed in a simple blouse and skirt, she looked less militant and more a victim; with each applause line, Terri could feel the pressure on McKinley Brooks.

"You are here," Mary said, "because you have chosen to believe in me. For that I feel deep gratitude and great humility. But in the larger sense, you have rallied for every woman who has ever felt the shame and tragedy of rape."

"That's pretty good," Richie remarked. "Universalize it. Make it bigger than she is."

Terri nodded. "It's fine for this. I just don't think it works for soliciting witnesses."

"Earlier today," the voice-over said, "Ms. Carelli and one of her lawyers, Teresa Peralta, made a last-ditch appeal for any woman to come forward who has suffered alleged abuse at the hands of Mark Ransom."

Making her appeal, Mary looked and sounded ra-

tional. Her expression was wounded, yet composed.
"She's good here too," Richie said.

When the camera shifted to Terri, her own face startled her; she looked tentative, disconcerted, more like a victim than the victim's lawyer. She felt herself flush. Then heard herself say, in a voice less firm than she remembered it, "as if she were partners with the man who raped her, she's hidden the rape inside her until she's become a different person."

When it was over, Terri sat on the couch with her hands folded, half listening to the sound of Elena's play.

"I don't know, Terri," Richie said at last. "I'm not sure that came off like you wanted it to."

He said this in a tone of concern, as if to help her do better next time. Except that Richie knew, as she knew, that next time would never come.

"I did the best I could."

"I know, Ter. I think it's just the wrong pitch, that's all. The woman you imagine sitting there with her husband and kid is going to look around her and decide not to reach for the phone." Richie gave a fatalistic shrug. "You can't really blame her. I think a lot of women get themselves in situations they know they should have avoided. I mean, put yourself in their place."

Terri did not answer. Finally, she said, "I think I'll just play with Elena for a while, check my messages on voice mail. Maybe someone will call."

"Sure." He paused. "What about dinner?"

"I'm kind of tired. Think you could fix macaroni and cheese? Elena would probably help."

"How about ordering pizza? I've got some work to do on the computer."

Terri looked at him. "Just no pepperoni, okay? Elena peels it off."

When the pizza arrived, only Richie's half was pepperoni. There had been no calls on voice mail. "Too bad," Richie said in sympathy. "But I think it really is like I said."

Four hours later, when Terri checked for the seventh time, there had been no messages at all, and Richie was asleep.

Silently, Terri undressed, put on a long T-shirt. She lay next to Richie in their bed, watching the red numbers of the alarm clock mark the minutes she could not sleep.

At one forty-five, she was still awake.

The telephone rang.

Terri started, and then tried to reach over the alarm clock to stop the ringing before Richie awoke.

"Hello."

Terri heard a faint hum, but no voice. Beside her, Richie was stirring. "What the hell . . ."

Terri placed one hand on his shoulder. "Hello," she tried again.

For a moment more, Terri heard the hum, and then a woman asked, "Is this Teresa Peralta?"

Terri felt herself tense. ‘‘Yes. It is.’’

‘‘I thought I recognized your voice.’’ There was a moment’s pause. ‘‘I’m sorry to call like this. But I couldn’t sleep.’’

‘‘How did you get my home number?’’

‘‘I started calling information everywhere in the Bay area.’’ The woman gave a shaky laugh. ‘‘If I hadn’t gotten Berkeley on my third try, I might have stopped.’’

‘‘That’s all right.’’ Terri hesitated. ‘‘Can you tell me who you are?’’

‘‘Yes.’’ Another pause. ‘‘My name’s Marcy Linton.’’

Terri thought for a moment. ‘‘The writer?’’

‘‘You’ve read me?’’

‘‘Yes.’’ Terri felt delayed surprise. ‘‘In *The New Yorker.*’’

‘‘That’s very nice.’’ There was a genuine politeness in the voice, as if, in the middle of the night, Marcy Linton was glad that a stranger had read her stories. ‘‘And, of course, I watched you on television. It touched me.’’

‘‘Yes?’’

‘‘Yes.’’ A final pause. ‘‘You were talking to me.’’

FOUR

THREE MORNINGS BEFORE the preliminary hearing, Teresa Peralta found herself in a rented Ford Escort with snow tires, steering through a valley in the Rocky Mountains—jagged peaks of black and white, wooded hillsides so steep they seemed to tumble toward the dirt road. To her left, a sheer embankment dropped to a glistening stream, whose gray and silver eddies were broken by logs or branches that had run aground in shallow water and dammed more clumps of driftwood behind them, white with new-fallen snow. The road ahead was covered with ice; in the morning sun, the white terrain was close to blinding.

Terri downshifted. She had not thought to bring sunglasses; she squinted at the road, steering gingerly, tense with the effort of driving for the first time on an ice-slick surface. A frightened deer skittered from the roadside at the sound of tires crunching, the hum of an engine. There was no one in sight.

As she drove, the mountains at the valley's end became higher and closer; it enhanced her sense of smallness and inadequacy. Her sole consolation was that she was learning to recognize those feelings and to fight her way through them. Marcy Linton, Terri was sure, must be even more apprehensive than Terri herself.

Linton was writing a novel, she had explained, in a cabin ten miles west of Aspen owned by her uncles. It was where she had brought Mark Ransom, she said, four years before. On the telephone, she had left it at that.

Twenty minutes farther, with the valley's end looming in her windshield, Terri found the gravel drive.

It wound to the left, down a hill, over a narrow bridge of railroad ties that crossed the stream, and then through more pine trees, until it ended in a circle looping past a wooden shed that housed a new Jeep Cherokee. By the shed were more trappings of rural life in winter—a mini snowplow, a stack of cordwood covered by a tarpaulin. To the side of the circle, a freshly shoveled stone walkway climbed a gradual hill, to the cabin.

It was two stories of wood and glass, with a stone chimney and an atelier, where, Terri assumed, Marcy Linton wrote. Through the glass front door, a slender woman peered out at Terri.

The woman was dressed for the outdoors—boots, jeans, green sweater—and her long strawberry-blond hair was pulled back. But the heavy clothes made her look too slight; there was something about her that seemed more suited to the city. As the woman stepped outside, Terri saw more clearly her pale skin, probing hazel eyes, and delicate face, pensive and lightly freckled. She was startlingly young.

"I'm Marcy Linton," she said. "I'm glad you could find me."

Her voice was clear but almost whispery. When she extended her hand, it felt fragile, as if Terri were cupping a bird in her palm. "Thank you," Terri answered. "I'm glad you could *call* me."

Linton gazed at her boots, as if checking them for snow. "Have you ever written?" she asked, and then glanced up at Terri. "I know that sounds foolish, and a little vain, but I think most writers survive partly by imagining how others must feel. The way you described my feelings was so perfect that it was like calling someone who already knew."

Terri shook her head. "I've never written—I wouldn't know how to start." She gave Linton a curious look. "I didn't expect you to be so young and to have written so much."

"I'm twenty-eight." Linton tilted her head. "And you?"

"Twenty-nine."

Linton looked off into the distance. After a time, she said, "Whenever I imagined talking about this, it was to a white policeman with the blank, somewhat cruel expression of an Aztec carving.'' She paused. ''I suppose I made him look like Ransom.''

Terri appraised her. Linton could put feelings into words, and Terri liked her instinctively. But they were still standing outside, as if lingering on the threshold of Linton's story, more painful than she made it sound.

''Do you have coffee?'' Terri asked. ''I'm pretty cold.''

''Oh, sure.'' Linton sounded chastened. ''Come on in.''

The inside was more elaborate than Terri had imagined: a stone floor of odd-shaped pieces; a marble fireplace; high ceilings; an expanse of glass window, which framed the mountains. There were animal skins on the floor, and above the fireplace, the head of an elk stared into space.

Linton followed Terri's eyes. ''My uncles kill things,'' she said. ''I can't work in this room.''

Terri nodded. ''I've never been able to imagine hunting. Or even owning a gun.''

Linton gazed at the elk. ''Oh, I own a gun now. But not for that.''

Terri paused a moment, wondering what next to say. ''Do you ski at all?'' she asked.

''Not really.'' Linton did not turn. ''I used to come here for the quiet.''

To Terri, Linton's voice carried a trace of sadness,

perhaps loss. Then Linton shrugged, as if to herself. "Do you like anything in your coffee?"

For an instant, Terri thought of Melissa Rappaport, making coffee as she avoided mention of Mark Ransom. Even here, where Ransom had come but once, Terri felt him as an unnamed presence who had broken the quiet, the reason Marcy Linton had a gun.

"Just black," Terri answered. "Thanks."

Linton disappeared.

Terri sat on a couch behind a heavy oak coffee table. On its lower shelf were two volumes of poetry, a thick book on impressionist painting, and a collection of Stieglitz photographs of Georgia O'Keeffe, which included several nudes. The volumes lent an urban sensibility, the slightest hint of female sensuality, as if to subvert the oppressive maleness of the room itself.

"He liked this room, he told me."

Reentering, Linton spoke in matter-of-fact tones. Her voice had none of Rappaport's pained ironic intellect; it was as if she were relating puzzling scraps at the margins of her memory, looking for clues to what had happened. She held a mug of coffee out to Terri, then sat on a heavy chair across from her.

"So," she asked, "will I have to testify?"

"Only if you want to." Terri hesitated. "We won't make you."

Linton considered that. Finally, she said, "But the

only way to help is to be a witness.'' Her voice was measured and subdued.

''Yes,'' Terri answered. ''I'm afraid so.''

Linton nodded, almost to herself; it was as if the silent gesture helped her absorb the truth. ''Will it be public?''

''If Judge Masters thinks it's relevant to whether Ransom tried to rape Mary Carelli.'' Terri hesitated. ''And if she's even thinking about throwing out the case, she'll want it public—for her own sake. To keep from getting pilloried as a biased woman judge.''

Linton sipped her coffee. ''That's a lot of pressure,'' she said. ''On the judge, I mean.''

There was something tired in the phrase, as if the thought of too much pressure on anyone made Linton feel enervated. Terri had first encountered Linton's short stories while riffling through *New Yorker*s in the waiting room of her obstetrician: lately, Linton's characters seemed to spend more time deciding whether to open their apartment door than they did on the other side of it. Terri, who admired Linton's sensitivity, found the increasing tentativeness of her people distressing, as if they bled strength from Terri herself. Yet, looking at Linton, Terri felt that whatever inner balance Linton had achieved belonged to *her,* and that Terri had no right to challenge it.

''There's a lot of pressure on everyone involved,'' Terri said at last. ''If you do this, it's got to be for yourself. Because everyone else in that courtroom will have their own agenda, and they're going to play for keeps. Even Chris, my boss.'' Terri hesitated. ''Perhaps Chris most of all.''

Linton stared at the floor. ''It's hard to know what to do with this.''

In these few stark words, Terri felt a deep loneliness. ''Do you think,'' she ventured, ''that we can just talk it through?''

Linton looked up at her. ''And afterwards, if I don't want to testify?''

''Then it never leaves here.'' Terri paused. ''I just stick it where I stick my own stuff. The things *I* never talk about.''

Linton seemed to search Terri's face. Then she said simply, ''Let me tell you about it.''

Why, Terri wondered, was she herself so much on edge. She took one deep breath, nodded, and continued to sip her coffee, watching Linton over the rim.

''I was twenty-four,'' Linton began, ''and three years out of Barnard. I'd come here to write the novel I'm hoping to write now.''

The clipped last sentence, Terri thought, had an undertone of damage. ''What is it about?'' Terri asked. ''Or is that a dumb question?''

''Not dumb, just difficult.'' Linton looked at her shoes again. ''Perhaps I'm a short story writer, not a novelist. Some people just can't do both.'' Linton glanced up at Terri. ''Mark Ransom could, of course.''

Terri hesitated. Part of Linton seemed disjointed, shaken beneath the calm. ''Did you admire him?'' she asked.

''As a novelist, yes. Our sensibilities were totally different, and his politics weren't mine. But page to page, he was a master of narrative and character. His characters weren't slight, at least not his men—he could make them struggle, breathe, quiver with surprise and change for twelve, thirteen hundred pages.'' Linton shook her head. ''We were nothing alike, and I thought there was nothing like him.''

''How did you meet?''

''Here, that one time. At a writers' conference.'' Linton's voice grew quiet. ''I timed my arrival in Aspen to coincide with two events—the beginning of my novel and meeting Mark Ransom.''

Terri felt puzzled. ''Did you expect to spend any time with him?'' When Linton looked somehow hurt, Terri added quickly, ''What I mean is that someone like Ransom must have had friends here, people competing for his attention, dinner plans in advance.''

A quiet pride crossed Linton's face. ''I'd already been published in *The New Yorker*. People knew my work.'' Then, as if to herself, she added softly, ''Young writers have no sense of proportion. If they *did,* they'd never write.''

Terri tried to imagine Mark Ransom caring about Marcy Linton's delicate fiction; it was like van Gogh being intrigued by Japanese watercolors. Finally, she asked, "Did Mark Ransom know your work?"

"He knew *of* my work." Linton's voice grew softer yet. "Before the conference, John Whitley, my editor at the magazine, called Mark himself. To tell him to 'take care of me.' " Linton looked away. "John is a very nice person. When he later asked if Mark had caught up with me, and I said yes, he looked quite pleased."

Again, Terri thought, a few oblique sentences conveyed much more: the small literary world to which Linton aspired; the naïveté of Linton's benefactor; her desire for approval; her fear of shattered friendships and notoriety had she denounced Mark Ransom as a rapist. Except for the exotica of Linton's chosen milieu, Linton had limned in a moment the dilemma of any woman raped by a respected man in a small town or university, or after an office party. It made Terri feel small.

"What is it?" Linton asked.

Terri shrugged off her depression. "Sympathy pains, I guess. I had a vision of this benign, white-haired editor, so pleased that Mark had honored his request, and how lonely that must have made you."

"John has black hair and is far too thin to look benign. But yes, I did feel lonely.

"The morning I saw John, my mouth felt swollen,

and I still hurt inside.'' Linton paused, staring down at her lap. ''When Ransom did it, I wasn't wet.''

Terri realized that she had crossed her arms. Quietly, she asked, ''How did it happen?''

Linton nodded slightly; the small gesture seemed irrelevant to Terri's question, as if Linton were reviewing some thought of her own. ''I was so vain,'' she said softly, ''to have published at twenty-three. I thought what I did with words was so extraordinary that even Mark Ransom would want to read them.''

Like her characters, Terri thought, Marcy Linton was having trouble opening the door. Terri waited, wondering how much of this reticence was the woman herself, how much she owed to Ransom. When Linton said nothing more, Terri asked, ''When did you first meet him?''

Linton seemed to be summoning a specific memory. ''It was the last night of the conference,'' she answered. ''At the bar of a glitzy hotel called Little Nell, jammed with writers and snow bunnies and slick men in ski clothes. But I found him right away, from the mellow voice and all that red hair. When I introduced myself to Mark, his smile of recognition thrilled me. *'Marcy Linton,'* he said, 'the most famous twenty-three-year-old writer since Sylvia Plath. John Whitley says you'll have even me reading short stories again.' He grinned down at me. *'Short stories,* of all things.' ''

Linton looked pensive, as if ashamed at some secret foolishness. "Except when I'm on some sort of literary high, I'm not very confident at social things—I'm more of the quiet observer type, I think. But the instant Mark clasped my hand, it was as if I felt connected to the confidence he gave off: bolder, almost brash.

"Suddenly it seemed right that America's most famous writer was interested in me.

" 'Maybe you don't *have* to read short stories,' I told him. 'I've just started my first novel.' "

" '*Good,*' he answered. 'Short stories are to novels what raisins are to wine—you can either shrivel your characters or let them breathe.' He laughed. 'I don't know what kind of metaphor that is, but it's how I *feel.*'

" 'Well, I'm going to let them breathe,' I answered. 'I just hope they don't get vertigo.' " Linton paused; her persona shifted from an excited twenty-four-year-old to the cautious woman Terri sat with now. "Listening to myself," she said with quiet irony, "I know why I never talked about this. My own bravado is far too painful to remember."

Terri waited, then asked simply, "What happened next?"

Linton touched her wrist, as if tracing a scar. When she spoke again, her voice seemed chastened by some hidden censor. "Mark looked at me for a moment. 'If you've just started,' he told me, 'I suppose I'll have to wait.' He sipped his drink and then, as if a new thought had just struck him, asked, 'Did you bring any pages?'

"God, I thought, he wants to *read* them. I was scared and excited, but more excited than scared. 'I didn't have to bring them,' I said. 'They're here, because *I'm* here. Living in a cabin, off by myself, until I finish.' " Pensive, Linton added softly, "I thought it made me seem more serious about the novel I'd just started. But what it must have told Mark Ransom was that I was available—away from the hotel, with no roommates and no boundaries, eager for him to think well of me."

Beneath the bulk of her sweater, Linton's frame appeared to settle, becoming smaller. "For a moment, as I remember it now, his eyes seemed to glitter. At the time, I thought that this was a moment when one writer recognizes another—older to younger, but members of the same species. Then, very politely, he said, 'I'd be flattered if you'd let me read them.'

"I remember imagining: What if Mark Ransom found a woman writer he admired enough to say so." Linton shook her head. "In the narcissistic way of young people who've been told they have talent but have yet to learn the limits of it, I began to imagine the bright dinner parties, the influential articles in the *Times* and *New York Review,* the great literary friendships that would start with this meeting. My own celebrity." Her voice, soft and clear, held a trace of self-contempt. "What a fool I was—how romantic, how unlike the people I've come to write about. It humiliates me just to think of it."

"Why?" Terri asked. "Were you supposed to be immune to dreams?"

"Not immune. But clear-eyed. Enough not to invest someone else with the power of my own fantasies."

Terri shook her head. "It's normal to look up to someone older, to want to be like them, or be close to them. It's just that for women, that can present a special problem. Because, in his mind, the man you've started to invest in may already have his fingers on the top button of your blouse."

Linton gazed at Terri. "We're supposed to know that," she said finally. "*You* must have always known that. But somehow I forgot."

"The penalty for forgetting," Terri answered quietly, "shouldn't be rape."

Slowly, Linton shook her head; once more, the gesture seemed to take her inward. "I offered to meet him the next morning, for breakfast. 'Don't worry,' he told me. 'I'd like to explore this country. If you'll be in tomorrow, why don't you let me find you?' He made it sound like an adventure. A game, almost.

"The next day, I was so excited that I could hardly write. I laid out all the bottles of wine my uncles had so that Mark could make his choice, then presliced some cheese and wrapped it in cellophane to keep from running around the kitchen when he got here, acting nervous like I do. About every half hour I would get up from my desk and look out the window for a car. It got so hard waiting that I almost called him.

"Around four-thirty, when I'd finally settled into my writing, there was a knock at the door.

"It was Mark Ransom.

"He had fresh sushi from town, and an expensive bottle of wine. 'First things first,' he told me. 'Put these in the refrigerator, and show me a quiet place to read.' "

Reflectively, Linton glanced upstairs. "I took him," she said quietly, "to the atelier. The place where I wrote.

"I had fifty pages waiting for him. Fresh and clean, worked and re-worked. The absolute best that I could do."

Her tone became flat, as if from the effort of memory. "He settled into my chair, leaning both arms on my desk, waving me away. He seemed totally intent on what I had written." Linton's voice fell. "I remember thinking that he wanted to know my work. To know *me.*"

It was strange, Terri thought, to listen to Linton after reading her stories. In her speech, as on the page, Linton was a minimalist: she conveyed her pain by indirection, in a few understated words. "You felt that he cared," Terri ventured.

Linton watched her. "What I felt," she said with equal quiet, "was that I had opened myself to him."

She turned to the fireplace. "I came down here, made myself busy. Opened the wine he had brought, to let it breathe. Started a fire. All the time wondering what he thought of my pages." She shook her head. "Writers have this great protection: unlike singers or actors, we don't have the terror and ecstasy of confronting our audience. But now I would, and it was Mark Ransom." Her voice lowered. "I felt so vulnerable.

"By the time he finished, an hour had passed, and it was dark." Once more, Linton shook her head. "When I heard his footsteps coming down the stairs, I wanted to run.

"He walked into the living room." Linton paused. "He just stood there, saying nothing. Giving me this enigmatic, knowing look. I couldn't stand the silence.

" 'So,' I said, 'should I throw it out?' When he didn't answer right away, I cursed myself: instead of sounding clever and self-confident, I was a supplicant, and the smile I pasted on to cover that felt like a rictus." Linton folded her hands. "I already felt naked, and he hadn't even touched me."

Terri gazed around the room. In the present, it was perhaps noon; through the windows, Terri saw that sunlight made the boughs of snow-covered pines glint with crystals, saw more sun streaking the jagged peaks on the far side of the valley. But what Terri imagined was a window blank with darkness, a room made close by firelight, dancing on the stone slabs and the skins of animals. A man with glittering eyes and a slender young woman, facing each other in silence, a few feet apart.

"What did he say?" Terri asked.

Linton stared at the fireplace. " 'Oh, I wouldn't throw it out,' he said, and gave this little smile. The smile gave the words an almost casual cruelty; what it said to me was that his answer was less about the merit of what I'd written than the pitiable way I'd asked the question." Linton turned to Terri, fresh pain in her eyes. "At night, when I still think about it, I wonder whether he'd intended all along to strip away my confidence."

Somehow, Terri felt the fragility of her own body. "And did he?"

Silent, Linton nodded. "In school," she finally said, "before I found writing, I was a pleaser. As a young girl, I stayed out of trouble, watched everyone else to know what to do and not do, killed myself to get the best grades I could. All to *please* other people." She paused. "When Ransom said that, it was as if he'd taken away my writing and I was a little girl again.

"All I could say was, 'Can we talk about it?' " Linton's voice returned to the present. "It sounded *so* pitiful.

"Mark just laughed. As if that, and *I,* were trivial.

" 'Of course,' he said. 'A little wine will warm me to the subject.' "

The first sliver of anger pierced Linton's voice. "It was so completely patronizing. As if he had to drink to work up any interest. But I was helpless to say, or even feel, anything like that." Her tone became bitter. "I poured the wine, like a waitress trying to please a customer. Like the pleaser I used to be.

" 'Go ahead,' he told me, 'have some wine, and sit. It's really not so bad.' " When Linton shook her head yet again, Terri saw it as a self-directed reflex of puzzlement and wonder. In a flat voice, Linton said, "That finished me."

"How do you mean?"

Linton seemed to swallow. "I've never liked to drink that much—it usually makes me queasy, not myself. But what he said made me feel like such a joke. I didn't *want* to feel like myself." She continued with painful slowness. "I sat next to him on that couch, put two glasses on the coffee table. When I filled my glass to the top, Mark Ransom smiled down at it."

Terri felt cold. There was a moment's silence, and then Linton spoke again. "He waited to start in on my pages until I'd finished a glass of wine and begun another." Linton hunched forward. "And then he told me what he thought."

"What did he say?"

"It wasn't just what he said, but the cold, analytical way he said it. He made my pages sound like a slide under a microscope—something with scientific interest but no life. Which, I've come to believe, has become the central problem with so many of my characters." Linton turned back to Terri. "When a good editor works with young writers, he or she will let them build some confidence—get some pages under them, speak only to what is most important. But Mark Ransom was more brilliant and incisive than any editor I'd known, and he was completely without mercy, scene after scene." Linton stared at the coffee table. "Every so often, between comments, he would pour us both more wine. And of course, I was grateful to drink it."

Linton, Terri realized, had turned pale. "By the time he got to his last comment," she said softly, "I felt paralyzed—with wine and with humiliation."

There was something missing, Terri realized, from what Linton had just said. "What," Terri asked, "was his 'last comment'?"

Linton touched her face. "What ruined the pages, Ransom told me, was the bloodless way I write about sex.

"I felt myself go numb. When I could finally speak, my tongue felt thick." Remembering, Linton bowed her head. "The scenes were about David, my boyfriend, and me."

Terri could think of nothing to say, and Linton

spoke again. " 'I *liked* that part,' I told him. 'It's *real.* They're both intellectuals, and so young, so inexperienced. They're still scared of feeling, and smart enough that they can hide it.' I felt desperate, almost pleading. 'Later in the book,' I said, 'they'll *know.* This is just the start.'

"It seemed almost to make him angry. 'It's like they're negotiating a contract,' he told me. 'Sex isn't an insurance policy, you know.' He stopped, taking one long look at me. 'What sex *is,*' he almost whispered, 'is spontaneity, and danger.' "

Linton was staring, as if transfixed by memory. "That one comment," she said quietly, "and I felt the whole thing turn on me. Everything he'd done was not just about my book, but about *me.*

"When he put his arm around me, the room started to spin."

Linton had begun to speak without expression. It was as if Ransom were about to touch her again; Linton had not stopped him in life and so could only remove herself in memory. She became close to inaudible. "I went stiff, felt too sick to struggle. And then, as if I belonged to him, he reached inside my blouse and put two fingers on my nipple."

Terri looked away; she found it easier to listen than to watch Linton's face. But when Linton spoke again, it was in tones not of hurt but of mild astonishment. "Do you know what he did then? With my nipple between his fingers, he took my face in his other hand and asked, 'Do you ever watch Laura Chase?' "

Terri felt herself freeze, did not know for how long. When Linton spoke again, she had been silently staring at the floor. "Are you all right?" Linton asked.

It reminded Terri that Mary Carelli had asked much the same question; when, Terri wondered, had she started losing her detachment? It made her feel as fragile as Linton sounded.

"No," she answered quietly. "This gets to me, and then I feel selfish. It's your pain, not mine. I'm just asking you to open it up to the world."

Linton shook her head. "Don't feel selfish. You just *feel,* that's all. It's why I'm opening up to *you.*"

You give me too much credit, Terri thought. She told herself to be a lawyer, get Linton talking again. "He asked you about Laura Chase," she said.

Linton looked at her another moment, and then her gaze grew distant. She nodded again, her body making a rocking movement, and briefly shut her eyes. "When he said that," Linton answered softly, "a shiver ran through me. It was like realizing that you'd missed the clues—that someone you've thought of as merely singular is, in fact, insane."

Linton's eyes opened. "Perhaps it was the fire, the stone floor, the elk head on the wall. Suddenly I felt like I was under the spell of something primitive. It was like being in a nightmare, yet being lucid, all at once. I saw his madness clearly, knew that it was becoming my reality. And then his thumb and forefinger tightened on my nipple.''

Linton turned toward the empty fireplace. ''That,'' she said slowly, ''was when I pulled away.

''His eyes got big. He simply stared at me, and then he smiled.'' Linton nodded, rocking herself. ''It was what he'd wanted me to do.

''I was still caught up in his eyes when he slapped me.

''My neck snapped back, and then I fell against the arm of the couch. I saw yellow flashes, tasted blood inside my mouth.

''He got up on his knees, waiting for my eyes to open. And then he ripped open my blouse.'' Her voice dropped. ''It was like it wasn't enough for me to feel him. He needed me to watch him.''

Linton closed her eyes. '' 'Shall I hit you again?' he asked softly.

''I couldn't talk, couldn't move. I just shook my head.

'' 'Then show me your breasts,' he said. 'And keep your eyes open.'

''My bra unhooked in the front.'' Linton's eyes opened. ''Even then, unhooking it was hard. My fingers couldn't move right.''

Terri wanted a drink of water, she found. But she couldn't speak. As if in a trance, Linton kept on talking. ''When I was uncovered,'' she said, ''he just looked at me. I had this crazy hope—if he liked my breasts, perhaps it would end there. I was so pathetic that I tried to smile at him. But my mouth was swollen, and I couldn't make it."

" 'That's good,' he said. 'Eyes open now.' His voice was soothing but impersonal, like a doctor's. And then I felt his fingers on the clasp of my jeans.

"When I began to wriggle, he slapped me again.

"I started to cry. *'Eyes open,'* he said angrily." Linton looked pale again. "He made me unzip my jeans, pull them off. Even to myself, I looked so thin.

"At first, he let me keep my panties on." Once more, Linton nodded to herself. "He opened my legs, forced his knees between them. I had to watch while he undid himself."

Linton's eyes were dry. Terri, watching, struggled for control. "When he was finished," Linton said quietly, "he told me to hold his penis while he pulled my panties down. To keep him hard.

"I did that.

"When he had me naked, he pushed me back. I felt his wool sweater, his face against my neck. And then I felt *him.*" Linton looked away. "He didn't care whether he hurt me."

Linton's voice became tired, as if with shock. "It hurt. But I was too afraid to close my eyes. I tried finding something to look at." She paused. "So I lay there, staring up at the elk head, while he had me.

"Afterwards, he made me cook him dinner. Without any clothes, while he watched me.

"I did that, still in shock, like a little robot homemaker. Then I cleaned up." Linton shook her head. "The more I moved, the more it hurt. And he just watched me.

"I was cleaning up the living room, wiping beneath the wineglasses, when I saw the stain on the sofa." She looked at Terri. "It was right where you're sitting now."

Terri could only stare at her. "I turned the cushion over," Linton said softly, "so my uncles wouldn't see the stain. For all I know, it's still there."

Terri got up, walked to the window. Her legs felt weak; perhaps, Terri told herself, she had been sitting too long.

"Would you like to go for a walk?" Linton asked.

Terri turned to her. "Is that all right?"

Linton nodded. "I need to stop this. At least for a while." She paused, touching her chest. "It's almost a physical thing. To talk about it hurts in here."

God, Terri thought, there can't be any more. She followed Linton to the hall closet, borrowed a ski parka and some boots, went outside.

It was crisp and still; the cold felt good on Terri's face. Silent, they began walking toward the road.

There was no sound except the crunch of their boots on crusted snow.

It was midafternoon, Terri realized. Daylong sun had warmed the pine boughs; once or twice the branches bent and their burden of snow fell to the ground, needles stirring with the fall. Terri and Linton walked side by side. For perhaps a quarter mile, neither spoke.

"When did he leave?" Terri asked.

Linton paused, staring out. "The next morning."

Terri let it go for a time. They reached the bridge of railroad ties; Linton stopped and leaned against the railing. Next to her, Terri watched the icy flow of the stream, listened to the water rush beneath them.

Terri turned to her. "Why did he stay?"

Linton shrugged. "Because he wanted to."

Terri kept watching her. Linton leaned forward, arms resting on the railing, cradling her chin. "It was as if," she said quietly, "he wanted things normal. To believe that I'd felt something more than pain."

"And you?"

Linton shook her head. "I was a shell."

Terri was silent.

"Have you heard of the 'Stockholm syndrome'?" Linton asked.

Terri nodded. "I think so. Isn't that where victims begin to identify with the kidnapper, because they're so afraid?"

"It was something like that. I was in shock, torn loose from my moorings. I wanted to pretend that nothing had happened. And at the same time, I was afraid of what he'd do if I asserted myself at all." Linton turned to Terri, hazel eyes full of confusion and self-doubt. "Can you understand any of this?"

Terri was quiet for a moment. "Yes," she said finally. "I can."

Linton turned to the stream. "That night, he slept with me. I couldn't sleep at all."

Terri tried to imagine lying in bed with the man who had raped her. It was like recoiling from a flame; the thought left a residue of shock.

"In the middle of the night," Linton said softly, "I felt him reach between my legs.

"It was semidark. The only light was from the bathroom; I'd gone to wash inside me, and left the light on and the door ajar. Like a child afraid of the night." Linton paused. "It hurt to be touched there.

"Suddenly he stopped. For a moment, I thought I was safe. Then he got up, pulled aside the sheets to uncover me. As he turned, his profile caught the light from the bathroom, and I saw that he had an erection.

"I lay there, stiff. But when he opened my legs, I reached out to him. So that he wouldn't hit me again.

"He pushed against me, trying to get in. I was wondering if it was dark enough to close my eyes."

Staring at the stream, Linton shook her head. "Then I realized that his penis wasn't hard."

Linton turned to Terri. "He flung my arms away, got back up on his knees, still between my legs. Just staring down at himself. He became so still that it frightened me. I didn't move, could hardly breathe.

"For a crazy moment, I thought he'd kill me. Because, somehow, I'd failed him." Linton was shivering in the cold. "And then, without a word, he gathered his clothes and went downstairs.

"I lay there for hours, a prisoner in my uncles' house, listening for sounds from below. The sun came up; there were streaks of light across the bed. Every once in a while I heard him pacing the stone floor. All I could do was pray that he would leave without wanting me again." Linton paused. "Then I heard him coming upstairs."

In her imagination, Terri heard Ransom's footsteps on the stairs. Felt herself waiting, as Linton had.

"I covered my shoulders," Linton said. "When I looked up again, he was standing at the foot of the bed.

"The look in his eyes was so peculiar: confusion, anger, fear. He stared at me as if I had tried to destroy him.

"Once more, I was sure that he would kill me.

"He came closer. Then he sat on the bed, placed one hand on my lips, and said in a whisper, 'You can never tell anyone.'

"I stared at him, and then I nodded. He looked into my eyes, as if deciding whether to believe me. Then he whispered, 'Good. Because that never happened to me before.'

"I didn't know what he was talking about. And then it came to me." Slowly, Linton shook her head. "He wasn't asking me to hide his rape," she said with quiet bitterness. "He was asking me to hide his failure."

Terri was silent. When Linton spoke again, her voice held a kind of amazement. "Even then, his only feeling was for himself. He left without saying another word."

Terri turned to her. "After that, what did you do?"

"I got dressed and sat down to write, as if it were a normal day. An hour later, I was staring at a blank page." Linton stared at the floor. "The scene I was writing was between a man and a woman, about to make love.

"For weeks, the book wouldn't come. I left here, took time off, tried writing different scenes. What I was really trying to do was lose myself in a story. Nothing worked. Mark Ransom had killed something in me—in life, and in fiction."

"You never told anyone?"

"I just couldn't do it." Her voice went flat. "It would make such a mess. Part of me felt, somehow, that I'd let him do it. Then, when I got away from here, it was almost as if it hadn't happened.'' Again, she shook her head. ''As you said, I just stuffed it somewhere. Sometimes the only way I knew that it had happened was how careful I was to avoid Mark Ransom. So *I* wouldn't feel dirty and ashamed.''

''And David?''

''We broke up. Before, I thought maybe I could let him get close—emotionally, that is.'' Linton paused. ''I just never did.''

Terri hesitated. Finally, she asked, ''Did you ever think of telling him?''

''Sometimes. But I never could really imagine it. David was a lawyer—shy about his feelings but very aggressive and literal about everyone else's rights. If I'd told him, he wouldn't have stopped there. And he would have taken what happened with Mark Ransom personally.'' Linton sounded weary, defeated. ''Sometimes I think men and women see these things so differently.''

Terri searched her face. ''The book,'' she asked. ''What was it about?''

The bitterness left Linton's face; its residue was another look, more distant yet profoundly sad. ''It was to be about David and me. Only a better, wiser version of us both.'' Linton's tone grew softer. ''Like many writers, I used fiction to bring order to the world, make life and people as I wished them to be. Including me.''

''And you're trying to write it again?''

"Yes. But it's not going well." The bitter smile returned. "I seem to have lost the feeling for it. Perhaps, as Mark Ransom suggested, I'm a writer of short fiction—'little people, little feelings, little stories.' "

Terri was quiet. Finally, she asked, "What do you call the novel?"

"Now? Nothing." She shook her head. "When I gave it to Mark Ransom, I called it 'The Pursuit of Happiness.' " She turned to Terri again, her eyes glistening. "I can't seem to be happy, if I ever was."

Terri did not know what to do or say, except to touch Linton's shoulder. "Marcy," she said gently, "you don't have to testify. No one will ever know."

For a time, Linton regarded her, and then spoke with equal quiet. "No," she said. "Maybe I'll never finish 'The Pursuit of Happiness.' But if I testify, perhaps someone else will understand why I'm so damned glad Mark Ransom's dead."

FIVE

"THAT'S A TERRIBLE STORY," Paget said.

They sat at a restaurant in the mountains above Aspen, one night later. Paget had flown out to help make Marcy Linton comfortable with him and to prepare her for what was to come. He had been candid and factual; although more reserved with Paget than with Terri, Linton was determined to testify. But watching Linton become the centerpiece of Mary Carelli's defense, Terri found herself resenting Christopher Paget for the relief he felt.

She looked around, pretending to enjoy the room. On another day, she would have. The restaurant Paget had managed to find was a long drive into the mountains and set off by itself; a rustic cabin that offered excellent food and, in the kennel just below, dog sleds for hire. Inside were candlelit tables, rough walls, and, through the windows, a view of snow filtering through the pines and aspens that covered the mountainside. They sat in a corner; the other tables were filled with twosomes and foursomes in jeans and boots and sweaters who had come for the food rather than to be seen. Beyond the murmur of the room, close and convivial, Terri could hear dogs yipping below, their cries echoing in the mountains.

"I'm sorry," she said. "I guess I'm not very good company."

"Oh, you've been surprisingly lifelike." Paget seemed to wince at his own words. "Forgive me. Sometimes I don't know what to say, when a simple 'What's the matter' would do nicely. What *is* the matter? Marcy Linton?"

For once, Terri thought, his intuition had failed him; she was better prepared for banter than for serious talk. She searched for something that would seem like enough to explain her mood and, at the same time, invite a change of subject. Finally, she said, "It's just how Richie sounded last night, I guess."

Paget tilted his head in inquiry. "How was that?"

"He's not happy about my being here." She smiled faintly. "I'm never sure anymore how attractive Richie really thinks I am, but he's absolutely certain that *other* men find me compelling."

Paget looked mildly surprised. "Me, for example?"

Terri nodded. "Uh-huh."

Paget seemed to consider that a moment. "You *are* compelling, of course. But that misses the point of our relationship. As professionals, or as friends."

"I know that. But Richie never will."

Paget stared out the window. His gaze was distant,

directed at the mountainside. "Sometimes," he said quietly, "people just need a safe place to go."

The waiter cleared their plates and wineglasses, took coffee orders. For once, Terri did not want dessert. She felt Paget watching her again.

"Linton's our one chance to win," he said finally. "And getting this out may well help her."

"That's much too easy." Terri stared at her coffee. "What gives us the right to play with other people's lives, for reasons of our own? What gives *me* the right to open them up like that?" Suddenly Terri needed to deflect the conversation. "Sometimes, I wonder if I was really made to be a lawyer."

Paget's smile was unimpressed but not unkind. "Is that what we were talking about—your fitness as a lawyer?"

She looked up at him, and then his smile disappeared. Softly, he asked, "What happened to you, Terri?"

She felt startled, confused. When she spoke, her voice sounded thin. "I became a lawyer. That's all."

Paget shook his head. "Something happened to you," he said. "If you're paying attention, as I've been, it's not even that hard to spot."

All at once, Terri felt exposed, angry at the tears she had to fight. "Can we go now?" she said. "I'm tired."

"Of course."

Quickly, Paget signaled the waiter, paid the bill. His manner was smooth and pleasant; the only change was that he let Terri keep to herself. On the way to the car, and for some time after, he said nothing at all.

The night was cold and dark. Through the windshield Terri could see a crescent moon; a black expanse of sky above the mountains; more stars than she could see in San Francisco, undimmed by fog or city lights. The only sound was the engine running.

They drove, two stiff and silent profiles, staring through the window at the dark. Terri felt herself hold on tight.

"I'm sorry," Paget said quietly.

Perhaps, Terri thought, it was the way he said it. She had curled up in the seat, tears running down her face, before she was aware that he had stopped the car.

They were at an observation point above the valley, a thousand feet of darkness.

"Are you all right?" he asked.

"No." Terri felt her emotions plummet in a free-fall with no end in sight. "I'm not all right. I haven't been all right for a long time."

Despite the tears, her voice was cold and clear.

"What is it, Terri?"

They sat there, Paget turned toward her, Terri staring out the window. It was easier that way.

"Five years ago," she said at last, "someone raped me."

He was quiet for a time. "And you've never told anyone."

Just look at the stars, Terri told herself. "It was stupid," she said.

Once more, Paget fell silent. Terri felt herself swallow, began again. "The man was a law professor in his forties—married, with two kids, and Hispanic like me. He'd done criminal defense in East L.A., worked with Cesar Chavez. Some of us saw him as a kind of role model." Terri paused. "Especially me.

"In my third year, a few months after Elena was born, he asked me to be his research assistant on a paper he was writing. I was flattered that he'd asked. But I did it because Richie had decided to add an MBA to his law degree, and we needed the money." She paused again. "From the start, Richie was jealous. The man was appealing in his way—black mustache, dark intense eyes—and Richie was sure that he was interested in me. But not so sure that he didn't want me taking his money."

Terri stopped, replaying the note of bitterness in her voice. So funny, she thought: her eyes were wet, but her throat felt dry.

"What," Paget inquired gently, "was this man's name?"

Terri hesitated; somehow naming him made it real again. "Urbina," she said at last. "Steve Urbina."

In the darkness of the car, Terri closed her eyes.

"If this is too much," she heard him say, "we don't need to talk about it."

There was a knot in her chest; she could not seem to get it loose. Talk about it, she told herself, as if it were a case. As if it were someone else.

"It was late Sunday afternoon," she finally said. "Richie and I had taken Elena on her first outing to Tilden Park. It was warm outside. We put Elena under a tree in one of those portable car seats while Richie and I ate our picnic. I was wearing a sundress, Richie his hiking shorts and a sweatshirt, and Elena had on a pink T-shirt that said 'Baby Power' or something foolish like that. I remember thinking that we were a family, and how glad I was that I'd decided to have Elena.

"We spent all afternoon there, remembering things about college and looking at Elena, who didn't do much but sleep and squall." Terri felt herself holding on to the memory. "But then babies don't *have* to do very much, do they?"

"I've never really had one," Paget said. "I envy you that."

"It was such a good day. We decided to go home, barbecue something on the roof of our apartment building, while Elena slept." Terri hesitated. "And then, after we put Elena in her bassinet for the night, we were going to make love.''

For a moment, Terri tried to recall her marriage to Richie before it began carrying the weight of her successes, his jealousies and fits and starts. It was more painful than she had allowed herself to know. She stayed there, lost in what she felt as Christopher Paget's infinite patience.

``When we got home,'' she said at last, ``there was a message from Steve Urbina.

``I'd forgotten to give him some research notes; could I drop them at his house?'' She shook her head. ``The thing I remember was that Richie was so pissed.

``I called Urbina and told him I'd be right over—it wasn't far. I didn't worry about him—I mean, he was a little flirty, but nothing serious, and home was where his wife and kids were. Actually, at the time I didn't even think about those things.'' Terri opened her eyes, looked out at the stars. ``And besides,'' she said in a flat voice, ``forgetting the notes was my fault.

``I went out the door, with Richie still angry.

``Steve Urbina's house was this stucco sort of Spanish place in Albany, with an apple tree in front. I got there in about fifteen minutes and hurried to the door.

``I was in such a rush to get back home that I tripped on one of his kids' tricycles.

"I was sitting on the walk with the notes scattered next to me and my sundress pulled up around my thighs, looking at my knee, when I realized he was watching through the screen door.

"It was strange for a second: he startled me, and I couldn't tell how long he'd been standing there. But all he said was, 'Let me take a look at that.'

"The scrape was pretty bad, with some surface bleeding. When he knelt beside me, I pulled my sundress down so that only one knee showed. 'We keep Band-Aids and Mercurochrome for the kids,' he said. 'That may need hydrogen peroxide too.'

"When I picked up my notes and followed him inside the house, I didn't hear anyone else.

" 'Mattie and the kids are visiting their grandmother,' he said. ' 'Fraid I'm the only nurse around.'

" 'It doesn't matter,' I told him. 'Just show me where the bathroom is, and I'll take care of this myself. It'll be practice for Elena.'

" 'Oh, come on in,' he answered, and steered me into his bedroom. 'Just sit on the edge of the bed, and I'll get the stuff from the master bath. I can't have you suing me for maintaining a dangerous condition on my own front walk.' "

Terri paused. "I was dumb," she said dully, "but he was so paternal, as some men can be, that I thought it made him feel better. I just sat on the edge of the bed.

"In a minute, he was back. He had cotton balls,

hydrogen peroxide, and a large Band-Aid patch. Very carefully—respectfully, almost—he waited for me to pull my dress up and then dabbed peroxide on the scrape.

"It stung—I flinched a little. He looked up at me, concerned, and asked if it hurt. When I told him 'A little,' his touch got even softer."

Terri looked down. "It wasn't sexual to me, but I remember thinking for a moment that his gentleness was nice, kind of warming." She paused, adding softly, "Richie was never that gentle."

She fell quiet for a time, suspended on the edge of what had happened to her. "When he put on the Band-Aid," she said finally, "he pressed down on each edge very carefully, to make sure it stayed on. And then he reached up beneath my dress and pulled my panties down."

There was something in Paget's perfect stillness that made Terri falter, as if the effort of his self-control tore something loose inside her. "It happened so fast," she told him softly. "Really, it was over before I could believe it."

Paget said nothing. She touched her eyes. "Maybe the worst part," she said at last, "is that I didn't do anything. I don't have any excuse—not like Marcy Linton. I just froze."

" *'No,'* I told him. And then he pushed me down on the bed and leaned his elbow against my throat. He was already standing between my legs. I was so easy for him.'' She shook her head. ''He was coming inside me before I even started to cry.''

Gazing out at the stars, Terri stopped herself from crying. ''Afterwards, he stood between my legs, staring down at me as he zipped up his pants. When he said that no one would believe me, I knew that he had done things like this before.'' She shook her head. ''He was far too confident, and he'd chosen his victim far too well.''

Terri swallowed again. ''Once I promised, he handed me back my panties. He just watched me while I put them on. He'd felt me respond to him, he said—that was why he'd done it. And then he told me it was time to leave.''

Terri leaned her face against the cold window of the car. ''I drove home in a daze, I don't even remember how. When I got there, Richie wanted to know what took me so long. He kept badgering me about why I needed to waste family time on Steve Urbina.'' Terri paused. ''I was so unresponsive that, in one of his lightning changes of mood, Richie suddenly became cheerful. He wanted to take a picture of me in my sundress. I remember trying to smile for him.'' Terri's voice became wondering. ''It's his favorite, he says. He still keeps it over his computer.''

Terri turned to Paget. ''That night, Richie fucked me twice. One for himself, I remember thinking, and one because I'd been at Steve Urbina's.

"I never told anyone. I couldn't explain, couldn't face Urbina." Her voice was parched. "I couldn't bring myself to even mention him. I wrote a one-page letter resigning my job, didn't go to graduation. I don't know whether I was more afraid of seeing Steve Urbina or I thought, somehow, Richie would know." Terri shook her head in wonder. "I felt it was my fault. That was why I became a rape counselor—to try to understand. What I learned was how many women this happened to, far more than most men seem to realize. But I could never talk about it. To anyone."

Pausing, Terri looked down. "Not only was I a coward, but I never seriously considered *not* being one. How did I ever ask Marcy Linton to do this?"

Paget watched her. "How can you have blamed yourself?"

"Because I let it happen." Terri paused. "Because I protected everyone but me."

Turning to the window, Paget gazed out at the night. "I hate that," he said softly. "I hate it for *you.*"

Almost to herself, Terri shrugged.

"Why," Paget asked finally, "did you never talk to your mother? You surely didn't think that *she* would blame you."

His tone was not judgmental; it was as if he wanted to understand her, and this was a piece that mattered.

"No," Terri answered, "I didn't think that. Looking back, I just didn't want to admit that I'd started doing what she'd always done—keeping things from Richie, keeping the peace. For both our sakes, I couldn't tell her that."

Paget turned to her. "Then who do you talk to?"

She thought for a moment. "You," she answered quietly. "I guess I talk to you."

SIX

TERESA PERALTA STEPPED from the shower.

Richie turned to look at her. It was strange, she thought; she had been naked with him countless times before, and yet tonight it made her edgy.

He put down the toothbrush, taking her in. "Coming to bed soon?" he asked.

She wrapped a towel around herself. "In a while. I have to dry my hair, take off my eyeliner. Unwind a little. It was a long flight and a longer two days."

Richie gave her the thwarted look she had come to know too well. "It's not like I've seen you much lately." His voice rose in complaint. *"I'm* the one who's your husband. Not Chris Paget."

Terri tried to understand why she felt guilty. "I know who you are," she said tiredly. "And I know you're my husband. In nearly six years of marriage, I've never *not* known that."

Richie was silent for a moment. Terri turned to the mirror, dabbing at her eyes with makeup remover. "Why didn't you call last night?" he asked.

Terri's guilt became defensiveness. "It was late, and I had a lot to think about." Terri paused. "If you were so concerned, you could have called *me*. I gave you the number."

"Was *he* with you?"

Terri stopped to look at him. "No," she answered quietly. "I just didn't want to call."

Richie put both hands on his hips. "I can't believe this."

"Then believe *this,* Richie. I've never been unfaithful to you, and I never will." Terri paused. "There's nothing you can do to change that, one way or the other. It's just the way I am."

Richie stood there watching her. In a lower voice, he said, "I don't want you working with him."

Terri felt a moment's anger, then felt tired. "You have an exclusive on my body, Richie. But you can't set the conditions under which I'm going to support you."

He flushed. "You know, that's a really telling remark, Ter. It's what you do—emotional abuse and economic castration."

It felt so unfair that Terri did not stop before she spoke. "When it comes to economic castration," she retorted, "you're a self-made man."

Richie stiffened; then, curiously, Terri thought she saw a fleeting triumph in his eyes, as if he had gotten what he wanted. Very softly, he said, "I don't know whether I'll ever forget what you just said."

"All that I meant to say," Terri answered wearily, "is that you should quit worrying about Chris and start worrying about Elena. *And* me."

"I thought our interests were synonymous." He stood straighter. "In a real family, Terri, that's how it's supposed to be."

Married all this time, Terri thought, and she was still not sure when Richie meant to be manipulative and when he was merely obtuse to any feelings but his own. She supposed it did not matter. "Let's stop fighting," she said. "Please. I just got home, and tomorrow the hearing begins."

He lowered his voice still further. "Your job. That's all you seem to think of now."

Terri picked up her hair dryer. "Tonight," she answered, "that's pretty much true."

She switched on the dryer, using its sound as a buffer. Richie lingered in the doorway of the bathroom, watching with an expression of stubbornness. Then he shrugged and turned away. Something in the gesture told Terri that their quarrel had not ended.

Terri stood in her transient zone of peace: the light of the bathroom, the drone of her hair dryer. Looked at herself in the mirror: the serious eyes, the first lines at their corners. Thought of Elena, sleeping in her bedroom, face lineless and untroubled, so much like Richie's that Terri still found it startling. And then her mind wandered again to Marcy Linton. To the way Mark Ransom had broken her down, used her fears and vulnerabilities until Linton felt a kind of paralysis. To whether Terri had any right to make her face a trial.

Tomorrow it would begin.

She finished. With more deliberation than normal, Terri put things away, hung the towel up. And then she breathed in, once, and walked into the bedroom.

Richie was waiting.

He lay propped up on one elbow, torso showing, half covered by the bed sheet. Even before he pulled the sheet down to make room for her, Terri knew that he was naked.

"Come here, Ter," he said. "It's no good for married people to end the night like this." He gave his most ingratiating smile. "Afterwards, I'll rub your back."

In the dim light from the lamp on Richie's side, Terri walked naked to the bed. "I'm really tired," she parried. "Think we can take a rain check?"

He shook his head, smiling as if to say that his insistence was well intended, that he knew what was best for them. "It's early yet," he answered lightly. "And I have to reclaim my territory."

"Really, I don't think that I could even come."

Persisting, his smile seemed to become an act of aggression. "Then we'll do the short version, rather than the deluxe."

What, Terri wondered, was the difference?

She turned out the light, slid inside the bed on her

stomach. Passive resistance, she thought; maybe he'll give up. She felt his hand lightly stroke her thighs; his touch was idle, aimless, as if he had nothing on his mind. Then it came to rest between her legs.

"Come on, Ter," he murmured. "Just for a little while."

His hand began to move again, small strokes where it had rested. Mentally, Terri shuddered.

As he touched her, Terri moved on her stomach, calculating the value of sleep. If she resisted, a quarrel would ensue. Richie could be relentless in his anger; the fulcrum of their marriage, Terri realized, was his uncanny sense of when her resistance would become fatigue. She could not afford to be tired; she owed Christopher Paget and Carlo, owed *herself,* the best she could offer as a lawyer.

How many times, Terri wondered, had Richie been inside her? How much would this time matter?

How long had she been dead this way?

Silent, Terri rolled over on her back. Richie's murmur of satisfaction seemed to come from some great distance. He would enter her without words, she knew; like many things, the act of sex was something that took Richie deep within himself, until Terri felt a bystander. She no longer thought of what they did as making love.

Sliding across her, Richie put his hands beneath her bottom, to move her as he wanted. She felt him push inside her. As he went as deep as he could, moaning his pleasure, she draped her arms across his back and wished that he were someone else.

The next morning, Teresa Peralta found herself with Christopher Paget on the fourth floor of the Hall of Justice, Mary Carelli between them, pushing through a lobby jammed with reporters.

Three broad-shouldered police ahead of them parted the crowd—reporters with microphones or notepads; photographers with flashbulbs; cameramen with minicams mounted on their shoulders, backpedaling to film the progress toward the courtroom. Terri glanced sideways. Mary Carelli looked composed and determined; Paget's expression was abstracted, removed from his surroundings, as if focused on the hearing ahead. In the last days, Paget's face or Mary's had been on the cover of four weekly magazines and on every network newscast; inside the courtroom waited the cameras of Court TV. Terri had hardly slept last night; she wondered if Paget had slept at all.

At the end of the green hallway she saw the double doors of the courtroom. From the side, reporters shouted questions, flashbulbs hissed, footsteps echoed off bare walls. In another minute or so, they would be inside, and it would begin.

Instinctively, she looked at the boy walking next to her: Carlo Carelli Paget, awkward but handsome in a coat and tie, looking so much like his mother that Terri thought some reporter would surely notice. Carlo turned to her, flashed the crooked, uncertain smile she had come to recognize; once again, Terri hoped that her advice to Christopher Paget would not damage a boy she had come to care about.

A flashbulb exploded in their faces.

She touched Carlo's arm, too quickly for anyone to see. Then she forced herself to look straight ahead, the dots of light from the flash still blurring her line of vision.

Thirty feet from the doors of the courtroom, Terri saw Paget turn at the sound of a question.

The noise had grown louder; the media people were backed against the doorways as if they had hit a wall. It was a red-haired woman reporter whose question had pierced the din: she slid behind the police and stood looking from Mary to Carlo.

"Who *are* you?" she asked Carlo again.

Carlo gazed down at her with a pained expression, as if trapped in an awkward social situation by a drunken and rude adult. "I'm Carlo Paget," he murmured.

Turning, Terri saw that Mary Carelli was stiff with alarm; Paget began pushing in front of her to get to the reporter. "He's my son," he snapped in a preemptive tone.

Carlo looked at him, as if startled. Then a slight smile of amusement crossed his face, relieving his look of tension. "I can't deny it," he said to the reporter.

The crowd kept moving toward the door. "What are you doing here?" the reporter asked. "Learning about the law?"

"No," Carlo answered calmly. "I'm thinking about medical school. In case I don't make the NBA."

Paget had stopped to watch him; it was as if, Terri thought, he was seeing who Carlo Paget had become.

"You don't want to be a lawyer?" the reporter asked.

From the side, a minicam moved in on Carlo. He glanced over, taking that in, and then looked back at the reporter. "Not at all," he told her. "I just want to be a son." He turned to face Paget and Mary. "Christopher Paget is my father, and Mary Carelli is my mother. And all I really have to say to anyone is that I'm very proud of them both."

The reporter was momentarily speechless. Touching Terri's arm, Carlo gave Mary a slight smile, shot a grin at Paget, and turned back toward the doors. Then they opened, and Carlo Paget walked through.

PART FOUR

THE PROSECUTION

February 10 – February 12

ONE

"ALL RISE," the courtroom deputy called out. "The Municipal Court for the City and County of San Francisco, the Honorable Judge Caroline Clark Masters, is now in session."

A handsome woman on the worst of days, Caroline Masters looked close to regal as she surveyed a courtroom filled by media representatives from around the world, with a small section reserved for members of the public who had lined up outside for the privilege of attending in hour-long shifts. More reporters watched in adjacent rooms fed by closed-circuit television; two cameras in each corner of the courtroom broadcast the hearing nationwide. On the steps of the courthouse, a coalition of women's groups carried signs and placards asking justice for Mary Carelli.

Mary herself stood beside Paget; the awe of finding herself in the cockpit of a crowded courtroom, charged with premeditated murder, showed in the way she grasped the table reserved for the defense. On his other side, Terri looked tired and troubled.

Carlo sat behind them in the first row; Johnny Moore had joined him and sat primed to feed Paget scraps of information for use in cross-examination.

Turning, Paget glanced at Marnie Sharpe. She looked pale. But her alertness of expression said that she was ready. Paget was certain that she, like him, had committed every pertinent fact to memory; had designed and redesigned lines of questioning; and had prepared herself against surprise. The one edge he carried to the courtroom was how much he had at stake.

From the bench, Caroline Masters appraised them both. The judicial frown she wore seemed the residue of pleasure and anticipation.

"Ms. Sharpe," she began, "Mr. Paget. A few ground rules. I suggest you listen carefully.

"First, the presence of television is a responsibility, not a chance to entertain. There will be only one 'personality' in this courtroom—and you're listening to her."

The judge paused, her voice becoming crisp and surgical. "Second," she continued, "we will be ruling on contested points of evidence—whether certain witnesses are relevant or other evidence should be made public—by holding private sessions in chambers. The transcript of those proceedings will be sealed, so as to avoid prejudice to all participants. If anyone alludes to the subject matter of those proceedings without my prior permission, this court will personally bring them before the disciplinary committee of the California State Bar.''

This, Paget knew, was a warning not to mention the Laura Chase tapes; James Colt; Steinhardt's recording of Mary; or the proposed testimony of any witnesses to Mark Ransom's sexual character until Masters ruled on them in private. The pressure of those issues, Paget thought, made even Masters seem apprehensive.

``Third,'' the judge went on, ``I reserve the right to pull the plug on all or part of these proceedings. If either the People or the defense makes an argument, or even asks a question, which I believe is designed more to create bias than to advance their legitimate interests, they will be severely penalized.

``Do I make myself clear?''

``Yes, Your Honor,'' Sharpe said.

Paget nodded. ``Quite clear, Your Honor.''

``Good.'' Masters looked down at Paget. ``Not to single you out, Mr. Paget, but you singled yourself out by asking for this. I expect exemplary behavior.''

``The court has every right to that,'' Paget answered mildly. ``From everyone.''

Masters raised her eyebrow. ``I'm sure *everyone*,'' she said with the slightest edge, ``is as aware of that as you are.'' She turned to Sharpe. ``I've suggested opening statements. Do you have one?''

"We do," responded Sharpe. She stepped to the podium, looking up at Caroline Masters, and the hearing began.

"*This,*" Sharpe opened, "is a simple act of murder."

Her voice quavered slightly, Paget thought, as if her larynx had been squeezed. But it was a good first sentence, and he was certain that the words themselves were crafted to get better.

"Mary Carelli admits shooting Mark Ransom to death. The one thing standing between the People and 'probable cause' is Ms. Carelli's story about *why* she killed him." Abruptly, Sharpe's voice was etched with scorn. "Or, I should say, her *stories.*

"Because if Ms. Carelli presumes to testify before this court, she must tell the court a far *different* story than she told Inspector Charles Monk."

This was clever, Paget saw: make Mary's credibility the focus of her argument; suggest that Mary will insult the court by lying; and then, in chambers, finish the job by asking to introduce a tape in which Mary admits perjury before the United States Senate. Next to him, Mary watched the prosecutor intently, as if preparing for cross-examination. Paget dared not look at Carlo.

"Let us start with the only things about which Ms. Carelli appears to have told the truth to anyone.

"Mark Ransom *did* contact her.

"Thereafter, Ms. Carelli *did* purchase a gun.

"She *did* come to San Francisco, at her own expense, without telling ABC or anyone else.

"She *did* go to Mark Ransom's suite with the Walther .380 hidden in her purse.

"And then, at about noon, Mary Carelli shot Mark Ransom to death.

"Right there, we have a probable cause for first degree murder." Sharpe paused for effect, and then her voice dropped. "And from there on," she added, "things get much worse for Ms. Carelli."

Caroline Masters leaned forward, betraying her interest. Terri was utterly still. The courtroom was far too quiet for Paget's liking.

"Mary Carelli claims to have purchased the handgun because of anonymous phone calls, to her *unlisted* number, which she failed to report to anyone.

"She says that Mr. Ransom lured her to the hotel room with information regarding Laura Chase." Sharpe paused. "On that point," she said dryly, "I will say nothing for the moment. I simply ask the court to keep that claim in mind.

"She says, even more fundamentally, that Mr. Ransom tried to rape her." The contempt returned to her voice. "That while maintaining an erection, Mark Ransom scratched her throat and leg and threw her to the ground. And then, in the ensuing struggle, that she shot him from a distance of two to three inches."

Sharpe paused and then began speaking in staccato sound bites, perfect for television. "Here is what we will show.

"There is *no* evidence of sexual arousal.

"The only skin beneath anyone's fingernails was found under *Ms. Carelli's*.

"There is no extraneous sign of a struggle.

"And as the medical examiner will tell us, Ms. Carelli's tale of shooting from two or three inches is off by at least two or three feet, rendering her entire story of the shooting implausible at best."

Sharpe stood upright, as if galvanized by sudden anger. "What Ms. Carelli appears to have done," she said with scorn, "is to fashion a fashionable defense from an issue which is far too real to far too many women to be so cheaply used." She turned to gaze at Mary. "Indeed, it seems that the only reason Ms. Carelli did not accuse Mark Ransom of child abuse is that she has reached the age of majority. For there is about as much evidence of child abuse as there is of rape." As she paused, the two women stared at each other. "Of course," Sharpe added quietly, "once one shoots someone else to death, one can speak without fear of contradiction. About the *dead,* one can say just about *anything*. The only boundaries are *this* one woman's sense of honor, and of truth."

Caroline Masters had begun to look impatient; her

expression said that she did not require rhetoric. But Paget could imagine all too clearly the first few moments of the evening news.

''Unfortunately for Ms. Carelli, there is more.

''At first blush, these discrepancies seem merely a grab bag of anomalies.

''For example, Ms. Carelli told Inspector Monk that when she arrived at Mr. Ransom's suite, the shades were drawn.

''We will produce three witnesses. One saw Ms. Carelli and Mr. Ransom sitting in a sunlit room with the shades up. The second witness saw Ms. Carelli draw the blinds herself.'' Sharpe's voice rose, became relentless. ''And the third saw Ms. Carelli outside the room. *After* Mr. Ransom died.

''Ms. Carelli told Inspector Monk that she called 911 as soon as possible.

''The medical examiner, Dr. Elizabeth Shelton, estimates that Mr. Ransom had been dead for the better part of an hour when Ms. Carelli placed that call.''

Suddenly Sharpe's voice grew quiet. ''*Ms. Carelli* claims to have scratched Mr. Ransom's naked buttocks in the struggle to defend herself.''

She paused again, speaking each word slowly. ''But Dr. Shelton believes that when Mark Ransom received the scratches, he was well beyond struggling. Specifically,'' she finished softly, ''Dr. Shelton believes that Mr. Ransom had been dead for a good half hour when Ms. Carelli chose to scratch the buttocks of a corpse.''

The audience emitted different sounds: shocked exclamations; murmured questions; the rustle of people turning to each other. Masters raised the gavel. The audience fell silent, waiting.

''Dead for a half hour,'' Sharpe repeated. ''The half hour, we will suggest, that Ms. Carelli was casting about for a story to tell.''

Sharpe focused her gaze on Masters. ''And what will all this tell *us?* That Ms. Carelli lied to the police, to cover her crime. Just as she must lie to the court.''

Masters's face was grim; Paget could not tell whether it was intended to foreclose the thought that Sharpe could prejudice her, or to express her determination that Mary Carelli could not lie with impunity.

''And what of motive?'' Sharpe inquired mildly. ''As a matter of law, we need not show one. Motive is not an element of the crime, and as to the elements themselves, we have more than enough for probable cause.'' Sharpe's voice rose again. ''But we *do* have motive. We will present that evidence to the court, in chambers, and ask the court to rule that it is admissible.''

Paget began to rise. Sharpe was skirting Masters's instructions, touting evidence the judge might not permit her to present in public. When he hesitated, fearful of drawing too much attention, Masters cut in. "On Mr. Paget's behalf," she snapped, "you've crossed the line. When I asked you not to talk about proceedings in chambers *after* the fact, I assumed that you would refrain from describing them *before* the fact. Or is there some distinction that eludes me?"

Sharpe had frozen. "No, Your Honor," she said in chastened tones. "I apologize for any error."

Masters frowned. "If that's what it was, Counselor. Move on."

But Sharpe had lost the force of her argument. She paused and then chose to wind up.

"Your Honor," she started again, "only one more thing need be said.

"Rape is a deep and serious societal problem. It should *not* be the issue *de jour* for a media-wise defendant, desperate to avoid the consequences of murder, eager to tell whatever story she thinks will work." Sharpe had recovered her confidence. "What Mary Carelli *says* is unworthy of belief. What Mary Carelli *did* is commit premeditated murder, and that is what the evidence will show." Sharpe stood straighter yet. "With respect, Your Honor, this court *must* find probable cause to hold Mary Carelli for the murder of Mark Ransom."

For a moment, she stood silent at the podium, gazing up at Caroline Masters. When she turned and walked back to her table, taking the room's energy with her, Paget felt respect and apprehension. Mary Carelli looked away.

"Listening to Ms. Sharpe," Paget began, "my first thought was that speeches are *not* evidence, and sound bites are not facts."

There was silence in the courtroom; Paget knew he already had the attention of the media. But Masters's narrow face registered displeasure, as if anticipating a personal attack on Sharpe.

"My second thought," Paget continued evenly, "was that rape is far too serious a matter to be treated as casually as the People have treated it this morning." He turned to Sharpe. "As serious a matter as the beating of a woman—the kind that leaves her bruised and in shock. And that is far too serious a *fact* to slip the prosecution's mind.

"Yet, somehow, it did."

Paget paused. "Listening to the prosecution's pastiche of circumstantial evidence, I was reminded of a somewhat troubling evening I spent a year or so ago.

"It occurred, of all places, at the movies."

Masters's shoulders moved, a small gesture of impatience. "I was with my son," Paget went on, and then turned to Carlo and Mary. "Ms. Carelli's son."

Mary gave him a slight smile of appreciation; behind him, Carlo nodded. Then Paget turned again, fearful of losing Judge Masters altogether. "The film concerned the assassination of a President, and it was Carlo's first exposure to the subject. And, like Ms. Sharpe's opening statement, it was gripping entertainment."

Masters seemed to sit back to see him more clearly, torn between curiosity and concern about Paget's choice of subject. Paget saw Sharpe half rise, searching for an objection she could put into words.

"The film's director," Paget continued, "managed to slice and dice every stray fact regarding the assassination until he came up with a compelling case that a conspiracy of Cubans, gay men from New Orleans, right-wing fanatics, CIA operatives, missile manufacturers, *and* the Vice President of the United States had murdered the President and then covered it up for thirty years, all with the assistance of countless members of Congress and the Chief Justice of the Supreme Court." Paget paused. "It was absolutely riveting entertainment. And like Ms. Sharpe's opening statement, its origin is circumstantial evidence." His voice slowed. "Circumstantial evidence," he repeated. "A dangerous thing, when it is left to brew too long in the fever swamp of a prosecutor's imaginings."

Paget gazed at Sharpe until her face was stiff with anger. "Movie theaters," he said coolly, "are the proper venue for fantasy and myth. *Not* courtrooms." He turned back to Masters. "Nor is any courtroom the proper place for the tissue of speculation Ms. Sharpe has just presented.

"I will not try the court's patience with a story of my own. Nor will I offer previews for all those watching of the evidence *we* will offer the court in chambers. I will merely offer the court one statement of fact, and make of the court one simple request.

"The statement is that Mark Ransom abused Mary Carelli. That is why she shot him, and that is what we will show." Paget turned to Sharpe again. "The request is that the court count how many times Ms. Sharpe's version of the facts turns gauzy under cross-examination." Paget paused, looking back at Masters. "And then," he finished softly, "I will ask the court to consider just whose credibility really stands at issue.

"Thank you, Your Honor."

There was silence; Masters looked surprised that he was finished. Walking to his chair, Paget found that what he felt was not relief but depression.

It was the spare approach: poke holes in the prosecutor's story; offer no story of your own; promise only to stick to the facts as they unfold. Viewed charitably, it could be read as prickly integrity. It was also, Paget knew, the only thing that was safe to offer Caroline Masters; Mary had no story that Christopher Paget could believe.

* * *

Taking the witness stand, Charles Monk sat with his head raised stiffly, turning to look about the courtroom. His face was devoid of all expression; to Mary, he had the unperturbed look of a snapping turtle that had stuck its head out and did not see anything of concern. According to Johnny Moore, he had testified in thirty-seven homicide prosecutions; thirty-six had ended in conviction. On the table next to him was the tape of Mary's interview, edited to delete the identities of Laura Chase and James Colt.

Quickly, Sharpe established that the tape was what Monk said it was; that it had been in their custody; that Mary had been advised of her rights—in short, that it was admissible. Stiffly, Mary watched the methodical grinding of a first-class prosecution team at work; when Monk began playing the tape, she felt helpless.

Sharpe had two purposes, Mary knew. To prove that she shot Mark Ransom, for there were no eyewitnesses to the crime itself. And, more devastating, to show that Mary had tried to mislead Charles Monk.

Snippet by snippet, Sharpe began to accomplish both. Mary listened to her own voice proving how foolish she had been.

Relentlessly, Mary's words began to support Sharpe's case. She had purchased the Walther after Ransom called. She had told no one of her trip to

San Francisco. She claimed that Ransom had attacked her after becoming aroused. She believed she had scratched his buttocks. The scratches on her body were Ransom's. She had shot him at very close range, with his hands on her wrists. She had noticed that the blinds were already drawn. She had called 911 as soon as possible. Her words came to her as sometimes cool, sometimes weary or confused, even angry once or twice. But always she sounded lucid. Her voice did not suggest a woman in shock; Mary, listening to herself as if to a stranger, was afraid to look at Carlo.

The courtroom was still.

When the tape ended, Mary felt heads beginning to turn, as if to reexamine her. Judge Masters eyed her with a new wariness.

They had *not,* Mary realized, played the 911 tape.

But then Sharpe and Monk were on to other things. Crime scene procedures; the presence of her fingerprints in several spots in the living room—an end table, a desk filled with stationery—as if she had been moving around the room at will. Only to her, Mary thought, would the woman Sharpe described sound trapped and desperate.

"In short," Sharpe's relentless voice was asking, "Ms. Carelli's fingerprints seemed to be all over the living room, on numerous pieces of furniture?"

"That's right."

"Was any of this furniture toppled?"

"No."

"Or damaged?"

"No."

"Or seemingly displaced?"

Monk shook his head. "No," he said slowly. His gold-rimmed glasses glistened in the light.

"Was the champagne bottle tipped over?"

"No."

"Or the glass?"

"No."

"Or the tape recorder?"

"No."

She placed her hands on her hips. "Put another way, was there anything in the room itself which suggested a struggle between Ms. Carelli and Mark Ransom?"

For a moment, Mary felt bewildered; she had not realized how the absence of evidence could be made to look.

"No," Monk answered calmly.

"Or anything which suggested other than that, prior to the shooting, Ms. Carelli and Mr. Ransom had simply been talking?"

"Objection!" Paget stood. "Calls for speculation. Lack of foundation."

"Overruled."

"No." Monk's deep voice sounded resonant, satisfied. "Nothing whatsoever."

* * *

Paget gazed at Monk with an air of puzzlement.

Watching, Terri felt as bemused as Paget looked; Monk was an experienced witness, whose testimony had consisted of Mary's own words and a series of simple facts. She did not know how Paget could attack him.

"Before you questioned Ms. Carelli," he asked, "did you send her to the hospital?"

For a split second, Monk seemed to hesitate; Terri guessed that the first question had surprised him. Very calmly, Monk answered, "No."

It was, Terri knew, the terse answer of an experienced witness; Monk did not wish to look defensive, or to temporize before he knew where Paget was going.

"As I understood your testimony," Paget said, "you saw no sign of a struggle, is that correct?"

Monk paused again. "Not in the room itself," he said. "No."

Turning, Paget glanced at Johnny Moore, now standing at the side of the courtroom. In less than a minute, Moore moved an easel to the center of the courtroom; suddenly the easel held a three-by-five foot photograph of Mary Carelli. There was stirring in the courtroom; the dark swelling on her cheek lent her eyes an air of shock. Judge Masters looked from Mary to the photograph as if at a double image; the well-groomed woman in the courtroom staring at herself as a battered victim. The contrast was striking.

"Do you recognize this photograph?" Paget asked.

"Yes." Monk spoke in measured tones. "It's a police photograph, from the crime scene. Blown up, of course."

"And is that how Ms. Carelli appeared when you first saw her?"

"Yes."

"That *is* a bruise on her cheek, is it not?"

"Yes."

"And her eye was swollen?"

Monk nodded. "Yes."

Paget raised an eyebrow. "Yet according to your testimony, there was no sign of a struggle."

"In the room itself," Monk responded. "That was what I said."

Pausing, Paget gave him an incredulous look. "In the room itself," he repeated. "If the coffee table had been chipped, would Ms. Carelli be on trial here? Or would you have charged her with vandalism as well as murder?"

Terri tensed. "Objection," Sharpe snapped. "The only purpose of *that* question was harassment."

"Sustained." Masters turned to Paget. "Don't even try to rationalize that one, Counselor. And don't insult the witness *or* this court by doing it again."

"Forgive me, Your Honor. I'll try to make the point in a less polemic fashion." Paget again faced

Monk. "Could you please look at the photograph, Inspector."

As Monk turned to Mary's bruised image, Paget backed away from it until he stood next to the witness stand. Together, he and Monk gazed at the picture like two visitors to a gallery. "Would you say," Paget asked conversationally, "that Ms. Carelli's face showed 'signs of a struggle'?"

Monk nodded. "With a bruise like that, physical violence is one possibility."

"As a result of your investigation, are you aware of any *other* possibility?"

"No," Monk answered carefully. "Not that we are *aware* of."

"And in fact, Ms. Carelli told *you* that Mark Ransom had struck her as she tried to defend herself."

"Yes. She did."

"But you didn't take her to the hospital."

Monk blinked; Terri saw that the change of subject had come so quickly that it seemed to undermine his confidence.

"No." Monk paused. "She said she didn't want to go."

Still gazing at the picture, Paget tilted his head. "Do you think that was a judgment that *this* woman should have made?"

Monk turned to him. "I thought she *could* make it, yes."

"Are you a doctor?"

Monk looked annoyed. "No."

"Do you know, for example, whether Ms. Carelli had a concussion?"

"No." For the first time, Monk showed some desire to explain. "When we got there, Ms. Carelli was calm, well-spoken, and sensible. The bruise on her face was not near as ugly as that blowup makes it appear. If *she* didn't want to go to the hospital, *we* didn't want to force her."

"But you didn't want to release her, either."

"Of course not." Monk frowned. "She'd not only killed Mark Ransom; she was the only person who *knew* what went on in that room."

"So forced with a choice between questioning Ms. Carelli or taking her to the hospital first, you questioned her. Is that correct?"

Monk hesitated. "Yes."

"How soon after arriving at the Flood did you begin to question her?"

Monk stared at the ceiling. "Roughly three hours."

"And where did the questioning occur?"

"The police station."

"What did you do with Ms. Carelli in the meantime?"

Monk hesitated. "For forty minutes or so, we kept her there. Mostly for the medical examiner."

Paget gave him a sideways look. "To take various tests?"

"Partly."

"Like fingernail scrapings?"

"Yes."

"And reexamining the scratches on the body?"

"Yes."

"So you had time to poke and prod Ms. Carelli for your own purposes, but no time to take Ms. Carelli to the hospital for the purpose of ensuring her well-being."

"Objection." Sharpe stood. "Misstates the prior testimony. Inspector Monk has already testified that Ms. Carelli didn't *want* to go to the hospital."

"Sustained." Once more, Masters frowned at Paget. "Stick to the facts, Mr. Paget."

"Of course, Your Honor." Almost immediately, Paget asked Monk, "So there were roughly two hours that Ms. Carelli spent waiting for you to question her?"

"Yes."

"And these were spent at the homicide bureau?"

"Yes."

"Alone?"

"Yes." Monk paused. "We tried to be sensitive to her rights, Mr. Paget. I'm sure we'd have heard from you if I'd detailed another homicide inspector to chat with her without Miranda warnings."

Paget stared at him. "Speaking of sensitivity, Inspector, did you bring in a rape counselor?"

"No."

"Or a doctor?"

"No."

"Or bring her any food?"

"I don't know." Monk paused. "I know we gave her some coffee."

"With cream and sugar, I hope." Quickly, Paget looked up at Caroline Masters. "My apologies, Your Honor."

Masters, Terri saw, wore a faint smile of amusement. "Respect, Mr. Paget, is never having to say you're sorry. Move on."

"Thank you." He turned back to Monk. "At this point," Paget asked, "did you know how long Ms. Carelli had been without sleep?"

"No."

"Or food?"

"No."

"You never asked?"

Monk hesitated. "Not directly, no."

"But you did know she'd been beaten?"

"She said she'd been hit. If that's what you mean."

"I appreciate the fine distinction, Inspector. Let me put it another way." Pausing, Paget pointed at the picture. "You *did* see that bruise?"

"Yes."

"And Ms. Carelli had already told you that Mark Ransom had tried to rape her."

"Yes."

"And you knew that she had shot him."

"Yes."

"It also appeared from the room that she and Mr. Ransom had been drinking champagne."

"Yes."

Paget looked from Mary to Judge Masters, then back to Charles Monk. "So at the time that you questioned her, at least as far as you knew, in the last eight or so hours, Ms. Carelli's only nutrients were champagne and coffee."

"I suppose so."

"And during those eight hours, you had reason to believe, Ms. Carelli had been struck, sexually assaulted, and forced to shoot someone."

Monk stared at him. "She *wanted* to answer questions."

"Wouldn't *you,* Inspector? Wouldn't any normal person who shot someone in self-defense want at least to say that?"

"Objection," Sharpe cut in. "That question is argumentative."

"Sustained," Masters said. But her face and voice told Terri that Paget's point was made.

Paget still faced Monk. "Are you familiar with the medical definition of shock, Inspector?"

"No." Monk was clearly nettled now. "But I have a layman's experience of shock, gained in twenty years of dealing with violent crime. And in my experience, Ms. Carelli had none of the loss of focus that *I* associate with shock."

Paget stared at him. "I guess we'll have to take your word for it—seeing that there was no doctor on the scene. But are you really comfortable trying to nail Ms. Carelli for discrepancies in what she told you, after eight hours of the trauma you've just acknowledged, without offering her so much as a Big Mac and fries?"

"*Objection,*" Sharpe called out. "This is a court of law, not a high school debate. Rhetorical questions have no place here."

"Mr. Paget," Masters said, "please show the rules of evidence some respect. And for that matter, give the court at least modest credit for intelligence. I got the message five questions ago."

Paget smiled. "Then I'll be happy to sit down," he said.

Sharpe stood. "A few brief questions," she said.

Masters nodded. "Go ahead."

Sharpe faced Monk. "Who terminated your interrogation?" she asked.

"Ms. Carelli."

It was a good opening question, Terri realized. Unable to attack the tape itself, Paget had undercut the basis for it—that Mary was equipped to talk at all. Now Sharpe would try to show that Mary was in full control.

Sharpe went on. "So Ms. Carelli felt free to decide not to answer any more questions."

"Of course."

"When she refused to continue, did Ms. Carelli seem disoriented?"

"Objection," Paget said. "We've already established the witness's lack of medical expertise."

"I'm not asking for a medical opinion," Sharpe retorted. "I'm asking the kind of questions any layperson is entitled to answer: 'Did Ms. Carelli seem confused?' "

"Overruled," Masters said. "The witness may answer."

"No." Monk paused. "I remember thinking that Ms. Carelli was unusually poised and very smart—remarkably so for a woman who'd just shot someone to death." Monk paused again. "The thing that really struck me is that she turned off the tape herself."

Listening, Paget did not change his expression. But Terri knew how much these questions had to hurt; the woman Monk described more closely resembled the cool voice on the tape than the battered face on the easel.

Sharpe moved closer. "Did Ms. Carelli ever ask for food?"

"No. As the tape indicated, she asked for water."

"Did she ever ask for a doctor?"

"No."

"Or for time to rest?"

"No."

Sharpe nodded. "After the end of the tape," she said softly, "did she ask for anything at all?"

"Yes." Monk looked from Mary to Paget. "Yes," he repeated. "She asked for a lawyer."

"This," Marnie Sharpe said on the television, "is a simple act of murder."

Terri and Paget sat in the library, reviewing Terri's notes to help prepare for Elizabeth Shelton. Reporters were clustered outside. They had shouted questions as Paget had driven Terri and Carlo into the garage: the questions were as much about Carlo's acknowledgment of Mary as they were about the trial.

Paget looked up at the screen; in dispassionate tones, he said of Sharpe, "She did well today."

Terri paused, sensing how the loneliness of the hearing must bear down on Paget when he had so much at risk. They had done little but work, avoided all personal subjects; now she wished that there was something she could do for him besides be a lawyer. "You did well too," she told him.

He shrugged. "You're kind to say so. But all I did was nibble at the edge. It's not nearly enough."

He sounded tired, Terri thought, and it was only

the first day. "A lot of it's up to Mary," she answered. "You can't kill this case on cross-examination. No one could."

"Let us start," Sharpe was saying in the background, "with the only things about which Ms. Carelli appears to have told the truth to anyone."

Terri watched her for a moment. Quietly, she said, "What *is* the truth, I wonder."

Paget leaned back on the couch, staring into the empty fireplace. Except for the lamps and the spotlit palm in the window, the room was dark; in profile, Terri could not read Paget's face. Finally, he answered, "I try never to ask myself that."

"Because you don't want to know?"

"Partly that." He turned to her. "It feels almost like superstition—that there's some reason that I *shouldn't* know."

"And the other part?"

"The other part is that knowing is impractical." He smiled faintly. "The truth might inhibit my imagination in constructing a defense."

"About the *dead,*" Sharpe was noting quietly, "one can say just about *anything.*"

"It's a funny game we play," Terri said at length. "It's not about the truth. It's about burdens of proof and rules of evidence—what the prosecution knows, whether they can prove it, whether we can keep things out or cast doubt on what comes in."

Paget nodded. ''That may be morally unsatisfying, on a human level. It's what I think civilians find so disenchanting—the feeling that a trial is Kabuki theater and *not* a search for truth.'' He shrugged. ''Of course, they forget that the system is freighted with other values, one of which is that a civilized society is *not* about retribution at any cost. If it were, we'd just skip trials and start tearing Mary's fingernails out until she told 'the truth.' Whatever *that* is.''

''Specifically,'' Sharpe was saying, ''Dr. Shelton believes that Mr. Ransom had been dead for a good half hour when Ms. Carelli chose to scratch the buttocks of a corpse.''

Paget looked up at the screen. ''If I can't do something with *that,*'' he said softly, ''Mary's close to finished.''

In Terri's mind, she heard Monk testifying again, tracing Mary's fingerprints as she drifted about the room at will, touching lamps, tables, drawers in a stranger's hotel suite. Doing what? Terri wondered. And was Ransom still alive, or dead on the floor?

''Do you think she's still lying?'' Terri asked Paget.

Paget stared at her. ''Yes,'' he said in a reluctant voice. ''At least in part. But I don't know *which* part. Nor do I want to.''

Terri considered him. ''I'm sorry,'' she answered softly. ''But I think I'd like to know.''

"Then do me a favor, Terri. Just don't tell me." He hesitated, then added softly, "I think it's enough to know the truth about our own lives."

Terri fell quiet for a time. "I keep wondering," she ventured, "what happened to the second tape. And, for that matter, to the Lindsay Caldwell tape."

For a moment, Paget looked upstairs, as if afraid that Carlo might hear them. "I have no idea," he finally said. "But seeing as how you've asked, I don't think the tape got lost by accident."

Terri stared at him. "Mary?" she asked.

Paget nodded. "I think so. But I really don't know how. And if that's so, I don't care to know. For my own sake."

On the television, Sharpe's opening statement drew to a close.

"What *I* care to know," Terri said finally, "is what happened in that room between Mary Carelli and Mark Ransom. Perhaps for *my* own sake."

Paget considered her. "But we never *will* know," he answered. "I just hope we never learn what's on that tape."

On the screen, Carlo's face appeared. Paget looked up.

Carlo gazed into the camera. "Christopher Paget is my father," he said simply, "and Mary Carelli is my mother. And all I really have to say to anyone is that I'm very proud of them both."

Paget shook his head. "God," he murmured. "I never wanted this."

The newsman's face returned. "The only comment from Mr. Paget or Ms. Carelli was a press release from Mr. Paget's office, which said only: 'Carlo Carelli Paget is our son. And all we really have to say to anyone is that both of us are proud of him.' "

"The phone was ringing off the hook," Paget said. "Mary and I decided quickly: no interviews on the subject of Carlo, or with Carlo. It's the first thing we've agreed upon in years."

Terri reflected. "I think she really loves him, in her way. It's just not a way I recognize."

Paget became pensive. "You know what I did when she first told me she was pregnant? I asked whose kid he was."

Terri looked at him. "That was a long time ago, Chris. Whatever you said doesn't matter now."

After a time, Paget turned to her. "I really am sorry to be keeping you from Elena."

"I miss her. But this will be over, without Elena thinking much about it." Terri paused for a moment, realized again that she was no longer quite sure where Elena's life was going. But there was nothing she could say to Paget, except to add, "It's Carlo I'm most worried about."

He gazed at her, as if to ask her something. Then he said simply, "I'm afraid of this hearing. For

Mary, for me, but most of all for him. I've taken such a chance, it seems.''

That was right, Terri knew; the Court TV legal experts were already second-guessing him, and there was more risk than they knew.

''Let's keep going,'' Terri said. ''I've got some thoughts about Shelton.''

TWO

WATCHING ELIZABETH SHELTON on the stand, Paget recalled that he had liked her instinctively.

Some of it, he decided, was her look of clear-eyed intelligence; she gave the impression of an inner balance in which no hidden angers or ambitions prevented her from being fair. The other part was the subtle sense that—as good a professional as she was—Shelton found her role in life the source of a certain amusement: her tailored suit and bright orange scarf signaled her awareness that she did not have to play medical examiner for a jury, and thus could reach into the closet for something she liked. It made Paget sorry that he did not know her in some other context and that *his* role was to try to discredit her.

But for now, he could only watch her help Marnie Sharpe build the bricks and mortar of a prosecution case.

In a few questions, Sharpe qualified Shelton as an expert in forensic medicine and criminology, with an extensive background in both, and then got to the heart of things.

"Did you examine the medical evidence," Sharpe asked, "with an eye toward corroborating Mary Carelli's initial story?"

Shelton folded her hands. "Yes. I did."

"And was there such corroborating evidence?"

From the bench, Caroline Masters watched intently. "With the exception of the bruise on her face," Shelton responded, "I found none."

"None," Sharpe repeated for emphasis.

Briefly, Shelton nodded; the reluctance of the gesture signaled her dislike for bombast. "That's correct," she answered.

"In a moment," Sharpe said, "I'll ask you to elaborate on that. But Mr. Paget's questions of Inspector Monk bring something else to mind. When you performed your various tests, Dr. Shelton, Ms. Carelli was present, was she not?"

Shelton nodded again. "For a time," she answered. "When I first arrived at Mr. Ransom's room, some of my work involved inspecting Ms. Carelli for signs of violence and other physical evidence."

"And that was when?"

"Perhaps one-fifty. A short time after Ms. Carelli first called 911."

"And did you speak with Ms. Carelli?"

"Yes."

"Could you describe that conversation?"

Shelton paused, looking gravely at Mary Carelli. "Among other things," she said quietly, "I asked her whether Mr. Ransom had penetrated her and whether she wished to receive medical attention."

"And what did she answer?"

"No. To both."

Sharpe nodded. "Could you describe her manner?"

Shelton seemed to reflect. "I would say that she seemed in some distress—still frightened a little. But quite sensible."

"In your opinion, did she exhibit signs of shock?"

"No." Shelton looked at Mary again. "We had a conversation, and the conversation tracked. She seemed appropriately concerned for her own situation."

Sharpe tilted her head. "Did she mention Mr. Ransom's situation?"

Shelton seemed to hesitate. "Her only mention of Mr. Ransom," she said, "was with regard to certain marks on her body—scratches, the bruise. Ms. Carelli attributed them to him."

"And do *you* attribute those to him?"

"I'm unable to. With the sole exception of the bruise on her face, the medical evidence simply does *not* support Ms. Carelli's version of events."

Sharpe nodded her satisfaction. "Could you

describe the procedures on which you base that conclusion?''

''Certainly.'' As Shelton half turned to Caroline Masters, Sharpe moved to stand only a few feet from her. The result seemed an intimate conference among the three of them, two credible professionals advising the finder of fact. It made Paget acutely aware of his gender, and of Mary's isolation.

''We start,'' Dr. Shelton went on, ''with what I would call Ms. Carelli's basic account. That is, her explanation of the physical evidence—which, as I understand it, has remained constant throughout.''

It was a shrewd introduction, Paget thought, and obviously rehearsed, for it carried the suggestion that Mary was a liar. Mary's narrowed eyes, watching Shelton, hinted at a sense of betrayal. As he turned briefly to Carlo, he saw that his son looked pale.

''She's good,'' Terri whispered.

''That basic account,'' Shelton continued, ''is relatively simple: that Mr. Ransom assaulted Ms. Carelli; that in the process he slapped her and scratched her thigh and neck; that during a pause in this same struggle, she was able to produce a Walther .380 from her purse; and that, as they wrestled for it, the gun fired into Mr. Ransom's chest from a distance of two or three inches.''

Shelton paused, briefly scanning the courtroom as if to ensure the attention of her audience. She had it, Paget knew; the room was still. "As to Mr. Ransom himself," she went on, "he was found lying on his stomach, with his pants down to his knees. According to Ms. Carelli, this was the result of his attempt to rape her, during which he achieved and maintained an erection." Turning to face Judge Masters directly, Shelton spoke softly but clearly. "There were also scratches on his buttocks. Again according to Ms. Carelli, she inflicted those scratches while fighting off the attempted rape.

"With *that* understanding of Ms. Carelli's account, I employed certain procedures myself, and worked with the crime lab in employing others."

Sharpe turned to Paget. "Will you stipulate, Mr. Paget, to Dr. Shelton's qualification to address work done by the crime lab? Or do we need another expert?"

Paget hesitated. But a second expert might only make things worse; better to take a chance that Shelton would at least be fair. "So stipulated," he answered.

Nodding, Sharpe paused a moment, further drawing in the courtroom and, more important, the judge. Unusual for her, Judge Masters had not spoken in some moments. Her expression was unselfconscious and utterly rapt.

"Could you describe for us," Sharpe asked at length, "each of these procedures."

Shelton nodded. "Certainly," she answered crisply, and turned directly to the judge.

"First, there are the scratches on Ms. Carelli's neck and thigh. Ms. Carelli says that Mr. Ransom made them. So we examined Mr. Ransom's fingernails for traces of skin."

"And what was the result?"

"We found none."

Sharpe's voice became more pointed. "And if Mr. Ransom *had* scratched Ms. Carelli, would you expect to find skin traces in his fingernails?"

"It's not a foolproof test. But yes, generally."

"Did you also perform that test on Ms. Carelli's nails?"

"Yes."

"And did the test work *then?*"

"Yes." Shelton spoke quietly, to Caroline Masters. "There were traces of skin beneath Ms. Carelli's fingernails."

Leaning forward, Masters asked her first question of the hearing. "Were you able to determine *whose* skin?"

Shelton shook her head. "No. Unless there's enough skin, we usually can't."

"Thank you. Go on, Ms. Sharpe."

Sharpe looked at Shelton with a faint, curious smile. "Did you find anything *else* under Ms. Carelli's nails?"

"Yes."

"And what did you find?"

Shelton paused. "Microscopic fibers of nylon."

Paget stiffened. Sharpe had never told him this; her smile had anticipated his own surprise. "In your opinion," she asked, "what is the origin of the nylon fibers."

Shelton turned toward Mary. Softly, she said, "There's no way to be certain. But they're consistent with Ms. Carelli's panty hose."

"And were there any traces of nylon under Mr. Ransom's fingernails?"

"None."

From behind him, Paget heard a low, tense buzz; the media people understood the wound that Shelton had just dealt Mary Carelli and now were poised for more.

"As you understood Ms. Carelli," Sharpe went on, "Mr. Ransom was sexually aroused during the alleged attack. Is that correct?"

"Yes."

"Did you attempt to corroborate that?"

"Yes." Shelton turned to Masters. "Prior to orgasm, and even intercourse, it's usual for the erect penis to emit a small amount of semen, sometimes enough to cause pregnancy without ejaculation. To determine whether that has happened, we swab the penis for any residue of semen."

"And did you do that," Sharpe asked, "with Mr. Ransom's penis?"

"Yes."

"And what was the result?"

"There was none." Shelton kept her eyes on Masters. "We found no secretion."

"Indeed, did you find any evidence, of any kind, that Mr. Ransom was sexually aroused?"

"No. None."

Sharpe stood straighter, moving back a couple of steps; both her tone and her posture bespoke a new command. "Let us move to the fatal gunshot wound. Originally, Ms. Carelli told Inspector Monk that she and Mr. Ransom had struggled with the gun and that it had fired into Mr. Ransom's chest from two to three inches. Was the crime lab able to form an opinion as to that?"

"Yes. It's not consistent with the evidence."

"When you say 'it' . . ."

"I mean that the gun was not fired from two to three inches or, in their opinion, from anywhere closer than at least two to three *feet.*" Pausing, Shelton turned to the judge again. "As you know from your own experience at the P.D.'s office, near gunshot wounds leave distinct residue."

"I *do* know," Masters said dryly. "From my own experience in cross-examining *you,* I learned great respect for gunshot residue. As I did for your skills as a witness."

The remark, pleasant yet somewhat Delphic, caused Shelton to smile but made Sharpe freeze for a split second, appraising Caroline Masters. When Sharpe began again, Paget sensed a shade less confidence. ‘‘Could you tell us what the powder marks in *this* case showed?’’

‘‘Yes. The weapon was a Walther .380, and the bullet was a Winchester Silver Tip—high-tech equipment, by the way. From two to three inches, *that* gun and *that* bullet would have left a distinct charcoal-gray circle of gunpowder on Mr. Ransom’s chest, several inches in diameter.’’ Shelton paused. ‘‘Here, there was no residue of powder. None.’’

‘‘And what do you conclude from this?’’

‘‘Start with this fact: the nearest that gun could have fired and left no gunshot residue is at least two feet and probably closer to three.’’ Shelton turned to face Mary. ‘‘From which we conclude that Ms. Carelli shot Mr. Ransom not from two or three inches but from two or more feet.’’

Mary’s eyes met Shelton’s. Between them, Sharpe nodded slowly, as if silenced by the gravity of what she had just heard. Then she asked softly, ‘‘And what about Ms. Carelli’s story of a struggle for the gun?’’

Shelton still gazed at Mary. ‘‘No sign of it,’’ she answered with equal quiet. ‘‘No fingerprints. No powder marks on Mr. Ransom’s hands. As you might expect had there been a struggle.’’

The courtroom was quite still. Paget knew why: the cumulative effect of Shelton’s crisp testimony and calm demeanor was devastating to Mary Carelli. It was hard for Paget to sit there as if nothing were amiss.

"On the tape," Sharpe asked, "Ms. Carelli said that she called 911 as soon as possible. Do you recall that?"

"Yes."

"And how long after that call did you arrive at the Flood?"

"Not long. Perhaps fifteen minutes."

Sharpe paused. "And how long, in your opinion, had Mr. Ransom been dead at the time you arrived."

"It's hard to be precise. But some little time—close to an hour, at least."

"On what do you base that?"

"His blood had begun collecting in his chest cavity. When the heart stops pumping, the blood flows to the lowest point in the body and stops there. It's really just a matter of gravity. But it doesn't happen all at once." Shelton paused. "In my opinion, the pallor of Mr. Ransom's skin suggested that the process had well begun."

"From which you conclude. . . ?"

"That Mr. Ransom had been dead at least one-half hour when Ms. Carelli called 911. Perhaps more."

"Do you know what Ms. Carelli *did* between the time that she shot Mark Ransom and the time that she called 911?"

Shelton still looked at Mary. Softly, she said, "I can only surmise."

"Indeed." Sharpe paused. "Which brings us to the scratches on Mr. Ransom's buttocks. Did you form a medical opinion as to those?"

Shelton's eyes flicked toward the judge, then looked away. As Masters stared down at her, Shelton's eyes fixed on some middle distance. "Yes," she answered slowly. "I did. After a great deal of thought."

"And what," Sharpe prodded, "was that opinion?"

Shelton turned to her. "That the scratches were inflicted *after* Mr. Ransom's death."

The courtroom murmur rose again and stayed suspended between crescendo and diminuendo, sustained by new voices and questions.

The gavel cracked. "This is a courtroom," Masters snapped, "not an audience participation show. If some of you don't get that, you can watch these proceedings on television, with everybody else." She turned to Sharpe, frowning as if the prosecution were at fault. "Proceed."

Sharpe nodded. "On what," she asked Shelton, "do you base your opinion?"

Shelton turned to Mary again; this time her gaze was reticent, almost an apology. "On the scratches themselves. Unlike the usual scratch, such as those on Ms. Carelli, there were no burst capillaries or other signs of bleeding.'' Pausing, Shelton seemed to exhale. ''From which I conclude that the blood in Mr. Ransom's buttocks had already departed. Because his heart had stopped beating.''

The courtroom was silent again. For the first time, Caroline Masters gazed not at Elizabeth Shelton but at Mary Carelli. Whose eyes had shut.

''Let us step back,'' Sharpe was saying, ''and take *another* look at the medical evidence. A look which follows the evidence itself, *not* Mary Carelli's story.''

Paget rose. ''Is there a question in there somewhere,'' he inquired, ''or is Ms. Sharpe about to announce her candidacy for higher office?''

Masters gazed at him. ''Is there an objection in there somewhere?''

''Yes, Your Honor, to the form of the question. I can't find it.'' Paget stepped forward. ''I've let Ms. Sharpe go on for over an hour, without objection. But when she begins to sound like Charles Laughton in *Witness for the Prosecution,* it's time for someone to remind her that *she* is not the witness and that speeches are not facts.''

''You've let Ms. Sharpe go,'' Masters rejoined, ''because her questions aren't objectionable. But speeches are.'' She turned to Sharpe. ''No preambles, Counsel.''

''Very well, Your Honor.'' Sharpe faced Shelton

again. ''Based on the medical evidence, Ms. Carelli shot Mr. Ransom from several feet, is that correct?''

''Yes.''

''So that, in your view, it is also possible that the blow to Ms. Carelli's face was *not* inflicted in a hand-to-hand struggle but in some other way.''

''Objection,'' Paget snapped. ''Calls for speculation.''

''I agree,'' Judge Masters said. ''But for what it is worth, I'll take Dr. Shelton's speculation.''

''Yes,'' Shelton said to her. ''It's possible. In my opinion, Ms. Carelli's bruise *was* caused by a slap to the face. But there is nothing to say *how* that slap was inflicted, or under what circumstances.'' She paused. ''Or even, necessarily, that it was Mr. Ransom who slapped her.''

''And in your view, there is nothing to show that Mr. Ransom was sexually aroused?''

''Objection,'' Paget said again. ''These questions have been asked and answered. Only this time they're leading.''

Masters nodded. ''True enough, Mr. Paget. But I'll allow Ms. Sharpe some leeway to summarize the evidence.''

''No,'' Shelton said to Sharpe. ''There's no evidence of sexual arousal.''

Sharpe paused. ''Nor,'' she said, ''do Mr. Ransom's fingernails suggest that it was *he* who scratched Ms. Carelli.''

"That's correct."

"Because the only fingernails with skin beneath them were Ms. Carelli's."

"Correct."

"And it was under *Ms. Carelli's* nails, not Mr. Ransom's, that you found traces of nylon fiber."

"Yes."

"Consistent with Ms. Carelli's panty hose."

"Yes."

Sharpe leaned back. "Based on the medical evidence, how would you characterize Ms. Carelli's story?"

Shelton gave her a considered look. "What I would say is that certain *parts* of Ms. Carelli's story—the gunshot distance in particular—are not consistent with the medical evidence. Everything else but the slap is unsupported."

Sharpe nodded. "Then let me pose you an alternative, based on the same medical evidence." She paused, voice rising in a rhythmic cadence. "Is it possible that Ms. Carelli murdered Mr. Ransom and did not call 911 until roughly forty minutes later, during which time she pulled his pants down, scratched his buttocks, scraped her own thigh and neck and tore her own panty hose, all the while concocting a phony defense of rape?"

"Objection!" Paget stood, walking forward amid the shocked murmur of those watching. "The question partakes of the fantasy I described in

Ms. Sharpe's opening statement. It's hypothetical, calls for speculation and, because it misstates, distorts, and selectively ignores the evidence, lacks any reasonable foundation. Put another way, it's moonshine.''

Judge Masters smiled thinly. ''And I suppose you don't like it, either. Most of what you say is valid, Mr. Paget—technically speaking. But we don't have a jury to protect from prejudice here, and I'm capable of according Dr. Shelton's response whatever weight I think it's worth.'' She paused. ''And for the record, I do think it's worth hearing.''

Turning, Paget saw Mary's face, suddenly fixed and white. Terri looked down; behind them, Carlo had a wounded, helpless expression. In the silent courtroom, Paget's walk back to counsel's table seemed to take too long.

He sat, arranging his face into a look of bored resignation.

''In my opinion,'' Shelton told Masters, ''the medical evidence is more consistent with Ms. Sharpe's hypothetical description than it is with Ms. Carelli's version of events.''

Sharpe nodded. With evident satisfaction, she said to Caroline Masters, ''That's all I have, Your Honor. At least for *this* witness.''

''Very well.'' Judge Masters looked at Paget. ''Does the defense have questions of this witness?''

''Yes, Your Honor. Quite a few, actually.''

The judge glanced at her watch. "We'll take lunch break, then. Back at one-thirty."

Without ceremony, Caroline Masters rose and walked off the bench.

The courtroom erupted. Paget stood there a moment, lost in thought. When he turned, Carlo had come to Mary and stood gazing down at her, trying to smile as she tried to smile back. They looked so much alike that it hurt Paget to see.

"Come on," he said to Teresa Peralta. "We've got work to do."

Paget rose from the defense table, walked forward a few feet, stopped to face Elizabeth Shelton. The spot that he had chosen was on the other side of Caroline Masters; as Shelton turned to face him, the judge watched them both. Until Paget spoke, there was no sound at all.

Quietly, he asked, "You don't know *what* happened between Mary Carelli and Mark Ransom, do you?"

Shelton appraised him for a moment. "No," she answered. "I wasn't there. I can only assess the medical evidence."

"So that you can't testify to whether or not there was a struggle."

"No."

Paget paused. "Or, for that matter," he asked

softly, "to whether Mr. Ransom attempted to rape Ms. Carelli."

"No." Shelton paused. "All that I can determine is whether the evidence tends to support Ms. Carelli's claim that an assault occurred."

Paget gave her a sideways glance. "Among that evidence is the swelling and bruise on Ms. Carelli's face, correct?"

"Yes."

"And at the time you examined her, you determined that this bruise had been forcibly inflicted."

Shelton paused; her intelligent face held a trace of puzzlement that she did not try to conceal. "Yes."

"And to your knowledge, the prosecution does not claim that Ms. Carelli *arrived* at Mark Ransom's suite in that condition, does it?"

"To my knowledge, no."

Paget nodded. "In your opinion, was the damage to Ms. Carelli's face inflicted by an open hand?"

"So I understand."

"By someone using his right hand?"

"Yes."

"And was Mr. Ransom right-handed?"

"So I understand."

Paget glanced up at Judge Masters. She was watching Shelton with an air of dispassionate interest; Paget imagined her remembering, perhaps without fondness, cases where Elizabeth Shelton had doomed Masters's clients to a verdict of guilty. He turned back to Shelton.

"Do you have a view," he asked, "as to whether the person who struck Ms. Carelli was right-handed?"

Shelton paused. It was a moment, Paget knew, where she could choose to hurt or help him: only Shelton knew whether or not she had an opinion, and unless she volunteered it, there was nothing Paget could do. His tension rose with each second of her silence.

"Yes," she said quietly.

"And what is that opinion?"

Shelton seemed to draw a breath. "That it is much more probable than not that the blow to Ms. Carelli was inflicted by a right-handed person."

Paget nodded. "And what are your reasons for that?"

"There are two, really. As a matter of habit, a right-handed person would strike such a blow with his right hand. The fact that it also involves violence, which in turn suggests spontaneity, reinforces the likelihood that the assailant was acting on instinct." Shelton paused. "The instinctive reflex of a right-handed person is obvious."

Paget watched her face. "There was a second reason, you said."

Quickly, Shelton glanced at Sharpe. "A more

marginal one,'' she answered. ''The blow was struck with considerable force. A right-handed person will have more power in his, or her, right hand and arm.''

Paget tilted his head. ''Incidentally, is Mary Carelli right- or left-handed?''

Shelton turned to Mary. In a cool, clear voice, she answered, ''Left-handed, I believe.''

Paget nodded. ''In your opinion, could Mary Carelli have inflicted this kind of damage by slapping herself?''

Shelton kept looking at Mary. ''That's *conceivable,*'' she finally said. ''But no, it's not very likely. It's never been my hypothesis that Ms. Carelli did this to herself.''

On the bench, Caroline Masters looked from Shelton to Mary. ''How many such blows,'' she asked, ''would it take to inflict more serious damage?''

Shelton turned, her face pensive. Paget sensed that, like Marnie Sharpe, Shelton was troubled by the thought that Mary was using the issue of rape to cover an act of murder but that, more than Sharpe, Shelton was also troubled by doubts she could not name. ''It's hard to say,'' she told Judge Masters. ''With repeated blows, the possibilities range from a fractured cheekbone, broken teeth, nose, or jaw, and, of course, a concussion.'' Shelton looked back to Mary. ''If the victim loses consciousness and falls, other injuries could result. Perhaps more serious.''

''What effect on the victim's consciousness and perceptions might such a blow cause?''

The judge was engaged now, Paget thought; Caroline Masters had not wholly lost the defense lawyer's habit of mind, and the question was a good one.

''Again,'' Shelton answered slowly, ''it's hard to say.''

''Would the possibilities include shock and an impairment of vision?''

Shelton considered her. ''Shock is a medical term, Your Honor, involving a cluster of symptoms I did not observe in Ms. Carelli. But some degree of disorientation is clearly possible.''

''So that the victim's perception of events, or memory of them, might be less precise?''

''That could happen, yes.''

''Thank you, Dr. Shelton.'' The judge turned back to Paget. ''Excuse me, Mr. Paget. The court was curious as to those points.''

''As were we.'' Paget wondered whether the judge's intervention was on Mary's behalf, out of concern for a possible victim, or whether Masters was settling some intellectual score with Shelton from another case. He moved closer to the witness stand, stopping when he had found his next line of inquiry. ''Following up on the court's questions, you take issue with Ms. Carelli's memory that the gun fired two or three inches from Mr. Ransom's chest, correct?''

''Yes.''

''But you concede that it *could* have fired from two or three feet?''

Shelton's voice turned colder. ''That would be the minimum distance, yes.''

Paget nodded. ''It is also true, is it not, that you cannot determine the angle from which the bullet was fired.''

''Not in this case, no.''

''Nor can you tell whether, at the moment of impact, Mr. Ransom was recoiling.''

''No.''

''Or leaning back for any reason.''

''No.''

Paget paused. At the margin of his vision he saw Mary hunch forward, as if to help him. ''So there is nothing in the medical evidence,'' he said, ''which precludes the possibility that in their struggle, the gun became pointed at Mr. Ransom and that he recoiled, shrinking away from it at the moment of discharge.''

Shelton gave him a calm, level gaze. ''I can't *preclude* it,'' she answered, ''but there are things which argue against that. Ms. Carelli claims that Mr. Ransom was wrestling her for the gun, and yet the only fingerprints we found on it were Ms. Carelli's.'' She paused, frowning. "Also, were he falling back with his hands in front of him, a shot from two or three feet would likely leave a residue of powder on his palms and fingers. We found none."

Paget hesitated. Shelton had just hurt him; lulled by her air of candor, he had forgotten how good she was. He struggled to find another question before he looked too rattled. "But you don't know," he managed, "whether Mr. Ransom was grasping the gun itself or Ms. Carelli's wrists."

"No."

"Nor do you know the position of his hands at the instant that the gun went off."

"No."

It was, Paget thought, the best he could do. "Let us move," he continued, "to other points of your direct testimony. You testified, did you not, that Ms. Carelli seemed lucid at the time that you first spoke to her."

"Yes."

"But you weren't present when Mr. Ransom died."

"No. Of course not."

"Then you have *no* understanding as to whether, from the moment of death until she called 911, Ms. Carelli was in shock. Or at least, as you put it, disoriented."

"No."

"So that, in contrast to Ms. Sharpe's hypothetical

scenario, in which Ms. Carelli spent that time in a state of hyperactivity, creating evidence and mutilating corpses, it is entirely possible that Ms. Carelli was seized by torpor and confusion."

"Objection," Sharpe cut in. "Mischaracterizes the prior testimony."

Masters gave her a quizzical look. "Does it? If so, not by much. Overruled."

"That is *possible,* yes." Shelton's voice became firm. "My answer to Ms. Sharpe's question was based on anomalies in the physical evidence. Anomalies which did not support Ms. Carelli's account of events between the time of Mr. Ransom's death and the call to 911."

"Speaking of which," Paget said, "have you ever heard the 911 tape of Ms. Carelli's call?"

Slowly, Shelton shook her head. "No. I have not."

Paget turned to Masters. "Your Honor, the prosecution has already stipulated to the admissibility of that tape. I would ask leave of the court to play it for Dr. Shelton."

"For what purpose?" Sharpe interjected. "Everyone acknowledges that Ms. Carelli placed the call and, moreover, that the call was *not* to Dr. Shelton. I don't know what you could possibly ask her about."

"It's simple," Paget responded. "Dr. Shelton has testified to Ms. Carelli's lucidity at the time of her arrival, based partly on her tone of voice and the content of her speech. I'd like her to compare her impressions of Ms. Carelli *then* to Ms. Carelli's earlier call to 911."

"I object," Sharpe answered. "We have not attempted to qualify Dr. Shelton as a voice interpreter. Or, for that matter, as a mentalist. Her earlier testimony was based on a doctor's physical impression of a woman sitting right in front of her."

"That's true," Masters answered, "but you also attempted to use Dr. Shelton's impressions, at least by implication, to cover Ms. Carelli's mental state for a good half day. I'm going to allow the tape to be played."

When Paget turned, Terri already had the tape recorder on the table in front of him. She smiled with her eyes: this line of questioning had been her suggestion. Beside her, Mary stared at the tape machine with a somewhat haunted look; Paget could not tell if this was because she did not wish to relive the moment of her call or was thinking of another tape, which she hoped never to see.

Terri switched on the tape recorder. As it spun, Paget suddenly saw Carlo, listening intently for the sound of his mother's voice.

The courtroom was silent.

"San Francisco Emergency," the male voice called out.

No one answered. The voice snapped again, ''San Francisco Emergency.''

There was yet more silence. Then, quite softly, Mary said, ''There's been an accident.''

In the courtroom, her tone was thin, uncertain. It was as if she were repeating a dream she vaguely remembered, to someone she did not know.

''What happened?'' the man asked.

''There's been an accident,'' she repeated. Her voice was weary; its tone said that her explanation was perfectly adequate and that he should listen more closely.

Listening, Caroline Masters narrowed her eyes, as if at some subtle alteration in her perception. The expression on Shelton's face was one of deep concentration.

On the tape, the man became more patient. ''What kind of accident?'' he asked.

There was a long pause. In a tone of disbelief, Mary said, ''A gun went off.''

Paget turned to Mary. Staring down at the table, she slowly shook her head. To Paget, the gesture bespoke a tragic wonderment, the helpless desire to reach back in time, change what had happened.

''Someone's been shot?''

''Yes.'' The voice quavered. ''I think he's dead.''

''Where are you?'' he demanded.

''The Hotel Flood.'' There was a long pause.

Then, in a tone of mystified apology, Mary said, "I can't remember the room."

"Who is this?"

"Wait," Mary interjected. "It's registered to Mark Ransom. A suite."

The last words held an odd note of relief, as if Mary had been frightened by a loss of memory.

"Who is this?" the voice demanded.

"Just come," Mary answered shrilly, and hung up.

When Paget gazed at Mary again, she had turned to Shelton with tears in her eyes. Shelton had lost color.

The audience was silent. A few shifted in their seats, some looked away. Paget was reminded of the eerie feeling he had once had, listening to the taped words of a flight crew in the moments before their airplane crashed.

Softly, he asked Shelton, "Does that sound like the woman you remember?"

Shelton gazed up. There was no good answer to the question; Mary's voice on the tape sounded shaky enough that to answer "yes" would make Shelton seem unfeeling. "No," Shelton said at last. "In person, she sounded somewhat different."

"How so?"

"When I saw her, she seemed to think slowly but to be in control." She paused. "The voice on the tape sounds more *distant,* I suppose. More overwhelmed."

"And the woman on the tape," Paget said, "was also much closer to the events the prosecution faults her for not remembering quite as well as it would like."

"Objection," Sharpe called out. "This time *I* don't hear a question."

"There was none," Caroline Masters said. "Do find a question, Mr. Paget. A proper one."

"Surely." Paget turned to Shelton again. "So you would concede," he pursued, "that her tone of voice in speaking to you does not mean that trauma didn't affect her behavior that evening—either alone with Mr. Ransom's body or answering questions from Inspector Monk?"

"I would concede that, for what it is worth." She gave Mary a cool, quiet gaze. "As Ms. Sharpe pointed out, I'm not a mentalist."

"Then we'll return to the physical evidence—which, I believe you testified, contained 'anomalies.' "

"Yes."

"And one of these anomalies was that, unlike Ms. Carelli, your test turned up no skin samples under Mr. Ransom's fingernails?"

"Yes."

Paget looked puzzled. "Did Mr. Ransom have long fingernails?"

Shelton paused. "No. Not at all."

"But Ms. Carelli did."

"Yes. In fact, she'd broken one."

Paget paused. "Isn't it easier to retrieve skin samples from someone with long fingernails?"

Shelton nodded. "Easier, yes. But it's common to do so with fingernails of ordinary length, from a man."

"Were Mr. Ransom's nails of 'ordinary length'?"

Shelton hesitated. "They were a bit shorter, I think. It appeared that he'd just clipped them."

"Might that affect the test?"

"It might, Mr. Paget. But if you take this line too far, one is left to wonder *how* Mr. Ransom managed to scratch Ms. Carelli."

There was a murmur in the courtroom; with one thrust, Shelton had stopped Paget's momentum and refocused attention on the prosecution's case. Stunned, Paget tried to summon a weary look, as if he had expected this. "It is nonetheless true," he said, "that your test doesn't always work."

"Yes. That's true."

"So that Mark Ransom could have scratched Mary Carelli and yet not collected enough skin beneath his nails to show up on his test."

"That's possible, yes." Shelton paused for emphasis. "But in the majority of cases, that test works. At least for scratches as deep as Ms. Carelli's."

Shelton had begun to fight him, Paget realized: partly out of professional pride and partly, he suspected, because whatever Shelton's doubt about the evidence, her experience told her that too much was wrong with Mary's story. He tried to search for a lower key. "One of the areas I found most troublesome," he said, "was that regarding Ms. Carelli's panty hose. I'd like to ask a few questions and see whether there might not be some other way to look at it."

Shelton gave a small shrug. "All right."

"You testified that you found nylon fibers, of the kind appearing in Ms. Carelli's panty hose, under *her* nails but not under Mr. Ransom's, is that correct?"

"Yes."

"And in part, it was based on that conclusion that you agreed with Ms. Sharpe that Ms. Carelli might have fabricated evidence."

"In part, yes."

Paget paused. "I don't know precisely how to broach this, Dr. Shelton, but putting on panty hose involves considerable effort, does it not?"

Shelton gave him a long, speculative gaze, which culminated in a slight change in her eyes. "It can," she said.

Paget nodded. "And in the course of that effort, it's a common thing for panty hose to rip."

Paget felt Masters's expression hover between interest and amusement, and then decide on interest.

Shelton's eyes narrowed slightly. "Yes," she said with an expert's gravity, "panty hose commonly rip." She paused. "At least in my observation."

"So that in the normal act of putting on panty hose, as Ms. Carelli did that morning, it would be possible to rip them."

"Yes. Of course."

"And it would also be possible, in the normal course of putting on panty hose, for Ms. Carelli to get fibers of nylon under her fingernails."

Shelton watched him. "Yes."

"Common, even?"

She hesitated. "I suppose not uncommon."

Turning, Paget nodded to Terri, whose questions these were. Then he looked out at the media people, crowding the benches between the cameras and behind the dock of the court. Perhaps half, as he already knew, were women; most wore skirts or dresses. "I wonder, Dr. Shelton, if you could cast an eye with me on the representatives of the media."

"Objection." Sharpe stood. "I don't know what diversion Mr. Paget intends, but we've moved far afield from the evidence surrounding Ms. Carelli's shooting of Mark Ransom."

"You really don't know what Mr. Paget intends, Ms. Sharpe?" Masters paused, eyes sweeping the press. "*I* know, and I'm curious about the answer. If only because this is yet another indignity to which women are subjected."

Sharpe flushed. "I don't find much amusement here, Your Honor."

"Nor do I, Counsel. And as I understand Mr. Paget's underlying point, it's very serious indeed."

"Thank you, Your Honor." Paget turned back to Shelton. "Taking a rough count of the press, I'd guess that around fifty or so are women. Would you agree?"

"I haven't counted. Sitting here, I see a number."

Paget nodded. "And what percentage of those women reporters," he asked softly, "would have nylon fibers under their nails if you subjected them to the same test that you administered to Ms. Carelli?"

Paget watched the faces in front of him focus on Elizabeth Shelton; beneath the particulars of the question, Paget sensed the press absorbing its subliminal impact—the instinctive fear of being falsely accused. "I have no idea what percentage," Shelton answered.

"But certainly some."

"In all probability. At least a few."

"None of whom, we can assume, murdered anyone on the way to the courthouse."

Shelton looked out at the faces as if searching for suspects. Without smiling, she answered, "I assume not."

"Thank you. Having eliminated the media as suspects, I'd like to return to Ms. Carelli. You've already agreed that she could have gotten nylon fibers under her nails simply by putting on her panty hose." His voice softened. "But it is also possible, is it not, that Ms. Carelli could have grasped the panty hose in an effort to stop Mark Ransom from pulling them off."

For a long time, Shelton simply stared at him. "Yes," she said finally. "That's also possible."

"And these various possibilities tend to undercut Ms. Sharpe's hypothesis that Ms. Carelli manufactured evidence."

Shelton looked pensive. "They *cast doubt,*" she corrected, "on one element of that hypothesis. But in addition to the absence of skin under Mr. Ransom's nails, we also have the absence of semen and the apparent infliction of postmortem scratches on Mr. Ransom's buttocks."

Paget nodded. "Let's take the semen first. That test is hardly foolproof, is it?"

"No test is. But in the vast majority of cases, erections cause secretions well before ejaculation."

"But not in all cases."

"No."

"And even in cases where there *may* have been secretions, your test is not one hundred percent?"

"No." Shelton sat straighter, a note of professional challenge entering her voice. "But you may have noticed, Mr. Paget, that your questions presume an unusual confluence of test failures. I believe that our tests are better than that and, for that matter, that *we* are.''

Paget paused. He was coming to the most delicate part of his examination; he could not afford to antagonize Dr. Shelton. ''I was not suggesting,'' he said easily, ''that you and your office are not highly professional. Merely that your office handles the cases you are given and that this particular prosecution case is highly circumstantial.''

Sharpe rose again. ''Mr. Paget complained about speeches. I'd like to register my own complaint. Particularly when Mr. Paget's only purpose is to attack the prosecution.''

Paget turned to Sharpe. ''My only purpose,'' he said, ''was to clarify any misunderstanding. In the course of which I thought it appropriate to distinguish between *Dr. Shelton's* professional competence and *your* case.''

Masters leaned forward. ''That's quite enough, Mr. Paget. Press on.''

''Thank you, Your Honor.'' Paget turned back to Shelton. ''Am I correct in understanding, Dr. Shelton, that a significant part of the prosecution hypothesis regarding fabricated evidence are the scratches on Mark Ransom's buttocks?''

Shelton considered him. ''It's a part, yes. I wouldn't care to characterize its significance.''

''But you concede, do you not, that you could be

mistaken—that the scratches could have occurred *before* Mark Ransom died.''

''Again, it's possible. But based on the lack of bleeding, the absence of damaged capillaries, I believe that the scratches occurred *after* Mr. Ransom died.''

Paget looked at her. ''Are you familiar, Dr. Shelton, with the procedures employed by paramedics in answering a call to 911?''

''Yes, I am.''

''And is there a uniform procedure in San Francisco County when they first attend the victim?''

''Yes. Unless the condition of the body makes it obvious that the person is dead, the paramedics *must* try to revive him or her. That means attempt to get a heartbeat, putting on pads.''

''And did they do that to Mark Ransom?''

''I understand that they did.'' Shelton paused. ''Mark Ransom had a single wound; under the guidelines, they could *not* conclude that he was dead.''

''And that would involve checking Mark Ransom's heartbeat?''

''Among other things, yes.''

Paget summoned a puzzled expression. ''But at the time you examined Mr. Ransom, wasn't he lying facedown on the carpet?''

''Yes.'' Shelton hesitated. ''My understanding is

that they rolled him over. But once they determined that Mr. Ransom was dead, they restored his body to the position in which they found it."

Paget nodded. "In other words, they found him on his stomach, flipped him on his back, and flipped him on his stomach again. Is that correct?"

"That is my understanding, yes. Less elegantly put."

"And in doing so, they had to handle Mr. Ransom's body."

Shelton's eyes narrowed. "Yes."

"The body of a man who, according to your report, weighed roughly two hundred and twenty-five pounds."

"That was his weight, yes."

"And they do all this quite rapidly, correct?"

"They *should*. On the assumption that the victim may still be alive."

Paget paused for a moment, looking from Caroline Masters, intent and quite still, back to Elizabeth Shelton. "Isn't it possible," he asked softly, "that the *paramedics* inflicted those scratches on Mr. Ransom's buttocks?"

Shelton stared at him a moment. There was silence; then, at length, she nodded. It seemed less an answer to Paget's question than a gesture of admiration. "Yes," she answered finally. "I don't know how likely it is, but that's possible."

"And, it is fair to say, the existence of that possibility undermines the hypothesis Ms. Sharpe posed to you?"

"To a point." When Shelton spoke again, her words were softer, directed at Paget alone. "But if Mark Ransom scratched Mary Carelli, and the paramedics scratched Mark Ransom, whose skin was under Mary Carelli's nails?"

The thrust was so perfect, its delivery so sincere, that Paget felt the entire painstaking cross-examination slide slowly out from under him. He did not need the courtroom murmur to know how badly she had wounded him. Was grateful, even, that it gave him time to think.

Masters's gavel landed. "Mr. Paget," she inquired. "Do you have anything more?"

"Just a couple of questions," he said casually. "You've named two possibilities for the origin of the skin beneath Ms. Carelli's nails. The first is that she scratched Mr. Ransom, which, although you posit it happened after his death, could have happened before. Is that correct?"

"Yes."

"You also posit that Ms. Carelli may have scratched herself in an effort to manufacture evidence."

"Yes."

"Isn't there a third possibility?"

Shelton gave him a guarded look. "Such as?"

Paget moved forward. "That in the struggle to

keep her panty hose on—in her struggle to prevent this man from raping her—Ms. Carelli scratched her own thigh.''

Shelton frowned a moment, staring at her lap; Paget felt her reviewing the evidence, less for this specific question than to ask herself what was fair. Then she looked up at him again.

''Yes,'' she answered softly. ''That's possible.''

Paget felt his own relief. ''Thank you, Dr. Shelton,'' he said. ''That's all I have.''

She nodded, giving him a faint smile, and then Paget sat down.

Sharpe was quickly on her feet. ''I was struck, Dr. Shelton, by something you said. I believe it was—and I paraphrase—that Mr. Paget's questions presume an unusual confluence of test failures. What did you mean by that?''

Shelton thought for a moment. ''What I meant to say was that for Ms. Carelli's account to be right would involve a sequence of botched tests and skewed judgments involving this office, as well as a high degree of coincidence.''

Sharpe nodded. ''Specifically, it would require the tests to have missed skin under Mr. Ransom's fingernails.''

''Yes.'' Shelton corrected herself. ''Although it's not uncommon that there is no skin to find.''

Sharpe frowned. ''But it would also,'' she prodded, "assume that the tests missed evidence of sexual arousal."

"Yes."

"And for Mr. Ransom to have no gunshot residue on his hands, despite Ms. Carelli's account of their struggle."

"Yes."

"And for him to be rearing back when she shot him."

Shelton nodded. "Yes."

"And for Ms. Carelli to have ripped her own panty hose."

"That's all true."

"And unless Mr. Ransom's scratches were caused by paramedics, it would also require for you to be wrong about *when* they were inflicted."

"Again, yes."

Sharpe looked incredulous. "Have you *ever* been that wrong?"

Shelton tilted her head. "I certainly hope not."

"And in your opinion, what does all that render Ms. Carelli's story?"

For a long moment, Shelton looked across at Mary. "Medically implausible," she said quietly. "To my regret, I simply don't believe her."

THREE

MARY CARELLI SEARCHED Carlo's face.

They sat at a corner table in the Café Majestic, an elegant Victorian room with ceiling fans and a pianist playing quietly in the background. As she had expected, the other diners shot them glances of recognition. But she had asked Carlo to dinner despite the possibility of this; the one thing that had disturbed her more than Elizabeth Shelton's last words was the way that Carlo had tried to cheer her.

Mary wished he had not come to court. But she did not want him to feel that his presence was a burden; Chris had made the decision, and it was done. "I haven't told you," she said finally, "how much it means to have you with me. The problem is that I'm not used to depending on anyone, so I end up feeling guilty." Smiling faintly, she finished: "Assuming that's a phrase I should be using."

She watched him attempt a smile of his own. As best he could, Carlo was trying to love someone he no longer knew; in the face of what Marnie Sharpe had placed before him, Mary found this both touching and painful. "You'll be all right," Carlo said finally. "Dad forced her to back off a lot."

The comment carried wistful undertones, as if Carlo hoped that his father's determination meant that *he* believed in Mary. But all that Mary could do was to tell Carlo that she believed in Christopher Paget. "He's doing a wonderful job," she answered. "He has a hard case, you know."

Carlo gave her a querying glance. "How do you mean?"

Mary steeled herself. Her job was to make him believe that she was unburdening herself, rather than trying to spare him something. "There are things I didn't tell the police," she said softly. "For reasons of my own. Chris's problem with me is that he's guessed that."

It hurt to see him struggling to be stoic and adult; once more, Mary questioned the delicate judgment involved in having Paget represent her. In a flat voice, Carlo asked, "Is it too late to tell him?"

"For some things, far too late." Mary paused. "Whatever my reasons *then,* Carlo, I have very good ones *now.* Please just accept that."

Carlo nodded slowly. "Okay."

Mary watched him wonder. She had not known how hard it would be to forfeit her son's trust, how deeply he had captured her. But she must leave Carlo with at least one parent to be proud of.

"There is one thing," she said, "that I do need *you* to know about."

It seemed to reach him. "You're my mother," he answered. "Whatever you need to say to me, it's all right."

By instinct, Mary shrank from thinking of herself in terms of need. But it was better for Carlo to think she needed him than to understand that it was his needs that were driving her. She put her hand on his. "There's a tape," she said, "of me talking to a psychiatrist. Mark Ransom had it."

Carlo had not yet learned Paget's pose that surprise was beyond his emotional range; alarm and confusion crossed his face before he found composure. "Does the D.A. know?" he asked.

"Yes. They think that's why I killed him." She paused. "There'll be a recess tomorrow or the next day. For a conference in chambers, while your father tries to keep the tape out of evidence."

"So Dad already knew?"

"*Now* he knows. But only because they found it." Mary kept her voice level; don't show him how hard this is, she told herself, or how scared you are of what Marnie Sharpe could do. "It concerns my time as a lawyer," she finished. "Things I'm deeply ashamed of."

"But to *kill* over it? That's what they think?"

"The tape would ruin my career." Mary gave a

thin smile. "I seem to have given some people the impression that would be enough."

Carlo shook his head; Mary could not tell whether it was in disbelief that anyone would think that or at what she had just told him.

"That *isn't* enough," she said softly. "Not to murder someone."

Carlo was silent for a time. "And the things Dad *doesn't* know. . . ?"

"Belong to me."

Carlo was staring at her hand, still on his. Then he turned it, so that her hand rested in his palm, and closed his fingers around hers.

His silent simple gesture brought Mary close to tears. "While Chris is trying to defend me," she said quietly, "there are certain things he doesn't ask and things he doesn't need to know. What I wanted *you* to know is that his problems as a lawyer are far worse than you can see. Worse, even, than he may know." Her voice grew softer yet. "For that you can blame me."

Mary saw his perceptions shift again, a kind of relief running through him. Realized, with sadness and satisfaction, how much this boy's sense of himself had come from Christopher Paget.

"He's been a good father," she said. "Hasn't he?"

"Yes. He has."

To Mary, he seemed glad of the change of subject,

and to know that he could speak well of Paget without offending her. As for her, she felt exhausted—anything was a better subject than the things she could not tell anyone, Carlo most of all.

"Does Chris have any kind of social life?" she asked. "I really have no idea."

Carlo's look mingled surprise with a certain amusement. "Do you mean a woman? Or just going to cocktail parties and stuff like that?"

"Women, I suppose." Mary paused. "I just wonder what he's been doing with himself all these years."

"He doesn't tell *me* much. But there are always one or two women around, usually good-looking and smart and with great jobs. He just never seems to get attached to them." Carlo shrugged. "Maybe some of it is that he's a parent, and a lot of the people he's gone out with don't have kids. But there's a part of him I think they never really get to see."

"Like me, I'm told." Mary smiled. "If you asked either of us to get in touch with our feelings, we'd probably need a map."

Carlo gave her a mischievous look. "Then for all either of you knows, you're still in love."

Mary laughed. "He's not *that* out of touch," she said in a facetious tone. "And the part of me *I* know about can't stand him." She paused again, voice softer. "It's funny, though. When I first knew Chris, I thought he was the most arrogant man I'd ever met, as strong-willed as I was, and certain of his own rightness. He seems so much more human now, more aware of his own flaws—even when he's being an absolute bastard.'' She smiled a little, shaking her head. ''The strange thing is, instead of liking that, it makes me a little sad. Like we've both gotten older.''

Carlo reflected for a moment. ''It's hard to think of him as older. To me, he's always looked the same. Ever since I first came here.''

His last phrase, outwardly careless, seemed to ask Mary why she had let him go. She searched for something else to say. ''What was Andrea like—his wife?''

''I don't remember much, except that I thought she looked kind of like you.'' He considered a moment and then shrugged; it seemed a teenage gesture of incuriosity, dismissing things that had nothing to do with him. ''I think they just kind of drifted apart.''

Mary nodded. Carlo had been young enough, and Paget sensitive enough, that the boy had never blamed himself. ''Perhaps he'll find someone else.''

''I don't know.'' Carlo seemed to reflect. ''The one I think he really likes is Terri, and she only works for him. Besides,'' he added, as if this closed the subject, ''she's got a husband and a five-year-old kid.''

Mary smiled. It was surely not her place to say what instinct told her: that Teresa Peralta was falling in love with Christopher Paget, husband or no, and whether or not Terri would ever permit herself to face that. ''Chris and Terri can still be friends, you know. It doesn't have to be passion.''

He gave her a wry look. ''Now you sound like Dad. Listen to him sometimes, and sex doesn't matter at all. Especially for me.''

Mary laughed. ''That's not how *I* remember Chris.'' The thought stopped her, and then other images ran through her mind—a night in Washington, an afternoon in Paris—much more bitter and more lasting. She stifled them, recaptured her smile. ''We were a disaster as a couple,'' she said. ''But when it came to picking a father for you, I did pretty well.''

Carlo raised his water glass. ''Then here's to all of us.'' He paused, then added, ''I know you're going to win, Mom.''

What she could not tell him, Mary thought, was that winning and losing had many faces. That when she had awakened the night before, sweating yet cold in a room that at first she did not recognize, her nightmare had been not of prison or disgrace but of Carlo Carelli Paget, listening to the tape they must never find.

Mary touched her glass to Carlo's. ''To all of us,'' she said. ''And, most of all, to you.''

FOUR

THE ROOM SERVICE waiter was a dapper Hispanic in his mid thirties, Paul Aguilar, with a black mustache, slicked-back hair, and a confident smile. The act of testifying before the world seemed not to bother him at all.

"Can you identify," Sharpe asked, "the woman you saw with Mr. Ransom?"

Her manner was relaxed; Paget guessed that she had worked with Aguilar extensively, and that he made a good witness.

"The defendant, Miss Carelli." Aguilar straightened in his chair, pointing at Mary. "Even without seeing her on television, Miss Carelli would be hard to forget."

"How gallant," Mary murmured to Paget. On the other side of him, Terri watched Aguilar intently; Paget sensed that he already concerned her.

"Once Mr. Ransom let you in, what happened next?"

"The usual thing. I asked him where to place the

champagne bucket, and he said the coffee table. So I put it there in front of Miss Carelli.''

"At that time, did Ms. Carelli say anything to you?''

"Nothing, except to thank me.'' He smiled, as if in pleasure at this brush with the famous. "She seemed very nice.''

"Was there anything unusual in her manner?''

"No. She was just like I'd expect her to be.''

"And how was that?''

"Classy.'' Aguilar seemed to wrinkle his nose at the word. "That's not exactly what I mean. Very poised, very relaxed, like someone who always knows what to do.''

Sharpe, Paget realized, was asking Aguilar to paint a word picture of a woman at ease, self-possessed and unconcerned. He made the snap judgment not to object.

"Did she seem worried about anything?''

Aguilar's shrug said that the thought had never occurred to him. "Not that I saw.''

"Or unfriendly to Mr. Ransom?''

"No.'' He gave a smile of bemusement, as if still deciphering Ransom's death. "She didn't look hostile at all. I thought they were friends, spending a few hours alone.'' He smiled again. "In my business, you see that a lot.''

On the bench, Masters frowned. "He's making this seem like a date,'' Mary whispered to Paget.

Paget turned to her slightly, still watching Masters. "I'd make it look worse by complaining," he whispered back. "Let's hope that this guy hangs himself."

"Did Mr. Ransom say anything?" Sharpe was asking.

Aguilar nodded vigorously. "I said something to *him* about how much I liked his books. So he told me that compliments like that were what kept him writing. He made me feel good I'd spoken up." He gave a sheepish smile. "I'm a room service waiter, you know. It's not my place to push myself on people."

With one innocuous question, Paget thought, Sharpe had made both Ransom and Aguilar seem more human. He felt Mary tense beside him.

Sharpe paused for a moment, as if preparing some ultimate thrust. "During this time," she asked, "did you happen to notice whether the sitting room blinds were closed or open?"

"Open. Definitely."

"And how are you so sure?"

Aguilar smiled. "Because I remember Mr. Ransom had a nice view of Berkeley, across the bay. So I looked out, imagining I could see my cousin's old house." He turned, explaining to Masters, "I used to spend a lot of time with him. My cousin, I mean."

Caroline Masters nodded. To Paget, her expression said that Aguilar's charm was lost on her;

quickly, Paget adjusted his impression of how far he could go on cross.

"Before you left," Sharpe continued, "did Mr. Ransom do anything else?"

"He signed the check, of course." Aguilar smiled again. "Then he gave me a nice tip, clapped me on the back, and winked."

"He winked?"

"Yes. Like to tell me he was lucky." He spread his arms, as if to affirm the pleasure of life itself, the understanding of one man for another. "You know, that he's alone with this beautiful woman and feeling good."

Masters's frown had deepened. She turned to Aguilar. "Are you sure he didn't have something in his eye?"

Aguilar looked puzzled, as if Judge Masters did not appreciate this moment of shared humanity. "No," he said. "It was a wink."

"I see," Masters said in her flattest voice. "Go ahead, Ms. Sharpe."

Sharpe gazed at her for a moment. When Terri turned to him, Paget whispered, "I don't think Caroline will be checking into the Flood very soon. At least not without bringing her own champagne."

But Sharpe was moving closer to the witness, with an air of expectancy Paget did not like. "Before you left," she asked quietly, "did either Mr. Ransom or Ms. Carelli say anything else?"

Aguilar nodded. ''Yes. Miss Carelli did.''

''And what did she say?''

Aguilar turned to Mary, as if Sharpe had trained him to do so. Softly, he said, ''To hang out the privacy sign.''

Sharpe paused, letting the moment sink in. There was a first faint murmur in the courtroom, and then Sharpe asked, ''Did Ms. Carelli say why?''

''No.'' A rueful shake of the head. ''If a woman wants to be alone with a man, I don't ask why.''

Sharpe nodded, as if he had said something profound. Then she turned to Masters. ''No further questions.''

Masters was gazing at Mary. As Masters looked away, Paget whispered to Mary, ''Is that true?''

Mary still watched Masters. ''Yes,'' she murmured. ''It is.''

Paget turned from the witness, listening as Johnny Moore bent forward from the first row, whispered his advice. Nodding, Paget stood and then walked toward Aguilar. ''Good morning,'' he said pleasantly.

Aguilar nodded; the impression was of a relaxed and friendly man in a service business, meeting another member of the public. ''Good morning, sir.''

''*Was* it morning,'' Paget asked abruptly, ''or afternoon when you went to Ransom's suite?''

Aguilar blinked. "Morning, I think. Late morning."

"And you worked from seven to five that day, correct?"

"That's my usual shift."

"That covers breakfast, lunch, and early dinner, correct?"

"Yes."

Paget gave him a curious look. "Have you any idea how many rooms you visited that day?"

"No."

"A lot?"

Aguilar furrowed his brow. "A fair number."

"If I told you that my investigator had checked the room service slips with your name on them and counted forty-three, would that seem out of line?"

"No. I keep busy—it could have been that many."

"Other than Mr. Ransom's suite, can you describe the occupants of any other rooms you served that day?"

"No." Aguilar paused. "It was fresher then. You know, the first time I talked to the police."

"But you also talked to my investigator, Johnny Moore, two days later. Is that correct?"

"I remember Mr. Moore. Yes."

"And do you also remember Mr. Moore asking the same question I just did: whether you recalled anyone else you served that day?"

"I guess so."

"And your answer was the same, wasn't it—you didn't remember anyone else, did you?"

Aguilar folded his arms. "I guess I didn't. These people were celebrities."

Paget moved close, ignoring the last sentence. "Nor," he asked softly, "did you remember whether anyone else had the shades up or down, did you?"

Aguilar began to look unhappy. "No," he said. "Mr. Ransom's room was the one I remember."

Paget nodded. In a tone of sudden understanding, he said, "Because you recalled looking out at Berkeley."

Aguilar leaned forward, as if eager to seize on the reason Paget had given him. "That's right."

"Do you make it a habit to look out at Berkeley? That is, when you get the chance?"

"When I think about it." Aguilar smiled. "The views in the Mission District, where *I* live, aren't so hot."

Paget smiled back. "Do you happen to recall," he asked pleasantly, "how many rooms you visited that day that had views of Berkeley from the tenth floor or above?"

Aguilar stared at him. "No."

"Twelve rooms," Paget said in the flat voice of authority. "And three suites. All with views of Berkeley. Does that sound right to you?"

Aguilar paused, giving him a trapped, wary look. "Could be."

"Must have been quite a nostalgic day for you," Paget observed.

"Your Honor," Sharpe called out. "That wasn't a proper question, and this has gone too far."

"It wasn't," Masters agreed, "and this has. Move it along, Mr. Paget."

The judge did not, Paget saw, look particularly annoyed. "Are you still quite sure," he asked Aguilar, "that *Mr. Ransom's* shades were open?"

"Yes."

"Because it is one of fifteen rooms you saw that day with a scenic view of Berkeley?"

"No." Aguilar's voice was emphatic. "Because of Miss Carelli."

"Miss Carelli." Paget stretched out the name. "Yes, she does seem to have captured your imagination."

Paget lent the last three words a faint sardonic edge. Caroline Masters caught it, he saw; a fleeting smile came and went. But Aguilar did not seem to follow him.

"Yes," he agreed, "I remembered her."

"How long were you in that room, Mr. Aguilar?"

Aguilar shook his head. "No way I can recall."

"You're trained, are you not, to get in and out of a room quickly?"

"Yes. People like their privacy."

"And all you had to do in this case was set down an ice bucket and two glasses, is that right?"

"And have Mr. Ransom sign the check."

"A simple job, right?"

"I would say so."

"So that if you told Mr. Moore that you had been in Mr. Ransom's suite for about a minute and a half, would that still sound right?"

Aguilar paused. "I guess so," he finally said.

"So that your testimony for Ms. Sharpe this morning is based on roughly ninety seconds in one of forty-three hotel rooms you visited that day. Is that correct?"

Aguilar's mouth set in a stubborn line. "I remember what I saw."

"And what you saw, you believe, was that Ms. Carelli seemed 'relaxed'?"

"Yes." Aguilar nodded. "She seemed comfortable with Mr. Ransom."

Paget stared at him. "Did they actually say anything to each other?"

Aguilar looked from Paget to Johnny Moore, sitting next to Carlo in the front row. "Not that I remember."

"Or say anything to you *about* each other?"

"No. Not that."

"Or touch each other?"

Aguilar stared at him. "No."

"Or even smile at each other?"

"No."

"In other words, each of them *talked* only to you, and *smiled* only at you, and yet you concluded they were 'relaxed' with each other."

"Mr. Ransom did order champagne, sir." Aguilar paused. "And then he winked at me."

Paget smiled. "Are you sure, Mr. Aguilar, that Mr. Ransom wasn't simply attracted to *you?*"

There was a ripple of laughter. Aguilar looked indignant. "Of course not."

"Really? But he *touched* you too, correct?"

"He clapped me on the back."

Paget shook his head. "I wasn't there, Mr. Aguilar, but it sounds pretty suggestive to me. Seems like a good thing you got in and out of there in ninety seconds."

The courtroom erupted in laughter. Sharpe was quickly on her feet. "Objection, Your Honor. Mr. Paget is badgering this witness."

"Really?" Masters asked her. "According to the testimony *you* just elicited, within a couple of minutes Mr. Aguilar served some champagne, sized up Ms. Carelli, observed the state of the windows, relived a few childhood memories, offered his views on literature, and did a little male bonding with Mr. Ransom. I'd love to know what happened in the other forty-two rooms."

Paget found himself laughing with everyone else.

Sharpe waited for the sound to die. "With respect, Your Honor, that summary is unfair to this witness. And it misses two central points: that the blinds were open when Ms. Carelli *arrived* and that, when Mr. Aguilar *left,* she asked him to ensure her privacy."

Masters nodded. "In my fascination with Mr. Aguilar's interpretive powers, I forgot to mention that I was sustaining your objection." She turned to Paget. "I understand your point, Mr. Paget: this witness's views regarding Mr. Ransom and Ms. Carelli are merely conjecture. Do you have anything else?"

Paget hesitated, disappointed; Masters's intervention, as favorable as it seemed, had saved the witness from potential devastation. Now he had to deal with the most difficult point of all. "It was your testimony, as I recall, that Ms. Carelli asked you to hang the privacy sign."

A vigorous nod. "That's right."

"After all this, are you sure it isn't possible that *Mark Ransom* asked you?"

"Positive."

Paget did not like the sound of that. "How can you be sure?"

"Because it stuck with me—Mr. Ransom winking, and then Miss Carelli *asking*. Like he *knew* it was going to happen, and she wanted that too."

Paget felt himself losing ground, asking questions he was not sure of in an effort to recoup. "Knew *what* was going to happen?"

"You know." Aguilar looked awkward. "Sexual intercourse. I mean, you couldn't read it any other way."

Paget tried to sound indignant. "Do you assume, Mr. Aguilar, that every time a man and a woman want to talk in private, it involves sex?"

"No," Aguilar protested. "I don't think that at all. But you see a man and a woman in a hotel suite at noon, the man ordering champagne and the woman asking to be alone, and you've got to figure the odds have just gone up. That's how *I* saw it, and *I've* got to figure that's how *Mr. Ransom* saw it. Which is why it stuck in my mind that Miss Carelli was the one that wanted privacy."

Paget felt like a fool. "You've got the edge on me there," he snapped, "by ninety seconds. But there are certain things you don't know, do you? Like whether Ms. Carelli simply wanted privacy to talk."

Aguilar eyed him. "No, I don't know," he finally said. "One way or the other."

"A judicious answer," Paget said coldly. He turned to Masters. "I'm through with this witness, Your Honor."

She nodded, giving Aguilar a speculative gaze. "Redirect, Ms. Sharpe."

"No, thank you, Your Honor." Sharpe smiled faintly. "Since my last objection, I've been content with the job Mr. Paget has done on our behalf."

* * *

"Which is it?" Terri murmured. "Ransom never got it up, or Mary the seductress?"

"Both," Paget whispered back. "Marnie's idea must be that Mary lulled Ransom into being all alone, then shot him."

Terri nodded. Together, they watched John Hassler take the stand.

He was a pleasant, open-faced man in his late forties, an insurance executive from Chicago with a twenty-year marriage and two teenage daughters. Sharpe added to this estimable life the fact that Hassler was a guest at the Flood on the day that Mark Ransom died, and then asked, "In fact, Mr. Hassler, weren't you on the same floor as Mr. Ransom?"

"That's right. I met him in the elevator, coming up from breakfast when he was checking in."

"You recognized him?"

"With that face and all the red hair? Couldn't miss him. So I said hello." Hassler shook his head sadly. "He was a nice man—friendly. Polished but very engaging."

"How long did you speak to him?"

"For five minutes or so. We were walking in the same direction, so he invited me into his room. I was curious about the suites, so we sort of checked it out together." He paused. "As I said, a nice man."

"What did you talk about?"

Hassler's expression mixed pleasure with regret,

as if reflecting that this was one of the last encounters Mark Ransom had with anyone. ‘‘He showed me the suite—which was quite spacious—and talked about some writers from Chicago whom he knew. He was very complimentary of them, and of the city. Then he looked at his watch and gave sort of an embarrassed smile. He said he wished that we could chat more but that he had to take a shower.’’ Hassler shot a glance at Mary. ‘‘He told me that a woman was coming to his suite in an hour or so, and he didn’t want to smell like an airplane breakfast.’’

‘‘Did he tell you why she was coming?’’

‘‘No.’’ Hassler paused. ‘‘But the way he looked and sounded, it wasn’t business. At least he didn’t give me any reason to believe it was.’’

‘‘Did he say whom he was seeing?’’

Hassler shook his head. ‘‘No. Just that I’d know her if I saw her. He sounded pretty pleased with himself—I must admit I was curious.’’

Paget glanced at Mary; through the stoic mask, her eyes flashed anger and contempt. On the bench, Masters wore a slight frown, directed at no one.

‘‘What happened then?’’ Sharpe asked Hassler.

‘‘Nothing. We just shook hands, and I went around the corner to my room.’’

‘‘How long were you there?’’

‘‘I had a business lunch at one, so it was maybe a couple of hours. I read some memos and worked the phones a little.’’

"Did you ever see Mr. Ransom again?"

Hassler looked down. "No. Later that night, after I heard, it was like someone walking over my grave."

"Did you ever see the woman who came to his room?"

Hassler hesitated. "Yes. I *think* so."

"Could you explain?"

Slowly, Hassler nodded. "It was about noon, and I'd gotten bored with the stuff I was reading. So I got up, yawning and stretching a little, staring out my window without anything much in mind.

"It wasn't a very good view. The Flood is shaped kind of like a block U, with two wings facing each other and surrounding an inner courtyard. I was on the end of one wing, so all I could see was the opposite wing and a few rooms on the right side of the U, where Mark Ransom was staying." Hassler paused. "I guess at some point it occurred to me to wonder which windows belonged to his suite. Seeing as how I'd been there."

"Did you do that?"

"Uh-huh. I began sort of counting windows, trying to remember how far along the back of the U his suite was." He paused. "That was when I saw her."

"Her?"

"Yes." Hassler glanced at Mary. "A woman, with long black hair. Standing in a window."

"What did she do?"

"She seemed to look out for a minute, as if she was staring at the bay. Then she pulled down the blinds, and I couldn't see her anymore." He averted his gaze from Mary. "But I figured it was the woman who'd come to see Mark Ransom."

"And why was that?"

"The position of the windows, for one thing. It seemed right."

Sharpe paused for a moment. "Was there anything else?"

"Uh-huh."

"And what was that?"

Hassler looked down. In a quiet voice, he said, "She was undressed."

There were whispers in the courtroom; quickly, Masters gaveled for silence, face grim. Paget's mind seemed to have gone blank. The one thing he could think of was Carlo.

Pausing, Sharpe showed no emotion. "I want to be clear on this," she said. "You saw her through a full-length window, am I correct?"

"Yes." Hassler glanced at Mary. "The woman I saw wasn't wearing anything. Nothing at all."

"How did you know that?"

Hassler looked away again. "There was a patch of black between her legs."

"Pubic hair," Sharpe said flatly.

Hassler sighed. His voice sounded feeble. "It was a long way off, but yes. Pubic hair."

Beneath the table, Paget realized, Mary's fingers grabbed his suit jacket. Her face was flushed.

"This window," Sharpe asked. "How many windows was it from the end?"

"Three, I believe."

Sharpe nodded. "And did we later show you Mark Ransom's suite, and three suites on either side?"

"Yes."

"And did you count the windows?"

"Yes."

"And what did you discover?"

Now Hassler looked quite miserable. "What I discovered," he answered, "was that Mark Ransom's sitting room contained the third window from the right."

Paget rose. Quickly, he said, "The window you looked at was at least one hundred fifty feet from your own, was it not?"

Hassler nodded; the look he gave Paget was half ashamed, half apologetic. "I would think that's fair."

"So you couldn't see her face, correct?"

"Not at all." He explained, "I *could* see height and coloring."

"Anything else?"

"Only that the woman was slender."

"Let me show you something."

Quickly, Johnny Moore had the easel out again;

another picture appeared, this time the distant color image of a dark-haired woman, gazing out a window at the Flood. "Your Honor," Paget said, "we're prepared to establish that Mr. Moore took this photograph through the window of Mr. Hassler's hotel room and that the woman in the picture was standing in Mark Ransom's suite."

Judge Masters turned to Marnie Sharpe. "Any objection?"

"Yes. I don't know what this is."

"True, at the moment. But I'm going to allow it, subject to proof. And unless you doubt Mr. Paget's word, you may wish to reach some sort of stipulation."

Sharpe frowned. "Very well, Your Honor."

Paget stepped forward. "Mr. Hassler, let me direct your attention to this photograph and then to the defense table."

Hassler looked from one to the other. "I have, sir. To both."

"All right. You'll note that *this* woman, although clothed, is standing in the full-length window, looking out as you described her. Does this approximate the view you had that day?"

"Yes. As I recall it."

"And can you identify the person in the picture?"

"No." Hassler looked embarrassed. "But like the woman I saw that day, her height and coloring resemble Ms. Carelli's."

Paget nodded. "So in your view, the woman in this picture bears the same resemblance to Ms. Carelli as the woman you saw?"

"Yes. It's hard to say, of course. But it could be the same woman."

"It could be, yes." For the first time, Paget smiled. "But actually it's Ms. Carelli's virtual twin. My associate, Ms. Peralta."

Masters gave a thin smile of her own. Paget turned to the defense table. "Would both of you mind standing?"

They did, Mary looking grim, Terri expressionless. "As you can see," Paget said to Masters, "the principal differences are Ms. Carelli's considerable height advantage, Ms. Peralta's lighter hair, and, as Ms. Carelli would be frank to admit, some fifteen years in age."

Judge Masters looked from the picture to Terri. "I've seen better likenesses, Teresa. But I suppose that's Mr. Paget's point. It's nice to have you in my courtroom, incidentally. Even in a nonspeaking part."

"Ms. Peralta will be speaking," Paget said, "when the defense puts on witnesses."

"Good, Mr. Paget. Not to denigrate your skills, of course." Masters paused. "I assume that you have more."

"Just a little." Paget turned back to Hassler. "Take another look at the picture, if you will. Given the distance between your window and those at the back of the U, can you even be certain that you're looking at a window on the precise same floor?''

Hassler cocked his head. ''Not from looking at this. No.''

''Or from looking through your window on the day in question? We are, after all, talking about a view from at least half the distance of a football field.''

Hassler considered that. ''No,'' he said finally. ''I can't be sure that I wasn't looking at someone on a floor above, or a floor below.''

''And in fact, didn't you assume that the woman you saw was in Mr. Ransom's suite because of what he *led* you to assume about his activities?''

Hassler looked confused. ''I'm not sure I know what you mean.''

''Let me put it another way. Would you have associated this woman with Mr. Ransom's suite if he hadn't implied to you he had some sort of date?''

Hassler's eyes narrowed. ''Maybe not,'' he said finally.

''Indeed, sitting here today, are you certain that the window you saw was the third window from the right?''

''I don't know.'' Hassler shook his head. ''After he was dead, these kinds of details become more important.''

''In truth, isn't what got your attention not the

sequence of the windows, or whose window it was, but the unexpected sight of a woman without clothes?''

Hassler looked chastened. ''It startled me, I'm sure.''

Paget paused. ''And attracted you?''

Hassler raised his head. ''I suppose so, Mr. Paget. Whoever it was, she was attractive. I'll admit to you that I didn't turn away.''

''Nor, after seeing her, did you count windows.''

''No.''

''So that you're not at all certain that the woman you saw was standing in Mark Ransom's suite.''

Hassler looked from Sharpe to Paget. ''No,'' he said in a hollow voice. ''I can't be sure.''

''Or even confident?''

''No.'' Hassler looked away. ''Not even that. What I saw was a naked woman. It could have been Mark Ransom's suite.''

''Or not.''

Hassler nodded. ''Or not.''

''It is also true, is it not, that you saw no one else through the window. *Not* Mark Ransom, or any other man.''

''That's true.''

''So that the faceless woman you saw could have been fresh from the shower, and quite alone.''

Hassler reflected. ''Yes, you're right. The woman I saw could have been alone.''

Paget paused for a moment. "Given all of these uncertainties," he asked, "and the potential prejudice to Ms. Carelli, why did you come forward?"

"I didn't *want* to." Hassler gave a helpless shrug. "But I met the man, and now he's dead. What could I do but tell the district attorney what I saw, and let them decide what to do with it?"

With a trace of weariness, as if his worst expectations had been confirmed, Paget slowly looked at Marnie Sharpe. Then he turned to the witness again. "Oh, you fulfilled *your* responsibilities," he said. "Thank you, Mr. Hassler. I have no further questions."

Sharpe was quickly up, an edge in her voice. "Did anyone, from either the police or the district attorney, coach you as to what you saw through the window of your hotel room?"

"Objection," Paget called out. "The scope of redirect is confined to matters addressed in cross-examination. Never once did my questions suggest that Ms. Sharpe suborned perjury."

Sharpe looked indignant. "Mr. Paget is deliberately misunderstanding, and overstating, the thrust of my question."

"Your Honor," Paget said to Masters, "let me make the thrust of *my* last question clear to Ms. Sharpe. My question implied—and I am now saying flat out—that it was shoddy for the People to prejudice Ms. Carelli's hearing by offering testimony which is at once so inflammatory and so flimsy. Period."

"All right, both of you." Masters turned to Sharpe. "I appreciate Mr. Paget's feelings, if not his every turn of phrase. We will likely never know *who* Mr. Hassler saw in that window, but we will surely *all* remember her mode of dress—as you no doubt intended."

Sharpe bristled; she had trouble, Paget realized, dealing with rebukes. "Our only intention," she said, "was to present evidence of what happened in that suite. I hope that the court will accept that."

"The court accepts that," Masters responded in a milder tone, "if not the probative value of this particular testimony. I'll allow the question, but I suggest that you wrap this up quickly."

"Very well, Your Honor." Sharpe turned to the court stenographer, a middle-aged black man who sat to the right of Masters. "Mr. Sanders, could you read back the question?"

He picked up the tape of paper from the machine, squinting at its shorthand symbols, and then read: "Ms. Sharpe: 'Did anyone, from either the police or the district attorney, coach you as to what you saw through the window of your hotel room?' "

Hassler shook his head. "No. Not at all."

Sharpe continued. "And what you described here is what you told our office on your own initiative?"

"Very definitely." Hassler paused. "I saw what I saw."

"And do you, despite the questions asked by Mr. Paget, continue to believe that it is more likely than not that the woman you saw was in Mark Ransom's suite?"

Hassler furrowed his brow. "More likely than not?" he asked Sharpe.

"That's my question, yes."

Hassler paused. "I'd have to say 'yes' to that," he finally answered.

Sharpe paused; Paget watched her decide that this was the most she could do. "No further questions," she said, and then Hassler left the stand, leaving Paget to wonder if the unclothed woman was Mary Carelli.

Edward Tench was a hawk-faced investment banker with dark-rimmed glasses, a crisply tailored suit, and an incisive air to match, as if he were accustomed to persuading conference rooms full of people to do what he wanted. He smoothed back his dark hair, straightened his red tie, and awaited Sharpe's next question.

"So that at about one o'clock," Sharpe asked, "you returned to your room at the Flood?"

"Yes," Tench answered. "I'd just finished an early business lunch and wished to call my office."

"And your suite was on the twenty-third floor. Mr. Ransom's floor."

"Yes."

"When you got off the elevator," Sharpe asked, "did you see anything?"

"Yes." Tench leaned forward, as if impatient with the structure of the questioning. "But perhaps I should explain its elevators. The elevator *I* took was at the far end of a long hallway, containing suites or rooms that face toward Berkeley. I was, I believe, two suites past Mark Ransom. So that I turned in the direction of his suite."

"Thank you," Sharpe said dryly. "And what did you see?"

"A woman, standing in front of the door to one of the suites."

"And what did this woman look like?"

Tench looked over at Mary. "From where I was standing, I couldn't see her face. But she was quite tall, about five feet eight, with long black hair."

"Do you recall what she was wearing?"

"I really don't, although I have the odd impression that she wasn't wearing shoes. What I do recall clearly is the shine of her hair, the way she carried herself—quite straight, like a model. There aren't many women who look like that from any angle."

A self-confident professional, Paget thought, determined to get the most out of what he knew, and then some. Without much material for cross, Tench would not be an easy witness—particularly, Paget added to himself, because the woman he saw was more than likely Mary Carelli.

"What did she do?" Sharpe asked.

"She stood there for a moment, staring at the door. Then, very abruptly, she stepped inside. It was as if she'd heard the elevator open and didn't want to be seen outside the room."

"Did someone let her in?"

"No," Tench said. "She let *herself* in."

For an instant, Paget imagined Mary Carelli standing in the hallway. But he could not imagine why she had been there.

"From her movements," Sharpe was asking, "did this woman appear to be injured in any way?"

"No, again. She moved very quickly." Tench paused. "I had the fleeting image of a dancer, perhaps a tennis player. A woman with confidence in her body."

"I'm going to enter a belated objection," Paget said. "I wonder if the witness could refrain from sharing with us his rich cultural experience and points of reference, and just stick to facts. Truly, I don't know whether this woman was a model, a dancer, an athlete or, for that matter, had recently had a steel rod implanted in her spine. And neither does this witness."

Masters smiled briefly and then turned to the witness. "In light of Mr. Paget's request, Mr. Tench, I wonder if you could confine yourself to what you actually saw."

"Of course, Your Honor." Tench looked vaguely thwarted. "I was only trying to be helpful. It's been my understanding that in the law, as with investment banking, one's experiences shape one's observations."

"Oh, they do," Masters agreed. "By the way, how long did you observe *this* woman?"

Tench seemed to reflect. "It couldn't have been long."

"Because from what you describe," Masters continued, "it sounds like ten seconds at the outside."

Tench looked nettled for a moment. "It was probably that."

"Oh, well," Masters rejoined. "One's experience can enhance the most fleeting observation. Press on, Ms. Sharpe."

Now Sharpe looked annoyed. It was a very good day for Caroline Masters, Paget thought, regardless of how the lawyers were doing; the first newspaper pieces about the judge were already starting to appear, and clips of her courtroom style would surely be featured on the nightly news. But how that might affect her, Paget could not guess.

"Your Honor," Sharpe finally said, "I wonder if I could ask Ms. Carelli to stand and turn her back to the witness."

"Mr. Paget?"

There was nothing he could do. "Certainly, Your Honor. Ms. Carelli would be pleased to turn her back to this witness."

Judge Masters smiled at one corner of her mouth. "Ms. Carelli," she said.

Mary rose, gazing at the witness. Then, slowly, she turned from him.

She could not help it, Paget realized; the image of a dancer or a model leapt easily to mind. For a strange moment, he remembered her standing naked in front of the Vasarely in his apartment, quite graceful and quite straight.

Now, in what seemed to be a lifetime later, Mary Carelli gazed out at the courtroom full of media people, come to watch her on trial for murder. She held her head high, kept her eyes still. Paget watched her face.

"That looks like the same woman," Tench said. "Or put another way, the woman I saw looked as Ms. Carelli does now."

Mary's face showed nothing. The courtroom was still.

"May Ms. Carelli sit?" Paget inquired.

"Of course," Masters said. "Thank you, Ms. Carelli. Any more questions, Ms. Sharpe?"

"None, Your Honor."

As Mary sat, she shot a querying look at Paget. How much does this hurt, the look asked, and what can you do with him?

Very little, Paget thought. He did not even rise from the table. In his most languid voice, he asked, "Tell me, Mr. Tench, was this nameless, faceless mannequin you saw for less than ten seconds in a dim hallway at least wearing clothes?"

There was a ripple of laughter. Masters raised her gavel and then thought better of it, looking over at Tench. His mouth formed a grimace in what, Paget thought, was meant to convey perfunctory amusement and a sense of his superiority.

Sharpe stood again. "Really, Your Honor, this isn't comedy."

"Far from it," Paget answered. "But this witness's powers of observation are so extraordinary that when he could not recall the woman's clothes, I feared the worst."

Masters's shrug suggested that her amusement was running low. "For the record, Mr. Tench."

Tench turned to Paget. "Yes," he said in a tone of weary condescension. "The woman was dressed."

"That's a relief," Paget answered. He turned to Masters. "Given that Ms. Sharpe wishes to avoid comedy, I have no further questions."

"Ms. Sharpe?"

"No." She looked at Paget with asperity. "There's nothing to ask."

"You may step down, Mr. Tench." He did so, looking irritated at his abrupt dismissal.

Masters, too, had begun to look annoyed. ‘‘Tempers seem to be fraying here,’’ she said. ‘‘I’d like a half-hour recess, and then we’ll meet in chambers. The topic will be certain evidence proposed by the prosecution to conclude their direct case.’’

The tape, Paget knew. But as Masters slammed the gavel, finishing public proceedings for the day, Paget found himself still wondering why Mary had left the suite. And then he turned to see his son, staring at his mother with new questions in his eyes.

No matter what doubts he had tried to plant today, Paget realized, the look on Carlo’s face told him how much Marnie Sharpe had managed to achieve.

FIVE

LIKE HER COURTROOM, the chambers that Caroline Masters used were borrowed: the tomes on evidence, treatises on trial practice, and bound jury instructions belonged to another judge, and the heavy furniture and green leather chair were unrelieved by any touch that was Masters's own. It did not seem to matter; three days into the hearing, Caroline Masters looked at home.

She leaned back in the chair, fingers interwoven beneath her chin, gazing thoughtfully at the tape recorder Sharpe had placed in front of her. The only persons present were Terri, Paget, Sharpe, and her assistant.

"The media," Judge Masters said, "don't know what they're missing. Which is precisely how I intend to keep it."

"What are we authorized to say?" Sharpe asked.

"Nothing. You'll tell the press, as I have, that these private sessions are to rule on disputed points of evidence. Period. You will not describe what the points are or what is in dispute."

Sharpe leaned forward. ‘‘It seems to me,’’ she ventured, ‘‘that Mr. Paget wants selective publicity—nationwide television for some aspects, and a lead-lined vault for anything that sheds some real light on Ms. Carelli.’’

‘‘This isn't about what Mr. Paget wants. It's about *my* quaint notions of decency.’’ Pausing, Masters looked at each lawyer in turn. ‘‘As I understand it, the parties intend to treat me to a tape of Ms. Carelli's psychoanalysis, another tape providing some distasteful insights into the relationship of a dead film star with a revered United States senator, and testimony from three women regarding Mark Ransom's sexual habits and/or his misuse of the tapes in question. If this stuff turns out to be admissible, I'll admit it. Until then, I'm more concerned with protecting the particular people involved than I am with the ‘people's right to know’—or, for that matter, the *National Enquirer*'s right to supplement their usual fare about Peter Lawford's final days and sex between women and apes.’’ She turned back to Sharpe. ‘‘Do I make myself clear?’’

Sharpe hesitated, as if to protest the focus on her. Then she nodded.

‘‘Good. Because if you feel like I'm picking on you, Marnie, you're right.’’ Masters's voice grew quieter. ‘‘Like half of America, I watched Ms. Carelli on *60 Minutes*. But unlike most of them, I knew precisely where the interviewer's questions came from. And I was forced to ask myself: Does Marnie Sharpe only care about the privacy of women who've *actually* been raped? Now, this morning, you wonder aloud about keeping information private which could cause great hurt to any number of people, before the court even determines that it's fit to be evidence.'' Masters glanced at the tape recorder, then back at Sharpe. ''I don't know what's on this tape. But if the press prints anything about it until and unless I decide that it's admissible, and I trace that story to your office, I will hold you personally responsible. Have I made *that* clear enough?''

''Yes,'' Sharpe said, with an edge in her voice. ''You have.''

Paget glanced at Terri, silently wondering whether these stringent procedures reflected the judge's reaction to the seriousness of the case, or something else. But Terri looked as surprised as he.

''During our private sessions,'' Judge Masters continued, ''it will be necessary to bring in a stenographer and have a record of what's said. But I intend to make this as comfortable as possible for the women who've come forward. This experience will be bad enough for them, and for my part, I think the courts should make every effort to encourage women who've been victimized to say so. Which means, among other things, that *I* will be the primary questioner. If anyone then wishes to ask anything for the sake of preserving the record on appeal, of course they may. But if I conclude that the particular testimony offered will *not* be used in open court, then I'll have that transcript sealed from the press to protect the women involved. As for the tapes, I'll play them *without* a stenographer, given that they speak for themselves." Once more, Judge Masters glanced at each lawyer. "Is that agreeable? If not, tell me now."

There was silence. Usually, Paget knew, the judge would be more observer than participant. He watched Sharpe calculate Masters's response if she objected; his own guess was that the judge would tell her to go to the court of appeals. But the hearing was going too well for Sharpe to risk alienating the judge, and Masters's resolve to guard the privacy of Mary and certain witnesses did not affect Sharpe's case on the merits.

"We have no objection," Sharpe responded.

"Nor," Paget said, "does Ms. Carelli."

"I would think not," Judge Masters said dryly. "How do you wish to proceed, Ms. Sharpe?"

"By playing this tape, Your Honor, which *does* speak for itself." Sharpe glanced at Paget. "I will say only that it is a tape of Ms. Carelli's psychoanalytic session with a Dr. William Steinhardt; that we found it in Mark Ransom's home in Key West; and that we are prepared to authenticate should the court deem it admissible."

"And I," Paget responded, "will say only that

the tape is so obviously privileged that the prosecution's sole purpose is to prejudice the court. Once the court has listened to it, that damage is done."

"I'm going to have to hear it, Mr. Paget. And then I'll hear your argument. You'll just have to trust my mental discipline."

"Thank you, Your Honor." Paget's response was formulaic; once Judge Masters heard the tape, her perception of Mary and her lawyer might be changed beyond repair, the contest for the judge's mind and sympathies lost.

As she switched on the tape, Sharpe seemed to wear a secret smile. At that moment, Christopher Paget hated her; what he felt was not the adversarial passion of a defense lawyer, Paget realized, but the visceral anger of the guilty at a prosecutor's pleasure. He sat back, trying to keep the shame and apprehension from his face.

"I keep having this dream," Mary said.

As before, her voice sounded naked, haunting; repetition did not lessen Paget's dislike of listening. "It's as if I shut it off by day, but at night I lose control."

Staring at the cassette, Judge Masters's face had none of its usual hauteur. It appeared that she did not wish to look at anyone.

"I'm in Paris," Mary went on, "at the church of St. Germain-des-Prés."

Her voice echoed in the room. With its dark wood

paneling, the window admitting one square of light, the chambers seemed charged by Mary's words with the character of a confessional. The lawyers were quite still.

"Why are you there?" Steinhardt inquired.

Mary's voice was quiet. "To ask forgiveness for my sins."

The voices went on: Steinhardt querying, Mary responding; both speaking softly, as if afraid they might be overheard. Caroline Masters looked away.

"Are they forgiven?" Steinhardt was asking.

"At first, I have no sign." As she described the dream, Mary sounded tired. "Then I go outside," she finished, "and receive His answer.

"Carlo is gone.

"In his place are two empty glasses. One for me, and one for Chris. And then I know."

"What do you know?"

"That Chris has taken Carlo, and that I must let him." Her voice was defeated. "That my sins are past redemption."

In silent inquiry, Masters looked up at Paget. He met her gaze, nodding. She studied his face a moment; then, with a self-conscious fixity, resumed watching the tape as the voices went on. At the corner of his vision, Paget sensed Sharpe interpreting the silent exchange.

"Who is Chris?" Steinhardt asked now. "And what are your sins—in the dream, that is?"

A long silence. "Do you know Christopher Paget?"

"I know *of* him. The young man who testified at the Lasko hearings."

"Yes." Mary paused. "Chris has Carlo now."

For a moment, Paget imagined that Terri's eyes shone. Then he remembered that she had never heard the tape.

"And your sins?" Steinhardt was asking.

"In the dream, or in real life?" Mary's voice became as cool as Paget remembered it. "Because in real life, sin has little meaning to me."

Caroline Masters's face was stone. In those few words, Paget thought, Mary had defined herself.

"The dream, then," Steinhardt said.

"You can't understand," Mary answered, "without some background. Did you actually watch the hearings?"

"Yes," Steinhardt said. "Like millions of others, I was fascinated."

"And did you watch my testimony?"

"With great interest."

"Then we need to start with one essential fact."

"What is it?" There was yet more silence, and then Mary's flat voice echoed in Judge Masters's chambers.

"I lied."

Masters's eyes narrowed: to Paget, the effect was

that of a contemplative woman putting the pieces together. But watching her face seemed better than living with his own thoughts. Helpless, he saw her listen to Steinhardt ask more questions, to Mary's answers.

"Then let me reassure you," Steinhardt was saying. "The tapes are for my use only, and only to assist me in your therapy. By state law, they are subject to the doctor-patient privilege, which I would ardently insist on even if there were no such law. So whatever you tell me is as confidential as if there *were* no tapes."

Masters raised her eyebrows at Sharpe. As though reminding the judge to listen, Sharpe angled her head toward the tape recorder.

As Masters turned, Mary confessed to perjury before the Senate.

To Paget, it seemed that Mary repeated the name of Jack Woods relentlessly, like a curse. Once more, Woods betrayed Paget's inquiry, sent a witness to his death. The memory of hating Woods returned to him, fresh and keen.

"All in all," Mary finished, "I told the truth a good deal of the time." She paused. "What I didn't tell Talmadge is that *I* had helped Jack do every one of those things."

Judge Masters's eyes showed nothing, looked at nothing but the tape recorder. Paget could not read her thoughts.

"You wanted to protect yourself?" Steinhardt asked.

As before, Mary sounded amused. "I wanted to stay out of prison. Even without that, the life I had worked so hard for would have ended if I had told the truth." She paused, voice softer. "And of course, I was pregnant."

Paget inhaled. He felt Terri stir next to him, moving closer.

"Did Chris know about you?" Steinhardt asked.

In the silence, Masters glanced at him. Paget saw that she instantly understood the implication: whether Paget knew about Mary's complicity and, more damaging, whether he, too, had lied to the Senate.

"Know what?" Mary answered.

The tape ended.

Without speaking, Masters went to the door and motioned in the stenographer. A round woman in her forties, she set up her machine in a far corner of the office, trying to be unobtrusive. As she did that, Masters settled back in her chair, still silent.

Sharpe broke the quiet. "This tape reveals Ms. Carelli's motives," she said. "And it suggests, regrettably, that Mr. Paget has a serious problem of ethics stemming from his own involvement in the Lasko matter and in the Senate hearings. Obviously, there is a second tape, which discloses much more regarding Ms. Carelli *and* Mr. Paget." She turned to Paget. "But *we* don't know where it is."

Paget said nothing. Masters waited until Sharpe looked back at her. "There's only one thing *I* want to know," she answered. "And that's what this tape is doing in a court of law."

Sharpe stared at her. "To listen to this tape," she rejoined, "is to know why Mary Carelli killed Mark Ransom. No one can say this tape isn't relevant to motive."

"Oh, it's relevant, all right. And if some court lets this into evidence, your chances of convicting Ms. Carelli go up about a thousand percent." Masters paused, stressing each syllable. "But there's just no way that *I* will. No way at all."

Sharpe sat straighter. "Without this tape, the court's proceedings are the shadow of truth. And determining truth is, or should be, our ultimate purpose. If courts become preoccupied with the *means* of justice, no one will believe that *any* court can serve the *ends* of justice."

Masters leaned forward. "Skip the pieties about 'justice,' Counselor. There's a psychiatrist-patient privilege in this state, and *this* tape falls as squarely within that as anything I can imagine." Her voice rose. "You've had me sit here listening to this woman's secrets, protected by law, without an argument worth making for getting this tape in. Your obvious and only purpose was to poison the court against Ms. Carelli and, it seems quite clear, against your opposing counsel. *That* is grossly unjust to both of them and contemptuous of me. Now do *you* fathom how *this* court feels about 'justice,' or should I spell it out for you?''

Sharpe looked pale. ''No,'' she said quietly. ''But I would just remind the court that, in a jury trial, I could ask a trial judge to rule without prejudicing the finder of fact.''

''I understand.'' Masters's voice became more level. ''But in my opinion, any judge who lets this in buys you two things: a guilty verdict at trial and a reversal on appeal. I suggest you try your case without it. As for me, I'll do my best to put this tape out of my mind.''

There was momentary silence, the reticence of lawyers in the presence of an angry judge. The stenographer finished tapping her machine and sat staring into space. ''Your Honor,'' Paget ventured, ''I assume this concludes the prosecutor's evidence.''

Masters looked to Sharpe. ''Does it?''

Sharpe paused. ''Subject to rebuttal witnesses.''

''In that case,'' Paget said, ''I intend to move for the dismissal of all charges against Ms. Carelli.''

Masters's expression said that this trial balloon, floated to test the judge's early sentiments, would get very short shrift. ''On what ground?''

''That the prosecutor's case, standing alone, does not support probable cause.''

''You must be dreaming, Counselor. As *People v. Souza* put it so succinctly, probable cause means simply 'more evidence for than against.' Don't embarrass yourself by filing a motion.''

How much of Masters's vehemence, Paget wondered, was the residue of the tape. ''I'll certainly forgo the motion,'' he answered politely, ''though I'm tantalized by the specter of victory.''

For the first time, Masters seemed to consider smiling. ''Don't let it keep you up,'' she said. ''Anything else, anyone?''

''There is,'' Sharpe cut in. ''I'd like to ask Mr. Paget if he intends to put Ms. Carelli on the stand.''

Paget hesitated. With each day of trial, the risk of exposing Mary to cross-examination seemed to grow exponentially; the night before, he and Terri had debated for an hour the merits of keeping Mary silent. But now that the prosecution had carried its burden on direct, Mary's only hope was to build an affirmative defense, close to impossible without Mary herself. ''My current intention,'' he said, ''is to have Ms. Carelli testify.''

''In that case,'' Sharpe rejoined, ''there's some unfinished business with respect to this tape.''

Masters looked curious. ''Such as?''

''Such as whether we can ask Ms. Carelli if she visited Dr. Steinhardt; or if a tape existed; or if Mr. Ransom had it; or why she didn't tell the police about any of this. None of which topics, it seems to us, are privileged in the least.''

''Perhaps not,'' Paget replied. ''But Ms. Sharpe

is attempting to evade the privilege by tricking Ms. Carelli into saying something about the tape—and thereby waiving the privilege against its disclosure—or by creating the aura of an undisclosed tape whose contents are unspeakably damaging.''

''As the court has already suggested,'' Sharpe said mildly, ''it's hard to imagine anything more damaging than the *actual* contents of Ms. Carelli's tape—unless it's her *missing* tape. And the law is clear: only the communications themselves are confidential, not the *fact* of the communications *or* the existence of the tape.''

Once more, Paget was forced to admire Sharpe's preparation: for every point where she lost ground, Sharpe had a second and third approach, and now had added a softer tone to mute the judge's anger. If Judge Masters ruled in her favor now, Mary's cross-examination would be even more brutal and dangerous, with the disclosure of the tape itself at risk with every answer.

''You can explore those areas,'' Masters replied. ''But questions like, 'Did you perjure yourself before the United States Senate,' or *any* question derived from the *contents* of the tape, simply will not do.'' She paused, looking from Sharpe to Paget. ''If this tape gets into evidence, it will be because Ms. Carelli waived the privilege by blundering on the witness stand. Understand?''

''In other words,'' Sharpe pursued, ''if Ms. Carelli testifies regarding the contents of the tape, or misrepresents them in any way, the People can play her tape in open court.'' She shot a glance at Paget. ''Or the *next* tape—if we find it.''

Paget's voice was clipped. ''I'm sick of Ms. Sharpe's insinuations. As for her suggestion, it's impossible to make a ruling in advance. Whether there's a waiver depends wholly on what's said.''

''That's correct,'' Masters responded. ''But if *I* think any statement by Ms. Carelli fits the formula that Ms. Sharpe has just proposed, there's a waiver. Because—and I must stress this before Ms. Carelli takes the stand—the law protects privileged communications, not the fact of perjury.''

''Forgive me, Your Honor,'' Paget said. ''But it seems that Ms. Sharpe has accomplished precisely what she set out to do: to plant the tape in this court's mind and to put Ms. Carelli at maximum risk.''

Masters shrugged. ''I've already reprimanded the prosecutor. But you *did* ask for this hearing, Mr. Paget.'' She turned to Sharpe. ''What I *will* do is take this tape into the custody of the court. For everyone's sake.''

''That's virtually unprecedented,'' Sharpe protested. ''Our office can take precautions to protect this tape.''

''So can I. Anything else?''

Sharpe hesitated. ''No, Your Honor.''

''Mr. Paget?''

''No, Your Honor. Thank you.''

''Then we'll adjourn until tomorrow.'' Masters paused. ''I don't know about all of you, but I've had quite enough.''

The stenographer left. Masters stood, and then, as if in an afterthought, turned to Paget. ''There is one thing I should say to you, Mr. Paget. It's this: You're as welcome in this courtroom now as you were before Ms. Sharpe played that tape. I don't care what you did or didn't know fifteen years ago, and I'm sorry Ms. Sharpe does.'' She glanced at Sharpe, and then faced Paget again. ''Personal lives are a complex matter, and it will be a pity if what's private between you and Ms. Carelli doesn't get to stay there. I know your son's here watching, and appreciate the pressure you're under.''

For a moment, Paget was speechless. He had been prepared for anything from Caroline Masters but compassion.

''I appreciate that, Your Honor. Truly.''

Masters considered him. ''There is, perhaps, one other thing I should say. In simple fairness, so that you can assess your alternatives.'' She paused again, then finished softly. ''You've done a very nice job. And you're losing this case.''

Paget stared into the martini glass. Straight up, no ice. His first in weeks.

" 'You're losing this case,' " he said to Terri, "does *not* require extensive analysis."

They sat at the Top of the Mark Hopkins, looking at the city as dusk fell. "Semantically speaking, no," Terri answered. "But it can mean either 'Your witnesses better be damned good' or 'Better cut a deal with Marnie while you've got the chance.' Or maybe 'Don't put Mary on the stand—you'll lose anyhow, and you'll just screw yourself up for trial.' "

Paget nodded. "I think it's one of the latter two. Maybe both."

"So do I. Unfortunately."

He smiled faintly. "It's one of the many things I like about you, Terri. You're honest."

She put down her wineglass, seeming to assess its contents. He could look at her then; the delicate face, crescent green eyes, the ridged nose that, Paget was sure, only she disliked. The woman he saw was smart and self-reliant, clear-sighted about everyone but herself.

"One problem," he told her, "is that Mary still won't take that deal. Even if they offered it."

Terri still gazed at her wine. "You kept the tape out," she said softly. "There was nothing more you could do."

"Caroline kept the tape out. At least for now."

She gave him a veiled look of worry; Paget watched her choose between sympathy and encouragement. "Tomorrow's our turn. We didn't expect to win now, remember? And Caroline did treat you well."

"She did, to my surprise." He paused, reflecting. "I find Caroline Masters completely inscrutable. I have the sense that something drives her besides sheer intellect, but I've no idea what it is. Or, really, who *she* is. It makes her impossible to predict."

"Then don't try, Chris. I don't think Caroline's your problem here, and you've got far too much to think about."

"I know." Terri's concern for him reminded Paget that she had worries of her own. "So how are things at home? And how's Elena?"

"Elena's great." Terri paused. "As for home, it's okay. Richie doesn't really understand the demands of this hearing—he takes it sort of personally."

Was there anything, Paget began to wonder, that Richie *didn't* think was about Richie? "That can be hard," he said.

Terri shrugged. "I just try to shut it off. Two weeks, and we're back to normal."

Her voice was flat. As if she heard herself, Terri asked, "How's Carlo?"

"Too quiet. I'm sure it's the implications about his mother and Ransom." Paget stared out the window. "More and more, I dread the day she takes the stand. Every time I drill her with questions, I find a new hole. Not to mention that Sharpe keeps coming up with new facts. It worries me, for Carlo most of all.''

Nodding, Terri sipped her wine, said nothing.

``Sorry,'' Paget said after a time. ``But if I don't say this stuff to you, it seems I don't say it to anyone.''

Terri looked at him. ``That seems to be our arrangement, Chris. In addition to doing trials, of course.''

``Lucky for me. Not only do you listen to me brood without visible boredom, but you come up with terrific lines of questioning.'' He smiled. ``You may have struck a death blow to the panty hose industry.''

He watched her smile back. It lightened his depression for a moment, and then he thought of the tape again, and Carlo.

Terri glanced at her watch. ``Melissa Rappaport should have checked in by now. I keep wondering if Caroline will let her testify in open court.''

``Probably not.'' Paget finished his drink. ``*I* just hope that Caroline remembers her whenever she remembers Mary's voice on tape.''

PART FIVE

THE DEFENSE

February 13 – February 19

ONE

"HE TOLD ME to undress for them," Laura murmured.

Her smoky voice sounded plaintive, more bewildered than angry. Caroline Masters looked from the tape to Terri.

"What is this?" she said quietly.

Terri paused, torn from her image of Laura Chase lying on a white couch in a white room, Steinhardt an unseen voice behind her. "Please listen, Your Honor. I think we can show relevance."

"And *did* you undress?" Steinhardt asked.

"Piece by piece." A long pause. "Jamie told me what to take off and how to move."

"How to move?"

"Yes." Her voice fell. "While they watched me, I danced for them."

"Danced?"

"Jamie told me how to move," she repeated. Laura did not seem to answer questions; it was more that she was talking to herself, or what was left of herself. Her voice sounded dead. ''When to turn around for them. What parts of me to uncover.''

Masters looked at Terri. ''James Colt?'' she asked.

''Yes.''

Slowly, Masters shook her head.

''What did you think about,'' Steinhardt was asking, ''while you were doing this for him?''

''That I wanted to keep drinking.'' Her voice stayed flat. ''We were in the recreation room of his friend's house. There was a bar there. They had everything they needed.''

''So you drank more.''

''Gin. Every time I took off something new. It helped me float away.'' Her tone became distant. ''When I slid my panties down, and turned around for them, I imagined that I was about to go swimming. With *her.*''

Masters's gaze seemed to turn inward; the effect was of someone who had removed herself. Terri's palms were damp.

''Then,'' Laura whispered, ''he asked me to touch myself.''

Paget and Sharpe's assistant looked at the floor. Marnie Sharpe sat with her arms folded. No one spoke.

''Touch yourself?'' Steinhardt asked Laura Chase.

''At first just my nipples. Then moving my hands, like I was discovering new parts.'' Another pause.

"After a while, he asked me to slide to the floor, and lean back against the bar."

"For what?"

"I masturbated. While they watched me."

The tape was silent.

"While I did it," Laura murmured, "I closed my eyes. Under my breath, so they couldn't hear, I whispered her name to myself."

Caroline Masters's eyes shut.

"Then someone put his penis in my mouth." Laura's voice became wispy. "I kept my eyes closed. I didn't want to know who it was.

"When he was through, and I opened my eyes, Senator James Colt handed me another drink."

Her tone was suddenly angry. The future leader of the free world, Terri remembered; that was what Laura Chase had called him, talking to Lindsay Caldwell. Lindsay had said it was the humor of a slave. But it was more than that: the phrase had a bitter irony. Terri's revulsion turned to anger.

It was all right, James Colt was saying. It was all right for Mark Ransom to treat Marcy Linton as his friends had treated Laura Chase.

Christopher Paget glanced over at Terri.

Don't get sidetracked, she told herself. You've got an argument to make. You asked to argue this yourself, and Chris agreed.

Laura Chase kept speaking.

"The second one stretched me out on the rug, and

opened my legs again.'' Her voice became distant. ''It made me think of that movie I made. Letting two men fuck me so other men could watch. I try never to think about that.''

''You bought up all the copies, didn't you?''

''I hope so.'' Pain deadened her voice again. ''But now it doesn't really matter, does it?''

There was silence, and then Laura's tone went cold. ''It stopped mattering a long time ago.''

''Tell me,'' Steinhardt asked softly. ''Did anything else happen?''

''The other one rolled me over.'' There was a long pause. ''He was hard again.''

''Rolled you over?''

''Yes.'' Laura's voice held a faint note of anger. ''They wanted to have me every way.''

Steinhardt's voice was quiet. ''That must have hurt you.''

''Not really. My father used to do that.'' Her voice became flat again. ''While it was happening, I looked up. Jamie was sipping his martini, watching.''

Caroline Masters seemed to inhale, and then she opened her eyes.

''I'm afraid,'' Steinhardt said, ''that our time is up.''

Slowly, Masters shook her head. From the tape recorder, Laura said in matter-of-fact tones, ''I may not be here next week.''

"That's all right, Laura. Just call my secretary, and we can reschedule. We'll certainly need to talk about this more."

There was the faint sound of movement: Laura rising from the couch. "You know what's so funny about it?" she asked. "I can never come. Except with her."

Her voice broke. There was one sob, then the convulsive sound of Laura Chase, breaking down.

The tape clicked off.

For a long time, no one spoke.

Caroline Masters touched her eyes. "Just what," she said to no one, "am I supposed to do with *that?*"

"Let us play it," Terri answered quietly, "in open court."

Masters thought for a moment. Then slowly, she got up from her chair and summoned the stenographer.

As before, the woman settled in an unobtrusive corner. "All right." Masters looked to Sharpe. "What do the People say?"

"That tape should be suppressed." Sharpe's voice had an undertone of disgust. "It may be appalling, but it's not relevant to anything."

Masters stared at the tape. "It's relevant to some things," she said. "Why Laura Chase killed herself. Who James Colt really was. How he felt about women. If I were a historian, I would strongly argue that Colt is due a hard second look. But I'm merely a municipal court judge.'' She paused. ''And, at the moment, I wish I weren't even that.''

''I may agree with you, as a matter of personal philosophy,'' Sharpe answered. ''But that has nothing to do with any issue in this case—which, after all, is about the death of *Mark Ransom.*'' Sharpe glanced at Terri. ''What the defense is trying to do is create a scandal which will deflect attention from Ms. Carelli's culpability. And, frankly, make this case expensive for the district attorney by alienating a family that still matters, a son who is running for governor, and all the people who believe that the country's finest moment was cut short by a plane crash.''

''The tape goes to who *Mark Ransom* was,'' Terri shot back. ''Our defense is that Mark Ransom was a tangle of sexual pathology, at the heart of which was a need for physical and mental dominance of women as symbolized by his obsession with Laura Chase. Any political damage to District Attorney Brooks *or* Ms. Sharpe is the incidental cost of a case *they* wanted to bring.'' Terri paused. ''I don't know how they can argue that the tape Mark Ransom played for Ms. Carelli—one that sexually aroused him in the moments before he attacked her—isn't relevant.''

''In other words,'' Sharpe said to Masters, ''make the victim so distasteful that it doesn't matter if someone murdered him. It's the world's tiredest defense strategy, Your Honor, dressed up as a feminist cause.''

Terri shook her head. ''Our strategy is to show this isn't murder at all, Your Honor. We ask that you not rule on the tape until you've heard all of our witnesses. Including the three witnesses Ms. Sharpe wants you to hear in chambers.''

Masters looked at her. ''But the only purpose of *that* is for me to rule on whether their testimony is admissible. And, therefore, can be part of the hearing on which the court determines probable cause.''

''That's why I suggest you wait to rule on *this*. We think that the testimony of our witnesses, *and* the Laura Chase tape, should be taken as a whole.''

''Who are they?''

''The first is Melissa Rappaport, Mark Ransom's ex-wife. The second is Marcy Linton, the writer.''

Masters nodded. ''I've read her stories. And the third?''

Terri paused. ''Lindsay Caldwell.''

Masters raised an eyebrow. ''What does Ms. Rappaport have to offer us?''

''A description of Mr. Ransom's obsession with Laura Chase, and with rape. Among other things.''

''What about Ms. Linton?''

''Mark Ransom raped her,'' Terri said softly. ''In Aspen, four years ago. He came to her cabin, under the pretense of a literary meeting, to commit rape.''

"And she's willing to say so?"

"Yes."

Masters looked pensive. "And Lindsay Caldwell?"

Terri tried to read her face. "Lindsay Caldwell," she answered quietly, "was the 'her' Laura mentioned. On the tape that I just played."

From the side, Sharpe turned to stare at Terri. Masters's eyes flickered. With equal quiet, she asked, "Can you explain the relevance of that?"

"Yes. Ransom told Ms. Caldwell that he had another, more explicit tape regarding her relationship with Laura Chase. He used it to arrange a 'meeting.' " Terri paused. "It was scheduled for the day after he met Ms. Carelli."

For once, Sharpe looked openly surprised; Terri watched her try to calculate the impact of what she had just heard. From the corner of her eye, Terri saw Christopher Paget's faint smile of approval, to assure her that she was doing well.

"Ms. Caldwell's also willing to come forward?" Masters asked.

"Yes. If you decide to let her testify in court, she will. In the meanwhile, we ask that you take all steps possible to assure that any appearance in chambers remain private."

Masters nodded, somber. "Of course."

"I admire Lindsay Caldwell," Sharpe put in. "But blackmail still isn't rape. Assuming that blackmail is what Ms. Peralta's implying."

"*Attempted* blackmail," Terri said. "*And* attempted rape."

Masters was gazing at the tape again. To Terri, she seemed unusually subdued.

"Explain your theory, Teresa. Step by step."

Terri nodded, organizing her thoughts. She was not as facile with words as Paget; what worked best for her was to be plainspoken. "In brief," she began, "Ransom's call to Mary Carelli was to blackmail her into being alone with him. The Laura Chase tape was something that excited him; he meant to use *Ms. Carelli's* tape to force her to have sex." Terri paused, speaking more deliberately. "When she refused, Ransom was already aroused by the Laura Chase tape. So he tried to rape Ms. Carelli, and she shot him in self-defense."

Masters looked from Terri to Paget. "How do you intend to acknowledge sexual blackmail without dealing with the existence and contents of Ms. Carelli's tape?"

"We have some thoughts about that," Paget answered. "But for now, I'd prefer not to share them with Ms. Sharpe."

"I think we're entitled to know," Sharpe put in, "if Mr. Paget intends some end run around the tape."

"What you're entitled to," Paget rejoined, "is what Mary Carelli gives you on the stand. As Judge Masters has already ruled."

Masters nodded. "I'm not here to force Mr. Paget's hand, Ms. Sharpe. You and I will find out together whatever it is she has to say. Then I'll decide if you can use Ms. Carelli's tape."

"And *this* tape?" Terri asked.

"I'm going to reserve ruling, Ms. Peralta, as you suggest." Masters gave her a thin smile. "Welcome to a speaking role, incidentally."

"Thank you, Your Honor."

Masters's smile faded. "As to your witnesses, I agree with Ms. Sharpe that Rappaport and Caldwell should be heard in chambers first." She turned to Sharpe. "Not so Ms. Linton. I want her testimony in open court."

Sharpe looked surprised. "Really, Your Honor, I'd request Ms. Linton also be heard in private. We need to explore whether her alleged experience was sufficiently similar to Ms. Carelli's supposed rape to qualify as evidence of a pattern on behalf of Mr. Ransom." She paused. "If this were a rape prosecution, it seems certain that the testimony of Ms. Linton would be excluded as too prejudicial to Mr. Ransom. At the Willie Smith trial, you will recall, the prosecution had three women ready to testify. The court excluded all of them."

Masters nodded. "I recognize the irony," she responded. "If Mr. Ransom had succeeded in staying alive, and you were prosecuting him for Ms. Carelli's rape, I would probably be forced to exclude Ms.

Linton altogether. As much as I disagree with the law as it now stands.'' Her voice grew quiet. ''But I don't have that problem, do I? Because Mark Ransom's dead.''

''That's correct,'' Terri put in. ''Under the Evidence Code, a victim's prior acts of violence are relevant to the question of self-defense. Including rape.''

''Truly,'' Masters said dryly, ''the law is a wonderful thing.'' She turned back to Sharpe. ''How many times, Marnie, have you asked a judge to help you prove rape by letting in testimony like Ms. Linton's?''

''Often,'' Sharpe answered crisply. ''And I've never won.''

''If you ever have one in front of me, you might try again.'' With another brief smile, Masters turned back to Terri. ''I'll hear Ms. Linton after Ms. Carelli. And please bring on Ms. Rappaport.''

Melissa Rappaport wore a gray suit and an expression of birdlike alertness, which, for Terri, did not conceal her humiliation.

She sat across from Caroline Masters, her back not touching the chair. Terri sat next to her, Sharpe a little farther away; at Paget's suggestion, he and Sharpe's assistant had stepped outside. The stenographer sat in her usual corner. Rappaport had yet to speak.

Caroline Masters had set aside her robe; suddenly her manner had none of the edge she reserved for lawyers. Her posture was relaxed, her tone business-like but pleasant, her expression one of mild inquiry. She seemed less a judge than a caseworker unraveling a complex family problem. It was a side of Caroline that Terri had not seen.

"I appreciate your coming," she told Rappaport. "The subject matter is inherently painful—human relations, and the turns they can take. Not to mention that this involves the death of a man to whom you were close, however complex those feelings might be." She nodded toward the stenographer. "I'm forced to make a record of what's said here. But please be assured that unless I have you testify, that record will remain sealed."

Rappaport merely nodded; despite Terri's best efforts to reassure her, it was as if she did not trust herself to speak. Terri was accustomed to the diminishing effect of courts, where the layman's every gesture bespoke some loss of self, but the difference between this woman in her own apartment and in Caroline's chambers was pronounced; even the nervous quickness of her movements seemed repressed. Her thumb and forefingers twisted an imagined cigarette.

"Your Honor," Terri asked, "would you mind if Ms. Rappaport smoked?"

The judge gave her a brief, quizzical look; she had

always hated cigarette smoke, and Terri knew it. "Would you care to?" she asked Rappaport.

"Yes. Thank you."

Caroline reached into the drawer and produced a standard glass ashtray. "It's Judge Brookings's," she explained. "When I borrowed these chambers, I found this filled with nonfilter Camels. You don't smoke *those*, do you?"

"No. Menthol cigarettes." Rappaport's voice took on a shade of irony. "The benevolent brand that sponsors women's tennis."

Caroline nodded. "Yes. I can just imagine Martina wheezing menthol as she jumps the net. But you may live longer—every time I hear Judge Brookings cough, I think of anthracite."

With a half smile, Rappaport watched the judge push the ashtray toward her. "It's an indefensible habit," she replied. "And, like so much of what we do, self-inflicted."

" 'Man is the complicating animal,' " Caroline said. "Do light up."

Rappaport put a cigarette in her mouth. Her fingers were stiff; it took several flicks of her lighter to summon a flame. Terri watched Caroline take this in, await Rappaport's first drag. Quietly, the judge said, "I'd like to hear about Mark Ransom."

Above the cigarette, Rappaport's eyes froze. Caroline went on: "Ms. Peralta can help out, of course. But this isn't a formal proceeding, so we can have a conversation without the artificiality of court. Essentially, I'd like to know what you'd say if you *were* in court, so that I can determine its relevance to Mr. Ransom's death. If there is any."

Rappaport hesitated. "I'm not sure what's even *potentially* relevant to Mark's death."

Caroline Masters appraised her. "According to the defense, his sexual profile. I understand generally from Ms. Peralta that he had an interest in 'male dominance,' to use her words."

Watching Rappaport, Terri felt as if she had betrayed this woman. "When we talked in New York," Terri said to her, "you suggested that, pretty much from the beginning, Mr. Ransom had some unusual desires. I don't think the judge is asking for every last detail—just a sense of what Mark Ransom's needs were, including his interest in Laura Chase, and how he acted them out."

Slowly, Rappaport nodded. The way Terri had phrased it put the focus on Mark Ransom, not her. It seemed to give her a way to talk.

"The first thing that I noticed," she told the judge in a toneless voice, "was Mark's obsession with Laura Chase."

She sounded like an anthropologist, describing the obscure rites of a tribe she had studied from a distance. But Terri could hear the resonance behind the words.

"You call it an obsession," Caroline said.

"Yes. He read everything that he could find." Rappaport paused. "But much of it was visual."

"Her movies?"

"Not just those. Magazines, fold-outs. Old calendars from when she was a starlet. Anything." Her voice became flat. "Nudes, of course, were especially valued."

Sharpe gave an impatient shake of the head. "Your Honor, this trip through the backwaters of a dead man's sexual thoughts is both ghoulish and irrelevant. The question is not whether Mark Ransom subscribed to *Hustler* but why Ms. Carelli killed him in that hotel suite. Surely it wasn't for looking at pictures."

It was a shrewd intervention, Terri thought, intended to embarrass Melissa Rappaport while disrupting any rapport between her and Caroline. Terri saw the same thought run through the judge's mind. In unruffled tones, Caroline said, "I find this very helpful. And I assume that Mr. Ransom's obsession with 'pictures' was focused on Laura Chase. Is that correct, Ms. Rappaport?"

Rappaport nodded. "Yes."

Caroline leaned forward. "Other than looking, did this interest in Laura Chase erotica take any particular form?"

Rappaport took another drag on her cigarette; exhaling, she studied the cloud of smoke as if it held some interest. "Sometimes, he would take out pictures and lock the bedroom door.'' She shrugged. ''I knew what he was doing—I'd had brothers, after all. But it seemed a bit arrested.''

She said it in disdainful tones, but then looked down; Terri imagined the humiliation of trying so hard to please Mark Ransom, at such loss of self, to be put aside for photos of another woman. As if she had the same thought, Caroline asked, ''Did you ever discuss that with him?''

''What was to discuss? You can fulfill your needs with photographs, or make love to your wife. But you can't do both.''

''How did you resolve that? Or did you?''

Rappaport gave a thin smile. ''Bondage. Of course.''

The startling answer hung there a moment; beneath its deceptive casualness Terri felt a lacerating self-contempt. She looked away, as did Sharpe. Only Caroline Masters seemed unfazed; ten years at the P.D.'s office, she had once told Terri, broadened one's sense of possibilities.

''Is there some way in which you associate that with Laura Chase?'' Caroline asked.

Rappaport looked past her. ''Mark did. He told me that bondage freed a woman to find what was sexual inside herself, as Laura had. That Laura would have liked it.'' Her tone became bitter. ''I tried to do what Laura would have liked.''

Terri winced at Rappaport's psychic dissonance—a woman of intellectual achievement, acting out her husband's fantasies of a movie star who inspired feelings in her of both contempt and inadequacy. But Caroline seemed to sense that compassion required her to be clinical. In an even voice, she asked, "Did what Mr. Ransom wanted follow any patterns?"

"Yes." Rappaport's voice was dry. "My subjugation, physically and emotionally. That was what excited him." She looked away. "Although afterwards he could hardly look at me."

"Do you know why?"

"No." Her voice dropped. "Once I even suggested something to try to please him, to help him not be ashamed. He just became upset. Because *I* was the initiator, I think."

"Did this go on throughout your marriage?"

"At some point, Mark lost interest. No matter what I did." Rappaport stubbed out her cigarette, grinding it to a nub. "So we went on to other things."

"The rape fantasy?" Terri asked.

"Yes." Rappaport looked directly at the judge. "I would come home, and Mark would pretend to rape me. I never knew when." She paused. "I think it was the surprise that he liked most."

"But this was consensual."

Rappaport's eyes shut. "Yes."

"Did he ever hit you?"

"No." Rappaport paused. "Not to hurt, and never without my consent."

Terri watched Caroline Masters take that in. "Mr. Ransom's preoccupation with rape," Caroline ventured. "Do you also relate *that* to Laura Chase?"

"Only at the end." Rappaport glanced at Terri. "But Ms. Peralta seemed to think this important."

"What is it?"

Rappaport paused, reached for her cigarettes. Terri remembered Rappaport's face when she had first described this encounter, her own feelings when she learned that it was Rappaport's last with any man. But Rappaport's response to Caroline suggested that it was something of marginal interest, thrown out to help Terri; only the tremor in her hand showed how much the memory still cost her.

"It was the last time Mark and I had sexual relations of any kind." As if steadying herself, Rappaport took a leisurely drag. "As before, it seemed that he'd been losing interest in me—that the rape motif had played itself out, as it were. This time, however, he'd added a little something. When he threw me on the bed, there was a film of Laura Chase on the VCR." She shrugged. "Visually, it was of very poor quality."

For an instant, Terri flashed on Steinhardt, talking to Laura Chase. Did you buy up all the copies?

Steinhardt had asked. I hope so, Laura had answered.

"A stag film?" Caroline asked. "With two men?"

Rappaport stared at her for a moment. "What I remember most about it," she said quietly, "was Laura Chase crying as they did it. That stuck with me, for some odd reason." She paused. "That, and Mark's renewed sexual vigor."

Caroline was quiet for a moment. "You said that was 'the last time.' You and Mr. Ransom separated after that?"

"Yes."

"As a result of this incident?"

"That and another." Rappaport put down her cigarette. "After he did that, Mark went to a bar with some friends. They stayed out late. He told me, when he arrived home drunk, of having a 'theoretical discussion' of certain sexual practices." She paused. "And then he wondered aloud if two of them could fuck me. While he watched."

Terri turned to her, startled. Rappaport looked quite composed, except that she did not notice Terri at all; quite suddenly, Melissa Rappaport seemed to be in a room by herself.

"Whatever Laura Chase did," she murmured, "he wanted *me* to do. I was never *real* to him. And neither, in the deepest sense, was Laura herself.

Dead or living, we were both about his needs and fears. We couldn't be ourselves."

Slowly, Caroline Masters nodded. But Rappaport did not seem to see her, and no one wished to speak.

Quietly, Terri said, "I think you can see the relevance, Your Honor. Except for the issue of consent, the use of the Laura Chase film in a fantasy rape bears striking similarity to the role of Laura's tape in Ransom's attempted rape of Ms. Carelli."

Caroline turned to her, as if grateful to be refocused on the law. "I understand the parallel, Teresa. As we agreed, I'm reserving judgment until you've called your other witness."

"Then I'll reserve my argument," Sharpe said. "But with the court's permission, I'd like to ask Ms. Rappaport one or two questions."

Masters looked at Rappaport; she sat with her hands folded, unusually still. Masters turned to Sharpe again. "All right."

Nodding, Sharpe faced Rappaport. "When you were discussing bondage, you mentioned that your husband 'lost interest.' Could you explain what you meant by that?"

Rappaport watched her. "What I meant by that," she said, "was that it—I—no longer excited him."

"By excited . . ."

Rappaport lit a cigarette. "By excited," she said coolly, "I mean to convey the opposite of flaccid."

Sharpe gazed at her. ''In other words, he no longer achieved erections.''

Surprised, Terri remembered with embarrassment that Paget had raised the question after Terri first saw Rappaport, and that she still did not know the answer.

''Yes,'' Rappaport said finally. ''Once or twice.''

''And it was after these failures that Mr. Ransom contrived the pretended rape.''

Where, Terri wondered, was Marnie going with this.

''Yes,'' Rappaport answered. ''It was.''

''You also mentioned that after bondage, he could hardly look at you. Did you associate this with guilt?''

''I don't know. Perhaps it was just embarrassment at what he seemed to need.'' Rappaport looked away. ''Or at what I was willing to do.''

Caroline, Terri saw, was looking at Rappaport with an air of concern. But in comparison to the woman Terri had met in New York, Rappaport seemed less highly charged, as if by acknowledging what had happened, she had started drawing out the poison.

''After he simulated rape,'' Sharpe was asking, ''did Mr. Ransom also have trouble looking at you?''

''Sometimes. Yes.''

Sharpe paused reflectively. ''You already indicated that the 'rape motif had played itself out.' Did that involve a similar loss of interest?''

Facing her, Rappaport seemed stronger. ''It involved a decline in frequency, if that's what you mean.''

''It's partly what I mean. But did it also involve impotence?''

It startled Terri. ''Did Ms. Rappaport mention impotence? I certainly don't recall that.''

''Mark *wasn't* impotent,'' Rappaport interjected. ''The time before the Laura Chase incident, he couldn't achieve erection.'' Her voice became bitter. ''But that was obviously due to the limits of *my* appeal. With Laura Chase to help us, Mark was every inch the man he wished to be.''

Sharpe shrugged, as if wishing to spare Rappaport further embarrassment. ''Thank you, Ms. Rappaport.''

Terri turned on the night-light, kissed the top of Elena's head. ''Good night, sweetheart. I love you.''

''Forever?''

''Forever,'' Terri answered firmly. It was a formula they had started; newly frightened by the concept of time, Elena had extracted a promise from Terri never to get old or die. It would not do to tell Elena that, tonight, Terri felt as old as her own mother.

She walked to the living room. "Long day," she said to Richie. "And another one tomorrow."

He sat at the coffee table, with index cards spread in front of him, coding them in red pen for input into his computer. Terri did not ask what plans this might involve; she had an almost superstitious fear of knowing, and Lindsay Caldwell was too much on her mind.

"Did you have time to put through that loan?" he asked.

Terri considered lying, to give herself the peace she needed. But she could not bring herself to do it. "I haven't signed the note yet."

His head snapped up. "Why not?"

"I still don't feel quite right about it."

"Damn it, I need that money for Lawsearch. You *know* that."

Terri felt the familiar weariness that seized her every time Richie wanted something. "And borrowing will gut my pension plan and tighten our cash flow. We're already maxed out on our credit cards and paying consumer interest without any end in sight."

He stood. "Look, Ter, this deal will pull us out."

"Then you should be able to find one more investor. Besides me."

His long appraising look ended in a distrustful half smile. "You envy me, don't you? You have to work for someone, and I have my own life."

Terri wondered yet again at how Richie could always change the subject, find some hidden and petty motive for her objections to his plans. "I don't work for *someone*, Richie. I work for you."

Richie shook his head. "We work for *each other.* Right now we can get by on what you make, and invest in the future." He paused, adding pointedly, "Besides, having me home is good for Elena. Don't leave her out of the family equation."

"I never do. But during your 'workday,' Elena's in day care. Which is another cost in our financial equation."

"Not during the summer. I figured out the other day that between June and September I saved us nearly two thousand dollars by working at home. Besides, she goes to public school this fall."

Terri moved to the couch and sat. "I'd like to look for another place," she said. "Somewhere near where we can afford to buy someday, and which has a public school we like. That way, Elena won't have to change schools."

Richie stared down at her. "We've got better ways to spend our money than moving, and the schools here are fine." His voice became accusatory. "I'm not going to do something with *my* daughter just because Chris Paget found some special school for his son and then fills your head with how great it all is while the waiter pours expensive wine. I'll be damned glad when this trial is over and we can have a family life without his fingerprints all over it.''

Terri did not trust herself to speak. Finally, she said, ''Why do you believe that I need help to worry about Elena? And why do you think I disagree with you just to cut you down? Because it isn't true, and it hurts to have you think that.''

The half smile returned. ''You always think I'm trying to manipulate you, don't you? Wear you down. There's a name for that, Ter. Paranoia.''

Terri rose from the sofa and went to Richie. She put both hands on his shoulders, gazing up at him. ''Am I real to you?'' she asked.

He gave her a defensive look. ''Real? You're my wife, Terri. You're a big part of my life.''

She shook her head. ''But am I *real* to you? Do I exist *outside* you? Does Elena?''

''Why are you attacking me, Ter?'' Quick as a stage actor, his shoulders slumped in her hands, voice conveying mystified hurt. ''We're a couple. We dream together, make love together, raise Elena together. We've made a family. Don't you see that every time you attack me it threatens that?''

Terri felt the numb helpless feeling creep over her again. She could think of nothing to say.

Gently, Richie kissed her forehead. ''Let's not quarrel like this, okay? It's no good for Elena.''

It was a familiar moment, Terri knew; the point

where she could not go on, where Richie promised her peace in return for giving in. Suddenly the words rushed out. ''Don't you see what we do? We both use 'family'—you to get me to do what you want, me to hide what I'm doing from myself.'' Her voice became pleading. ''I'm dead inside, Richie. I don't *feel* anything.''

He stared at her. ''You're tired. It's no good for you to talk when you're tired—you lose perspective. Get some sleep.'' He paused. ''Even better, wait till this trial is over and things are where they used to be.''

Terri found she could not go on. She turned and walked out the door.

What, Terri wondered, am I doing? She was half-way down the hall before she knew that she was headed for the fire escape, to get some air. Richie did not follow; he knew that he did not need to.

The night air was cold. Slowly, Terri climbed the catwalk to the fourth floor. She stopped there, looking across the street at the student housing where they once had lived. They had not come, Terri realized, very far at all. And then she felt the tears on her face.

Why, she wondered, do men never seem to cry? Even the best ones, and even at the worst of moments.

She stayed there long after her tears had stopped, listening to the crickets in the cool night air, remembering the five years that had brought them to where they were. Tried to imagine the next five years, and then Elena's life to come.

She knew why she was afraid to do this. It was easier to keep busy day to day, the future no farther than next Saturday's matinee with Richie and Elena, or a picnic to which they took Elena and a friend from day care. Snapshots of a family, with both parents' arms around Elena. Pictures that hid, rather than revealed, the truth about her marriage.

At what age, Terri wondered, would Elena start absorbing the subliminal message of things unsaid and unfelt? At what point in childhood would she start to become like Terri, without ever choosing for herself? For what, when she was older, would she hold Terri to account—the marriage that Terri had stayed in, or the marriage that she had left? And with what damage would Terri send her to a marriage of her own?

She could find no answers. Standing there, Terri realized that she was tired and cold.

She had a trial to worry about, she told herself, Lindsay Caldwell to shepherd. The process did not stop because some defense lawyer had started to face her life.

She went back inside. Richie was still in the living room; the stacks of cards seemed only to have changed their sizes, some smaller and some larger.

"I agree with you," she said slowly. "We shouldn't talk until the hearing's over. And then we should talk seriously."

He looked up, eyes newly alert. "About what?"

She gave an apologetic shrug. "Maybe we both should take a little time off. To think."

His eyes narrowed. "Time off from work?"

"Time off from us."

He stood, his tone suddenly aggressive. "That we should separate, you mean. Why don't you just say that?"

Terri felt suddenly confused. "Live apart," she temporized. "Just for a while."

" 'For a while.' " His voice rose. "You'd do this to Elena, without even listening to me or going to see a counselor. Just walk out."

Already Terri felt guilty. "This *is* about Elena. Even if we're apart, we can always see a counselor."

Richie watched her with an odd, superior smile. "You're not being practical, Ter. We can't afford to separate."

"What do you mean?"

"I'm not leaving this apartment. Not while I've got a business to get up and running." His voice became cool. "If you pull the rug out from under me, I figure a court awards me around two thousand a month in interim support." He paused. "More, if they give me Elena."

It startled her; the conversation had spun out of

control, with Richie pushing it into realms she had not contemplated.

"They'd never do that," she managed.

"Because you're a woman? Before you go running off, Ter, wake up and smell the coffee." His tone turned harsh. "The women's movement has arrived. Courts look at who the real parent is, not just gender. In *this* family, your role has been to provide, and *mine* to care for Elena."

Terri could not shake the sense of unreality; she seemed to have entered a world she did not believe in, armed only with a lawyer's rote responses. "I never *asked* you not to work."

The smile reappeared. "But you agreed to it, and I relied on that. And that's all I'll need to tell the judge."

Terri felt herself trembling at Richie's rising air of confidence. With a sudden terrible clarity, she knew that he had been planning for this moment, perhaps for a long time.

"I'm very slow," she said softly. "But once I learn something, I remember it."

He nodded. "This is ugly, Ter. I don't like even imagining it. But if you're going to bring it up, we should talk about reality."

Terri looked at him: the slender frame, the curly hair, the face in which she once had seen such life and imagination. The face of her husband, her adversary.

"I've got another witness in the morning," she finally said. "I'd better get some sleep."

"Sure." His voice was gentle now. "When I come to bed, I'll try not to wake you."

Terry felt something shiver inside her. "Please," she said.

That night, with Richie asleep beside her, she wept again.

In the morning, Terri found him in the kitchen. The coffee was already made.

He handed her a cup. "French toast coming up," he said cheerfully. "Your favorite."

She took the coffee, sat at the kitchen table. "Want some milk for that?" he asked. "Or half-and-half?"

For a long time, Terri merely looked at him. With sudden pitiless comprehension, she saw the moment for what it was: the sweetness after the storm, calculated to help her pretend that nothing had happened. "I may not be real to you," she said quietly, "but what you understand about me, you understand very well."

He turned to her, expression hovering between relief and apprehension.

Terri stood. "I'd tell you not to threaten me with Elena, Richie. But it may be far too late."

"I didn't threaten *you*. It was *you* who wants to separate."

"Don't twist things." She shook her head. "You

told me to face reality. The sad reality of our marriage is that you're always three moves ahead of me, and I still can't bring myself to believe that there even are moves to make.''

He stared at her. ''What exactly are you saying?''

''That you don't love me. And that I haven't loved you for a long time, and hid that from us both.'' Terri paused. ''If you want to blame me for something, blame me for that.''

He flushed with anger. ''Don't bullshit me, Ter. It isn't our marriage. You had this alleged breakthrough when you started spending time with Christopher Paget.''

Terri walked silently to the sink, tossed the coffee down the drain, turned to face him again. ''Chris and you don't belong in the same conversation. First, you're nothing alike. Second, this has nothing to do with him. It's all about *you.*''

''I can't believe that.''

''Believe it. It's *you*, Richie. You, and the fact that you can never accept that it's you. And never will.''

He was silent; for the first time, Terri saw the panic in his mental calculation. ''It's about Elena, Terri. Our daughter, remember?''

She felt a surge of anger. ''Didn't you hear me? Don't use Elena to cover for yourself or to blackmail *me.*'' She paused, lowering her voice. ''I've got a case to try, and I'm going to do it right. For as long as I'm doing that, you've got me to support you. As long, that is, as you don't touch me."

Terri turned and went to wake Elena.

Watching Caroline Masters greet Lindsay Caldwell, Terri thought that they seemed like members of the same species, who recognized each other without ever having met. Caroline's manner bespoke a respectful sense of how difficult Caldwell must find this; Caldwell's quiet command seemed tempered by the knowledge that she could not control what Caroline did. Both spoke softly; neither smiled.

"Did they get you past the press?" Caroline asked.

Caldwell nodded. "They took me through the underground garage and then up a private elevator. I felt like plutonium."

"Which you are, in a way." Caroline Masters paused. "Unless I decide they have to, I don't want the press to ever know that you were here."

Caldwell glanced at Sharpe. "I appreciate that," she said, and the four women sat, Caroline behind her desk, Terri next to Caldwell, Sharpe a few feet back.

They were a strange assortment, Terri thought. Sharpe's alertness suggested some deeper tension, whereas the case appeared to have drawn from Caroline an unforeseen reserve of empathy. As for Terri, she still felt her inexperience. But at least all three were lawyers; here in chambers, Caldwell, with her tawny hair and chiseled profile, familiar only as an image on film, seemed startling.

Caroline faced her. "Tell me about Mark Ransom," she asked.

Caldwell nodded briskly, as if she appreciated the judge's directness and would be equally direct. In the corner, the stenographer sat poised over her machine. "It's quite simple," Caldwell began, "and quite painful. Twenty years ago, shortly before she died, I had an affair with Laura Chase. Mark Ransom found out."

Caroline's face was expressionless. "Did he make clear how he intended to use what he knew?"

"It was clear to *me,*" Caldwell answered coolly. "And he made it *very* clear that he was in control."

Caroline seemed to appraise her. "When you say that what Ransom knew was 'painful,' " she finally asked, "do you mean something about the affair itself. Or do you mean the fact of it?"

For a moment, the two women looked at each other; to Terri, their silence had a sudden unspoken intimacy. "Not the fact of it," Caldwell answered. "It was confusing to me then, but I've come to terms with that part. People's sexuality can cover a wide range, and my range, it seems, made being with Laura a possibility—at least for that time. No, what was painful was that the circumstances were so tied to Laura's death." Caldwell paused, as if still processing the memory, and then went on. "The affair began two weeks before Laura shot herself, with Laura looking out for me at a time I badly needed someone. One week later, I abandoned *her,* out of fear of Laura's needs and my own sexuality. Her suicide completed the chain of cause and effect. *That's* the pain Mark Ransom touched."

Caroline's gaze was still level, unfathomable. "I've listened to Laura's last psychiatric tape," she finally said. "A few days before she died, three men used her with a callousness that was equaled only by the psychiatrist who listened to her." Her voice grew quiet. "What I've just told you can never go beyond this room. But it's something you should know. Before you start apportioning blame."

Terri looked at her in surprise. For the moment, Caroline seemed to have set aside the murder of Mark Ransom; her exchange with Lindsay Caldwell had the unsparing directness of two women concerned with matters deeper and more intimate than a criminal proceeding. Caldwell shook her head. "I was with Laura when James Colt called her," she answered quietly. "Both Laura and I knew what he intended. I left anyway."

Caroline folded her hands. "We've been speaking of blackmail," she said. "For Laura to put her decision on you was a kind of emotional blackmail. You didn't force Laura to go with him. Or to kill herself."

Caldwell looked away. "Mark Ransom touched one other thing," she finally said. "Although he may not have known it."

"Which is?"

"An hour before she killed herself, Laura called me, drunk and desperate." Caldwell's voice fell. "I rejected her again."

Caroline watched her. Softly, she asked, "Did you think Ransom knew that?"

"I didn't know. He certainly knew enough." Caldwell still gazed down. "I thought perhaps she'd called Steinhardt that night, and that Ransom knew that. I still don't know whether that would have made me feel better, or worse."

"But you wanted to know."

"I've *always* wanted to know. As much as I feared exposure, *that* was why I would have seen Mark Ransom."

Caroline was quiet. "It may be beside the point," she said at last, "but I believe in personal responsibility for personal choices. You were what—nineteen? Laura let *herself* go." Her voice hardened. "But if we're adding links in some chain of cause and effect, add Steinhardt and James Colt—or Laura's father, for that matter. It's not germane to Ms. Carelli's culpability, but the suggestion that Mark Ransom found *that* tape exciting is almost as appalling as the suggestion he was using it for sexual blackmail."

"And they are *both* suggestions," Sharpe pointed out. "Not *facts*. Nor defenses to premeditated murder."

Caroline Masters turned to Sharpe. "I'm not here to bail out Ms. Carelli. But it's probably fortunate that the prosecution isn't required to show the human decency of the victim." Once more, Caroline faced Lindsay Caldwell. "As the issues of guilt which must occupy Ms. Sharpe are confined to Ms. Carelli, perhaps we should turn to the nuts and bolts of your conversation with Mark Ransom."

Caldwell leaned back, looking out the window. "I was surprised when he called," she finally said. "But the first thing I really remember was when he said that he'd been hearing so much about me.

" 'From whom?' I asked him.

"He hesitated, then he answered, 'Laura Chase.' "

Caldwell paused. "I was at my beach house in Malibu," she said slowly. "In the living room. My husband was sitting next to me.

"When Mark said that, I started—quite literally. I remember looking over my shoulder. Roger was reading a novel by Philip Roth, half smiling to himself.

"In the most normal tone I could manage, I said, 'Really.' And then Ransom began laughing." Caldwell's voice became low and angry. "The conversation had hardly begun, and I'd already told Mark

Ransom that there was someone in the room with me and that I was scared of Laura.

" '*Really,*' he repeated. 'Specifically, what Laura told me is that you're the most beautiful and sensitive lover she had ever been with.' It chilled me. And then his voice took on the unctuous tone of someone giving an exaggerated compliment. 'Coming from Laura, that's quite extraordinary, don't you think? It certainly impressed *me.*' "

Terri turned to glance at Caroline. But the judge's gaze had moved to her hands.

"The odd thing," Caldwell went on, "is that beneath the syrupy surface he sounded angry. As if knowing about Laura and me had thrown him off balance.

" 'Of course,' Ransom went on, 'toward the end, Laura had very poor luck with men—or women, it seems.' " Caldwell shook her head. "And then he said, in a horrible joking tone, 'The confusion must have killed her.' "

Caroline Masters looked up. "What did *you* say?"

"Roger glanced over at me. I realized that I'd been talking for some time and that he was becoming curious. So I said in the driest voice I could master, 'That's very droll, Mark. Where are you getting your material, the *Reader's Digest?*'

"Ransom laughed again. 'My Most Unforgettable Lesbian'? No, my material comes direct from Laura. In her own voice.'

‘‘Almost by reflex, I said, ‘Then I hope she called collect.’ ’’ Pausing, Caldwell looked at the judge. ‘‘It was so strange: I was trading black jokes with Mark Ransom about my affair with Laura Chase, trying to keep Roger from noticing how intimidated I was by whoever was on the other end.

‘‘ ‘No,’ Ransom told me. His tone was suddenly serious. ‘But I paid for it quite handsomely.’

‘‘Roger was looking at me now. ‘What rights did you buy?’ I asked Ransom.

‘‘Ransom’s voice got very quiet. ‘Literary rights,’ he said. ‘To the tapes of Laura and her psychiatrist.’ ’’

Caldwell paused again, looking at Caroline Masters. ‘‘For a moment,’’ Caldwell told her, ‘‘I forgot where I was. I don’t even know what I said. But for the rest of my life, I’ll never forget what *he* said next. ‘‘ ‘Laura seems to have loved you,’ he told me. ‘And you seem to have left her to her fate. Which, as it happens, is the subject of my book.’

‘‘For a time, I could hardly speak. ‘What,’ I managed, ‘is the book about?’

‘‘ ‘Laura’s suicide,’ he told me. ‘The days and hours before she pulled the trigger. I mean to answer the question ‘‘Who Killed Laura Chase?’’ ’

‘‘ ‘Who *did?*’ I asked, and then I realized Roger was staring at me.

‘‘More quietly yet, Mark answered, ‘Whomever I choose, Lindsay. Whom would you suggest?’ ’’

Terri watched Caroline Masters imagine what Terri could see clearly: Caldwell in the beach house Terri had visited, trying to conduct one side of the conversation for her husband's benefit while she listened to Mark Ransom exhume the guilt of twenty years. Caldwell's voice turned dull, as if at the memory of her helplessness.

" '*What* would *you* suggest?' I finally said to Mark.

" 'That you listen to my tape of Laura, talking about you.' His tone became intimate. 'Then you'll give me a very private interview. If you're sufficiently cooperative, I may even consider you an "editorial consultant." '

"Roger had gone back to reading Philip Roth. 'Is that necessary?' I asked Ransom.

"There was a long silence, and then he said, 'Only if you want the tape.'

"I felt sick. 'Why?' I asked.

"He was quiet again. 'Remember that little quarrel we had about Laura,' he asked, 'at the Yale symposium on "Women in Film"? You called me "the poet laureate of the centerfold," I believe.' "

Caldwell crossed her arms, as if hugging herself. "Something in those two sentences," she said to Caroline, "was as frightening as knowing he had the tapes.

" 'Yes,' I told Ransom, 'I remember.'

" 'I found you terribly arrogant,' he went on. 'But

I didn't know then just how well *you* knew your subject. So I thought it was time that we have a much more intimate chat about Laura. *And* about centerfolds.' "

Caldwell sounded tired. "If I'd had any doubt at all about what he wanted," she said, "that ended it."

" 'That's not my favorite subject,' I said.

" 'But it's *mine,* Lindsay. Because I've always wanted to interview someone who slept with Laura Chase. And hearing from Laura about how it was to sleep with *you* suggests that you have much more to offer me than I could ever have imagined.'

"I couldn't think of anything to say. When I turned to look at Roger, he was smiling at his book again. And then Mark Ransom said, 'I want you for an entire day. Alone. I promise, of course, to bring the tape.' "

Caldwell's voice became wearier. "I agreed to see him. At a hotel room in Los Angeles. It would have been the day after he met with Mary Carelli."

Caroline was quiet for a time. "And you never told your husband?"

"Only in the narrowest sense. After I hung up the phone, Roger asked who it was. I told him it was Mark Ransom and he wanted to sell rights to a book about Laura Chase." Caldwell shook her head. "It wouldn't come to anything, I told Roger—it wasn't my kind of material, and Ransom wasn't my kind of writer. But I was going to meet him anyway.'' Caldwell's voice fell. ''After all, I said to Roger, we were only talking about one day out of my life.''

Caroline leaned back. ''Why,'' she finally asked, ''are you willing to come forward now?''

Caldwell seemed to ponder the question. ''My reason has changed. When I first spoke with Terri, I was certain that the police had found the tape, or soon would. That my secret was out.'' She paused. ''And I desperately wanted to hear what Laura had said.''

''And now?'' Caroline asked. ''The tape is missing. Unless and until it's found, you're the only one who knows what happened between you and Laura Chase.''

Caldwell gave her a level look. ''That's true,'' she said finally. ''But I also know what happened between *Mark Ransom* and me. And knowing that, I know who Mark Ransom was.''

''And that makes silence difficult.''

Caldwell nodded. ''Until Steinhardt's daughter sold Ransom those tapes, *I* was content to live with what had happened. Because the only living person it hurt was me. That's not true anymore. Now Mary Carelli's on trial for murder, and the tape may surface anyway.'' She paused again, looking at Caroline Masters with an air of fatalism. ''If you decide that what I know is relevant, I'll tell Roger and my son and daughter. And then I'll testify for Ms. Carelli.''

Caroline Masters bent forward, as if in private contemplation. Terri could almost read her thoughts: that the matter of Mark Ransom was far more complex than she had imagined; that she did not wish to harm Caldwell or Melissa Rappaport; that she no longer saw the trial in terms of her own role.

"May I pose a few questions?" Sharpe asked.

Almost unwillingly, Masters turned to her. "Of course."

Sharpe pulled her chair closer, facing Caldwell.

"Do you know where the tape is?" she asked.

Caldwell shook her head. "No. I don't."

"Do you have any idea what might have happened to it?"

"No." Pausing, Caldwell looked puzzled. "I wish I did."

Sharpe cocked her head, as if equally bemused. "Did Mr. Ransom ever demand sex for the tape?" she asked.

"No. Not in so many words."

"Did he propose any kind of sexual activity between you and him?"

Caldwell stared at her. "Did he say, 'I'll trade the tape for sex'? No. Did he have to? You wouldn't ask if you'd been on the other end of the telephone."

"I understand. But don't you agree that, in the literal sense of his words, Mark Ransom could have been asking you for information—albeit of a very intimate kind?'' Sharpe paused. ''Perhaps pushing you, as journalists sometimes will, but after nothing more than the most sensational book he could write?''

Caldwell flicked back her hair. ''Only if you believe that when a man says to a woman, 'I'd like to stay the night,' the literal sense of his words is that he admires your living room couch.'' She paused, adding in sardonic tones, ''Perhaps pushing you, as men sometimes will, but only for a good night's sleep.''

The sudden stinging irony startled Terri and seemed to snap Caroline out of her private reverie. Sharpe flushed, and then assumed a tone of exaggerated patience. ''The literal sense of words *does* matter if you're in a court of law. I've prosecuted any number of rape cases where the man claimed that 'no' meant 'yes.' If that kind of Orwellian twist were evidence of guilt or innocence, one of those men would no doubt be raping another woman even as we sit here.''

''Don't *you* twist this,'' Caldwell snapped. ''The only reason Mark Ransom didn't try to rape *me* is that Mary Carelli shot him first.'' Caldwell's voice turned calm but very cold. ''The curious thing about his call was how clear it was to me, whatever words he used, that part of Ransom's very sick thrill was that I was a successful woman and a feminist. Like you, I assume.'' Caldwell paused. ''I can't help but wonder how *you* would have felt, Ms. Sharpe, if Mark Ransom had placed that call to you.''

Sharpe pulled back, staring at Caldwell with an odd, hurt expression. ''That's completely unfair.''

''Is it?''

Caroline leaned forward. ''I understand your point, Marnie. *And* Ms. Caldwell's. Do you have anything more?''

It took a moment for Sharpe to turn from Caldwell. ''Only an observation,'' she said quietly. ''We have no explicit request for sex, no blackmail which can be proven. And certainly no rape. Quite literally, Mr. Ransom did not come within four hundred miles of Ms. Caldwell. So all we're left with is a long-distance call that *Ms. Caldwell* conducted in a deliberately obscure manner and that is evidence of nothing more than Ms. Caldwell's private pain. Which is how it should remain—private.''

Terri leaned forward. ''That goes to the weight of the evidence,'' she replied. ''*Not* its admissibility. The court should allow Ms. Caldwell to testify fully and completely. Ms. Sharpe can cross-examine. After that, the *court* can decide how it sees Mr. Ransom's call to Ms. Caldwell—which, as she points out, bears as much resemblance to a request for information as rape does to a honeymoon.''

''The problem,'' Caroline rejoined, ''is that it

doesn't resemble rape, either. Which is Ms. Carelli's defense.''

Terri felt Caroline deciding against her, reached for a new argument. ''Ms. Carelli's defense,'' she responded, ''involves this man's sexual character, and his sexual agenda in contacting Ms. Carelli. Which, as Ms. Carelli can attest, involves the same supposedly 'ambiguous' approach Mark Ransom used with Ms. Caldwell.''

''But we're looking for admissible evidence on which to decide whether Ms. Carelli acted in self-defense and therefore can defeat probable cause. You'll admit, Teresa, that we're nowhere near what could be considered a 'similar act' to rape.''

''It depends on *which* act we're talking about.'' Terri shifted ground again. ''Let me suggest this: that the court wait until the entire defense case is in before ruling on whether Ms. Rappaport, Ms. Caldwell, and the tape of Laura Chase can be part of the record on which the court decides the issue of probable cause. That ought to assure the broadest information and perspective when the court *does* rule.''

Caroline gave a small smile. ''Never face today,'' she said, ''what you can put off till tomorrow. If you're losing, that is.''

Terri smiled back. ''Never rule today,'' she answered, ''if your ruling may be better tomorrow.''

Caroline's smile faded, and then she nodded

slowly. "All right, Teresa. You've preserved your position for the moment. I'll rule after your remaining witnesses." She turned to Caldwell. "I apologize for keeping you in limbo, Ms. Caldwell. But from the court's perspective, Ms. Peralta's request makes enough sense to honor it."

Caldwell nodded. "I understand."

"I hope so." The judge turned to Sharpe. "In the meanwhile, Marnie, if any new tape involving Ms. Carelli, Laura Chase, *or* Ms. Caldwell comes into your possession, you are to notify me immediately." She paused for emphasis. "Immediately, and privately. Because if *any* of these tapes is made public, and it's the doing of the prosecution, I'll be inclined to see that as a deliberate denial of due process. The sanction will be to dismiss this case. And in dismissing it, I'd feel impelled to set forth why."

Sharpe looked startled. "Is it really necessary," she asked, "for the court to assume responsibility for safeguarding so much evidence in such an extraordinary way?"

"It's necessary for my own sense of decency. For which *I* take responsibility." Caroline turned back to Caldwell. "If I decide to rule for Ms. Peralta, I'll give you reasonable notice. So that you can tell whomever you need to tell."

"Thank you," Caldwell said. "At some point, I may tell my family, regardless of what happens here.

But whether and when is something I need to work out for myself.''

Caroline was quiet. ''In the end,'' she answered, ''I may force you to. That's a decision that weighs heavily on me. But it's part of being a judge. So perhaps you can indulge me while I give you the perspective of a judge.''

''Of course.''

''Sexuality *does* involve a wide spectrum. But you couldn't have known that at age nineteen. And as simple as it seems, many people find facing that difficult at *any* age.'' Caroline's voice slowed, as if to make sure Caldwell heard her. ''For almost twenty years as a defense lawyer and now a judge, I've been mired in questions of guilt and innocence—moral as well as legal. Of all the people involved with Laura Chase's death, your wounds seem by far the worst to me, and you have by far the least to answer for. Forgive yourself.''

Caldwell looked surprised. Abruptly Caroline stood, extending her hand. ''Good luck, Ms. Caldwell.''

Caldwell took Caroline's hand. ''And you,'' she said softly. ''Thank you.''

Caroline called her deputy. Within a minute, Caldwell and Terri, accompanied by two bailiffs, were in a freight elevator, silently thinking their separate thoughts.

Finally, Caldwell turned to her. "You were good, Terri. She was going to rule against you, I think."

"I think so too."

They got to the underground garage. Caldwell's limousine, black with opaque windows, was parked by the elevator. The bailiffs stood back; Caldwell's chauffeur waited on the other side of the car. "It seems," Caldwell said to Terri, "that I'll leave as I came, anonymously. It's a luxury I don't often get."

Terri was quiet, then she said, "I don't know how to thank you."

"You needn't thank me, and you needn't feel responsible. Really, I had no choice."

Terri watched her face. "At least Caroline Masters tried to make it easier," she said at length. "Much more than before, I'm really coming to admire her."

"You *should* admire her—she's an admirable woman." Caldwell paused, and then added softly, "But I think there's something else—a particular sensitivity. Something personal, perhaps."

Before Terri could question her, Lindsay Caldwell touched her shoulder. "I wish you well," Caldwell said, "with everything."

Caldwell disappeared into the limousine. Terri watched it drive up the exit ramp, a black car with an unseen passenger, and vanish.

TWO

TELEVISION FLICKERING IN the background, Christopher Paget poured Mary Carelli a glass of red wine.

"You still like Chianti, I imagine."

"Since even before you knew me." Her voice was dry. "Of course, I've learned to like better Chianti since I lived in Rome."

To Paget, the remark had a rueful undertone, which mingled pride in what she had accomplished with fear that it would soon be gone: to remember Rome was to acknowledge that she might never see it again.

Paget raised his wineglass. "To Rome."

Half smiling, Mary touched her glass to his. "To Rome," she said. "And to getting through tomorrow."

They sat in Paget's library on Sunday evening, the end of four days spent rehearsing Mary's testimony, while Terri handled Rappaport and Caldwell and then prepared for Marcy Linton. For the first two days, they had crafted Mary's testimony, confessing error or doubt when necessary; carefully treading through her interview with Charles Monk; designing, editing, and discarding verbal formulas until they found the answers they wanted. And then Paget had devoted the weekend to tearing those answers apart.

Now it was dark outside, and they were finished.

"You've worked hard," he said. "All you have to do is stay alert but calm."

Mary's smile became ironic. " 'Alert but calm,' " she repeated. "So easy to achieve. And such a perfect approach for a premeditated murderer."

For Paget, the remark had a surreal quality: a mordant joke from a calculating woman from whom he could not demand the truth, and in whose truthfulness he could not believe. But the most eerie part was that he could hear the comment either as a veiled confession or as understated bitterness that Sharpe—and perhaps Paget—believed her capable of murder.

"I think Caroline's ready to listen now," he said finally. "Whether she lets them testify or not, Rappaport and Caldwell have made an impression. Which means that Judge Masters is thinking about who Ransom was, rather than just wondering who *you* are."

Of course, Paget thought, *I* wonder who you are. But he did not say that: while their preparation was shot through with the fact of Mary's lies, they had treated that as an intellectual problem, and each other with civility. After four days, the two things Paget knew for certain were how facile and self-disciplined Mary Carelli still was.

As if in counterpoint, her face now appeared on television: first as a young witness before the Senate, then as a woman charged with murder. "Tomorrow morning," the voice-over said, "Mary Carelli faces the most critical moment of the hearing and, perhaps, of her life. The moment when she takes the stand."

Mary gazed at the screen, and then at Paget. "Don't worry," she said. "I won't blow this. Whatever else you think, you should know me well enough to know that."

The remark was matter-of-fact, but there was steel beneath it. "Just don't underestimate Marnie Sharpe," Paget answered.

Mary stretched her legs. "I've been studying her, Chris. I know exactly how she'll be."

Paget nodded; he could too easily imagine Mary, removed from all emotion, dissecting Sharpe while she went about her business. That her business was to prove Mary a murderer would make Mary all the more determined.

"I'm sure," he remarked, "that Marnie's every quirk is coded on your brain."

"It is." Mary's voice went cold. "I won't let her nail me."

"I believe you."

Her ironic look returned. "Yes? About that I suppose you do."

Paget smiled. But all that he believed in was Mary's resolve; he was far too skeptical of her innocence not to worry. He wished that he could fast-forward his life to the end of her testimony, find their defense still viable, their secrets safe from Carlo.

The seamed face of a prominent defense lawyer had appeared on Court TV.

"It's such a mistake," he said, "to put her on the stand. But then this whole strategy is a mistake. If Christopher Paget loses *here,* he's got no surprises left for trial. To me, this defense looks like a play written by a gifted amateur—flashes of brilliance, but a plot that won't fly. I think he's far too close to the case to be objective."

Paget turned off the sound. "We've done all we can," he said quietly.

Mary turned from the television. "We have," she said. "I should leave in a while."

She looked suddenly tired, Paget realized, and a little sad. Like a woman with nowhere to go.

When she glanced at the television again, the picture had changed. A much younger woman, she stood in intimate profile with Christopher Paget, in the moments before he testified in the Senate. And then Carlo's face appeared.

"Did you see the cover of *People?*" she asked.

He nodded. "Carlo. But I didn't read the article."

"They don't have much yet." Mary paused. "It's just as well that my parents are dead."

Paget nodded, lost in thought.

"Do you ever wonder," Mary asked softly, "what would have happened to us without the Lasko case?"

Paget gazed at her. "Without Carlo? Or with?"

"With, I suppose." Mary looked down. "That was a good night, Chris. A good weekend."

"It was." Paget contemplated his wine. "But it's impossible to project from a single weekend. We're so very different, after all."

She raised her eyes. "But could my *life* have been different? Would *I* have been different?"

Paget thought for a time. "I don't want to sound like a moralist," he answered, "and certainly not tonight. But by the time we made love that weekend, you'd already committed yourself to helping Jack Woods. Once that was done, the whole thing had an inexorable quality." Pausing, he switched off the television. "The truth, I think, is that people keep on being who they are and what they want. I don't think the fact that two people encounter each other truly changes either one. It may change their *lives,* perhaps, but not their essential selves."

Mary fell quiet. "You and me, you mean."

He nodded. "You and I made each other's *lives* wholly different. But that was because we encountered each other head-on, and then proceeded to be precisely who we were. As Malraux observed, 'Character is fate.' ''

She studied him. ''Carlo didn't make just your *life* different, Chris. He made *you* different.''

Was that true? Paget wondered. Had Carlo made him any better, any wiser and more loving, than the man Paget's parents had sent into the world? ''Perhaps,'' he said finally. ''But then *children* are different.''

The thought led him again to Carlo: how this trial might change his view of his own parents and, more subtly, of himself. It took Paget far away from Mary.

''I'm sorry,'' she said at last. ''For everything. More than you'll ever know.''

He looked up at her again. At that moment, fifteen years fell away; he saw her as she had seemed to him in Washington, making love on the weekend before he had learned what she had done. ''I know you are,'' he answered. ''I *do* believe that.''

She searched his face, as if measuring the truth of what he said, hoping for something to take away from all that had happened. And then, very simply, she said, ''Thank you.''

As they watched each other, something changed.

It would have been possible, Paget knew for an instant, to reach out to her. To put aside their past and suspend all disbelief. To make love for a night, escape from fear. People do these things for different reasons and then, in the morning, leave the moment and their needs behind. He knew that Mary and he could do that. Knew, as he looked into her eyes, that part of Mary wanted to.

He did not know what stopped them. History, perhaps. Perhaps, for him, there were other reasons.

"The one thing you have left to do," he told Mary, "is sleep."

For another moment, she simply looked at him. "I'll call a cab," she said.

The courtroom was dense with silence; the extra reporters Judge Masters had admitted to hear Mary Carelli stood at the back of the room. Carlo and Johnny Moore watched from the front row; intent, Terri took notes.

Outside, groups of women with a sprinkling of men among them chanted and held a banner that read: RAPE IS NOT A RIGHT. Facing them, separated by the width of the concrete walkway leading to the door of the courthouse, a group of counterpicketers carried signs reading: JUSTICE FOR MARK RANSOM; THE VICTIM IS NOT ON TRIAL; DON'T MURDER THE FIRST AMENDMENT. The doorway was guarded by police; more police lined the rear of the courtroom.

"And why did you agree to see Mark Ransom?" Paget asked Mary.

The question was critical—it would determine the course of Mary's testimony and the line of Sharpe's attack. Sharpe did not move; even Caroline Masters's gaze, intent and unblinking, underscored the moment. Only Mary looked calm.

"He had a tape," she answered. "Of a session I had with a psychiatrist in Beverly Hills. A Dr. Steinhardt."

At the corner of his vision, Paget saw Sharpe tense with surprise. "Why did you visit Dr. Steinhardt?" he asked.

"Because I was in deep emotional pain." Mary paused, but her gaze at Paget did not falter. "There were things I had done—hidden things—of which I was deeply ashamed. I had no peace of mind."

Paget heard whispers exchanged behind him, saw Sharpe half rise in her chair, looking from Mary to Masters. But Masters, staring openly at Mary, did not see Sharpe.

"And you described those things to Dr. Steinhardt?" Paget asked.

Mary's face was a mask of shame. "In as much detail as I could." Her voice fell. "I thought it was in confidence."

"And why was that important to you?"

She looked down. "Because what I told him was so deeply personal."

Sharpe's body, Paget saw, was taut with repressed energy—concern that Mary's fear of secrets might gain sympathy, eagerness to argue that Mary had opened up the tapes herself as evidence. "And how,'' Paget asked Mary, ''did you feel when Mark Ransom described the contents of the tape?''

''I was devastated.'' The memory appeared to drain her. ''After he hung up, I went to my bathroom and vomited.''

Paget paused, as if letting her collect herself. ''Did Ransom say what he thought would happen if he disclosed the tape?''

''Yes.'' Mary raised her head. ''He said that it could ruin my reputation, and my career.''

''Did you agree?''

Mary nodded. ''That was why I saw him,'' she said quietly. ''To ask him—beg him, if necessary—to leave my past life where it belonged. In the past.''

''You felt that desperate?''

Mary's eyes shut. ''The things he knew tortured me. That's why I went to Dr. Steinhardt.''

Paget turned to Judge Masters. ''Might we have a bench conference, Your Honor?''

Masters looked surprised, as if still caught in Mary's testimony. ''Yes. Of course.''

Quickly, Sharpe and Paget approached the bench. Glancing toward the crowded room, Masters leaned forward, to speak out of earshot of Mary, the reporters, the microphones of Court TV. Paget felt the cameras follow him to the bench.

''What is it, Mr. Paget?''

''Ms. Carelli has said all she intends to about the

tape. She's acknowledged that it exists; that it would damage her reputation and career; and that it was the reason she agreed to see Ransom. Which, we strongly believe, is an adequate substitute for disclosure of the tape itself—both from the standpoint of its impact on Ms. Carelli's actions and from simple fidelity to the truth. And because she's said nothing about the specific contents of the tape, Ms. Carelli has *not* waived her right to protect her conversation with Dr. Steinhardt."

"If this is fidelity to the truth," Sharpe said in muted tones, "then we should replace the scales of justice with Pinocchio. Ms. Carelli has *finessed* the contents of the tape, omitting *why* it was so harmful—that she lied to the United States Senate—while gaining sympathy for Mr. Ransom's exploitation of this nameless secret. For all that appears on the record, Ms. Carelli was ashamed of cheating at Monopoly."

Paget turned on her. "Does *that* end careers, Marnie, and ruin reputations? If you got caught cheating at Monopoly, would *you* throw up?"

"Only if I were looking for sympathy," Sharpe retorted, turning to Masters. "She's opened up the tapes."

"Regrettably," Masters answered, "*you* opened *this* up—when you got my permission in chambers to ask essentially the same questions Mr. Paget just asked. He's simply preempted you. If you want to play those tapes, you'll have to induce Ms. Carelli to say more than she has."

"Thank you," Paget said quickly. He walked away, leaving Sharpe still staring up at Masters. As Sharpe shrugged, Paget gave Mary a silent nod; one corner of her mouth formed the briefest of smiles. Glancing at Carlo, Paget saw his face relax.

"Please continue," Masters said.

Paget nodded. "Let me ask you this, Ms. Carelli: why did you bring a gun to Mr. Ransom's suite?"

"To protect myself."

"But why did you feel the need?"

Mary folded her hands. "His telephone call to me was filled with sexual innuendo and sexual blackmail."

"Could you be specific?"

Mary's shrug lent the suggestion of a shudder. "It wasn't just the words he used," she said quietly. "It was his tone—sniggering and systematically degrading. He expected a 'private interview.' He was going to 'interview' another 'famous woman' in Los Angeles. He wanted us 'back-to-back,' so that he could 'compare notes.' We could even discuss 'freedom of choice' and a woman's 'right to privacy.' " She shook her head. "Each word made my skin crawl."

Paget glanced up at Masters, as if to underscore the connection to Lindsay Caldwell. Then he asked Mary, "And what did you conclude from this conversation?"

"What Ransom so clearly *wanted* me to conclude," Mary answered coolly. "That he would trade the tape for sex. And that he would hurt me if I didn't."

Sharpe was on her feet. "Move to strike that last answer, Your Honor. It's wholly speculative—the witness is claiming omniscience regarding what Mark Ransom never said."

"Sustained." Masters turned to Mary. "We want the facts, Ms. Carelli. Please leave the interpretations to me."

Slowly, Mary nodded.

Moving forward, Paget asked, "Did you *intend* to trade the tape for sex?"

"I didn't *want* to." Her voice fell. "I just wanted to talk him out of it. Beyond that, I didn't really know."

"And yet you brought a gun."

"Yes," Mary looked at Masters. "But *not* to kill him. Because he frightened me."

"Then why didn't you tell the police?"

Mary paused, touching her eyes. "Because I didn't want anyone knowing what was on the tape."

"Is that also why, after Mark Ransom died, you *still* didn't tell the police about the tape?"

"Yes. It is."

"Didn't you think that the police would find any tape that Mr. Ransom had?"

"That's logical, of course." Mary turned back to Caroline Masters. "But I was in shock."

Paget nodded, satisfied. By asking the questions a skeptical judge or cross-examiner might ask, he was depriving Sharpe of points while helping Mary restore her credibility. And though Masters understood all this, she was plainly prepared to listen: Terri had done her job, and now Mary was doing hers.

"Is it your understanding," Paget asked, "that there are actually two tapes of you and Dr. Steinhardt, and that the prosecution has only the first?"

"That's my understanding, yes."

"Do you know the whereabouts of the second tape?"

Mary looked at Sharpe. "No," she said emphatically. "I do not."

A slight edge in Mary's voice hinted anger at the question; if she knew what had happened to that tape, Paget thought, then Mary was a gifted liar. But, of course, she was.

"In fact," Paget said, "Ransom didn't bring *any* tape, did he?"

"No tape of *me*." Mary looked troubled. "He did bring a taped session between Dr. Steinhardt and Laura Chase. Her death was to be the subject of his next book."

There was a stirring in the courtroom; until this moment, the press had not known about the tape of Laura Chase.

Now Sharpe was on her feet. "Your Honor," she interjected. "The People request a bench conference."

The two lawyers met in front of Masters. "That tape has not yet been admitted," Sharpe said. "Mr. Paget phrased the question indirectly, so that Ms. Carelli could slip in Laura Chase before I saw it coming. I didn't know that we'd invited her."

"What *are* your intentions," Masters asked Paget, "now that Ms. Carelli has so neatly summoned Laura from the dead?"

"To describe the contents generally," Paget said, "*without* mentioning James Colt." His voice quickened. "Laura Chase is dead; it's Ms. Carelli who has a claim on our compassion. And as Your Honor knows, the Laura Chase obsession goes to the heart of Mr. Ransom's sexuality. It's a central part of what Ms. Carelli says happened here—"

"The sexual acts described are quite different, Mr. Paget."

"True. But the obsession is all of a piece. And that's what triggered Mr. Ransom's abuse of Ms. Carelli."

"According to Ms. Carelli," Sharpe put in, "that unimpeachable source of truth."

"Save it for cross," Paget retorted, "where Mary can answer you."

Masters raised her hand. *"Enough,"* she said. "I'll allow a very general description. As Mr. Paget points out, there's no privilege here. And Mr. Ransom's sexual proclivities are clearly relevant to the defense. Let's get back on the record.''

"Thank you,'' Paget said. Briefly, he nodded to Terri, and then faced Mary again. "Ms. Carelli, could you generally describe the contents of the tape?''

"Yes.'' Mary's voice was soft. "It involves a weekend Laura Chase spent with three men in Palm Springs. The men involved her in a series of sexual activities—exhibitionism, at first.'' Mary paused. "And then two had sex with her while the third watched.''

Watching Mary, Paget felt and heard the crowd reaction—bodies stirring, exclamations. The judge cracked her gavel, and there was silence again. "Why did Mr. Ransom bring *that* tape?'' Paget asked.

"What he *said* was that he wanted to discuss his new book on Laura Chase. Of which that supposedly was an integral part.'' Again, Mary hesitated. "He intimated that if I interviewed him on *Deadline,* it might help him forget *my* tape.''

"What did you say?''

"That he'd misled me. That he'd held back the tape to continue his blackmail.'' Her voice grew faint. "His answer was that we should listen to the Laura Chase tape and then talk about it.''

"And did you listen to Laura's tape?''

"Yes." Mary looked away. "He made me."

Paget cocked his head. "Was that after Mr. Aguilar appeared with the champagne?"

"Yes."

"And did you ask Mr. Aguilar to hang the Do Not Disturb sign when he left the room?"

"I did. Yes."

"And why was that?"

Mary turned to Caroline Masters. "I was there against my will," she said softly. "Because Mark Ransom knew things I didn't want *anyone* to know. The fact that Mr. Aguilar saw us was upsetting enough; I didn't want to have a cleaning person come in and see us talking." She paused. "And when Mark Ransom described the Laura Chase tape and then told me I had to listen, I knew I didn't want anyone walking in on *that*. I was far too ashamed of what was happening."

"You didn't make that request of Mr. Aguilar just to be alone with Mark Ransom?"

"Not in the sense that *he* interpreted it." Mary's voice hardened. "I don't want to disappoint Mr. Aguilar, but I consider Mark Ransom to have been the most twisted and distasteful man I have ever known."

Paget was silent for a moment, letting Masters absorb that. "Could you tell us," he asked, "what this 'twisted and distasteful man' tried to do once Mr. Aguilar left?"

"He tried to rape me." As if to answer some unspoken doubt, Mary turned to Caroline Masters, repeating softly, "Mark Ransom tried to rape me."

"Could you explain what happened?" Paget asked.

Turning again, Mary stared into some middle distance. "It began when he played the tape." Her voice became quiet now, almost frightened. "It was awful. As Laura Chase danced for these men, and then started touching herself, Mark Ransom grew more excited. When the sex acts began, it pushed him over the edge."

"Could you describe that?"

Mary's look of fixity lingered: it was as if she were replaying a tape of her own, searching for precision. "He began to drink quickly," she finally answered. "Glass after glass. I had the odd feeling that I was watching a perverted *Alice in Wonderland*—that if Mark Ransom could step through a looking glass and find himself with Laura Chase and those three men, he would have given up his soul."

There was another murmur from the spectators. Sharpe stood again. "The same objection, Your Honor. If anything, Ms. Carelli is taking more liberties than before."

Masters turned to Mary. "I agree with Ms. Sharpe, and I'm striking the last sentence of your answer. Just tell us what happened."

Mary shifted, folding her arms so that she seemed

to hug her own shoulders. "For a moment, it was as if I weren't there anymore. He sat there listening, an odd smile on his face, just sat looking at me. Like he was hearing music from very far away—something beautiful, which he might never hear clearly. And then he put his hand on my knee.

"I pushed his hand away, looked up at him in surprise." She paused. "When my eyes met his, his gaze moved to his lap. Slowly, to make sure that I followed him.

"There was a bulge in his pants.

"It was as if we'd *both* stepped through the looking glass." She turned to Masters, speaking in an embarrassed tone. "I'm sorry, Your Honor. But what he said then, very soft and very low, was, 'I like fucking women I've seen on television. It's like I've made them real.' "

Masters gazed down at her. "It was so hostile," Mary told her. "They say that for some men sex is an act of violence, not of love. What I felt then was that Mark Ransom wanted to commit an act of violence—against me, and against who and what I was: a successful woman whom other women might actually admire." Her voice grew harder. "Mark Ransom hated women unless they were subservient. That's why forcing me to listen to Laura Chase's degradation excited him. That was why he wanted to break my will."

Paget saw Sharpe begin to rise once more, then

think better of it. "What did you say to him?" he asked Mary.

"No." Mary still faced Caroline Masters. "I said *no.*"

"And Mr. Ransom's response?"

"That if I had intercourse with him, the tape was mine." She turned back to Paget, finishing softly. "But if I didn't, my secrets belonged to the world."

"And you still refused."

Mary paused. "Not at first. I was too scared."

"What did you say?"

She looked down. "That I'd help him promote the Laura Chase book."

"But he didn't accept that?"

Mary shook her head. "He told me that was the *other* thing I'd do for him." Mary's voice fell. "After I undressed for him, like Laura."

"And you refused?"

"Not really." Her voice became puzzled. "It was more like an instinct. I knew I couldn't let him make me be Laura Chase." She turned to Masters, her words coming in a rush. "It wasn't a rational thing. It was a felt thing. I remember thinking that it would never end—that if I gave in now, he could force me anytime he wanted me, until my life wasn't worth living. I thought of all I'd done to become who I am, to stand for something. And then for a split second I thought of all the women who've given in to men like Ransom—whether for a job, or for their children, or for money to get by on, or just because they were too frightened to resist.'' Her tone hardened. ''Some deep instinct made me want to fight back, no matter what. It was as though if I gave in, I'd lose *myself*. Forever.''

In that moment, Paget imagined the people watching on television, imagined McKinley Brooks calculating the political cost of prosecuting this woman as he felt her intensity, saw her impassioned profile gazing up at Masters.

''What did you do?'' Paget asked.

''I grabbed my purse. I wanted to leave before I *thought* more than I *felt*. To leave while I was still *me*.'' Mary seemed to swallow. ''And then Ransom spun me around.''

Paget stepped forward. More quietly, he asked, ''What happened then?''

Mary straightened her skirt, the reflex of a woman imposing order on her own emotions. To the side, Paget saw Carlo again, face tight and miserable. The courtroom was silent.

''I was still holding my purse.'' Mary's voice was quiet but clear. ''Suddenly he was on top of me, pulling down my panty hose, as Laura Chase described two men having sex with her while the third one watched.''

There was a nervous cough in the courtroom.

''It was almost unreal,'' Mary went on. ''Some part of my senses registered Laura Chase's voice,

Ransom's face, the champagne on his breath. I still remember those things clearly.'' She touched her forehead, as if searching for some lost detail. ''Another part fought him by instinct. But it's as if *that* woman lost her memory to shock. All that I can retrieve are fragments.''

Paget nodded. ''Was your memory keener when you talked to Inspector Monk?''

Mary shook her head. ''No. It's not a matter of memory, but of trauma. If anything, the trauma was more debilitating when I was with Inspector Monk.''

Glancing up, Paget saw Masters's unblinking gaze at Mary, as if by sheer intensity she might divine the truth. The hearing seemed to weigh on her now; she seemed less inclined to arid wit, more troubled by judgments yet to be made.

''Do you recall,'' Paget asked Mary, ''how you received the various injuries described by Dr. Shelton?''

''Some. Not all.'' As Mary turned to Sharpe, her voice became cold and precise. ''The only thing that I can say with certainty is that I did not inflict them *after* Mark Ransom died. *Any* of them.''

The last phrase rang with anger and conviction; so far, Paget thought, Mary's demeanor was close to perfect. ''Is there any injury you recall more clearly than others?''

''Yes.'' Mary touched her cheekbone. ''The first blow to my face. I recall that very clearly.''

‘‘And why is that?’’

‘‘Because it was slow, deliberate, and brutal.’’ She paused. ‘‘And because Ransom seemed to take such pleasure in it.’’

Paget saw Caroline Masters lean forward. He could almost trace her line of thought; this was the injury Elizabeth Shelton could not explain, inflicted by a man with a taste for bondage and simulated rape.

‘‘Could you describe the blow?’’ he asked Mary.

‘‘Yes. I was on my back. He had one hand on my chest, pinning me to the floor, staring at me with a hatred so intense that, for a moment, I stopped struggling.’’ Mary’s tone grew quiet. ‘‘That moment—and the look he gave me—has stayed in my mind like a freeze-frame. And then he hit me.’’ She stopped, as if at the shock of memory, and then, slowly and pointedly, added, ‘‘Just as I told Inspector Monk.’’

To his left, Paget saw Marnie Sharpe frown; Mary was doing well, he knew, and this was the one piece of evidence for which Sharpe had no ready answer.

‘‘How did Mark Ransom’s blow to the face affect you?’’

Mary’s voice became toneless. ‘‘My neck snapped back, my head hit the floor. A jolt of pain went through my skull and eyes. It got dark—I think perhaps he’d started choking me.’’ She stopped as if puzzled. ‘‘It was like I’d blacked out. The next thing that I remember is my legs spread apart, and Ransom kneeling between them. His pants were down.''

''What did he do?''

Mary gazed at the back of the room. ''He'd stopped,'' she said quietly. ''His head was cocked to one side. And then, in the background, I heard Laura Chase's voice again.'' Mary's own voice filled with wonderment. ''He was *listening* to her. As if he were listening for a cue.'' Masters gave Mary a pensive look; as Paget had intended, Mary's comment resonated with Rappaport's last encounter with Mark Ransom. And then Mary added, ''As I *also* told Inspector Monk.''

That was good, Paget thought; Mary's testimony had begun to highlight the points where her statements to the police were congruent with the physical evidence or the account of other witnesses. With each moment, the misstatements stressed by Sharpe began to seem more petty and unfair.

''Did he have an erection?'' Paget asked.

''Yes.'' For a moment, Mary closed her eyes. ''As he listened to Laura, he held it in his hand.''

''Did he seem ready to penetrate you?''

Mary's eyes opened. ''Yes.''

Masters leaned forward. ''Could you describe,'' Masters asked quietly, ''how it happened that Mark Ransom was shot? In the most factual terms you can manage.''

Mary turned to her, as if startled by her intervention. "Mark Ransom was shot," she finally answered, "because he stopped to listen to Laura Chase."

Masters's brow knit. "Could you explain that?"

Mary nodded. "As he listened, it was like a respite. I had a moment of clarity—heightened awareness, almost. I felt the strap of my purse in my hand. All at once, I remembered what was inside it." Pausing, Mary sounded bemused. "A gun. The gun I had bought."

She made it sound, Paget thought, like an object of wonder and horror. "How did you get it out?" Masters asked.

Paget was helpless now; he had not expected Masters to interrupt the flow of their questions, rehearsed until it seemed natural. "I heard Laura's voice," Mary answered. "She was saying something like, 'He wanted them to have me every way.' And then it came to me.

" 'You can take me,' I told him. 'I'll let you do it, any way you want.' " Mary's voice became bitter. "He looked so pleased—my consent to being degraded was what he'd wanted most. And then I said, 'But only if you use a rubber.' "

Masters's look suggested surprise, perhaps unease at Mary's presence of mind. "How did he respond?"

"By laughing." Mary paused. "And then I said there was one in my purse.

"It seemed to startle him. Before he could answer, I started to reach in my purse." Mary's voice became tired. "When he pushed me back again, the gun was in my hand." She stopped abruptly.

"What happened then?" Masters asked her.

Mary stared at her hands. "His hands were on my wrists, grabbing. I kneed him." Mary's lips parted, mute, and then she said softly, "The gun went off."

Masters watched her. In level tones, she asked, "How close were you?"

Mary shook her head. "I don't know anymore. I just don't know."

"But you told the police two to three inches."

Mary shrugged, as if helpless. "I did the best I could," she said wearily. "I was trying to answer what they asked. I didn't know how they could make a wrong answer look." Her shoulders drew in. "I'd kneed him. He could have been falling back when the gun went off. I accept that what I thought was wrong. I wish I could tell you why. But I can't."

Paget saw tears in Mary's eyes. But her gaze at Caroline Masters was unblinking. In a soft voice, Masters asked, "His hands were never on the gun?"

"Perhaps they were. But I never told the police that. Because what I remembered was his hands clamped on my wrists."

"Did you close the window shades?"

Mary seemed not to notice the abrupt change of subject. Her voice was leaden. "Yes."

"Before the gun went off, or after?"

"I think after." Mary paused. "After, everything that happened is so vague. My only association with the window was that I was ashamed of what had happened. I know that doesn't make any sense." She shook her head, as if at an afterthought. "I was wearing clothes, though. He never got my clothes off. So I don't know who that man saw."

"Mr. Hassler," Masters said. "Was it you that *Mr. Tench* saw? Outside the room?"

In Mary's silence, Paget felt the slow dismantling of their preparations. It was as if the judge had required a closer sense of Mary than Paget could supply. "I think so," Mary said at last. "I think for a moment I was going to get help. But then I went back to the room without doing anything." She sounded bewildered. "I seem to have an image of being outside the door, not believing what had happened. That if I went back inside, he would be fine and the nightmare would be over."

Caroline Masters remained silent, waiting for more. Mary, stripped of the careful framework she and Paget had constructed, seemed to have started free-associating. From the corner of his eye, he saw Marnie Sharpe, intently scribbling notes.

"I felt I was sleepwalking," Mary went on. "I remember drifting around the room, moving from thing to thing. Touching each piece of furniture as if to find out what was real. I did everything but look at him.'' She paused, gazing up at Masters. ''You see, it was so horrible the way he died. Staring down at me with the life slipping out of him, as if I had hurt his feelings. When I wake up at night, that's what I remember. That, and pushing him off me, feeling from his weight that he must be dead.''

''But if you had to push him off,'' Masters asked, ''how was it you shot him from at least three feet away?''

Mary shook her head; the movement had a dazed quality. ''Perhaps he fell forward. But I don't know. I just don't know.''

''Were your panty hose already torn?''

''Yes.'' There was pain in Mary's voice. ''God, yes. Maybe *I* ripped them in the struggle, but yes. Afterwards, I wasn't capable of anything. Even sensible things. When I called 911, it was like just enough fog had lifted to see the telephone.''

''Did you scratch Mr. Ransom's buttocks?''

''I must have—we were struggling.'' Her voice rose in sudden anger. ''But *not* when he was dead. That's ridiculous. It's sick. The prosecutor's whole case is sick.'' Sharpe looked up from her notes. ''Sick,'' Mary repeated to Sharpe. ''But then ambition is a sickness. *I* know.''

As Sharpe stared at her, a murmur rose from the press. Paget sensed that Mary's sudden challenge would become a defining moment in their memory of the hearing.

"Ambition may be a sickness," Sharpe said to Masters. "But murder is a crime. I object to Ms. Carelli's efforts at distraction."

Masters turned to Mary. "Whatever your emotions, Ms. Carelli, I will ask that you confine your answers to the questions asked."

"I *do* have emotions, Your Honor. I *have* been charged with murder. It's hard to be dispassionate. Or to feel apologetic to Ms. Sharpe." She paused. "But I will try, at least, to be responsive."

"Responsiveness," Masters said dryly, "will suffice."

The judge's shift of mood, Paget realized, was meant to signal that she was finished. "Might I ask a few questions?" he inquired.

"Of course, Mr. Paget." Masters smiled faintly. "Ms. Carelli is *your* witness, and I appreciate that my intervention here has been out of the ordinary. But I wanted to keep Ms. Carelli on track, and Ms. Sharpe from having to object."

Mary seemed to gaze at them with the passivity of exhaustion. The effect was far different from that of the poised woman who, unknown to those watching, had lied to the Senate: *this* woman was more flawed, more human, and, somehow, much more real. It came to him that beneath her seeming discursiveness and pain, the core of Mary's responses to Caroline Masters had been as flawless as was possible—every inexplicable act explained as trauma, each inconsistency blurred by shock and confusion. Suddenly Paget saw where he should go next. "When the police came," he asked, "did they offer you a doctor?"

"Yes." Mary lowered her head. "But I didn't want anyone touching me. I told them that."

"Did they then suggest a rape counselor?"

Mary shook her head. "No."

Paget was quiet for a moment. "When had you last eaten?"

"The night before." She paused. "That morning, I was too upset to eat."

"Did the police ask you *that?*"

"No."

Paget nodded. "So at the time they questioned you, you hadn't eaten for almost twenty-four hours."

"Yes."

Paget tilted his head. "How does going without food affect you?"

"I feel weak. It makes me impatient." Mary looked at Sharpe. "To me, that's how I sound on the tape of the interrogation—hungry and exhausted. I become a one-note person."

"Is that *all* you felt—hunger and exhaustion?"

"No. I felt disoriented." Her voice fell. "I was

answering questions to answer them. Even when I didn't *know* the answer. By the time I asked for a lawyer, it was the only thing I could do.''

Paget turned to face the courtroom—the cameras, the reporters standing in the back, the sheriff's deputies guarding the door. Then he saw Carlo, sitting in the front row, expression soft and focused on Mary, as if to get her through this.

Paget faced her again. Quietly, he asked, ''Did you murder Mark Ransom?''

Mary straightened on the witness stand, raising her chin. ''No,'' she said. ''I did not.''

''What *did* you do?''

''Defend myself. Because he wanted to abuse me. Because I was so terribly frightened. Everything that was happening, everything about who Mark Ransom was and what he wanted from me, scared me to my soul.'' Mary's voice grew quiet. ''I didn't want to lose myself. That was why he died.''

Paget was silent for a moment, and then he nodded. ''Thank you,'' he said. ''That's all I have.''

Sharpe walked toward Mary, her right hand clasping the barrel of Mary's gun.

''What's she doing?'' Terri whispered to Paget.

''Psychological warfare, I think. She wants to make Mary hold the gun.''

Sharpe held the gun out to Mary. ''This *is* yours, isn't it?''

Mary stared at her. She did not take the gun. "It looks like mine."

"It's been identified as *yours.*" Sharpe thrust the gun toward Mary. "Take a closer look."

Mary gazed at the gun as if it were a foreign object. "It wouldn't help," she said quietly. "I don't know guns. And I'd rather not touch this or any gun, ever again."

Sharpe paused. Abruptly, she asked, "You'd never owned a gun before, had you?"

"No."

"And you didn't buy this one until *after* Mark Ransom called you?"

"I think so."

"I *know* so." Sharpe walked back to the prosecution table, put down the gun, and then turned. "The reason you gave Inspector Monk for buying *this* gun is that you'd received threatening calls, correct?"

Paget tensed; Sharpe had immediately headed for one of Mary's lies. On this, and other points, he had coached Mary to give the minimum answer, so as not to lie further.

"Correct."

"How many calls were there?"

Mary hesitated. "Two, I think."

"You *think?* The calls disturbed you so much that you bought a gun, and you don't remember how many?"

Mary folded her hands. "If that's a question, my answer is the same: I think there were two calls."

"You do remember the sex of the caller, I assume."

Mary nodded. "It was a man."

Sharpe placed her hands on her hips. "Then please tell us, in as much detail as possible, what this man said in his threatening call or calls."

It was what Paget had feared: that Sharpe would ask an open-ended question, requiring Mary to embroider the fictions she had already told. Mary straightened on the witness stand. "I don't recall precisely. But he said something about watching my house. That was why I bought the gun."

Sharpe gave her a skeptical smile. "He didn't happen to mention Laura Chase, did he?"

Paget half stood, thinking to object to the sarcasm. And then Mary said coolly, "No, he didn't. So I'm almost sure that it wasn't Mark Ransom."

There was another murmur from the courtroom, a cough that sounded like stifled laughter. Sharpe stopped, staring at Mary. "Did you think it was *anyone* you knew?"

"No."

"If you had thought that, you would have reported them, correct?"

Mary hesitated. "I believe so, yes."

"But you didn't report the call at all, did you?"

"No."

Sharpe paused. "Wouldn't it have *had* to be someone you knew?"

Paget saw the apprehension register in Mary's eyes. "You mean," she said calmly, "because my telephone isn't listed?"

Sharpe looked surprised. Mary had preempted her question and the trap that lay behind it. "Yes," Sharpe answered. "Among other things."

Mary nodded. In a tone of sympathetic puzzlement, she said, "I can't explain that, either."

Paget almost smiled. What stopped him was the look on Masters's face; her eyes seemed to narrow, as if she had registered how clever Mary was.

Terri had seen the same thing. "This would be better if we had a jury," Terri whispered. "Mary should just take her lumps and go on."

Terri looked tired, Paget thought. "You're right," he murmured back.

"In fact," Sharpe was asking Mary, "you never told anyone about the calls, did you?"

"No."

"Not the police, or friends, or anyone at ABC."

"No. No one." Mary paused. "Not even the person who sold me the gun. I didn't want to sound paranoid."

"Was that it? Or was it hard to describe calls you never received?"

It's not that hard for Mary, Paget thought to himself. "The problem isn't describing them," Mary told Sharpe. "That's *not* the reason."

Sharpe gave her a cynical once-over. "Didn't you buy the gun for the specific purpose of confronting Mark Ransom?"

The answer, Paget knew, was yes. "No," Mary said firmly. "The reason is that the calls reminded me that I was a woman who lived alone. Just as I told Inspector Monk." Mary paused, tilting her head. "You prosecute rape cases, don't you? Don't a lot of your cases come from women who live alone?" A final pause. "Or," Mary finished in a soft voice, "from a woman who has been *trapped* alone?"

Sharpe turned to Caroline Masters with a weary expression. "Your Honor, would you again explain to Ms. Carelli that her purpose is to answer *my* questions, not to give speeches or pose questions of her own—rhetorical or otherwise."

Masters turned to Mary. "There *are* rules here, Ms. Carelli. You should confine yourself to giving Ms. Sharpe *answers* she doesn't like. So that she can ask more questions that *you* don't like."

Mary smiled faintly. "All right."

"All right?" Sharpe repeated in sarcastic tones. "If it's all right with you, Ms. Carelli, let's discuss another matter you never reported to the police—that

Mark Ransom had a tape or tapes that were damaging to you. You failed to mention that, correct?''

''Objection,'' Paget interjected. ''I already asked that question, and Ms. Carelli already answered. Imitation may be the sincerest form of flattery, but repetition is harassment.''

Sharpe turned from Paget to Masters. ''I can well understand why Mr. Paget wants to sweep this under the rug. In fact, the first hour of his examination swept so many things under the rug that he needed a shovel. But he can't inoculate Ms. Carelli against cross-examination—particularly on a foundational question to establish the premise for questions Mr. Paget never asked.''

''Speaking of speeches,'' Masters rejoined, ''your last sentence was sufficient. Ms. Carelli can answer the question.''

Sharpe turned to Mary. ''Yes,'' Mary answered promptly. ''I failed to tell the police.''

''And in fact, you led them to believe that your sole purpose in seeing Mark Ransom was professional.''

Mary paused. ''By omission, yes.''

''By omission? Didn't you tell Inspector Monk quite an elaborate story about the news value of the Laura Chase tape, and your interest in the ethics of buying and selling people's secrets?''

Mary straightened in her chair. ''What I said was

true,'' she answered quietly. ''What I didn't tell Inspector Monk was that the secrets Mark Ransom proposed to buy and sell included my own. Because, as I said, I was deeply ashamed.''

Once more, Sharpe seemed to slow, and then find another angle of attack. ''Didn't you also invent fictional dialogue for Mr. Ransom? Such as him telling you that truth is more important than privacy or sentiment, for the dead and for the living?''

Mary looked at her calmly. ''He *did* say that. Laura Chase was the dead. *I* was the living.'' She paused. ''Mark Ransom was using Laura Chase's secret for money, and mine for sex.''

Sharpe nodded curtly. ''Which must be why you told Inspector Monk that you were surprised to find Mark Ransom alone. You *did* say that, didn't you?''

''Yes, I did.'' Mary paused. ''As I said, I didn't want to admit to blackmail.''

''Is that also why you told Inspector Monk that you expected Mark Ransom to bring a publicist?''

Mary paused. ''Yes.''

''*That* wasn't a mere omission, was it? It was a lie.'' Sharpe paused. ''A lie, deliberately invented to cover your purpose in coming.''

Masters turned to Mary, as if awaiting her answer. ''I don't know *why* I said it,'' Mary answered, ''except that I was frightened and confused.''

''But you didn't expect a publicist, did you?''

"No, I did not." Mary paused. "Nor did I go there intending to shoot Mark Ransom."

Sharpe turned to Masters. "I move to strike the last sentence of that answer as unresponsive."

"Granted." Masters turned to Mary. "Again, Ms. Carelli, confine yourself to answering the question which is asked." She gave a thin smile. "After all, this is municipal court. We have higher standards for responsiveness than do presidential debates."

There was a ripple of laughter from the gallery. But Paget did not join it; the faintly slighting comment signaled Masters's resolve to let Sharpe take her shots at Mary unimpeded by verbal sparring. The first flicker of worry crossed Mary's face. "I apologize," she said to Masters. "Being charged with murder is quite emotional. I'll try to repress that."

"Please do try. For your own sake." Masters turned to Sharpe. "Go ahead, Counsel."

Perhaps, Paget thought, he alone felt a new chill in the courtroom. "Let's talk," Sharpe said quietly, "about Mark Ransom's erection. Or erections. How many did he have—one or two?"

"Penises?"

"No." Sharpe's voice held a lethal patience. "Erections."

"I don't understand."

"You told Inspector Monk that Mark Ransom got

an erection while listening to the Laura Chase tape, correct?''

Mary nodded. ''He wanted me to see the bulge in his pants.''

''How long was that before he tried to rape you?''

Mary looked puzzled. ''I don't know when he first got it. I only noticed when he touched my knee.''

''And how long was *that* before he tried to rape you?''

''Perhaps five minutes.''

''What's Marnie's thing about erections?'' Paget whispered to Terri.

''You can forget penis envy,'' Terri whispered back. ''With Rappaport, as I told you, she was hinting at impotence. She knows something—or thinks she does.''

Paget nodded. ''I don't like this at all.''

Sharpe moved closer to Mary. ''And when he dropped his pants, you testified, he also had an erection.''

''Yes.''

''And quite a memorable one, in that you recall him stroking it.''

''I remember that, yes.''

''In fact, you now remember more about that erection than you recalled for Inspector Monk—to whom you said something like, 'It was an erection. I didn't stop to notice how special it was.' ''

Mary paused. "I was in shock," she answered. "Days after, some details became clearer."

Sharpe's voice was staccato. "Why not how your panty hose ripped? Or why you closed the window blinds? Or what you were doing in the hallway? Or your reasons for wandering around the suite? Why Mr. Ransom's erection?"

"I don't know." Pausing, Mary seemed to search her memory. "I suppose certain details etch themselves on your brain out of sheer horror, and when the shock wears off, they have this awful clarity." She turned to Masters. "Mark Ransom stroking his penis while listening to Laura Chase describe her violation was one of those. And it defines him to the core."

"Move to strike the answer as nonresponsive," Sharpe said.

For a moment, Masters was silent, appraising Mary. "Denied," she said in a casual tone. "At the risk of sounding like far too many men, you asked for an erection, and you got one."

Again, there was muffled laughter. But Masters did not smile, and Paget, watching her, did not care for what he saw; something in her words and manner suggested her awareness of Mary's powers of invention, and the damage that Steinhardt's tape had already done.

Sharpe pressed on. "Was that the same erection

as the 'bulge' you described, or a different one? In other words, was Mr. Ransom continually aroused from the time that you were sitting on the couch?''

Once more, Mary hesitated. ''I didn't watch that, obviously. But I think so, yes.''

''And between the time you first noticed his erection and the time you shot him, how long was it?''

''I'm not sure. Ten minutes, at least.''

''And during those 'at least ten minutes,' you say, Mark Ransom tried to talk you into sex.''

''Yes.''

''And pushed you to the floor.''

''Yes.''

''And struggled with you.''

''Yes.''

''And tugged at your panty hose.''

''Yes.''

''And pinned you under him.''

''Yes.''

''Then slapped you.''

Mary's voice became tight. ''Yes.''

''Scratched your throat.''

Mary nodded. ''*Yes*. To all of that.''

''And, after all that, stopped to listen to the voice of Laura Chase.''

Mary touched her forehead. ''Yes,'' she said softly.

Sharpe stared at her. ''And during all that time, and all those strenuous and distracting activities, this fifty-six-year-old man achieved and maintained an erection.''

Mary stared at her. ''I didn't think of it that way. I really don't know how to answer that.''

Turning from Mary, Masters gave Sharpe a puzzled look. ''Maybe,'' Terri whispered, ''Marnie just wants to discredit Mary's story.''

Paget shook his head. ''I don't think that's it. She *did* mention the possibility of a rebuttal witness, didn't she?''

A look of concern crossed Terri's face. ''Yes. She did.''

But Sharpe had begun a new line of attack.

''You acknowledge telling Inspector Monk that you shot Mark Ransom from two to three inches, don't you?''

Mary nodded. ''Yes. I've tried to explain my state of mind at the time.''

''And you also told the police that Mark Ransom's blinds were closed when you came to the suite, correct?''

With Sharpe's second question, Paget saw with alarm where this was going. Sharpe would force Mary to trace every change in her story to some police discovery.

''Objection,'' he called out. ''Asked and answered. How many times must Ms. Carelli repeat her testimony on direct?''

As Sharpe started to speak, Masters held up her

hand. "I'm going to let this go awhile, Mr. Paget. Ms. Sharpe can make her point."

"Yes," Mary answered promptly. "That was what I first recalled."

"But you heard Mr. Aguilar testify otherwise."

Mary stared at her. "I did."

"And now, this morning, you acknowledge closing the blinds."

"The day Mark Ransom died, I was in shock. My recollection comes back in bits and pieces."

Sharpe gave her a look of open disbelief.

"And shock, I believe, is the reason you give for the delay in calling 911 estimated by Dr. Shelton."

"As best I understand my own actions, yes."

The courtroom was dead silent now. Paget saw Masters's eyes sweeping back and forth with each question and answer, as if watching a tennis match.

"But when you spoke to Inspector Monk," Sharpe pursued, "you said you called as soon as possible."

Mary hesitated. "That's what I thought at the time."

"Isn't it true that your story changed *after* you heard Dr. Shelton's account?"

"As a matter of the sequence of events, yes. But that's not why I testified as I have." Mary paused, turning to Masters. "Again, it's a matter of piecing together what happened."

"But you already acknowledged omitting any mention of the tape."

Slowly, Mary faced Sharpe again. "As I explained, the contents of the tape were painful."

"So painful that you hid the tape's existence until we found it."

Mary leaned forward. "That's a way of putting it," she said coolly. "But I wasn't just hiding from you. I was hiding from everyone but Dr. Steinhardt, the man I chose to trust with my own guilt and shame. What I did with Inspector Monk, in my confusion and shock, was follow the habit of years."

"Lying, you mean."

Mary flushed, faltered for a moment; Paget could feel her trapped awareness that Caroline Masters knew of her perjury. Then, very softly, "That's not what I meant, Ms. Sharpe. And you know that."

Sharpe slowly shook her head. "What *I* meant," she said with equal quiet, "is that you adjust your story not because your memory revives but to accommodate the testimony of other witnesses. And *you* know that."

Caroline Masters turned to Mary; to Paget, her expression was an odd combination of skepticism and regret. "That's not true," Mary told Sharpe. "What I *do* know is never to expect compassion. Not from you."

Sharpe stared at her for a moment. Then she shrugged, as if anything Mary said to her now was too self-serving to require a response. Despite himself, Paget admired that: by some effort of will, Sharpe was mastering her own sensitivity to attack, making herself cooler and more controlled.

"Speaking of compassion," she said, "you claim to have been wandering in the hallway—at which point Mr. Tench saw you—in contemplation of seeking help for Mr. Ransom. But you didn't *get* help, did you?"

Mary lowered her gaze. "Not then, no. As I said, it hadn't become real to me."

"Hadn't it? Isn't the *real* reason you were in the hallway to determine whether anyone had heard a gunshot, so you wouldn't be caught falsifying evidence?"

"No." Mary half rose in the witness stand. "That's not true."

"Really. Isn't *that* also why you closed the blinds—so you wouldn't be caught fabricating evidence?"

Mary seemed to brace herself. "According to your witness Mr. Hassler, I must have been fabricating evidence in the nude. But that struck me as so senseless I've decided not to 'adjust my story' to accommodate nudity."

There was a murmur from those watching; a bark of laughter. Paget saw Sharpe stiffen with anger. "No," Sharpe retorted, "what happened is that you undressed to disarm Mr. Ransom, and then shot him. After *that*, you closed the blinds. That *is* what happened, isn't it?"

"It is not." Mary's face was ashen, but her voice was edged with contempt. "Except in your own fantasies. And, perhaps, Mark Ransom's."

"Mr. Ransom *has* no fantasies. Tell me, Ms. Carelli, did you begin to wander about the room, determining the 'reality' of certain pieces of furniture, *after* you closed the blinds?"

Mary stared at her. "I honestly don't remember."

"You don't recall when you touched both end tables, the bookshelf, and the desk."

"No."

"Or why your fingerprints appear on the handle of the desk drawer."

"No."

"What *was* she doing?" Terri whispered to Paget.

Tense, Paget kept his eyes on Mary. "I have no idea."

Sharpe paused. "Weren't you, in fact, looking for tapes of your session with Dr. Steinhardt?"

Mary's eyes widened in surprise. "I was *not,*" she said finally, "looking for tapes."

"Didn't you find one tape? And then destroy it?"

"When?" Mary's voice was shot through with incredulity. "How? Flush it down the toilet? As you must know, I never even entered the bathroom." Mary seemed overcome with anger. "Mr. Paget's opening statement was right. The prosecution's case is like a satire of conspiracy theories, written by a lunatic. But then it requires so much more imagination to convict someone who is innocent. Unless, of course, *you're* fabricating evidence.''

By instinct, Sharpe moved forward. The sound from those watching was muted; Paget could almost feel them squirm with tension. Masters's gavel cracked.

The two women froze, looking up at Masters. Her face was angry and closed. ''That's enough,'' she snapped. ''I appreciate, Ms. Carelli, that Ms. Sharpe's cross-examination is intense. But your comment is unacceptable. To *me.*'' Her voice grew quiet. ''I'm out of patience. The next outburst will be followed by a contempt citation.''

Mary turned to her. ''Forgive me, Your Honor. But those accusations are very difficult for *me* to accept. It's very hard for me to summon the one-way deference Ms. Sharpe seems to require while she tries to destroy my life.''

From the public section, someone clapped abruptly. Masters's tone was cool. ''The deference *I* require is to the court, from and among *all* participants. As for whether you receive justice here, that's on my head, not Ms. Sharpe's. You may find it reassuring that mere charges—hers *or* yours—impress me not at all.'' Masters paused. ''The sole question before this court is whether there is sufficient evidence of probable cause. And I will decide that question as wisely and fairly as I know how.''

Mary's face softened. When she nodded, it

seemed less an acceptance of Masters's power than of her desire to be fair. "I apologize," she said quietly.

The judge gazed at her a moment and then said, "Please continue, Ms. Sharpe."

Sharpe moved in again. "Let us return, Ms. Carelli, to the tapes. Did Mr. Ransom describe what was on them?"

"Yes. He did."

"Did he suggest to you, in words or substance, that the tapes reflected on your honesty and veracity?"

Mary looked from Paget to Sharpe. "He did not *suggest* that. No."

Sharpe moved closer. *"Do* the tapes reflect on your honesty and veracity?"

"Objection." Paget stood. "I'd like a bench conference, Your Honor. Immediately."

Masters nodded. "I would expect you do."

Sharpe and Paget walked briskly to the bench. They kept their voices low. "What's the next question?" Paget demanded of Sharpe. " 'Bigger than a bread basket,' or 'Does it start with a vowel or a consonant?' " He turned to Masters. "If Mary has to answer questions like those, there *is* no privilege. And if Ms. Sharpe throws out any more hints—like 'Did the tapes concern your service as a government lawyer?'—there'll be investigative reporters crawling all over Mary's life."

Sharpe shook her head. "That was *not* the question I asked, Your Honor. The question I asked was whether the embarrassment and pain to which Ms. Carelli already testified relates to a failure of veracity."

Masters leaned forward. "We three *know* what the tape relates to. But that tape, and its contents, are not properly part of the record. And those questions aren't proper, either. Unless Ms. Carelli raises the contents of the tape themselves, I'm instructing you not to ask about them. Or, more devious, what Ransom *said* about them. Understood?"

Sharpe nodded. "Yes, Your Honor."

The two lawyers left the bench. "What was *that?*" Paget murmured.

Sharpe gave him a fleeting sideways glance, and then shrugged. "Never up, never in," she said, and turned to face Mary Carelli.

In an even tone, Sharpe said, "Our next subject, Ms. Carelli, is the moment you shot Mr. Ransom."

"All right," Mary answered. "But for the record, I don't remember it as the 'moment I shot Mr. Ransom.' I remember it as the end of a struggle, when the gun went off." She turned back to Masters. "You see, I don't recall *shooting* him. And I didn't *plan* to shoot him. I just wanted him to stop."

Good, Paget thought; it was another step back from murder, and one they had worked on together.

"Semantics aside," Sharpe said, "he let you reach into the purse unimpeded. Is that your testimony?"

"I told him that I was reaching for a condom, Ms. Sharpe. I'm sure he wasn't expecting a gun."

"How did you ever reach the gun? Hadn't he pinned you to the floor?"

Mary hesitated. "That's true," she said in a patient tone. "But when I told him about the condom, he took his weight off me."

"How did he do that?"

"I don't know, really." Her voice became weary. "But the hand he'd slapped me with was free, obviously. Perhaps he leaned on *that*."

Sharpe's brow furrowed. "But when you pulled the gun, he was essentially on top of you."

"Yes."

"Too close to extend your arms in front of you."

"Yes."

Sharpe walked back to the prosecution table. She returned holding Mary's gun.

Silently, she placed it on the front rail of the witness box. "Could you show me," she asked, "how you held the gun and how close it was to your body?"

For a moment, Mary simply stared at the gun. Then she squared her shoulders, took it in both hands, and pointed it at Sharpe with her wrists bent to her chest. ‘‘Like this,’’ she said coolly. ‘‘As best I remember.’’

Sharpe eyed the gun. ‘‘He was still on top of you, correct?’’

‘‘Yes.’’

‘‘But he permitted you to pull a gun from your purse, clamp it in both hands, and assume the rather awkward position you’re demonstrating now.’’

Mary held the gun steady. ‘‘He didn’t permit me to do anything,’’ she answered. ‘‘As I said, he grabbed my wrists.’’

‘‘While he was still on top of you?’’

‘‘Yes.’’

Sharpe cocked her head. ‘‘Could you describe your relative positions?’’

Mary placed the gun on her lap. ‘‘It happened so fast,’’ she said.

‘‘Just your best memory.’’

Mary’s eyes narrowed. ‘‘He was kneeling between my legs, leaning forward. Both hands were on my wrists.’’ She gave a melancholy shrug. ‘‘That’s what I remember.’’

‘‘And as he grasped your wrists, the ‘gun went off,’ as you put it.’’

‘‘Yes.’’

Sharpe looked puzzled. ‘‘Didn’t we just skip a step?’’

‘‘Skip a step?’’ Mary asked carefully. ‘‘I don’t know what you mean.’’

‘‘I mean the step where Mark Ransom obligingly

released your wrists and catapulted backward so that you could shoot him from at least three feet.''

The question was delivered with subversive innocence, in a tone so bland that it underscored the absurdity Sharpe meant to suggest. The buzz from the spectators was like a delayed reaction.

''Jesus,'' Terri whispered.

Paget kept watching. ''No. I think it's all right.''

Mary stared at Sharpe, face quite composed, her perfect stillness commanding silence in the courtroom. ''As I told you,'' she said calmly, ''I don't remember everything. But Mr. Ransom was a very tall man, and I expect his *arms* were three feet long. And I think they were extended, pinning my wrists to my chest.'' She clasped the gun between her breasts, aiming at Sharpe again. ''Like *this.* So you see, the bullet could have traveled close to three feet if he'd never even flinched.''

There were muted exclamations. Sharpe looked stunned.

''She walked right into that one,'' Paget whispered. ''Wonder why she believed that Mary and I wouldn't think of it?''

Terri turned to him. ''I wonder if it's true.''

Looking up, Paget saw Masters's faint smile at Mary. ''All that matters,'' he said, ''is that *Caroline* wonder.''

But Sharpe had recovered. ''He was leaning forward, you said. Not backward.''

Mary put down the gun. "I don't know, Ms. Sharpe. Somehow the gun went off, and somehow the bullet traveled two to three feet. All that I know for certain is that I didn't mean for it to happen." She shook her head. "I only meant to scare him. To make him stop."

Sharpe placed her hands on her hips. "Isn't what happened that you bought this gun planning to shoot Mark Ransom, came to the Flood and killed him from a safe distance—after which you closed the blinds, scratched yourself, tore your own panty hose, and scratched Mark Ransom's buttocks, in an effort to claim rape? Isn't *that* what happened?"

"It's nearly over," Paget whispered to Terri.

"Pardon me," Mary said politely. "But didn't you skip a step? The part where I slap myself?"

Another, deeper sound. Terri murmured, "You know, I've never seen anyone quite like her."

Neither, it was clear, had Marnie Sharpe. "I didn't," Sharpe finally said. "Because when you pulled the gun, Mark Ransom swung at you by instinct. And then you shot him, just as you intended. *That's* what happened, isn't it?"

Once more, Caroline Masters turned to Mary. Pausing, Mary folded her hands. "No," she said calmly. "That is *not* what happened. Mark Ransom tried to rape me, and I defended myself." Mary's voice grew quiet. "A gun went off. But as tragic as that is, I'd defend myself again."

Slowly, Sharpe shook her head in silent disbelief. Then, in a tone of dismissal and contempt, she said, "No further questions, Your Honor."

"She survived," Terri murmured to Paget.

Paget nodded. "Yes. She did."

It took a moment for Masters to turn from Mary. "Redirect, Mr. Paget?"

Paget stood. "No questions," he answered. "None at all."

Masters nodded. "You may step down, Ms. Carelli."

Mary stood stiffly, seemingly unsure that it was over. She was still for a moment, as if preparing for the reporters outside, the cameras, the people who wished to cheer her, to revile her, or simply to collect her autograph. Then she walked across the courtroom, composed again, as she had been that day fifteen years before, leaving the Senate.

THREE

Mary flashed on the screen, pointing the gun at Marnie Sharpe.

Paget and Carlo watched in the library. "In a tense confrontation," the narrative began, "Mary Carelli held her own with Prosecutor Marnie Sharpe. Refusing to wither under repeated attacks, Ms. Carelli fought back at the end of her testimony, dramatically affirming her innocence."

Carlo turned to Paget. "She *was* good," Carlo said.

He seemed to need reassurance, as if doubting the evidence of his own senses. "Very good," Paget answered.

He fell silent. He could not say to Carlo that Mary had *needed* to be good simply to survive; that drama was not innocence in the eyes of Caroline Masters; and that in the unsparing calculus of evidence—the relentless accretion of fact upon fact—Sharpe's attack had been telling. Nor could Paget say that the secrets Caroline Masters already knew, and that he hoped Carlo would never know, might have damaged Mary beyond repair.

"Do you think the judge believed her?" Carlo asked.

Carlo now seemed to have the caution of a lawyer, rather than the fierce loyalty of a son. It was painful to see. "Your mother gave her reason to," Paget answered. "Tomorrow morning, Terri puts on Marcy Linton. By this time tomorrow evening, Caroline Masters will know that Mark Ransom raped a defenseless young woman."

Carlo looked hopeful; it was as if he, too, would then be persuaded. "After that, the judge should *know* that my mother's telling the truth, don't you think?"

"Caroline's hard to read. But it will at least make Mary more credible, and much more sympathetic." Paget switched off the television. "This trial has been hard for you, hasn't it?"

Carlo shrugged. "In a way."

A glancing phrase, Paget thought, which held much more: children are meant to learn ambiguity and moral complexity in some other place than the trial of a parent, to never learn their parents' secrets, or even that they have them. "Like most of us," Paget said, "your mother has done things that she's ashamed of. But that doesn't mean that people shouldn't believe her. *All* the women who dealt with Mark Ransom seem to have suffered for it."

Carlo was quiet. "Do you think she'll ever tell me what was on the tape?"

Inwardly, Paget flinched; the conversation made him feel like a hypocrite, using Mary as a shield. "If she never did," he asked softly, "would you stop caring about her?"

The question seemed to give Carlo pause. He shook his head. "It doesn't have anything to do with me, really. Or her and me."

Perhaps, Paget thought, his son would never learn that the tape had everything to do with Mary and Paget, Mary and Carlo, and why Paget had raised him. "Then let it be. The hearing will be over soon." Paget paused. "Perhaps it will have taught you to be less like me—judgmental to a fault—and better able to separate the mistakes people make from their worth as people. As someone like Terri seems able to do."

Carlo gave him a curious look. "She talked you into letting me come, didn't she?"

"Terri?"

"Uh-huh. Because you've never done a one-hundred-eighty-degree turnaround on any 'no' I can remember."

Paget smiled. "I've always believed that consistency is a virtue. Of course it was Terri."

Carlo smiled back. "I know you, Dad. From *me* you've got no secrets."

Paget was quiet for a moment. "Just one or two," he said.

Teresa Peralta sat on the couch in Mark Ransom's suite, gazing at the bloodstained carpet.

It was six-thirty; at seven, she was meeting Marcy Linton at a nearby hotel, to prepare for the most important day in court she might ever have. But an hour before, on impulse, she had called Marnie Sharpe for permission to visit the suite again. Sounding tired from her cross-examination of Mary, Sharpe did not question her, leaving Terri to question herself.

Why was she here?

The truth, Christopher Paget had told her, was something he wished never to know. All that mattered was that Sharpe never find the second tape.

Where was it?

Terri sat back, reflecting.

Where, for that matter, was the Lindsay Caldwell tape? If Ransom had failed to bring that as well as Mary's second tape, despite his promise to both women, why had Sharpe not found the missing tapes in his home with Mary's *first* tape?

Terri stood, eyes moving across the furnishings.

Why, in the moments after Mark Ransom died,

had Mary gone from the end tables to the bookshelves to the desk? Leaving fingerprints on each.

Because she was looking for the tape, Marnie Sharpe had suggested. That was wrong, Mary answered; she was in shock, wandering aimlessly. Not sure of where she was and what she was doing.

Terri opened the drawers of one end table, then another. A telephone directory. A Gideon Bible. Nothing else.

The bookshelf was no different. One drawer, empty. A few volumes of coffee table literature. Banal and impersonal, suited to a room where people came and went.

She found herself gazing at the bloodstain.

What had happened here between Mark Ransom and Mary Carelli, in the moments after Paul Aguilar had brought them champagne? Was Mary the naked woman standing in a distant window? What was Mary Carelli doing in the hallway when Edward Tench had seen her? While, inside the suite, Mark Ransom was lying dead.

Turning, Terri walked slowly to the desk.

On top were a pen, blank paper. She opened the drawer.

Empty, except for stationery and envelopes, imprinted with the address and logo of the Hotel Flood. A shield with a script *F*.

Closing the drawer, Terri gazed out at Berkeley, as Paul Aguilar claimed to have done.

Elena was there. Having dinner with her father while Terri worked again.

He was the care provider, Richie would tell the judge.

The unfairness of it seized Terri by the throat. *She* should raise Elena. At least she saw Elena as someone outside herself. As a person to be nurtured.

She turned away, standing over the stain Mark Ransom's death had left, lost in her own thoughts.

Finally, she looked at her watch.

Six-fifty. It was time to go; Mary's defense depended on Marcy Linton now, and there was much to do.

Terri picked up her purse and left the suite.

In the hallway, a uniformed policeman waited at the elevator Edward Tench had used. Terri turned toward it and then stopped, glancing at the mail slot.

She had stood here with Chris and Johnny Moore on the morning they first saw the suite.

What was Sharpe's point, Terri had asked, about Mary being in the hallway?

No idea, Chris had answered. And then he had made a bitter joke: "Probably figures Mary found herself with a half hour to kill, scribbled a few postcards on Ransom's rear end, and then mailed them to all her friends."

Terri turned and reentered the suite.

She walked to the desk. Opening the drawer, she took out an envelope, studied it, pensive. Then, without quite knowing why, she slid it in her purse.

She stood still for another moment. Then she hurried from the suite toward the elevator, to meet Marcy Linton.

"I can't find the tape," Johnny Moore said. "And neither can Marnie Sharpe."

He sat with Paget in the stern of Paget's sailboat. It was night, and the boat was docked; this time it was Paget who had felt too confined to meet inside. The lights of San Francisco climbed the hills behind them; more distant, the towers of the financial district glowed against the black. The night was quiet, still except for the muffled sounds of the city, the lapping of water against the hull. Moore and Paget drank beer.

"Mary had to have gotten rid of it," Paget answered. "Somehow."

Moore shrugged. "So Sharpe thinks, my sources tell me. And so *I* think. But the police combed every scrap of garbage at the Flood, and everywhere the garbage went. They even tore Ransom's toilet apart. Although, as Mary points out, there's not one bit of evidence that she even entered Ransom's bathroom."

"Yes," Paget murmured. "She was too busy touring the hallway."

Moore sipped his beer. "I've thought of the mails, of course. As has Sharpe. But with all its considerable advantages, the D.A.'s office hasn't found it. There's just no evidence that Mary sent it anywhere. Even assuming she could have."

"Not even care of ABC?"

"Not to ABC. Not to herself. Not to anyone." Moore paused. "Which leaves us with the notion that Ransom hid it somewhere and that Mary's telling the truth. As hard as that may be for you to believe."

"I haven't had much practice." Paget gazed out at the city. "They've checked Ransom's homes, of course."

"And his banks. And with any friend who claimed him." Moore paused. "Of course, unlike Mary, Ransom was at liberty. There's all sorts of places a clever man can hide something the size of a tape. Which, although I don't mean to press it on you, also enhances Mary's claim."

"You think it's destroyed?"

Moore shook his head. "No way that Mary could do it. And no way that Ransom wanted to. It's out there, somewhere."

Paget was silent.

"I'm sorry," Moore said softly. "I wish I could give you some peace of mind. At least while you're trying this case." He paused. "Better yet, I wish I could tell you I'd destroyed it."

"I'd never ask you to do that, Johnny."

"You wouldn't have to."

Paget was quiet for a time. "It's enough," he said finally, "that you've been looking after Carlo."

"No trouble. It's the nearest I'll ever come to having a son." Moore paused. "It's mostly rides to basketball, and he plays a good game."

"I'm sorry to be missing it."

Moore was silent. Finally, he asked, "Did he tell you about the other day?"

"I'm not sure."

"Someone from *US* ambushed him after the basketball game, with two TV reporters right behind him, cameras and all. Wanting to talk about his childhood."

"What did he do?"

"Just stared at them. I chased them off."

Paget felt a surge of anger, then of shame. "He never told me."

"He doesn't want to bother you. What with the hearing."

"Bother me? He's my son."

Moore gazed at him. "That's why he didn't say anything."

Paget fell quiet again.

"About Ransom and women," Moore said finally. "Still nothing. I begin to think there's nothing to find."

"What does *that* mean?"

"No idea, and such a loss to womankind." Moore tilted his glass to Paget. "Here's to Mark Ransom's undying potency. Now that he's dead, that is."

FOUR

SOFTLY, MARCY LINTON SAID, "Mark Ransom raped me."

The courtroom was still, tense, as crowded as for Mary herself; present for the first time, McKinley Brooks sat behind Marnie Sharpe. Moving closer to the witness stand, Teresa Peralta asked, "Could you tell the court how it happened?"

"Yes." Dressed in a simple skirt and a high-collared blouse, Linton was pale but composed. Her quiet voice had the edge of repressed emotion. "We were in the living room of my uncles' cabin. Drinking wine while Mark Ransom took apart my writing."

"He was critical?"

The word made Linton pause. "Brutal. His clear intention was to strip me of every scrap of self-respect."

Terri saw Sharpe rise to object to the answer, then hesitate. Quickly, Terri asked, "Did he succeed?"

Linton seemed to reflect, as if examining the extent of the damage. "He humiliated me. When he offered me wine, I wanted it." She gazed past Terri, as if explaining herself to the gallery. "I was twenty-four, and I'd been so proud. Had so looked forward to having Mark Ransom read my writing. And then he made me feel like nothing. Like I, and what I cared about, were contemptible to him."

Terri waited for a moment. "Who provided the wine," she asked, "you or Ransom?"

"Ransom. I didn't really like to drink."

"But you wanted to on this occasion?"

Linton nodded. "As he tore me apart, Ransom kept pouring, and I kept drinking."

"How did you feel?"

"Numb." Her voice grew quieter. "But that was better, really."

Terri nodded. She had prepared Linton carefully: despite an inability to sleep, and the burdens of carrying Mary Carelli's defense, Marcy Linton was facing her ordeal with composure. But that did not seem to diminish her ethereal quality; with her pale skin and slender frame, the sense of devastation Linton conveyed did not seem self-pitying but merely factual. Marnie Sharpe watched her without taking notes.

"Did any of Ransom's comments," Terri asked, "concern the subject of sex?"

"Yes," Linton answered. "At the end, after he had torn apart everything else, he ridiculed the 'bloodless' way I wrote about sex."

On the bench, Caroline Masters's gaze never moved from Marcy Linton. That was good, Terri thought. Her own role was merely to help Linton trace the parallels to what Mary Carelli had said: when Linton's testimony was finished, neither Caroline Masters nor anyone else should doubt who Mark Ransom was. If Terri did her job, by evening there would be no pickets seeking justice for Mark Ransom's memory, and Brooks and Sharpe would know how much this case could cost them.

"Did you answer him?" she asked Linton.

"I defended my writing, yes." Linton paused, distractedly touching her hair, more auburn than red in the fluorescent lights. "The scenes he mocked were about me and someone I loved. I told Ransom those scenes meant a lot to me."

The phrase had a valedictory note of sadness, Terri thought, that no lawyer could teach and even Mary Carelli could not replicate. "What," Terri asked, "did Ransom say after that?"

" 'It's like they're negotiating a contract,' he said. 'Sex isn't an insurance policy.' For a minute he seemed angry, and then he looked up and down my body. 'What sex *is,*' he almost whispered, 'is spontaneity, and danger.' " Linton paused. "Before I could answer, he put his arm around me."

Caroline Masters's posture was stiff, unnatural.

"What did you do?" Terri asked.

Linton stared past her. "I couldn't move, felt

sick.'' She shook her head. ''It was like being drugged. I knew what was about to happen, but I couldn't seem to stop it.''

''In what way,'' Terri asked quietly, ''did Ransom first touch you? Sexually, that is.''

Linton looked down. ''He reached inside my blouse,'' she said quietly, ''and touched my nipple.'' Her eyes shut, as if to protect herself from those who watched and listened. ''Then he took my face in his other hand and asked me, 'Do you ever watch Laura Chase?' ''

There was a release of sound, a low collective gasp. Caroline Masters made no move to silence it. She looked stunned; even Terri, who was prepared for the answer, felt shaken by it.

''What did you do?'' Terri asked.

''I shivered.'' There was a first tremor in Linton's voice. ''It was as I told you—the fire, the darkness, the elk on the wall. When he said the name Laura Chase, it was as if I'd been trapped in some primitive ritual, by a man who was insane.''

The courtroom was silent again. ''What did you do?'' Terri asked.

''I pulled away.''

''And then?''

Pausing, Linton shook her head. ''His eyes got so angry,'' she said softly. ''But he smiled, as if I'd pleased him. Then he raised his hand, very slowly, and slapped me across the face.'' Linton began rocking. "My neck snapped back. As I fell back on the couch, I saw yellow flashes. There was blood in my mouth."

Slowly, Terri turned to Sharpe, and then to Caroline Masters. Sharpe's gaze seemed inward, reflective; Masters's mingled compassion and deep thought.

"What happened next?" Terri asked.

"He rose to his knees, waiting for my eyes to open. And then he ripped open my blouse." Linton's voice echoed with disbelief. "He told me to watch him do it.

" 'Do you want me to hit you again?' he asked.

"I couldn't talk or move. So I shook my head." Linton's voice trembled now. "Then he told me to show him my breasts. And to keep my eyes open."

"Did you?"

Linton nodded, mute.

"I'm sorry," Terri said softly. "We need an audible answer for the record."

"I showed him my breasts," Linton said tonelessly. "And I kept my eyes open."

Terri ached with sympathy. She remembered that Linton had tried to smile at him, hoping that he would stop, but that her bruised mouth had hurt too much to move.

"What did he do then?" Terri asked.

"He made me unzip my jeans. Then take them

off.'' Once more, Linton's eyes shut. ''Then he told me to hold his penis while he pulled my panties down. So that I could keep him hard.''

Terri felt drained. For the first time that day, she glanced at Christopher Paget. He watched her for a moment, and slowly nodded.

She turned back to Linton. ''What happened then?'' she asked.

''He hurt me.'' Opening her eyes, Linton seemed bewildered. ''The way he did it was *meant* to hurt me. For days I hurt inside.''

''Physically, you mean.''

''Yes.'' Linton paused. ''Emotionally, the hurt has never stopped.''

Terri watched for a moment. ''While he was raping you, Marcy, what did you do?''

''I lay there, staring up at the elk.'' She shook her head. ''I was afraid that if I closed my eyes, he'd hit me again.''

The whispers in the courtroom were quiet, deferential. Sharpe was scribbling on a legal pad; it might have been notes, Terri thought, except that the penstrokes seemed aimless. Then Terri caught Mary Carelli's split-second gaze, perhaps only imagined the smallest of smiles. If you get off, Terri thought coldly, you will owe a lot to Marcy Linton. And to me. She turned back to Linton.

''When it was over,'' she asked, ''what did Mark Ransom do?''

Linton looked down. ''He told me to cook for him. Without clothes.''

''And did you?''

''I was afraid of him.'' Linton's voice became a monotone. ''And he wanted to watch me.''

The last sentence, with its silent weight of fear and humiliation, lingered there.

''Are you still afraid of him?'' Terri asked.

Slowly, Linton nodded. ''He didn't just rape me,'' she finally said. ''He *changed* me. What he left behind was instinctive fear—of life, and of *him*. I know I can never stop him, no matter how many times he wants to do it.'' Her voice fell. ''I don't believe he's dead. Really, I can't believe it. He's been inside me far too long.''

Terri watched her. Softly, she asked, ''Why didn't you defend yourself?''

Linton gave a helpless shrug. ''I just didn't. I couldn't. He was too strong, and I had no way to defend myself.''

''Do you wish you could have?''

''Oh, yes.'' Linton's voice became stronger. ''Much more now, even, than when it happened. Because I know what scars he left behind.'' She paused again. ''It's terrible to think about hurting someone else. But in the balance of a life, Mark Ransom lost his right to be safe from hurt when he decided to hurt *me*.''

Terri nodded. ''Since then,'' she asked, ''have you taken steps to protect yourself?''

''Yes.'' Raising her head, Linton added quietly, ''I bought a handgun.''

The courtroom was still. Terri waited before asking her last question. ''Why,'' she asked, ''did you come forward now?''

Linton seemed to hesitate. But when she answered, her voice was clear and firm. ''Because the only way left to defend myself from Mark Ransom is to tell the world *who* and *what* he was. Because women should do that for other women.'' Marcy Linton turned to Mary. ''And because what Mary Carelli did, *I* should have done.''

Rising to cross-examine Marcy Linton, Marnie Sharpe looked tentative. It was as if she were gazing at the specter of doubt.

''Good afternoon, Ms. Linton.''

Linton nodded. ''Good afternoon.''

Watching in the silent courtroom, Terri thought how strange Sharpe must find this. Sharpe had a visceral hatred of rape; she had spent her professional life protecting its victims. Cross-examining a victim seemed to slow her; when she spoke, her voice was gentler and faintly sad.

''Let us agree,'' she said to Linton, ''that Mark Ransom visited your home. And let us further agree that you and he had intercourse on the specific occasion that you just described. And that after that you cooked him dinner. All right?''

''All right.''

''When did he leave?''

Paget turned to Terri. ''How did she know to ask *that?*''

Terri shook her head, watching Linton. Softly, Linton answered, ''The next morning.''

''The next morning? How did *that* come about?''

Linton looked away. ''He wanted to stay. I was afraid to argue.''

''And where did he sleep?''

''With me.'' Linton hesitated. ''At least some part of the night.''

Sharpe nodded. ''Was there some reason,'' she asked, ''that Mr. Ransom did not spend the *entire* night in your bed?''

Linton flushed. ''He went downstairs.''

It was uncanny, Terri thought with apprehension; Sharpe seemed to know what to ask, question after question. ''Was there a particular reason,'' Sharpe asked, ''that Ransom went downstairs?''

Linton's shoulders drew in. ''He tried to make love to me.''

''Did you resist him?''

''No.'' Linton shook her head. ''I was afraid.''

Sharpe paused. ''Fearful enough,'' she asked quietly, ''to act like a lover?''

"Objection," Terri called out. "Ms. Sharpe is dragging the witness through needless pain, to no point. We've already established the act of rape and the fear that it caused. How long does the prosecution intend to spell out the forms that fear can take?"

Sharpe turned to Masters. "There *is* a point to this, Your Honor, which the People will make clear if necessary. Even on the record to date, the issue of consent justifies exploring whether Ms. Linton's subsequent actions are truly consistent with rape. But in fairness to this witness, I'll confine myself to a few more questions."

Masters nodded. "All right, Counsel."

Terri sat down, appraising Sharpe with concern. "There's nothing you could do," Paget whispered. "Caroline has to let her cross-examine."

Terri leaned toward him, still watching Sharpe. "Marnie knows what happened, and I don't know how. Marcy hasn't spoken to her. Or anyone, that I know about."

Sharpe had turned back to Linton. "Did you respond," she demanded, "as if you and Mark Ransom were lovers?"

Linton stared at her. "I didn't want him to hurt me."

"So you pretended?"

"Yes."

Sharpe folded her arms. "Then why," she asked, "did you and Mr. Ransom not have intercourse?"

Linton hesitated. "Because he couldn't."

"Couldn't what?"

Gazing at Sharpe, Linton seemed to regather strength. "Maintain an erection," Linton said quietly. "That was why he went downstairs."

Sharpe paused for a moment. "Was he embarrassed?"

"Oh, yes." Her voice rose. "But it wasn't just embarrassment. It was fear and anger."

"What did he say?"

"He made me promise not to tell anyone. Told me that he had never failed before." Linton's tone grew bitter. "It was as if I'd taken something from him. I suppose he considered his performance on the downstairs couch much more of a success."

It was, Terri thought, a nice retort. But Marnie Sharpe looked calm enough.

"Thank you," she said. "No further questions."

Paget glanced at Terri. "What was *that* about?" he asked.

Terri shook her head. "I'm going to try something," she said, and was back on her feet.

"Before Mr. Ransom raped you," she asked Linton, "you resisted him, correct?"

"Yes. I did."

"What was his reaction?"

As Linton gazed at her, Terri saw the comprehension in her eyes. "It seemed to excite him."

"And slapping you seemed to excite him also."

Linton nodded. ''His eyes almost glittered. I think that was why he made me watch him and do things for him. He liked *forcing* women, dominating them.''

Terri nodded. ''And so the second time he wanted sex, you took the line of least resistance.''

''Yes.''

''You didn't struggle.''

''No.''

''He had no excuse to slap you.''

''No. I didn't want to give him one.''

Terri paused. ''Instead you reached out for him, correct?''

''I was frightened.'' Linton's voice fell. ''So I put my arms around him.''

''And what happened?''

''He lost his erection.'' Linton shook her head. ''It was so strange.''

''Is it? Isn't the only difference between the two incidents that the rape—when he achieved penetration—involved violence and abuse? Whereas the time that he failed, you pretended to be his lover by consent?''

Linton was silent for a time. ''Yes,'' she said. ''That is the *only* difference. But then Mark Ransom hated women.''

''But then Mark Ransom was a *rapist,*'' Terri answered. ''It seems that when you reached for him, you saved yourself from more than just a beating.''

Masters raised an eyebrow. "Was that a question, Ms. Peralta?"

Terri turned to her. "It was a *comment,* Your Honor. I *have* no further questions."

Masters looked from Paget to Terri. "Is Ms. Linton your final witness?" she asked.

Terri glanced at Paget. "Yes. Pending the court's decision on the admissibility of the testimony we tendered in chambers."

Caroline Masters nodded. "I'll hear argument on that at nine tomorrow morning." Turning, she faced Marcy Linton. "You're excused, Ms. Linton. And speaking for the court, your appearance here is very much appreciated."

Nodding, Linton stepped down. To Terri's hopeful eyes, she looked no worse—perhaps better—than when she had come. And then, as she had the night before, when Terri had told her of Steve Urbina, Marcy Linton put her arms around Teresa Peralta.

Terri parked her car in front of Mary Carelli's hotel.

It was dusk, the end of a silent drive from the courthouse. From the passenger seat, Mary looked out at the cluster of reporters, waiting for some final comment. "I wonder if I'll ever see them the same," she said. "Let alone be one of them."

Terri was exhausted, she realized: partly by Linton, partly by the tension of preparing to argue that

Rappaport and Caldwell should be heard in open court. After a time, she said, "At least they should be friendly."

Mary nodded. "It was a good day—my best, probably. Thank you for that."

"You're welcome. But it wasn't me. It was Marcy Linton." Terri paused. "It's hard to feel elated. From Sharpe's questions, she's saving a surprise for us."

"Still, you *did* find Linton. Despite my considerable doubts." Mary turned to her. "You had something you wanted to ask me about?"

Terri waited for a moment. "The missing tapes," she said finally.

Mary's eyes narrowed. "What about them?"

Terri's stomach felt tight. "I'd like to know where they are."

Mary stared at her. "Why do you care?" she asked coolly.

"Because we need to find them before Sharpe does. And because I don't want Chris or Carlo hurt even more."

"Did Chris send you on this mission?"

Terri shook her head. "Chris has had to shut everything out, just to be able to defend you. This is for me."

Mary smiled faintly. "I thought as much. Do you have any ideas?"

Terri nodded. "Two, actually. One general and one specific. My general theory is that you got rid of them."

Mary's face turned hard. "And your specific theory?"

Terri felt herself take a deep breath. "That after Mark Ransom died, you put them in an envelope and dropped them down the mail slot."

For a moment, Mary was quiet. "You give me great credit for presence of mind."

"Yes. I do."

"Too much, and yet not enough." The mirthless smile returned. "What, for example, did I do for postage? Which, incidentally, pretty much rules out any foreign destination."

Terri looked at the reporters. A group of four hovered in the half-light a few feet from the car. "You had stamps in your purse," she said finally. "Or Ransom had some."

"Really? And after I picked Ransom's pockets for stamps, to whom did I address it? Myself?"

Terri shook her head. "The police would have found it."

"True, I'm not *that* foolish. But then where did it go? Surprisingly, I'd forgotten my address book. And any address I knew by heart probably would be somewhere Sharpe would think to look."

The conversation was becoming murky, unreal. Despite the sardonic edge in Mary's voice, her eyes were curious and quite intent; Terri could not tell whether this curiosity was about Terri herself, with whom she was playing some abstract game of mental chess, or about something else.

"That's what worries me," Terri answered. "Where you sent it."

Mary gave a short laugh. "Here's what would worry *me*. If I addressed an envelope in my handwriting, and then stuck the tapes inside, it would be like a signed confession. All Sharpe would have to do is find it."

"The tapes," Terri asked. "Plural?"

Mary shook her head. "It was *you* who said 'tapes.' I just repeated it. But it does point out another small problem with your theory: motive. The only tape that really hurts *me* was found at Mark Ransom's home." She paused, still watching Terri. "Is there anything else?"

Terri shook her head.

"No? Then thank you for the ride." Mary put her hand on the door handle, and then turned back. In a cold, quiet voice, she said, "Don't *ever* assume that I haven't thought of Carlo."

She snapped open the door and got out, closing it behind her with fearful gentleness. Then she walked toward the hotel, smiling at reporters as she answered their questions.

FIVE

THE LAWYERS SAT clustered in Caroline Masters's chambers, awaiting her decision on Rappaport and Caldwell.

Glancing around her, Terri saw dark circles under Marnie Sharpe's eyes. The media reaction to Marcy Linton's testimony had been to present Mark Ransom as a sexual predator: whether because of that, or private qualms, Sharpe looked as if she had not slept. Pensive, Terri turned back to Caroline Masters, the conversation with Mary Carelli still echoing in her mind.

Caroline nodded to the stenographer, then to Terri. "The witching hour has arrived, Ms. Peralta. Let's hear your argument."

Terri paused to compose herself. "This issue is critical to our defense," she began. "Because the relevance of both witnesses, *and* of the Laura Chase tape, is now very clear.

"First, Ms. Rappaport.

"Our defense is not simply that Mark Ransom attempted to rape Mary Carelli, but that he was impelled by a serious personality disorder: an obsession with Laura Chase, and a need to demean and dominate women which was so strong that it seems to have driven his sexuality.

"The man that Mary Carelli describes was sexually stimulated by a tape of Laura Chase engaged in sex with two men. The man that Melissa Rappaport describes was aroused by a *videotape* involving precisely the same thing."

Pausing, Terri saw that Caroline Masters listened with care, felt Sharpe intently watching. "Melissa Rappaport," she went on, "describes a man who required fantasies of bondage and rape to assure sexual performance. The man *Mary Carelli* describes was a rapist who beat her. And the bridge between these two women is Marcy Linton, whom Mark Ransom beat and raped and with whom, when she later feigned consent, Mark Ransom could not perform."

Terri's voice became quiet. "By the time he got to Mary Carelli, Mark Ransom knew what worked for him. But his 'journey of discovery,' as it were, began with Melissa Rappaport.

"Finally, Melissa Rappaport proves the relevance of the Steinhardt tape of Laura Chase to Mark Ransom's sexual *modus operandi*. The videotape had pictures, the Steinhardt tape words—Laura's own voice. But that was the only difference."

Sharpe, Terri saw, was scribbling furiously. She felt herself gaining confidence.

"Last," she said, "there is Lindsay Caldwell.

"Ms. Caldwell has shown great courage. Like Ms. Rappaport, she is willing to come forward, at whatever cost, because what she has to say is important."

Pausing, Terri saw Caroline's troubled look. Terri's voice became stronger, more emphatic. "Mary Carelli says Mark Ransom tried to blackmail her. So does Lindsay Caldwell.

"Mary Carelli says Mark Ransom wanted sex. So does Lindsay Caldwell.

"Mary Carelli says Mark Ransom hated women." Terri slowed her words, softened her tone. "And so does Lindsay Caldwell.

"Ms. Sharpe says that Mary Carelli is not credible. Can she say that about Melissa Rappaport? She cannot. Can she say that about Lindsay Caldwell? Again, she cannot. And then Mary Carelli *will* be credible, well beyond Ms. Sharpe's ability to argue otherwise."

Terri turned to Sharpe. "With respect, Ms. Sharpe's only hope is to bar their testimony—both here and, if necessary, at trial. Because if those two women testify, and become part of the record in *People v. Carelli,* the People will lose." Terri faced Masters again. "Except that, in reality, the *people* win only if Ms. Carelli wins. Because only the testimony of these two women can present a true account of who Mark Ransom was. And that is what the *people* deserve."

Pausing, Terri felt the passion in her voice. ''The problem with proving rape, Your Honor, is that too often there are no witnesses. The victim faces the rapist alone, and then must face the trial alone. And so, too often, cannot carry the burden of proving what was done to her.

''That need not be. It is time for the law to acknowledge that every woman abused by a rapist can bring us closer to the truth.'' Terri paused again. ''As can, so clearly, Melissa Rappaport and Lindsay Caldwell. The court should let them be heard.

''Thank you, Your Honor.''

From the corner of her eye, Terri saw Paget smile; even more encouraging was Caroline Masters's seeming introspection. And then Caroline said to Sharpe, ''I won't need argument,'' and Terri, stunned, knew that she had lost.

Caroline leaned forward. ''That was ably presented, Teresa. I regret having to rule against you. But I must.''

Stricken, Terri listened as Caroline went on. ''Let us start with the Laura Chase tape. No privilege protects it, so that the only question is relevance. I've permitted Ms. Carelli to testify generally as to what is on those tapes.'' She paused, adding quietly, ''Without naming names.

''Here, I should digress. I'm appalled by the contents of that tape. And I'm personally appalled that its protagonist, a man who sought the presidency, was so lacking in humanity as to disqualify him from an office which requires—or should require—empathy for the pain of others.''

Caroline's face was hard, her voice incisive. ''But the man is dead; his family survives. *Their* pain is worth considering. And I'm equally appalled by the use of Laura Chase's most painful and private moments, her confession to a psychiatrist, in the name of 'truth.' That not only hurts the living—Ms. Caldwell comes to mind—but even the dead deserve better.'' Caroline paused. ''Laura Chase was used quite enough in life. No one asked her if she would also like to be used in death. Her entitlement to dignity did *not* die with her, and this court will not kill it.''

Abruptly, Caroline stopped herself. Looking at Terri, she spoke more quietly, ''I don't fault the defense for arguing relevance. If I agreed, none of what I just said would matter. And if the sexual acts described on the tape were similar to those Ms. Carelli attributes to Mr. Ransom, I *might* agree. But they aren't, so I don't.

''I feel much the same about Ms. Rappaport. To testify regarding her marriage to Mark Ransom would be to humiliate herself in public. *If* the acts Ms. Rappaport described were the same as those described by Ms. Carelli—rape, as in the case of Ms. Linton—I would agree with the defense that it might suggest that Mr. Ransom was prone to rape.

But the heart of Ms. Rappaport's humiliation is that her actions were consensual. Which is the precise reason that her humiliation is irrelevant to Ms. Carelli's defense. At least as a matter of law.''

Caroline stopped, folding her hands. ''And then,'' she said slowly, ''we have the matter of Ms. Caldwell. Each of us may have our private view on whether Ms. Caldwell did anything 'wrong.' Hopefully, our understanding of sexuality is broader and more humane than it was twenty years ago; certainly a nineteen-year-old can't be held accountable for the suicide of someone as complex and tormented as Laura Chase. But, absent extraordinary circumstances, that private matter should remain Ms. Caldwell's to live with, in private. Without becoming 'the woman who killed Laura Chase.'

''She is willing to forgo that right. I will not ask her to. I agree that her testimony suggests that Mr. Ransom's feelings about women were lamentable. But misogyny and blackmail do not prove rape.'' Pausing, she turned to Terri. ''Indeed, they may even suggest a motive for murder.''

That was right, Terri knew. She watched as Caroline Masters leaned back in her chair, as if to finish. ''Finally,'' Caroline said, ''there is fairness to the prosecution. It is hard to listen to Ms. Rappaport and Ms. Caldwell without developing a certain feeling about Mark Ransom. However, we are not in the business of deciding whether murder victims deserve to die, but simply whether murder was committed. I've tried to put their testimony out of my mind. It will not be part of the record on which I determine 'probable cause.'

"That's all. On the question of whether Ms. Carelli has proven her affirmative defense, I'll make my finding based solely on the testimony of Ms. Carelli and Ms. Linton."

Terri turned to Paget, the disappointment washing over her. He gave a small shrug: you've done your best, it seemed to say—we'll have to win without them. But, to Terri, the gesture did not quite cover the worry he felt.

Sharpe was leaning forward, as if to seize the moment. "Given that the defense has rested," she said in tones of confidence, "the People ask the court to enter a finding of probable cause without further proceedings. If the court needs argument, I can make it now."

"I *will* set a time for argument," Masters responded. "But you mentioned a possible rebuttal witness. You've decided not to call anyone?"

Pausing, Sharpe looked openly concerned. "Is that really necessary, Your Honor? I'm confident we've shown probable cause on the ample record which exists. Whether Ms. Carelli and Ms. Linton raise a reasonable doubt should be reserved for the jury at a subsequent trial."

Masters raised an eyebrow. ‘‘You *do* have a witness ready, correct?’’

Sharpe hesitated. ‘‘Yes. One.’’

‘‘But you'd prefer not to give Mr. Paget a preview of the utter devastation he or she will cause at trial. Is that it?’’

Slowly, Sharpe nodded. ‘‘Not unless the court is in doubt on the issue of probable cause.’’

‘‘I won't say *what,* if anything, the court is in doubt on. And I ask you not to read anything into my suggestion, other than my preference for a complete record on which to make whatever mistake I'm about to make. But that's up to you.’’

The dry remark reminded Terri that Caroline, too, faced political consequences, however she ruled; unlike traffic offenses or disorderly conduct, it was the kind of case that could cost her reelection. But it was the consequence to the district attorney that seemed to have struck Marnie Sharpe; her face was somber.

‘‘Thank you, Your Honor.’’ Sharpe hesitated, as if making a final decision. ‘‘We're prepared to call our witness now.’’

Masters glanced at her watch. ‘‘I'll hear him at ten o'clock. Meanwhile, we're on break.’’

Terri and Paget were in the hallway outside chambers before they could speak. ‘‘I'm sorry,’’ she murmured. ‘‘I'd begun to believe we could win.’’

‘‘Maybe you got through to her anyhow,’’ Paget

said quietly. ‘‘Hopefully, that’s why she’s making Marnie call Mr. or Ms. X.’’

‘‘Whoever it is,’’ Terri answered, ‘‘we’re about to find out what it is that Marnie’s always known.’’

Terri took an elevator to the first floor, avoiding reporters.

Here, the Hall of Justice broke into a maze of bleak green corridors. She followed one, then turned down another, until she found an empty telephone booth.

Glancing over her shoulder, she ducked inside.

There was a telephone directory, but the overhead light was broken. Terri squinted at the pages under ‘‘United States Government’’; at length, she found the heading ‘‘Postal Service.’’

What did I do for postage? Mary had asked.

Beneath the heading was a page-long column of telephone numbers—area post offices, express mail, complaints, employment verification. The only one that looked promising was ‘‘Dead Letter Branch.’’

I’m not so foolish, Mary had said, *as to mail them to myself.*

This was foolish, Terri thought. But the conversation with Mary would not leave her; Mary’s chilly exercise in logic was either a heartless game, played to no purpose, or designed to trace the rigor of Terri’s thoughts.

They were not very rigorous, Terri knew. But she

was certain that her opening premise was the same as Marnie Sharpe's: that Mark Ransom died in possession of the tapes.

Terri picked up the telephone and dialed.

"Dead Letter Branch," a woman's voice answered.

Hesitating, Terri formed a vision of her: black, substantial, and middle-aged, phlegmatic from years of inquiries.

"I have a question," Terri ventured.

"That's why we're here, ma'am."

"What I wanted to know is what happens if someone mails something but forgets to put the whole address on. Or any address at all."

"It depends." The woman coughed. "Sorry, but I can't seem to kick this cold. Anyhow, some things we just throw out. It depends on whether we think they have value."

"How do you determine that?"

"We open the parcel. If it's just a letter, and we can't tell where it should go from looking at it, we get rid of it. If it looks like something of value, we keep it for a while."

"How long?"

"Usually three months."

It was about five weeks, Terri thought, since Mary Carelli had shot Ransom. "What happens then?" she asked.

Terri heard the stifled sound of a repressed sneeze.

"Then we sell it at auction," the woman answered. "If it doesn't sell, then we give it away or throw it out. Why, what did you lose?"

Terri paused, trying to envision the fate of Mary's tape at a public auction. "Cassette tapes," she said finally. "Like for a car stereo."

"Yeah, we might keep them."

The voice was becoming bored and taciturn. Once more, Terri hesitated. "If I described them, could you take a look?"

There was silence. "Didn't you already call about tapes?" the woman asked. "A few weeks back?"

Terri was stunned. "No," she said finally. "It wasn't me. I've never called before."

"Would there have been postage on them?"

"I don't know," Terri replied.

"Well, *this* isn't the lost and found, ma'am. If it had no postage and you want it, you got to go to the post office and look yourself. You know what zip code this got mailed from?"

"I know it was Nob Hill."

There was silence, then a sudden loud cough. "I think that's Station O," the woman wheezed. "Van Ness Avenue. You might go look there."

The witness was a round-faced man with thick glasses and a blond fringe of hair. His face was reflective but good-humored; his voice—deep, slow, and authoritative—had the trace of a southern accent. There was something quite gentle about him.

"Who," Terri whispered to Paget, "is Dr. George Bass?"

Wary, Paget watched him. "I don't know."

"And you're a psychiatrist," Sharpe was asking, "licensed in the state of Florida?"

Bass nodded. "That's correct."

Paget felt Mary touch his arm, suddenly tense. "What's *this* about?" she demanded.

"Just let me listen," he snapped. "If this guy's Ransom's psychiatrist, I'm about to object."

Sharpe moved forward. "And was Mark Ransom one of your patients?"

Bass nodded. "Whenever he visited Key West. He started about four years ago, and our last session was about three months back."

"When Mark Ransom first visited you, Doctor, what reason did he give?"

Bass looked faintly sad. "At first, it wasn't any reason he gave, so much as what he talked about."

"And what was that?"

"Women, and his feelings about them." Bass frowned. "It took me some time to get to what *he* saw as the root of the matter."

"And what was that?"

Bass paused. "Impotence," he said quietly.

"Mark Ransom could no longer achieve intercourse with a woman."

There was a sudden startled buzz. Paget was on his feet abruptly. "Objection," he called out. "Is the witness speaking from personal knowledge? Because if not, his testimony is hearsay, and I request that he be excused."

"Your Honor," Sharpe responded, "Ms. Carelli is claiming an attempted rape by a man who, Dr. Bass now tells us, was impotent. Surely Mr. Paget is not claiming that Mr. Ransom lied to Dr. Bass about *that.*"

"I have no basis for knowing," Paget responded. "Nor does Dr. Bass. The court should not hear his testimony."

Caroline Masters leaned forward. "It may seem archaic, Mr. Paget, but as a matter of evidence, Mr. Ransom's admissions on this subject are deemed so embarrassing as to be reliable. This witness may help shed light on Mr. Ransom's state of mind, and the question of sexual capacity is important. Overruled."

Sitting down, Paget could see the fear in Mary's eyes at Masters's ruling: Bass already looked like a good witness, and Mark Ransom's supposed impotence went to the heart of her defense. "No wonder," Terri murmured, "that Johnny couldn't find any women."

Silent, Paget wondered how long Sharpe had

known this. Before Melissa Rappaport had appeared, he realized, and perhaps even before the indictment. It turned his understanding of the case upside down.

Sharpe was moving closer to the witness. "Was Mr. Ransom's impotence the result of some physical incapacity?"

Bass shook his head. "Mr. Ransom told me that he was capable of having an erection, but that he became flaccid whenever he attempted intercourse. Understandably, Ransom felt that he was not the same man."

"And this upset him?"

"To put it mildly. His chosen self-image was one of virility. It took a number of sessions before he could admit this, even to me."

Sharpe nodded. "And to what do you attribute Mr. Ransom's impotence?"

"According to Mr. Ransom, or my own analysis?"

"Your own analysis, Doctor."

Bass nodded. "The superficial answer is that Mr. Ransom disliked women. But the result of that hostility was guilt and ambivalence. About himself and his own sexuality." Pausing, Bass removed his glasses. "Mark Ransom wanted to subjugate, and even humiliate, women. But in his subconscious, he felt he had to inhibit himself. The ultimate result was impotence. You can view it as a kind of sexual policeman, dispatched by his conscience."

Terri leaned close to Paget. "Are we supposed to feel *sorry* for him?"

Slowly, Paget nodded. "At least see him as human," he murmured. "Marcy Linton hurt them—if not with Caroline, then with the public. Sharpe means to turn all that around on us."

"To what do you attribute Mr. Ransom's hostility toward women?" Sharpe was asking.

"In part to his feelings toward Siobhan Ransom, his late mother. She was a domineering woman and seems to have served as an archetype for any woman he perceived as strong and aggressive—those of independent accomplishment, or ardent feminists. Women who he believed might dominate him, or criticize him, or simply not think well of him. As I say, Mark Ransom was a frightened and vulnerable man."

To his left, Paget felt Mary's rising anger. The testimony regarding impotence was eating through her self-control; she stared at Bass with barely repressed rage. Once more, against his will, Paget wondered what had happened in Mark Ransom's suite.

Keep your concentration, he told himself. Look for a line of attack.

"How serious," Sharpe was asking, "did you consider Mr. Ransom's sexual problem to be?"

Bass looked grave. "Extremely serious, and very deeply rooted. At the time of our last visit, he had not been able to have intercourse for nearly four years.''

Paget saw Caroline Masters's eyes widen. Sharpe waited a moment. ''And did Mr. Ransom specify to you,'' she asked quietly, ''the last time in which he achieved intercourse?''

''It was the same occasion that *he* blamed for his impotence.'' Pausing, he turned to Masters. ''The rape of the young woman you saw yesterday—Marcy Linton. After that, Mark Ransom became impotent.''

The courtroom was silent. Softly, Sharpe said, ''No further questions.''

Rising from the defense table, Paget saw Mary's sudden look of defeat. Behind her, Carlo stared at his shoes. Paget felt their reactions as his own; with her final question, to his utter disbelief, Sharpe had pointed Marcy Linton's testimony back at Mary Carelli.

Slowly, he walked toward Bass.

''You mentioned Siobhan Ransom as an archetype,'' Paget began. ''Did Ransom develop a counterarchetype? That is, was there a particular woman who he imagined represented his *needs?*''

Bass watched him for a moment. ''Yes. The actress Laura Chase.''

Paget felt a spark of hope. ''So he mentioned her in analysis?''

"Frequently."

"And what role did Ms. Chase play in Mr. Ransom's psychic landscape?"

Idly, Bass tapped his glasses. "In shorthand, she represented security and sexual fulfillment. The Laura Chase he invented in his mind would have done anything to please him. She not only would have catered to his sexual desires but, equally important, she would have *admired* him."

Paget gave him a curious look. "Did he specifically associate Laura Chase with sexual performance?"

"Yes." Bass sounded rueful. "He came to believe that with Laura Chase, he would have been the sexual man he wished to be. He saw her as someone mysterious, yet available; a woman who wanted to maintain a distinct and exotic role that was not in competition with him."

"Is it fair to call this preoccupation with Laura Chase a fetish?"

Bass nodded. "In a sense. It's not at all uncommon, Mr. Paget, for men with doubts about their sexuality to seek arousal through fetishes or rituals. I don't mean to sound insensitive, but the incident with Ms. Linton traumatized him. He was deeply afraid of failure."

Paget felt himself slow down. "Did Mr. Ransom also have a preoccupation with rape?" he asked.

"Yes. It was part of his desire to subjugate women."

"Is it fair to say that rape is a crime of violence rather than of passion? As evidenced by the blow to the face he inflicted on Ms. Linton?"

"I would agree, yes."

"And it's true that Mr. Ransom derived sexual stimulation from physically abusing women? Also as evidenced by Ms. Linton?"

"That is possible. At least it is consistent with his psychology."

Paget moved closer, glancing up at Caroline Masters. "It is even possible, is it not, that he might view slapping a woman's face as a way of achieving and/or maintaining an erection?"

"Yes. That also would be consistent."

"So that we have now identified two factors which helped Mr. Ransom achieve erection: striking a woman, and his fetish for Laura Chase. Is that correct?"

Bass gave him a thoughtful gaze. "Those could be factors."

It was time, Paget thought, to take a chance. "Did you ever become aware that Mr. Ransom had obtained tapes of Laura Chase's sessions with her psychiatrist, Dr. Steinhardt?"

"Yes." Bass looked defensive. "I don't approve, incidentally. I'm here because my patient was killed, and because Ms. Sharpe was quite insistent. In fact, I find it quite ironic to be here discussing Mr. Ransom's confidences.''

''I understand,'' Paget said. ''But fairness to Ms. Carelli requires that I pursue this. Specifically, did Mr. Ransom tell you that he had obtained the tape described by Ms. Carelli—one in which Laura Chase described having sex with two men?''

Bass nodded unhappily. ''He did. Yes. He was quite excited about it.''

''Did Mr. Ransom believe that this tape might restore him sexually?''

''Objection,'' Sharpe called out. ''The question asks Dr. Bass to speculate.''

Caroline Masters gave her a droll look. ''People who live in glass houses, Ms. Sharpe, are likely to get glass in their eye. Carry on, Mr. Paget.''

''That would be speculation.'' Bass paused. ''But yes, I think so. I do know that once Mr. Ransom got that tape, he stopped seeing me.''

All at once, Paget understood the doctor's rueful tone: Mark Ransom had chosen Laura Chase as a substitute for therapy, gone down what Bass believed to be a sad and fruitless path. ''But after that, Doctor, he *did* see Ms. Carelli. So let's briefly reprise your testimony. Slapping women helped Mr. Ransom stay erect, true?''

''So it seems.''

"The Laura Chase fetish also helped Mark Ransom stay erect?"

Bass nodded. "It was a primary source of stimulus, yes."

"So isn't it quite possible that stimulated by the Laura Chase tape and by slapping Ms. Carelli, Mark Ransom could have tried to rape her?"

"It's possible, yes. But after Ms. Linton, that would have put Mark Ransom at great risk of personal embarrassment." Pausing, Bass glanced at Mary. "It's difficult to envision him taking that risk with a woman like Ms. Carelli."

"But weren't women 'like Ms. Carelli'—independent women of achievement—the very type of women Mark Ransom despised and wished to subjugate?"

"True, on one level." Bass shifted on the witness stand. "But to me, the operative word is 'fear.' The man I saw was far too mired in fear to attempt penetration with an unwilling woman."

Paget's voice went cold. "That's called rape, Doctor. Which is the *third factor* we've identified as a sexual stimulus to Mr. Ransom."

"Indeed," Bass said. "But I saw the man for almost four years, and what you describe is hard for me to imagine."

It stopped Paget again. He stared at Bass, feigning incredulity, while he tried to think of a way to end on a better answer. ''But isn't it possible,'' he finally asked, ''that Mark Ransom could have achieved an erection under circumstances that would convince Ms. Carelli she was going to be raped, including the infliction of a blow to the face, whether or not he could actually do it?''

''That's possible, yes.''

''Or whether or not, in the end, he intended to even *try* penetration?''

Bass looked at Sharpe, then turned again to Paget. Slowly, he answered, ''I suppose that's also possible.''

When Paget glanced up at Caroline Masters, her gaze was cool. But there was nothing more that he could do.

He turned back to Bass. ''I have no further questions, Dr. Bass. Thank you for your patience.''

Walking back to the defense table, Paget saw that Sharpe was already on her feet.

''During the four-year period of Mr. Ransom's treatment,'' she asked Bass, ''did he ever discuss raping anyone?''

Bass shook his head. ''No. As I said, the consequence of his attack on Ms. Linton tormented him. His fantasy concerning rape, when he acted it out, came at a great cost to *both* people involved.''

''Did he indicate any predisposition to rape anyone again?''

Bass paused, looking at Mary Carelli. "No. None."

Sharpe nodded. "In fact, did Mr. Ransom talk of sexual contact with *anyone?*"

"No one."

Sharpe paused for a moment. "Did he ever mention Mary Carelli?"

Bass shook his head. "If he had a particular interest in Ms. Carelli, I was not aware of it."

"Thank you, Dr. Bass. No further questions."

As Caroline Masters excused her last witness, Sharpe walked to the prosecution table with an air of satisfaction. Watching, Paget felt disheartened.

From the bench, Masters faced the lawyers again. "I'd like to compliment both prosecution and defense on an admirable presentation of the evidence. I'll hear final argument at ten o'clock tomorrow morning."

Abruptly, she banged her gavel.

"All rise," the courtroom deputy called out, and Caroline Masters left the bench, the sudden tumult of the courtroom trailing after her, the legacy of Sharpe's final witness.

PART SIX

THE COURT

February 19 – February 22

ONE

TERESA PERALTA pulled up in front of the post office.

She sat in her car for a moment, watching the pedestrian traffic on Van Ness. It was one o'clock; men and women on lunch breaks filed in and out of restaurants and shops and the stereo outlet across the street, in no particular hurry. The desultory rhythm of normal life seemed alien to Terri; the day was unseasonably warm, and the brightness of the sun surprised her.

The cloistered world of a trial was unnatural, she realized; a forced obsession which so consumed its protagonists that they thought of little else. For two weeks, the hearing had been her life; the witnesses her chief concern; Christopher Paget and Caroline Masters and Marnie Sharpe and Mary Carelli her human reference points. She had watched them stumble, grow, confront the relentless pressure of the courtroom and of life in the third person—watching their every act replayed on television—until, finally, it was almost finished.

Chris was shut in his office, trying to adjust his thoughts to the testimony of Dr. Bass, refusing all calls from the press so that he could outline his final argument to Caroline Masters. Later, Terri would listen and offer advice. There was just one more thing she needed to do.

This would come to nothing, she believed. But if the tapes had not been destroyed—and while Mary had motive to destroy them, she lacked the means—Chris and Carlo were still at risk. If Terri could not find the tapes, at least she would know that.

Getting out of the car, Terri felt the breeze on her face, took in the vehicles that passed, the people in the crosswalk, the sounds of engines and car horns, the random buildings—some tall, some low, their irregular height like the rooftops of a toy city, built by a child. After she saw Chris, perhaps she would pick up Elena early from day care, drive her to the beach. They both needed that.

Terri walked into the post office.

It was dim, musty-smelling. Ten or twelve people waited with sullen detachment for three postal clerks to process their mail or retrieve a package. The bearded man in front of her hummed tunelessly, passing time to his own inner voice.

The beach was a good idea, Terri thought. Once the hearing was over, she would be free to spend time with Elena and deal with Richie.

She checked her watch. One-fifteen.

What was Caroline doing now? she wondered. Calmly nibbling on her usual salad, having made up her mind? No, Terri thought: Caroline might already have decided how to rule, but she would not be serene about it. The hearing, and the people it touched, seemed to weigh on her now. She would be thinking of those people as much as her career or even Mary; she could cause the machinery of justice to release them by freeing Mary Carelli or, with Mary, send them all to trial.

Terri would not, she decided, wish to be Caroline Masters.

She shuffled forward, imagining the moment when Caroline announced her decision. The thought led her to another: even less would she like to be Christopher Paget.

They had lost, Terri believed. Lost with the final witness.

"Next," a man's voice called.

Terri looked up in surprise. There was no one in front of her; a pleasant-faced Japanese postal clerk looked at her expectantly.

She walked up to the window. "Sorry," she said. "Absentminded."

"Sure." He was looking at Terri with an intelligent, curious expression; for the first time, it struck Terri that her face might be recognizable to strangers. Then he asked, "What can we do for you?"

Terri hesitated. "I'm looking for a lost package.

Something with an incomplete address, or the address missing. It got mailed from Nob Hill, we think.''

Perhaps, Terri thought, she only *imagined* that he looked curious. ''You didn't mail it yourself?'' he asked.

Terri shook her head. ''No, a friend. We think she stuck it in the mail by accident.'' Feeling awkward, Terri joked, ''She's absentminded too.''

The man seemed to study her face. Then he smiled. ''You'd be amazed,'' he said. ''What was in there?''

What had she told the woman in Dead Letters? ''Cassette tapes,'' she answered. ''Like for a stereo.''

He looked thoughtful. ''I might have noticed that. We get some good stuff back there, and I play music all the time in my car. Offhand, I don't remember tapes.''

Didn't you already call about tapes, the woman had asked, a few weeks back?

''Can I take a look?'' Terri asked.

He hesitated. ''There's no one back there now.''

Terri smiled. ''I promise not to take anything that's not mine. All I'm looking for are cassette tapes, really. Maybe in an envelope marked 'Hotel Flood.' ''

He thought for another moment, and then shrugged. ''We have a lot of things. I might have missed it.'' He motioned her around the counter. ''Come on back—you've got an honest face.''

Terri followed him down a hallway to an open room with metal shelves full of packages and a three-foot stepladder next to the door. ''This is it,'' he said cheerfully. ''If you find what you're looking for, come get me.''

''Thanks,'' Terri said. Somehow, being in the room made her quest seem real. Her skin tingled; she did not dare look around her until the clerk had left.

She should have told Chris she was coming.

It was all right, she told herself. Chris was distracted enough. He did not want the tapes found by anyone else; if they were anywhere Sharpe or the media could get them, he would choose to have them first. And if Mary lost, and went to trial, it was all the more important that Terri find them.

Look systematically, she told herself. Don't become frenzied, glancing from shelf to shelf, and don't leave anything to chance. Then you can forget this.

There were shelves on three walls.

The first row of shelves took a half hour. She spent the time bending, stretching, using the stepladder, until her back hurt. She found a baseball glove, foreign currency, several watches, a box full of religious tracts, a cookbook with handwritten recipes stuffed in several pages. The scraps of lives, but no tape.

Once more she climbed the stepladder, peering over the top of a new shelf.

"Find anything?"

She turned atop the ladder. The clerk stood in the doorway.

"Not my stuff," she said. "But a couple of nice watches."

The clerk laughed. "You must really want those tapes. This room reminds me of the army. It's depressing."

Terri smiled. "If I start to need air, I'll let you know."

"Okay." He paused. "These tapes, they're not the Grateful Dead, are they?"

Terri shook her head. "No."

"Too bad. I really love the Dead." He went back to his customers.

She turned, resting on her arms, and glanced at the top of the next shelf over.

There was a ripped letter-size envelope, Terri saw, with a rubber band around the middle. Inside the envelope was the outline of a small rectangular object.

At least it was the right size, Terri thought. She paused, debating whether to break her discipline of a systematic search, and then climbed down the stepladder.

She slid the ladder sideways across the floor, then climbed it again, peering at each shelf as she went.

She got to the top, gazing down at the envelope. Finally, she picked it up.

It was light in her hand. When she turned it over, she saw the logo of the Hotel Flood with a line drawn through it.

Her hands began shaking. As she removed the rubber band, it fell to the floor.

She reached inside the envelope.

There was not one rectangle, her fingers told her, but two. She pulled them out.

Tapes.

Staring at them, Terri saw the Roman numerals. But it was a moment before she could accept what she was holding.

The first tape, she knew from Steinhardt's code, was of Laura Chase. Which meant that the second was Mary Carelli.

She stood there clutching the tapes, wishing that she had not come. Then she slowly climbed down the stepladder with the tapes and the envelope.

The rubber band was by the ladder. She picked it up, put the tapes in the envelope, and wound the rubber band tight around it.

The clerk was serving a customer. Terri walked behind him. "I found it," she said quietly.

He turned, smiling, and took the envelope from her hand. He glanced at it and looked up again.

"Amazing," he said. "Goes to show what they say about perseverance."

He might not have noticed how strange she had sounded, Terri thought. She saw his customer watching them. "I guess so," she said. "Thanks for your help."

"Oh, you'll have to sign for it. We can't just let stuff go."

He left for a moment, returning with a sheet filled with descriptions of parcels, a column for signatures and addresses. His index finger rested on a line headed "Tapes, Flood." "Here," he said.

Carefully, Terri signed the index, the tapes held in her right hand. "Thanks," she repeated.

"Sure." He looked at her again. "Don't I recognize you from somewhere?"

Terri managed a smile. "I have that kind of face," she answered, and left.

TWO

CHRISTOPHER PAGET found it hard to concentrate.

He walked to his window, gazing out at the panorama of the city—the green rise of Telegraph Hill, houses and apartments seeming to climb up its side; the sweep of piers with their luxury liners and tour boats; the blue expanse of bay. Since he was a child, Paget had loved this city, counted himself fortunate to live here; as an adult, he had taught Carlo to love it too, exploring its vistas and its nooks and crannies—a neighborhood Italian restaurant in North Beach, pocket parks with swings and slides, places to walk on Sunday morning for croissants or blueberry muffins.

On a normal day, these thoughts brought him contentment. Being part of a place that Carlo now wished to be part of made him feel that his life had added up to something, was not just about himself and how he had made his way. He no longer saw his decision to raise Carlo as something done for a lonely child: it had created a depth of happiness and pleasure that would have been beyond him on his own.

Whatever else the accident of Mary Carelli had brought him, their careless weekend in Washington had brought him Carlo. Christopher Paget was lucky to be Carlo's father; looking at the city, defined by the days they had spent together, reminded him of that.

But today the view gave Paget little pleasure, and less peace.

From the beginning, he had believed Mary guilty of something, in some degree or another. Everything he knew about her, and every twist in her story, told him she was hiding something deeper and more obscure than what had happened on the day Mark Ransom died. But Paget had forced himself to focus simply on what the prosecution could prove. If he put Sharpe's case to an early test, he had reasoned, perhaps he could extract Mary from danger before the prosecutor learned what Paget himself did not know—by finding the tape or otherwise. And Marcy Linton had made a difference; there were times, despite himself, when Paget gave Mary's account some credence.

Now George Bass had shaken him to the core.

It wasn't merely the damage to Mary's defense—though Paget could see that in the faces of the media people as he had left the courthouse, hear it in the shouted questions he had ignored. Nor was it that Johnny Moore's failures now made sense, or even that Sharpe had transformed Marcy Linton—at least in some sense—into a prosecution witness. What was so painful was the realization that in spite of his best professional efforts and all that he knew about her, Paget had still wanted to believe in Mary Carelli.

Why blame Mary? he thought. She is who she is; only a fool invests in believing his client. Even when the client is the mother of your much-loved son.

Especially then.

Now there would be a trial, he believed, another ordeal for Carlo to bear. Searching for motive, Sharpe might find the tape: even if it was inadmissible, sooner or later someone from the media would ferret it out. There was no chance that the lucky reporter would conclude that hurt to Carlo Paget outweighed the boost to his or her career, piously cloaked in the public's right to know. And in the meanwhile, Carlo would be besieged by questions from all sides, and worst of all his own: whether his mother had killed Mark Ransom not because of rape but to save her own career, and then coolly lied about it until the lies entangled her.

There was a soft knock behind him.

As Paget turned, Teresa Peralta appeared in the doorway.

"Do you want to talk," she asked, "or should I come back?"

She looked as troubled as he was, Paget thought. "Stay," he answered. "I'm not functioning very well. Perhaps you can help."

Just her being there would help. But Paget could not tell her that. Too much of what he felt was no longer about Terri the lawyer, as good as she was, but about Terri the woman.

"Is it Bass?" she asked.

Paget nodded. "He seems to have set off a chain reaction. In the past hour, I've covered Mary, Carlo, the tapes, and my own monumental foolishness. I haven't come up with a line of argument."

She closed the door, stood leaning against it with her black purse clasped in front of her. "Tell me the worst part," she said.

Paget was silent for a moment. Then he asked, "Did you ever love someone so much it hurts?"

Terri nodded. "Elena."

"For me, it's Carlo. It's the only time I've let myself feel like that—perhaps I thought that loving a child was safe." He shrugged. "Loving someone is never safe. There's too much that can happen."

"And you're worried about what will happen to Carlo."

"To Carlo, yes. Perhaps, more selfishly, to Carlo and me." He paused. "I don't want this to go on for him. And I keep worrying about that tape. What on earth could have moved Mary Carelli, of all people, to bare her soul for a tape recorder?"

Terri watched him. "You're still afraid they'll find it, then."

"If they have a reason to keep looking. An ongoing prosecution will do nicely."

Terri's shoulders drew in. Softly, she said, "They won't ever find it, Chris."

Her tone was very subdued and very certain. "Because Mary destroyed it?" he asked.

"No. Because I have it."

Something in her voice kept Paget from saying anything. Slowly, Terri took an envelope from her purse.

She walked across the room and placed it in his hands. "There are two tapes inside," she told him. "One is Laura Chase, talking about Lindsay Caldwell. The second is Mary."

He stared down at the envelope. "How long have you had these?"

"For less than an hour." Her voice was still quiet. "I found them at the post office."

Paget looked up. "Mary told you?"

Terri shook her head. "I figured it out. After Mary shot Ransom, she put them in a blank envelope and slid them down the mail slot. That's what she was doing in the hallway."

"Then she lied about that too." Paget touched his eyes, slowly shaking his head. "If she was cool enough to do *that,* God knows what else she did. And lied about."

Terri walked away from him, sat in a chair, looking out. "I shouldn't have told you," she said. "Not today."

Paget shrugged. "You didn't want me worrying anymore—at least about the tapes. And you reasoned, correctly, that any decent defense lawyer wouldn't let this keep him from arguing the evidence before the court."

She looked up at him. "Do you want *me* to do the argument?"

"No. You've done far too much already." Paget's brain was sluggish, he realized; it was only as he spoke that it came to him that Terri was at risk. "You got these tapes yourself?" he asked.

"Yes. There's a storeroom for mail without postage."

Paget looked from Terri to the envelope and to Terri again. "They made you sign for them, I imagine."

"Yes."

"Then they can trace this to you."

"I suppose so." Her voice and eyes were steady. "Better me than you. Or Mary."

Paget sat next to her. Quietly, he asked, "Why did you do this?"

She was silent a moment. "Because I like Carlo," she answered. "And I like what you've done with him. He's been hurt already, and I didn't want him hurt anymore. Now, perhaps, he won't be."

"But you've got your own life, Terri, your own career. I didn't want you involved. Not like this."

Terri looked down. "I have trouble drawing lines sometimes. I know that. But if it were Elena, and me, wouldn't you have done the same thing?"

Paget gazed at her; the still, silent profile, the face he had learned to trust. "Then leave it at this," he said. "You gave me the tapes, and your responsibility ended. You didn't know what I'd do about them, and I never said. But you assumed I'd keep them safe."

Terri smiled faintly. "Did I?"

"Yes, you did. And that's what you'll say if you're ever asked. For my own peace of mind."

Her smile faded. "All right. If that's what you want."

"It's very much what I want."

They sat next to each other for a time, Terri staring out the window, Paget at the envelope. At length, she asked, "Can I help with your argument?"

"In a while." It was only when he spoke again that he was certain. "After I listen to this tape."

She looked over at him. "You want to do that? Now?"

"I can't *not* do it. Tomorrow, the next day—I'd have to listen to it, Mary's feelings aside." He paused. "I don't like this. But she's lied to me about too many things for far too long for me to worry about *her* feelings. And who's to say that Steinhardt was the only other person who knows what's on the tapes? If it concerns me, and what we did in Washington, I have to know.''

''But why today?''

''Because until I hear it, I can't think about anything else.''

Terri touched his shoulder. ''I'll leave, then. Call me when you need me.''

He gazed at her. Softly, Paget asked, ''And what if that's now?''

Her eyes filled with confusion. As if sparring, she said, ''You don't want me to know what you'll do with them.''

''True.'' He looked away. ''But you can know that I listened.''

Terri's eyes did not move from him. In a quiet tone, she asked, ''Why do you want me here?''

''As I said, I feel squeamish about Mary. But I just don't want to be alone with this.'' Suddenly Paget felt embarrassed. ''All my life, I've never leaned on anyone. Tomorrow I'll go back to that. I suppose, for a day, I'm borrowing you.''

She nodded, silent. After a time, she reached into the envelope, pulled out a tape. ''It's this one.''

Paget stood, walking to the credenza behind his desk, and produced a portable tape player. He put it in front of them. Inserting the tape, he briefly looked at Terri. Then he pushed the button.

As Paget sat next to Terri, Steinhardt asked, "Did Chris know about your involvement with this man Jack Woods?"

The tape crackled with static. Steinhardt's words had a ghostly quality; it reminded Paget of driving late at night through the Pennsylvania hills during a college trip he had made across the country, the distant voice of an evangelist the only sound that could come from his radio.

"What do you mean?" Mary asked quietly.

Steinhardt hesitated, as if confused. "Your involvement in obstructing the Lasko investigation."

"Yes." Mary's voice became a monotone. "He knew about that."

There was a long silence. "But as I recall his Senate testimony," Steinhardt said slowly, "he supported you."

"No," Mary corrected. "Chris *lied* for me."

Paget felt Terri glance at him, look away. Listening to Mary's taped voice, saying through the static what she never thought he would hear, was haunting. But at least, as Mary had described this tape, he had already heard the worst of it.

"Do you know why Chris lied?" Steinhardt asked.

More silence. "I know of one reason," Mary answered. "The night before we testified, I told him I was pregnant."

"With Carlo, his son?"

The silence became longer. "With Carlo. Yes."

"When you told him, how did he react?"

"We met by the Jefferson Memorial at night, so at first I couldn't really see his face. But his words were clear enough." Her voice turned briefly sad. "He thought Carlo wasn't his. He suggested I consider an abortion."

"And what did you say?"

Her tone sounded bitter. "That he must not think very well of me. And that I was keeping Carlo."

Paget's eyes shut. He felt Terri touch his arm. "It's all right," she murmured. "That was all so long ago. You couldn't know who Carlo would be."

"Then you didn't want an abortion?" Steinhardt asked Mary.

"That's what I told Chris." There was another pause, and then Mary's voice became muted. "But if he hadn't covered for me, what choice would I have had? Carlo would have had no father, and a mother in prison."

"Did you tell Chris that?"

"No." Another pause. "I knew I didn't need to."

"Why was that?"

"Because I felt him start to take in the reality of it—that I might be pregnant with his child. He began to look at me differently, to ask how I felt." Paget heard an ironic smile in Mary's voice. "He even said I should sit down. Like an inexperienced new father, not knowing what to do, amazed at the wonder of it all.''

Listening, Paget felt the moment again: the darkness outside the memorial; the woman he did not trust but who might have life inside her; the sense that his own life was about to change. He still felt shaken by it.

''Did you love him?'' Steinhardt asked.

Paget sensed Terri's gaze. ''Yes.'' Mary's voice was cool. ''As much as I can love anyone.''

''You think you're not capable?''

''Not head over heels. Not to the point where I lose control, or lose sight of what I want. I can't let myself.'' Another pause. ''I've never known whether that's a virtue or a fault. It just is.''

''Did you think that Chris loved you?''

''I don't know. In a lot of ways, Chris was *like* me—he's very cool and controlled.'' Mary's voice fell again. ''It surprised me when he wanted to raise Carlo.''

Next to Paget, Terri slowly shook her head. ''Mary never knew who you were,'' she murmured. ''She still doesn't.''

''Perhaps he did love you,'' Steinhardt was saying. ''Perhaps *that's* why he helped.''

''Oh, it was partly out of feeling for me, I think, *and* the baby I was carrying.'' Her tone changed again. ''And partly because I could help him send Jack Woods to prison.''

‘‘Did you offer him that?’’

‘‘I didn’t have to. He knew that if he covered for me, I would help him ruin Jack.’’ Another pause. ‘‘And *I* knew how much he wanted that. Because I knew how much he hated Jack.’’

Paget turned to Terri. ‘‘She did understand me,’’ he said softly. ‘‘Much better than you think.’’

‘‘But you testified *before* Chris did,’’ Steinhardt probed. ‘‘You didn’t know what he would say.’’

‘‘It was better that way.’’ Mary’s voice turned cold. ‘‘Watching me testify, Chris saw what I could do to Jack. And he also knew that if he turned me in, I would be forced to protect myself instead of repeating my story at Jack’s trial.’’ She paused again. ‘‘All Chris had to do was lie about me, and he would save a pregnant woman and destroy Jack Woods. I still don’t know which one he wanted more.’’

Paget’s surroundings—the airy office, the panorama of the bay—seemed to vanish. All that he could imagine was Mary in the sterile room Terri had described to him, telling their secrets to a tape recorder. ‘‘She told me the truth,’’ he said to Terri. ‘‘This tape does no more harm to her. But it would have ruined me.’’

‘‘And Carlo,’’ Terri answered. ‘‘Imagine him listening to this.’’

‘‘Jack Woods,’’ Steinhardt was asking Mary. ‘‘What happened to him?’’

‘‘All the things that would have happened to me.’’

Mary's voice turned grim. "He pleaded guilty rather than face a trial. Three years in prison were the least of it. His career was ruined. He couldn't even practice law."

"They took away his license?"

"Yes." Mary paused. "Much worse, they took away who he was. When he got out of prison, he was no one."

"Did you ever see him again?"

"Of course not." Mary's tone was ironic. "By then I was on my way. In one day, Chris Paget and I destroyed Jack and launched my career in the media."

"Do you feel guilt about that?"

"Not about *that*. Jack had blackmailed me into helping him because of what I already knew, until I was in far deeper than I ever wanted. I owed him nothing." Mary hesitated, voice softening again. "No, Doctor, I'm here for another reason. One we haven't even touched on."

Something in her tone made Paget tense. "Is it about Carlo?" Steinhardt asked.

"Partly." Her voice was hesitant. "But it's also about Chris. And me."

"That dream," Steinhardt said. "You're in the church in Paris, asking forgiveness for your sins. Is your sin giving Carlo to Chris?"

There was a long silence. "Yes," Mary answered softly.

"Has Chris been a good father?"

"I think so." Mary's voice sounded parched. "I've tried to stay out of the way. After years of trying to keep him away from Carlo."

"I don't understand, then. You believe Chris to be good with Carlo. And in the dream, you're asking forgiveness *before* you give Carlo to Chris. Not after."

There was a long silence. "You're an intelligent man, Doctor. But there's something I haven't told you. Or anyone."

"And what is that?" Steinhardt asked.

To Paget, Mary's silence was like the intake of breath. Then, very coolly, she answered, "Chris isn't Carlo's father."

The next moment was a blur. Terri's pale, stricken face. Feeling himself bend forward. Steinhardt's dry voice, asking the next question as if nothing had happened.

"Who *is* the father, then?"

Another silence, as if Mary could not bring herself to answer. Through his shock, Paget felt Terri's hand on his arm. "Jack Woods," Mary answered in a trembling voice. "Chris's enemy. The man we sent to prison."

"Oh, Chris." Terri's voice was anguished. Looking up, Paget saw the tears in her eyes.

It doesn't matter, he wanted to say. But he found he could not speak the words. Or any words at all.

"Why didn't you tell Chris?" Steinhardt asked.

Through the static, Mary's voice was faint. "At first, I wanted him to protect me. So I let him think the baby was his, to save myself."

"And later, when you gave up Carlo?"

"Chris flew to Paris, full of worry. He'd seen how Carlo was, living with my parents. I'd tried to put it out of my mind, tell myself it was temporary. Chris couldn't do that." Her voice was soft. "We sat at a café in the shadow of St. Germain-des-Prés, the cathedral in my dream, while he begged me to give him Carlo. And when that didn't work, he blackmailed me. For the son that was never his."

Paget covered his face. Some deeply irrational part of him wanted to turn back the clock and erase the tape from his mind. But when he felt Terri reach for it, he grasped her hand. "It's too late," he said softly. "For fifteen years, it's been too late."

The tears ran down her face. "I did this," she murmured. "I did this."

He shook his head. "*I* did. When you were younger than Carlo is now." He saw Terri swallow; the tape spun inexorably on—silence, then static, then silence again.

"Did you think about telling Chris then?" Steinhardt finally asked. "In Paris?"

"I couldn't bring myself to do it." Her voice fell. "I took the coward's way out. I tried every way I knew to discourage him. Just as I'd refused any help from him once Carlo was born. But this time, nothing worked.'' The irony returned, this time mixed with sadness. ''He was Carlo's father, he told me. He was willing to sacrifice his marriage to save him—his own reputation, even. And mine.''

''How did that make you feel?''

''That Chris would do anything he had to do.'' Her voice softened again. ''And that in the end, I'd given Carlo the right father.''

''The right father,'' Paget murmured, ''for Jack Woods's son.''

As Terri took his hand, Steinhardt spoke again. ''Was that why you let him go, Mary?''

There was silence. ''I let him go,'' she finally answered, ''because Chris made me think. About who he really was, and who I wanted Carlo to be.'' Her voice became sad, yet certain. ''You see, I realized that Chris wasn't really like me, after all.''

In the quiet that followed, Paget shook his head. ''Then what is your sin?'' Steinhardt asked.

''That I could let my son go,'' she said softly. ''And that I lied to Chris twice. The first to save myself, the second to save Carlo.''

''Did you feel you were saving Carlo?''

''I thought of my own childhood. What Chris said about the damage to Carlo scared me.'' She paused. ''But not enough to give up my career. Only enough to give up Carlo, and to use Christopher Paget one more time. And the only thing I can say to myself is that when I did it, I was thinking more of Carlo than of either Chris or me."

"Have you thought of telling Chris *now?*"

There was more silence. "I always do," she said, in muted tones. "But I tell myself that it would hurt them far too much." She paused again. "They love each other now. With every day I allow to pass, it would hurt them more."

"Then why are you so troubled?"

"Because I could lie about that. Because I could do what I did. Because I'm not troubled enough." Her voice fell. "Because there's something missing in me, and always will be."

Through his anger and anguish, something in Paget found the words both sad and frightening. On the tape, Steinhardt asked, "How does that make you feel?"

"Free," Mary answered softly. "Free, and very alone. Like no one can touch me." There was another pause; for a moment, Mary sounded close to tears. "What Chris could do for Carlo, I could never do. I could never feel enough. I only feel enough to stay away from them. To not face what I've done."

Perhaps, Paget thought, Mary was crying, but too quietly to be heard. Then Steinhardt asked, "Where are you going?"

"I'm leaving." Mary sounded weary, but composed again. "I came here wondering if I should tell Chris the truth. But I can't."

"That's not the only reason to seek help."

There was a final silence. "There's no help for who I am," Mary said quietly. "And never will be."

Terri let go of Paget's hand. A moment later, at the margin of his consciousness, he heard her switch off the tape.

Paget sat there alone.

The central act of his life, the raising of a son, had no more meaning than his lies to the Senate. They were the acts of a fool, mired in vanity and self-deception.

Did you ever love someone, he had asked Terri, so much that it hurts?

Elena, she had told him, and Paget had answered, For me, it's Carlo.

Jack Woods's son.

He did not realize that he was crying. Then Terri took him in her arms, pressing his head between her breasts, her face resting on the top of his head.

"I'm so sorry," she whispered.

When he looked up at her, she brushed the hair back from his forehead with her fingertips. "What can I do?" she asked.

"I need to be alone with this," he said. "It's a lot to sort out."

She nodded. "What will *you* do?"

"I have no idea." He paused. "About anything."

Terri let him go. For a moment, she stood next to

him, hand resting on his shoulder. Then she started toward the door.

She stopped there, turning. "She's right, Chris. You're not like her. That's why it all happened."

He could think of nothing to say.

"I'll be in my office," she told him and left, closing the door gently behind her.

THREE

WITHOUT MAKEUP, Mary's eyes seemed hollow, her face drawn. She had the strung-out look of a woman too wired to sleep. Finding Paget at the door seemed to startle her, as if the hearing had eaten through her nerve ends.

"What do you want?" she asked.

Paget simply stared at her. Softly, he said, "You seem to have lost your tolerance for surprises."

Mary stared from the doorway, like a woman wrenched from her private space by someone who was threatening her. She made no move to ask him in. "Shouldn't you be preparing your argument?" she asked.

"I seem to be having trouble with it."

Her eyes narrowed. "And you've come here for my help."

"In a manner of speaking."

She paused, waiting for him to say more. He said nothing.

Finally, she stepped aside. The gesture was grudging, almost angry. When he walked to the middle of the suite and turned to her, she still held the door.

"You might want to close that," he said.

Slowly, she did. She stood, gazing at the doorknob, as if reluctant to face him. There was a new fragility to her movements, Paget thought.

Turning, she squared her shoulders. "*You're* behaving strangely," she said.

"Am I?"

"Yes." She paused. "I really don't appreciate this."

"What, precisely?"

"Your just showing up. What is it you want?"

Paget gazed around him, choosing a place to sit. The drapes were drawn; there was nothing of Mary in the antiseptic room. It was as if personal possessions were clues, to be hidden from intruders.

"The truth," he answered. "I'd prefer to hear it sitting down. But you can stand there if you like."

He walked to the couch and sat, gazing up at her with a look of mild interest. "You can start anytime," he said. "I've got till ten o'clock tomorrow."

Her mouth opened to speak, closed again. "What is it, damn you? Bass?"

Paget watched her. "I'm not here to discuss why I want the truth. I simply want it."

"Then you can leave. You already have the truth." She folded her arms. "Your cross on Bass was right. Whatever Ransom could or couldn't do, I was frightened.''

''No,'' Paget said softly, ''you were rational. And once I understood that, I knew the reason you delayed in calling 911.''

''And what is that?''

''To cover up the murder you'd been planning.'' To Paget, his own voice seemed to come from a distance, very calm and very polite. ''There *is* one point you can help me with. What were you doing in the hallway?''

''I was in shock, damn it.'' Mary stood rigid, clenching her fists, voice rising as she spoke. ''Do you find some pleasure in tormenting me? Wasn't the trial enough for you?''

''No. It wasn't.''

''Please, Chris, *leave.*'' Her voice sounded brittle. ''Leave me alone. I don't want you here. The place I need you is in court.''

''But I can't leave.'' Paget spoke with exaggerated patience, as if to a child. ''You haven't answered my question.''

''There *is* no answer.''

''Oh, I'm sure there must be.''

''Why? Because you've been talking to your diminutive friend, Ms. Peralta?''

Paget raised his eyebrows. ''What does Terri have to do with this?''

''Will you *stop.*'' The first edge of Boston Italian

appeared in her speech, as if her persona were unraveling. "I can't remember *what* I was doing."

"It may come back to you." Casually, Paget took the tape from his pocket and placed it on the coffee table, still looking up at her. "Why don't you think for a moment."

As if by reflex, Mary drew up her hands. Her face was white.

"Of course, you may not remember what's on *this,* either." Paget's voice became softer yet. "Five years is a long time in the life of a parent. And it's one third of the life of your son."

Mary turned to the window. In the silence, she was stiff and still, and then her shoulders began trembling.

Paget stood. "Look at me, damn you. You had the courage to kill a man. All that you did to *me* was change my life. It shouldn't be too difficult to look me in the face."

Silent, Mary shook her head. She did not turn. The tremors ran through her body.

"I lied for you," Paget continued. "I left Washington because of you, abandoned the career I'd wanted. I let my marriage founder and raised Carlo as my son, because of you. And now, because of you, I've found out what a joke it's all been."

Mary's head bent forward. Her body shook in spasms now, but still she made no sound.

"*Look* at me," Paget demanded. "You can use

people, or kill them, or just warp their lives. People aren't real to you—*I'm* not real to you. You don't see anyone apart from what you want. For you, the only excuse I or anyone has for living is to serve as your pawn. So the least you can do is look at me.''

Mary's back straightened.

Slowly, she turned to him. Tears ran down her face.

Paget struggled for self-control. It took all that he had; he felt no pity, but his voice was still soft. ''Forgive me if I sound harsh,'' he said. ''But I just found out that you arranged for me to raise Jack Woods's son as mine. And you know how *I* hate surprises.''

Mary tried to speak, could not. Her hands touched her chest in a posture of grieving and shock.

''You're a remarkable woman,'' Paget said. ''You helped me send Carlo's father to prison to save your own career, and used *his* son to make me help you. It's hard to put a name to that.''

''Don't you *know,*'' Mary burst out, ''why I went to Ransom's suite?''

''Of course. To kill him.''

''No.'' Through her tears, Mary's voice shook with pain and anger. ''To do anything he wanted. So that you and Carlo would never hear that tape.''

Paget was silent. ''It's touching,'' he said finally, ''to consider the sacrifices you've made on my behalf. The guilt may be too much for me to live with.''

Mary seemed to blanch. She half turned from him, face wet with tears, arms crossed as if to hold herself in. Her shoulders quivered; she looked desolate and alone.

Paget did not move or speak. He simply watched her; his sole expression was one of distaste.

All at once, Mary sat down on the rug.

Her face bent to her hands; there was one convulsive sob, and then the sounds that followed were like keening. Whatever had happened with Ransom, the lies and torment that had come from it had pushed her to the edge. Now, at last, the second tape had shattered her: the Mary Carelli that Paget saw was the one woman he had never imagined.

Paget waited until the keening stopped. Walking across the room, he stood over her, holding the tape in his hand.

"Then tell me." The quiet in his voice was anger, barely controlled. "Everything. But not until you look me in the face."

For a long moment, Mary's face stayed in her hands. Then her face rose to meet his gaze. "It wasn't *me*," she said, "who did those things with Ransom."

"The things you say Ransom wanted? Or killing him?"

Mary swallowed. "The things I did for him," she said at last. "Only killing him was me."

"Then tell me," he repeated.

Slowly, Mary nodded. "All right," she answered quietly. "But I can't talk about this with you standing over me."

Paget stifled a harsh response. He thought of pulling her up, then decided that he did not wish to touch her.

After a moment, he sat cross-legged on the floor, several feet from her. "You can start," he said, "with Ransom's first call."

Mary looked at her hands. "It was simple," she said at last. "Ransom described the tapes and said he'd give them to me." Her voice became muted. "One meeting at a time."

"Was he more specific?"

"He said that I had a choice. He could undress me in public or in private." Her tone turned bitter. "He wanted to be fair with me, he said. I should understand that in private, I would do anything he asked me to do. So I shouldn't assume that my 'private exposure' would be any less humiliating than 'public exposure.' "

"And you agreed?"

"No. I took his number and said that I'd call back. When I put down the telephone, my hand was shaking." Mary hesitated. "Then I went to the bathroom and threw up. Just as I said in court."

Mary paused for breath. When she began speaking again, her voice was weaker. "I couldn't imagine it: how this man could have *those* tapes; why he needed to do this to *me*. I couldn't sleep that night. I thought of everything—the Lasko case, Steinhardt, my career, Carlo. Even you. And then, after that, I imagined what Ransom must want." Her eyes shut. "In the morning, I called him back."

"What did you say?"

"That I would meet him." Mary's eyes remained closed. "If he gave me my choice of tapes."

For the first time, Paget hesitated. "You asked for the second?"

"Yes."

Paget fell silent. After a time, he asked, "Why did you buy the gun?"

Mary's eyes opened. "Because I was afraid," she answered simply. "Once we were alone, I didn't know what he would do."

Paget searched her face. "The night before, you came to see us. After eight years."

"I came to see Carlo." Her gaze was steadier now. "It was *me* who said that I'd meet Ransom in San Francisco. I was still torn about what to do. I thought, in a strange way, that seeing Carlo might help me."

"How?"

"Enable me to go through with it." Abruptly, she looked down. "If you and Carlo found out the truth, then no good would have come of letting you believe he was your son. I wanted to believe that good had come of it."

"And did you?"

"When I saw Carlo, I knew that he was happy. It made up my mind. Because I knew that good *had* come of it." Her voice fell. "Until now."

Paget looked past her, struggling for calm, felt his grip tighten on the tape. For this moment, he told himself, put your emotions aside. First you should know the truth.

"What happened," he asked, "when you got to the room?"

Mary still stared at the floor. "Ransom opened the door. He didn't say anything. Just looked at me, with a strange smile on his face. His expression was almost gloating, and yet I felt the tension beneath it. It was like walking into a nightmare.

"He still wouldn't talk. I put my purse on the coffee table, where I could reach the gun." Hesitant, she tried to look at Paget again. "Then I asked him to play the tape for me. *My* tape."

"And did he?"

Slowly, she nodded. "Listening to it—my voice, Steinhardt's questions—brought back how I'd felt. When I couldn't look at him anymore, he put his hand on my breast, like he did with Marcy Linton." Her gaze broke. "And when I didn't take it away, Ransom knew we had a deal. He'd never had to say a word."

Paget's stomach felt hollow; since Bass's testimony, he had not eaten. He found that he could not ask questions.

"The first thing he said," Mary told him softly, "was that we would share a bottle of Roederer Cristal. Because Laura Chase drank Cristal with her lovers. After she undressed for them." Mary touched her eyes. "Once the room service waiter left the suite, I knew that I would have to take off my clothes. That was why I asked him to hang the privacy sign."

Paget was silent. Mary had stopped crying; her shame seemed beyond tears. "Ransom put the tape between us," she murmured, "and watched me undress.

"When I was naked, he motioned me to the couch, to sit facing him. He positioned me in a certain way." The sudden anger in her voice was like the memory of hate. "He wanted to see each part of me, he said, without having to tell me what to show him. Because the tape I was about to hear demanded my total attention."

"Laura Chase," Paget said softly.

Mary nodded, still looking away. "I was to listen carefully, he said, while he inspected me. So that I could do for him what Laura had done for James Colt." Mary paused. "Then he made me drink a toast to Laura Chase."

Mary seemed to shiver again. Drained of defiance or calculation, she looked tired and too thin. But her narrative had taken on a relentless quality; Paget had wanted the truth, and now she would spare neither of them. "I sat there, listening to that tape: Laura Chase describing in a lost voice what she had done for those men, what they had *made* her do.

"With each act she described, Ransom would smile at me and then slowly move his eyes across my body." Mary paused again; for a moment, her voice was thick. "By the time the tape was over, the champagne was almost welcome.

"He still didn't speak. I sat there in his silence, watching him look at each part of me, taking his time. There was an almost casual cruelty in it, as if he were making sure that degrading me still held interest for him." Mary raised her head. "Then he smiled," she finished quietly, "and started to rewind the tape."

Mary's eyes stayed fixed on Paget. "He didn't need to say anything. When the tape finished rewinding, I would be standing in front of him, doing what Laura Chase had done.

"I asked him to close the blinds. 'Do it yourself,' he told me. 'That way I can see how you move.' "

Her voice had become flat; to Paget, it made what had happened seem inexorable. "I went to the window," she said. "Below me was the city, people going about their normal lives. I stood looking out, wishing I was one of them, not wanting to turn and face Mark Ransom. That was when John Hassler saw me."

The mood had shifted again; the flat words held an understated horror and, beneath that, irony—Mary had lied about what Hassler saw, but the scene as Hassler witnessed it was more illusion than truth. Softly, Mary said, "Then I heard Laura's voice again, and pulled down the blind.

"When I turned, Ransom stopped the tape.

" 'You're already naked,' he told me. 'So when I turn on the tape, I want you to start dancing. Please listen to Laura carefully.' Then he smiled again, and said, 'I want Laura Chase to be your teacher.' "

Mary swallowed again. "He tried to sound casual, in command. But I'd started to feel something desperate beneath it—as though if I got it wrong I would break some spell. Before, I was disbelieving, angry, ashamed. Now I felt frightened.

"When I began moving for him, he took his penis out.

"I felt like a courtesan. Dancing to make him hard, as Laura told me how." Color came to her face. "I did whatever Laura Chase did, desperate to be as Ransom imagined her, until I felt more like Laura than me. It was like losing my soul."

Paget shook his head. "Why did you do all that?"

Mary gave him a silent prideful look, the first semblance of her former self. "The tape he made me dance for would destroy Carlo," she said simply.

"And the tape I didn't ask for would destroy *me*. I wanted them both."

"But to keep on . . ."

"I was alone with him." Mary looked at Paget steadily. "As Mark Ransom watched me dancing, standing with his penis in his hand, I knew he was insane. I was afraid of what would happen to me if I couldn't make him hard.

"I kept listening to Laura. When Laura touched herself, I touched myself. And when it was time to slide down the wall and masturbate for Mark Ransom, I did that too." Her voice became callous, almost brutal. "It's not the first time a woman has pretended to come. Women my age were taught to be actresses for men, in all sorts of ways, first by our mothers. It was like a tribal skill, still there when I needed it. I was merely glad that Laura Chase had kept her eyes closed.

"When I felt his penis enter my mouth, I knew that it had worked." She paused. "I began to suck him. Just like Laura on the tape."

All at once, Mary stopped talking.

She pulled up her knees, hugging them close to her. Paget watched her force rhythmic breaths through her body, in and out and in again, until the quivering ceased. When she looked up, her face was naked once more: it was as if the long repression of her feelings had exhausted her. The wetness in her eyes was fresh.

"That was when it happened," she said quietly.

Her voice had changed again. It was sadder and softer, one human speaking to another; for once, appearing vulnerable seemed less like a choice she had made than all she could do. It made Paget feel a kind of dread.

"*What* happened?" he asked.

Her eyes opened wide, as though comprehending something for the first time. "As I sucked him," she said, "his penis started turning soft.

"He began cursing me in a strangled voice, telling me to suck harder. Nothing worked." Stopping, Mary took another deep breath. "I looked up at him. The back of my head was against the wall, his penis still in my mouth. He was staring down at himself. His eyes were angry and frightened all at once." She paused again, voice lower. "When his gaze met mine, his penis slipped from my mouth.

"He looked down again, watching himself shrivel.

"I was afraid to look away. I stayed very still, trapped between Ransom and the wall, watching with him. Every second he grew smaller scared me more.

"I was still watching when he slapped me.

"I looked up, stunned, eyes blurring with tears. He slapped again, looked down at himself, slapped me again, looked at himself. Like slapping me would make him hard.

"I spun away, the room turning black in front of me, began crawling toward the coffee table. In the background, Laura was still describing what they did to her. It made me crawl faster. When I looked back, he was still staring at himself.'' Her voice sounded shaken. ``Tears were running down his face.

``It stopped me. I just knelt there by the coffee table, naked, watching him as he cried.

``Then he saw me.''

Mary's gaze was fixed; she seemed to be looking not at Paget but at Mark Ransom. ``The rage and humiliation came to his eyes. He stared at me like an animal, face red with anger, pants around his ankles. It was like he felt too much hatred to speak.

``He began walking toward me.

``His pants were still down, and his movements were jerky, almost bestial, as if his failure had swept away whatever made him human. Then he raised his hand again.'' Her voice took on a visceral intensity. ``There was something primal about it—an absence of limits. Before, he wanted to punish me, to help make himself hard. Now he wanted to destroy me.

``Looking at each other, we both knew that.

``I grabbed my purse.'' She stopped again: in her silence, Paget felt the combustible moment when Mark Ransom's pathology triggered Mary's will to survive. ``My fingers were numb. I could barely get the gun out.

``When I turned with it, still shaking, he was maybe six feet from me.

"His eyes widened." She paused at the memory. "For an instant, he just stood there. Then he started toward me again. He seemed so enraged that he could imagine nothing else but reaching me."

Mary's voice became staccato. "I was still on my knees. 'Stop,' I called out. He didn't.

"Now he was four feet away. I still couldn't shoot." Her eyes closed. "And then he called me a worthless cunt.

"All at once, I hated him enough to shoot.

"Maybe I could have stopped him—his pants kept him from moving fast. Maybe I could have shot him in the leg. It didn't matter anymore." Pausing, Mary shook her head. "All that abuse and then, with a single word, he made me the same person *he* was." She stopped again, and spoke her next words slowly and distinctly. "The only thing I cared about was killing Mark Ransom.

"My hands stopped shaking. He was four feet from me when I shot him in the heart."

The new calm in her voice gave Paget a chill. Her eyes opened again, staring past him. "He didn't so much fall as stop. His eyes were blind with shock. It was as if he were no longer in the room, and I was no longer there.

"He slumped a little. His face became sad, almost puzzled. Then he crumpled, sitting on the floor.

"Tears came to his eyes again. The last thing he

did was mumble a single word.'' Mary's voice filled with wonder. '' 'Laura.' He whispered the name 'Laura.'

''The blood drained from his face. I knew he was dead before he had fallen backward.

''Suddenly I was alone.

''I tried to take it in. A moment before, Mark Ransom might have killed me. Now he was a corpse with his pants around his ankles.'' The tone of wonder returned. ''I was sitting next to him, naked in a strange hotel suite, with a tape filled with secrets sitting on the coffee table.''

Paget tried to imagine it. But there were too many layers—shock, horror, shame, and disbelief—for him to understand how Mary could have coped. As if by reflex, he looked at the tape in his hand.

Her gaze followed his. ''I had killed a man,'' she said slowly. ''For a prosecutor, my tape would explain why. But without my tape, there was no explaining his naked genitals, exposed so I could please him. Or the tape of Laura Chase.

''On some level, even through my shock, I understood all that. It was like being under anesthesia but still conscious.

''I never really had a plan. It came to me in pieces—jumbled, out of order. The only thread was that I had come there to conceal the tape, and now I had to conceal why I'd come.''

Her voice was thin, emotionless. It was as if she

had been drugged and now was trying to reconstruct actions she dimly remembered and barely understood.

"It all seemed too hard," she said. "For a moment, I thought of giving up, just telling the truth. Then I thought of Carlo." She paused. "And, of course, myself."

There would be no more tears, Paget thought. She was too spent for emotion or, it seemed, dissembling. There was nothing left to hide.

"Finally," she went on, "I forced myself to look at Ransom. He was lying there, mouth open, sprawled on his back like someone who had died in the middle of dressing himself. And then the first thought came to me: there was no explaining *anything* with Ransom as he was." Her voice turned cold. "I couldn't explain why he was half naked, or why I was naked with him. Let alone why he deserved to die.

"I remember being angry. What he had done to me was not just a violation of my body, but of *me*. And yet I could tell no one.

"He *violated* me, I kept thinking. He deserved to die, I told myself—what he did was worse than rape." Her voice filled with discovery, as if replicating the moment. "Rape," she said simply. "The first cousin of sexual blackmail. The only explanation I could give them.

"But how had he gotten me there? I wondered.

He could be a rapist, but not a blackmailer. And then I remembered: he was writing a book about Laura Chase.

"Of course, I thought—*that* was why you came. For a *story*. To hear him play that tape.

"I suppose it was like writing a play. It explained my presence, Laura's tape, the cassette player. And when I looked down at him, remembering his pathology, I realized that Laura's tape would help explain why he was naked."

Through his grief and anger, Paget felt a kind of fascination. "So you rolled him over," he said softly. "Because a rapist would have been on top of you."

Mary met his eyes and then slowly nodded. "He was heavy," she said softly. "I had to reach beneath his buttocks to flip him over. That was when I left the scratches, and broke my nail."

Paget touched his forehead. "I said it was the paramedics."

"*Sharpe* said I did it to fake a struggle. Not even *I'm* that cold. I hated touching him."

Paget felt his eyes close, heard a sliver of shame in her voice. "Once he was on his side, I gave him a push. He fell sprawling like a rag doll, more limber than in life, his buttocks in the air." She paused, and then added, in a tone of surprise, "As I looked at him, my story became real.

"I felt a surge of crazy energy. Don't *feel,* I told

myself—just *do*. But I didn't know *what* to do.'' Her voice slowed, as if she were reliving the process of thought. ''He hadn't penetrated me, of course. But I didn't know what that meant. So I thought of all the things a rapist might do before penetration, and did them.''

Paget imagined her, standing naked over Ransom's body: half horrified, half rational, trying to think her way to freedom. His eyes opened. ''You scratched yourself,'' he said.

''Yes.'' She paused. ''And put a run in my panty hose. I didn't think about getting fibers beneath my nails.''

Paget found himself trying to think with her, floundering and desperate, knowing little of police work. Quietly, he said, ''There were still the tapes.''

After a time, Mary nodded. ''I knew that. But I couldn't think anymore. Not until I got dressed.''

She looked bemused. ''It was strange,'' she said quietly. ''He'd taken so much from me. But with clothes on, I was more myself. Only Mark Ransom was naked.

''I walked to the coffee table and picked up the tape.

''I stood there, the tape clutched in my hand. Somewhere out of reach was another tape, which could ruin my life. But the tape I was holding would ruin Carlo's, and yours.'' She stopped for a moment, adding quietly, ''Once I got rid of it, I could tell them I was only there because of Laura Chase, and hope they never found the other tape.

"One by one, I clicked off the possibilities.

"I couldn't throw my tape out the window. If I tried to flush it down the toilet, the cassette might get stuck there." She paused. "I'd started checking my watch, trying to fight the panic I was feeling. And then, for some reason, I remembered the mail slot in the hallway."

Mary began speaking faster. "In a kind of frenzy, I began looking for an envelope. I was too rushed to worry about fingerprints. Too panicky to look first where it was logical to look—the desk.

"I got to it last. When I opened the drawer, there were envelopes.

"Then I saw the other tape. I thought it might be *my* other tape, and that Ransom had been listening to it. But I didn't know; Steinhardt's numbering system meant nothing to me. I couldn't listen to it myself—I didn't have time, and I'd leave fingerprints on the cassette player.

"I just grabbed it.

"There was a pen in the drawer, but I couldn't use it—fingerprints again. All at once, I saw how stupid I was being. If I mailed it to myself, and they arrested me, the police would find it before I did." She paused, catching her breath. "And then something more basic came to me. I had no stamps.

"I started shaking.

"I couldn't stop myself. I took a pen from my purse and crossed out 'Hotel Flood' on the envelope. I stood there trembling while I tried to imagine the fate of an envelope with no postage and no return address, wending its way through the postal system."

Mary stopped, shaking her head. "I had no idea. The only image I could fix on was some bureaucrat sorting mail at the post office, uncaring and uncurious, throwing out the tapes because no one had sent them and no one could receive them." Mary gave a small, mirthless smile. "So I decided to put Carlo's fate in the hands of the government. The one thing that never occurred to me was that *his* fate was Lindsay Caldwell's."

Silent, Paget stared at the tape he held. She saw that and looked away.

"I put them in the mail slot," she said softly. "Just before that pompous investment banker got off the elevator.

"When I went inside the room and closed the door behind me, I knew I was out of time.

"I didn't really have a story. Only fragments." She paused again. "When I called 911, all I had were my own resources. As you've been so fond of pointing out, that was hardly enough."

For a moment, she was silent. Then she looked up at him again. "Of course," she said quietly, "I also had you."

His eyes met hers. "Why?" he asked. "Because you could manipulate me?"

"You underestimate yourself, Chris. You're the smartest lawyer I know. I also counted on your feeling for Carlo." Paget saw her hesitate, the shame in her eyes becoming a question. "I believed you'd protect the tapes better than anyone. And that, God forbid, if you ever heard them, you'd make sure that Carlo never did."

For a long time, Paget looked at her without speaking. "Fifteen years ago," he finally said, "I wasn't sure if Carlo was mine. But after he came to live with me, I stopped wondering. I didn't want to anymore." His voice grew softer. "My life may have disappointed me, partly on account of you. But at least I had a son."

The quiet words seemed to devastate her. Her shoulders slumped, and she looked away. "Withdraw as my lawyer, Chris. You don't have to go to court tomorrow."

"Do you think that will fix things, Mary? Knowing what I know? Holding this tape in my hand?" He paused, voice lower. "And it would be like telling the world you're guilty."

She gave a tired shrug. "I wonder if that's any worse than living with *this* has been. And I *am* guilty, I suppose. Because I'll never know whether I needed to kill him."

"Nor do I. If that matters."

She straightened, as if gathering strength. "I lied to you. You owe me nothing. I ask only that you never tell Carlo what you know." She looked into his face, a quiet plea in her voice. "I'll plead guilty, if you like. But destroy this tape, Chris. Please."

Paget watched her, not answering. Then he stood. "You've no right to ask for anything, Mary. But you're certainly free to hope."

He turned abruptly, and left.

FOUR

"HOW'S IT GOING, Dad?"

Carlo stood in the entrance to the library. He was trying to sound casual, Paget realized, but he had the abstracted gaze of someone who had spent the afternoon in thought, and his voice was too quiet. Paget did not want to look at him.

"I'm pretty tired." Paget stared at his drink. "I have a lot to think about."

His voice was not welcoming, nor did he wish it to be. He did not know what he would do about anything: reassuring Carlo was beyond him, and he did not have the resources to lie. All that he wanted from anyone was that they want nothing from him.

But Carlo could not know this. He walked inside, flicking on the illuminated chandelier. "This room is pretty weird without the lights."

Paget sipped his drink. "I'm capable of finding the switch."

Carlo paused, as if deciphering his mood. Quietly, he said, "You think she's guilty, don't you?"

Paget did not turn. "If you really care to know, Carlo, I'm sick of thinking about her at all."

"Jesus." Carlo's voice rose with sudden strain: it still had the lightness of youth, but there was something new in it. "Why do you hate her so much? What did she ever do to you?"

The words had an angry timbre that Paget had never heard from Carlo and yet touched a chord of memory: it was like that of Jack Woods on the last night they had faced each other, with Mary Carelli—their lover—standing between them. The thought made Paget turn to Carlo.

The boy he saw now startled him. His face was older; it had the look of a man whom Paget had despised. The blue eyes were not Paget's at all.

How, Paget wondered, could he have failed to see it?

"It's as she's always said," Paget replied. "I'm an insensitive bastard."

Carlo stared at him, as if at a stranger. "You think she's guilty," he repeated.

Guilty of a thousand things, Paget thought. Guilty of this moment, as he faced the son who was no longer his and yet who felt the anger of a son. "You were the one who wanted to be there," Paget said. "What do you want from me now? To tell you that she's wonderful?"

Carlo reddened. "What are you angry at *me* for? *I* didn't ask for any of this. Or for either one of you."

Paget caught himself, expelled a long breath. "I know you didn't," he said tonelessly.

Carlo watched him. "You've been surprised in court before. You can't just fall apart on her."

"Who said I'm falling apart? I'm just sick of people leaning on me."

Carlo stiffened. "Like me?"

"Like your mother. It seems I've spent my life cleaning up her messes." Paget lowered his voice again. "It's complicated, and much too personal. You wouldn't understand."

"Try me."

Paget shook his head. "No," he said softly. "Thank you."

"You mean you'd rather take it out on me." Carlo's voice was raw. "Do you think you're alone? This hasn't been any day at the beach for *me,* you know. *She's* my mother, and I have to live with *you.*"

"I'm sorry I've been such a burden." Paget answered politely. "Would you rather not live here?"

Carlo shoved his hands in his pockets. "Would you like me to go?"

The boy's words quivered with pain and anger. "I didn't want to have this conversation," Paget said. "I *don't* want to have this conversation."

Carlo turned from him. "All I wanted was to talk to you. It didn't have to be about *her.*"

The stark request took Paget by surprise. For a

moment, he saw not Jack Woods but a lonely seven-year-old boy.

"I'm sorry," Paget told him. "This case has taken a lot out of me. Too much, it seems."

Carlo looked down at him with Jack Woods's eyes. "Mark Ransom was a piece of shit."

Paget shook his head. "This isn't about Mark Ransom."

"Then what *is* it with you and her?"

"History."

"Fifteen years is too long to hold a grudge." Carlo paused. "She doesn't hate *you.*"

"You don't know anything about us, Carlo. It was a mistake for me to do this. Perhaps it's best if Mary gets another lawyer."

Carlo stared at him. *"Now?"*

"Yes."

"But you can't do that. Not on the last day."

Paget faced him again. "She and I have already discussed it. She left it up to me."

Carlo paused, trying to absorb the implications. "What is it that I don't know?"

There was no use in lying. "Quite a lot."

Carlo sat down. Softly, he asked, "Did she admit killing him?"

The conversation was so pointless, Paget thought: the central issue between Paget and Carlo's mother was not Mark Ransom's murder, and had never been.

"She *did* kill him," Paget answered. "The question was whether she killed him in self-defense."

" 'Was,' " Carlo quoted. "So now you don't think she's innocent."

The anxious questions annoyed Paget—he no longer cared whether Mark Ransom had deserved to die. But the only way to explain that to Carlo was to tell him the truth: Your mother lied to the Senate. She lied to this court. I covered for her fifteen years ago, and tomorrow, if I'm still her lawyer, I'll have to cover for her again. And by the way, you're not my son. I just found out she lied about that too.

"I don't think she planned to kill him," Paget said. "But I question my effectiveness. So does she."

"Because of that psychiatrist?"

"No. Because of *us.*"

" 'Because of *us,*' " Carlo repeated. "What has *she* ever asked you for? You sit here telling me what a burden she is, and she's never even been around. And now that she is, and really needs you for once, you treat her like dirt."

Paget stood. "I *will* not talk about this, damn it."

"We're going to." Carlo rose to face him, voice trembling. "*You* drove her away, didn't you? She was never welcome here—"

"*Stop this,* Carlo. Right now."

Carlo shook his head. "*I* never had a mother because *you* never wanted me to have one. You wanted me to yourself. And now that I may lose her again, you won't lift a finger.'' Carlo paused, catching his breath, and then spoke more slowly. ''I always looked up to you. But now I see how selfish you are. You say you're sick of my mother? Well, I'm sick of *you.*''

Paget clenched his fists, rigid with hurt and anger. ''You have no right to be sick of me, Carlo. You don't know how little right you have.''

Carlo's face was a mask of pain. ''Don't talk down to me. I don't respect you enough to listen.''

In one angry motion, Paget picked up his drink glass. Carlo's white face was three feet from him. Paget suddenly turned and flung the glass at the palm tree outside.

As the window shattered, Carlo flinched but did not move.

''Then you won't have to listen,'' Paget said softly, and left the house.

Teresa Peralta's headlights cut the darkness.

The beach was deserted. A full moon lent the ocean a touch of light, silver on obsidian, shimmering at low tide. But the sand itself was dull black, as if stained by an oil slick. At its edge, perhaps a hundred yards away, Terri saw the lone figure of a man, staring out at the water.

There were no other cars. She parked where the cement ended, got out. The man turned at the sound of her car door slamming.

Terri moved toward him, sand giving way beneath her feet. The night was still warm; she hardly felt the breeze in her face. The rolling tide was a deep susurrus of sound.

The man stood waiting, as if uncertain of who she was. His hands were shoved in his pockets; backlit by the moon, he looked slender and solitary. As she came nearer, she saw that he had not changed from court; his shirtsleeves were rolled up, and his tie and collar loosened. He looked much too young to have lived the life he had lived and to bear what it had brought him now. All that she wanted to do was hold him.

She stopped two feet away, looking up into his face.

"It's all a mess," Christopher Paget said.

Terri nodded. After hours of aimless driving, he had called her on his car phone, ostensibly to explain why he had not called her before; he had told her just enough for her to sense that beneath his emotionless words, Paget felt lost.

"The beach is where *I* come," she told him, "when it gets to be too much. But never at night."

Paget gazed at her. "Was there trouble with Richie?" he asked.

Terri hesitated. It was she, not Paget, who had suggested that they meet; it was not the night to explain her relationship to Richie, and there might never be such a night. Best to stick to the simple truth—that Richie had not objected much—and omit the reason: that Richie had commenced a relentless campaign to keep her, appealing to her sense of family while reading one self-help book after another, swearing that their marriage could be healed if only Terri tried as hard as he was trying. It made her weary, and guilty about her dead emotions. She felt as though by asserting herself she had changed him, so that now he—and Elena—deserved the second chance Terri was not sure she wanted to give. Letting her leave without complaint was part of the new Richie: if Christopher Paget would ever be one of Richie's weapons again, Terri sensed, it would be after she was bound to the marriage once more, perhaps by the second child Richie had begun to press for.

"Richie was fine about it," she told Paget. "He knows we still have work to do." She paused, looking into his face. "Do we?"

He gave a weary shrug. "I don't know."

"What happened, Chris?"

Paget did not answer. He turned from her, hands still in his pockets, and began walking along the edge of the water. Terri understood that she was to walk with him; they moved in silence, tide lapping near their feet, the Golden Gate Bridge to their back, scattered car lights moving slowly across it. To their left was a rocky hillside; above them, the sprawling stucco houses of Seacliff overlooked the water, much as Terri imagined an Italian hill town. Paget did not seem to notice; he was silent for a long time, and when he began to speak, he gazed at the sand in front of him.

He talked for perhaps an hour.

He told her everything. His voice was uninflected, yet unsparing of himself or anyone else. When he had finished, they had turned back toward the Golden Gate, and Terri was exhausted.

"What will you do?" she asked.

"I don't know." He paused. "It's like something's broken. I don't even know where to start."

Terri watched him for a moment. "It's so unfair, Chris. I feel that for you."

"Carlo?"

"Everything."

Paget gave a tired shrug. "Carlo doesn't know," he said. "If I'm looking for perfect justice, I suppose I'll have to look somewhere else. Mary seems to have that particular market cornered."

Terri moved closer. "She *is* his mother, Chris. When a parent isn't around, kids invent a person who makes them feel better about that. I think that's what Carlo must have done with Mary."

Paget's repeated shrug seemed the only way he had to slough off feeling. "That's how God made it big, I guess—by not being seen. So why not Mary?"

He was trying to sound fatalistic, Terri knew, but

his voice had a weary undertone of bitterness. She waited him out.

"It's eight years of questions," he said finally. "We never really talked about his mother, or *why* he was living with me. Tonight was like a dam bursting." He paused, then, his voice lower, as if he was talking to himself: "Christ, what a fool I was."

Terri moved closer to him. "But there's nothing you can do about the past." Her own voice grew quieter. "Just as I wish I'd never found the tapes but know there's nothing I can do now. Just as there's nothing *you* can do to put off tomorrow."

Paget looked away. "God, I wish there were."

"But there isn't." She paused again. "You're going to have to deal with Carlo, and with Mary. But first you're going to have to keep on living with yourself. And whatever you do tomorrow will be part of that."

He turned away from her, toward the ocean. It was a gesture not of dismissal but of thought. Terri watched him stand there, framed by moonlight and black water. When she felt it was time, she moved beside him.

"You've been a lawyer for almost twenty years," she said. "Lawyers protect their clients."

Paget did not turn. "I wasn't her lawyer," he replied, "when I lied to the Senate."

"But you are now, Chris. Mary may not have told

Caroline the truth, but it's at least as close to the truth as Marnie's version.'' She paused. ''Whatever Mary did to Ransom, it wasn't murder. She was battered, degraded, and deeply frightened—close to breaking, it seems. What she did was somewhere between manslaughter and self-defense, and I doubt even Mary can know which one.'' Her voice gained intensity. ''Think of her as just a client, if you can. How much does a woman have to take before killing a man is self-defense? Does she have to know to a moral certainty that he would *kill* her? For *me,* what he had already done, and what he was threatening to do, is more than enough.''

''She *lied,* Terri. As always.''

Terri waited. ''Do you mean that she lied to Caroline,'' she asked, ''or lied to you? Because if her sin for these purposes is that she lied to protect herself in court, you'd be the first to say that clients do that all the time. It's only *your* sin if you were part of it.''

''You know I wasn't.''

Terri nodded. ''Then there's no problem of ethics here. You can argue the evidence. Or Sharpe's lack of evidence.''

''And cover for Mary again.''

''You can avoid that, Chris, by pulling out. You've got the right. But if you do, she won't just lose in *this* hearing. People will believe you're withdrawing because she's guilty of murder.'' Terri paused again, then finishied quietly: ''And as much as I dislike her, I don't think she is.''

''It's a little hard for me to care.''

Terri hesitated. ''She *did* try to protect you, in her way. At least with Ransom.'' She gazed at him intently. ''I'd guess that most of the people you've defended are far more guilty than Mary. If you let this happen to her, that will become part of what you take from this. Do you want that?''

Silent, Paget bent to pick up a piece of driftwood. For a moment, he turned it in his hand. Then, as if gauging its capacity for flight, he slowly turned and flung it out to sea.

''It's not Mary I'm worried about,'' Terri told him softly. ''It's you.''

He turned to look at her. In the semidark, she could not read his face.

''It's Wednesday night,'' she said. ''On Friday morning, you're going to wake up and start living with what you've learned. But you'll also have to live with what you've done. How would you rather face Mary and Carlo?''

''I don't know.'' His voice was equally quiet. ''Really, I don't.''

She moved closer to him, fingertips touching his shirt. ''You may not be there for Carlo, or Carlo for you. How will you feel then, if you've abandoned

Mary? And if you and Carlo still want to be together, dropping Mary will have made that harder. Impossible, perhaps.''

``Ah, Terri . . .''

His voice, soft and despairing, trailed off to nothing. In the moonlight, his face seemed unspeakably sad.

``Carlo loves you,'' she said. ``And he expects things from you. For better or worse, *you're* the person he's *learned* to expect things from.'' She paused, trying to find a way to reach him. ``It may not be fair, Chris, but Carlo told you the truth as he understands it. The only thing worse than abandoning his mother is what you'd have to tell him to justify yourself.''

Paget did not answer. Terri reached up, touching his face. ``Finish this, Chris.'' Her voice was soft but clear. ``Be yourself for one more day. Then you can choose who else to be.''

FIVE

THE NEXT MORNING, Paget and Carlo rode in silence to the Hall of Justice.

Paget had not slept. The sun cut into his eyes; he had turned off the radio to banish the cheery morning voices. Carlo—it hurt Paget not to think of him as his son—preserved a taut and edgy quiet. Paget could not tell whether Carlo was upset about their rupture and his own part in it; afraid that speaking would increase Paget's withdrawal; or restrained by some reflex of manners. Carlo did not ask what Paget would do.

Paget could not have answered him. The ebb and flow of feeling had become an undertow; he was not sure enough of himself to reassure anyone else. He had never felt this lost.

As they approached the Hall of Justice, he glanced at the profile of the boy who sat next to him. Carlo's thin face had become handsome with age, but his eyes were bleak as they swept the warehouses and parking lots and treeless sidewalks, as if looking for something he could never find. His face seemed so familiar, Paget thought, and yet so strange.

It was like the death of a parent. When his mother had died, and then his father, Paget had felt a shift in the world that was beyond his ability to change or comprehend. They had given him little but money, one part of Paget knew, but nonetheless they were the touchstones of his life—the first people he had tried to love and, because he had tried to love them all their lives, the people who made him think most deeply about the nature of love, the limits of understanding, the curse of mortality.

Now there was Carlo. He had believed in Carlo and himself much more than he had ever believed in his parents, believed from the perspective of adulthood, as someone who had chosen to be a father, drawing on the lessons he had learned from being a son. He and Carlo had redeemed the shortfall of his family in a way that was mysterious to him: his fathering of Carlo was like a gift of understanding he had sent his parents, when it was far too late to do it any other way. But then he had believed that his parents, and Carlo, were kin.

It was too much to assimilate now, if he ever could, that the end of Paget's family had been Paget himself. Or that his attempts to redeem the past and his highest hopes for the future—his vanity, perhaps—had been focused on the son of Jack Woods and Mary Carelli.

And yet here Carlo was, still sitting next to Paget, as he had for the past eight years.

Carlo watched the street as if it were a war zone. Mary was arriving by herself; as they parked and got out, Paget sensed that the boy was looking for his mother. Whether they would drive her was the one question that Carlo had asked; when Paget said no, he had lapsed into silence again.

On the steps, Paget and Carlo edged through the media gauntlet. The reporters pressed too close; their open mouths and hectoring questions reminded Paget of a drunk in a bar, demanding his attention, oblivious to the fact that he wished to be alone. As with yesterday, their questions centered on Dr. Bass or on what Paget would next argue. As with yesterday, Paget did not answer. He had ceased to care about them.

The only thing he noticed, at the edge of his vision, was Carlo.

Silent, the boy glanced at him as they pushed through the crowd. This time, Carlo said nothing to the press in defense of his mother; Paget had become certain that Carlo feared pushing him over the edge. The thought unsettled him: Paget's last eight years had been devoted to helping Carlo to trust and to feel safe. To be a source of worry to Carlo violated some deep instinct; the residue was guilt, and then anger at Mary.

Why was he here?

The weeks since Ransom died had changed him. Waiting for the elevator reminded him of taking it with Mary on the night the police had brought her in, their encounter with the media just moments away. Now, alone with Carlo, he felt like a different man: as they walked down the corridor, the memory of his first appearance here, on the day he had demanded this hearing, was like a dream. Entering the courtroom, he wished that he had never entered it before.

Yet they were all here. Reporters, their faces now familiar. Terri sitting calmly, with her notepad in front of her, as if their conversation on the beach had never happened. If Terri wondered what Paget would do, she gave no sign. Last night, she had tried to help him by speaking to his heart, and now she would try to help by acting like a lawyer.

Next to her was Mary.

They had not spoken since he left her hotel room. Now she turned to watch him coming toward her. Her expression, a surface calm covering deep watchfulness, triggered yet another image: it was how she had looked when Paget entered the Senate hearing room and she had not known what he would say or do. Paget first saw the difference—a certain fatalism—when he drew within a few feet of her. She gave an almost imperceptible shrug, an indication that she was resigned to whatever happened, and did not much care.

He sat next to her without speaking. She turned away, as if she knew to leave him alone. But he felt something deeper from her: buried shame, and quiet apology.

In a moment, Caroline Masters would enter, and nothing else would matter.

Sharpe sat poised at the prosecution table. She had the tensile alertness of a lawyer ready to argue her biggest case; it was odd, Paget thought, how the past twenty-four hours had opened a gulf between them. He no longer felt like a lawyer, or even like himself.

Looking past her, Paget saw McKinley Brooks.

Unobtrusive, the district attorney sat on a bench behind Sharpe. Save for the day of Linton's testimony, Paget had not seen him since Mary had turned down the offer of a plea bargain and Brooks had filed murder charges. The reason Brooks was here now, Paget knew, was politics: he would get a feeling for the courtroom and for Judge Masters, to add to the soundings he no doubt had taken from his precinct leaders and in the neighborhoods. He sat with his hands folded on his stomach, inscrutable as Buddha; catching Paget's gaze, he gave a small smile, which did not reach his eyes. The stakes were too high, Paget thought, for Brooks to pretend otherwise.

"All rise," the courtroom deputy called out, and Judge Caroline Masters ascended the bench.

She, too, looked different. At the beginning of the trial, Masters would commence the day with an alert, expectant look that bespoke some inner pleasure; she was a woman at the height of her powers, and they were finally being stretched a little closer to capacity. But now there was something muted about her: her face was somber, her expression inward. Paget could no more read her thoughts than he could those of McKinley Brooks.

He had expected Judge Masters to give some preface, tracing her expectation for the argument with incisiveness and a certain dry wit. But Masters did not do so. Nodding to Sharpe and then Paget, she said simply, "This is a great responsibility. Please do your best to help me."

It was far better than a speech. When Sharpe approached the podium, her manner was respectful, and her opening words were soft.

"For the district attorney, as well, this case is a responsibility which has occasioned great thought. We have tried to address the issues responsibly and thoughtfully, and will try to do so now."

It was effective, Paget saw; she had caught the judge's mood and would not oversell her case. Caroline Masters, he realized, was not the only person who had grown.

"Mary Carelli," she said in the same quiet voice, "killed Mark Ransom. She admitted that long ago. And unless she can show self-defense, that killing is a murder."

It was strange, Paget realized: that was what he had said to Carlo at the beginning of their terrible—perhaps fatal—argument. Turning to Carlo, Paget saw pain etched in his face, as if he were hearing a chorus of voices arrayed against his mother.

"As the court knows," Sharpe went on, "proof of motive is *not* an element of murder. But as this court also knows, Ms. Carelli had a compelling motive." Here Sharpe paused. "A tape," she said succinctly, "which could ruin her life."

Alone among all who were there, Paget could hear the tape that no one but Terri had heard.

"All that stands between Ms. Carelli and probable cause," Sharpe said, "is whether she has proven self-defense."

The silence was complete. Sharpe had them now; she knew better than to raise her voice. "Ms. Carelli has *claimed* self-defense. But her attempt to prove that has proven only that she is unworthy of belief.

"The formal caption of this case is 'People versus Carelli.' In reality, it has been 'Ms. Carelli versus the evidence.' For the only thing that supports Ms. Carelli's *story* is Ms. Carelli's *word*.

"The court must consider, then, what Ms. Carelli has proven her word to be worth."

Better than Marnie Sharpe, Paget thought, *he* knew the answer. But in his own reaction, subjective as it was, Paget felt the shrewdness of Sharpe's argument. Short of proving Mary a murderer, Sharpe could prove her a liar. People—including judges—do not care for liars.

"Mary Carelli asks this court to believe her, just as she asked the district attorney to believe her before we brought this case. We therefore ask the court to learn from us, just as we learned from Ms. Carelli." Sharpe paused. "Learned, and kept learning, until we had no choice but to charge her with murder."

Caroline Masters leaned forward, frowning as she followed Sharpe's argument. She did not look at Mary Carelli, nor Mary at her.

"Part of what we learned," Sharpe said, "is that Mary Carelli cannot be believed.

"Ms. Carelli told *this court* that she visited Mark Ransom's suite because he had a tape—a tape so damaging that Ms. Carelli's lawyer insisted that it be suppressed. And yet, before we found that tape in Mark Ransom's home, Ms. Carelli had never mentioned it to us. Instead she invented an elaborate story about visiting Mark Ransom solely to hear a tape of Laura Chase." Sharpe lowered her voice. "Invented a story, coolly and plausibly, within an hour of shooting Mark Ransom dead."

There was a low murmur in the courtroom. Sharpe had given her argument a new and compelling thrust; rather than focus on the evidence, she would erode all sympathy for Mary, as a woman or as a victim.

And perhaps, in the process, root out any sympathy Sharpe herself might feel.

"But the discovery of the tape," Sharpe went on, "answered all the mysteries of Ms. Carelli's story.

"We discovered that Mary Carelli had bought a gun after Mark Ransom first called her. Because, she said, she had received threatening phone calls.

"We thought it strange that these calls had driven her to that point of fear and yet that she had never revealed them to anyone. But when we found the tape, we also found the answer: Mary Carelli bought the gun to kill Mark Ransom. Because he had the tape."

Sharpe paused again; her pauses, as well as her voice, had fallen into a rhythm. Paget felt it sweeping away Mary's fragile story.

"After she brought that gun to Mark Ransom's suite, and shot Mark Ransom to death, Mary Carelli told us that he had tried to rape her.

"We thought it strange that there were no secretions on his penis."

There were no secretions, Paget suddenly realized, because—afraid for her life—Mary Carelli had sucked Mark Ransom's penis until he had gone soft.

The judge's frown had deepened. As if encouraged, Sharpe's tone became mordant.

"We thought it strange," she said with lethal clarity, ''that Ms. Carelli had scratches on her neck and thigh and yet that *Ms. Carelli,* and Ms. Carelli alone, had skin beneath her fingernails.''

''We thought it strange that the scratches on *Mr. Ransom's* body seemed to have been made when he was dead.

''We thought it strange that Ms. Carelli claimed to have shot Mark Ransom from a mere three inches and yet left no gunshot residue.''

Sharpe paused again. ''Perhaps, in fairness, I should amend my statement. Those of us without training as pathologists thought these things strange. But Dr. Elizabeth Shelton merely found it grisly. For she concluded, as *all* of us concluded in the end, that the medical evaluation best supports the thesis that Ms. Carelli had murdered Mr. Ransom, fabricated the evidence, and accused a dead man of rape.''

Sharpe raised her head, looking only at Masters. ''A dead man,'' she repeated softly, ''who, when he was alive, was impotent.''

The courtroom was still. Once more, Christopher Paget felt the truth that others did not know. Unwittingly and with reason, Marnie Sharpe had strung Mary's lies into a larger lie of her own invention: that Mary Carelli had gone to Ransom's suite intending to kill him. Mary had gone, Paget knew now, not to commit murder but to do as Ransom wished, to protect the son she had first sought to protect by lying to Paget himself. But Sharpe continued relentlessly, telling the truth as she understood it.

"The man who Mary Carelli swore had tried to rape her was incapable of raping anyone—"

"How do you explain Ms. Carelli's bruise, Ms. Sharpe?"

It was Caroline Masters; she had interrupted as if speaking Paget's thoughts.

"We don't know *how* she got it," Sharpe replied calmly. "What we *do* know to a moral certainty is that Ms. Carelli did *not* get it in the way she described to this court. And because we have been able to expose her other lies, Ms. Carelli's entire story rests on a bruise we cannot explain."

Masters raised her eyebrows. "That is *not* a mere anomaly, Ms. Sharpe. From the photographs, it appeared that Ms. Carelli had been beaten."

Beaten, Paget thought, in Mark Ransom's final frenzy. Because he failed to turn hard.

"What we *think,*" Sharpe replied, "is that the truth is hidden in some part of the story Ms. Carelli cannot tell us, for fear of admitting guilt. My own theory is that Mr. Ransom struck her when she pulled out the gun. But the heart of the matter is this: Ms. Carelli cannot use one unexplained fact to avoid trial on a charge of murder."

Sharpe paused for a moment, peering at Judge Masters to see if she was satisfied. Masters looked back at her in silence; when Sharpe resumed again, the awkward interlude had leeched some certitude from her tone.

"With so little to say for *herself,*" Sharpe told Masters, "Ms. Carelli has tried to portray Mark Ransom as a man too despicable to merit justice, or even our concern.

" 'Why bother with the evidence of murder,' her tacit message goes, 'when the *man* I murdered was such a swine.'

"Ms. Carelli *says* Mark Ransom tried to blackmail her into having sex. But she said that only *after* we found the tape—after Ms. Carelli was committed to a defense built on rape.

"How can we believe Mary Carelli about *anything?*"

Mary's face did not change. But her eyes, fixed on the table in front of her, bespoke her hopelessness and despair. Paget imagined her memories—undressing for Ransom, posing for him naked on the couch—as she heard Marnie Sharpe call her a liar.

"So they offer Marcy Linton," Sharpe went on, "to try to persuade us of what Mary Carelli cannot.

"Without Marcy Linton, Mary Carelli would have no defense at all."

But there could have been Melissa Rappaport, Paget thought, and Lindsay Caldwell. He wondered if Caroline Masters could dismiss them from her thoughts as easily as she had swept them from the case.

Compassion had crept into Sharpe's voice. "None of us who saw her," she said, "will forget Marcy Linton. Nor is there any cause to forgive Mark Ransom for what he did to this young woman. But we are not here to prosecute a dead man for the rape of Marcy Linton."

Sharpe paused again. "Indeed," she went on quietly, "it seems that Mark Ransom had already prosecuted himself. For *that,* Dr. Bass explained to us, is why this man was impotent.

"Impotent," she repeated. "Impotent from the moment he raped Marcy Linton to the day that Ms. Carelli shot him."

Her voice rose for the first time. "That," she said with new assurance, "is the *only* truth Mary Carelli ever told us—that she shot him. And the truth of that shooting is that it was murder."

But the truth of the shooting, Paget knew, lay in the moment that Mark Ransom had pressed Mary Carelli against the wall with his penis in her mouth and watched himself turn soft; the moment when Mary Carelli became the focus of his rage. Assuming, of course, that Mary had finally told the truth.

"Everything else," Sharpe went on, "is false. The story Mary Carelli spun to excuse that shooting is a web of lies. And now, at last, it has hopelessly entangled her.

"That is just. Mr. Paget may use words like 'miscarriage of justice.' But the only result worthy of those words would be to free Mary Carelli on the basis of her testimony.''

There was a passion in Sharpe's voice now. She grasped the podium, as if to rein in her emotions. ''This is *not* a feminist cause, Your Honor, and Mary Carelli's lies were not an accident,'' she said. ''Mary Carelli told these lies because she is a murderer. We ask the court to enter a finding of probable cause.

''Thank you, Your Honor.''

As she turned from the podium, Paget felt the complex skein of his own emotions—fatigue, deep anger at Mary, admiration of Sharpe's effort, disquiet at the hidden injustice of what she had said. And then he saw McKinley Brooks nod toward Sharpe, as one lawyer to another who had done all she could, and done it well.

When Caroline Masters spoke, Paget realized that moments had passed while he sat unmoving in his chair. He felt Mary turn to him in mute appeal, Terri's hand on his arm.

Masters's tone was ironic, but there was puzzlement beneath it. ''Mr. Paget,'' she said, ''perhaps you would care to say a few words on Ms. Carelli's behalf.''

Paget looked up at her. There were no notes in front of him; he had prepared none.

''Perhaps a few,'' he said.

* * *

Walking to the podium, Paget faced Judge Masters.

It was a strange moment: Caroline Masters must have sensed that she had not yet heard the truth, but Paget alone knew what it was. As if she read his thoughts, the judge said coolly, "What really happened here, Mr. Paget?"

He paused for only a moment. "Mark Ransom abused Mary Carelli," he answered.

The judge leaned forward, as if to scrutinize him. "I admit that Ms. Sharpe can't cover all the bases. It even strikes me that something may have happened in that hotel suite *other* than premeditated murder. But really, Counselor, Ms. Carelli's account is nearly as flawed as Ms. Sharpe suggests. Diaphanous, one might even say."

All at once, Paget felt the hearing move to a new level of reality: the judge was less offended by lies than interested in a truth she had yet to hear. Tell me, she seemed to be saying, why finding for Mary Carelli would be right.

It was just as well, Paget thought, that he had nothing prepared. But it took him a moment to find somewhere to start: he would not lie to Caroline Masters, or ask her to believe the lies that Mary had told in court.

"Mark Ransom beat Mary Carelli," he began. "We know that.

"Mark Ransom beat and raped Marcy Linton. We know that."

Paget paused, looking from Sharpe to Masters. "No one here doubts Ms. Linton. But the prosecution has ignored the striking parallels between Mark Ransom's treatment of Marcy Linton and of Mary Carelli.

"First, he used whatever leverage he had to get them alone—in Ms. Linton's case, the reading of a manuscript; in Ms. Carelli's, the playing of a tape.

"Second, he used alcohol to dull their reactions.

"Third, he used psychological abuse to make them vulnerable."

Paget's gaze fixed on Caroline Masters. "And fourth," he finished quietly, "he used physical abuse. Because that's what excited him."

His voice rose. "*Every one* of these elements had happened to Ms. Linton. *Every one* of them was part of what Ms. Carelli told Inspector Monk. And yet, until this hearing, Mary Carelli had never heard of Marcy Linton."

Caroline Masters folded her hands, gazing fixedly from the bench. Paget had Masters's attention now, he sensed, and that of everyone in the courtroom. Feeling the dense silence behind him, he searched for where to take this: away from Mary, he decided, to the man she killed.

"Marcy Linton," he said quietly, "had told no one. It's a tragedy repeated across this country, countless times a year. We can never know how many women let sexual abuse go unpunished, fearing the shame we visit on them. So that we never know who these men are.

"But now, because Mary Carelli shot Mark Ransom, Marcy Linton came forward. And so at last we know just who and what Mark Ransom was.

"In Mark Ransom's twisted world, there was no room for any woman to be a person, rather than a projection of his fantasies.

"For Mark Ransom, women had no thoughts, no feelings, no *life* apart from his need for them." Quiet scorn entered Paget's voice. "And once one understands that, how fitting it is that his ideal woman had been dead for twenty years.

"For Laura Chase there can be no questioning, no hope, no awareness of all that women have perceived. Nothing, in short, to mar Mark Ransom's image of compliance."

Paget's eyes locked on Caroline Masters. "Mark Ransom died because, in the end, he could not turn Mary Carelli into Laura Chase." Paget paused once more, letting the thought sink in. "And *that* is the deeper truth that George Bass left with us."

Paget nodded to Marnie Sharpe. "Ms. Sharpe called Dr. Bass to testify to impotence. But what he stayed to give us, based on intimate knowledge, was an indelible portrait of the man Mary Carelli encountered in that suite.

"The man," Paget repeated, "whom Marcy Linton has described to us.

"A rapist.

"A man obsessed by Laura Chase.

"A man who derived pleasure from beating women.

"A man who blamed Marcy Linton for his supposed impotence.

"A man determined to reassert himself sexually.

"A man who, armed with the Laura Chase tapes, was searching for a victim in the hope that abuse and fetishes would make him the 'man' he used to be.

"A man who, by the time he fixed on Mary Carelli, had become a sexual psychopath." Paget paused, adding quietly, "A tinderbox, waiting to explode."

Behind the bench, Caroline Masters shifted. It was time, Paget knew, to return to Mary Carelli. "But *that* man," he added quietly, "met the wrong woman. Or, one might say, the right one.

"The only question is whether Mary Carelli acted in self-defense.

"Ms. Sharpe says that Ms. Carelli is unworthy of belief. We can debate the niceties of circumstantial evidence. But all that we can determine, where none of us but Ms. Carelli knows the truth, is all the different theories that trial lawyers can evolve.

"So let us look at the *essence* of what Ms. Carelli says.

"Ms. Carelli says that Mark Ransom beat her. She has the bruises to prove that.

"Ms. Carelli says that Mark Ransom abused her sexually. *We* have Marcy Linton, and Dr. Bass, to say that is the truth.

"That much we *know*.

"Ms. Carelli says that, at some terrible moment of violence and abuse, she shot Mark Ransom out of fear for herself." Paget stood straighter. "Ms. Sharpe would say that we have only Ms. Carelli's word for that. But who among us is the better judge?

"Can we now stand here in this room and pass judgment on *her* judgment at the moment that she killed him? We cannot.

"Mary Carelli faced that moment alone.

"Now Mary Carelli has come before you to claim self-defense. Ms. Sharpe says that Ms. Carelli cannot be believed. But the most credible thing Ms. Carelli says—the central truth of this case—is that Mark Ransom was an abuser of women.

"Because Mary Carelli met him, he changed her life forever. But because *he* met Mary Carelli, hers is the last life Mark Ransom will ever change."

Paget stopped to look at Caroline Masters. "I cannot consider that a tragedy. Except, perhaps, for Mary Carelli.

"Nor, Your Honor, should this court find it to be a crime."

Caroline Masters gave him a querying, troubled

look. ''The law,'' she said, ''defines what is or is not a crime. And this *is* a court of law, not an outlet for our passions or beliefs. Yours, mine, or anyone's.''

Paget nodded. ''True, Your Honor. But at its best, this is also a court of justice.'' He hesitated; the law was against him, and there was no point in evading that. ''When this proceeding began, you said that probable cause was *not* a daunting standard. I acknowledge that. And therefore I must acknowledge that as a matter of law, this court can find against Mary Carelli and there is nothing *I* could do.''

Paget raised his head. ''But that would *not* be justice.

''It would not be just to condemn Mary Carelli to a further trial. Because what we have proven here is that this is *not* a case where the prosecutor can prove guilt beyond a reasonable doubt. They do not have the evidence.

''Instead they rely on the law of probable cause to induce the court to let them go to trial. And there, amidst the passions of a jury trial, they hope to win a conviction they cannot support.''

Caroline Masters remained impassive; how was he to reach her as a person, Paget wondered, without offending her as a judge? ''This court is bound to apply the law,'' he said. ''But this court is *not* required to measure out the law like some apothecary.

For the law is meant to be not a dry prescription but an expression of what is just and moral.

"On *this* evidence, the just result—the moral result—is to let Mary Carelli go free. For in the end, there is too much to say that the Mark Ransom she describes is the man that she encountered, and nothing to say that he was not." Paget paused for the last time, speaking slowly and clearly. "As terrible as it was, what Mark Ransom brought upon himself in that hotel suite was justice. This court cannot improve on it."

Without more, Paget sat down.

Of the next few moments he had only impressions: Caroline Masters's gavel cracking; a softening in Carlo's face; Mary's murmured thanks; Masters leaving the bench; the crowd releasing its tension in a cacophony of sound.

None of it seemed real; he knew only that he believed what he had said. For now, that would have to be enough.

It was Terri, touching his arm, who brought him back. "You can go on now," she said.

He turned to her. For a moment, he watched her face, as if searching for something more to believe in. "To where?" he asked.

SIX

IT HAD BEEN some time since Christopher Paget had thought about Andrea, who once had been his wife.

In the chaos of the courtroom, his bewildered words to Terri had been swallowed by sound. The media had converged before he and Carlo could speak; all that Paget could do was begin pressing toward the hallway, with Mary, Terri, and Carlo carried by the throng that followed. On the steps of the Hall of Justice, Johnny Moore had managed to tell him that he was taking Carlo to school; Paget had time only to suggest that Terri leave with them. Reporters had shouted questions from all sides.

It had seemed wrong that he was not with Carlo. But he was not yet sure what either of them would say, and this was not the place to say it; part of him was simply glad that Johnny could get Carlo away from this. The boy had disappeared in the crush, and Paget and Mary Carelli had faced the cameras alone.

Mary had been uncharacteristically subdued. All that Paget recalled her saying was that she was grateful for what he had done and that the rest was in Judge Masters's hands; she did not proclaim her innocence or even ask for understanding. Then she had disappeared into a limousine, giving Paget a last backward glance, and he was alone with them.

He had said almost nothing; his closing argument, he told them, was what he meant people to remember. He did not add that he himself could hardly remember what he had said. Their faces were a blur.

He had driven home by instinct.

The quiet house had felt deserted, like a place preserved as a museum to some life no longer lived there. Climbing the stairs to his bedroom, he had stopped at the sight of the canopied bed.

Andrea had chosen it. The bed was not to his taste, but when she had gone to Paris, leaving Paget and Carlo in a third-floor flat not suited to a child, she had not taken it. In the semidaze that followed, Paget had kept it; there was a boy to worry about, too many other things to brood on for Paget to replace a bed. The bed had remained until getting rid of it seemed a reaction to pain and disappointment Paget simply wished to put aside; since then, there had been no woman in his life so permanent as to see Andrea's presence in it, or express tastes of her own. The bed had become an artifact.

Now the memory of Andrea was clear and sharp.

Paget stood there in the doorway, staring at the bed until he understood his thoughts.

It was the tape: Mary's voice, telling him that Carlo was not his son, had taken him back to the moment in time when he had decided that the boy needed him, no matter what. Now, pausing in the doorway, he felt himself standing on that threshold again. Time changed for him: Mary Carelli was seven years in the past; Andrea Lo Bianco was his wife again; some other life, now unlived and irretrievable, was still possible for him. Perhaps when Andrea's career was over, and they could look at things anew, they might decide to have a child. There were still times between them that seemed so good.

The moment passed.

He had no idea where Andrea was now; he had let her vanish from his life without a trace. It made him feel shallow and unreal. He had loved her enough to envision a life with her; now she could die without his knowing. He saw her in his mind, a dancer who carried herself so much like Mary, the mother of the son he had not then known.

Except that it was eight years later; Andrea was gone, and Carlo—the boy he now knew well—was not his son at all.

He walked to his dresser, opening the top drawer.

The tapes were inside. It was where he had hidden them, minutes before Carlo had found him downstairs, drinking alone in the darkened library. He still did not know what to do with them.

About this he could not talk to Terri. He could not

tell her what he feared: that if the tapes were traced to her, and Paget had destroyed them, Terri would share his culpability. Only by putting Terri at risk could he ensure that Carlo would never hear the tape.

He no longer controlled his life, Paget thought, or even how he felt about it.

He slowly shut the drawer.

Where would he go? he had asked Teresa Peralta.

Paget found himself staring at his calendar. He had always kept it on top of his dresser, to remind him of his schedule, and Carlo's. But he had never flipped it to February; gazing at January, he saw that it was checkered with Carlo's basketball games. Paget had recorded them in December, when the schedule first came out, to remind himself. Now January read like a trail of broken promises; Paget had not seen a game since Carlo's mother shot Ransom.

How would Caroline Masters rule? he wondered.

Tomorrow, at two o'clock, Masters would announce her decision. He did not try to guess what she would say; he knew only that as of today, he had made his final argument as Mary Carelli's lawyer.

Today, February 20th. The first morning he had awakened knowing the truth about himself and Carlo.

He flipped the calendar to February.

February 20th was Carlo's final game.

Had Johnny taken him there? he wondered.

It did not seem likely; how could the boy make

himself play basketball? And yet, this morning, he himself had argued Mary's innocence. Every age has its own terrors; often we respond as we are taught. If Paget had made himself go to court, then Carlo, seeing this, might force himself to play. Or perhaps, long ago, the boy had started to respond like Paget. For better or for worse.

Where was he going?

To a basketball game. He had nothing else to do.

Arriving at the game, Paget felt disoriented.

The gym, the red banners with ACADEMY PREP lettered in white, the changing tide of the game itself, were like shadows at the periphery of his mind, the crowd noise like distant signals on a crystal set. But the usual parents were scattered in the bleachers, their faces familiar from the games before Mark Ransom died. Sitting alone, Johnny Moore looked up in amiable surprise.

"Taking the afternoon off?"

"At least." Paget sat down. "Do me a favor, Johnny. If you're planning to kill someone, wait a week or so. And don't murder anyone I know personally."

Moore seemed to know better than to smile. They watched the game in silence.

Amid the red uniforms, Paget saw Carlo.

His face was damp with sweat. He ran down the court to set up for defense, sweeping the thick black hair back from his forehead, glancing at the melee of red and blue uniforms and then up at the time clock. He did not see Paget.

Paget realized that he had been quiet for some moments. Turning to Moore, he asked, ''How has he played this year?''

''Well, as I said.'' Moore kept watching the game. ''Carlo's more improved than anyone—he plays hard all the time, really responds to pressure. He's the one on the team who's got real character.''

Paget hesitated. ''He hasn't said much about it. I figured he wasn't doing well.''

Moore shook his head. ''He's turned into the player other kids respect. Watching, you'd never know what was happening to his mother—he wouldn't let it show. He just kept getting better.''

''I wonder if that's good.''

''How would you have him be? Really, Chris, you'd have liked watching him. He loves to play under pressure.''

Paget was quiet again. Then, nodding toward the blue uniforms at the other end of the court, he asked, ''Who are the bad guys?''

''Woodland Prep.'' Moore focused his attention on the team in blue. ''See the black kid?''

''Uh-huh.''

''That's Tony Farrow. He plays a game most of these kids don't even understand.'' Moore smiled. "It's a shame you missed the *last* Woodland game."

Paget turned to him. "I'm not sure I heard about that."

"Carlo won the game off Farrow." Moore's voice warmed. "Snatched an offensive rebound out of Farrow's hands, got him to buy a fake, slid past him under the basket, and flipped the ball in over his head as the buzzer sounded. It was one for the highlight film."

Where have I been? Paget wondered. Where have *we* been? He lapsed back into silence.

Most of the first half of the game came to Paget as a collage of images—long periods of introspection, interspersed with sudden moments when Carlo, bursting into action, left an imprint on Paget's retina and brain. The score was not important; Paget was not part of the crowd. It was Carlo the person, not Carlo the player, that registered with Paget. The boy alone kept him from thinking of the past, or Mary Carelli, or what Caroline Masters would decide.

Carlo played harder than anyone.

The game transformed him. He seemed eager to be lost in it, to find himself again in the ebb and flow of bodies; the sudden shifts of emotion; the strategy and errors and spontaneity. His body still did different things at different times, and his shot was not yet consistent. But the still boy with the quick tongue and lazy grin, the one who could seem to occupy an entire couch with no hint that he would ever move, played with an intensity that Paget had not seen. He stole the ball; blocked shots; turned rebounds into baskets; shouted encouragement or advice. He and the black kid, Farrow, seemed to have something going; when Farrow shot an elbow to his ribs, fighting for a rebound, Carlo simply shook it off. But a few plays later, in a melee beneath the basket, Farrow doubled in pain; Carlo emerged from the crush with the ball and a twitch at one side of his mouth which, just for an instant, transformed his stoic face. And then he was off down the court, the first awkward step accelerating into a fast break in which Carlo, passing, sped suddenly past the last defender so that when the ball came back to him he was under the basket alone. He seemed so much faster; when he put the ball in, there was no one within ten feet. The stands erupted.

By what alchemy, Paget wondered, had Carlo made himself this good?

The moments came quicker: Carlo knocking the ball from Farrow's grasp, then launching it down the court into a teammate's hands. Carlo blocking a jump shot so hard that he spiked it to the floor. Carlo sinking a shot of his own, nothing but net. Only Farrow looked better.

Part of Paget could not believe that Carlo had come so far. His mind was still suspended between now and eight years prior; fresh as yesterday was the small dark-haired boy who was afraid to go outside, who snatched vainly at the rubber ball the first time Paget threw it. But between then and now were a thousand baskets, shot at the hoop Paget had put up in the backyard, first seven feet high, then eight, and finally the full ten. The sound of Carlo's basketball banging on cement still echoed in Paget's ears.

Carlo drove suddenly to the hoop, drawing a foul as the buzzer sounded to end the third quarter.

For the first time, Paget looked at the scoreboard.

Woodland led by a point.

Carlo walked to the foul line. On the opposite side of the gym, the Woodland kids jeered and stomped their feet to rattle him. A red-haired kid with big ears half rose from the Woodland bench and yelled, "*Choke.*"

It made Paget angry. For a moment, he thought of a frightened young boy on a Boston playground, telling Paget that other kids would not play ball with him because he was no good. But Carlo did not seem to hear.

He looked calmly at the basket, the ball in the air. It arced into the basket, barely hitting metal.

Carlo's second shot hit only net. He watched it without expression. Then he turned to the red-haired kid who had jeered him, and gave him the crooked grin that Paget had known for years. But now it was the grin of a competitor, triumphant and without malice. Carlo trotted toward the bench, smiling to himself. Academy led by one.

The boy who was Paget's son, but not his son, was becoming a young man. Paget was no longer sure he knew him.

In the fourth quarter, Carlo felt Tony Farrow taking over.

The game was Carlo's world now. All that he cared about was the next eight minutes. The thought of winning consumed him with a fierce purity.

But Farrow raised his game to where no one else could reach it.

He was six feet two, incredibly quick, completely without nerves, and headed, Carlo was certain, straight for the NBA as soon as he got his driver's license. And he was everywhere. A fall-away jump shot; a drive; a three-point shot; even a tip-in. Mike Stanley, who was guarding Farrow, could do nothing with him. Carlo and Academy kept close with fast breaks, but suddenly Woodland was up by three.

There was one minute left.

Turning to the bench, Carlo saw Coach Mack call a time-out. Carlo glanced up at the clock; fifty-five seconds.

He did not look toward the stands. He knew that his father was not there; he did not want to distract himself by wishing otherwise.

On the way to the bench, Carlo turned to Mike. ‘‘Tired?’’

Mike shook his head. ‘‘It’s just that this guy’s Jesus Christ.’’

‘‘Yeah,’’ Carlo said, ‘‘I saw the movie. Mind if I try guarding him?’’

Mike hesitated, and then looked relieved. ‘‘It’s fine with me. Just don’t tell coach that.’’

They reached the sideline. Carlo grabbed a towel off the bench and wiped the sweat from his forehead. ‘‘What is it?’’ Coach Mack demanded.

Carlo gave him a level glance. ‘‘Let me take Farrow. Mike’s knee’s acting up.’’

Mack turned to Mike. ‘‘Is that right?’’

Mike shifted from foot to foot. ‘‘Just a little. Not enough to come out.’’

‘‘I want to do this,’’ Carlo said. ‘‘I really want this guy.’’

Mack looked from one to the other. ‘‘All right,’’ he said to Carlo. ‘‘You know what you need to do.’’

Carlo nodded. The coach no longer barked at him; he had learned that Carlo did not like or need it.

When they ran back onto the floor, Woodland was inbounding the ball, and Carlo was facing Farrow.

A dreamy smile crossed Farrow’s round face. ‘‘You?’’ he murmured.

‘‘Uh-huh.’’

Farrow stood with his back to Carlo, poised to break, staring at the blue-shirted teammate who stood out of bounds at half-court, ready to throw the ball inbounds. Three feet behind Farrow, Carlo tried to keep loose, running through what Woodland might do.

Farrow broke abruptly.

The ball floated to where he should have been. But Carlo had broken too, bumping Farrow with his hip as they sped toward the ball. For two steps, Farrow staggered.

It was enough.

The ball bounced free, and then Carlo got there in full stride. He hurtled toward the basket with three headlong bounces; the quicker Farrow was just fast enough to hack him as the ball left Carlo's hand.

As the ball fell through the basket, Carlo's right wrist went numb.

He winced, grasping it. Beneath the screaming from the stands, Carlo heard the whistle. *"Foul,"* the bearded referee called out. "Blue, number twelve."

Farrow stepped to his place beside the line. There was something almost perfect about him, Carlo decided. Short haircut, large brown eyes, smooth skin, a face of broad planes. Gazing at the basket, Farrow could have been contemplating the moon, with a mild and somewhat dreamy interest.

As Carlo stepped to the foul line, the other ref gave him the ball. He, too, was bearded and middle-aged; before the game, thinking jokes might help him forget his mother's dilemma, Carlo had dubbed the two referees "the Smith Brothers." But nothing was funny now; his wrist hurt too much for him to shoot well, and the joke reminded him of how scared he was for Mary.

The stamping and jeering began again.

The pain from his wrist became nausea in the pit of Carlo's stomach. It was foolish not to have eaten, when last night he had not slept. But today he could do neither.

"Choke," the jug-eared kid yelled again.

Shut it out, Carlo told himself. Shoot as if there were no pain.

He breathed in, once. Then he cradled the ball in his palm, feeling its pebbly surface as he had a thousand times before, eyes focused on the hoop. The jeers became white noise.

He flinched as he shot.

But the ball had already left his hand. The arc was not flawless, merely good enough. It rattled the metal and fell through.

Carlo looked at no one now. He did not think of smiling. There were forty seconds left.

Backpedaling up the court, Carlo held his wrist loosely at his side, keeping three feet between himself and Tony Farrow.

Woodland took its time. The point guard crossed the center line, looking from right to left. They had a set play, Carlo saw. He tried to guess what it was.

The last game, they had set a screen; Carlo had diagnosed it, but Farrow had twisted in the air, sucking Carlo into a two-shot foul. Sooner or later, Carlo knew, the ball would come to Farrow again.

When it did, there were twenty seconds left.

This time, Carlo guessed, Farrow would do something different.

Farrow stood with the ball two feet in front of Carlo. Carlo crouched, hands raised in front of him, knees flexed.

Farrow suddenly drove the lane.

He was at full speed in less than two strides. But Carlo had guessed right again. He was a foot in front of Farrow, blocking his angle to the lane, when Farrow pulled up and shot a fifteen-footer before Carlo could even stop.

The move had the silken perfection of a dance routine, practiced until it involved only muscle memory and the certainty of instinct. The shot was far too good to miss.

Carlo watched it fall through the net.

With fifteen seconds, Woodland led by two.

Coach Mack screamed for time-out. But when Carlo ran to the bench, the coach was under control.

"Nothing you could do," he said to Carlo.

"It's okay," Carlo answered. "They just bought themselves some overtime."

At some point in the season, Coach Mack had learned to smile. "Your wrist okay?"

"Fine." Carlo hesitated. "If it's in the plan, I still want the ball."

Mack nodded. "It's in the plan." He drew the team around him. They leaned forward, faces drawn and intent. "We'll get the ball to Carlo," he said, and gave them the play.

The whistle blew, and then Academy inbounded the ball. Carlo danced in the wing, feinting to keep Farrow off balance, waiting to make his break.

When he broke for the lane with five seconds left, the ball was there for him.

A great pass, perfect timing. But when he spun to drive, Tony Farrow slapped his wrist so hard he heard the sound before he felt it.

The whistle blew.

Carlo doubled over in pain. That sonofabitch Farrow had done it on purpose. "Two shots," the referee called out.

The game was on Carlo's shoulders, where he wanted it. With his wrist hurting the way Farrow wanted it.

Still bent over, Carlo tried to flex his wrist. It felt stiff. He straightened, keeping his face impassive, and walked slowly to the line.

Two shots. He had to make them both.

Carlo knew from experience that the wrist would swell. It would lose all flexibility; he would have to miss practice tomorrow and ice it. Except that there was no more practice; this game was the end of their season. Tomorrow there was only the courtroom, and his mother.

At both sides of his vision, three players lined the key. A blue uniform, then a red, then a blue again, poised to fight for a rebound should Carlo miss. To his right was Tony Farrow. The Woodland kids were stomping again. There were three seconds left.

Forget about it. Just concentrate. Look at nothing but the hoop: screen out the score, the noise, the pain in your wrist. Screen out anything else in your life.

By the time he shot, all he saw was the basket.

Pain ripped through his wrist to his elbow.

The ball bounced on the metal rim, once, then twice more, each time closer to the inside of the rim. The angle of the last bounce was right; the ball rattled within the rim and fell through the net.

The crowd erupted. Carlo never changed expression. But his hand felt like a catcher's mitt. He guessed the truth then; Tony Farrow had fractured his wrist.

One shot to go.

He did not really blame Farrow. He had not meant to break anything. Farrow was just exploiting a weakness, putting the pressure on Carlo by forcing him to shoot fouls with a wrist that hurt. That was the game; people who thought basketball wasn't a contact sport weren't watching hard enough. It was what his father, joking, had once said about law.

What to do about his wrist?

He would have to shoot differently. He could no longer flip the ball with his hand; he must push more with his arm.

The gym was hushed now; it was as if Carlo's first shot had sucked the air out of it. The jeering had stopped.

Just one more.

Carlo straightened at the foul line. He breathed in again, breathed out, felt loose. His vision narrowed to the net.

He held the ball at chin level, cradled in his left palm. Then, with his right hand, he pushed it toward the basket. His eyes stung. But he could see that the trajectory looked decent. Just slightly to the left side of the basket.

It hit the inside left of the rim.

Good, Carlo thought.

The ball bounced, hitting the back of the rim, circling around the edge of the basket. Then it paused, teetering on the rim, and fell to the floor without passing through the net.

There were groans, cheers, a brief scramble where Tony Farrow got the ball. Then the Woodland players gathered in a knot, celebrating.

Carlo bent forward, head down, palms resting on his knees. He had no feeling in his wrist now.

He had lost the game.

Teammates filed by, patting him on the back. The

coach put his arm around him. "You're the best we had," he told Carlo. "If I had to lose, I'd want to lose with you."

"Thanks," Carlo said. He did not look up; he needed time to gather himself.

He felt Tony Farrow standing next to him.

Pull yourself together, Carlo.

He looked up. "Your hand okay?" Farrow asked.

"Fine." Carlo shrugged. "It doesn't really matter. Season's over."

Farrow was staring at Carlo's wrist. It had swollen visibly; the skin near his hand seemed discolored. Then Farrow looked at Carlo again, his face solemn. For once, it seemed that someone was home in there. "Man," he told Carlo, "you turned out to be a player."

Carlo nodded. "I figured you didn't want to play alone."

It made Farrow smile. He hesitated a moment, as if to say more, and then extended his left hand.

Carlo shook it.

"See you next season," Farrow said, and was gone.

Next season, Carlo thought. Where would he be? He felt empty.

"Care to go to dinner?" someone asked.

It was his father. His tone was matter-of-fact, as if he had picked up Carlo after practice.

It surprised him. For a moment, Carlo recalled

the first time he could remember meeting this man, and he had seemed so tall. It made him feel like a child again. But it was surely still the pain that stung his eyes.

"Better take me to the hospital first," he said.

The beach looked different than it had the night before.

Terri had expected it to be shadowed by her meeting with Christopher Paget. But they had left no trace. The late-afternoon sun glistened at the water's edge, fuller at high tide. The sound of the waves was deep and lulling.

She sat in a small cove carved into the cliffside, sheltered from the wind. Elena played at her feet. With a child's solemn concentration, she arranged toy people in various formations around pieces of plastic furniture. There seemed, Terri realized, to be a mother, a father, and a little girl; she wished that she could see into Elena's mind. Then Paget broke into her thoughts once more.

He would, she was certain, never again represent Mary Carelli. But Terri thought his final argument had been all that Mary could have asked. Perhaps it was because Terri knew, as others did not, that Paget had spoken to the truth of what Mary had done; perhaps Terri only imagined that he had reached Caroline Masters. But Caroline's last comment, a warning against passion, struck Terri as Caroline's warning to herself.

Terri might be inventing this. Lawyers, their fears unrelieved for days on end, come to read too much into the silences and stray comments of a judge: sometimes, Paget had once quoted Sigmund Freud, a cigar is only a cigar. At least Paget had taken the part he could control to the end. But she was far less sure that the part Paget could not control—the trial of Mary Carelli and the ordeal of the tapes—would end with Caroline Masters. For a moment, she wished that *life* were a tape, which she could fast-forward to tomorrow, so that she would know that the hearing was over.

The tapes.

It scared her now, though she would never say that to Paget. But if he had destroyed them, and they were traced to her, the district attorney might hold her at fault. Paget would try to protect her, Terri knew, but it would hurt her career were the tapes to vanish. And Terri's career, it seemed, was the only security she and Elena had.

She turned back to her daughter.

Elena was talking to her plastic people. "You sit *here,*" she insisted, "and Daddy sits there."

"Who are you talking to?" Terri asked.

"You. You're sitting next to Daddy."

"And where do you sit?"

"Right there," Elena said triumphantly, and placed a plastic child between its plastic parents.

A child, Terri thought sadly, ordering the world of adults. Terri had been certain that she had given Elena no sign of her conflicts with Richie; now she searched her mind for times when she had. She found none. But Elena must have some intuition; she had spent an hour at this game of family, far beyond her usual attention span. Terri had seldom seen her so intent.

Let her be, Terri told herself. At least for a while.

Thoughtful, Terri gazed down the beach.

It was a workday afternoon. The beach was not crowded: mothers with children; a couple or two; a few singles who were used to being alone, and so walked or sat by themselves. A shirtless student type threw a Frisbee for his collie to retrieve, his bare skin stretching as he threw, as if there were hardly enough to cover his slender frame. The collie trotted eagerly into the surf, returning with the Frisbee in his mouth; he shook the water from his coat as he ran toward his master. It reminded Terri that Elena kept asking for a dog.

She turned back to her daughter. Elena had moved the figures again; now they sat at a kitchen table. The child was still between her parents.

"Do you like playing that?" she asked.

"Yes." Elena stopped, staring at her plastic family, and then looked up at Terri. "Why are you so mean to Daddy?"

Her daughter's voice was part inquiry and part accusation; there was an eerie certainty in it, as though Elena knew she was speaking an indubitable truth.

Terri was momentarily speechless.

Keep it neutral, she told herself; don't seem defensive or annoyed. Sound as if you're merely seeking information.

"How am I mean to Daddy?" she asked.

Elena did not answer. But her voice still held conviction. "Daddy cries, you know."

"Have you seen him?"

Elena shook her head. "No. He doesn't want to cry in front of me. He does it when he's alone, after you hurt his feelings."

Terri felt herself stiffen. Quite calmly, she asked, "Then how do you know?"

"Because he tells me." Elena's voice held a kind of pride. "When we're alone, and he tucks me in at night, we talk about our feelings."

Terri recognized the note in Elena's voice now: the false wisdom of a child, flattered by the contrived confidences of a manipulative adult. Anger ran through her like a current. When she spoke again, it was without thinking. "Daddy shouldn't say those things to you."

"He *should.*" Elena shook her head, almost angrily. "Daddy says I'm old enough to know things."

She had been foolish, Terri realized. This could not—should not—be resolved between Elena and herself, but between adults with enough compassion to know that, deep inside themselves, children wish to be children.

Terri wanted to confront Richie right away. But it would not do, she realized, to leave abruptly with this conversation fresh in Elena's mind: the child might see the cause and effect.

"Can I play with you?" Terri asked.

All at once, Elena's mood changed. "Okay," she said, and smiled up at her mother.

For a half hour, Terri forced herself to remember that she had come to play with her daughter. They did that, talking about everything and nothing, until the breeze grew too cold for a child.

As they drove home, Terri half listened to Elena. Her mind felt as cold as the breeze had been.

Richie was in the kitchen. At the sight of Elena, he bent to her and flashed an incandescent smile. "How's my sweetheart?"

His voice was almost crooning. Perhaps it was her mood, Terri thought, but something about it made her skin crawl. "Can you put away your toys?" she asked Elena, and watched the little girl scamper down the hallway. She was unusually cooperative, Terri thought; she found herself wondering if, subconsciously, Elena had begun trying to keep her parents happy.

"How was *your* day?" Richie asked. "Court all right?"

"Fine." Terri's voice was cool. "And yours? Or did you spend it crying?"

Richie looked startled, and then tried a puzzled half smile. As he looked at Terri, it died there.

"The funny thing," she said conversationally, "is that you never cry. Sometimes I'd feel better if you did. But the deepest feeling you can dredge up is self-pity, and that's only to manipulate me. Of course, Elena doesn't see that yet."

Failing sun came through the window. It was dusk: facing Richie, Terri felt darkness closing around them. He watched her in silence. "Quit being abusive," he finally said. "People express their emotions in different ways, you know."

"What have you been telling Elena?"

Richie folded his arms; Terri saw the faintest glint of satisfaction in his eyes. "Lainie's a smart little girl, Ter. Not even a parent can keep her from seeing the truth."

There was something frightening, Terri thought, in the way Richie appropriated a five-year-old to corroborate his view of things. "Elena's not some extension of you, Richie. She's her own person."

Richie gave her a knowing smile. "I get it. You've always resented it because Lainie is so much like me, and now you're blaming *me* for that. Well, I'm sorry, Ter—that's just how it is."

Terri stared at him. "What have you been saying to her?" she repeated.

She saw the calculation run through Richie's eyes: how much to say, what spin to put on it. "I'm just being a parent," he said coolly. "I want Lainie to know the difference between real love and false love based on images."

"Oh, and what *is* real love? I'm not sure I'd recognize it."

"Then let me explain it to you." Pausing, Richie spoke with exaggerated patience. "Real love is when people make a commitment to family and carry it out, even through the bad times. It's the opposite of this stage you're in with Christopher Paget, an infatuation with surface instead of substance." There was an edge beneath his monotone. "I feel sorry for you, Ter. If you don't learn to understand yourself, you'll go from crush to crush, never finding the happiness you'd feel from accepting me as I am."

"At least you'd be free of someone who doesn't deserve you." Terri stopped there; what she felt was too deep for sarcasm. "Don't you understand? I never *cared* if you were the world's greatest promoter. That was *your* dream. I just wanted us to live a real life."

He shook his head. "As soon as you got a law job, you changed. All of a sudden you were afraid I'd be a bigger success than you, that you'd look small next to me." He threw his arms open. "Nothing makes you happy. It's like right now. You want me to parent Lainie, and then you complain when I do. I can never win.''

Terri shook her head. Softly, she said, ''You always win, Richie. But this time I won't let you. Not with Elena.''

Richie placed his hands flat on the kitchen counter. ''Lainie's not like you, and she'll never see me like you do. She's imaginative, like me. We communicate on levels you don't understand.'' His voice filled with authority. ''It just is, Ter. You should rise above your jealousy and learn to see how good I am for our daughter.''

Terri could not answer. All that she could do was let reality sink in—his deep certitude, his irreparable self-involvement. He would always see Elena in terms of his own needs, and if one of his needs was to use Elena to maneuver Terri, he would do that without hesitation, certain it was best for Elena. Perhaps, Terri realized, *that* was the most frightening perception of all. Richie was *not* merely calculating: some unfathomable part of him could make himself believe what he was saying.

''I'm leaving you,'' Terri said.

Richie stiffened. They stood there watching each other, two still figures in the semidark. The silence felt like a caught breath.

''You can't do that,'' Richie said at last. He made his voice calm. ''Not without counseling. I'll set up an appointment. Six months down the road, we'll see where we are.''

It took her a moment to believe what she had already said, another to tell him what else she believed. ''You have an uncounselable problem, Richie. And so do I.''

Richie looked wounded. ''What is so wrong that we can't fix it?''

His voice was suddenly plaintive; it made Terri sad, and sorry for what she had said. But she *had* said it now. ''You can't see other people as separate from you, Richie,'' she said softly. ''I can't change it, and I won't fight it.''

''You can *help* me, Ter. That's what marriage is about.''

His shoulders slumped. He looked so alone, Terri thought, and then she remembered Elena. ''No,'' she answered. ''Only *you* can help you. It's too late for us, and I have Elena to think of.''

His voice rose. ''If you were thinking of Elena, you'd give her an intact family.''

Terri felt her throat constrict. ''It's all I ever wanted, Richie—a family. But there's a difference between 'intact' and 'healthy.' We're no good for Elena.''

The room was dark now. Richie moved closer. ''It's not up to you to say what's good. It's up to a judge, and he'll listen to me.''

''And what will you tell 'him'?''

"That *I've* been the caretaking parent while you've worked long hours with a man who just may be your lover. That I want Elena." He paused; the smile that followed seemed a reward for his own cleverness. "That I can't provide care for her without sixty percent of your income."

"That's crazy."

His voice filled with triumph. "It's the *law,* Ter. I've checked it out. And even if you get custody, you think it's easy to find a man who wants to raise someone else's kid? You'll be alone."

Terri kept her own voice steady. "I don't love you," she said. "I don't think you're a good father for Elena. I don't think our 'family' is good for Elena. So if I have to be alone, I will. And if I have to fight you for Elena, I'll do that too."

"You'll lose." He paused, words softer. "But don't worry, Ter. Every other weekend, I'll let you see my daughter."

It was near the surface now: the fear that had kept her prisoner here. Some stranger, a man or a woman she did not know, would decide whether Terri could raise Elena and, in deciding, would set the course of Elena's life. Richie would make himself be smooth and plausible; how could Terri explain to a judge how things really were? Somehow she would have to be more determined than Richie in his relentless quest for control. But even the thought made her tired.

She forced herself to speak slowly and evenly. "I'm taking Elena and going to my mother's. We need to decide what to tell her."

Richie moved closer, biting off his words. *"We're* not telling her anything."

"We should. And we should do it together."

He was standing over her now. In the dark, she could barely see his face, and only because it was so near. "We're not telling her anything," he repeated. "And you're not going anywhere."

His voice contained an anger she had never heard before: it quavered with his failure to control her.

She tried to step past him. He moved with her, blocking her way. Terri felt her own voice shaking. "I am, though. Please, don't make this worse."

"You don't understand, Ter. I'm not letting you do this."

She felt her heart race. All at once, she had to do something. She put her hand on his shoulder, pushing gently so that he would stay where he was, trying to move past him.

"You bitch," he spat out.

She froze as his hand jerked upward in the darkness, poised to hit her. *"Don't,"* she managed.

"Do you still want to leave, Ter?" His hand stayed up, ready to strike unless she shook her head. "Or are you ready to talk?"

Terri was silent. As his hand rose higher, she

flinched. *"Don't,"* she cried out again, and turned, running to the kitchen wall.

She heard him move behind her. Hands against the wall, she fumbled for the light switch. When she flicked it on and turned again, Richie was two feet away, his hand still raised, blinking at the light.

Terri was breathing hard. "Do it, Richie. Do it twice. That way the family court won't miss it."

Crimson spread across his face. But his hand did not move.

Terri looked into his face. "At least you weren't abusive, I used to tell myself. Not like my father with my mother." She stopped herself, catching her breath. "Now I know why. Before I ever met you, I was trained to give in. The only difference between you and my father was *me.*"

Richie was silent, flushed, staring.

"But not anymore," Terri finished quietly. "Whether you hit me or not, I'm leaving. And if you *do* hit me, I'll make sure it's the last time you'll ever hit anyone."

He gaped at her, and then anger became another expression— embarrassment, exposure. His hand dropped to his side.

Don't let him see your fear, Terri told herself. She knew that this was not over; with Richie, things were never over until he won. Her only goal was to leave the house with Elena.

Terri made herself stand straighter, as if certain he would not strike. "I'll think of something to tell Elena," she said. And then she walked past him, going to get their daughter, not looking back.

Carlo gazed at the cast on his wrist. "Guess I can't do homework," he said.

They sat in a grill both had always liked: Paget for its wood and its white tablecloths, reminiscent of old San Francisco; Carlo for its cheeseburgers. Paget sipped his martini. "At least you can keep up with your reading," he answered. "Just flip the pages with your left hand."

Carlo gave him a brief smile. "Sympathetic, aren't you."

"When you're truly maimed, Carlo, get back to me about homework." Paget nodded toward Carlo's empty plate. "I thought you managed that cheeseburger rather neatly."

"I was *hungry*. The emergency room took forever."

It was true enough. In the two hours they had spent waiting there, the traffic in urban tragedy had been harrowing: a battered woman with her face bruised and one eye swollen shut; an elderly man comatose from a hit-and-run; a young Hispanic shot in what Paget guessed was a botched drug deal. Paget and Carlo had watched these horrors in silence; the parade was deadening, and an emergency room was nowhere to talk about what lay between them. A harried doctor had finally looked at Carlo's X rays, sheathed his wrist in a plaster cast, told him to come back in two weeks, and sent them into the night. But the aftershock of the emergency room stayed with them; they had said little about anything, and nothing about Mary. Their brief exchange about Carlo's wrist felt more like reflex than conversation.

They lapsed into silence again. But it seemed that neither wanted to leave; perhaps, Paget thought, both felt that rushing home would underscore their awkwardness and cast them back into the shadow of tomorrow's ruling. What, Paget wondered, was Caroline Masters thinking at this moment? Or, for that matter, Mary Carelli?

He ordered coffee for himself, dessert for Carlo. The boy gazed around the room, toying with his unused spoon. Paget wished he knew what to say. But what he knew, and Carlo did not, felt like a weight. He had not been able to think things through.

Carlo eyed the spoon. Without looking up, he said, "You were great today. It's good you did that for her."

"Honestly, Carlo, I'm not sure who I did it for." He paused. "Remember that first night, when you said I shouldn't take the case?"

"Uh-huh. I didn't think you believed in her."

Paget nodded. "I'm sorry for that. But I did the best I could."

"I know. I was there."

Paget watched his face. "Some pretty tough things were said last night. Some of them by you."

Carlo averted his eyes for a moment. But when he looked up, his gaze was steady. "Before, I was always able to count on you."

"I'm not a robot, Carlo. This involves my feelings as well as yours."

"But you were ready to desert her." Carlo paused, struggling to explain. "It wasn't just about *her;* it was about *you*. If I can't depend on you to be you, what can I depend on?"

"Do you think you were fair?"

"No. I was angry." Carlo hesitated. "Do you think *you* were fair?"

"No. But I think I deserve a break from you." Paget leaned forward. "This case is a strain on me, for reasons you don't understand. But never, ever have I wanted you not to have a mother. What I wanted was for you to be happy and secure."

Carlo's look became more open. "I always have been," he said quietly. "Until now. I don't know what's happening anymore. I don't know what all this is about."

The simple words threw Paget off track. He thought again of a seven-year-old boy with no certain future, nor any sense of being loved. Paget had tried as hard as he could to make the boy sitting in front of him different from the boy he had been; it shook him to think that this might be lost. ''It's about your mother and me,'' Paget answered. ''There's too much in the past. At some point, you'll have to accept that I don't feel about her as you do, and that she doesn't feel for *me* what she feels for you.'' Paget paused. ''Just as it's all right with me that *you* love *her.*''

''Because any mother is better than no mother?''

''No. Because you and Mary can have something, and I think she wants that very much. If I don't put myself in the way.''

Carlo raised his head. ''I won't let you.''

''Then neither will she.'' Paget paused. ''But I can't be her lawyer, Carlo. If she loses tomorrow, I'll help her find someone else.''

After a moment, Carlo nodded his acceptance. Quietly, he asked, ''Do you think she *will* lose?''

''Yes. I do.''

Carlo took that in. ''If she does,'' he finally said, ''it won't be your fault. I had no idea how good you are.''

''I never told you?''

''No.'' Carlo's face remained serious. ''After today, I don't think anyone could have done better. It'll help me accept whatever happens.''

Paget was quiet a moment. In some small measure, he realized, Carlo had lightened the burden he felt.

''I'm sorry I missed your season,'' he said at length.

Carlo shrugged. "You can't help that. It's fine."

The last words triggered a memory. They had been watching Mary on television, Paget recalled, emerging from the Hall of Justice on the night Ransom died. How was the game? Paget had finally asked. Fine, Carlo had answered simply. And for the days and weeks since then, Carlo Paget had tried to make things fine.

"You played hard," Paget said. "I was proud of you today."

Carlo looked across at him, as if he had much to say, much more to ask. But all that he said was, "Thanks, Dad."

Two words. Paget did not know why they filled his eyes with tears. "I really do love you, Carlo. Quite a lot."

Carlo gave him a puzzled smile. "It was only a game, Dad. I'll get over it."

Paget managed a smile of his own. "Sometimes parents lack perspective," he said.

It was past ten when they got home, close to eleven when the telephone rang in Paget's bedroom.

It was McKinley Brooks. "We've asked to see Judge Masters tomorrow morning," Brooks said without preface. "Ten o'clock. She requested that I give you notice."

Brooks's voice was somber. "In chambers?" Paget asked.

"No. In open court. We've invited the press."

Paget glanced at the drawer where the tapes were hidden. "What's this about?"

"Can't tell you. You'll have to hear it with everyone else. Assuming you don't know already."

It was Terri; they had traced the tapes, Paget guessed, found her signature. Terri was in trouble, and Brooks intended to make the most of it. "It's too late for games, Mac. If you intend to introduce new evidence, or do anything that would embarrass anyone, you should audition in private."

"It's too late for *that,* Chris. Open court it is, by order of the Honorable Caroline Clark Masters. See you there."

Brooks rang off.

Paget sat on the end of the bed. They would accuse Terri of obstruction, he supposed. And, of course, Paget. For the district attorney, it was a no-lose situation: righteous indignation if Paget had destroyed the tapes, public clamor for their disclosure if he had not. Either would put pressure on Caroline Masters to rule against Mary Carelli. All that it required was indifference to Teresa Peralta—Paget himself, he was sure, had long since ceased to matter.

What Brooks did not know was what the second tape would do to Carlo.

For an instant, Paget wanted to call Terri. But he knew what she would say—destroy the tape for Carlo's sake—and that he would refuse. It was best to spare her a sleepless night.

Paget opened the drawer. Slowly, he took the tapes out, staring at them for a moment. Then he put them in his briefcase.

There was one thing he could do. If Brooks started in on Terri, he could ask for a recess, and give the tapes to Caroline Masters.

He picked up the telephone and called Mary Carelli.

SEVEN

To Paget, the courtroom seemed bleak.

It was packed; McKinley Brooks had alerted the press to his last-minute appearance. Brooks sat next to Sharpe at the prosecution table, hands folded across his stomach, wearing the serene expression of someone schooled in self-control. Sharpe seemed less taut than usual; Paget guessed that, this morning, she had no role to play. But there was a gravity to her expression, as if she were about to witness something of moment. Neither looked at Paget or Mary.

Carlo sat behind his mother; Paget had thought of no way to keep him from coming. The boy looked openly worried. Paget had not told him of his suspicions, but the absence of explanation told Carlo enough.

Nor had Paget told Terri. He had waited until this morning even to say they were going back to court; she had looked startled, as if she instantly saw what would happen. Now, sitting next to her, Paget saw the bruise of sleeplessness beneath her eyes: he rebuked himself for how much this case, and all that she had done for Paget and Carlo, already had stolen from her.

Only Mary looked calm.

That was odd, Paget thought. Mary alone knew Paget's suspicions; last night, he had told her of his surmise that Brooks had traced the tapes and of his own desire to surrender them if asked. She had been silent for a time. "You have no choice," she said finally. "If Terri hadn't found them, Brooks would have. You can't very well hang her out to dry."

That had been all. Her expression now was simply resigned; she was caught in a trap of her own making, and would not complain about it. Nor would she let anyone else see what Paget had seen: her feelings were private, and she would go down clinging to them. The rest was out of her hands.

All of them, and the press, waited for Judge Masters.

She was taking her time. That was peculiar; Caroline Masters ran a punctual courtroom. But it was ten minutes past ten. Perhaps, although Paget doubted it, she was relishing a last grand entrance before returning to the obscurity of traffic offenses and petty lawsuits.

"All rise," the courtroom deputy called. "The Municipal Court for the City and County of San Francisco, Judge Caroline Clark Masters presiding, is now in session."

Judge Masters walked to the bench, tented her hands in front of her, and looked directly at Brooks. Her aquiline features held no curiosity: what Paget imagined seeing was challenge and a dash of apprehension. "Well," she said to Brooks, "what is it?"

Brooks stepped forward. "I would like to be heard, Your Honor, on a matter of some importance. I believe it will be worth the court's time."

Masters's expression went opaque. "Of course, Mr. Brooks."

Instinctively, Paget touched the briefcase at his feet, glancing at Terri. When she turned to him, Paget knew that she had guessed as he had.

"I have the tapes," he whispered.

Her eyes widened. "Why?"

"Because it's my responsibility."

She stared at him. "But what about Carlo?"

"I know. But there's nothing for it."

As Brooks stepped to the podium, Paget turned to watch.

"Six weeks ago," Brooks began, "in this city, a prominent woman journalist shot and killed America's most famous writer. His death raised the most fundamental questions: Why are the victims of crime so often forgotten? And how do we treat a woman whose defense—attempted rape—cannot be proven?"

Brooks's voice became reflective. "These are difficult questions," he went on. "The result has been a difficult hearing. Inside the courtroom, it has required this court to make the most delicate judgments, demanded of Ms. Sharpe an extraordinary degree of skill. And outside the courtroom, it has divided men and women of good will.

"As district attorney, I have felt both the pressures of the courtroom and the ambivalence of the community. I have heard the people of this city debate the evidence, question Ms. Carelli's innocence, challenge the sensitivity of my office to the genuine mistreatment too many women face. To them, I have said, 'We believe in women's rights far too fervently to allow them to be abused. For we cannot believe Mary Carelli.' "

Brooks paused, his face becoming almost sad. "But no amount of professionalism in court, no amount of soul-searching at night, has stemmed the unease this case arouses. There are many who question whether the legal process can handle such a case—where the evidence is circumstantial, the issues so emotionally charged, the stakes so high, our belief in justice so fragile. But in the end, our office cannot be dissuaded by fear of the consequences." Brooks paused again. "Political, or legal.

"Whatever passions some people may feel, if the evidence justifies a case, our office must bring it. We did so here. Many have castigated us for that. But now, having listened to the evidence before us, we have the opportunity to restore their faith in our judgment.''

Mary's face had turned grim. ''He's going to offer up you and Terri,'' she murmured to Paget. ''What better way to show I'm guilty than to point to guilty lawyers.''

But Paget had been watching Caroline Masters. ''Wait,'' he whispered.

''We have heard Marcy Linton,'' Brooks continued. ''We have brought forward Dr. Bass. And we have had time to reflect.

''On the current evidence, we must concede that conviction is uncertain. Our only certainty is that far too many people will believe that *any* verdict—including the guilty verdict we seek—is unjust. Thus, even as we have pursued this case in court, we have searched for something that would prove our case and persuade the doubters of its justice.'' Brooks paused again, glancing at Paget.

''The tapes,'' Mary whispered.

Paget did not answer. He could only watch, helpless, waiting for Brooks's next words.

''We have found nothing,'' Brooks said softly. ''We now believe there is nothing to find.''

Paget stared in surprise. The media people seemed like faces in a frieze.

Only Brooks looked serene. ''We therefore move to dismiss the case, and ask the court to discharge Mary Carelli.''

The courtroom burst into sound.

Paget could not comprehend. Mary turned to him, lips parted. Only Caroline Masters did not appear surprised.

She cracked the gavel, waiting for silence. Brooks waited calmly at the podium.

"I must concur with you," she told him. "It seems likely that, however it occurred, Mark Ransom mistreated Ms. Carelli. That may not defeat probable cause. But it suggests that a jury should not be asked to find her guilty of murder and, if asked, should not do so. Your decision does you credit." She turned to Sharpe. "As did Ms. Sharpe's performance before this court."

Brooks nodded. "Thank you, Your Honor."

Masters faced Mary Carelli. For a long moment, she seemed to appraise her, and then she spoke the final words. "Case dismissed, Ms. Carelli. You are free to go."

The courtroom stirred again. Quickly, Judge Masters looked from Brooks to Paget. "Mr. Brooks, Mr. Paget, there is one more matter I wish to speak with you about. Ten minutes from now, in chambers."

She cracked her gavel. Paget glanced at Terri; when he looked up again, Caroline Masters had disappeared.

The rest was white noise. Reporters ran for telephones, snatched portables from their briefcases. The cameras zoomed in on Mary Carelli.

She was weeping.

She stood alone, not covering her face. For an instant, she reached toward Paget, pulled back. Then Carlo was there, putting his arms around her. When he turned to murmur thanks to Paget, one arm still around his mother, he was crying as well. Their faces, Paget thought, were so much alike.

He felt a hand on his elbow.

It was Terri. Her face was drawn, and she did not smile. "You did it," she said.

Paget stopped himself from holding her. "*We* did it," he answered. "And you're all right now."

When they filed into chambers—Brooks and Sharpe, Paget and Terri—Caroline Masters asked them to sit.

"You did the right thing," Masters said to Brooks.

Brooks gave her a Delphic smile. "I hope the press sees it that way."

"I'll help them, McKinley. I can talk about this now." She gave a dry smile of her own. "Do you prefer the word 'courageous' or 'sensitive'?"

" 'Courageous,' thank you. 'Sensitive' sounds too effete for a prosecutor."

"I thought as much. I'll stick with 'courageous.' "

Paget felt an undertone in their exchange, something unsaid. But he was still too dazed to sort it out: it seemed that he had lived so long with the Carelli case, and the specter of the tapes, that he could not accept that it was over. He kept the briefcase close to him.

Caroline Masters drew back in her chair. "I have a private concern," she said. "It began in this room, and I'd like it to end here. The matter of the tapes." She turned to Brooks again. "Given that you've dismissed the case, it seems that the two Steinhardt tapes I have—Laura Chase's and Mary Carelli's—are no longer evidence. Would you concur?"

Brooks gave her a quick, knowing glance. "I would."

Masters looked at him for another moment. "There were two things about this case," she continued, "that I found particularly troubling. The first is the pain that it inflicted on Ms. Linton and, prospectively, on Ms. Rappaport and Ms. Caldwell. But Ms. Linton's testimony was the only way Ms. Carelli could make her defense. It's sad, but if the law does not allow corroboration—as in establishing Mark Ransom's sexual pattern—too few sex crimes will ever be proven, and too many women will continue to be abused. So there is no help but for public testimony.

"But that isn't true of these tapes. If I let them out, some other writer will turn a profit on Laura Chase or—after this trial—on Mary Carelli." Masters paused. "I assume, McKinley, that what happens to these tapes is a matter of indifference."

Brooks shrugged. "To *me*. Maybe not to Ms. Steinhardt."

Masters gave a thin smile. "Then perhaps I should ask Ms. Steinhardt whether I should burn them, or simply cut them to shreds. But I won't. What I *will* do is give Ms. Carelli's tape to Mr. Paget. Out of this entire mess, *that's* the justice I'm most certain of."

Paget fought back his surprise. "For one," he said quietly, "I appreciate that."

Masters nodded, then turned to Brooks. "As for the tape involving Laura Chase and James Colt, I'm leaving it in your custody. I'm sure that everyone can trust your discretion until such niceties as ownership get sorted out."

Brooks smiled. "Of course."

Masters faced Paget again. "Which brings me, Mr. Paget, to the two *missing* tapes: the second Carelli tape and the one regarding Lindsay Caldwell." Masters glanced briefly at Sharpe. "I won't ask if you know where they are—I can't think of any reason for a defense attorney to turn them over. But if there *was* a reason, there isn't anymore. Not after today."

Slowly, Paget nodded. He could think of nothing to say.

Caroline Masters looked at him intently. "I suppose some journalist can argue that by lying, Ms. Carelli brought the 'truth' down on herself. But Lindsay Caldwell deserves better."

"I agree, Your Honor."

"I thought you would." She turned back to Brooks. "I take it you've no further interest in *those* tapes, either?"

"None."

Judge Masters stood abruptly. "Then that concludes our business. You did well, all of you."

They began to file out the door. Paget was the last. When he turned, Caroline Masters was already sitting.

She raised an eyebrow. "Yes?"

"I was just hoping, Your Honor, that I'll see you again."

The thin smile flickered. "In municipal court? I would hope not. For both our sakes." The smile faded. "But there *is* one more thing I'd like to say to you."

This time, Paget smiled. "It's too late to tell me that I'm losing this case."

Caroline Masters did not smile back. "Mary Carelli," she said softly, "is a very lucky woman. That's what I meant to tell you."

Leaving chambers, Paget saw Marnie Sharpe alone at the drinking fountain. He walked over and stood beside her.

"What happened?" he asked.

"We dismissed the case." Pausing, Sharpe fixed

him with a level gaze, reading his face. "Or do you mean what *really* happened?"

"Yes."

She turned, glancing down the corridor outside chambers. Brooks and Terri were talking some distance away, waiting for their partners; their faces seemed amiable enough, the look of lawyers whose conflict has been settled. Sharpe shrugged. "I suppose you'd be the last to tell anyone," she finally said. "Perhaps I can give you the condensed version."

"Please." Paget looked at her. "So what *did* happen?"

"Caroline. Yesterday afternoon, she called us."

Some part of Paget had guessed this much, but it still surprised him. "What did she say?"

"That Dr. Bass's testimony had made her rethink excluding Melissa Rappaport and Lindsay Caldwell." Sharpe's voice took on a slight edge. "My mistake, obviously. And that—'probable cause' aside—the case was too murky for Mary Carelli to go to trial. About which, now that it's over, I'm not entirely sure she's wrong."

"And that persuaded Brooks?"

Sharpe smiled without humor. "There was more. Caroline had two choices, she told us. The first was to throw out the case and take the risk of being reversed on probable cause, thereby looking like a bad judge. The second—which she claimed to like better for her own sake—was to reopen the hearing and allow Rappaport and Caldwell to testify. But after *that,* the electorate might return Mac to private practice.'' Sharpe's voice became a sardonic mimicry of Caroline's. ''Of course, she told Brooks, that was sometimes the price of pursuing a case one believed in. But she was giving him a third choice: dismiss the case, and she would help him look like a statesman.''

Paget pondered that. ''It's not a bad suggestion, you know. Between Linton, Rappaport, and Caldwell, a jury would have hated Ransom. Mac might have ended up wishing Caroline *had* thrown out the case.''

Sharpe glanced back over her shoulder; Brooks and Terri were still talking. ''He knew that,'' she said quietly. ''And there was something else. The tapes. He didn't want the Laura Chase tape out, given the impact on James Colt's family. That's why he was willing to let Mary's tape go.''

''A prudent career move, I would think. What with James Colt junior running for governor.''

Sharpe nodded. ''Mac could imagine the next D.A. walking over his grave. He spent some time wondering which choice Caroline would make if he refused her, then decided to take her up on it. The right decision, I suppose.''

Paget nodded. ‘‘If Mac *hadn’t* bitten, I wonder which choice she would have made.’’

‘‘Oh, I always knew—I’d seen her with those women in chambers. I just didn’t tell Mac.’’

‘‘Will you tell *me?* Now that it’s over.’’

Sharpe considered him for a long time. ‘‘Caroline was bluffing,’’ she finally answered. ‘‘She’d have thrown out the case and taken her chances. But she’d never have put those two women through testifying in public—especially Caldwell.’’

‘‘You think so?’’

‘‘I’m sure so.’’ Pausing, Sharpe gave the wintry smile again. ‘‘Caroline said that to kill the case, that’s all. She just wanted to be sure about those tapes.’’

EIGHT

THAT EVENING, Christopher Paget watched himself on television for the last time.

The news began with McKinley Brooks on the courthouse steps, poised and in command, explaining how he had weighed the evidence against the importance of the issues. The story quoted Caroline Masters as calling Brooks's decision "courageous" and "appropriate." As Paget had wished it, his own time on camera was brief: he thanked the district attorney, expressed his admiration of Judge Masters, and was finished.

"As for Ms. Carelli," the newswoman went on, "her comments were uncharacteristically subdued."

Mary appeared on-screen. Her face showed relief but no elation, and she looked too tired to smile. Microphones jabbed at her from every angle. Carlo stood next to her.

"I would like to thank Christopher Paget," she began, "who gave to my defense more than I ever wished to ask."

She paused there; as the camera zoomed in, she

seemed to search for words. ''I would also like to thank all those who supported me,'' she finally said. ''Especially those women who came forward to testify—Marcy Linton most of all. In a case like this, regrettably, it seems that there is no other way to defend yourself.

''As for me, I'm relieved. I will always think about Mark Ransom's death, but I hope that you will forgive me if I don't wish to talk about it, except for the issues it raises. For me, it's done.

''In three days, I intend to fly back to New York and resume my life.'' She paused again, voice lower. ''But when I do, it will be with special thoughts of my son, Carlo Carelli Paget. Thoughts too private to share, and too deep not to acknowledge. Like his father, he is more than I could have hoped for.''

Watching, Paget saw the smile on Carlo's face. Mary glanced at him, then softly finished: ''That's all I have to say.''

She had been true to her word. The crowd had parted for her; she had stepped into the limousine without looking back.

Now, hearing the doorbell, Paget knew that it was she.

She stood in the doorway. The black limousine was double-parked outside. ''Is Carlo ready?'' she asked.

''Almost. He's just out of the shower, I think.'' Paget hesitated. ''Would you care to come in?''

“Do you mind?”

Paget looked at her for a moment. Then, slowly, he shook his head.

They walked into the library.

Mary studied the palm tree for a moment. “Carlo told me about that tree,” she said. “Before, I couldn’t imagine why you didn’t cut it down.”

Paget shrugged. “I was waiting until he went to college.”

She turned, studying his face. “Are you going to tell him?”

“No. I’m not.”

She paused. “Why?”

Paget looked past her. “Because we put too much time in,” he finally said, “believing we were father and son. So now we are.”

Her body seemed to relax a fraction. “I don’t know what to say to you, Chris.”

“Trying would be pointless. Everything you could have said was on that tape.” He paused. “I know much more than you ever could have told me. The good, and the bad.”

She looked down. “What about Carlo and me? I’ll want to see him.”

“Then see him. Just arrange it between you and Carlo. You and I are quits with each other, Mary. At last, and as we should be.”

Slowly, Mary nodded.

In their silence, Carlo came down the stairs. He

smiled at them both, looking happier than he had since Mary had killed Mark Ransom. Perhaps, Paget thought, happier than he had ever been; his mother and father both loved him, and they meant each other no harm.

"You're very handsome," Mary said. "You carry yourself like Chris."

Carlo smiled again. "Can't help *that,*" he told her. "But my friends say I look like you."

"Oh, well," Paget said.

Mary smiled. "Ready for dinner?" she asked her son.

"Always."

They headed for the door, Paget following them, Mary looking fondly up at Carlo. She stopped in the alcove, as if seized by a sudden thought.

"Can I talk to Chris for a second?" she asked Carlo.

"Sure."

Carlo went out to the limousine. Mary looked after him, and then turned to Paget.

"Yes?" he asked.

She hesitated. "Do you remember on the tape, when I told Steinhardt I'd have aborted Carlo if you hadn't bailed me out?"

"Of course."

"That was true." She paused again, and then added softly, "So when you look at Carlo, and think that you see nothing of yourself, remember that."

* * *

Later that night, Paget decided to burn the tapes.

He took them to the library. Then he threw logs in the fireplace, lit the kindling. He had time, he reasoned; Carlo and Mary planned to stay out late.

For no particular reason, he started by burning the Lindsay Caldwell tape. Tomorrow, perhaps through Terri, he would find a way to tell Caldwell that her secrets now were her own: what she chose to do with them was hers to decide, just as Paget was deciding for himself. He picked up the first tape of Mary.

He paused for a moment, watching the fire burn. How many times, he thought, had Carlo watched with him, caught by the sinuous dance of flame against darkness. Then he began pulling the tape from its spindle.

When the front door opened, Paget started.

It was Carlo.

He heard his son walk to the library, drawn by the firelight and the crackling logs. By instinct, Paget picked up the second tape. Mary, saying that Carlo was not his son.

The boy stood in the entrance. "What are you doing?" he asked.

There was nothing he could say now, Paget knew, but the truth.

"Burning this tape." Paget paused. "After this, there's one more."

"The one about my mother?"

“No,” Paget answered. “The one about *me* and your mother.”

Carlo hesitated. “Can you do that?”

“It’s not evidence anymore, Carlo. All that’s left now is a source of pain. I’m free to do as I wish.”

Carlo looked at him steadily. “Then can I hear it? I’m your son, after all.”

“You are, Carlo. But you’re also becoming an adult. And part of that is accepting that your parents are people apart from you, with their own lives and their own failings.” Paget paused. “Yesterday you asked me to help your mother. Today I’m asking you to help us both. By living in the present, and letting us put the past to rest.”

Carlo looked at him. It was so strange, Paget thought, to face Carlo with the secret of his birth clutched in one hand, asking as a favor for himself the forbearance that, if only Carlo knew it, would keep the boy’s world intact. But he could not tell him: in the end, Carlo’s happiness would rest on his compassion for his parents.

“I’ll always wonder,” Carlo said.

“Try not to. For you, your mother and I are what we are to you today. Nothing else matters.” Paget paused again. “Unless, of course, you make it matter.”

Carlo looked pensive. “What would *you* do, Dad? If you were me.”

Silent, Paget gazed at the second tape. Then he

tossed it, underhand, to Carlo. For an instant, the moment reminded him of that first day in Boston, when Paget had thrown this boy a red rubber ball. Except this time, of course, Carlo caught it.

"I'd help me burn this," Paget said.

Carlo gazed at him another moment, then at the tape in his hand. "How long has the first one taken you?" he asked. "You were never very mechanical."

Paget smiled. "It skips generations. My father once built a ship in a bottle."

Carlo hesitated. Then he sat on the rug, Paget sitting next to him. They faced the fireplace, backs against the coffee table, as Carlo and Paget unspooled their tapes.

"I'll bet you planned on doing this without me," Carlo said.

Paget turned to him. "Why *did* you come home early? Nothing wrong, I hope."

"Nope. But my mom and I are doing something this weekend. We got to the end of dinner, and I just wanted to be with you."

"Why?"

Shrugging, Carlo gave Paget a fleeting smile. "Who knows?"

They sat there next to each other in companionable silence, unspooling the tapes of the past. When Carlo was finished, he held the tangle of tape in front of him. Then he stood and silently tossed it into the fire. The tape seemed to wither with the heat, crackling, and then it disappeared in flame.

Together, they watched it burn, and with it, the truth of Carlo's birth. It was right, Paget thought, that this was so. For what Paget had learned from Carlo was that being a parent was not about ties of blood, any more than starting a family can assure love among its members. These bonds are ours to make, Paget knew; we define them, day by day, by who we choose to love and how we choose to love them. And, by these choices, define ourselves.

Paget glanced over at his son. Perhaps, Paget thought, Carlo might have learned as much from the tape. But the lesson of the tape was for Paget to know; Carlo would learn it in his own way. The capacity to love, he already had.

Paget threw the first tape after Carlo's. They watched it vanish in the flame.

"There," Paget said. "It's done."

That night, for the first time in weeks, Paget slept soundly.

In the morning, Carlo went out with Mary. Paget stayed home.

He had a lazy breakfast, avoiding the newspaper. Then he drifted to the deck. There was little on his mind, and that was as he wanted it. It was time, as his friend Larry Colvin once had put it, to let his soul catch up with his body.

The morning sun was bright. A few sailboats flecked the bay; in the foreground, homes of pink and white stucco glistened in the light. Paget found that he liked San Francisco again.

But there was much to get used to. In the measure of his life, he had gained Carlo, and much had been lost. He did not yet know what it all meant. In two years, Carlo would go to college; Paget would be happy for him, and their house would be empty.

The doorbell rang.

It was a reporter, Paget thought, or a delivery. He debated not answering, then went to the door.

It was Terri.

She was dressed in blue jeans and a blouse, and looked wearier than yesterday. Paget smiled at her. "The case is over," he said. "You get to go home. Sleep, even."

She hesitated. "I'm a little at loose ends right now."

Paget nodded. "Sometimes that happens after a trial." He paused for a moment. "I was just out on the deck. Care to join me?"

Terri still seemed hesitant. "Maybe for a while."

Something was wrong, Paget thought. He decided not to ask.

They walked to the deck. Terri went to the railing; she leaned on it with her palms, gazing out at the bay. A light breeze rippled her hair.

She was quiet for some time. Paget watched from behind; she squared her shoulders, staring intently at the water.

"Are you all right?" he asked.

Terri did not turn. "Yes and no," she finally answered.

Paget moved beside her. He stood there, watching with her. When she turned to him, her eyes seemed large and very grave.

"I've left Richie," she said.

The realization washed over him. Terri had not come for his help, or his advice. She had simply come.

"Is this all right?" Terri asked.

He struggled to find words. "I'm forty-five years old," he said at last, "with a teenage son. You're newly separated. And you work for me." His voice softened. "Any counselor in America would tell you I'm a bad idea, and that you just need time to see that."

Terri watched his face. "But how do *you* feel?"

They looked at each other, each afraid to speak. With his next words, Paget knew, she would stay or go.

"This won't be simple," he said at last.

"I know that. I've got a thousand warnings of my own." Terri paused. "But all that we could ever do, Chris, was wonder. Now we can find out."

A moment passed. And then, sudden and warm, the surprise of his good fortune made Paget smile. "You'd make me live in Richie's shadow?"

"Please. As soon as possible."

As her grin cracked, clean and white and sharp, Paget laughed aloud.

"All right," he said. "But first I have a question to ask."

"What?"

"Is *this* what your mother would have done?"

"No-o-o." Terri leaned back, shaking her head slowly, smiling up into his eyes. "This one's for me."

ACKNOWLEDGMENTS

There are a number of people to whom I owe a great deal. Those who contributed important background information include Bill Fazio and Frank Pasaglia of the District Attorney's Office in San Francisco; Homicide Inspector Napoleon Hendricks; County Medical Examiner Dr. Boyd Stephens; defense attorney Jim Collins; and my colleague, Randy Knox. Dr. Norman Mages was a valuable sounding board when I applied my lay psychology to several of the characters. And Al Giannini, also of the District Attorney's Office, not only provided me with stimulating advice before I began writing but gave me important guidance once the manuscript was done. They deserve a goodly share of the credit for verisimilitude on matters such as medical and criminal procedure; any errors or omissions are my own.

There is no greater favor a writer can ask of a friend than to be an objective and critical reader. A book in progress can feel quite fragile; it is of immeasurable assistance to have readers who are supportive but honest. Because my fiancé, Laurie Anderson, my close friend and partner, Philip Rotner, and my great pal and literary agent, Fred Hill, were discerning judges of the strengths and weaknesses of my first draft, *Degree of Guilt* is a far better novel. And there is no finer editor than Sonny Mehta—incisive, patient, and devoted to bringing out the best values of the manuscript from the day that he first read it.

Finally, this book would not have happened the way it did without Alison Porter Thomas. That she typed the manuscript was the least of it: page to page and scene to scene, she was a gifted critic of language, characterization, and dialogue. I cannot ever thank her enough.